THE
WICKED
AND THE
JUST

The Wicked and the Just

J. ANDERSON COATS

HARCOURT
HOUGHTON MIFFLIN HARCOURT
BOSTON NEW YORK 2012

Harcourt is an imprint of
Houghton Mifflin Harcourt Publishing Company.

www.hmhbooks.com

Text set in Celestia Antiqua and Letterpress Text
Design by Christine Kettner

LIBRARY OF CONGRESS CATALOGING-IN-PUBLICATION DATA

Coats, Jillian Anderson.
The wicked and the just / by Jillian Anderson Coats.
p. cm.
Summary: In medieval Wales, follows Cecily whose family is lured
by cheap land and the duty of all Englishman to help keep down the
"vicious" Welshmen, and Gwenhwyfar, a Welsh girl who must wait
hand and foot on her new English mistress.
ISBN 978-0-547-68837-4
1. Wales—History—1063-1536—Juvenile fiction. [1. Wales—
History—1063-1536—Fiction. 2. Middle Ages—Fiction.
3. Prejudices—Fiction.] I. Title.
PZ7.C62927Wi 2012
[Fic]—dc23
2011027315

Manufactured in the United States of America
DOC 10 9 8 7 6 5 4 3 2 1
4500344053

To Michael and Owen

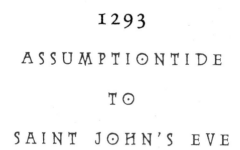

1293

ASSUMPTIONTIDE

TO

SAINT JOHN'S EVE

TONIGHT at supper, over capon and relish, my father ruined my life.

He smiled big, scrubbed his lips with the end of his cloak, and said, "We're moving house."

"Thank the Blessed Virgin!" I sat up straighter and smoothed my kirtle. "I'm weary to thimbles of Coventry. Will we be back at Edgeley Hall in time for the Maypole?"

"No, sweeting. We're not going back to Edgeley. We're moving to Caernarvon."

"*What* in God's name is *that?*"

"It's a town in Wales."

I'm in my chamber now. I will never speak to him again.

Unless he buys me a new pelisson for the journey.

I'll not go to Caer-whatsit, not while there's breath in me.

I'll not eat. Not till my father gives up this foolish notion. At supper, I enter my uncle's hall with my nose in the air and sit at my father's right and sniff as the plates pass.

Betimes I glance at my father to see if he notices, but he's too busy loading his gob with sowce so grease-slick shiny it catches rushlight, and pies with crusts that dissolve at the touch.

I eat in silence. But everything tastes as bitter as wormwood.

So I refuse to speak to him. Not one sweet word from his beloved daughter, his only living child, the light of his otherwise meaningless life.

My father merely smiles and remarks to the saints, "My, how delightfully quiet it's become."

I've no wish to resort to manipulating him, but it's rapidly becoming necessary to end this worrisome notion of moving with a slightly underhanded blow.

So I confront him in the public of the hall with my most piteous Salvo-eyes and wail, "How can you do this to me? I'll die an old maid! There won't be a suitable man for leagues out in the wilderness!"

"A pity you were not born a boy, sweeting," my father replies. "What a King's Bench lawyer you would have made."

And then he arranges for our household goods to be brought to Caer-whatsit by pack train.

An unwelcome feeling is coming over me. This might really be happening. And there might be naught to do for it.

Alice and Agnes pull me into the hearth corner, their eyes as big as trenchers. They want to know if it's true, if we're really leaving. I cannot speak, not even to Alice, who gave me her only ribbon to cheer me when Salvo went lame, nor to Agnes, who has held her tongue about how I kissed Wat the groom last May Eve.

Coventry was bad enough when we came here last Easter. Filthy and crowded, not a patch of green anywhere. Only for a while, my father promised, since already we were straining my uncle's hospitality. Only till we got Edgeley sorted.

Now this. Giving up his birthright to live among savages. Dragging me away from my two dearest friends and any chance at all of making a decent marriage. All with good cheer, no less! I'd think ruining a family would weigh heavier on a father's conscience.

My father may be going mad. Apparently I'm the only one who sees it.

Says my uncle William: "No service owed for your holding? Neither here nor overseas? Only twelvepence a year and that's all? Blast it, what fortune you have!"

Say my cousins: "Hey, Cesspool, how will you keep your precious undershifts clean now?" "Poor Cesspile, you'll have to give them up for want of lye!" "Cesspit, you'll tell us how the Welsh lads kiss, won't you?" "That's if you make it back alive, eh, Cesspile?"

Charming. You'd think that one being a squire and the other a journeyman goldsmith would make them too grown-up to mock my name. You'd be wrong.

My aunt Eleanor is the only one with something sensible to say: "Oh, Robert, how can you take a young woman into that den of vipers? Leave poor Cecily here with me."

I seize my father's sleeve and beg, "Please, Papa, couldn't I stay?"

But my father only laughs, big like church bells. "I would miss you far too much, sweeting. Besides, it's perfectly safe. I wouldn't put you in danger for all of Christendom."

One morning in April just after Easter, my father rents a cart and hires a man who smells of cabbage to drive it. Most of our belongings will follow us by pack train, but my father would bring the valuables with him. The pewter and a strong-box are hidden among some of our simplest goods, and those will keep us till the pack train arrives.

The cart fills up fast. Our things are stacked two and three bundles high. I direct two of the townsmen to load my coffer into the wagon. The coffer contains my most treasured possessions, so I know my father would want it with the valuables.

Salvo limps out of my uncle's townhouse. He stumbles over the doorframe and heaves his way to the cart, where he collapses against the wheel. I kneel and pet him, and he lifts his tail high enough for a single friendly whap.

Then I peer into the wagon crammed back to front.

Salvo whines quietly, nose on paws.

This won't do, so I climb into the cart and shift the bundles and crates, but the stacks I make grow so high that the goods will end up in the mud at the first deep rut.

Salvo closes his eyes. His sides are still fluttering.

My father is arguing with the carter. As usual, it's up to me to make things right.

I catch one of the townsmen by the sleeve and tell him that my coffer should be removed from the wagon to the pile of goods being brought later. The space it leaves is just big enough for Salvo, and I bring his sackcloth bed from my uncle's hearth with my own hands.

My relations turn out to say farewell. My uncle William clasps wrists with my father and tugs cheerfully on my veil. My aunt Eleanor kisses us again and again, sobbing into her handkerchief. She leaves wet smears on my cheeks.

Alice and Agnes cling to my elbows and weep. My two friends are all that has kept my exile in Coventry bearable.

I embrace them both and whisper, "I'm coming back. I'll not be in that dreadful place forever."

They weep harder. They don't believe me.

The wagon is loaded. All is ready. My father embraces my aunt and uncle once more while I hold on to Alice and Agnes as though Hell's great maw has opened beneath us.

Alice and Agnes and I lean together in a tight knot and pledge to be friends forever, no matter how far apart we are. Their shoulders are warm and wisps of their hair tickle my cheek and I'm choking out my promise because I'm going to wake up tomorrow and Alice's elbow won't be jammed in my ribs and Agnes won't be there to lend me a length of thread when mine goes missing in the dim.

As I climb into the wagon, Alice catches my sleeve. She presses a soft folded packet into my hands and whispers, "We want you to keep it. To remember us."

I weep as Coventry rolls out of view. I am like the saints who were sent into the desert to be killed by infidels.

I run out of tears and rub my stinging eyes. The wagon jounces along a rutted track, hitting rocks and chuckholes. I have a blurry view of the carter's faded hood and the oxen's rumps, and Salvo is heavy on my feet.

There's something in my hands. The packet Alice gave me. I unwrap it and my throat closes up tight.

It took us a year, all three of us perched like dolls shoulder to shoulder, bent over one long frame. My fingers throb just looking at the two dozen saints lined up before the throne of God.

Alice was keeping this altar cloth we made to present to Saint Mary's in Coventry at Whitsuntide.

Instead she gave it to me.

To remember them.

As if I need an altar cloth for that.

When dusk is falling, we stop at an inn. Supper is a meat pasty with stale crust and some small beer in a wooden vessel. I'm so hungry that I eat the pasty in three bites without thinking too hard on what might be within.

Then I find a hair in my teeth.

I must share a pallet with two alewives. They both snore like pigs. The fleas devour me toe to crown.

Once we're stuck in Caer-whatsit, I will go to Mass as

faithfully as an abbess and confess my sins every quarter-day. If Hell is anything like this journey, I want to be certain of my soul.

I'm restless all night, and I rise even ere dawn and watch the whey-pale daughter of the house blearily stir the fire to life. After she drags herself away, I wrap up tight in my cloak by the struggling fire and stare hard into the flames.

Right now it's lambing season at Edgeley, and I should be on the uplands watching the little darlings frisk and stagger. I should be admiring the clean cuts of the moldboard as the plowmen follow the oxen up and down the strips. I should be sowing my garden behind Edgeley's kitchen with rue and madder.

"How are you holding up, sweeting?" My father glides out of the darkness and nudges my foot cheerfully.

"Fine."

"That well, eh?"

His good humor makes Edgeley seem even farther away.

"Oh, Papa, why do we have to go to Wales?"

My father kneels at my elbow and squints into the fire. "I'm trying to decide what answer to give you. The one I'd give a child who needs to hear everything is well, or the one I'd give a grown girl who can cope with a bit of the world's ill."

"I'm not a child, Papa."

"Very well." He sighs like a bellows. "I lost the suit."

"Oh, Papa, no! They found against your claim to Edgeley? How could they, when you ran it so well for so long?"

He shrugs sadly. "Simple. Roger is my elder brother. The manor goes to him. I must wish him well of it."

"I wish he'd never come back." I fold my arms. "I wish the infidels had *eaten* him."

My father stiffens. "Watch your tongue, Cecily. Your uncle Roger is a Crusader who followed his Grace the king to liberate the Holy Land."

"And when he comes back, he liberates *your* land," I mutter.

"Sweeting, come here." My father holds out his arms and I'm so tired and heartsore that I shift into his embrace as if I'm six again and scared of the bull. "I'm not happy about it, but such is the way of the world. In Caernarvon, I can get a burgage for twelvepence a year without any military service due, not foreign or domestic. It's all I can get if I'll not have the humiliation of being a steward on a manor I was once lord of."

"What about me? Thimbles, Papa, Edgeley was to be mine! Now I don't even have a dowry!"

My father hugs me tighter. "You let me worry about that, sweeting. In the meantime, you'll be lady of the house once we have our burgage."

Lady of the house. Keys at my belt. Servants doing as I bid them. Like my mother once, at Edgeley.

"Besides, Roger has no heirs, and he still gets those spells from so many years beneath the Crusader sun." My father looks pensive. "If we live quietly in Wales for a few years, who knows? I might find myself in possession of Edgeley after all, as will you and your husband when I'm gone."

That year in Coventry was bad enough, chewing my fingers to pulp and waiting for assize judges and King's Bench lawyers. That year within walls was merciless without Plow Monday or Rogation, without Alred's Well and Harcey's Corner and my mother's grave in the churchyard, where the yew trees grow in thick.

I'm ever so weary of endless green fields and priory floors and travel bread. I want to go home. To Edgeley.

But every turn of the cart's wheels takes us a little farther away, so I ask the carter if he knows anything about the Welsh.

"Oh, aye, demoiselle." His breath smells like onions. "A tricky lot, those. Say one thing and do another. Can't trust 'em farther than you can throw 'em."

Charming. We're going to be murdered in our beds.

"Are they . . . Christian?" I whisper.

The carter smacks his lips. "After a fashion, I suppose."

Even better. We're going to be murdered in our beds by infidels.

My father must not be aware of this. He can wield a falchion and knows a goshawk from a sparrowhawk, but he can be rather dim betimes.

"Oh, demoiselle, beg pardon. It was a poor joke." The

carter smiles like a dog that's used the hall floor as a privy. "Aye, the Welsh are Christian and hold Our Lord and His Holy Mother as sacred as we do."

I pull my hood over my head. At Edgeley I heard Mass every day surrounded by Edgeley people who tilled the fields and drove the beasts and never once looked me in the eye.

"And don't you worry, demoiselle," the carter rushes on. "The Welsh are harmless. It's been ten years since his Grace the king subdued the land of Wales, and there are over a dozen good Englishmen in Caernarvon's garrison. Walls like Jerusalem. Caernarvon's the last place there'd be trouble, mark me."

Today I'm driving the cart.

Well, I'm holding the reins and keeping the oxen while my father and the carter rock and grunt and heft a wheel back onto the road.

The oxen's mouths pull at the strips of leather, as if all they want is my hand to guide them.

As if I'm holding the reins of the whole world.

I could grow accustomed to driving.

When we arrive in a town called Chester, my father hires a guide who has the temper of a sunburned boar. He smells like one, too. My father says we need him to pass safely, though, for he knows the Welsh tongue and every path within a day's ride.

"The Welsh tongue?" I frown. "You mean . . . they don't speak as we do?"

My father shrugs. "They're different from us in many ways, sweeting. Why do you think the king wants us there? How else will they learn to behave?"

At dusk, we stop at a rickety thatchpile house. A woman comes to the door and speaks to the guide in a tangle of sound that makes no sense, but our guide answers in a like manner. Then he tells my father that she's offering hospitality, and my father bids the guide to thank her.

This must be the Welsh tongue. When the guide speaks again I listen carefully, but it's as if someone stretched out his tongue with red-hot pincers and left it to dry in the sun. The sounds he makes are not like proper words at all, and I'm glad when he speaks in good English once more.

I suspected my father mad ere this, but I know it certes now. If the Welsh cannot even speak properly, we have more work before us than I wish to do.

It's late afternoon, right about the time we usually knock on someone's doorframe and request the hospitality of what passes for a hearth in this misbegotten land, when my father reins in his palfrey next to the cart and points.

"There it is, sweeting."

"*That's* Caernarvon?" I put a hand to my mouth. "Saints, Papa, it's *beautiful!*"

No one said anything about a castle. And not just any castle. Possibly the loveliest, most elegant castle in all of Christendom. A wall of gray stone lit orange by the sunset, thin window-slits, high towers. And bands of purple stone threading through the gray like the finest embroidery. Where the castle leaves off, there spans a wall studded with towers. It looks like a subtlety of stone.

"But I thought . . . I thought the Welsh . . ."

My father chuckles. "The Welsh didn't build this, sweeting. His Grace the king did."

His Grace the king has excellent taste.

Even the beasts seem to hurry. We stream down an incline toward a river mouth where boats bob against a series of docks, then we curve around the docks to the south. Little wonder. I can see no gate, only towers that bristle from the wall like cloves in an apple.

As we pass the docks, one of the brawny lads unloading a barge looks at me. Right in the eye, without dropping his gaze or ducking his chin. As if he's my brother. Or my sweetheart.

Tenants at Edgeley would never dare such a look. They all know better.

But I am a long way from Edgeley and there is naught to do for any of it.

We arrive before a massive gate, and the men guarding it approach my father to parley. My father hands over some silver and they nod us through. Above us, the city walls are as wide as several men lying head to toe. The walls are dark and damp and cold, but thick.

It would take a lot to get through walls this thick.

What opens up within the walls does not look like Coventry. There are no townhouses overhanging the roads, blocking out the sun. There are no muddy gutters and middens.

There are open spaces greening with furze and narrow plots with new-turned furrows waiting for May planting. Unfinished townhouses rise golden like solid honey, and older houses, gleaming white with limewash, sweep up from green plots.

I can have a garden here. Just like at Edgeley.

My father looks smug. "More to your liking, sweeting?"

"It's not Edgeley. But I suppose it will do. For now."

The street we follow veers slightly to the left and ends abruptly with the city wall. We pass one cross-street, then another, ere the guide calls gee and directs us down the endmost street.

The castle is massive now. I can just see a curve of tower and a tangle of scaffolding when we lurch to a stop.

"What do you think, sweeting?" My father gestures to a house that rises tall and graceful out of a tidy yard. The bottom part is stone, the top timbered with bright limewashed panels.

"Is that our house?" Not a mud-and-thatch midden-hole, and certes a hand up from my uncle William's crowded lodgings in Coventry.

But by no means is this Edgeley Hall.

My father smiles. "Welcome home."

A thickset woman of middle years answers my father's knock. She is Mistress Tipley. She and the servant have been caring for the place through the winter, and she thanks the saints that we've come through safely.

Mistress Tipley looks suspiciously like a chatelaine, when I'm to be the lady of this house.

At least she is speaking English.

"Sweeting, I must go see the constable," my father says. "Let him know we've arrived and find out what he requires of me. Mistress Tipley will show you the house."

My father swings back astride his horse with a faint groan, then bids the guide bring the cart into the rearyard and unload. I'm left in the foyer with Mistress Tipley regarding me as though I'm a child threatening the wall hangings with my damp little hands.

Being the lady of this house was promised me. I put my chin in the air and tell her, "I can show myself the house. You may go."

Her face reddens, but she bobs her head and disappears.

Abovestairs is a chamber halved by heavy curtains. I claim the half at the rear of the house as my own; my father can have the other. There's a pallet on the floor, but I sincerely hope my father doesn't think I'm sleeping on the floor now that we're here. We can stay at an inn with real beds until the pack train arrives.

I throw open my window shutters and gasp. The view is stunning. The sun is all but down and the land across the shimmering water is a rich, glowing purple. Boats bob and creak below, tethered to docks that run along the city walls. In our rearyard is a scattering of outbuildings and animal pens and a kitchen garden greening like a meadow.

If I'm not murdered, this might not turn out so badly after all.

I trudge belowstairs in search of a place to rest my cart-rattled bones, and I come upon the hall. Salvo is already asleep before the hearth, where a girl about my size is raking the coals. She's dressed in unbecoming gray wool that has been patched and repatched with tight, careful seams.

The servant, like as not. And I am the lady of the house. Like my mother once, at Edgeley.

I wave a hand at the girl and say, "Fetch me some wine."

Rather than leaping up and skittering toward the kitchen, the girl regards me so fiercely that my belly seizes up. Her eyes are dark as currants and unblinking as a bird's.

I stiffen from jaw to fists. "You will bring the wine. Then you will beg my pardon."

The servants at Edgeley would never have dared to so much as raise their eyes to me.

And this girl is fighting a smirk.

"I am the lady of this house," I say in small, bitten-off words, "and you are dismissed from it. As of right now. Be gone!"

I wait for her to cower and plead, but she merely looks at me as steadily as a saint. At length she returns to raking.

"Did you not hear me?" I wrench the grate rake from her hand and haul her to her feet. "You will leave at once!"

The girl's expression hardens. For a long moment she does naught, neither word nor deed, and I'm about to prod her with the rake when she turns on her heel and marches toward the rear of the house.

I'm looking for a place to hang the rake when the girl returns with Mistress Tipley, and the crone is bristling like a sopping cat. "Gwenhwyfar is going nowhere. Now give her the grate rake and let her get on with her work."

"She's ill-mannered," I reply, "and unfit for this house."

"What's unfit for this house?" my father asks as he plods into the hall and tugs at his gloves.

"Her." I level a finger at the girl as she studies her bare feet.

My father runs a hand through his hair. "Cecily, please. We're all weary. Let it lie."

I sharpen my voice. "I'll not have her in this house."

My father sighs. "If it'll make you feel better, sweeting, mayhap—"

"My lord, begging your pardon," Mistress Tipley cuts in, "but if you dismiss Gwenhwyfar, you may as well dismiss me, too."

I turn on my father like a whipcrack. "She's lying! She cannot leave!"

Mistress Tipley draws herself up straight. "I've breathed town air much longer than a year and a day, so I can come and go as I see fit. I'm here for wages, and with the borough's leave. If this arrangement doesn't suit you, my lord, I'll gather my things and be gone by first light on the morrow."

My father blinks. "Christ, no. Mistress Tipley, please. Let's not be rash. Of course Gwen—Gwinny—of course this servant shall stay. And so shall you. And *no more*"—my father gives me a warning look—"will be said of it."

The girl, Gwinny, slices a triumphant look at me as Mistress Tipley hands her the tool. Then she kneels once again and begins to rake around Salvo in long, taunting strokes.

I sulk on the bottom step of the stairs. I will see that crone Tipley on the street by midsummer. Her and her precious Gwinny. No one makes a fool of Cecily d'Edgeley and gets away clear.

A KNIGHT and his daughter, she said. No mistress.

More fool I, to have thanked God for small blessings too early.

No mistress, and new English might be bearable. No sniping. No accusations of familiarity with the master.

No insistence that I live in this town. In this house.

But what I get is worse again, and from a girl no older than I who stands there hands on hips, eyes narrow, brazen as a cold-water drench. As if this is her house already. Her grate to be raked. Hers from splinter to beam.

Wait for the master to slap her senseless. But he does not.

Expected a lot of things from new English. Did not expect to be ruled by a brat.

Long winter days, and I should have known better than to grow accustomed to the blessing of stillness. To grow to love the way quiet could fill space. To close my eyes one too many times and think mayhap new English would never arrive, mayhap this place could stay waiting forever.

Now it's spring, English are here, and I could kill the brat a hundred different ways.

Could strangle her with one of her foolish ribbons. Dump hemlock in her breakfast porridge. Push her down the stairs. Would be no different than killing a rat.

She is English.

The lot of them should burn.

MY FATHER refuses to get us into an inn. When I presented a clear and thoughtful argument, his eyes bulged as if I had spit at the king. Then he said blather-blather-"silver" and blather-blather-"ruinous" and ended the discussion. It appears that cushioning his beloved daughter's poor bruised body is not worth a few measly pennies, so I must sleep on the floor. On the pallet. With all the fleas.

I want my bed.

My father says the pack train like as not won't arrive for another fortnight. If it's not waylaid.

Even in Coventry I slept in a bed.

I must have been more tired than I thought, for I awaken to Prime ringing. Mayhap they are Christian here.

There's a bucket of washing water in the corner. I splash some on my face, brush and plait my hair, then slide on my gown. It takes hardly any time to ready yourself when there's no one to hide your shift or tease you about your shiny forehead.

My tread echoes in the chamber. In this morning light, the space spreads out like sown fields. No elbows to bump. No feet to trip over. It's just me.

Agnes talked too much and Alice couldn't keep a secret to save her soul from Purgatory, but it's all I can do to swallow down my tears. I take out our altar cloth and sit for a long time on the floor, tracing every stitch with my fingers.

But the lady of the house cannot sit and mope. I rise, hide the altar cloth beneath my pallet, and head belowstairs. In the hall, there's bread on the trestle table and I fall on it like a hungry raven. Mistress Tipley bustles in, adjusting her wimple. She picks up the market basket near the door.

The lady of the house does the marketing.

I must sort out a way to get rid of Mistress Tipley.

"I'm coming with you," I inform her.

She blinks rapidly. "Demoiselle, you must be tired after your—"

"I'm coming with you." I look her in the eye till she huffs.

"Very well," Mistress Tipley replies, "but we must leave now."

I lead her into the street, where women lug buckets of water and men sweep refuse into the gutter.

And I remember where I am.

I will be murdered as sure as God hates sin. Some big hairy Welshman will beat me to death with my own market basket. I shouldn't even *be* here; I should be at Edgeley Hall throwing sticks for Salvo's grandpuppies and stitching my bridal linen.

But the passing townsfolk do not lurk or creep or even menace. Most greet Mistress Tipley. In English.

The last place I expected to hear the English tongue is this back-end of Christendom's midden.

We have been walking forever. Mistress Tipley is either lost or daft, or possibly both. I match her pace and say, "Surely we must be at the market common by now."

"It's not a market day," the old cow tells me. "We're just going on the rounds."

"But how can you market on a day that isn't market day?"

Mistress Tipley sighs. "It's a privilege, demoiselle. Hurry, I'm busy today."

Charming. Next she'll be telling me the mayor is a heathen Turk and wine flows through the gutters and this place isn't in fact full of cutthroats and barbarians.

We stop at the bakery. The baker is just lowering his stall-front into a counter and propping up the awning when Mistress Tipley trundles up. The smell of bread is divine.

She pulls out a linen-wrapped parcel and slides it across the counter. The baker counts five wads of bread dough and places the parcel beneath the counter, then he withdraws four cross-stamped rounds from a shelf behind him.

"Half a penny, mistress." In English. Like any of my neighbors at Edgeley.

Mistress Tipley arranges the bread in her basket and pays the baker.

"Why only four?" I ask. "You gave him five loaves. Why do we not get five in return?"

"Castellaria," Mistress Tipley replies as she herds me into the street. "Everyone must contribute to support the castle garrison."

I cannot think of men I want better fed than those of the castle garrison.

Mistress Tipley bustles up the street like a hen. She does not seem to worry about being murdered.

At the coster's counter, Mistress Tipley buys a pan of onions. The coster weighs the pan and says, "That's a penny, mistress."

No one is speaking Welsh. I haven't heard a word of tongue-pull since our ill-humored guide took his leave.

I ask the spicer where he's from.

"King's Lynn, demoiselle." He hands a small packet of pepper to Mistress Tipley.

"You're an Englishman, then."

The spicer chuckles. "Of course I am! Where else would I come from?"

"Er." I gesture around. "Wales?"

The spicer roars laughter as if I've made the most uproarious jest ever in the annals of jesting. "Wales! Oh, saints, listen to the little maid! Did you fall off the turnip cart this morning, or are you laughing in your sleeve?"

I clench my fists. It's a decent guess, as we're in the thick of Wales. But for some reason it's high amusement to mock poor Cecily who asked an honest question and expected an honest answer.

Mistress Tipley swallows her rude laughter and pulls me up the street. I'm itching to ask what's so funny, but I will not give her the satisfaction of mocking my ignorance, too.

We're heading toward the house when I see *him* again. The lad from the docks who seems to think it proper to look upon me squarely. And as he drives past on a rubble cart, one sturdy bare foot resting easily on the foreboard, sure enough, he does it again. He looks right at me, and this time he *smiles*.

Mannerless vermin like him would be cartwhipped at Edgeley.

Not soon enough, we get back to the townhouse. I follow Mistress Tipley down the greenway to a rearyard that's frightfully mucky. But it's my duty to know it well, so I pace it off while holding my hem out of the mud.

The kitchen takes up a good portion of the yard and houses a massive cookfire and several trestle tables. Alongside the mud-splattered kitchen wall is a small roost for hens, and a pig keep. A pigling trots to the pen's rail and grunts hopefully as I near. I haven't any scraps for him, but I scratch his back with a stick of kindling. Next to the lovely garden are a shed and a covered space where two barrels sit empty. The yard ends abruptly at the city wall, which rises like a shield stuck in earth.

Standing in the yard between house and wall is like being folded into your father's embrace after losing at chess or delivering a particularly harrowing confession.

I never thought I'd like walls so much, not after looking over Edgeley's rolling yardlands.

But Caernarvon is not Edgeley. It can never hope to be.

So I'm glad for the walls that stand between me and all that is without.

We go to Mass. I wear my second-best kirtle and my cloak trimmed in fur, despite the sun roasting me like a Michaelmas goose.

Though my father has not yet taken the oath, the burgesses welcome him into their midst with back-slaps and bellowed greetings and extended wrists. Their wives cluck over me, and I duck my chin and flutter my lashes in case they have comely sons who might pay me favor.

They are English, to the smallest babe.

I'm beginning to wonder if there are any Welsh at all in Caernarvon.

When I lead Mistress Tipley out to do the marketing after Saturday Mass, she does not turn onto Palace Street toward the baker's shop. Instead she plows up the big main street toward the city gate. I suffer walking at her elbow and ask, "Are you lost? Palace is behind us."

"Today is market day," Mistress Tipley says, "and the market proper is held without the walls on the common, so we must go there."

Market day, at least, makes sense. Unlike so many other things here.

When we reach the city gate, a massive trestle bars the way through the dark arch. A straggling queue stretches along the walls and curves out of sight. There's no space to get past the trestle save a single gap near the wall, and that space is blocked by a big serjeant bearing a long knife.

Two men sit at the trestle. One guards a wooden box with thick hinges and a sturdy lock. They, too, have knife-hilts clearly pushing back their cloaks.

Mistress Tipley nudges me from behind. "Come. We're not required to pay murage."

She approaches the serjeant and taps his elbow. He steps aside, nodding politely. Ere I can speak, she seizes my sleeve and drags me forward, wrinkling my plum-colored gown.

"This is the daughter of the Edgeley house," Mistress Tipley tells the serjeant. "You will be seeing her as well."

Edgeley House. I must admit it has a music to it.

The serjeant inclines his head to me, then pushes aside the first few men in line so that the old cow and I might pass. The men mutter in tongue-pull.

I stand very still. Surely they'll not murder me while an armed serjeant stands within a knife-slash.

The Welshmen don't even look at me. To a man they push their hoods back and study their bare feet while Mistress Tipley brushes past them, towing me by the sleeve.

Outside the gate, the Welsh appear like worms in cheese. The bridge and fields are crammed with them. Tongue-pull and singsong English ring all around like birdcalls. You can't turn around without roughening your elbow on homespun.

Mistress Tipley plows through the Welsh so briskly that it's all I can do to follow. The poor wretches plod like oxen, even the children, as if this is a quarter-day and not a market day when all the shopkeepers have their awnings out and ribbons on their poles and criers are hawking everything from meat pies to smoked fish.

There's a worn path leading past the castle, and a long queue of Welsh people stretches beyond the gatehouse and the wharves. They're bearing boxes and crates, packs and satchels, animals on tethers and wheelbarrows piled with graying vegetables.

They must be from the countryside.

Mistress Tipley does not join the queue. She strides purposefully to the front amid a flurry of elbows and shoves. I hurry to catch up.

The queue is held up by a trestle that bars the mill bridge, much like the one beneath the castle gate. Three men sit at the trestle. One has a strongbox. Another has an array of eggs, spun fibers, fish, apples, and cheeses in baskets both on the trestle and at his feet. Several armed serjeants stand in the only gap.

"Come," Mistress Tipley says over her shoulder. "There's no toll for us." To the serjeant she says, "Edgeley of Shire Hall Street."

The serjeant nods and stands aside. As we move past the trestle and onto the market common, the first Welshman in line drops something in the strongbox. It clinks like metal.

One of the men at the trestle marks the Welshman's shoulder with chalk and the serjeant steps aside to let him pass.

How sensible. A toll to keep the riffraff out.

So the Welsh are only permitted near the walls once a se'ennight and they must pay for the privilege.

Mayhap I will not be murdered after all.

On the market common, the Welsh kneel before their wares spread out on homespun. Mostly they offer milk and meat, but some have cured hides and rolled fleeces and wool in skeins. The wool is rough and grainy, hardly fit for monks. Our wool at Edgeley was ten times better.

It's a charitable thing indeed for the burgesses of Caernarvon to allow these folk and their pitiable goods near the walls in the first place. The Welsh ought to thank the burgesses on bent knee for the opportunity to trade with the English in the shadow of their walled town.

Mistress Tipley buys a sack of oats and a big wedge of cheese, then she says we must go to the wharves to get the best fish. She leads me past all the lambs and cattle to the edge of the common, to a board straining beneath baskets of fish.

The fishmonger scrambles to his feet and pushes back his hood. "A health to you, mistress." He speaks properly, but barely so, for his words are made singsong by tongue-pull.

"Five of your best sparling," says Mistress Tipley.

He fumbles through a big covered basket and pulls

out fish by the tail. Three are shiny and gray-green, but the others are stiff like planking. And they smell.

Mistress Tipley had better not think I will be carrying those fish.

She shakes her head. "Your best."

"They're the best I've got," he grumbles. Then he straightens and adds, "If it pleases you, mistress."

"Half price, then," Mistress Tipley says. "Those two aren't fit for anything save a stew."

I'm sure as anything not eating them. I'll give them to Salvo. He likes foul dead things.

"Naught wrong with them," the fishmonger insists. "Just listless from being at the bottom of the basket."

"Then a levelooker shall decide," Mistress Tipley says firmly. "The judges at Piepowder Court won't mind settling the matter."

I giggle. Piepowder. Mayhap the judge is a baker and you're amerced in sacks of flour.

The fishmonger growls something in tongue-pull, then sighs. "Very well. What'll you give for them?"

Mistress Tipley squints. "Twopence."

"I'd rather have the sack of oats that your daughter there is holding."

I jerk back as though he hit me. That he could even *think* such a thing, much less speak it!

"Twopence," repeats Mistress Tipley.

The fishmonger looks bellysick. "Please, mistress. Lastage is the worst tax of the lot, so there are no costers out here."

Let him rot. That'll teach him some manners.

"Twopence or nothing."

The fishmonger closes his eyes for a long moment. His jaw is working. Then he deliberately pushes back his ratty cloak and drops a hand to a knife-hilt.

I choke. I freeze. I cannot even stumble out of his reach.

"Don't." Mistress Tipley's voice is steady, her posture rigid. "That's trouble you don't want."

I garble out a prayer in an undertone. I will stand before my Maker ere my Ave is done.

"What you want is to finish this trade," she goes on in a voice even I can tell is too calm. "Then there'll be no trouble."

The fishmonger's wrath falters and his shoulders slump. At length he drags his cloak over the knife-hilt. "I . . . I just haven't the coin . . ."

Now that the knife is out of sight, I manage to tumble behind Mistress Tipley like a days-old puppy.

". . . it'll be county court because of the blade . . ."

Mistress Tipley regards him steadily. "What blade? I've come for fish. Twopence for sparling."

The fishmonger gapes like a pardoned man on the gallows. At length he pleads, "Half the oats, then. Half for all five sparling, plus a handful of herring. Your handful."

Mistress Tipley puts a thoughtful finger to her chin, and it's obvious now that she's not fit to do the marketing.

There's naught to consider with such a bargain. He's offering easily fivepence worth of fish for a piddling halfpenny's worth of oats. And after the fright he put on me, the wretched brute deserves to come up short.

"Very well," she says. "Half."

The fishmonger piles the fish into a cloth she holds out, penitent now, babbling like a lackwit. "A blessing on your kindness, mistress, for I've two little ones to feed, and with all the tolls it's enough to drive a man to—"

"Shhh!" snaps Mistress Tipley, and she jerks her chin at me.

The fishmonger bobs his head, smiles, cringes like a whipped hound. "You are kind indeed, demoiselle, and God Almighty and all the saints will reward you for it."

An Ave ago, this wretch was ready to gut me like a fish. Now he's heaping blessings on me. And pulling his cloak firmly over the knife-hilt, hoping I'll forget.

I don't, though. When we pass the toll table on our way out, I tug on a serjeant's sleeve and whisper in his ear.

"He had what?" The serjeant draws back, startled. "Where?"

I gesture toward the wharves, trying to look frightened. It isn't hard.

"Good work, lass." The serjeant nods to his fellow and they peel away from the toll line, pawing through Welsh people and drawing their weapons as they go.

Soon there's shouting and commotion and the slushy

sound of fish dumped on the ground. More shouting, then a cry of terror and the thrash of struggle.

I smile as I follow Mistress Tipley back toward Caernarvon, despite the black look she's giving me. Somehow I'm not as frightened anymore.

THE brat never looses me ere sunset. Most days it matters little.

On market day, it means we starve.

The last few shopkeepers will be drawing down their awnings and folding up their counters by the time I reach the market common.

Only one thing to do.

Promised Gruffydd I would not. But we must eat, and this is what they've left us.

Down the road, beneath the dark grave of a gate, toward the mill, bracing myself. Deep breaths. Steady on.

Knuckles against the weathered rearyard door. The Cadnant laps quietly below.

A face, doughy and wroth, peers through a cracked door. "Whaddaya want?"

"Oats."

The doughball's eyes flick up and down. Then he gives a greasy smile. "Threepence."

Open my hand. There he is. Staring out, hair like the waves, becrowned. Bastard has the gall to smirk, even cast in silver.

He is why.

It is he who reduced us so.

Turn the penny over. The cross is better. Must think of the saints, though. Not the churchmen.

"How much for a penny?"

"A curse," the doughball spits. "Filthy whore. I've been amerced enough today."

Turn. Walk away. Won't limp here. Not beneath walls of bone and stone.

"Unless . . ."

Keep walking. Already know what he'll want for a miserable half-sack. Back along the path, head down, feet raising dust.

Squeeze the penny tight. Mayhap hurt him whose likeness is stamped here, can men of silver hurt.

Toward Porth Mawr. With luck it's not too late and he'll have something left. Sun isn't completely down yet. Mayhap, since the Porth Mawr mill is farther from the walls. But English watch him more closely for that very reason.

"Three measures," whispers the miller through the crack in his rearyard door. "And you did not get it from me."

"Crown measures?"

"Christ, yes. What else?"

Stuff the sack through the crack. A rustling, and the sack returns dangling from a grizzled hand. It looks empty still. Weak and limp. The levelookers must have been here today.

Peer in. Oats at the bottom, a finger's depth.

Crown measures.

It's all I can do to keep from stuffing them in my mouth. Handful after handful, oats clinging to my lips. Feel full. Just for a moment.

Give the penny one last squeeze, my thumb over his face. Press hard. Hurt, silver king. Die.

"Now get gone," the miller hisses, "ere I'm amerced again."

Hug the sack. Hug it close.

The lot of them should burn.

The path unfolds, some last hints of sun at my right. Skirt fields, fine greening swaths of oats and barley. Mustn't tread there. Watchers are about. Traitors all. Like their miserable fathers.

Should be Gruffydd's. And men like him. Every handswidth. Instead it belongs to burgesses. Given by a king who had it to give because he took it. Sown with blood. Every handswidth.

Woods are nearing. Stumps and holes in waves where the timber gangs have been. English always need wood. Firewood. Castle scaffolding. Townhouses.

Gallows.

Timber gangers never want for coin. Smug bastards with their steady wages and their woodboon and their wretched quarter-day feasts on the borough's penny. Hand-picked by the English, every man, to keep the rest of us jealous and compliant.

At the top of the rise is a dull bulk of shadows. Hidden. They'd have to care to find us.

Shoulder through the curtain. The fire is down to embers, and next to it Mam lies on her pallet. She looks dead. Just a pile of threadbare blankets. The one I got from the porter for showing my tits. The one Gruffydd got for spading up and sowing the first mayor's curtilage garden. And the one that smelled like Da for almost a year till the dirt crept up from the floor and the mold crept down from the walls to take him away from us one last time.

Go to her. Kneel. Her eyes are clenched closed. Her face is lines all cracked like thirsty ground. Her bone fingers pick at the blankets. She is never warm.

Rise. Legs throb all the way up, throb and ache and feel wobbly inside, bones of water. Turn from her, quiet. Mustn't wake her. Feed the fire enough ill-gotten sticks to keep it sputtering. Mash a small handful of oats into gruel. She'll be hungry when she wakes.

Lift the gruel spoon, watch the liquid oats dribble. Almost more than I can bear, empty as I am. When I'm at the brat's, the chatelaine does what she can—a wedge of bread at midday, a covert mug of ale—but there's naught to do for Crown measures and market penny.

Drink some watered mead. Tricks my belly into feeling full.

"Babies."

Crawl to Mam's side. "I'm here. Please be still."

"They're coming." Mam's eyes are flat like coins. They have not looked in years. "They'll take everything. The herds. The pewter. They'll kill my babies. They'll kill my poor little lambs."

Mam's eyelids flutter and her limbs begin to thrash. Slide a bit of wood between her teeth and press her shoulders against the pallet till the shaking dies away.

"Your babies are alive." Pitch my voice calming. "Sleep now. They're alive."

Mam's face is bloodless. Tug the stick from her sagging jaws. Cover her with blankets. Spoon some gruel into her mouth.

Your babies are alive. Every time, I lie. We are alive in body, my brother and I. English should have put us to the sword, though. Spared us this.

Muck out the byre, toss the leavings on the midden, then haul bucket after bucket of water. It's long past dark when everything is set. A bucket of water at Mam's right hand. Her knife carefully sharpened and cleaned. Chips for kindling the fire and wood enough to keep it burning all day. Her privy rags and bucket, dumped and squeezed and scrubbed. A pottle of mead, nigh empty.

Now, with God Almighty's help, Mam might live another day.

Drink mug after mug of water. In the blackest part of night, I will rise so I can be at the brat's house by dawn to haul water and cook pottage and listen to the lackwit prattle on about how unfair it is that she must sit so still while the buttermilk bleaches her freckles.

I've DRAGGED one of the hall benches into the frontmost chamber, the one with the big windows that open onto Shire Hall Street. Most likely it's meant to be a shop of some kind, or a workroom. It's the only place I can spin or sew in peace. If the pack train ever arrives, I'll set up my embroidery frame here. It'd be perfect but for the flies and the smell of the road out front.

My father clumps in crowing like a cock. "Oh, my girl, get dressed! They're waiting on us even now."

"A moment, Papa." I'm squinting at a particularly tricky curl of a peacock's tail. "Let me finish this stitch."

My linen is jerked from my hands. My father tosses it onto the bench and pulls me up by both wrists, grinning like a fool.

"Hey! Papa—"

"Hay is for horses, sweeting. Now go put on your surcote. Quickly now."

I weave my needle into the corner of my linen and bundle the lot into my workbasket. "What's the hurry?"

"The Coucys have invited us to dinner. Now go!"

Right. Yes. There was someone by the name of Coucy at Mass. Bark like a mastiff and hands like a smith. I put on my yellow surcote with the vine stitchery around the collar and off we go.

Up the road. Toward the High Street.

We stop before a door twice my height that's set in a building all in gray stone, four stories' worth.

The Coucys live on High Street in a house of gray stone.

I suddenly realize my hair is a mess.

A girl in a homespun apron lets us in. We're led into a paneled hall and given hippocras. My father beams down at me and pets my plaits, putting them in further disarray.

"Edgeley." A sun-browned man fills the entryway.

My father crosses the room with big strides and clasps the man's wrist, then inclines his head. "My lord, you are kind to invite us. We are honored to take meat at the table of Sir John de Coucy."

Sir John nods. "You're most welcome to Caernarvon."

"Thanks to the goodwill of *honesti* like yourself."

"Well, don't think it comes cheap," Sir John replies to the wall behind my father's head. "You'll take the oath as soon as we can convene. By quarter-day at the latest."

My father blinks. "B-but that's midsummer."

"So it is. Sooner the better, eh?"

A woman and a girl come through the doorway after Sir John. The girl is about my size and has hair that flutters about her waist. It's the color of sunlit flax.

My hair is plaited. It's the color of wet sand.

I hate this girl already.

She is called Emmaline. When I'm presented, she smiles at me, and I mark that her teeth are more crooked than mine. This pleases me.

At table, I'm seated next to Emmaline, so we must share a cup of wine. I manage to refrain from spitting in it since my father is watching me like an unpaid gaoler.

We're served stuffed pigling and gingerbread. Gingerbread! I eat two whole pieces and I'm reaching for a third when my father kicks me under the table. I reluctantly pull my hand into my lap.

While the apron girl is clearing away the pewter and horn, Emmaline asks her mother, "May I show Cecily my embroidery?"

"Of course you may," says the harridan, so I'm obliged to follow Emmaline abovestairs.

The walls of Emmaline's chamber are tinted a delicate shade of orange. There's a cushioned windowseat and a brazier that smells faintly of sandalwood. A small table stands near the bed, and on it are a brass bowl and ewer, some vials, a scattering of combs, and a bronze looking glass.

At my house, I sleep on the floor.

Emmaline goes to an embroidery frame beneath the window and unpins a length of linen. "I'm working this veil for my brother's wife. Do you think she'll like it?"

She's holding out the linen, hopeful as a dog with a stick,

so I take it carefully in both hands and pretend to care. The stem stitches look loose, like gallows-rope, so I sneak a quick peek at the back. The knots are a mess, all tangled and lumpy.

I grin outright. I can do better work with my feet in the dark.

"I spent all winter on it," Emmaline says proudly. "My brother and his wife live in Shrewsbury, but they're coming to visit this summer."

"Ugh, why?"

Emmaline looks puzzled. "Why not?"

I gesture around. "Who would set foot in this town if they could avoid it?"

"You mean Caernarvon?" Emmaline cocks her head. "But it's a lovely place! You've come in spring, true enough, and it's a bit gray now, but come summer you'll fall in love with it."

"What about . . ." I grimace. "The people. Who live out there. Without the walls."

"The Welsh?" Emmaline smiles as if we're sharing a secret. "Don't be troubled by them. Most newcomers find them odd at first, but once you know them, they're charming. They have the most beautiful children, and you should hear them sing."

Somehow I doubt that Emmaline has ever been within spitting distance of a Welsh person, much less been saddled with an ill-mannered one as a servant.

The apron girl appears at the top of the stairs bearing a tray loaded with honey wafers.

Honey wafers *and* gingerbread. Sir John ought to change his name to Croesus de Coucy.

Emmaline sits on the bed and holds out the plate of wafers. I take a big handful and cram them in my mouth without anyone to say me nay, while Emmaline's happy chatter about the Eden that is Caernarvon flows over me like rain over feathers.

I have a bellyache. Emmaline's company must have upset my digestion. I retire to the floor of my plain, cold, untinted bedchamber with a cool cloth over my eyes and a mug of weak small beer infused with chamomile.

I'm better by supper, and I grumble belowstairs to eat sparling and cabbage with antler spoons.

Up the street, Emmaline is eating honey wafers and wasting gold thread on that excuse for a veil.

"So," says my father, "a nice surprise at dinner today."

I sniff and stab at my sparling.

"You're always complaining how much you miss Alice and Agnes. I thought you'd welcome the company of another young female."

"That girl isn't Agnes or Alice."

My father lowers his meat-knife. "You will be pleasant to Emmaline de Coucy. Her family built this borough. Sir John was one of the first Englishmen here."

I wrinkle my nose at my trencher.

"Cecily." My father's voice has an edge I shrink from.

"Very well. I will be pleasant."

"She would make you a very good friend," my father says as he tears off another piece of bread. "Invited to an *honesti* home within a fortnight of arriving—I barely believe such fortune. The saints are looking out for us, sweeting, to bring us into the graces of the town's elite. To say naught of my taking the oath by midsummer, when I thought Martinmas at the earliest. Almost six months early! It's most fortunate, and we must make of it what we can."

My father can make what he wants of this place. It'll be all I can do to run this house and keep my gowns in good repair and not get murdered until we can go home to Edgeley Hall.

God is merciful to sinners! The pack train just arrived! And at its head is Nicholas, my elder cousin.

"Cesspit!" he crows, hopping down from his palfrey and throwing his arms about me. He smells like horse and sweat and sweaty horse, but I hug him hard. It's Nicholas, the lop-eared oaf who puts horse apples in my shoes and hides my hairpins, but my throat is choked up as if I've swallowed too big a bite of pie.

"I could really use a mug of your strongest," Nicholas says, clasping my father's wrist, "but first let's set this lot to their labor." He gestures to a group of ragged men hovering like locusts at the corner of the house among the crowd of laden mules. "I hired them without the walls. Will they understand a word I say?"

My father shrugs. "Usually there's one or two who will."

"Very well." Nicholas bawls at them, as if they're hard of hearing. "Unload the mules. Put things where my lord of Edgeley"—Nicholas claps my father's shoulder—"bids you. A penny per man when you've finished."

One of the laborers steps forward and speaks in tongue-pull to the others. I freeze right there in the yard with Nicholas's arm still about my waist.

It's *him*. The one who *looks* at me.

Of course he'd be a Welshman. I should have marked him by his stabley manners and his scruffy gray tunic that's laced all crooked, revealing far too much in the way of dirty collarbone.

I ought to bid Nicholas knock his front teeth in, just on principle.

But Nicholas is already halfway inside, telling my father of the journey and the river crossings and an inn in Chester where the girls did some shocking things. I turn and follow ere *he* has a chance to look at me.

My father sits at the trestle table with Nicholas and laughs and brags and hears the news, so it's my task to tell the laborers what goes where. In my own house and with two armed men present, the laborers wouldn't dare try to murder me. But I'm on my guard nonetheless.

I don't look at the men. I look at what each is bearing,

then point with sweeping gestures and use small words so mayhap they'll understand. Hall. Kitchen. Abovestairs. Workroom. They nod and duck out and do as they're told. Like dogs.

Dogs do not murder.

The laborers heave and haul and tote from midmorning well into the afternoon. They sweat like oxen and they're twice as filthy, but by sunset our little house actually looks like a house. There are cooking pots and fireplace tongs and linens and saints be praised, my bed is finally here and strung together.

As soon as one of the men brings up my coffer, I carefully lay our altar cloth within, next to a bunch of dried flowers from Edgeley's garden and my mother's handkerchief, the one she pressed to my bleeding palm when I tried to imitate her slicing bread on a trestle I could barely see over.

When the mules are unloaded, the laborers look and smell like an army of pigs. One poor wretch has jammed his thumb so badly it's turning purple. They line up in the gutter while *he* hovers at the front door, waiting to be paid. Like as not he's looking at me even now, but I'm stringing my embroidery frame in the workroom and ignoring him for the beast he is.

And I can ignore pretty well.

Apparently my father can, too, for it's quite a while ere he groans up from the trestle and clumps outside while pouring coins into his hand. He sifts through them, then drops a halfpenny far above each sweaty palm. By the time my father gets to the one who *looks*, there's a lot of grumbling down the filthy line.

"Beg pardon." His English is singsonged by the tongue-pull. "A penny was promised us for this work."

"You were promised nothing of the sort," my father replies. "Half a penny is more than you deserve, so get gone lest you'd have the Watch on your backsides."

I come to the window in time to see a shadow of rage move across the boy's stubbly jaw. Half a penny might be more than they deserve, but I'd be wroth too were I denied what was promised me.

But he only grunts something in tongue-pull to his mangy fellows and they troop down Shire Hall Street in a cloud of sweaty dust.

At supper, we celebrate with a haunch of mutton with sage. The trestle is set properly with linens and pewterware. I sleep like a babe in arms in my own bed.

God is indeed merciful to sinners.

Nicholas is here two whole days ere he works up the courage to lay out the terrible news. My thieving uncle Roger has posted banns. He will marry a girl half his age at midsummer. Which means there could be an heir to Edgeley Hall by next Easter.

I could be stuck here forever. And there'd be naught to do for it.

I wonder just how much penance I would have to do for praying her barren.

My father is taking his burgess oath ere the month is out. I have nothing to wear.

There's the green kirtle that was small on me last year, which hovers around my calves as though I'm a ratty little waif. I may as well brand UNMARRIAGEABLE on my brow. The yellow surcote has a gravy stain in the lap that no amount of fuller's earth can remove, and the alkanet kirtle is barely fit for rags.

My father cannot think I'll stand before the whole town wearing one of these excuses for a garment.

As soon as I've finished supervising Mistress Tipley doing the marketing, I go down the road to the common stable just within the walls. My cousin is there, brushing his palfrey.

"Nicholas." I lean prettily on the stall. "You love me, do you not?"

"I do, Cesspit. You're my favorite cousin."

I'm also his only cousin, but that's a tired jest. "How much do you love me?"

Nicholas combs the horse's flank with long, chuffing strokes. "Not enough to do whatever it is you want of me."

"I only need someone big and strong to escort me around this filthy place."

"And?"

"And . . ." I make my voice small and sweet. "And lend me the price of a new gown."

Nicholas pops up over the horse's rump. "Hellfire, Cesspool, do I look like a man with the price of a gown?"

"All right," I grumble. "Be mean and pinch your pennies. But come with me. Please? You're going to miss me sorely."

He groans and tosses the comb onto a ledge, mumbling something unflattering about women. I let his remark fall, though. Doubtless he secretly likes ferrying me around. I must look fair upon his arm, and if Fortune favors him, people will mistake me for his sweetheart.

We head up High Street and turn on Castle, where I spot a swinging sign bearing a faded ship. At the counter is a falcon-faced graybeard measuring cloth nose to fingertips. He looks up as we approach.

"G'morn, my lord. Have you come for wool?"

"Something suitable for a gown," I jump in, ere Nicholas can ruin things. "For a special occasion."

The merchant glances at Nicholas, who nods. Then the merchant turns to me and holds out the wool he's been measuring. "There's this, just back from the fuller. A good tight weave."

It's just minnet. I frown. "What else have you?"

"This ochre is fair." The merchant brings out a scrap.

I pet it and it's like sand. "Surely you've something better."

The merchant glances again at Nicholas. My cousin

shrugs. Then the merchant holds up a finger and disappears into the shop. In a moment he's back with the most beautiful bolt of finespun I've ever seen. It's the color of fresh blood and as soft to the touch as a lapdog. I pet it and pet it. I cannot take my hands off it.

"How much?" I ask.

"Fifteen shillings a yard."

I blink. Even Nicholas looks a little stunned. Horses can cost less. "W-well, I'll take it. My father will come with me on the morrow to settle up."

"Beg pardon, demoiselle, but without some kind of surety, I cannot hold the wool for you. I could sell it to half a dozen buyers by the morrow. It's right off the boat from Flanders."

I must have this wool.

"Nicholas, what do you have of value?"

"Sorry, Cesspile, all I've got is gold plate," my wretch cousin snipes in a most flippant way.

I must have this wool.

The merchant holds the bolt close to his heart like an only son. Nicholas folds his arms and leans on the window frame as if this is boring somehow.

I swallow hard. "How about an altar cloth? All stitched in gold thread? It has two dozen saints. Took a whole year to make."

The merchant shrugs. "I'd have to see it."

"Nicholas, my dearest cousin, the kindest and most self-less Christian ever to—"

"Yes, yes, I'll go fetch it," Nicholas grumbles. "Where is it?"

"Folded in the coffer in my chamber. Nicholas, you are simply the most—"

But he's striding up the street like his cloak is afire. One little favor and he's worked himself into a lather.

In less than two Credos, Nicholas is back with a familiar packet that he slaps hard into my belly. I ignore him and unfurl the altar cloth like a grand banner. The merchant makes an approving little noise and puts out a hand.

I hesitate.

The linen is soft as a mare's flank. The saints are peaceful all in a line. Alice and Agnes would never speak to me again if they knew.

I push it into his hands all at once. "Take care with it. It's dear to me."

The merchant folds the altar cloth into a tidy square. "This'll be enough to hold the wool. You'll get it back when I've been paid in full. Your father will return on the morrow to pay?"

"Oh, indeed, my lord," I reply. "Mayhap even today. The sooner, the better."

But as the merchant begins to unfurl the wool for measuring, a tall cock of a man slides up to the market counter and smiles all teeth at Nicholas.

"You are a foreigner," the cock-man says to my cousin.

Nicholas frowns. "What do you mean?"

"And trading on a Wednesday. Amerced a penny." The cock-man holds out his palm.

Nicholas squares up. "I made no trade."

The merchant draws back, clutching his bolt of finespun. "I knew not, Pluver. I swear I didn't."

"I made the trade." I step before Nicholas and glare a brace of daggers at this wretch Pluver. "My father is Robert d'Edgeley, and I will see you cartwhipped for your baseless threat against my kinsman, you filthy swine."

"Robert d'Edgeley." Pluver squints thoughtfully. "Newly of Shire Hall Street. Not yet admitted to the privileges and still a foreigner. That makes you a foreigner, too." He holds out his hand. "A penny."

"I've no idea what you mean," I reply through my teeth, "but I'll not give you a single blasted thing merely at your word."

The merchant has withdrawn and stored the bolt of finespun out of sight.

"You are a foreigner trading on a day that is not Saturday, the recognized market day in Caernarvon," Pluver explains, as if I'm a halfwit. "You are amerced a penny for this trespass. In my hand, or it'll be Court Baron before the bailiff."

I sneer. "I'm not a foreigner. I market every day with Mistress Tipley and she said we owe no market tolls. She said only the Welsh must pay tolls."

Pluver seizes my wrist and it stings like sin. Nicholas starts toward Pluver, but the brute says, "One hand on me and I'll haul you in for assault, lad, and then you're waiting on his Grace the king's itinerant justice. Six months at best."

The filthy swine drags me through alleys and greenways. My hem is a mess and my wrist afire. If anyone ought to be hauled before Court Baron, it's Pluver. We go up and over and up to a tall timber building in the shadow of the castle. It's the Justice Court and no more than ten doors from my own.

Nicholas is my shadow till we arrive, then he mutters something about bringing my father and disappears like an angry ghost.

Justice Court is lit by braziers and two big windows with ornate shutters. There are lecterns and rustling clerks and the moldy smell of damp parchment. I'm sat on a bench and told to keep still. The bailiff barks at me whenever I so much as shift.

My backside is sore. I could do with a cup of wine.

My father arrives, Nicholas on his heels. I leap up and move to throw my arms about my father, but he curtly bids me sit and pulls Pluver and the bailiff into the corner. They mutter like conspirators.

I sit. My father will demand they apologize for the rough way they treated me. For putting hands on me right in the street like they might some red-handed felon.

It's several Aves ere my father returns with the bailiff

and Pluver. I rise, brush dirt from my gown, and prepare to receive my apology with grace and dignity.

". . . appreciate your discretion and understanding in this matter," my father is saying to the bailiff. "You have my word it'll not happen again."

I smooth my hair and glare at Pluver.

"As soon as your daughter has begged my pardon," Pluver says to my father, "she can be quit of this place. Doubtless you of all men have no desire to see the inside of Justice Court right now."

Nicholas will explain. He'll tell my father how I was goaded into defending him and ill-served as a result.

But Nicholas won't even look at me. His back is turned. Like everyone else's.

"Papa, I—"

My father squeezes my elbow and fixes me with such a look that I grit my teeth and mutter to my toes, "Begging your pardon, my lord."

The words taste of sulfur.

Pluver has agreed to forgive the amercement for trading on an unlawful day since no trade was actually made, but I am being amerced a half-penny for calling an official of the borough a filthy swine. It's been entered into the *rotuli* and everything, and I will be required to present myself at Court Baron to answer for it.

Now in the sight of God and Crown, I'm a slanderer. I will die an old maid surrounded by twenty cats.

My father steers me out of Justice Court by the elbow and propels me up Shire Hall Street. "What were you thinking? Haven't you the sense God gave a goat?"

"Papa, I—"

"Do you realize the weight of this matter? How will this look to the *honesti* who vouch for my good name before mayor and community?"

"It's not my fault!"

"And whose fault is it?" My father is turning purple. It's most unflattering. "Christ, Cecily, that levelooker was ready to bring *Nicholas* in! Nicholas, who taxed the goodwill of his lord to safely bring our belongings all the way out here!"

I pull my arm free. He's hurting me. "How was I to know? How could you let them treat me like one of the Welsh? Amercing me for *trading*."

"That half-penny is coming out of your clothing allowance, Cecily, and going right to alms for the poor. And you'll stay in the house a solid se'ennight."

"That's fine!" I shout back. "Because I don't want to even look upon you for *twice* that long!"

I'm in my chamber ere I recall that the wretched merchant still has my altar cloth. *Our* altar cloth. And God only knows how I'll get it back now.

I cannot bear to stay housebound for a whole se'ennight, so at cockcrow I busy myself with things that will put my father in a kind and favorable mood. I air all his linen and replace the birdlime flea-traps in his chamber. I make a whole pottle of the sage wine he favors, then I brush all the snarls out of Salvo's tail.

When my father comes in for supper, the trestle is perfectly laid. The pewterware shines. The pottage is still steaming. There's even a bunch of violets tied with twine arranged on the broadcloth.

For a while, the only sounds are chewing and the snick of meat-knives. I wait till my father has emptied his mug and poured himself another. Then I clear my throat.

"I regret that Nicholas almost got amerced. I'll ask his pardon when he's back from the Boar's Head."

My father snorts quietly. "What in God's name were you even trying to do, you silly creature?"

"My garments are a mess. I thought to get some decent wool to make a gown for your burgess oath-taking." I give him Salvo-eyes. "I would hate to reflect poorly on you."

"What a sacrifice for you," my wretched father drawls.

I stab at my supper. If he would mock me, I'll not speak to him for a fortnight this time.

"Sweeting." My father lowers his meat-knife. "Until I take the oath, we're foreigners. It may seem difficult to believe, good English that we are, but until I have the privileges we're legally no better than the Welsh."

"What of Mistress Tipley? Why can she market freely?"

My father takes a heaping bite. "She cannot, unless she

buys for this house. This house has privileges that we don't. Not yet, anyway."

I spear a turnip cube with my meat-knife. Foolish town rules. Foolish townspeople.

"So you must mind yourself better, at least till I'm admitted to the privileges. You're damn lucky the bailiff believed your tale of misadventure."

"I knew not, Papa. I truly didn't."

"I know you didn't, sweeting. Just as I know you truly did not expect me to pay fifteen shillings a yard for finespun."

I groan. "Very well. Let me put on a sackcloth smock and roll around in the midden."

My father laughs aloud.

"It's not funny! They'll all be watching. Do you not want me to look like a burgess's daughter?"

My father closes his mouth abruptly. Hitting him square in the pride rarely fails. I want to remind him that my favorite color is green, but I dare not risk his changing his mind. At length he licks his lips and mutters, "Mayhap . . . mayhap you might wear her vellet gown."

I gasp. "You're jesting."

"I'm serious as the grave."

My mother kept the gown wrapped in lavender-sprinkled linen and took it out every quarter-day to brush it and flick it with holy water. It's as close to indigo as the likes of us dare get, brought all the way from some southern place near the Pope's front courtyard. It must have cost a small fortune.

I've not seen it since she died.

"Th-thank you, Papa."

My father grunts and turns back to his meat.

She'd let me touch it only after I scrubbed my hands twice in the ewer and dried them on clean linen. The gown looked vast lying on the bed, yards and yards of sleek cloth, and it was softer even than newborn lambs or kittens.

I'd beg my mother to put it on and show me how it looked, but she'd just shake her head and smile and wrap it back up, laying it reverently in the coffer, as if it belonged to a saint.

CANNOT get without the walls quickly enough. Step lively till the gray stone beast is all but gone among the trees.

Through the doorway curtain, shoulder first. It's stifling in the windowless steading. There's a fire. Gruffydd is feeding it sticks.

My little brother has fresh bruises across his forearms and his feet are black as soot.

Little. Gruffydd hasn't been littler than me in years. But he's still my little brother, even if I must look up at him.

Didn't expect him till Sunday. He said he'd been hired to cart stone for a se'ennight, and the lads would be staying at the quarry to save the walk. The quarry is heavy work, but at least the wages are certain. Not like standing idle without the walls waiting to be hired by burgesses to do donkey-work for a pittance.

Move to hug him, but he holds me off with a simple embrace about the shoulders. Gruffydd says I should not touch him, for he's always covered in road dust and town filth, but even when he's just out of the river he puts me off.

"Hey, Gwen." He presses a hand to his lower back and grimaces. "Please tell me there's supper."

"No quarry, I take it." Pull out the bread the chatelaine gave me, the stale round I've been saving since midday.

Mouth waters, but I tear off a piece for Mam and hand him the rest. "You look like Hell's own castoff."

Gruffydd grins at me lopsided as he wolfs down the bread. "You too."

"What happened with the quarry?"

"Burgesses."

Tear the bread into pieces for Mam. "Bastards all."

He shrugs. "I take what they give me. They're the ones with the coin."

"They hired that lapdog Tudur Sais again, didn't they? And you said naught and let them."

"What would you have me do?" Gruffydd asks wearily. "Raise Cain? End up like Maelgwn ab Owain? His youngest finally died. She didn't weigh much more than a hearthcat at the end."

Kneel, check Mam. Her breathing is steady. Stay knelt, even when there's naught more to check.

At length, Gruffydd says, "I saw Dafydd on the wharves. He asked after you."

"We are not speaking of Dafydd now." Shoot to my feet, glaring. "We're speaking of how you must not let the likes of that slavish hound Tudur Sais take all the best work, especially when that work was already promised to you!"

Gruffydd smiles sadly. "I know not what you did, but Dafydd is absolutely besotted with you."

If Gruffydd knew what I did with Dafydd, he'd beat him senseless instead of playing errand boy.

Turn away. "Doesn't matter what I did. I'll not marry him. That's the end of it."

Gruffydd flings a hand. "Because of me? I'm not a child, Gwenhwyfar! I can look after myself."

Today's quarry incident would suggest otherwise.

"Saints, how many times must I say it? To you, to Margaret, to Dafydd himself? Must I carve it into my forehead? The answer is no!"

Gruffydd shakes his head. "And Marared is so kind to you. She says naught when you arrive late at the townhouse. Slips you food. Stands up to the master, if what I hear is true."

"Margaret. That's what she calls herself within the walls." Snort, roll my eyes. "If Margaret Tipley chooses to be kind to me, it should be because I work hard and do as she bids me. Not because she used to plait Mam's hair, and certes not because she'd see me wed to the only son of her dearest friend."

"It's because she'd see the burgesses humbled and made to follow the law," Gruffydd says. "And she'll always be Marared to me."

"She cannot be, not in there. Not as a burgess running-dog. And she's in no hurry to leave."

"I'll not throw stones at anyone for how they made their way when the English came," Gruffydd replies quietly, "nor how they must live now."

Only so many times I'll suffer this discussion.

Hold up my coin cross-side out. Gruffydd takes the hint

and pries up the hearthstone. There's a moldy scrap of wool beneath. He unwraps it carefully on his palm. Together we count. Five. There are five silver pennies all together.

"It's not enough," he murmurs. "They'll take something."

"May God strike them down." Can barely speak for choking.

"They can distrain what they like should we not pay," Gruffydd says. "Damn taxmen will be here any day now."

Rub my eyes. Head hurts. Smoke rises like a shroud, silts me down.

My little brother's hands are cut up and sown with splinters. They hang limp at his sides like some lord's kill.

He should be wearing rings. Sitting at the dais of Pencoed and riding the land his by right. He is not, though, and he'll not be. Not now. Not ever.

Nicholas is leaving for Wallingford. I drag my feet while walking him to the door. "You'll come back soon, will you not?"

"If I can, lass, but my lord has little business here."

I study my felt shoes and swallow hard. The house is so much fuller with him in it, belches, bootsteps, and all.

Nicholas smiles suddenly, lighting up like a Candlemas altar. "I nearly forgot to tell you the joyous news, Cesspool. Alice de Baswell is wedding Adam Baker at Lammas. *Your* Alice! The mousy little thing got herself a husband, can you believe?"

She'll have flowers in her hair and her mother will make her the loveliest gown and away she'll go with her comely new husband and I'll miss the whole thing. The ceremony at the church door and the bride ale and the bedding revels. Alice, who sings like an angel and taught me to cheat at tables.

And here's me, adrift in the wilderness without half a yardland in dowry and waiting for the Crusader sun to finish off my uncle so I can go home.

Nicholas is still grinning like a halfwit, as if he's paid me some sort of favor, so I make myself smile. "Godspeed." I squeeze his forearm. "Ride safe."

He yanks my plait with one hand and unties my

apron with the other. Then he winks and he's out the door, down Shire Hall Street. Ere long he's just one of the crowd, and I lean against the doorframe watching all the strangers go by.

An affeerer for borough court comes to the house to remind my father that I'm due in Court Baron for my offense against the levelooker Pluver.

My father stabs me with a quick glare and tells the affeerer that we'll be there.

It's cruel for my father to throw that incident back at me. It's dustier than Adam.

When the affeerer is gone, I slam down my spindle and huff. My father pulls out a whetstone and his meat-knife, so I huff again, louder.

Finally he gets the hint. My father is truly not the brightest-eyed dog in the pack. He sighs and asks, "What is it, sweeting?"

"If I'm to be dragged into court and humiliated, I'd have some justice for my own loss."

"And what would that be?" He shings the blade down the stone and doesn't even look at me.

"The merchant kept the altar cloth I gave him for surety," I reply indignantly. "That's thievery."

My father snorts. "Sweeting, I'm more worried about our future right now than about a strip of linen you embroidered. We'll discuss it after Court Baron. I want no trouble with the law here. Especially not ere I've taken the oath."

"But Papa, they'll—"

"Look at it this way, sweeting," my father cuts in. "A burgess of Caernarvon has a better chance than a foreigner of getting your whatsit back. Does he not?"

It's very annoying when he has a point. I've no liking for his thinking he might be right too often. But I say naught, kiss his prickly cheek, and pick up my spindle, because I want my altar cloth back more than I want to be right.

Court Baron is held in the churchyard. My father holds my elbow firmly as if I'll flee. He's in a foul humor. It's as if *he's* the one who was provoked into slandering a borough official, who was roughly treated and spoken to unkindly by small-minded brutes.

There's a big crowd around the portal of Saint Mary's down at the end of Church Street. At the top of the steps is a trestle, and sitting at it are two men. One I recognize as the bailiff from Justice Court. The other is as sun-browned as the guide who brought us here, and looks like a mouthful of vinegar.

I stand beneath a yew tree for a gasp of shade.

They start calling plaints.

Oath-breaking, amerced a penny. A dog tore up someone's curtilage garden, amerced twopence. The master, not the dog. Someone's pig wandering the streets. I can feel my hair growing.

A beardy burgess all in graceful saffron is called up for breaking a contract, but he isn't two moments before the trestle ere the bailiff intones, "Trespass forgiven, no amercement."

"By God, there will be!" A Welshman leaps from the crowd and lashes a finger at the beardy burgess. "This man sold me sheep with the murrain and passed them off as healthy! I demand justice!"

My father's hand tightens on my elbow.

I stand on tiptoe and crane my neck. Mayhap there will be a scandalous brawl right here in God's yard.

No luck. Serjeants fall on the Welshman, seize his arms, and force him still.

The bailiff points at him. "Amerced twopence for slander."

The Welshman is turning an interesting shade of red. "You'll regret it, by your beards. You'll regret your every last act sooner than you realize."

"Serjeants, put him out." The bailiff flicks his fingers. "Without the walls. Where he belongs."

The serjeants drag the Welshman out in a flurry of elbows and scraping of heels that seems awfully harsh for a man merely seeking justice.

And my turn is coming.

When I'm finally called, my father pushes me forward

with a firm hand between my shoulder blades. I have to walk through the big mob of scofflaws like I'm one of them.

I stand before the bailiff and the sourpuss. I clasp my hands and push my lip out the smallest bit like I'm innocent as a babe. Poor Cecily, motherless little lamb, victim of a woeful misunderstanding.

My father is yammering about the respect he has for borough government and how he would rather die than break one of its laws out of malice and his firm commitment to attaining the privileges to defend laws such as this one and his close friendship with *honesti* like Sir John de Coucy.

Poor little Cecily. Let her keep her halfpenny. She has learned her lesson.

The bailiff sits up straighter. "What did you say men called you?"

"Edgeley, my lord. Robert d'Edgeley."

Even the sourpuss is alert now, and he and the bailiff tilt their heads together and mutter.

"Of Shire Hall Street? Down from Justice Court? White timbered house?"

"Yes, my lord." My father seems confused. But that's nothing new.

The bailiff mutters something to the clerk, then announces, "The borough forgives Cecily d'Edgeley her amercement. In light of your taking the privileges, Edgeley, and staying in that house. Is that clear?"

My father nods, but he still seems bewildered. "Thank you, my lord."

The bailiff smiles at me. "Go on, now, lass."

I twitch my hem and take my father's elbow merrily. Poor motherless Cecily has hoodwinked the fools at borough court!

There's a distinct murmur in tongue-pull as the clerk scritches something on the *rotuli,* but the serjeants clear their throats and fidget with their knife-hilts and the churchyard falls quiet so the borough can finish handing out justice.

1293

SAINT JOHN'S DAY
TO
MICHAELMAS EVE

ELLET is heavy. It's like wearing a hundred soaking cloaks.

But my mother put this gown on once. She rustled it over her head and tightened the lacing.

This gown seemed as vast as Heaven once. But when I slide it on, it extends a mere fingerlength beyond my wrists and pools just slightly on the floor. Some places are bulgy. Others hang in folds. But mostly it fits.

Then I try to walk, and I catch my toe in the hem and fall into the wall.

I wager a whole shilling my mother never fell into any walls.

My father is waiting in the hall. When I appear in the doorway, he gapes at me like a landed eel. "Glory, when did you grow such? Were you not playing dolls last month?"

I laugh and tug my hem. "Papa, don't be daft!"

"By God, but you are her image." He mutters it, hoarse, as if she left us yesterday and his knees are raw from vigil.

I hold my breath and will him to say more. Anything. To tell me her favorite flowers. Whether she liked sweets. What she might have thought of this place, of what he goes to do today.

"Well, we'd best be off," my father finally says, and yet again all my willing comes to naught.

Even though the castle is a stone's throw from our door, my father has hired horses so that we might arrive as befits our new station. We ride up Castle Street toward the King's Gate, and we're just crossing the weed-choked castle ditch when my mouth falls open.

The castle wall that faces the town is not made of the same purple-banded stone as the town walls or the rest of the castle. It's made of sturdy wooden palisades limewashed and stained to ape the stone. The wall still rises so sheer and high it hurts my neck to look at the top, but I held Caernarvon to be a great massive pillar of stone, solid as an anvil and mighty as a saint's resolve.

The castle is not as it seems.

The sentries at the King's Gate nod us through. Inside, the purple-banded parts form a meandering, drunken shell that's still webbed with scaffolding and awash in mud.

Edgeley and its greening yardlands are a world away, like something from a nursery story.

My father dismounts before a wooden hall that's ochered a deep red, and I do likewise. It's not made of purple-banded stone, but at least it makes no pretense of being something it's not.

A man with a falcon-sharp face and a heavy gold chain about his shoulders beckons my father to the front of the hall. My father squeezes my elbow and departs, so I slump on a bench and cinch my arms over my belly. No one sits next to me. As other burgesses take seats, I catch sight of Emmaline de Coucy and her parents across the aisle.

Emmaline is wearing a gown of the red Flanders fine-spun that nearly got Nicholas amerced and landed me un-justly in Court Baron. She lifts a cheerful hand when she sees me.

I face forward.

Even petting my mother's vellet does not cheer me. See-ing that finespun on Emmaline's back puts me in mind of my stolen altar cloth, which puts me in mind of Alice and Agnes and how far away they are. How far away Edgeley is.

My father places his hand on a wood-bound book held out by the gold-shouldered man and swears to maintain the privileges of Caernarvon and conduct the town's business thoroughly and a lot of other things I pay little heed to be-cause I'm too busy wishing the castle were more like it should be and wondering who's noticing me since I'm wearing my mother's gown and hating Emmaline for her sleek, effortless plaits while mine look hagstirred from the buffeting wind off the strait.

The gathered burgesses abruptly raise a cheer. My father clasps wrists with the gold-shouldered man, then steps into a crowd of burgesses who all clap him on the back or clasp his wrist or both.

Good. It's done.

I rise and shake out my gown. There's a clammy skin of

sweat over my whole body. My hair is heavy and damp on my neck.

Something seizes my arm. My father, and he's grinning like a well-fed monk.

"Oh, sweeting, it's set and sealed! I couldn't be happier!"

I could. If a runner brought word that my uncle Roger was dead and we could go home to Edgeley. If I had that dratted gown of finespun on Emmaline's back, which is rightfully mine. If I had a mouthful of wine.

"It was lovely, Papa," I lie. "Where are the horses?"

My father beams down on me. "It's not over, sweeting. Whenever they swear in a new man, they must check that the town's liberties haven't been encroached upon, so we must walk the boundary stones."

I look down at my clean blue hem. My vellet hem. My mother's hem.

I am sweatier than a pig in Purgatory.

For all that the privileges of Caernarvon are costing me, they'd best pay off to the hilt.

It's hotter than perdition. I have been walking forever. If I were a saint, I'd be a martyr by now. Saint Cecily, scorched to death on a forced march.

I trudge behind my father, step after miserable step. My slippers are ruined beyond salvage, so I labor to keep my hem off the ground. There is less mud out here, but the vellet across my arm feels like a cartload of masonry bricks.

We seem to be walking a circuit around the town walls. We keep passing these bits of quarry-stone poking out of the ground like teeth in an old man's head.

By all that's holy, why must this town be so large?

Someone falls into step at my side. A wineskin appears before me, hovering like some strange trick of a heat-addled mind.

If it is a trick of my mind, it's one that pleases me. He's got hair like a blackbird's wing and a careless smile and the most charming dimple.

My hands are shaking, but I take the wineskin and raise it to my lips. No wine comes out. He laughs and uncorks the bung, then offers it again.

If God Almighty had any mercy at all, He'd let me melt through the desolate wasteland below my feet ere making me face this comely stranger before whom I've just made a fool of myself.

"Thirsty work, this," he says, "and you seem thirstier than most. Would I had something for you to ride."

The wine is bitter and warm, but I drink it so I'll not have to look at him, or speak. Then I hand the wineskin quickly back.

My father has noticed my new companion and drops back to take my elbow, which he holds much too tightly. "Edward Mercer. A health to you."

"Oh, come now," my wine-saint replies. "You must call me Ned if we're to be neighbors."

He says it to my father, but he looks right at me.

My father snorts so quietly that I'm certain he's merely clearing dust from his throat.

My wine-saint is still smiling at me. My father would flay me alive should I call a man I'm not wed to by his Christian name, but my father would also not want me to be ill-mannered.

So I smile at the mercer. At Ned.

"And welcome to the privileges, Edgeley. How does it feel to be a friend of the king?"

My father worms his way between Ned and me. My elbow is fiery where the vellet scratches.

"It'll feel better when those privileges begin to take effect. I put down quite a sum on murage just getting my household through the gate."

"Well, you're free of those tolls now. The king does not wish to burden his friends here with such bothersome details. We'll let the Welsh maintain the walls and roads, right?"

"So there is actually some advantage to being here?" I ask, partly because I'm interested but mostly because Ned will have an excuse to speak to me directly. "It's not just where all the castoffs and vagabonds end up?"

Ned winks at me and my father's hand on my elbow tightens enough to burn. "Why, demoiselle, you couldn't drag me back to York, God's honest truth! I can charge their lot what I like and they must pay, for they're not permitted to trade outside the Caernarvon market. Not even an egg can pass from one neighbor to another without the both of them being dragged into borough court and amerced."

Saints, but Ned has a shivery smile. I cannot look upon him without feeling all hot and sloshy.

"The sheriff of Caernarvon cannot even peek beneath the canvas on any of my loads, and all it costs me is keeping this place safe, which I'd do anyway." Ned half draws a short sword at his belt and adds, "There isn't the Welshman born who'd dare touch me."

My father shifts enough to block Ned and loudly asks how the borough enforces trading restrictions. Ned speaks of chalk and levelookers and county court in a voice smooth and mellow like a summer evening. Even so, listening to them is tedious. Would that they would stop talking about tolls and start talking about something important. Like whether I can have another drink from Ned's wineskin, and when this barbarous death-march will be over.

My father is now a burgess of Caernarvon. Friend of the king. The mayor leads the other burgesses through our house in a long, meandering line while bearing a rather heinous-looking mace over his shoulder.

Ned is among them, all leather boots and a finespun woolen mantle. He winks at me and I get a bellyful of shiveries.

My father shows the burgesses his sword and falchion. He shows them the sacks of barley and millet, the salted meat, the bins of peas and turnips.

The mayor approves. My father's stores are sufficient and his weapons sharp. The burgesses give a rousing cheer and my father grins as if he just made peerage or sainthood. They clap him on the back and paw his shoulders and crowd around until I cannot tell him from any of the others.

THE brat sets me to cleaning her blue gown. Mud clings like stolen goods to a thief's hand.

Off they went, the pair of them. The master and the brat. Back they came clad all about in town privilege.

Knew it would happen. It's why they came here. It's why any of them come here.

But watching them ride upstreet made what happened at Pencoed yesterday and nevermore all in one gasp. Horseback English, a decree from their king, and my first taste of foreign rule went down bitter and clear.

One more burgess. One more friend of the king. One more stone in those purple-banded walls.

The mud has worked into the very weave of the wool. It'll take lye and scrubbing to bring it clean.

As a burgess of Caernarvon, my father has been endowed by the king with some cropland. It's without the walls and comes with Welsh people to till it. It's been sown since March with oats, so all that's left to do is weed and chase away crows. That job is done by a sullen little boy whose only words in English are *bastard, whoreson,* and *rot in Hell.*

I go with my father to look at the land. He stands hands on hips and gazes over the greening yardlands as if they're Eden. "Of all the privileges that come with this place, sweeting, land without tenure is the cream."

"I like Edgeley better," I say.

"I owed service for Edgeley," my father replies. "I had to be ready to go armed where my lord bade me at any time, for any reason. This land I hold of the king for twelvepence a year. That's all. It's that simple."

I still like Edgeley better, but my father is grinning so big as he walks among the rows of plants and ruffles their leaves as he might Salvo's ears that I say naught.

Mistress Tipley is hollering at me to help with the brewing. My shutters are closed so I can pretend not to hear. I tiptoe down the stairs, past the hall—where my father would notice me and bid me go help the old crone—and out into the glorious sunshine.

Down the street I stride, dodging puddles and horse apples. It's a fine day for justice, and I cannot wait to taste it.

Now that my father has the privileges, I will have what is due me.

There's the shop, just as I remember it. I've been waiting for this moment for se'ennights. I'll march up, rap at the counter, and demand what's mine. The merchant will be vengeful but pale, but all that's good and right is on my side and he'll reluctantly pull my altar cloth from behind the counter and pause just a moment with sublime regret ere putting it in my deserving hands.

I will tell him how fortunate he is that I am such a good Christian that I will not haul him before Court Baron for theft, and he will gibber in gratitude for his good name. It will be most embarrassing for him, with all of Caernarvon watching.

I cannot wait.

The awning is down, but the sign is different. It's not the merchants' ship. It's a spool of thread and a needle. A tailor's shop.

I freeze in the gutter, my hem in the mud. I check and recheck. Yes, it's the right stall, between the empty building and the house with faded crates full of dead herbs.

An amiable redhead comes to the shop window-counter and asks if he can help me with something.

"Wh-where is the merchant?" I ask. "This used to be a merchant's shop. Where is he?"

The redhead shrugs. "Gone. One too many unlawful trades. The borough revoked his license. His loss is my gain, though."

I turn on my heel. Muddy road is flashing beneath my feet. My fists are stiff at my sides. I round the corner of Shire Hall and knee an illegally kept pig out of my path, then slam our gate hard enough to echo.

I find my father in the hall and shout, "How could you?"

My father looks up from a bowl of chestnuts, bewildered. "Do what, now?"

"He's gone, he took it with him, and now I'll never get it back, never, and it's your fault, Papa. You're the one who let him go, and I'll never forgive you for it!"

"Sweeting, I—"

"It's all I had left of them! Now I don't even have that much! It's gone forever, just like they are!"

My father puts aside the bowl. "What are you on about?"

"My altar cloth," I sob, and collapse in a weeping heap at his feet. It's best that I'll never see Alice and Agnes again, for they'll never forgive me this.

There's a muffled groan, then a heavy shape sinks at my side and there's a warm weight over my shoulders. My father has put his arm around me and I fall against him, hugging him and sobbing.

"Forgive me, sweeting," he says, holding me tight. He

smells like leather and dust. I sob harder and hide beneath his arm. "You can make another one, though. A better one."

Just because a thing is new doesn't make it better.

But I say naught and let him hug me, all pokes of leather and scratchy wool and strong embrace like city walls about my shoulders.

After Mass, Emmaline de Coucy invites me on an outing.

She knows a little place where the river pools, where there's shallow water for wading and a good grassy place for rest and food. She played there often as a child, pretending to be queen of the water sprites with her shift hiked up to her knees.

Emmaline leans in close when she tells me this, glancing at her parents sidelong even though my father has snared them in a conversation they seem to be reluctantly tolerating.

There's nothing I want more than to sniff and tell her not for all the damask in Damascus would I pass one more moment in her wretched golden company than I'm forced to.

But the air in the townhouse is like curdled cream and everything smells of sweat, and I'm ever so weary of the square of street that's visible from the workroom window.

So I agree. Emmaline squeals and claps her hands and bids me meet her by the gates as soon as I'm ready.

Back home, Mistress Tipley is clarifying lanolin. There's a massive fire in the rearyard and she's leaning over a potbellied kettle. Her face is as red as the Adversary's backside and she's sweating fit to drown.

I come into the rearyard to get my shoes from the stoop, and the old cow aims the stirring paddle at me.

"Here, stir this. I must get more firewood, and the lanolin will burn if it's not tended."

My father has gone to Watch and Ward. He'll not be back till sundown. I breeze past her toward the greenway as if she's speaking Welsh.

Mistress Tipley hisses like a cat. "You don't think to leave, do you? There are fleeces to roll and wool to comb. They must be ready for the Saint Margaret's market."

I'm already up the greenway and almost in the street when I hear her holler for Gwinny to come take the paddle, and by then it's too late. She'll never find me in the crowd.

Emmaline waits at the gate. A knot of people I don't recognize stand with her. The man has Emmaline's flax-colored hair. The women are veiled, but one has a sharp face like a wolfhound, and she curls her lip at me and smirks.

"Oh, Cecily, I hope you don't mind," Emmaline says. "My brother and his wife and our cousin would come with us. And our maids, of course. It's too nice out to keep the servants inside all day."

The maids are elegant girls in plain wimples who stand like statues at a proper distance, hands folded, chins tucked. They hold baskets that smell faintly of bread.

"Do you not have a maid?" Emmaline asks, peering over both my shoulders. "We can wait for her."

"Her?" snickers the wolfhound. "A *novi* with a maid? Hardly."

"Now, cousin, don't be unkind," Emmaline says cheerfully to the wolfhound. "Cecily cannot help it if she's new to the Principality. Not everyone has the good fortune to grow up here."

I breathe deep and harness all my hating. I'm to be pleasant to Emmaline de Coucy, and that means not taking her wretched cousin down a peg.

"As a matter of fact, I do have a maid," I reply, just short of haughtily. "She's poorly today. I bade her stay abed."

Emmaline is all concern. "Summer chills are the worst. We'll pray for her health. Shall we go, then?"

I nod. Best get it over with. I trudge like a penitent a pace behind them, just in front of the maids.

Without the walls, big spans of green open up. Naught but plots of summer-bright crops stretching out for leagues, all endowed to burgesses. Emmaline directs us across the mill bridge and tells us to follow the river.

Emmaline's brother is called William, and he is tall and long-limbed with a friendly, crooked smile. He inclines his head politely and asks, "How do you find Caernarvon?"

"We found it same as anyone, I reckon," I reply, a little bewildered. "The road from Chester that runs along the water."

The wolfhound snorts. "Lackwit. Any fool knows how you *find* it. He means how do you *like* it?"

My whole face is hot and scorchy. I would give anything short of my immortal soul to reply to this viper as she deserves, but I'm to be pleasant to Emmaline de Coucy.

I turn away from Emmaline's wretched cousin. To William I choke, "Fine. I like it fine."

William smiles lazily and paws my shoulder like a mother cat. "Don't mind Elizabeth. She's living proof that girls should never learn to read."

William's wife is called Aline. She narrows her eyes at me and then makes a show of taking William's elbow. Then she glances at Cousin Evilbeth and they trade cruel smiles.

"We're almost there." Emmaline points at a dark smudge ahead. "Look, where those willows are thick."

I hurry ahead of the others. Aline says something to Evilbeth as I brush past, and they both giggle.

Let the hens cackle. I would put my feet in the water.

It's shady beneath the willows, dapply-cool. The river moves slowly here and murmurs over round rocks. Even the air feels lighter, and there's a breeze.

All at once I'm back at Edgeley, splashing in the creek that turned the mill-wheel and held tiny silver fish that girls could catch in their handkerchiefs if they had patience enough.

It's just like home.

Then I see them.

Across the stream, half a dozen ragged men in homespun are gathered close like sheep in a storm, their heads bent together.

I freeze.

They're deep in conversation. I cannot hear any words over the stream's murmur, but their lips are moving.

"Hey!" William leaps past me like a roebuck, his short sword drawn and brandished. "I'll see the lot of you in the stocks for a se'ennight!"

One of the men shouts something in tongue-pull and they scatter in six directions. William is knee-deep in the stream when they're all out of sight.

"Bastards," he mutters as he wades out. He slams his sword into its scabbard and squishes up the bank.

I crane my neck, but naught remains of the men save swaying branches and trampled mud.

I hurry to catch up with William. "I agree with you. Welshmen should all be put in the stocks."

He shrugs, but his face is still dark. "Men who follow the law ought to be left to their business. Those who break it must pay."

"Standing on a riverbank is unlawful?" My father certes does not want to see the inside of Justice Court again.

"It is for Welshmen," William replies grimly, "should they gather in groups. Twice over, should they be armed. As that lot was."

All at once the world seems very large, away from

the castle and town walls and armed sentries who incline their heads.

Emmaline does not seem shaken. She even hums as she spreads a blanket where the grass is dry and bids the maids set out pasties and apple tarts and slices of cold meat and cheese. Piles and piles of everything, straight from the kitchens of Croesus de Coucy.

I drop to my knees and pick up two pasties and a tart. Evilbeth puffs out her cheeks like a pig. I take a third pasty and stick my tongue out at her ere I can stop myself.

Aline is still standing, her arms cinched tight as a girdle. "It's not safe here. Let's go back."

"They're gone, love," William tells her. "Half a league from here by now. Welshmen want no part of the law, believe me."

"They were here," Aline insists. "They might come back."

William eats a pasty in two bites. "Not today."

"You don't know that. Who can know what they're capable of?"

If Gwinny is any indication, the Welsh are quite capable of airing linen and laying fires and scooping dog leavings onto the midden.

"Come now, Aline," Emmaline says. "Surely you've seen Welshmen ere this. You've been staying in Shrewsbury for months."

William sighs. "Really, love, Em's right. You may as well fear the cattle."

"You're cruel to mock me." Aline wrings her hands in her sleeves. "Both of you. I would go home. Not just Shrewsbury, either. Home to England."

I grab two wedges of cheese and another tart. I've not even put my feet in the water and this whiny little mouse would drag us back to the sweltering town merely because she fears her own shadow.

William takes her hand kindly. "I should never have allowed you to come. The fault is mine. But Belvero and Whetenhale would never spare me to bear you home to War- wick, or even to our lodgings in Shrewsbury. The part of the fifteenth we collected back at Easter was barely adequate, so the October sum must make up for it."

"I'm weary to death of hearing of this fool tax!" Aline shakes off William's hand and folds her arms like an ill- mannered child.

I'm weary to death of hearing her fool voice, but I'll not be rude about it.

William selects the biggest apple tart, gently untangles Aline's arms, and tucks the pastry into her hand. Her surly pout cracks, then she cuts her eyes to him and takes a bite. He grins and plants a smacking kiss on her cheek.

If we were still at Edgeley, there would be ten kind, comely souls like William lined up outside the door, every man of them begging for the chance to become the heir to a well-run manor like Edgeley.

But we're not at Edgeley.

I shove the last of a tart into my mouth and tromp down to the river. I kick off my shoes and pull up my hem just the smallest bit. The ground is cold and moist, the water deliciously freezing. Like balm against my sweaty feet.

I take out my handkerchief and peer into the creek for fish, just as I used to do on the bank of Edgeley Run.

When I risk a glance behind me, William and Aline are feeding one another tidbits and Evilbeth has taken out her spindle. Emmaline stands apart, gazing toward the angry purple mountains that rise sheer and stark to the south, one hand gently stroking the broad leaf of some bushy plant.

I've seen that look ere this. My father has it as he strolls town and castlery, whistling just as cheerfully as he did walking Edgeley's yardlands.

It's midafternoon when we pack up to leave. At least, they do. I'm still in the stream shallows with a wet hem. The trees dapple shade on my hands and bone-cold water ripples around my ankles and I never want to go back to the dank rotting town, never.

"Come, Cecily!" Emmaline calls as she hands the hamper to her maid. Her feet are rubbed pink, without even a line of mud beneath her toenails to betray her.

Evilbeth rolls her eyes and mutters to Aline, who grins.

God save me from being a shrewish harridan when I'm grown.

I look around one last time, drinking in the graceful

limbs and the gentle murmur of water over stones. I never thought to memorize Edgeley Run like this. I never knew it would be needful.

I'm glad to know this place is here.

The others are already disappearing among the trees and I hurry to catch up. William strides at the fore, Emmaline is a few paces behind him, and then come Evilbeth and Aline, with the maids trudging at the rear. I whisk past the maids, then push past the two shrews. I've just shouldered past Emmaline when the bushes shudder.

Men rise out of the brush like ghosts, at least a dozen, on both sides of the deer track.

Behind me, a girl screams.

William drops a hand to his sword.

But ere he can draw it, the men pelt him with rubbish. Rotting turnips, handfuls of mud, horse apples, all flying in a stinking wave from every side, splattering, smearing, whacking, and thumping. The men jeer and shout in tongue-pull as they throw.

William holds both arms over his face to ward off the barrage. He's cursing like a drunken carter.

A handful of muck splatters my gown just above the knee. Slimy green and brown, God knows what.

"You miserable misbegotten *brutes!*" My voice is shrill and brittle. "I will see you all *hang* for this!"

But the men have already vanished, leaving naught but waving branches and a vile midden stink.

William straightens, lowers his arms. His tunic is motley with chunks and smears of refuse. Something pulpy caught him upside the head and clings in gobbets in his hair. He looks like a mad leper thrice-spurned by God.

Emmaline rushes to his side and makes to seize his shoulder, then pulls away. She looks a little greensick. "William! Are you sound?"

He skins off his hood and wrings murky liquid from it. "It'll avail them not a bit. Not one bit."

I turn to William and bare my teeth like an animal. "Hang them. Hang them all."

He uses his hood to wipe rotting muck from his arms and chest. "I regret your gown, demoiselle. That was not meant for you."

I sputter. I stammer. I stomp and kick the brush. I've sworn enough curses to earn a hundred Aves at my next confession. And I have to bite my tongue to keep from earning a hundred more.

"They're getting bolder," William says with a grim laugh. "Last time it was just words, and words these days are enough to get a Welshman amerced."

A splatter of muck on sky-blue linen. Stains mocking fuller's earth already, and my father as miserly as a miller in debt. I shake my skirts and a shower of filth tumbles down. "A curse on every Welshman ever born. God be praised they're not permitted within the walls. Caernarvon is almost tolerable without any Welshmen in it."

"We will go house to house to collect this tax, *hafod* to *hafod* if need be." William draws his sword and nods us down the path. "No man wants to pay his taxes, but the Welsh must put their share forward, same as the rest of the realm."

We walk in silence for some time. William's bootsteps squish. Evilbeth and Aline creep like cats and leap at the smallest sound. Even Emmaline walks on her brother's very heels. William grips his sword till his knuckles whiten.

"I warned you," Aline snivels. "It's not safe anywhere in this dreadful place."

"It's not common for them to harry a *taxator*," William says over his shoulder, "but it's not unheard of. It's getting worse, though."

"You're a *taxator*?" I ask. "When did his Grace the king call another tax?"

William snorts. "This is the tax of the fifteenth that was called two years ago, demoiselle. Wales is not easy to tax. But his Grace the king will not give up. He beggared himself bringing the Welsh to heel. High time they repaid it."

"My father won't be happy to hear from you," I tell William. "He was on his knees with his paternoster for blasphemy for a whole se'ennight the last time he was assessed."

"Your father has naught to worry about," William replies. "Burgesses in the Principality are never subject to taxation."

"They're not? Not ever?"

"Heavens, no!" William laughs. "Nor are they required to pay a penny in tolls, not even market tolls."

I've passed that trestle on the mill bridge dozens of times, dozens of Saturday markets, and skimmed past the Welsh lined up for leagues with their grubby coins and wads of butter and baskets of eggs.

They must want to trade at the market pretty badly to stand in line for so long and part with their goods to pay tolls.

William insists on seeing me to my door. Aline is one massive scowl and Evilbeth is drawn tighter than a bowstring. Emmaline squeezes my arm and thanks me for coming.

"We shall have to meet again," Emmaline says cheerfully, as if William is not covered in filth and the rest of us skittish as colts. "When your maid has recovered, you'll come to my house and we'll spin."

Yes. My maid. My nonexistent maid.

I try to seem pleased at the prospect as I hurry toward my door. When I look over my shoulder, I catch Evilbeth's cruel, knowing smile.

POOR girl is almost dry. She lows as I milk her, but there's naught to be done for the heat that parches the soil.

There's even less to be done for Crown measures and market penny, and God help you should you seek redress. Fanwra from down the vale may never recover from that month on the gatehouse floor.

Almost a bucket of milk. Mayhap it will be enough. Silver in their palms and mayhap they'll leave us our cow. Part is better than naught. Even taxmen must know that.

Bucket in my hand sways like a hanged man as I set off toward that eyesore on the strait. Handle digs into my palm, gritty.

Take the long way. Fewer Watchers. And with any fortune, Dafydd will be waiting on the other path, the one the timber gangers use.

Saturday, and the roads are full of dusty feet and baskets on backs. Fall into step with them. Say naught. None of us do. Plod toward the castle. Toward the swarm of souls without the walls on the market common.

Horseback English ride, pressing horseflesh through the queue. Step away from hooves and heels. They watch, not us but our goods. They watch our hands to make sure naught passes between us. If we trade away from the walls, they're denied their share of our sweat.

If we trade away from the walls, they amerce us and take more.

English at the trestle looks me up and down. "Lastage, and market penny."

"Half measure milk instead?" My words in their tongue are purposefully stumbling, purposefully broken. It's never good to let them know what you know.

"Silver," says trestle English. "Or be gone."

Could bribe him. Others do. A heaping Crown measure, and the need for silver is suddenly weaker. But betimes the "gift" disappears and still they demand silver.

Slam the coins down before him. The whole trestle shudders. Horseback English turn, poised like wolfhounds. Trestle English narrows his eyes as he slides the coins into his palm.

Brace for the blow, standing to like a foot soldier. Some take special pleasure if you beg or cower.

But trestle English merely reaches across to chalk me, to keep the levelookers off. Mustn't flinch. Not a hairsbreadth. The milk will spill, and part is better than naught.

He chalks me across my tit, cups it, squeezes, smiles. Stand to. Not a hairsbreadth. Stare through him.

Eyes are stinging. Must be the dust.

Sway past the trestle, into the market beneath the walls. Find the other dairy girls, chalked over the tits same as me, the cheeses and butter and endless buckets of milk already ripening in the sun.

Flies in my milk. Scoop them out, cover my pail with what's left of my cloak.

And he comes through the crowd, damn him, golden and glowing like a war-band chief. My penance for a lapse in judgment I'd have back at any price.

Pull my hood over my eyes and slump, but it's for naught. Dafydd is already heading toward the dairy row.

"They charged me double toll again," he says cheerfully. "You can be sure it'll go in my next petition to the king. I'll tell him, 'Your Grace, not only is it unlawful, but I'll be obliged to court my beloved in my smallclothes.'"

He means to make me smile, so I try for courtesy's sake. But the walls cut a harsh shadow across the market, even at midday.

Dafydd kneels, pretends to examine the milk. "If they're resorting to such petty tricks, the nerve I hit is raw. My petition will eventually be granted. They cannot keep me out forever."

It isn't. It won't. They can.

"Caernarvon won't change unless we make it change," he whispers. "There's naught in the king's law that says a Welshman cannot take a burgage. All this ill is just the burgesses guarding their privileges. Changing anything takes strength, and I know no one stronger than you. I need you."

Choke on a sound, an animal sound. All the strength in

the world did naught for Da. "Changing anything takes sacrifice, and that's a luxury I cannot afford."

"When we're successful, you'll be able to afford all the luxuries to hand, and some you just dream up."

"That's not what I meant."

"I know." Dafydd lifts my chin with two fingers. "I love you. I want you as my wife."

Flinch. Remember despite myself. His gentle hand sliding up the small of my back, his warm breath against my neck.

Look down. My knees dig into sun-baked dust. A chalk gash over my tit.

Shake my head, curt, like a fist to the jaw.

"Why not?"

Two pennies poorer and naught to show, horseback English watch my hands, and above us all rise those purple-banded walls that can be seen for leagues.

He must notice how my eyes slice over the market, for he sobers and says, "It just wants one crack, Gwenhwyfar. Just one crack and then time will do its work."

It does want a crack. One dealt with knives and fists and red, raw anger. One dealt with the gallows in plain view. English understand naught else.

Pull my hood over my eyes, stare into the milk. Dafydd takes the hint and rocks to his feet. "Right, then, I'm off. But you'll see me again. I don't give up easy, you know." His voice softens. "Not for the things that matter."

Linen shuffles, and he's gone. Risk a glance after him.

Hate him for that square of shoulders, that proud, lovely stride.

This is why, Dafydd. Because you're a fool.

They come at night. Man-shaped shadows, sleek like wolves and faceless in the dark. By morning, something English will be in ashes or hamstrung or torn to pieces or just plain gone. They've come for Peredur's son, and Gruffydd ap Peredur goes to the door to give them his regrets.

"This is not the way." Gruffydd glances over his shoulder at Mam and me. "Too much risk and naught to gain."

"Your father thought otherwise." The voice without the door is harsh, disparaging.

"Aye," Gruffydd replies, equally cold. "Look what it got him."

Somewhere in the rafters is Da's spear. Slid there to wait by some comrade lost to memory while Da still hung from the walls. But Gruffydd does not look up. He meets the gaze of the hooded shadow and does not flinch or beg pardon when he tells the men to go with God, that for everyone's sake they were never here.

Gruffydd's tread is heavy as he makes his way fireside and collapses on his pallet.

Lie back on my own pallet as the fire sputters its last orange breath. Mam next to me sleeps as if she's dead already. Stare hard into the thatch, trying to make out some stray wink of steel. Just so I know it's still there.

Beastly-hot air drafts through my shutters. I'm in bed wide awake. My bare skin is damp, my bedclothes are damp, and Gwinny's going to have to air the linen again today because I'm sick to bleeding death of this sticky-foul cling of damp cloth.

I rise and open the shutters. The sky is a most lovely shade of deep blue. It was never this blue at Edgeley.

The house is silent. There are no thumpings in the rearyard, so no one has risen to prime the kitchen fire. It must be very early.

I should just go back to bed. But then I'll have to lie in mucky-damp linen.

I struggle into a shift and put on my bedrobe. I pad belowstairs into a hall that's much cooler than my chamber. By the rear door, there are two buckets full of water. Just as there should be.

Gwinny may be difficult, but at least she's a decent-enough servant.

The rearyard is deliciously cool. Salvo sleeps against the kitchen wall, sprawled like a dogskin rug. I check his water pan, then lift my leaky watering bucket off its peg, dip it into the bigger bucket, and swing it dripping toward my garden.

That's when I see the child.

The little urchin is wearing naught but a sleeveless shift and she's standing smack amid my neat rows of herbs. Her fat fists are crammed with bright blue borage.

"Yook," the herb-trampler tells me, "fow-ers."

My garden is pulverized. Stalks crushed, smashed, pulped, uprooted. Chunky little footprints criss and cross through the disaster, and in case there is some doubt as to who the culprit might be, this little thing is filthy knees and elbows and—saints preserve me—mouth.

The urchin smiles. She holds out the crushed borage, dirt dangling from the roots.

"You must be one of those tenscore Glover creatures from next door," I mutter. "Your rotten brothers throw mud at my laundry."

She smiles and opens her hand. Mangled borage falls at her filthy feet.

"You need to go home. Go away. Shoo. Back where you belong." So I can see what can be salvaged of this mess.

I point to the greenway that leads to the street out front, but the child makes no move to obey. Instead she stomps her stubby feet in what's left of my tansy.

God save me ere I have any babies. They are grabby, clingy little beasts who steal your figure and always want a ribbon or a wooden sword. And who sometimes make you die bearing them.

"Come with me, then." I rise and unstick my shift from my backside, then head down the greenway. The child doesn't follow. She's uprooting fennel and flinging it and chortling.

I consider dragging her by the wrist, but then she'd squawk and bring not only the house but all of Shire Hall Street to gape and snicker at me in my sweaty underthings when I haven't even washed my face or put a comb to my hair.

Cringing, I hoist the urchin up, one hand beneath each armpit, and hold her at arm's length. She doesn't protest. In fact, she giggles as if we're playing some game. I stagger through the greenway into the Glovers' dooryard, lower her gritty little feet onto the hearthstone, dust off my hands, and head up the path.

There's a pattering and she's right behind me, treading on my heels, grabbing at my bedrobe.

"No. You stay here." I shoo her back to the hearthstone as if she's a halfwit baby Salvo. "Stay. You stay."

She sucks in a big sobby breath and lets it out as a throaty whine that steadily grows in volume.

The sky is still a deep night-blue and all the buildings are black. Caernarvon is utterly still, like we're the only souls within.

She is really quite small. Too small to know better than to throw mud at laundry.

"Very well." I hold out a hand and she leaps at it. I am the most selfless Christian in all of Christendom. "Let's go back to my house. What are you called?"

The child doesn't answer. She's obviously not the sharpest little knife in the Glovers' brace.

As soon as we're back in my rearyard, she's tumbling away like a fat wobbly puppy. By turns she's carefree or intent on tiny things like dew on the greenery or the dregs in the pigling's trough. She giggles like a drunkard and spins like a whipping top.

I cannot imagine chasing a baby all day if this is what they're like, but whenever she runs up and hugs me, a sticky embrace made fierce and swift like an attack, I always hug her back.

The sky is still a deep sapphire when the row next door starts. There's a lot of thumping and the clatter of feet and someone shrieking like a lost soul. The Glovers must have risen and found themselves a child short, though how that's noticeable I know not.

I tighten my bedrobe. "Come, let's go find your mama."

"Mama," echoes the baby, and she takes my hand and toddles with me up the greenway, through the gutter, to her door.

No one answers my knock for several long moments, then a tousle-head boy peers out. He gives a great whoop and throws the door wide.

"It's Nessy! Mama! Nessy's here!"

Mistress Glover is at the door in moments; she scoops up the baby and squeezes her tight. Even with her great swarm of children, Mistress Glover kisses this small one and pets her hair and coos and embraces her again and again.

Then Mistress Glover turns her petting on me and hugs me across the shoulders as much as she can with children hanging off both arms and crowding at her skirts. She thanks me up to the heavens for bringing back her lost lamb, who she thought for sure was down the well or in the mill-pond or beneath the hooves of some beast.

I peel myself free and smooth my hair. "She was in our rearyard. I live next door."

"Oh, dear." Mistress Glover hoists baby Nessy on her hip. "I hope she didn't do you any ill."

My borage. My tansy, my fennel, eyebright, rue, lady's mantle, coltsfoot. All gone. A whole year's worth of herbs, stomped into pulp by small feet.

But Mistress Glover is regarding me doe-eyed as if I'm a saint and running a hand again and again over Nessy's thread-thin hair as the child snuggles against her mother's shoulder, so I grit a smile and say, "No trouble, Mistress Glover. Really."

My father presents me with a piece of fine linen. He struts around like a peacock, proud of his largesse.

"Now you can make a new altar cloth," he says cheerfully.

"A better one." And he stands there with his chest puffed out waiting for hugs and squeals.

I don't want a new altar cloth. I want my old one.

I hug him and thank him. I cannot muster squeals, but he doesn't seem to notice.

When he leaves, I pin the linen on my frame. It's soft and smooth, a clean panel just waiting for saints and holy figures, vine borders and spirals.

I stare at the linen and my throat chokes up. So I unpin the cloth, fold it carefully, and retrieve my spindle. It's possible to spin and cry. I've done it many times.

It's been raining for a solid se'ennight. This place has no seasons. Even summer is winter here.

Ned Mercer calls just as dinner is ending. His black hair is damp and tousled from the mist, and he asks my father if he might take me on a walk since the weather has finally turned from deluge to heavy gray.

Gracious, but he is lovely on the eyes.

And I am wearing a kirtle with two different stains on it.

My father squares up like a mastiff. "I think not, Mercer. Cecily is very young, and—"

"Can I go, Papa?" I know my father is thick, but not so thick that he doesn't notice a comely suitor doing his work for him. "Please? Getting out of the house would do me much good."

My father pauses. The war between paternal smothering and scrabbling for position in this backwater is plain in his every line.

Finally he says, "If you'd have it so. And only because you'd have it so. Mistress Tipley goes with you."

Ned inclines his head politely. My father calls Mistress Tipley, and in a moment she appears in the hall in a jingle of keys that rightfully belong at my belt.

I force down a scowl. A man should never see you scowl till after you're married. My mother used to say that whenever I was surly, but I rarely saw her so much as frown.

I kiss my father's prickly cheek, then Mistress Tipley, Ned, and I squish into the dull gray chill.

My hands are shaking. I grip my cloak and try to hide the worst stain, a dark gravy patch from breakfast.

Ned moves easily at my side, graceful as a wolfhound. He's speaking of the weather. I'm glad for it, since my throat is stoppered firmly and I couldn't speak to save my neck.

Mistress Tipley huffs and pants to keep up. Already she has fallen a stride behind. I take big steps to match Ned's pace even though I'm almost trotting.

Ned walks me past his townhouse, a brilliantly ochered structure across from the church. Through the window, I see a workroom much like my own, only this one is tinted a strong and living green. There's a big trestle table, and seated there is a well-groomed apprentice busily sorting skeins of silky-looking yarn.

The whole room smells like ginger and wool.

I could very much get used to it.

I'm fussing with some transplanted seedlings in my garden when Mistress Glover appears at the fence.

"Have you seen Nessy?" she asks.

"Sorry, no." And thank goodness for that.

But then I notice that her eyes are wild and her face is as pale as her wimple.

"I haven't seen her since breakfast," Mistress Glover whispers. "And she likes your house, so I thought . . ."

I rise and dust off my hands. "She's not here. Are you sure she's not just hiding from you? Playing a trick?"

Mistress Glover shakes her head. "Nessy is too small for tricks. Besides, I've searched the house from top to bottom. The lads have been up and down the street. No one has so much as seen her."

"She has to be somewhere nearby," I say soothingly, but my stomach is full of odd little pangs. "Let me ask my father if I can help you look."

Not only does my father give permission, he joins the search himself. "She could not have gotten without the walls on her own."

My father underestimates Nessy's ability to get places she isn't supposed to be.

But by sundown, we've knocked on every door and searched every empty lot and outbuilding. Mistress Glover is all but raving and Master Glover quietly sits on the threshold drinking claret. There's nary a sign of a lost baby anywhere in Caernarvon. It's as though she's vanished from God's green earth.

Nessy Glover is still missing. Hue and cry has been raised, but a formal search of the town by the constable himself and both bailiffs has turned up nothing.

Today they're dredging the castle ditch and both millponds.

The town is so tense, I nearly forego supervising Mistress Tipley's marketing. Men mutter in doorways and women don't tarry long at the well. Even children move about quietly. No frantic patter of feet and no shouting in street or yard. I breathe easier when we're safely home.

I search our rearyard for the fifth time, Salvo limping at my heels. Mayhap an impish golden head will pop out from behind the rain barrel, chortling nonsense baby words and oblivious to the panic she's caused.

No luck.

Around midday, Ned turns up on my doorstep. I've been changing the linen and my hair is in a state. I start frantically smoothing stray tendrils behind my ears, but he says, "I beg your pardon, demoiselle, but today I've come for your father. We must question the Welshry." He's slapping a sturdy blackthorn cudgel against his palm.

"But why?" I'm still fighting my hair into some kind of order and covertly biting my lips to redden them. "My father says Nessy couldn't have gotten without the walls."

"Unless one of those—people—abducted her," Ned replies with a tight, forced smile. "So we must, er, question them."

God only knows why anyone would want to steal a baby, troublesome creatures that they are. But I don't tell Ned this. Instead I bid him Godspeed and try to enjoy the back of him when I see him and my father off.

Caernarvon is still as a graveyard. Usually the streets are bustling and the gate is crowded, but the serjeants have closed the murage trestle and only burgesses may pass.

I know not what else to do, so I take a loaf of sweet bread to Mistress Glover's house. One of her sons silently shows me to the hall. The whole room is packed with women and the trestle is loaded with stews, cakes, and even a haunch of mutton studded with cloves. Mistress Glover sits ashen and dry-eyed at the hearth, her flock of sun-browned children arrayed like quiet dolls at her feet.

I stay as long as I can bear, then escape home.

My father isn't back from questioning the Welshry till long past curfew. I'm dozing before the banked hearth, but I leap up to hear the news when I hear him banging down the corridor.

Just one look at him and my heart sinks. They've not found her. Not even a trace.

My father is muddy to the knees and his forearms are badly scraped. He tosses a blackthorn cudgel into a corner and curtly bids me go to bed.

Dim, but growing louder every moment, is a clacking of clappers and the echoey thudding of drums. I make it to High Street in time to see a scruffy Welshman being rattle-and-drummed toward the castle by a crowd of raging townspeople. The bailiffs ride grim-faced and the Welshman must stagger behind them since he's tethered by the wrists to their horses, but he's hollering his innocence with every stumbling step.

At supper, my father is in high spirits and answers my question ere I can even ask it.

"Black Reese of Trecastell," my father tells me. "A vile brute of a highwayman who haunts the king's road to Chester, but he'll hang for the abduction and like as not murder of Nessy Glover."

"Like as not?" I ask hopefully. "They haven't found her body yet?"

My father shakes his head and pours himself a mug of undiluted wine. "Black Reese swears he's never laid eyes on the girl, but the bailiffs have him in the darkest hole in Caernarvon. He'll confess soon enough."

"Do you suppose he really did it?"

My father shrugs. "No reason he wouldn't."

I chew my bread thoughtfully. "If he did abduct her,

what does he gain by denying it? Would he not instead demand a ransom?"

My father bangs his mug down. "Jesu, Cecily, the burgesses are doing the whole castlery a favor by sending this cur to meet his Maker."

"But isn't it unlawful to—"

"Enough! The man is guilty of *something!*"

I nod slowly because I know better than to challenge that tone, but if Black Reese is to be hanged for something, it should at least be a crime he's actually committed.

THE priest's boy comes to the door. He asks if I know of anyone in the vale who is missing a baby.

Long past sundown. On my feet all day. Wrung out like a rag. But the word stills my hand on the kettle.

"Baby?"

The servant nods. "Girl-baby. Two milk-teeth on top. She doesn't say a word, so they don't know her name. Yellow curly hair. Like a little angel, they say."

"They?"

"A herdsman out in Llanrug found her. Cadwallon ap Goronwy. His wife is called Gwladys. No one they know recognizes the little lass. They've no idea what to do. They're too old to raise another." The boy shakes his head. "Poor little thing. Her mam and da must be frantic."

Girl-baby. Curly yellow hair. Like a little angel.

It cannot be. It's too far. And without the walls.

It has to be. Her mam and da *are* frantic.

Release a long breath. "The baby belongs within the walls. She's an *honesti* baby."

The boy crosses himself, babbles a string of oaths. "Christ help us. What'll I tell the herdsman?"

"Tell him . . ." Grit my teeth. No way out but through.

"Tell him to bring the baby to the Saturday market and hand her over to the gatemen."

The boy gapes. "I'll not! You're mad!"

"English will praise the Almighty to find the baby alive." Press a hand to my eyes. "Besides, would it be better for English to find the baby at Cadwallon's steading? They'll go croft to croft soon enough."

The boy shudders, reluctantly nods, takes his leave.

By dying firelight, look down at Mam curled like a stringy corpse beneath her blankets. *Honesti* mother had better thank God on her knees for the safe return of her child. It's a lot more than some mothers get.

MY FATHER has been given an office of charge. He says it's almost unheard of that a burgess so new to the privileges is entrusted with responsibility in the borough government, and he does his mad capering dance the length and breadth of my workroom before all the neighbors of Shire Hall Street.

I would we had better shutters.

He is now Officer of the Town Mills. He is charged to regularly visit the two mills, the one on the Cadnant and the one at Porth Mawr. He's to survey the grindstones and ensure that the millers take no more than their due and that the quality of the flour is acceptable. The Officer of the Town Mills is also required to regularly ride through both the castlery and the Welshry to ensure that no man has a handmill, and if any man is grinding his own grain, to bring him before borough court for amercement.

My father is very proud of his office of charge. We have a haunch of mutton and sage wine to celebrate. His office will give him something to do and keep him out of trouble. And hopefully out of my workroom, too.

Mistress Tipley and I are heading home with the day's bread when we hear an earsplitting shriek near the gate. I fling the bread at Mistress Tipley and fly toward the clamor.

Just within the gate is Mistress Glover—hugging Nessy!

Townspeople crowd around, cheering, blessing the baby, patting both Glovers as they hug and squeeze their errant child. I can barely see Nessy through the welter of arms and bodies, but her cheeks are pink and she's squealing merrily just as I remember.

I grin big as market day. God is merciful to sinners.

Nearby, three serjeants form a well-armed ring around an elderly couple, who cringe and glance about uncertainly. One of the serjeants clears his throat and says, "Master Glover?"

Mistress Glover looks up over Nessy's blond head. Her eyes are streaming and cold like a wolf's. "They'll hang with Black Reese."

I frown. If Nessy is safe, surely the burgesses will let Black Reese go.

The old woman says something in Welsh angled like a question. Her voice is a panicky stutter. The old man chimes in with a protest, calm but desperate. But the serjeants pay them no mind and jerk them toward the gatehouse.

Nessy appeared in my rearyard and tore up my garden. No one marched me off to be hanged when I brought her home.

I press close to Mistress Glover. "Mayhap we should ask them how they came to have Nessy."

"They *took* my Nessy," Mistress Glover growls. "When you're a mother, you'll understand."

"Look at her," I insist. "Nessy has been gone a fortnight

and there's not a scratch on her. It wouldn't be right to hang them with no cause. What if they *helped* Nessy?"

Mistress Glover looks down at her pink, healthy child for a long moment, then nods reluctantly. The elderly couple are manhandled before her and both begin a frantic chatter in Welsh.

"Speak properly!" Mistress Glover shrieks, and both of them cringe and fall silent and gesture with gnarled hands.

"I don't think they can," I say into the quiet that's descended.

"Then they hang!"

Mistress Tipley pushes to my elbow and bobs her head to Mistress Glover. "They're saying they found the baby eating turnips in their garden. They live all the way out in Llanrug and none of their neighbors recognized her. They had no idea she belonged within the walls or they would have brought her sooner. They beg you to show mercy."

I stare openmouthed at Mistress Tipley. She can understand Welsh!

"Nessy looks well fed," Mistress Tipley adds, "and look how clean her face and feet are."

Mistress Glover scrubs at her wet cheeks. "Oh, you lot deal with them!" And she turns on her heel and bustles up High Street with Nessy peeking over her shoulder.

I turn a pleading gaze on Master Glover while Mistress Tipley glowers at him, hands on hips, and at length he bids the serjeants to release the couple. The two poor souls lean on each other, faint with relief, then fly through the city gate as if the Adversary is seeking them.

If it had been my baby returned hale and plump, all but back from the dead, I would have at least thanked the people who fed and tended her.

Even if they were Welsh.

IT'S all over the Welshry. Gwladys and Cadwallon of Llanrug were as good as dead, accosted at the city gate with the baby they'd been wringing their hands over. The baby they'd been tending with the last of their milk and borrowed oatbread.

The *honesti* baby that castle English have been threshing the Welshry to find.

Gwladys and Cadwallon of Llanrug were as good as dead, sent to their fate by naught less than my foolish belief that English would celebrate the baby's safe return more than they'd demand vengeance for her disappearance.

But Gwladys and Cadwallon were spared because of an English girl who spoke for them brassy as you please right before castle English who would have strung them up then and there.

Mayhap they helped Nessy, she said. It wouldn't be right to hang them without cause.

And castle English stayed their hands.

They're saying it was the brat. *My* brat. Brattily Bratly of Shire Hall Street.

Gwladys and Cadwallon live. Their home intact. Limbs aright. Not even a bruise. For no other reason than the kindness of the brat.

Wait for her to crow and preen. But all she does is wrap a honey cake and bid me take it to the *honesti* baby next door.

The brat wraps the cake so carefully that it's hard to recognize her work.

For the second time in a year's worth of saints, my father has ruined my life.

"I've had the most joyous tidings!" he crows at supper over his plate of trout.

"Uncle Roger has died and we can go home to Edgeley?"

My father serves me a dark look. "No. Mind your tongue."

I bow my head and try to look sorry.

He brightens as he reaches for the nef. "The good news is that the lady de Coucy will be helping you learn to get along among the ladies of Caernarvon. On the morrow, you're to present yourself at her door at the ringing of Sext. Be sure your chores are done in the morning."

"Papa, no! I don't want to!"

My father pinches two fingers of salt from the bow of the small wooden ship and dumps it in his visorye. "Your opinion on the matter is acknowledged. The ringing of Sext. Don't tarry."

"I know all about how to run a household!"

"It's got naught to do with running a household, sweeting," my father says. "I might have taken the privileges, but there is more to being a burgess than I realized. I'll not have you at a disadvantage. Since you get on so well with Emmaline de Coucy, her mother has agreed to take you under her wing. So you will be attentive." His voice sharpens. "And well-mannered."

I nod miserably and push my trencher away. I'm not hungry anymore. "It'll serve no purpose. When we go home to Edgeley, I'll need none of these foolish town customs."

My father blinks rapidly and chokes. He must have taken too large a bite.

As Sext rings, off I dutifully go. A servant answers the door and directs me to the solar, where Emmaline is ruining linen with her disastrous needlework and the lady de Coucy is spinning. When she sees me, the lady sets aside her work with a faint jingle of keys. She's blinking rapidly, as if a dairy-maid has entered the solar, or mayhap her cow.

"Saints," the lady mutters, eyeing me up and down. At length she puts together a smile and gestures me in.

My father did not raise a cow. I lift my chin. I straighten my shoulders. I walk like a queen through the solar to stand before her, and I regard her steadily.

"Emmaline," the lady says, "what did this girl do wrong?"

Emmaline bites her lip, toys with a trailing stitch. She meets my eye and shrugs the tiniest helpless shrug ere saying, "The walk . . . and the look."

"Dare I hope you've even been to a town ere this one?" the lady asks wearily.

I unclamp my teeth from my bottom lip. "Coventry, my

lady. We spent a year there. We were waiting to go back to Edgeley Hall, but—"

"Right, yes. That grubby little manor in the midlands." She wrinkles her nose as if she's caught a whiff of manure. "Your father is a burgess of Caernarvon now. For good or ill, you're one of us, and by all that's holy you will not bring shame on this town."

I nod because I'm to be attentive and well-mannered, but may God Almighty strike me down ere I become anything like the ladies of Caernarvon.

The lady de Coucy puts me through my paces as though I'm a mastiff whelp. Walk. Speak. Roll over. Not like that! Bad girl! Nones is ringing when she finally lets me leave. It's all I can do to incline my head ere fleeing from her solar like a loosed felon.

I stomp up High Street, kicking rocks and hating everything because I'll be at her mercy every wretched Monday and there's naught to be done for it thanks to my father's conniving.

I look up and see *him*. The miserable Welsh vagrant who *looks*. He's driving a timber-laden cart toward the city gate. The horse strains against its collar and the load lists dangerously beneath the tethers.

I'm sweeping past, nose in the air, when a cart wheel hits a puddle and a curtain of filth sluices up and drenches my gown and it's too much and I whirl on him like a soaked cat.

"Saints above, look what you've done!"

He barely spares me a glance, harried as he is and tangled to the elbow in reins. "Demoiselle?"

"As if it isn't bad enough that— How *dare* you?"

He manages to still the horse, but the load slides drunkenly with each jerk of the cart. "Beg pardon, demoiselle. Bad roads."

He certes doesn't look sorry. And there's naught I can do for it. There's naught I can do for a lot of things.

I glare at him with all my hating, trying to kill him where he stands, but it isn't working. He's waiting like some half-witted hound, not seeming to notice how much I'm hating him.

Waiting. And shifting uncomfortably and glancing at the castle every few moments as if it's a boot poised to kick. "Er, by your leave, demoiselle?"

He's a head taller than I and strong enough to break my neck with one throttle, but he cannot leave till I say he can.

An English person has spoken to him and now he must await his dismissal. Like any dog.

And there's naught he can do for it.

"Demoiselle?" He tries that smile, but something in my face must stay him because he squares up and fixes his eyes over my shoulder as if I'm my father. "By your leave?"

I put a finger to my chin and hold it there, pretending to consider. Then I stare back at him, right in the eye, till he looks at his bare feet and not at me. Not anymore.

"Mayhap," I drawl, "if you ask nicely."

"*Please,* then, demoiselle." There's an edge to his voice, no hint of plea. "I'll certes be thrashed as it is."

Good. May it cut to the marrow.

"Very well, off with you," I say, and it's not out of my mouth ere he's whipping the horse into a smart trot. He does not look back.

I breathe in deep and smile for the first time since Sext.

I'm holding the reins of the whole world.

Going to Mass is now a critical part of my day, since I can walk past Ned's townhouse twice without it seeming untoward. From without, Ned's house smells of bread and woodsmoke. Betimes the shutters are open and I can peek inside.

What slivers of workroom I can see are clear and tidy; floors shining, walls wiped, the trestle clear and waiting. Nothing like Edgeley when my mother came to live there. Despite the passage of years, she'd tease my father about the bench she'd had to peel her backside from and the pewterware with dregs caked at the bottom those many years ago, and he'd gallantly sweep a hand over Edgeley's hall, now clean and humming and cheerful, all the better for its lady.

When I peek in the windows of Ned's townhouse, I must admit I'm a little disappointed. There wouldn't be much for me to do. I would gain a house like Edgeley was. There would be no need to make this house into Edgeley.

RHYS Ddu of Trecastell has still not been released from the gatehouse. It's hard to know whether to curse or cheer. Fewer men deserve hanging more.

But the gallows on the market common cannot tell felon from hero. They both hang the same and end up just as dead, especially when the hand on the rope does not change.

Know not when I first notice. Watched burgess land no longer opens up with endless nodding furrows of oats and barley. The crops are shriveled now, poor things, sodden and pulpy and twisted, as if the Adversary himself whispered in their little ears. Field after field. The ravens circle overhead, searching in vain for a stray kernel or grain. Betimes a priest walks among the furrows, flicking holy water and begging the Virgin to have mercy and intercede with the Almighty to lift the damp.

They'll still have to bring the harvest in. Some of it must be salvageable.

Gruffydd waits for me at the wood-edge long after twilight, thumbs hooked over his rope-belt, kicking dust.

Fall into step beside him. "They'll be hiring for harvest work any day now. You'll be at the front of the queue, right?"

He nods. His cheekbones stand out like fence rails.

English fret and mutter. The master spends days at a time at his stolen land, comes back pale and drawn like a corpse. The barges pole in from Môn with fewer sacks every day, and they pass the common wharves that stand idle to tie up at the Havering wharf, the Whetenhale wharf, the Grandison wharf. Grain that lands on private wharves, burgess wharves, might as well not even be.

And still Gruffydd meets me when day is dying slowly over the stone-and-mortar eyesore. Every day. Bite my tongue and bite my tongue until finally I demand, "You stood aside, didn't you? For one of those blasted toady—"

"They're not hiring for harvest work."

Stop. Close my mouth. Stammer, "Wh-what?"

"No harvest work." He gestures helplessly at the pulpy fields, the crumbly, damp furrows. "I'll try the wharves. The burgesses import most of their grain from Môn anyway."

Gape at him. "The wharves? Jesus wept, we haven't the silver for a bribe that big! Especially not when there's no harvest!"

Gruffydd hitches a shoulder. "Have you a better idea?"

Burn them. Burn every last damn one of them.

Let out a long breath, then dredge up a smirk. "At least we'll get to watch the bastards starve."

Gruffydd squints at the horizon. "If anyone starves in the Principality, it won't be them."

"We don't need their wretched barley. There's the cow. Milk and butter and cheese."

"For now." He smiles sadly. "Until the taxmen come. Then back she'll go to Pencoed. Or mayhap Plas Newydd. All the old estates are filling up with distrained beasts."

The old estates. *Your* estate, Gruffydd. And men like you.

"We'll buy her out of lien ere winter." Say it forcefully, as if force will make it so.

"Dafydd had a horse distrained against tenpence at the Easter collection," Gruffydd replies. "When he went to redeem it, Whetenhale told him fifteen."

Roll my eyes. "But that's Dafydd. He may as well brand himself and spare them the trouble."

"Go ask Fanwra down the vale how much they demand for her cow. Or Maelgwn ap Tudur, or Llywelyn ab Owain, or—"

Fling a gesture, and Gruffydd falls silent.

"Very well," he says at length, "if we cannot afford a workboon for the wharves, I'll . . . I'll find something. I just . . . I cannot bear to take work from any man with little ones to feed."

Da went out. Da never came back. Little ones learn to feed themselves. Little ones learn to *fight*.

"We need the silver, too." Speak quietly, because he means it. "We have Mam."

Gruffydd nods. "I'll find something."

Little ones look after the littler ones.

Take my brother's arm. It's warm and rough and dusty, his elbow bound with a ragged, blood-smeared cloth. He places his hand over mine for a long moment ere he pulls away.

My FATHER has learned about the outing Emmaline de Coucy invited me on after Mass. He leaps around my workroom like a mad fool, crowing with joy. Right before the big windows for all the neighbors to see.

My father can be such a trial betimes.

"And you'll invite her here, of course," he says. "You mustn't slight her by not returning the courtesy. You'll invite her, along with her cousin and sister-by-marriage and—"

"What? No!" My whorl clatters to the floor. "Please don't make me!"

My father frowns. He's going to insist because they're the Coucys. I cast about for something with half a chance of staying his hand.

"The linen is stained, the walls are plain white, the floor wants a scrubbing with sand, and there isn't a candle in the place." Square in the pride. "What would I even serve them? I would shame you, Papa, offering turnip broth and blackberry wine to daughters of the *honesti*."

My father folds his arms. "Honey, for wafers. And a mazer of good wine. But the walls stay white and we'll keep using pine knots and you can help Mistress Tipley scrub the floor and wash the linen."

Splendid. They'll take one look around this miserable

hole and mutter how presumptuous the *novi* are, placing themselves beside those who built the borough. Emmaline's coming would be bad enough. Aline and Evilbeth will split their girdles laughing, and their maids will snicker in chorus like chantry.

Oh, thimbles—the maids!

They'll know I lied about having a maid the moment they arrive, regardless of whatever perjury I come up with. And they'll laugh till they cry ere ensuring that every soul in this town knows of my airs.

Gwinny shuffles into the workroom with the broom. Her gray smock is stained with God knows what and tattery at the hem. She smells like goat.

No. There's no way.

My other choice is to stand humiliated before the sly and blackhearted daughters of the *honesti*.

All Gwinny has to do is hoodwink them for a single afternoon, but she must look the part.

I hurry abovestairs and rummage through my coffer till I find a moss-green kirtle given me last New Years by Alice's mother. The wretched gown bunches strangely beneath the arms and the color makes me look like a sick frog, but the cut is stylish and there are no patches and it doesn't smell of goat.

Even now, Saint Peter is recording this act of charity to my credit in his book.

I skip into the workroom waving the kirtle like a battle standard. "Gwinny!"

She sweeps around Salvo, long and even, and chuffs dirt out of the corner.

"Gwinny. Gwin-ny!"

She pulls the mound of debris into a pile, then looks me right in the eye as if we're the same.

Just as that mannerless wretch of a laborer did, the one who unloaded the pack train and *looked* at me right in my own yard. The one I cowed in the street. The one who'll not soon look at me again, should he have wit enough to study his lessons.

I wind my fists into my apron and make myself smile. "You're a fortunate girl, Gwinny. I'm giving you this gown."

Her brows dip. Her lashes flutter. And then she smirks. She actually smirks, the ill-bred hound!

At length she lowers her chin and the look is gone, replaced by the drum-tight mouth and blank birdlike eyes.

"You'll get your penny same as always." I hold out the folds of pond-colored wool. "This isn't payment. It's a gift."

Gwinny eyes first the garment, then me. She reaches hesitantly for the gown. I thrust the lot into her arms and beam.

"Good girl. Now put it on and let's see how it looks."

Once on Gwinny's back, the gown falls in graceful folds to the floor and the cuffs hang just over her wrists. And by all the saints if the color doesn't make her eyes glow like fish-ponds just after the weirsman's brush.

"There!" I clap my hands and grin. "Splendid. Oh, saints, mayhap this'll work. You hardly look Welsh at all!"

Gwinny stiffens as if she got a cold-water drench. She skins the gown off, leaves it in a pile on the floor, and puts on her gray smock once more. Then she goes back to sweeping.

I scoop up the kirtle and fling it at Gwinny. "Put that on! How dare you insult me so basely? Spurning a gift, a gift that's worth what you earn in a year."

Gwinny makes no move to catch the gown. It hits her shoulder and slides to the floor. She toes the folds of wool and closes her eyes for a long moment.

Then she retrieves it, strips off her filthy smock, and slides into the new garment slowly, as though it's a shroud.

"Good." I fold my arms. "For shame, Gwinny. Treating me this way when I seek to help you."

She collects her old goaty smock, folds it, and places it near the rear storage chamber.

"That new gown will be on your back tomorrow," I tell her, "and the next day, and the day after that."

She nods without looking at me and retrieves the broom.

I mutter a rapid prayer to any saint listening. Please let the *honesti* girls be fooled. Otherwise I will have to move house again or take up residence in the cellar.

Mayhap they won't come. Mayhap they won't want to be

seen with a *novi*. Mayhap Emmaline's father will forbid her. Mayhap William will forbid Aline.

If God Almighty has any mercy, none of them will come.

They all come. They bring their embroidery. Now we're sitting here in stifling silence while I try to think of things to say to daughters of the *honesti*, two of whom keep smirking and snorting and snickering whenever they glance my way.

Even their maids brought needlework. Margery and Maudie and May. The three maids sit in a row like little poppets on a bench dragged in from the hall. They sew shifts for their mistresses while my "maid" stands in the shadows like an effigy, smelling vaguely of straw.

Please don't let Gwinny ruin this. All she has to do is be still.

We've already spoken of the beastly weather. The way heat clings to floorplanks and leaves skin damp and sticky. We've spoken of William, Emmaline's father, my father, and Evilbeth's betrothed.

Now it's quiet. Sickly quiet. The kind of quiet that makes you stare at your needle and try to ignore the hair prickling at the back of your neck.

I clear my throat. I cannot stand it. "So . . . what are you all doing for Michaelmas Eve?"

Emmaline frowns. "Well, what else is there but—?"

"Nothing," Evilbeth cuts in. "That is, naught but silent

prayer and contemplation. And fasting. We fast and pray to honor the saint. Alone."

"But, Bet, you've forgotten the bonfire!" Emmaline wriggles and grins like a child on her year-day. "Oh, you'll love it, Cecily, there's naught else like it all year! There'll be cider and music and dancing, and if you're brave, you can put chestnuts in the fire and divine who your future husband will be!"

"As if that's likely," Aline mutters, squinting at a stitch.

Evilbeth glares at Emmaline, but Emmaline doesn't notice because she's toying with her half-finished veil and gazing dreamily into the hearthfire as if it's Michaelmas already.

I dredge up a smile. "That sounds lovely. At Edgeley, we'd crack nuts in the church. We could do that here."

"We could," Evilbeth drawls, "if we were *novi* and didn't know any better."

"I fancy a honey wafer." I leap to my feet and throw my linen blindly onto the bench. There's a tiny metal sound like my needle coming loose, but I pay no heed. "We have them all the time, so I'm sure there's a big pile in the kitchen. Gwinny!"

She shambles out of the shadows, tripping over her hem. She looks worse than usual, stains on her new gown and big dark rings around her eyes.

"Fetch the honey wafers from the kitchen," I say in slow, careful words. "Bring lots, because we always have enough to spare. And bring the wine. We're thirsty."

Evilbeth is smiling. My hackles go up like angry crows.

"*That's* your marvelous maid?"

"Yes." I cannot find my needle, so I pretend to stitch with small violent stabs.

"And of course she's one of *them*."

I'm burning to demand what business it is of hers, but I'm to be pleasant to Emmaline de Coucy and my father will flay me where I stand if I'm rude to any of the *honesti*.

Especially a Coucy.

"I should have known." Evilbeth snorts. "*Novi*."

"How can you trust one in your house?" Aline shudders. "Are you not worried she'll steal? Or break things?"

"The king would have the Welsh live cheek by jowl with us," Emmaline puts in, drawing her needle clear. "Within the walls and full privileges as burgesses. My father says there are already Welsh burgesses in Harlech."

Evilbeth sniffs. "It'll never happen in Conwy."

"A Welshman was supposed to live in your house, Cecily," Emmaline says. "Dav-ith something. Petitioned the king and everything. That's why your father was admitted so hastily."

Gwinny appears at the door, a plate of honey wafers balanced on her arm. In her other hand is a pewter mazer.

I can smell the honey wafers clear across the workroom. My father is still bemoaning the cost and swearing I'll not see another drop of honey till my wedding, but it's worth every penny because *I* am Croesus today.

As Gwinny approaches, I gesture to the coffer I lugged in from the hall and arranged before the benches, as if it's always there for the piles of honey wafers we always have.

Gwinny bends to set down the mazer and the platter of wafers tips. They're sliding, the whole pile, toward the gritty floor that never did get scrubbed with sand.

"No!" I lunge for the platter but instead catch Gwinny's wrist. She startles and corrects too much and the wafers fly like leper bread, scattering at the *honesti* girls' feet.

Evilbeth brays donkey-laughter and Aline cackles like a hen. Even Emmaline is tittering behind her hands.

I stare hard at the floor. At the wafers scattered there like fat straws.

All the honey in the house. Every drop.

"Gwinny, you clumsy ox!" My voice is high and choked. "I should have you cartwhipped! Look what you did!"

"No matter," Emmaline says cheerfully. "There are more wafers in the kitchen, right? She can just fetch another plateful. Here, Margery can pour the wine."

Gwinny studies her dirty bare feet, begging to be kicked and slapped into martyrdom for making a fool of me before these viperous *honesti* who built this vile town but haven't the manners God gave a goat.

Evilbeth snorts. "*Novi* and their airs. This little baby ought to unpack her dolls and go back to the nursery."

"Gwinny," I finally manage, "pick up the wafers. Margery can pour the wine."

As Gwinny kneels and collects the wafers, Evilbeth prods her shoulder with one slippered toe and shakes her head.

"Worthless," Evilbeth mutters, then narrows her eyes at me. "I'd dismiss a servant of mine on the spot for something so disastrous."

If I were really the lady of this house, I'd dismiss Gwinny in ten different ways and kick her rump on the way out. But as long as Mistress Tipley stands for her, and my father stands for Mistress Tipley, I'm stuck with them all.

I shake out my fists. I swallow till I'm fairly sure my voice will come out level. "Gwinny, I'll fetch the wafers from the kitchen. Give me the tray. You are excused for the day. Off with you."

She goes, and I make it to the rearyard ere angry tears get the better of me. I lean against the house and sob and hate Evilbeth as hard as any good Christian dares.

Then I take the platter into the kitchen, pick off the debris clinging to the wafers and stack them artfully back on the platter. They look a little mushy, but these girls deserve no better.

I splash water on my face, take a breath, then carry the tray back to my workroom.

My father had better appreciate all I'm doing for him.

Black Reese of Trecastell has turned up badly beaten near Llanfair, one of the very places he used to haunt to rob innocent travelers on the king's highway.

One of his arms hangs limply from the shoulder and his right leg is broken in two places. His tongue has been cut out and his face is swollen and purple. He draws breath in short raspy bursts when he's not coughing up blood.

Of course my father must relate this over supper. I push my trencher to arm's length.

County court conducts an inquiry. The bailiffs say they released Black Reese the very day Nessy Glover returned home, but the Welshry cries foul and demands that the porter of the city gates be called as an oathgiver to confirm the bailiffs' account of Black Reese walking out of the gatehouse in the same condition he went in.

The sheriff reminds them that Englishmen are not required to give evidence against other Englishmen when accused by Welshmen.

The bailiffs scoff that such a beating could come from any cudgel and that tongues could be cut out by any blade. Highwaymen make enemies of all, say the bailiffs, and such an accusation defames the borough when there's not a shred of proof.

That's when a Welshman seizes the plaint roll from the clerk and rips it to pieces, and the whole of the Welshry begins raising a row.

The sheriff shuts down the inquiry on the spot, and when he reopens it the next day, every man of the castle garrison stands behind him in a glowering, white-tabarded wall.

Black Reese dies halfway through the inquiry, but with

his tongue cut out he wasn't able to make oaths anyway. After deliberating for half an Ave, the sheriff rules misadventure and fines the Welshry for presentment, since Black Reese was one of theirs.

For the next se'ennight, my father does not ride the Welshry in search of handmills. He says he's feeling poorly, and he recuperates while honing his blade and carving a grip into the blackthorn cudgel that surely should have gone onto the midden after Nessy Glover's safe return.

Ned calls. He'd take me on a walk around the city walls. I turn my best Salvo-eyes on my father and he grunts his permission. While we wait for Mistress Tipley to wrap her bulk in her voluminous cloak, Ned thaws my father's icy scowl with an amusing tale of three Welshmen who attempted to arrange a buy-naught in the Conwy market. People were too frightened to refuse paying the market-penny, though, and someone turned them over to the bailiff, so the three poor wretches ended up rattle-and-drummed into the strait up to their necks and left there for two whole days.

My father is smiling by the time we depart.

Ned sets his usual stiff pace, which I can now easily match. Mistress Tipley is left well behind us, puffing and heaving in a most unflattering way. We turn up High Street and head toward the twin-towered gap in the wall that rises twice and thrice my height.

"The Water Gate," Ned says, smiling in that knee-melting

way. He strips off one glove and whistles with two fingers. A head bobs above us, then a rope ladder tumbles down. "You've not seen Caernarvon till you've seen it from the walls."

The hemp fibers are wet. And slimy. And the ladder sways like a three-wheeled cart and I'll fall and break my neck.

"Oh. You're frightened." Ned's face falls. "That's well enough. I just wanted . . . Never mind, it's naught."

"It isn't naught!" I crane my neck to catch his hangdog gaze. "Please tell me. Please?"

Ned glances at me sidelong through a windwhipped lock of hair. "It's just that I come to the Water Gate whenever I need some peace. And I wanted to share it with you because you're the only girl who . . . But I'd never see you frightened. Not for anything."

Something dear to him, and he's sharing it with me. And only me.

I seize the first rung. The ladder smells like pulp and brine. I take a deep breath and look up, and up and up.

A heavy hand falls over mine.

"I think not." Mistress Tipley pulls me away from the ladder and faces Ned, hands on massive hips. "You first. I'll follow the child up."

Ned shrugs. "As you would, mistress." And he shinnies up the rungs of rope like a squirrel.

I ignore Mistress Tipley and seize the ladder boldly, even through the stink of wet hemp will be on my hands till Christmas. Hand over hand I climb, clinging tight and not looking down. The ladder does sway like a three-wheeled cart, but I do not fall.

Ned helps me onto the wall. There's a walkway that runs behind the notches an armslength wide. The wind off the strait whips my hood back. He holds my hands longer than he needs to, rubbing my palms with his thumbs.

Caernarvon is below me now, rooftops and roads and patches of green all bound by the thin gray wall. Beyond are fields bristling with winter wheat, and farther away are dark purple jags where the mountains meet the sky.

The town does not look solid from up here. It seems naught but a jumble of toothpick thatch and parchment wall that I could grind beneath my heel while it begs for clemency. Or I could put my arms around it and protect it, like a child with a block castle when the dog walks by.

Mistress Tipley is still climbing the ladder. Her face is white as lye and her eyes roll around. She clings to the rungs midway up, as if the whole town is sinking.

"I can see why you like it up here," I say, and silently celebrate that my words don't come out choked or stuttery and I don't sound like God's greatest fool. "You have such a view of everything."

"You'd be surprised how many people have no liking for the walls," Ned replies, leaning on the stone in a way that lets our elbows touch. "I'm pleased you're not one of them. I didn't think you would be. You're too clever and brave."

My father thinks I'm restless and headstrong. The lady

de Coucy thinks I'm crude and dull. But Edward Mercer, burgess and *honesti* of Caernarvon, thinks I'm clever and brave.

"There's where I want to go, though." Ned gestures across the strait. "Anglesey. That's where the money is. That's where the *grain* is."

I parse his meaning. I want to seem clever. "We don't grow enough food here, so if you have extra grain over there, you could sell it at the Caernarvon market. You're a burgess, so there's no toll."

Ned grins at me, and hot shudderies clamor in my middle. *Thimbles*, but he is fair to look upon.

"Got it in one, demoiselle." He smiles slyly. "You know, a lot of men have no liking for clever girls. Me? I've no liking for girls who have vapor for brains."

Behind me, Mistress Tipley is struggling near the top of the rope ladder and Ned turns to help her onto the wall walk.

Now that she's here, Ned keeps a proper distance, but I can still feel the warm circle of touch on my elbow where he leaned against me. He is still speaking of Anglesey grain, but he often glances past Mistress Tipley and winks.

I am clever enough to know what this means, and betimes I am even brave enough to wink back.

Mucking the byre when I hear hooves on turf and a clatter in the yard. Hooves are never good. Hooves mean they've come.

Seize Mam's pallet and heave. It slides backward and my knees pop and stab pain. She stirs, groans, flails. Drag Mam on her pallet into the byre, just behind the woven wall.

Make it almost to the hearth ere the doorway curtain is torn away. Three men, and they must stoop. Stand my ground behind the firepit, chin up.

"Householder." One has a roll of parchment that he holds up to doorlight and squints at.

"Gruffydd ap Peredur." Never give them more than they need, and besides, know better than to tell them that Gruffydd is my brother and not my husband.

English peers at his list. "In arrears. The total owed is a shilling and threepence. The amount collected in June, threepence. Your man owes his king a shilling, sweeting."

They're leering, all of them, and they're treading in their heavy boots right where Mam's pallet was.

Lick my lips. "Fivepence we have."

"Movable goods assessed in the summer of the king's twentieth year: one cow, a dozen sheep, a pig, a set of bed linens, a cauldron, and a pewter spoon." English scans, lip curling. "Take the cow."

One produces a rope, strides to the byre, loops it about the cow's horns. When he leads her out, she nearly steps on Mam.

"And where's the fivepence, sweeting?"

I almost tell him how high he can hang himself. Just for that surge of righteous bravado that goes to your head like claret and puts the moment squarely in your hand.

Then I remember June. What that moment will cost.

So I kneel. Pry up the hearthstone. They're hovering. Crowding in. Hot and sweaty and damp.

Se'ennights of scrubbing and burned forearms. Fingers like bones from cold water, scaly and red as the Adversary's.

Hand over the packet of coin. Se'ennights, and it's gone in an eyeblink. Tucked into a fine wool tunic and bound for the English king's coffers. From him it came and to him it goes.

"Tell your man he'll have a chance to get his cow again when what's due the king has been paid," English tells me. Then they swing up on their horses and disappear, the cow trundling peaceably behind.

Tomorrow she'll be in some Watched field. She and all the other cattle taken against their king's tax. Past her I'll walk to the brat's, barely looking, for even intent is enough to land you on the gatehouse floor.

All that coin still owed, and back they'll come at Easter.

God only knows what they'll see fit to take next.

1293

MICHAELMAS

TO ☉

CHRISTMAS EVE

VEN ere I open my eyes, I know what day it is. Despite the dim light, I can make out the plinking of a lute and the high, shrill notes of a whistle beyond my window, and the whole house smells like roasting goose. It's Michaelmas!

I leap out of bed and wash, then I slide through the curtain into my father's chamber and check the bunting hanging from his window.

This far up, I can see over the rooftops of Caernarvon, row after row, all the way to the city wall and into the green beyond. The first hints of gold morning are broaching Saint Mary's, and the thatch roofs light up like firebrands.

Heavens, but for all its barbarism, this place is not without beauty.

Down below, in the yard out front, Mistress Tipley and Gwinny have laid out our largesse already. There are trestles with rows of steaming custards and piles of small birds in pasty crust for the fairgoers to help themselves. It will all be gone by Tierce, but we'll be the talk of Shire Hall Street for the sheer volume of food we've provided.

I go belowstairs and into the yard. At the trestle, Gwinny arranges fried lamprey in neat rows. Her cheekbones leap out of her face and her hand lingers over the meat, almost a caress.

No tenant at Edgeley ever looked so raw.

I comb my hair behind my ears. "Have something, Gwinny. Whatever you want. It's Michaelmas."

Gwinny hovers a hand over the pasties stuffed with spiced meat, easily the costliest and richest dish on the trestle. Then she cuts her eyes to me.

I nod cheerfully.

Without ceremony, Gwinny eats the pasty in two bites and licks her fingers. It's gone so fast I almost bid her take a second one. When I turn toward the house, her hand flashes between the table and her apron, but I say naught and head inside.

My father is rosy with ale and it isn't even Tierce. He bids me perch on his knee and pours pennies into my hand.

"Take Gwinny and go have fun, sweeting," he slurs, "but stay out of trouble."

I plow outside and grab Gwinny by the sleeve ere he sobers up enough to realize just how much coin he gave me.

In the street, I loose Gwinny's sleeve and we regard one another. Her bad humor will completely ruin my Michaelmas, but if she goes back to the house, my father will notice. He'll be upset that I'm roaming the city alone. And he'll come find me, drunk as Noah, and make a scene that will leave me twice humiliated before the *honesti* girls and him before Court Baron for disturbing the king's peace.

I sigh and gesture toward the road, and Gwinny looks as pleased to go as I must look to bear her company.

In High Street, we enter the fair proper, a solid wall of liveliness that chokes the wide street with stalls, carts, beasts, and children. There are baskets and woolen elbows and horse's rumps and glory but it's the Michaelmas fair!

And I have a handful of silver burning a hole in my palm.

I am in a better humor already.

I buy a big wedge of pandemain and slurp down mulled wine, giving Gwinny whatever I cannot finish. The treat seems to put her in a better mood, which cheers me all the more. I pet the silks and fondle the brocades and watch a trained monkey mimic a knight, a bishop, and a fine lady. I buy a new needle and a tiny packet of cloves and I'm eyeing a fine copper cloak pin for my father when I catch sight of a wretch I'd hoped never to see again.

On the corner, oozing among hawkers and dirty-footed shepherds, is Levelooker Pluver. The one who seized Nicholas and made me infamous before Court Baron with false charges.

Pluver wears a fine orange surcote and a tall floppy hat wrought in yellow. It looks like turds of butter. He's torment-ing a ragpicker, rooting through the poor wretch's rags and dumping them into the mud.

"That filthy swine," I mutter as Pluver seizes the ragpick-er's mangy hood and grinds it underfoot with one elegant boot. "Someone ought to teach him to study his lessons."

At my elbow, Gwinny snorts softly. "Will not happen."

I turn to her, chin high. "It should."

"What do you care?" Her voice is bitter like wine too soon from the cask.

"Justice," I say firmly.

Gwinny squints at me for a long moment ere she snorts again. "Mayhap. But given by who? You?"

I match her cool tone. "Mayhap."

She's fighting a smile, and it makes me want to slap her senseless. "You. Right. We'll see."

And Gwinny's off through the crowd like a hearthcat on the hunt, past shoulders and bundles toward Pluver, who is upending the poor ragpicker's cart. She glances over her shoulder and smirks as if she's caught me playing with dolls. Then she puts herself before Pluver and asks loudly if he's yet amerced a one-eyed brewster whose ale is watered and not up to scratch, and worse, has no license from the borough.

And it hits me—Gwinny is distracting him. She's daring me to teach him a lesson, as I said I would.

My father does not want to see the inside of Justice Court again.

But there's no filthy swine who deserves justice more than Pluver, and Gwinny will have to swallow that smirk.

I know just how to do it.

I circle wide, darting through the crowd and craning my neck, pretending to hunt for someone. Gwinny slants only one glance at me, then fixes her eyes on Pluver and raises her voice. Soon I'm behind Pluver, and his yellow-turd hat slides back on his greasy head as he aims gestures at Gwinny.

It won't really be stealing. He'll get his foolish hat back. Eventually.

In one motion, I rise on tiptoe, wick the hat from the filthy swine's fat head, and whirl it beneath my cloak as if I'm adjusting the drape. Then I move away as though I'm still hunting for someone, craning my neck and seeming peeved.

It's a few moments ere Pluver realizes he's bareheaded in a crowd of fairgoers, but by that time I'm watching from a good stone's throw.

Gwinny flings her hands up as if she's lost patience with Pluver, then stomps into the crowd. Pluver is patting his head and glancing around like a chicken with too much seed. He kicks at the mud and peers behind baskets and carts, all the while touching his head as if the hat will reappear through sorcery.

The ragman grins like a schoolboy as he rights his cart and scoops up sopping rags.

When Gwinny appears at my elbow, I move my cloak just enough that she can see the hat's fat yellow crown. She barely looks at it, though. She's staring at the ground, brow in knots, jaw working.

"You did it," she finally murmurs, as if I gave her a month off with double wages. "One of your own. And you did it."

"Not one of *mine*." I nod us toward the city gates, away

from the scene Pluver's making. "Justice for those who deserve it."

When we pass a massive dull-eyed hog tethered to a cart, I jam the levelooker's hat over the hog's ears and keep walking.

"Right enough," Gwinny mutters, "but how will anyone know the difference?"

I laugh outright. "Not by the smell!"

We move through every single handswidth of the fair. Gwinny isn't afraid to walk past the shady stalls that abut the city wall, the ones with goods of dubious provenance and therefore the best prices. She isn't even shocked that I suggest it. She doesn't protest that it isn't safe.

I suspect she wouldn't be afraid of climbing the city walls, either.

The sun is burnished and falling ere Gwinny and I return to the townhouse. Our shadows run out before us, tall and wispy like the banners of an invading army. Two faceless girl-shapes, heads lumpy from piled plaits, gowns fluttering about their feet like massive butterflies. They are so alike that betimes I must glance to be sure it's still Gwinny at my elbow, and not Alice or Agnes or Emmaline de Coucy.

Even though it's frigid in the workroom, I'm spinning before the window and ignoring my father. He's being completely unreasonable, denying me permission to go nutting. He says it's too wet and I might fall ill, but he says it while glancing at the blackthorn cudgel that's still propped in a corner.

Honestly, you'd think he's forgotten that the sheriff gave the ringleaders of that scene in county court a se'ennight on the gatehouse floor to study their lessons.

"Iiiiiiit's of a fair young maaaaaaaiden who's walking in the wood," I sing, badly, at the top of my voice so it will echo into the hall where my father is. *"Her voice was so mel-o-di-ous, it charmed him where he—*Oh, hey, Papa."

"Hay is for horses," he growls, gripping the doorframe. "What are you doing?"

"Singing." I smile and let my whorl spin. "Like Paul and Silas did while they were in gaol."

"They also prayed," my father replies through his teeth. "Try that. And you're not in gaol."

"Am I not? Can I go nutting, then?"

My father is growing steadily redder. "You're leagues too old to be fooling with such childish things."

"Fine." I tease out more woolen fibers. In a fortnight he will tell me I'm not old enough to go Catherning with the women, even though Mistress Glover already said over the fence and ten thousand bobbing blond heads that I could join her and Mistress Sandys and Mistress Pole.

My father's bootsteps clump down the corridor. I give him time to pour some ale and settle before the fire and let Salvo curl against his feet.

Then I warble, *"For if you stay too laaaaaaate to hear the plowboy siiiiiiiing, you may have a young faaaaaaarmer to nurse up in the—"*

The front door slams hard enough to shake the shutters. My father storms past, and by the look of him he's heading to the Boar's Head.

"Spring," I finish softly, and I let the whorl twist back and forth like a hanged man.

I enter the lady de Coucy's solar and drop my backside on the uncushioned bench reserved for me, but the lady drags me up by the wrist. She cannot believe I just shuffled into her presence like a plow horse after everything she's been trying to teach me.

"On my first day, you said my walk was wrong," I protest, and immediately wish I could have it back because it's not well-mannered in the slightest and the last thing I need is my father wroth with me when I'm trying to get him to buy me a new gown and all he can speak of is how we're going to eat this winter.

The lady puts one hand to her temple as if pained. At length she snaps her eyes up and demands, "What would you do if John de Havering walked through that door right now?"

She's regarding me so intently that I know she means to trap me. Should you behave toward a Crown official as if he's a borough official, God help you. Should you address someone as "my lord" instead of "your Grace," you may as well dump a privy bucket over his head.

Behind her mother's back, Emmaline catches my eye, then inclines her head and makes a tiny curtsey.

"Er . . . curtsey?"

The lady de Coucy's brows come down. "Do you even know who John de Havering is?"

I parse and parse. Surely my father has talked about him, mayhap even invited him to our house. Is he the sheriff? One of the other officers of charge? Surely not the constable of the castle—

"Oh, saints!" The lady groans and flings her arms wide. "He's only the justiciar of the Principality of North Wales, you ignorant girl! By the Virgin, I know not how you'll ever manage this if you're such a lackwit that you cannot even remember the simplest things."

"Mother, please!" Emmaline tugs on the lady's sleeve. "She's really trying! Mayhap all she needs is a little more help. I can go to her house and—"

"No!" The lady de Coucy rounds on her like a mastiff. "No, you'll not be seen . . . Sit down, sweeting. And *you.*" She turns to me with knuckles upraised, but at length she lowers her arm and regards me as if I'm a sodden kitten that's just been sick in her lap. "No. It's not your fault. Poor motherless thing. It's not your fault you were raised in a byre by a ham-handed oaf."

If John de Havering walked through that door right

now, I'd spit on him just to see the look on this shrill harridan's face.

She's naming borough and Crown officials, and she gives me such an eyestab that I echo them after her in as frosty a tone as I dare. Because my father may be a hamhanded oaf, but I'll not have it said that he raised a lackwit who is not clever and brave enough to hoodwink a shrew with vaporheaded compliance.

Sacks appear one by one in our shed. They're full of milled barley and wheat and oats. I ask my father about them. He says the millers give him grain as part of his office of charge.

The millers must like him mightily if they gave up a share of the thumb's depth they've wrung from everyone else.

It darkens earlier now that the season has changed. Mayhap the millers will be more accommodating, now that it's harder to be seen.

Knuckles against the door. And wait.

The Porth Mawr miller peers out. "You again."

Hold up the sack without a word.

He puts out his hand for the penny, for my se'ennight's worth of sweat.

Jab the coin into his hand.

The miller leaves the door ajar while he clunks about within. Then he thrusts out the sack, and it sways in his meaty grip like a wrung-neck chicken.

The sack is light. As if it's empty. Peek in. There's barely a dusting.

"Th-this isn't half what my penny brings." My voice is low and raw.

The miller spits. "It's what your penny brings now, after that worthless harvest. What will you do, call the Watch?" He laughs, ugly. "Off with you."

Raise my voice. "Give me my due."

"God rot your filthy soul, you ungrateful—"

Something hits my back hard and I'm pushed into the mill and harsh commands echo and feet scuffle in straw and my sack gets ripped from my hand and I'm face-first against the wall, gasping for breath.

A forearm across my shoulders and a hand at my lower back hold me pinned. Limewashed wattles gouge my cheek.

"Right, then, miller. Is this girl a burgess, pray tell, or are you trading on an unlawful day? And after sundown?" A cough of laughter. "Even better."

The arm at my shoulders pivots and a hand reaches beneath my underarm and cups my tit. Hot breath dampens my ear. Nipple gets pinched. Rubbed.

"What else can I amerce you for?" Heavy bootsteps clump across the room. "Will I find sawdust in these sacks?"

Something smashes. The miller cries out in dismay. Then there's a heavy sound, like a quartermeasure sack hitting the floor, and laughter. Several men, including the one pinning me.

The miller will get a fine. English will give me irons and time on the gatehouse floor. Or worse.

"I've done naught wrong," the miller says, but his voice quavers beneath a try at strength.

More laughter. Whoever's holding me rubs his groin against my backside, slow and deliberate. My hipbones grind into the wattle. He grunts softly.

"I believe I'll let the constable decide what you've done. He'll taste this flour and—"

"Saints, this sack of flour has opened, my lord." The

miller's voice is shaky. "I have no use for it. Why do you not, er, dispose of it for me? I would be in your debt."

Grip stray strands of wattle. Press my forehead against the wall. His grunting grows louder and the hand on my tit squeezes and rubs.

"Come. This mill is in order. Except for that open sack. Leverdon, take it to my shed."

Wince at one last grind of hips as he rocks away. Footsteps echo, and there's a whuffle of door.

"Whore, this is your fault! Show your face here again and I'll make you sorry!"

The miller seizes my collar and arm, gripping so tightly I cry out. Stumble out the door as he throws me.

Land, hard, on rocky ground. Lie crumpled there a long moment. Then struggle up and limp home.

Full dark now. Empty belly. Empty hands.

Gruffydd pushes roughly through the steading's doorway. "Dafydd's with me. Don't even start, hear?"

Bristle at my little brother ere I get a look at Dafydd. His face is raw and bruised, and he limps inside while Gruffydd hovers at the curtain, peering out.

Blink and blink and finally find my voice. "Wh-what happened?"

"I was well met last night," Dafydd growls. "Hauled out of bed and cudgeled something fierce. My door kicked in. My whole place sacked. Thatch everywhere."

"Jesu, why?"

Dafydd smirks. "My prospective neighbors within the walls wish to inform me that continuing to petition the English king for a burgage in Caernarvon is an endeavor to be conducted at my peril."

Fight to stay calm. Know not what else he expected. Especially after what happened at county court.

"You cannot stay." Say it kindly, but brooking no refusal. "They watch this place. Because of Da. They'd love an excuse."

"I'll certes put that in my next petition to the king. 'Your Grace, mayhap it would interest you to know that the officials who govern in your name visit the sins of the father upon his innocent children.' It'll go right after 'It troubles me to report that Caernarvon's gatehouse is enchanted. Upon leaving, men are rendered invisible for a fortnight, then turn up fatally beaten. At least, that's what your bailiffs would have you believe.'"

"Please." Regret my soft words already. Giving Dafydd anything is like oil on fire, and nay is easier said in blade-edged tones. "If they find you here, we'll all *wish* for time on the gatehouse floor."

Dafydd moves to rise, but Gruffydd at the doorway gestures him down.

"Nothing yet," Gruffydd reports. "Mayhap we lost them. That's enough, Gwen. Now's not the time."

Fold my arms. "Oh, come now, it's not the first time the

burgesses thrashed him, is it? Nor will it be the last. And I've no liking for this trick—"

"Gwenhwyfar." Gruffydd's voice is low and fierce. He's angled in the doorway like a beast in the furze. "Enough."

They're both muddy to the knees and covered in brush. Tense like foxes at the horn. Neither of them is smug.

This is not a trick.

Let out a long breath and summon brook-naught words, but one sidelong look at Dafydd and my voice betrays me with its catch. "The English will not tolerate your antics forever."

Dafydd straightens. "So be it. It's unlawful, what they're doing, and someone has to stand against them or the king will never know."

It makes no sense to stand when it will change nothing.

Gruffydd leans inside, eyes wild. "Go. Now. They're coming up the hill."

Dafydd runs a hand down my cheek ere I can pull away. His touch is warm and gentle, curse him.

By the time English cudgel into my house, Dafydd is gone into the greenwood while Gruffydd and I stand elbow to elbow, bracing to be questioned.

My FATHER is having winter firewood loaded into our rearyard. Cartload after cartload, and all I can hear is clumping hooves and blasphemy and the clatter of wood on wood.

I have never made a more crooked seam, not even ere the age of reason.

They must be quieter.

I stomp through the hall and into the rearyard to make them. The back door rattles on its leather hinges when I kick it open.

It's *him*. Of course it is. The one who *looks*. The one I made study his lessons, right in the middle of High Street.

He's chopping a massive heap of wood. With one smooth swing of his ax, he splits a piece, then reaches for another chunk while rolling the ax behind his shoulder. By the time his ax is upraised, the next piece of wood is on the block and ready for splitting. Again and again, fluid as a carole dance.

The last time we met, he was not sorry. He stood there in the High Street not being sorry for my gown or my convenience or his own brazen behavior in defiance of the king, who asked us to come here to teach them to behave.

Today he will be sorry.

I hook my hands behind my back and saunter toward him, swaying my hips and pushing my chest out. I stand just out of the way and watch him swing the ax up and bring it down.

He glances my way, startles like a cat, then whips his eyes back to his task.

He does not *look*. He *dares* not look.

And there is naught he can do for it.

"G'morn," I say sweetly.

"Better to you, demoiselle." He does not break rhythm or turn in my direction.

"What are you called?"

The ax comes down crossways, glancing off the chopping block. As he recovers and hoists the blade onto his shoulder, he mutters, "Gruffydd ap Peredur, demoiselle."

"Griff-ith," I repeat in my flattest English way.

He grimaces, shakes his head the smallest bit, then brings the ax whistling down.

I peer at him as if he's a hairy insect in my porridge. Let's see how he finds being looked at.

Under my scrutiny, his cuts become steadily less even and betimes he must chop the same piece twice. Betimes the ax must rest on his shoulder while he fumbles for another piece of wood.

"Begging your pardon, demoiselle," Griffith says to his chopping block, "but is there something you've come for?"

"Not particularly." I idle around to his other elbow, all hips and teases of ankle. "I've a right to be in my own yard, do I not?"

He scrubs a wrist over his eyes while the ax weighs down his shoulder. "Right aye, demoiselle."

I let him chop several more pieces, reveling in every wavering upswing and crooked cleave. One piece he must cut thrice, and he nearly crops a finger doing so.

"One reason we're here is to teach your lot to behave," I muse. "The king would have it so. And you're always looking at me. It's really quite rude. As if you really haven't studied your lessons at all."

The ax comes down hard, the blade half-buried in the chopping block. It takes Griffith nearly an Ave to work it free. Once he does, he looses a long breath and begins his rhythm anew.

"There must be some mistake," he finally mutters. "I've no idea what you're speaking of."

"Oh, I think you do. You're always looking at me. Now, let's see here. What could the reason *possibly* be?"

Griffith's expression darkens. He grips and regrips the ax, but when he speaks, his voice is quiet and level. "I must get on with my task, demoiselle. By your leave."

"Mayhap you look at me because you think I'm comely." I twitch the hem of my gown as if I'm going to lift it.

A look of panic crosses his face and he swipes a chunk

of wood, heaves the ax onto his shoulder, brings it down fiercely. Another piece, then another, as though all the demons in Hell are driving him like a mule.

"Do you?" I brush his shoulder with my handkerchief and he leaps as if stung. "You'd best answer."

"I . . . cannot . . ."

"So you think I'm plain." I make my voice all warpy like I've been weeping and throw in a stifled little sob for good measure. "I think I'll run into the house crying. My father will doubtless wish to know what's amiss. And he'll look into the yard to see what could possibly—"

"Oh, Christ, no!" Griffith sinks the ax into the chopping block and drops to his knees at my feet. "Demoiselle, please! I beg your pardon! Forgive me!"

I look down on him, right in the eye. And I smile. "Again."

Griffith closes his eyes, there in the mud on his knees.

Where he belongs.

"I beg your pardon." His voice is raspy, uneven. "Forgive me."

"Much better." It occurs to me to pat his head as though he's Salvo, but instead I angle my hand down in the *free dog* command. "Right, then, on with your task."

It takes Griffith most of the day to cut the wood. He cannot regain his rhythm. He's too busy glancing at the back door as if it's the gallows.

Ned comes to supper. My father is warming to him, for he tells highly amusing stories and always brings a pottle of very good hippocras.

Tonight Ned has a good tale of a Welshman who thought to avoid paying market penny by means of trickery. The Welshman wanted to sell goats outside the borough market, so he had a handful of reeds that he sold for the price of a goat, and if you bought his reed you'd get the goat for nothing.

As the bailiffs fell upon the Welshman, he protested that it was quite legal to sell reeds without license. It did not avail him, though. The Welshman's goats were distrained and he sits in the gatehouse awaiting gaol delivery, accused of defrauding the borough.

Tonight, along with his customary wine, Ned brings us a goat. She's in the rearyard tethered to the pig byre. Soon we'll have cheese every day, and mayhap some extra to sell at the market.

I sit at Ned's right. Beneath the trestle he leans his leg against mine.

I am warm to my core.

Then Gwinny tips a platter of custard in Ned's lap. He leaps to his feet and curses like a wharfside ganger. My father nearly bursts his belt laughing.

"Gwinny!" I gasp for words. "What—how could—?"

I'm still stammering like an addlebrain when Gwinny

serenely topples a mug of wine into Ned's boots and flicks gravy onto his surcote as she wipes up the spill.

Ned makes curt apologies to my father and leaves in a huff. He doesn't even glance at me on his way out.

If I wasn't unmarriageable ere this, I certes am now. And it's all Gwinny's fault, the clumsy lackwit.

She will pay for this.

Despite Mistress Tipley's feeble protests, I set Gwinny to shoveling the privy, scrubbing pots with lye, scraping hair from skins. While she's at her labor, I follow her from chamber to kitchen to hall, shouting how she ruined me and how she'll never get a moment's peace in my house and how fortunate she is that I cannot give her any worse than she's already getting. Gwinny leaves every day pale and wrung out, limping, hands bleeding.

It's naught she doesn't deserve. And she'd best get used to it, for I'll be cold in my grave ere I forgive her this.

Aline and Evilbeth are leaving Caernarvon. Emmaline begs me to come over and see them off with her.

"I'm going to weep and weep," she explains in a quavery voice. She clutches a handkerchief with stitches so uneven I can see them a league away.

I can think of no sight more welcome than that of those two vexing shrews growing smaller on the horizon, so I agree.

There's a knot of riders before the Coucy townhouse, but Aline and Evilbeth have not yet mounted. They stand with Emmaline shoulder to shoulder, their foreheads pressed together, clutching one another's forearms.

Promising, like as not, to be friends forever, no matter how far away they are.

Finally, reluctantly, they pull apart.

"Godspeed," I say civilly, nodding to Aline and Evilbeth. It's surprisingly easy to be pleasant now that they're leaving.

"I'm going to miss you both so much," Emmaline chokes out.

"You'll see us this time next year," Evilbeth replies. "Remember? For my wedding?"

Emmaline sniffles. "I suppose. In the meantime, Cecily will keep me from missing you."

Evilbeth cackles. "You certes won't have to worry about her getting married out from under you."

I glare at her ere I can stop myself, but Evilbeth only barks out a harsh laugh. She must have heard about Ned.

Rot that Gwinny, anyway.

Evilbeth and Aline mount their horses and ride with William and his companions out of Caernarvon. Tears stream down Emmaline's face and she dabs at them with her dreadfully stitched handkerchief. Even though I've never been happier to see anyone leaving, Emmaline's tears are making my own eyes sting.

So I say, "Would you come to my house, Emmaline? I must comb fleeces, but you could help."

Emmaline brightens, but the lady de Coucy pulls her toward the gilded Coucy townhouse and says stiffly, "Emmaline is occupied. You mustn't presume on people like that. Go on, now."

I'm burning to ask the lady de Coucy if a good woman of Caernarvon refuses comfort to a friend who's obviously in need of it.

But that wouldn't be well-mannered or attentive, so I stomp all the way to the townhouse, thanking God Almighty and all the saints that these customs will be easy to forget once I'm back home at Edgeley Hall.

On Saturday, while I'm supervising Mistress Tipley's marketing, I catch sight of Ned's russet cloak whipping into an alleyway. Mayhap I can salvage his attention. Mayhap all is not lost. I duck in behind him to beg his pardon for Gwinny's unforgivable behavior.

And I freeze.

Ned has a girl pinned to the wall and she's weeping something in Welsh while he scrabbles with the folds of her gown.

He looks fierce and terrible. Not at all fair to look upon.

I back out of the alley and walk home so fast my legs tangle in my skirts and I stumble unattractively. The hall is empty save for Salvo curled on his pallet near the hearth. I sink next to him and run my fingers through his warm gray hair, and he whuffles in his sleep.

Salvo came to Edgeley with my mother when she wed my father, and the hound did not like her out of his sight. My father says Salvo had to be tied in the hall for the first month of their marriage, so sure the poor beast was that his mistress was in mortal danger behind the bedcurtains.

My father is better than he could be, but my mother could not have known that when she stood with him at the church door.

But now I know something about Edward Mercer. And I'm too clever and brave to let it stand.

The linen my father gave me lies folded over my embroidery frame. Betimes I take it out and pin it, but then I only stare at the smooth, creamy expanse.

I keep waiting for my father to ask when I'm going to embroider something on it, but he seems to have forgotten he ever gave it to me.

Mistress Tipley comes into the hall. "Edward Mercer is here to see Cecily. He'd take her riding."

My father looks up over the knife he's sharpening. He's smiling, wary but interested.

There's naught like justice well served.

I make a greensick shudder. "Tell him to be gone. After what he did, I'll have no part of him ever again."

My father lowers his knife. His whole face goes granite. "What did he do?"

Mistress Tipley's eyes are wide. "Naught, my lord, I swear it. I've been with them every moment."

"Please don't make me speak of it." I cast my eyes down, pitch my voice calm with just a hint of disgust. "The mere thought of him turns my stomach."

I watch my father carefully over my mending. Sure enough, his face is darkening to that dangerous shade of plum and his fists are flexing like a plowboy's. He rises, rams the knife into its scabbard, and storms from the hall. I jumble my linen into a wad and hurry to the workroom window to get a good view.

By the time I crack open the shutter, Ned is already in the middle of Shire Hall Street, flat on his back in a shin-deep patch of mud. My father advances, wroth as a sunburned hog, with fists at his sides while Ned scrabbles back on his elbows.

I wonder if Ned will still like clever girls in an Ave.

My father hauls him up by the collar and bawls, "You worthless cur, don't you ever get within a stone's throw of my daughter again unless you want more of the same!"

"Wait—I know not—"

"If you value your manhood, stay off my doorstep! Now be gone!"

The front door clatters. I slam the shutter home and dash headlong for the hall. By the time my father huffs back to the hearth, I'm on the bench with my mending, all big eyes and curious frowns.

"Whatever happened, Papa?"

"Naught, sweeting," he gruffs. "He'll not bother you any longer. Should have known better. But it's done now."

I narrow my eyes and smile to myself.

Gwinny slides into the hall and begins to sweep. She is smiling narrow-eyed like me.

I think of the girl in the alley, tear-streaked, mud-hemmed, sobbing in Welsh.

Mayhap Gwinny is just as happy as I am to see Ned get his justice right in the middle of Shire Hall Street.

Mayhap what she did at supper was not an accident.

Later, when she's clearing up the bread and cheese, I seize her sleeve. "You knew about Edward Mercer, didn't you?"

She swipes some crumbs into her palm. "How could you not? He's infamous."

My stomach rolls.

"I'm glad you spilled all those things on him," I say firmly. "And I . . . regret that you were punished for it."

Gwinny stacks trenchers without looking at me. "Well worth it. Justice for those who deserve it."

Like Levelooker Pluver.

And there is naught like justice well served.

"I'd take back your punishment if I could," I tell her, and I mean every word.

She flings crumbs into the fire, stoops to give a stray crust to Salvo.

"Gwinny?" I take a breath. "Thank you."

Gwinny swivels, regards me as if I just offered her an ell of brocade. At length she nods, reluctant, as if she's heard something she never wanted to hear.

GRUFFYDD brings some bread. Gnarly. Half moldy. He won't say where it came from. Have learned not to ask.

Most of the wretched bread soaks in hot water for Mam. Cold saps the life from her. It takes more to keep her going in winter. More food. More fire. More cheer and old tales from nursery. More lies.

What's left we eat, Gruffydd and I. We crouch near the fire across from Mam. We do not speak. We say it's because we might disturb her. It's really because we don't want to speak of what's left to speak of.

Crown measures.

Men like Tudur Sais.

Pencoed's English lord.

When Gruffydd lifts his bread to take a bite, I mark the red crescents around his fingernails.

His fingers are bleeding. They have not bled in years. Not since his first few se'ennights of hard labor when we all wept in our sleep.

Seize his hand, hold it firm when he struggles to withdraw. Peer close. The skin around his fingernails is torn bloody. He's biting every finger till it bleeds.

This is not from labor.

He pulls his hand back. "Let it lie. I'll not speak of it."

"It's the wharves, isn't it?"

Gruffydd bites a finger.

Mutter a swear. "Walk past those Chester merchants twice and they think they own you. They might as well, since the Crown turns a blind eye to—"

"I *should* have paid the boon and worked the wharves! Then I wouldn't . . ." Gruffydd scrubs a hand over his face. "I have work. For now, anyway." He laughs mirthlessly.

Eye him. "Beg pardon?"

"It should have been simple work. And it was, until the daughter of the house decided on some sport." He swallows hard. "I did naught wrong. But it won't matter, will it?"

Christ help us.

"Thank your saint, she tells me. My father has all kinds of work that needs doing, and you're just the man for the job." Gruffydd laughs again, hollow. "It's only a matter of time ere someone comes into the rearyard. All he'll see is a burgess's daughter alone with a Welshman, and she knows it well."

Fist up both hands. "Quit. Don't go back."

Gruffydd doesn't reply. We both know why.

"There's other work. There *has* to be."

"Not if I say one of them nay. Especially not if I say *her* nay."

Sink back on my heels.

Mam's low, throaty breathing seems very loud.

Slide next to Gruffydd and put an arm about his shoulder. My little brother buries his head in my neck and his whole body shudders with a muffled sob.

He wept when they came for Pencoed. He wept when Mam stopped knowing who we are. He wept every night of that first month when he stood without the walls in the shadow of Da's swaying corpse, waiting for work.

I squint into the rafters until a telltale wink of steel looks back.

A FORTNIGHT ere Christmas, Nicholas comes roaring up before the house. He's brought a packet of royal missives for the mayor of Caernarvon, and he's permitted to remain until Epiphany.

There's a young man with him, and it's several moments ere I recognize my younger cousin. Henry actually looks like a man, furry across the cheeks and broad through the shoulders. Not the hare-toothed oaf with tousled hair and dirt beneath his nails who told one too many landlord's-daughter jokes.

I embrace them both twice and bring each a mug of hot cider while my father bids them come near the fire to tell the news.

"Mother's piles are acting up again," says Nicholas, as if my aunt Eleanor would like this information made public. "The miller's wife bore twins and had to swear her fidelity on the gospels. Agnes got married. I reckon there's some hope yet for you to unload this minx of yours, Uncle Robert. Someone saw the Adversary in the wheat field. Oh, and Father's brand-new bay mare went lame. I warned him not to buy from that . . ."

Agnes got married.

I slip out of the hall and drift into my workroom even

though it's withering cold, and I sink down before my empty embroidery frame.

They're both wives now. When they'd merely been far away, they seemed within reach. Now that they're married, they're gone for good, no matter what we promised.

Bootsteps behind me. Nicholas clumps into the workroom and shudders dramatically. "Brrr! Why do you not come by the fire, Cesspool?"

"That's all right. I like it here."

Nicholas kneels at my elbow and studies my empty frame. "She's happy, you know. Agnes. Alice, too. They live just around the corner from each other. In and out of each other's kitchens all day."

Just like a man to say the wrong thing and not know it's the wrong thing.

But Nicholas seems to realize something is amiss. "Mayhap this will cheer you."

He offers a small parcel of grubby linen. Within are skeins of embroidery thread. A whole fistful, every color I could want. Even gold and silver. Good thread, too, not that coarseweave that bloodies your fingers. I squeal and clap and throw my arms about him.

"I know you were deprived of an altar cloth," Nicholas says with a smile. "Nothing could replace that, of course. But this will help you with another one."

Nicholas pulls plaits and laughs too loud and blames farts on Salvo, but he'll be here to hang the holly and ivy and light candles and offer me his elbow when we walk to Christ's Mass.

Henry has come to see Caernarvon. Nicholas has told him of the liberties and privileges given to burgesses, and Henry is weary of waiting for the chance to become a master goldsmith in the Coventry guild.

My father decides to show Henry the sights. After a little pleading on my part, my father relents and permits me to join them. We pass the Justice Court, the Boar's Head, and the murage trestle, my father rattling on about no tolls and cheap labor, until at last we find ourselves without the walls at the endowed cropland.

Henry stands openmouthed at the neat furrows of icy clods. "All this is yours?"

"Twelvepence a year," my father says. "No service owed. Held by simple burghal tenure."

Henry whistles low, shakes his head.

From somewhere nearby I hear a small noise I cannot place, so I move into the furrows and seek it. It sounds like a lost puppy, mournful and urgent. Mayhap my father would allow me to keep it. Salvo might enjoy a little company.

I top a small rise and stop short. Lying in the dirt, bound wrist and ankle, is the boy whose task it is to ward away crows. There's a filthy gag in his mouth and he struggles against his bonds. His hair has been so harshly shorn that his scalp is half torn away. Even his eyebrows are gone.

"Hey, Papa." I force my voice even. "Papa, Henry, I think you should see this."

My father and Henry cut the ropes in a trice and help the poor lad to his feet. He scowls at them and shakes off their hands, muttering in Welsh.

"Who did this to you?" my father demands.

The boy stares mutely, defiantly.

"It was those whoresons with blackened faces, wasn't it?" My father mutters another foul swear that unfortunately I don't quite catch. "Bastards think they can wreak violence on the few of you with half a measure of loyalty, do they? I shall see them punished, mark me."

"He will," I assure the boy. "He helped put all three of those women in the stocks last month, the ones who tried to sneak into the market without paying the toll. And those lads that sank that barge at the Grandison wharf. The bailiffs are still tracking down whoever carved those, er, offensive pictures into the city gates, but my father thinks the Porth Mawr miller knows who did it, so he's being questioned even now. Whoever it was, though, God help him. I doubt there'll be much left of him to hang."

The boy squints at my father and mutters something that sounds like *tooth-dee-din,* which I take to mean thank you.

"Back to your labor, then," my father says in a gentler tone. "Not your fault, lad. Mind yourself, though. Watchers are hard to come by."

The boy stumbles away through the furrows. Just looking at his clotted scalp makes my head throb, but soon the poor lad will have justice. My father will see to it.

My father needs some sacks of grain moved into the shed. I know just the man for the job.

I send one of the Glover boys for Griffith, and as always, he comes trudging up Shire Hall as if being led to the gallows. As he passes the house, Griffith looks up at it as if it will eat him bone and toenail, and when he sees me at my father's window he quickly drops his gaze.

I flutter my fingers and stare him into the rearyard. He does not look up anymore.

Gwinny is sweeping my chamber. I can hear the scratch of broomstraws on the floor as I sail down the stairs, tying my cloak and pulling on gloves.

The cold is searing outside the hall. I bounce on my heels in the storage chamber and rub my hands while my father gives Griffith his instructions. He speaks loud and slow and repeats himself thrice.

Then my father clumps back inside. He doesn't see me in the shadows, and I give him plenty of time to settle himself before the hearth with a mug ere I hitch my gown up just enough and stride into the rearyard.

"G'morn, Griffith," I say sweetly, even though the cold is crippling and it's hard not to curl into myself and shudder.

He freezes, his back to me and a sack on his shoulder. It's

heavy. I can tell by how he's listing. His whole body slumps like one great sob.

I smile. "I wonder how your lessons are coming today."

Griffith's gloves have no fingers and he has no cloak, merely a tunic that's seen more than one winter. His cheeks are already burned red and his ears are twice wrapped in wool, but still his hair tangles out like ribbons.

"Demoiselle," he finally says, "would you not rather be in by the fire? This weather is not fit for dogs."

It's rising Tierce. It's cold enough to freeze the beard off an icon. Yet he stands with a hundredstone weight on his shoulder while his rag-wrapped feet sink ever deeper into mud clods because he dares not answer and dares not ignore.

"Doubtless no," I purr. "I have *all* morning."

Griffith grimaces as he shifts beneath the weight. "By your leave, then? Should I get this finished, I can—"

"Are you *looking* at me again?"

He opens his mouth. Closes it. Shakes his head once, curtly.

I perch on the kitchen stump and get on with my teaching.

IT'S better when she's gone. Can pretend this house is Pencoed and it's my floor to sweep. My linen to hem. My hearth to stoke.

Pencoed was taken, though. Bastards took everything.

Wouldn't have it different. Having now means kneeling then. Kneeling before them, taking their king's peace.

Da would not. So English took everything. Even his life.

Cold. Bone-biting cold. Must sweep for warmth. All the dim corners and forgotten places.

Must close those rotten shutters.

Lean out to seize the straps. And see them. Gruffydd and the brat.

It grieves me to say it, she says with a smile of pure venom, but you're just not learning anything at all. What *would* the king say, could he see us now? Mayhap you'll never learn, no matter how much you study your lessons. Mayhap you're just not capable of it. I wonder what we'd have to do with you then.

Gruffydd is red and sick and scuffing the icy ground and not looking at her and it's *her,* it's the brat, she's the one plaguing Gruffydd and it's worse again than he ever let on and God help me I'll kill her dead and go to the gallows and not a vile

English soul in this Godforsaken town will hire Gruffydd's labor again and Mam will starve and freeze and die.

Lean against the wall. Gasping.

He was ready to kill them all with his toy spear when they came to seize Pencoed and Mam threw a blanket over us and told us to make no noise, not a sound, and I held my hand over his mouth and gripped him still while he fought to get free and things crashed beyond the wool and Mam wept and men shouted and I whispered over and over for him not to be afraid, that all would end up well.

Liar.

Rock away from the wall. Storm to the garment rod. Gowns hang there. Shifts. Hose and slippers and ribbons and surcotes.

Rose gown is on top. The one I put a thousand-thousand stitches into till my eyes hurt, and with no thanks. No notice of my bleeding fingers.

Seize that rag by the collar and rip. It tears in two with a satisfying groan and I laugh and sob and kill it some more, till it's dead in pieces on the floor. Sleeves like slain birds. Wrought hem like a gallows noose.

Throw its corpse down. Pick up the yellow gown and tear.

The lot of them should burn.

SOMETHING'S HAPPENING in the house. There's clunking and banging and the strangest other sound. Groaning?

Mayhap Ned has returned to try his luck against my father's rage.

Griffith is all but in tears. I've only permitted him to move three sacks. And I could easily stretch this work out all day. Whether I will or not I haven't decided. I sweetly promise to return as soon as I'm able and I swish all hips into the house.

The hall is quiet. My father is nowhere in sight, but Nicholas dozes before the fire in the big master's chair he's dragged from the trestle. Salvo sleeps on his feet.

The strange noise is clearer in the hall. It's not a groaning sound at all. It's a ripping sound.

Something is being torn abovestairs.

I take the stairs two at a time. At the curtain, I stop cold.

I cannot be seeing true.

There is clothing everywhere.

No. No, there are *pieces* of clothing everywhere. My garment rod is empty and there are skirts across the bed and sleeves on the floor and a leg of hose dangling from the shutter and scattered about are scraps that might have once been ties or hems or girdle lacings.

Gwinny stands in the middle of the wreckage, panting as if winded from a sprint. Her fists are stiff at her sides and both clutch handfuls of wool scraps. She looks poised to attack, like a mad dog or a boar.

Christ and all the saints but she will pay! And not just at Court Baron.

I seize her wrist and haul her from the room as hard as I can. She bangs an elbow on the doorframe and cries out.

"After all I've done for you, too!" I leap the last two stairs and heave her toward the hall. "My father will be furious and you will be *cartwhipped*."

Nicholas blearily rocks into a sitting position and Salvo creaks aloft his gray head.

I throw Gwinny before Nicholas and howl, "I've had all I can bear from this servant my father won't let me get rid of. I'd have her punished for ruining my garments!"

Nicholas blinks and rubs his eyes. "I'm sure there's naught wrong with your foolish gowns."

"She tore them all!" I lash a finger at Gwinny as if dealing the mark of Cain. "Every last thing I own is in ribbons!"

Gwinny says naught. Her eyes are red, as if it is she who's been wronged and betrayed.

Nicholas frowns and stretches. "This is something your father should—"

"My father isn't here!" I glare at him with all my hating. "Are you not a man? Punish her!"

"Wait here," Nicholas says grimly, and he goes abovestairs. When he returns, his face is terrible. He towers over Gwinny and demands, "What would make you do such a thing?"

Gwinny looks at me long and level, then turns her eyes to the floor.

"*Cart. Whipped.*" I snap each word as I cannot Gwinny's neck. "She has devils in her."

Nicholas's face is black as sin. He takes Gwinny by the elbow and roughly tows her out the rearyard door.

KNOW what's coming. Not afraid. Keep my eyes down, though. No need to make it worse.

The cold is blistering. Fingers stiffen in instants. Wind makes a mask of my face.

Oh, Christ. Gruffydd is by the shed, something on his shoulder. Catch his eye and shake my head. He must not step into this. The brat cannot know this matters to him.

Put both hands on the kitchen wall. Not afraid.

Brace.

A stripe of fire across my back. Curl my fingers against the wattles. Dig nails in.

A second blow over the first and I cry out. A third. Salted daggers carve from shoulder to backside, curling beneath my arms, nipping ribs. Christ help me, I'm dying on my knees in the snow while leather sings and my back opens and my throat goes raw and little ones look after littler ones no matter what the cost.

It's over ere I know it. Gwinny is sobbing in a heap in the snow. Mistress Tipley flies out of the kitchen, her sleeves still rolled to the elbow, and she falls to her knees at Gwinny's side.

"Happy?" Nicholas asks me curtly. He turns on his heel and strides into the house.

Griffith stands in the shed's doorway, gripping the frame as if it's the neck of something deadly. He starts toward Gwinny, then hesitates, cuts his eyes to me.

I will not be trifled with. That's the lesson he must study over all the rest.

I follow Nicholas into the house, but I don't stop in the hall. I don't even acknowledge his shaky voice offering me a drink of undiluted wine. I stomp abovestairs, grinding my toes against every step.

There are rags all over my chamber. Rags, where once I had gowns.

I kneel, collect a few scraps of rose wool. These stitches were strong, too. Tiny and doubled-up. Some of my best work, and like as not Gwinny's too. Now the edges are frayed and tangled. They'll not even be stitched back together in this state.

I close my eyes.

Later today I will show this mess to my father and he will shrug unhelpfully and give me the usual nonsense about how every penny he has will go to keeping us in bread this winter and there's no coin to spare for frivolities—that's how he'll put it, *frivolities,* as if my whole *life* isn't in tatters—and what's wrong with the gown I'm wearing, anyway?

Later today I'll have to go to the Coucy house. The lady de Coucy will eye my ragged cuffs and explain to me for the better part of an afternoon why ragged cuffs will mark me a *novi* and no good lady of Caernarvon should be seen outside wearing clothing in ill repair and I'd know that if I paid half a mind to her but apparently I'm too ignorant to even listen properly.

I gave Gwinny a gown. We saw justice done to a filthy swine of a levelooker who abused his position of power in the borough. She even helped me fend off the unwanted advances of a known scoundrel who sought to take advantage of my youth and gentle nature.

And this—this!—is how I'm repaid.

Gwinny will curse the hour she wronged Cecily d'Edgeley.

I don't give Mistress Tipley the chance to give her a soft task, tucked away in some warm corner of the kitchen. I call Gwinny abovestairs to clean this mess.

It seems forever ere there's a dragging on the stairs, then Gwinny appears at the curtain. She's the color of new cheese and she moves like a stiff puppet on strings.

"Pick it up." I kick a crumpled sleeve at her. "Pick it all up, damn you. Every last scrap."

Gwinny does not bend over to retrieve the wool. Instead she crouches and feels about till she gets it in hand. Then she rises like a water bird, her teeth gritted and her breath in gasps.

"All I had." I swallow and swallow but my voice is still warpy. "All I had that was mine. And only mine. And now I have naught. Because of you."

Gwinny leans heavily against the wall and falters, then she makes a garbled sound and collapses to the floor.

I jab her shoulder with my toe. "Get up, you lazy thing, else I'll give you such a cartwhipping that your grand-children will feel it. You're fooling no one with this dis-play of—"

"Merciful God Almighty!" Mistress Tipley crosses the room in three big strides and shoves me away from Gwinny.

I hit the wall hard, then rock away sputtering, "How dare you?"

The old cow glares up at me like a serpent from Gwinny's side. "How dare *you,* you wicked girl? Now help me get her on the bed."

"*My* bed? I don't think so."

"Fine, is it?" Mistress Tipley mutters to Gwinny as she tugs and wriggles Gwinny's gown over her head. "You most certainly are *not.*"

Gwinny makes no sound as Mistress Tipley pulls off her

garments. She lies on her side facing the wall. Her hair spills like a matted hide around bony gray shoulders.

"Come here, girl," Mistress Tipley snarls at me, "and see what you wrought."

I don't have to come. I can see from here.

Gwinny's back is covered with a grid of cuts. Most are a fingernail's depth with edges that curl apart like long, gaping mouths. Where the worst cuts cross, the skin is peeling away in a limp triangle. Her whole back is a deep, angry red, smeary with blood and striped across with angry purple jags.

"No," I finally whisper. "I—I didn't do this."

"You most certainly did. Now help me get her into bed."

I hesitate. And hesitate. Then I pick up Gwinny's feet. They're freezing cold and rough like stones. Mistress Tipley gingerly hoists Gwinny beneath the armpits and we shudder her onto my bed, where she lies like a wet sack.

On my clean linen.

Gwinny moans something in Welsh. Mistress Tipley pets her ragged hair and dabs a rag wetted in my washwater against the cuts on her back. Blood fills the cleaves and stripes down her back, staining the linen.

I did not do this.

Gwinny would be fine had she not wantonly destroyed my property.

I stomp belowstairs and into the hall, and my father bids me a spry good morrow when I take my place at table before a trencher of maslin. Henry grunts a greeting through a mouthful of food, but Nicholas is nowhere in sight.

My father prattles about his foolish office between bites, how the millers are desperate cheats who'll do anything to avoid borough court and how Welshmen do any number of clever things to hide their handmills when they hear he's nearby, which just shows how well he's extending borough justice to the Welshry.

My father must not know yet.

I eat quickly, then excuse myself. He'll find out soon enough, and my father in a temper is pure wrothfulness, not justice.

I go to the workroom and sit before my embroidery frame. I pin and repin the length of linen my father gave me, then I unwrap my skeins of Christmas floss and try to imagine where to begin, what image to make.

It's no use. I give up on the linen and retrieve my spindle from beneath a wadded cloak in need of mending.

I tease out some wool, let the whorl drop. The fibers twist on themselves, and in a while I have a strand of yarn the length of my hand.

In the time it took me to make this strand, Gwinny tore apart every gown I owned.

I throw the wool and spindle across the room with a howl and hate Gwinny and her whole family and weep and hurl the half-mended cloak at the wall for good measure.

Someone will hear me and come. My father, or mayhap one of my lackwit cousins. They'll come to the workroom door with brows furrowed and ask what the matter is, and I'll weep and mourn my loss and they'll see justice done.

The moments stretch like year-old honey. Laughter from the hall, the clatter of crockery. No one comes.

My father does not throw Gwinny into the gutter when he learns what she has wrought. He does not even devolve into ranting. Because while I'm sulking in the workroom, Mistress Tipley plies him with claret and spins a fairy story about spats between girls, how easy it would be to overreact to something this silly, how things like gowns can be repaired, how he has a reputation in the borough to consider.

So he merely whistles low when I shake handfuls of rags in his face, and he jokes that he ought to hire Gwinny as one of his mill enforcers. He laughs aloud when I demand that he take Gwinny to Court Baron for recompense for my wardrobe, and he chides Nicholas for whipping a maidservant so hard. When I'm ready to boil over, my father gives that rotten Gwinny a clean-struck penny for her troubles. The hospitality of his hearth, he says, is hers till she recovers fully.

In the same breath, my father tells me I'm stuck with my one remaining gown unless I grow two handswidths during the winter, and even then he might just bid Mistress Tipley give me something of hers. Then he tells me to stop my caterwauling and mend my underclothes because no one has any business putting eyes on them anyway.

I'm in my workroom now. I cannot wait till tomorrow, when Griffith will be here to mend the byre fence and study his lessons.

1293–1294

CHRISTMAS

TO

ASSUMPTION EVE

T'S CHRISTMAS. The holly and ivy are up. There's strong cider waiting when we get back from Mass and the Yule log stretches all the way across the hall, so we must step over it. I can close my eyes and everything is as it should be, all the mingled smells of roast goose and woodsmoke and bitter evergreen, the wind twittering, the crunch of feet in snow, the crackle of fire.

Then I open my eyes.

Nothing is right.

The goose is roasting, but it is Mistress Tipley's hand on the spit. Not my mother's.

Nicholas and Henry are cheerfully drunk on Rhenish and aqua vitae. They are planning to go out mumming later, which will inevitably devolve into misrule. They might even remember to wave to me through the window when they go, and they will come back pink and laughing and full of furtive looks and guffaws and secret jokes that they will tell me are not fit for my ears.

The holly and ivy are up, as crooked as only drink-addled male hands can make them. My mother would have straightened the greens, primped them, and tied tiny ribbons to the ends.

My father hasn't spent a Christmas sober since she died,

but this year he is staggering about town visiting houses, bringing a year's worth of good fortune with his dark hair. He says it's a civic duty. It's really just a way for him to get into the homes of the *honesti* even for a moment.

The same wind clattering about the eaves blows over her grave far away at Edgeley, and my wretched uncle and his mewling girl-wife will not place a bough of yew on the grassy patch that had all but sunk to ground level when we left for Coventry.

I am playing draughts with myself on the board my mother gave me the year my first milk-tooth fell out. I make a move, then turn the board and make a countermove.

There will be frumenty, figs, and all the plum pudding I can eat, but nothing is really quite right.

My mother was born on this day. She would go about with red ribbons in her hair. We'd play draughts and drink cider and sing ballads while the snow battered against Edgeley's tight walls and mourned about its door.

Not a day goes by when I don't think of her, but on Christmas I wear red ribbons in my hair and commend her soul to God.

I mend before the fire. Stitch by stitch, trying to put my wardrobe back together.

Gwinny lies up in my chamber behind shuttered windows and beneath piled bedclothes. Not only is her back in tatters, she's become feverish.

Just like my mother.

It's no use. Gwinny did her work too well. I can sew most of the cloth back together, but all the seams will show.

I hold up a bodice. It looks like Gwinny's back, all cross-hatched and frayed.

All of Edgeley prayed for my mother. *Pater noster qui in caelis es.* My father on his knees before the high altar for days at a time, unshaven, hollow-cheeked, gray from hunger. *Ave Maria gratia plena.* Saint Alrida's bell ringing to beg the saints to intervene on her behalf, day and night, day and night. *Miserere mi Deus.* Me in the corner with my hair in plaits, curling into a smaller ball and clutching my wooden paternoster while the household tiptoed past.

I go abovestairs and peek into my chamber. Gwinny lies motionless on my bed. Her back is covered with a fragrant poultice.

She must have known what I would do. She must have known the punishment would be severe. Nicholas even gave her a chance to explain.

Justice for those who deserve it.

Pater noster qui in caelis es.

Toward the end, they brought me to see her. My mother sweated and twitched beneath a mountain of bedcovers, too weak to do more than let her gaze fall upon me. The room was hot and close and damp. My father knelt at my mother's side, hands clasped and pressed against his forehead. His lips were moving and his cheeks glistened. My aunt Eleanor wept openly at the foot of the bed. The priest thumbed his beads in the shadows, the hall servants wrung their hands in the corridor, and all of Edgeley prayed.

Gwinny is alone here. No one to sit vigil by the bed. Mayhap even now someone worries over her, watches the door for her to burst in all surly frowns and blank bird-stares. That poor soul has no notion what became of her, where she might be.

Mayhap it's a child.

I bow my head and pray for Gwinny, as Edgeley prayed for my mother.

Mistress Tipley insists I help tend Gwinny. She says she has enough to do running the household that she cannot spare much bedside time.

"I can run the household," I tell the crone primly, but she just guffaws in that rude way of hers and hands me a rag and bowl.

I gather the shredded linen that no one has any business putting eyes on and stomp up to my chamber. As I drag the stool next to the bed, Gwinny glances over her bare shoulder with a look that's almost pleasant, but when she sees it's me and not Mistress Tipley, a hard look falls over her face like a curtain.

"I see you've come to reckon if I'm still alive," Gwinny says. "Sorry to ruin your game."

I gape. "What? No! I didn't wish you dead!"

"Deny it, then."

"I swear it on the Mass. I never wished you dead. Not once. Not *ever*."

Gwinny eyes me as if I'm on a spicemonger's scales. At length, she replies, "Right, then. You've done your good deed. Now you can go."

"I cannot. Mistress Tipley says I must tend you."

"I've no need for it. Go play lady of the house somewhere else."

"I'm trying to show you kindness," I say in little, bitten-off words, "and you are repaying it with scorn."

Gwinny laughs aloud. "God save me from any more English kindness!"

"I gave you a gown! We shared marchpane and wine at Michaelmas!"

She regards me levelly. "I spared you from standing at the church door with Edward Mercer."

"Exactly! I thought we'd reached . . . well, an understanding."

Gwinny snorts. "Oh, I understand. I understand quite well."

I frown. "So . . . you're sorry for what you did?"

"I asked the master's pardon. He has given it. He considers the matter closed."

"What about my pardon?" I brandish the tattery lengths of linen at her. "How could you do this to me? What have I ever done to you?"

Gwinny stiffens. "Don't you mock me."

"Or what?" I swallow and swallow to drown the warp in my voice. "What else do I have that you can destroy? Sorry to ruin *your* game, Gwinny."

In slow degrees, she pushes herself onto her elbows, wincing with each small movement. "In truth? You'd know what you've done to me?"

"In truth," I repeat firmly. "Because I want to hear you admit it before Almighty God. That I did naught. That it was spite and envy that made you do such a terrible thing."

Gwinny's jaw is working and she mutters something in Welsh. At length she sighs. Long, as if she's picking up something heavy. "If you say it's so, it must be so."

I lean back on the stool. "Good. Then do we have an understanding?"

She nods. She doesn't look at me.

"Here. You stitch these." I push a handful of linen scraps at her. "Something to pass the time."

When she shifts to take the linen, the poultice slides off her shoulder, revealing a long cut the color of day-old meat.

I did not do that.

Gwinny's stitches are tight and careful. Even flat on her belly, she matches me stitch for stitch, and ere it's time for dinner, we've put together most of a shift.

Mayhap I will forgive her. It's what my mother would have wanted.

* * *

My father takes Henry to meet formally with the mayor and the foremost *honesti*. They are very interested in having a goldsmith in Caernarvon, and there is a newly built townhouse in Palace Street they would have him view. If they find Henry agreeable, he could be living here by this time next year.

Mayhap I will speak to Emmaline about him.

Nicholas departs for the Boar's Head, so once again I'm alone, forced to spend another tedious day tending Gwinny. I have an armload of undergarments still in need of repair, but when I get abovestairs I find her asleep. The poultice is gone, and her cuts stand out against her flesh like claw marks from some unholy beast. The whole room still smells of pine and juniper. I stand shivering for many long moments to be sure Gwinny isn't playacting, but at length I sigh, toss my torn-up shifts on the coffer, and slip through the curtain.

The house is deadly still. No one will be home till supper.

I pace the landing like a tethered hound. My footsteps creak and echo. At length, I go into my father's chamber. There's his curtained bed and a stool with a tunic thrown haphazardly atop. Beneath the window lies the locked coffer containing my mother's gown and Heaven only knows what else that once was hers. I kneel before it for a long moment, my fingers tracing the lock.

Belowstairs, the workroom is cold and empty. My embroidery frame stands like a naked skeleton by shuttered windows that leak slats of thin gray daylight.

The hall is dim at the corners. The fire crackles and the trestle gleams with each flicker of orange light. Salvo on his pallet snores like a bellows.

Out in the rearyard, the kitchen windows glow. Mistress Tipley is holed up there, drinking small beer with her feet on the grate and dozing like an aging cat.

I go back to the workroom and throw the shutters open. A wall of crippling cold air drafts in, but so does a block of daylight, pale but steady. I pin my father's length of linen to my frame, take out my charcoal stick, and begin to sketch.

"Get down here!" My father, bawling like a boar. It's most unflattering. "That was Sext just then! You should be at the Coucys!"

I fold a half-stitched shift. Then I unfold it, smooth out wrinkles that aren't there, and fold it again. "Coming!"

"You'll regret it should you make me come up there!"

To my undergarments I mutter, "As if you'll get off your arse before that fire." Then, louder, "I said I was coming!"

I stand on tiptoe to drape the shift across the garment rod. "You deaf old badger."

Gwinny props herself on her elbows and watches me fidget and fuss with the shift. Mistress Tipley says it'll only be another few days ere she's well enough to get out of my bed and resume her duties.

"Do I look ill to you?" I ask Gwinny. "I could pinch my cheeks to redden them. And I can hoarse up my voice."

Gwinny shakes her head.

"Ahhh, you're right. He'd make me go even if it meant dragging myself from my deathbed. Anything to nuzzle up to those rotten *honesti*."

"You—don't want to go?" Gwinny sounds surprised.

"By all the saints, no!" I step into my felt slippers because I'll get an earful should I arrive barefoot. "I'd rather muck every pig-keep in Caernarvon."

Gwinny regards me with a mule-skinner's measuring gaze. "She'll make you one of them. Townhouse lady, servants all around."

"It's what my father wants." I scuff my heel. "He'd see me one of them."

Gwinny draws back, frowning.

"Cecily! *Now!*"

I tuck stray threads under my cuffs. I may not know my lord from your Grace, but I was raised with enough courtesy not to mention someone's ragged cuffs or call her father a hamhanded oaf.

Bootsteps creak on stairs.

I grab my cloak and fly for the door. My father glares me a warning as I hurry past.

On my way down Shire Hall Street, I drag my feet. I count chuckholes. I watch shiny green flies buzz over horse apples. For one sweet stone's throw, fifty-four steps if I make them small and Lady de Coucy–sanctioned, I can do what I will.

AFTER she's gone, shift—ow—margin—ow—by margin—ow—till I'm facing her coffer, her garment pole, the
tiny shuttered window.

The brat will be gone till Nones, and she'll return in the
foulest humor. The master will lecture her on how her ill
temper is imprudent since it may offend her benefactor. He
would have his privileges go straight to the bone, not merely
lie skin-deep. He is *novi,* but men like him rarely stay *novi*
for long.

Were it anyone but the brat, I might pity her.

Till Nones, then, peace.

Awakened by a shuff-shuff far away. The chamber is
bitterly cold, even with the hall brazier brought up by Margaret. The sun's slant is narrower now, like a child's slice of
pie. Not much peace left. Close my eyes. Flatten my hands
beneath my chest for warmth.

Shuff-shuff. Shuff-shuff.

That had best not be what I think it is.

Grit to my feet. Handswidth by handswidth. Glide to the
window as if my spine is kindling.

Gruffydd is threshing barley in the shed. Shuff-shuff as
the flail comes down, sings across the floorboards, snaps up.

And she'll be home any moment now.

Too risky to shout. Cannot whistle. Work my fingers around the edge of the shutter and bang it against the house until Gruffydd pauses, glances around, then looks up. He grins like a sunrise, waves the flail.

Belowstairs, the front door slams and the brat's shrill voice rings out for the master.

Cringe my arm up in tiny jagged bursts, jab a thumb at the rearyard door.

Gruffydd frowns, makes a bewildered gesture.

Belowstairs, the master calls the brat into the hall. He bids her look in on me ere she starts her spinning or sewing or what-have-you, and listen for the laborer in the rearyard to be finished so the master can pay him.

Fling one last helpless finger at the rearyard door as Gruffydd steps out of the shed and shrugs expansively.

The stairs begin to creak, footfall by footfall.

Turn from the window. Lurch toward the bed. Must get clear ere she makes it up here, catches me looking.

Because then she will puzzle it out.

And Gruffydd will get worse again by tenscore at her hands.

Shuff-shuff. He's back to flailing. Shuff-shuff. The master has all kinds of work. Shuff-shuff. Say them nay and reap the whirlwind.

By the time the stairs fall silent, I'm on the bed facing the wall. Feigning sleep despite the agony spreading through my back. And praying to any saint who's listening.

Shuff-shuff. Go pick up your spinning. Your sewing. Shuff-shuff. For Christ's sake, leave him be.

The stairs begin to creak again, growing softer as she descends. She tells the master she's going to check on the laborer's progress.

Oh, little one. I tried.

Shuff—

How dare you look at me like that? Her voice is a whip-crack, like leather against tender skin. You'll study your lessons or you'll be very sorry.

Grip the brat's bed linens. Bury my face in them, so I cannot hear her bait my brother. Press tighter, so no one can hear me weep.

MY FATHER storms into the house bareheaded and reeking of smoke. His tunic is singed and his face is blackened with what seems to be soot. As he grumbles through the hall, what he mutters is not fit for my ears, so I try to catch every black word of it.

"Water," he growls over his shoulder as he clumps abovestairs. "Hot."

Charming. I get Mistress Tipley to haul up a basin of steaming water.

At suppertime, my father huffs into the hall wearing a clean tunic and surcote. His face and hands are pink-scrubbed, but he still smells faintly of smoke.

I don't tell him this. Instead I pour him some ale and ask, "Do you think it might rain?"

"Hope not. There's to be a hanging."

Just my fortune. Finally something interesting happens, and I haven't a thing to wear.

My father has a faint ring of purple shadowing his right eye. He obviously did not scrub his face as thoroughly as he thought.

The gallows stands on the market common, and it'll be nearly impossible to get a good view. All of Caernarvon has turned out to see two poor devils hang.

On the mill bridge, there's a man in a trencher-shaped helm wearing a white tunic crossed in red. He rests one hand on the pommel of the sword displayed plainly at his hip. At the end of the bridge, I can see two more men in white tunics, and another few near the gallows. It's easy to spot them because people skirt them like they've got the pox.

Even the castle garrison have come to watch the hanging. I'm pleased the king saw fit to grant them leave.

In Coventry they hanged a thief once, and the crowd bawled loud enough to deafen a post. But this hanging is curiously silent. There's no baying and howling, despite the size of the crowd. Every soul in the Welshry must be on the market common.

I draw closer to my father.

When we reach the end of the mill bridge, two men-at-arms fall into step on either side of us. My father opens his mouth, but one of them shakes his head curtly.

"Save your breath. Captain's orders."

My father cuts his eyes over the crowd. "Surely they wouldn't dare. Not in the very shadow of the walls."

The man-at-arms shrugs. "Best not to tempt them. Besides, it's not just you, is it?" And he tips his chin toward me.

My father grunts something like agreement, and now the crowds part for us as the men-at-arms lead us to the foot of the gallows, to the place usually reserved for victims of the condemned.

I brought some rotten cabbage from the shed wrapped in old sackcloth, but now I'm not sure I want to throw it. Not up here. Not in front of every soul in the Welshry. Not even with men-at-arms at my elbows.

There's a crunch of wheels on dirt as the condemned are rolled toward the green on a cart. I hop and weave, but it's no use. All I can see are two dirty hoods.

I let the cabbage roll off my fingertips and stomp it into the mud.

"What did they do, Papa?" I ask, wiping my hands on the sackcloth.

My father does not answer, but one of the men-at-arms mutters, "Crimes against the borough, demoiselle. Don't worry, though. You're perfectly safe."

He says this as he grips and regrips his sword-hilt and runs his eyes over the crowd.

The cart heaves to a halt before the gallows. The condemned stumble out and drag themselves up the steps, closely flanked by more men-at-arms. Both prisoners' faces are streaked with soot, as if they escaped a house fire on the breath of God.

Two nooses stand out against the crisp sky. The condemned stand beneath the dangling ropes.

The crowd is buzzing now. Not hollering. Not baying for blood. Muttering. Fidgeting. And though those gathered keep a healthy distance from the men-at-arms, I can feel thousands of eyes on us up here, in the very shadow of the gallows.

Two men-at-arms no longer seems like a lot, even though they're built like mastiffs and armed with daggers and broadswords.

The hangman cinches a noose tight over the neck of the first man, then the second. The first one says something in Welsh, something calm and bold, something that redoubles the crowd's murmur and turns more eyes to us than ever.

I grip my father's elbow.

The hangman puts a hood over each man's head, then steps back to the tether. There's a drawn-out swiff of rope and both men sail into the air, wriggling like worms on a fishhook.

The crowd falls utterly still, as if they're deep in prayer.

My father insists we stay till the bodies cease swaying. When we finally leave, much of the crowd remains. Some are kneeling as if it's a vigil.

The men-at-arms escort us to our dooryard. One offers to stand post outside for a few days, but my father thanks him and says him nay.

"This," my father says, gesturing to the house, "I know they wouldn't dare."

The man-at-arms shifts beneath his leather armor. "I've been here long enough to know better than to guess at what the Welsh will and will not dare."

My father laughs and sends him and his fellows on their way. I watch the men-at-arms disappear around the top of Shire Hall Street, then I go into the rearyard and put both hands on the walls that keep things like sooty felons and the need for armed guards safely without.

When I arrive at the Coucy house for my se'ennight's bad-mouthing, I find the lady de Coucy arranging strips of linen and foul-smelling pottles in a basket.

"Oh, you're leaving." I clasp my hands and study the floor so she cannot see my good cheer. "Beg your pardon. I'll just be off."

She pulls a bright cloth over the basket and reaches for her cloak. "You'll be coming with me. Emmaline, too. It's nearing Mistress Glover's time."

"Time for what?"

"For her child to be born, silly girl."

I step back. "I—I'll just be in the way."

"Nonsense, Cecily. Helping at a birth is one of the most important things a good woman of Caernarvon does."

It's Mistress Glover's hundredth child. Like as not she just has to sneeze for the baby to come out.

Emmaline takes my elbow. "Mayhap we'll be allowed to hold the baby!"

Mayhap I'll be allowed to hide in the garden shed.

Mistress Sandys is already at the Glover house when we

arrive, as is Mistress Pole. They're fluttering up and down the stairs bearing lengths of linen and basins of water. Someone has brought a relic to aid in the birth—a girdle that Emmaline swears belonged to Saint Margaret—and draped it reverently over the mantel.

The moment the lady de Coucy walks into the Glover house, she takes charge of everything. She sends Emmaline abovestairs with some rosewater for Mistress Glover's brow, and she gives me the task of opening and untying. Leaving even a single knot tied might tangle up the baby or wrap the cord about its neck, and a closed door or shutter could stop up the birth canal. It would be all my fault. So I throw open every shutter and untie every knot in the house, down to the laces in Saint Margaret's girdle on the mantel.

After I finish, I edge into the shadows of the hearth corner. Borough ladies wick by me, eyes to their footing or their burdens. Betimes they mutter in hushed voices that put me too much in mind of a sickroom for my liking.

I haven't a paternoster, but I whisper a prayer for Mistress Glover.

Then there's a thin, spindly cry from abovestairs. A baby's cry.

Emmaline appears at the bottom of the stairs. Her hands are clasped and she's bouncing like a wagon on the low road. "Oh, come and see, Cecily. He's just the sweetest baby in all of Christendom!"

Babies ruin your garden, even when they aren't yours. They get lost and worry you ill, even when they aren't yours.

But I follow Emmaline abovestairs and into the bed-chamber, where Mistress Sandys has just lifted the tiny baby dripping from a basin. She dries him off and wraps him tightly in crisp white linen, then tucks him into his mother's elbow.

The baby is a deep glowing pink. He isn't stinky or screamy. He looks weary but content.

Emmaline shyly asks if she can hold the baby. Mistress Glover hands him up and Emmaline settles him in the crook of her arm as if he's wine from water.

"Would you like to hold him next, Cecily?" Mistress Glover asks.

I shake my head violently and the women laugh, but not in a mocking way. Then Mistress Pole says she'd never even held a baby until the moment her eldest was placed in her arms, and Mistress Pannel cackles when she says she tiptoed around her eldest's cradle for a whole fortnight after he was born, afraid to wake him. She'd have to pick him up then, she explains, and she was sure she'd drop him and break every bone in his body.

The good borough ladies laugh and brag and best one another with outlandish stories, and it isn't long ere we've all drawn stools around Mistress Glover's bed. Someone produces a flask of claret and starts it around. Mistress Glover smiles and closes her eyes while Emmaline hums a lullaby and sways the baby like a dancing partner.

Mistress Pole places the flask in my hand without thinking twice. She does not seem to notice that I'm a *novi* who will never be one of them. The wine is strong and sweet. Not bitter at all.

I've saved what I can of my tattered wardrobe. I manage to piece together two shifts, two pairs of hose, and my bedrobe. What's left is a mass of fibers that cannot even be unraveled, tied together, rerolled into a skein, and rewoven. They are finely spun, expensive rags.

So I do what you do with rags. I bundle them up for the ragman.

I find him at the market one Saturday, the same wizened ruffian whom Gwinny and I avenged when Levelooker Pluver was plying his odious trade. We surely got the best of Pluver that day. I laughed like a madman when Pluver finally found his hat crushed beneath that hog's filthy trotters.

Neither Alice nor Agnes would ever have done anything so clever and brave. They would have pressed hands to mouths and fretted about being caught.

The ragman offers me a penny for my bundle. I tell him I cannot take less than five, and show him the quality of the rags.

He chitters like a jay, rubs them, then asks toothlessly, "What possessed you to stove up such fineries?"

I pet the rose wool. I could be *wearing* this gown, and thinking about it still makes me want to kick something.

But I toe a line in the dirt and quietly reply, "I know not what I was thinking."

Gwinny is finally well enough to leave. Mistress Tipley tries to persuade her that it's too late for her to walk home, that the men with blackened faces do terrible things to collaborators, but Gwinny shakes her head firmly.

She totters into the hall, stiff like a lance. I'm grinding bits of beechnut hull for dyestuff. She nods to me as she fumbles with her cloakstrings.

"Gwinny."

She's halfway out the door, hands already balled in her cloak against the cold, and she winces as she sidles back into the hall.

I put aside the beechnuts and approach her. She lifts her chin. She does not cringe, but she seems to be bracing for a blow.

I untangle her hand from her cloak and lay her wages in her palm. Three pennies that catch firelight.

Gwinny gapes at the coins. The bird-look falters and she begins blinking rapidly.

Then she inclines her head, fists a hand about the pennies, and disappears into the deepening winter twilight.

MAKE no haste. Couldn't if I wanted to, but I don't. What awaits me at the steading will be the same regardless of haste.

It'll be bad. Scavengers will have been at the corpse.

She'll have died alone, weeping for her babies.

That is what the brat will pay for. Whatever the cost.

Uphill takes months and years. Must move in tiny margins. Mustn't bend. Scabs are still raw enough to tear.

Cannot smell the corpse yet. Mayhap the cold holds it down.

Limp inside and blink. There's fire.

Go cold all over because fire means Gruffydd has foregone labor to tend Mam and it'll be se'ennights ere he sees even half a chance at a penny again.

But it's not Gruffydd who rises from the shadows. It's Fanwra from down the vale, and she gestures shyly to Mam.

"She's a tough old girl," Fanwra says in her wispy little voice that makes me think of baby birds and dry grass.

"You're kind to come."

Fanwra worries her ratty sleeves. "Gruffydd asked me to stay with her. There's not much I'd deny him."

Her words hang there, waiting for me to dignify them,

to bless her devotion. Not in this lifetime, though, nor in any spare moment of the hereafter.

"You're kind to come."

Fanwra finally flutters toward the door, muttering well-wishes and prayers for Mam. The moment she's gone, I sink in fits and measures to my knees while keeping my mince-meat back in a rigid column.

Mam whimpers for water. The leather bucket is empty. Look at it and look at it, as if one wrung-out plea will make it fill itself. Then rise, every margin a blade of fire, and edge downhill toward the creek with the bucket swaying from my hand like a hanged man.

They come at night. Gruffydd goes with them. He darkens his face with ashes and pulls Da's spear from the rafters without flinch or hesitation, as if he'd known where it was all along. His eyes scream like jewels from the soot.

The others say little. They stand without the door, flat against the steading. A mass of shadows, men and weapons, curves and angles and blades.

Don't see them. Don't know them. Cannot betray them.

Da went out. Da never came back. They left his body on the walls till naught but scraps were left.

Gruffydd wears no cloak. Cloaks catch and snag on brush. He shivers already.

My little brother. The boy who once wept for injured

hares and maidens ill-served in nursery tales. Now there's down on his cheeks. Scars across both hands.

Da went out, called up by his prince. Da stood with the prince when he fell at Cefn-y-bedd, and all Wales with them. He stood after, while men submitted in droves to save themselves, their lands. He stood against their king till English hanged him from the walls of Caernarvon.

They come at night and Gruffydd follows, disappears into darkness.

A SE'ENNIGHT after Candlemas, we always feed the poor in honor of my mother.

At Edgeley, tenants filled the great trestle tables in the hall and spilled out into the yard. Every man, woman, and child in the village left full to bursting. Meat and ale, bread and cheese. Wine for the reeve. Cakes for the children. Whatever was left we sent home with each family, wrapped up in linsey.

When we return from Candlemas Mass, I ask my father how we'll feed the poor this year when our house is so small.

"Oh, sweeting, it'll be hard enough to keep our bodies and souls together till spring." He runs a hand through his hair. "And it isn't as if this is Edgeley, where the tenants would be at the door with pitchforks should I think to go against custom."

I frown. "You mean we aren't going to feed the poor this year?"

"I'll pray for them, sweeting. These people aren't my tenants. There's no custom binding me to them."

The custom doesn't bind us to the tenants. It binds us to her.

But he's got that don't-make-me-cuff-you look about him, so I duck my head like a good girl and say naught. Instead I wait for him to put on his boots and pick up his questioning cudgel and go out to officer the mills. I hide behind the garden shed until Mistress Tipley lumbers into the yard privy, then I dart into the kitchen and liberate three big loaves from the trestle. I put on my cloak and find Gwinny plaiting hemp in the hearth corner.

"Can you walk? I'm going without the walls and I'd have you with me."

"What for?"

"I'm feeding the poor."

Gwinny's eyes jerk up as though I've crowned myself dunghill princess. "You are not."

My mother had hair the color of a new-brushed roan. She was always moving, never still, and she walked chin up with a jingle of keys, with Salvo ever her shadow.

I hold up the bread.

Gwinny lays aside her task and rises in stiff margins. "If you say it's so, it must be so."

"Does that mean you're coming?"

Gwinny smiles in a way I'm not sure I like. "Wouldn't miss it."

It's rising Tierce. Midmorning is achingly cold and the color of wallstone. The bread in the satchel against my back is no longer warm and grows heavier by the moment. The serjeant at the trestle marks Gwinny at my elbow, but I meet his eyes steadily until he steps aside and lets us through.

Outside the gate, I drift a few paces, then stop ere I even

get across the quay bridge. I didn't think this through very well. I haven't the first idea where to even look for the poor.

"You still want to feed the poor?" Gwinny stares into the distance, her hair snarling into her eyes. I nod and she says, "Come."

She leads me toward the market common. Along the trodden toll path, huddled like piles of wet laundry awaiting the clothesline, are whole families with cheeks like slack sails, and graybeards with fingers all knuckle. Dozens of men, women, and children, and I have but three loaves.

"The poor," Gwinny says expansively, gesturing. She's appraising me sidelong, not quite smiling.

She's waiting for me to run away screaming.

The poor are ashen and malodorous. They're not like the poor of Edgeley. Those were people I knew. Every one of them. Down to their livestock. They were a part of Edgeley and therefore mine. But these poor wretches are living skeletons, something straight out of a sermon on sin. If I stay too long in their company, I'll end up one of them.

But I'll not give Gwinny the satisfaction of leaving. Besides, I'm not here for her.

I slide my satchel off my shoulder and fumble with the bread. Nearby is a gaunt mother of two tiny redheads who are covered in rashy scabs. I tear off a chunk of bread and hand it to her.

She gapes and stammers something to me in a voice that sways like a bird on the wing, then breaks the bread in two and hands one piece to each child. She closes her eyes as they gulp it down.

Some of the poor, the stronger ones, rise and lurch toward us, and Gwinny says something to them in Welsh in a sharp, no-nonsense voice. They stop and retrace their steps, some mutinous, some hopeful.

"I told them to make a queue," Gwinny says to me, "and that you'd go along and give everyone something."

So I do. I break off pieces as equally as I can, placing bread in every palm that's put toward me. They eat as if they've never seen bread ere this. As if they'll never see it again.

When the bread is gone and my satchel twice tipped for every last crumb, I smile and shrug and look to Gwinny to say something to them. She does, and when she's finished, I gesture to the city gate and she falls into step at my elbow.

I cannot recall ever running out of food when we fed the poor at Edgeley.

"This isn't even the worst of it," Gwinny says quietly. "These are the ones with strength enough to crawl to the common to beg."

My mother was always moving, never idle, and had she been starving on the roadside with me beneath her arm, she would have gone without so I could feel full just for a moment. She would have wept to see me hungry, to have no way to feed me.

"Why?" Gwinny asks, so quiet the wind nearly takes it away.

"Why feed the poor?" I ask, and she nods. "Er, because they're hungry?"

Gwinny frowns as though she's heard me wrong. "Because they're hungry."

I nod firmly, because I don't trust my voice to speak of my mother. Especially not today.

Back at the townhouse, my father is roaring at Mistress Tipley for taking the bread that was to last us the better part of a fortnight, and Mistress Tipley is cowering before the hearth and blubbering that she didn't take the bread and cannot imagine where it has gone.

As usual, it's up to me to make things right.

When my father pauses to take a breath, I clear my throat. "Papa, I know what became of the bread."

All three turn toward me—my father in rage, Mistress Tipley in mute hope, and Gwinny in disbelief. But I'm no fool. I'll feed the poor, but I'll not take a thrashing for them.

I blame the one creature in the house guaranteed never to feel my father's temper.

"Please don't be wroth with him, Papa," I say, "but I saw him coming out of the kitchen with the bread in his mouth, and when he saw me, he just gobbled it down ere I could get it away from him. I tied him up after that, but he must have eaten the other loaves ere I caught him. He's just so hungry, poor beast. Like the rest of us."

My father's color is still high, but his fists are sliding to his sides and relaxing. He looses a long breath and mutters something to Mistress Tipley that might be an apology or permission to depart. Either way, she bobs her head and all but flies out of the hall.

I go to the rear storage chamber to fetch my father a mug of ale, but when I see the level in the barrel, bring him half a mug instead. My father sulks on one of the trestle benches and glares at Salvo, who lies against the warm hearthstones in dreamless sleep.

We eat naught for dinner, and for supper there is only watered maslin and some old squishy turnips that smell like unwashed hose.

I bite my tongue, though. If I'm hungry, someone else isn't, and I'm that much closer to her.

Rain and cold have killed the winter crop. Not just here, but on Anglesey, too. The barges have stopped poling in after Nones.

The prices at the market jump to twice and thrice the summer rates. On one Saturday alone, there are three knife-point robberies and a whole rash of petty thefts.

Even though no victims were English and none of the assaults were carried out on market grounds, my father assigns one of his mill enforcers to escort Mistress Tipley and me when we market. He is called Geraint, and he has curls that beg to have hands run through them. He is the tallest of the mill enforcers by a head and muscled like a bulldog.

I must admit I like having Geraint along. Not only is he fair to look upon, the toll-table queue falls away like meat from a bone when we approach. So do the poor who still crowd the market path. The ones strong enough to crawl there.

I pray for them, then I thank God Almighty and my father and the millers of Caernarvon for the modest surplus in our rearyard shed.

Not long after Prime, Gwinny comes into the workroom, where I'm mending a massive tear in one of my father's tunics. "The lady de Coucy sent for you."

I groan. "But it isn't Monday! Why in thimbles does she want to see me *now?*"

Gwinny shrugs, but I don't expect an answer from her. And the good Lord knows my father will raise Cain should I ignore a summons from the oh-so-important Coucys, so I put on my cloak and head up the road.

A mousy servant answers my knock and shows me to the solar. The lady de Coucy is spinning, so I discreetly clear my throat. She looks up and startles.

"Saints! Child, what are you doing here?"

I bite down on the smart-mouthed retort that will make its way back to my father and end in trouble I don't want. "You sent for me."

The lady de Coucy slowly shakes her head as if I'm a babbling halfwit or speaking Welsh or both. "Why under Heaven would I send for you? Now be gone. I'm busy."

"But . . . you . . ." I stifle a grin and nod politely and hustle out of the room ere she changes her mind. I'm so delighted that I've been spared an afternoon of harangue that I'm halfway up High Street ere I reckon why Gwinny would tell me the lady de Coucy wanted to see me when she obviously didn't.

When I get to the townhouse, Gwinny is shivering in the gutter out front. I approach her, but ere I can speak she says, "You're wanted at the Glover house. Mistress Glover hopes you'll mind the baby while she sleeps."

"Mayhap in a moment," I tell her, "because first I'll know why you . . . told me . . . What is that sound?"

Shuff-shuff. Shuff-shuff.

I crane my neck to peer down the greenway at the garden shed, but Gwinny puts herself firmly in my path.

"I must have been mistaken. Mistress Glover said to hurry."

It's a flail against the shed floor. And that can mean only one thing.

"How do I know you're not, er, *mistaken* again?" I ask in a voice of honey. "Mayhap you should run over there and be sure."

Gwinny shakes her head. "I'm not. Just go."

She's standing like a mastiff between me and the greenway. I move to pass her and she puts herself in my path. I slide to one side and she matches me, smooth and even, as if we're dancing.

And it dawns on me.

"You don't want me in the rearyard, do you?" I fold my

arms and smile. "That's why you sent me to the Coucy house. And that's why you'd trap me under the Glover baby."

Gwinny lifts her chin. She makes no reply, but she's girding herself as if she'll tackle me if need be.

I smile again, slyly. "You're sweet on him, aren't you?"

"No! I—I—"

Gwinny is usually so calm and deliberate. It's amusing to watch her redden and stammer in a mix of Welsh and English.

At length she closes her mouth, draws a few long breaths. "To think you almost had me hoodwinked. With your pitiful nod to justice and your feeding the poor. More fool I, thinking you were any different from the rest. Especially the likes of that shrew in the gilded townhouse you cannot complain of enough."

I stiffen. "I am nothing like her!"

"You will be." Gwinny narrows her eyes. "You're already well on your way."

"Name one thing she does that I do!"

"Murder!"

"I—*What?* Are you *mad?*"

Gwinny's words are clipped and haggard. "Your hands won't be on the rope, but mark me, his blood will be on your hands. A fine little game. You just love your little game. To *Hell* with you *and* your Goddamn game!"

The blasphemy is shocking enough that I step away, into the gutter. Gwinny looks a heartbeat away from weeping or throwing a fist, but one wrong word and she'll do much worse.

"Whose blood?" I gesture toward the rearyard. "His?"

She doesn't answer, but she doesn't have to.

"What is he to you?" I ask quietly, because she's crying now, but by no means is she getting out of my way.

"My brother," she chokes, "and he's all I've got, rot you! He's all I've got and he's going to end up dead because of you!"

We're in the churchyard, my father and I, and before us is her grave, freshly mounded with dark damp earth. My little white hand is tight in his big brown one, and he's holding it hard enough to crunch my bones to powder. He whispers, mayhap to me and mayhap to himself, "Just you and me now, sweeting. You're all I've got."

I draw back, pull my cloak about my shoulders. Gwinny's stance relaxes but she never takes her eyes off me. "What did my brother ever do to you, to deserve death?"

"But he *doesn't* deserve death!"

"*Then why are you doing this to him?*"

I toe the mud that's caked on my shoe. "Er . . . he needed to . . . I . . . well . . ."

Gwinny presses a hand to her forehead. "So it's true. You'd call down the wrath of Caernarvon on an innocent man just for the sport of it. Jesus wept. You should be grateful all I could do was rip up your worthless clothes."

For an instant I see scraps all over my chamber. Scraps, when once I had gowns.

Gwinny took the whipping of her life—for vengeance.

"I—I never would have let it go that far!" I protest. "You must believe that! I would have put a stop to it ere they *killed* him!"

Gwinny swipes at her streaming eyes and cries, "How?"

"Well, I'd just—just—"

And I shut my mouth. Because I am too old for nutting. Not old enough for Catherning. Girls do not go mumming. Walk this way your Grace my lord—

I turn on my heel and hurry into the townhouse, down the corridor and abovestairs and onto my bed and under the bedclothes. The window is shuttered, but I can still hear the muffled shuff-shuff of the flail hitting the shed floor.

1294

ASSUMPTIONTIDE

TO

SAINT JOHN'S EVE

NE of the tenscore Glover lads appears in my garden unannounced at dawn and spades the whole thing up. He is sullen and grumbly, but he makes a good shift of it. It's early for planting, but I take a chance and sow the fresh cold earth with seeds and cuttings. Ere midmorning, there are neat rows marked with stakes and tiny linen flags.

It's hard to make things grow here, harder than Coventry and twice as hard as Edgeley, where everything green sprang up even where it wasn't wanted. But there's something about coaxing life from ground that shrugs at you, that makes you tend it with fish guts and holy water, coddling it as if it's an old sick hound. It matters more. You harvest every blade and seed and grain. You cherish what the earth bestows.

Soon I will have tansy, rue, and coltsfoot.

This year, I will put up a baby fence.

It's Easter. I've been a whole year in the king's borough of Caernarvon.

My wretched uncle Roger is still hale and still lord of Edgeley. The Crusader sun has not yet finished him off. There's still hope, though, for there's been no smug announcement of a birth or even a quickening. My new aunt is not much older than I, but may she remain childless till she's gray as a mule's back-end.

My father offers frankpledge for our street every month and never misses Court Baron. He says he finds borough service most rewarding. He swaggers down Shire Hall like lord of the manor. It's as if he's forgotten Edgeley even exists.

That cur Edward Mercer has kept his distance, but he hasn't taken an interest in another girl. Mayhap he is pining for me. None of the *honesti* girls looks twice at him, and their fathers are never far away when he's about.

Edward Mercer is still shivery-fair to look upon, especially when he flashes that carefree smile, but the shivery only lasts a moment and does not blur my vision.

Mistress Tipley still holds the keys and directs the kitchen. I've not given up, though.

We walk the liberty stones, every burgess and his family. The mayor leads the procession bearing his big mace, the priest at his elbow flicks holy water, and we all tromp dutifully after, trying to keep the mud from our finest clothes.

Up rise the city walls, steep and solid and grand like holy Jerusalem. The view from down here is so different from that atop the walls. Down here there are no glowing rooftops, no endless fields. Down here there is only mud and stone. Up there is utterly out of reach.

Not till I pass through the gates do I feel like myself again.

* * *

Just after Compline, my father calls, "Come here, sweeting. Come look at this."

My chamber is dark and I'm just about to undress for bed. I put my obviously restitched bedrobe over my shift and slip through the curtain to my father's chamber.

He's at the window. The shutters are flung wide and the sky beyond is a rich, deep blue, nearly fallen to black. The land is black, though, and across it lie hundreds of flickering sparks. The tiny dots of orange cover the ridge and spread like pinpricks into the dark distant hills.

I lean against my father's shoulder. He's warm and solid and smells faintly of horse. "It's pretty. What is it?"

"The Welsh herdsmen are burning carcasses," my father replies. "Every beast that has murrain must be killed and its body burned."

"So much fire for one little animal."

"We would not see one beast burning, sweeting. Those are bonfires. Dozens of animals must be destroyed. Hundreds."

My father puts his arm about me and I lay my cheek against his shoulder while the hills glitter and twinkle as if all the stars have fallen.

When time comes to hire a man to clean out the shed, I send one of the Glover lads for Griffith. The poor wretch comes up Shire Hall Street like a soul into Purgatory.

He knows what happens to him here. And yet he comes anyway. He dares not cross me. The cost is too high.

The cost of many things in Caernarvon is too high. That's a lesson both of us have studied.

I bid Mistress Tipley give Griffith his instructions, then I spy on him from my chamber window as he carries crates and sacks from the shed.

At first Griffith cringes with every snap and rustle. He even drops a crate when Salvo lurches outside to drink from the rain barrel. But after a time his whole body loosens. He ceases looking over his shoulder and lingering within the shelter of the shed. He shoulders his burdens with an easy grace that's lovely to watch. He even whistles. When he sweeps the shed floor, he twirls the broom like a dancing partner and flourishes his ratty cloak.

I withdraw two pennies from my father's strongbox and bid Mistress Tipley give them to Griffith for his labor.

Her eyes get big. "Twopence? For merely cleaning the shed?"

"And whatever bread that's idle in the kitchen," I tell her firmly.

"There isn't—"

"Give him mine. I'll go without."

When the old cow trundles outside, I hurry abovestairs and watch from the window. Mistress Tipley hands the coin to Griffith along with a linen-wrapped parcel. Griffith glances about furtively as if something's going to pounce, then takes a whiff of the parcel. He says something disbelieving to Mistress Tipley and she shrugs.

Then Griffith inclines his head and departs through the greenway, carefully stepping over my garden.

I'm curiously warm. As if there's something sweet and delicious baking deep in my vitals.

As if I'm holding the reins of the whole world.

It's raining. Again. Little wonder naught grows here. We ought to sow the fields with fish.

I'm finally ready to stitch. It took innumerable sharpenings of my charcoal stick and three washings, but the design is right at last.

It's the Holy Family. They're on their way to Nazareth. Saint Joseph is holding the Christ Child while the Virgin prays at the roadside. The road winds through a stand of thick woods, and beyond the woods is the sea. High in one corner is Caernarvon, castle and town.

It took us a whole winter, but we turned out an altar cloth that all but marched off the linen. Three of us, shoulder to shoulder before a single frame, giggling, pushing, drinking cider till we lined up for the privy. All three of us together for the last time, not knowing to cherish it, thinking we'd be together forever.

But they're lost to me, and Emmaline de Coucy cannot

sew a straight seam to keep her soul from Purgatory. A pity I cannot ask Gwinny. My undergarments are stitched as tight as wine casks.

So this piece will be my own. It will take me longer, but every stem stitch and knot, every curl and vine and wallstone, will be mine alone.

I sort through the thread Nicholas gave me and choose a deep brown for Saint Joseph's robe.

THE brat is in an ill temper. She's had me sweeping and tidying the hall since sunup, cleaning out corners I've cleaned thrice.

There's a knock at midmorning, and in come the Shrewcys. Mother and daughter, and both have baskets over their arms.

The brat smiles and bids them enter, but she's stiff as a days-old corpse and her smile is too cheerful.

Stand in the corner as she bade me.

Mother Shrewcy wrinkles her nose and asks has the brat never heard of garlands? The brat's smile goes frozen. She opens her mouth in a way that makes me brace for the scolding. But the brat ducks her head and says she merely forgot and begs Mother Shrewcy's pardon.

Saints, that I was fool enough to agree to your education, grumbles Mother. At least your boorish father knew enough to beg the right woman. You'd best not shame me, girl. I mean it.

As Daughter Shrewcy entreats the brat to try harder, the brat's ancient dog limps into the hall and noses Daughter's hand. Daughter shrieks and whips her hand away, pulls out a handkerchief, wipes her fingers.

Send that mongrel out of doors, Mother snaps.

The brat pets the dog's gray head and says, The poor creature is as old as the hills. The damp's not good for his bones.

Put him out, says Mother firmly, and the brat squares up like a toll-table serjeant.

We are nowhere near your grubby little manor, Mother goes on in a blade-cold voice. Those who think to become *honesti* will do well to remember where they are and whose favor they need.

The brat blinks hard, kneels, puts her arms around the dog's neck. Forgive me, she whispers to the beast, then walks it at its shambling pace into the rearyard.

She's gone for many long moments. Slip into the rear chamber, peek into the yard. The brat idles near the kitchen, knotting, reknotting, and unknotting a length of rope around the dog's neck.

Mother and Daughter in the hall discuss whether the brat's table linen ought to be replaced or mended.

The brat brings a pan of water to the dog, pets its head, picks at tangles in its hair.

Daughter Shrewcy comes to the rear door and tells the brat that Mother Shrewcy is waiting and it's time to show the master her walking.

The brat heaves herself up and scowls murder at the kitchen. Then she fixes that false, pained smile and trudges inside.

Have seen that look ere this. Know it, down to my white-hot core.

She walks the way they tell her. She holds her feet, her shoulders, her hands just as they do. The master looks on as if she's made of gold. The brat's smile does not change, unless it grows sharper. As if anyone within an armslength would end up bloodied should that look leave her face and flow through her fists.

She could be one of them. Townhouse lady, servants all around.

It's what everyone wants but her.

BECAUSE THERE is the off chance I might enjoy myself, my father has forbidden me from Midsummer porch vigil at Saint Mary's.

"Midnight is too late for you to be out alone," my father says. "If I didn't have Watch and Ward, I'd be happy to escort you."

"You're *always* on Watch and Ward," I sulk.

"They've stepped up the guard. The whole castlery is a tinderbox since the murrain, to say naught of the Welshry. And then there's the October collection of the tax of the fifteenth drawing nearer. I'm sorry about porch vigil, sweeting. Mayhap next year."

"But Emmaline de Coucy is going to porch vigil!" This is a lie, but it's a lie square in the pride.

My father straightens his cloak. "I believe I said you nay. Don't make me repeat myself."

I put on my best air of offended but obedient dignity, for I have every intention of sneaking out after Vespers and sitting on the church porch until the souls pass by. I want to know right away if my uncle Roger will die in the coming year.

I can barely believe my fortune when my cousin Henry rides up in a splatter of mud a whole month early. I sail out to greet my dearest cousin, call for a Glover lad to take his horse to the common stable and for Gwinny to bring him the coldest buttermilk in the house. When Henry is resting in the big chair with his feet up and his throat wet, I ask him pretty as you please if he plans to attend the Midsummer festivities in our fair town.

"Would that I could, Cesspool," Henry replies, "but the foremost *honesti* will be here tonight to discuss my prospects for taking the privileges."

Thimbles and pins! Not even Fortune will take my side.

My father leaves explicit instructions to me in Henry's presence that under no circumstances am I to leave the house for porch vigil and that it'll be Henry's hide as well as mine if he is disobeyed.

Henry warns me with a single look, then bids Mistress Tipley fetch our second-to-last cask of ale from the cellar.

I defy my father by sitting in the rearyard and throwing hempseed into the mud. It's supposed to grow and my future husband is supposed to come rake it behind me. All it's doing is giving the pigling something to root for.

At dusk, Henry calls me inside and banishes me to my chamber with an awkward but genuine apology and the assurance that the hall will be no place for me tonight. And judging by the houndlike singing and hallooing and laughing that fills the house as the pillars of Caernarvon arrive to discuss Henry's prospects, he may be right.

Exiled, I throw my shutters open and lean out my window as far as I dare. I can see only a shade of the rear wall of Saint Mary's, but mayhap I'll catch sight of the souls on their way to the porch. Mayhap my uncle's soul will be among them. Then my father will be back in possession of Edgeley. By Christmas I could be walking the same floorplanks my mother once trod, and Salvo could be buried at her feet when his time comes.

In an Ave, I'm bored.

So I sit at the top of the stairs and listen to the goings-on in the hall, trying to piece together how Henry is doing, how the burgesses are taking to him.

How good a chance there is that he will become our neighbor.

Apparently they took quite well to him. The *honesti* have extended an official invitation to my cousin Henry to consider the privileges of Caernarvon. He has accepted. He will take the oath at Christmas and move into the townhouse on Palace Street.

Henry goes on at length about how envious Nicholas is and how Nicholas swears as soon as he gets his spurs he'll come to Wales and take so much of that twopenny land that he won't be able to ride its boundaries in a day. Baby Henry has finally beaten Nicholas to something, but I'm still trying to catch them both.

Now that Henry will be our neighbor come Christmas, I cannot wait to show him the market and the Water Gate,

Saint Mary's and the wellheads and the place where the Seiont pools cold and quiet, where small fish come to nibble your toes.

The evening ere he leaves for Coventry, Henry clears his throat and casts about and does worse than ruin my life.

He ends it.

Henry ends my life with the black news that Thomas d'Edgeley was born to my wretched uncle Roger and his worthless slip of a wife on May Eve.

My father cheerfully throws on his cloak, seizes Henry by the elbow, and calls over his shoulder that they're off to the Boar's Head to drink to the babe's good health.

I sit at the empty table and stare into the dying hearthfire.

It's gone.

The snug little hall with its brand-new chimney, the glowing garden, the dovecote, the turn of stream where quiet fish would gather in a silvery cloud. The pasturage where goats would crowd their necks through the fence for a handful of clover. The churchyard with its ancient yews and graves. The swing, swaying from an oak limb, that my father made from a length of hemp and an old cart-slat.

Edgeley was to be mine. My mother promised all of it to me on my saint day when I turned seven and she let me carry the keys on a piece of twine tied about my waist from Prime till Compline. I could open every chest and door and lock. I spent every moment of that day at her side, hurrying to match her calm, swishing stride, and Salvo followed us both.

At Vespers I was hiding from her in the dovecote, clutching the keys together to keep them from clanking. She had the grooms combing the yard for me, as it was long past my bedtime. The poor lads called and called, but they were grown and had forgotten the best places to hide. I could have stayed where I was till the Last Trumpet, and I planned to. I could not bear for the day to end.

My father came out as far as the trough and promised me the whipping of my life should I not immediately present myself before him, but I held the keys tighter and moved not a margin.

My mother finally came into the yard herself, holding up the horn-paned lantern. "Cecily, sweeting, one day it will all be yours. Every post and barrel, and there won't be a day that goes by that those keys aren't at your belt. You must be patient."

One day felt like the morrow when she said it. I came out and put the big ring of keys in her keeping. And I did get the whipping of my life.

And ere the season turned, we buried her.

Edgeley is his now. The rotten usurper mewling at his girl-mother's breast. It's all his, every post and barrel.

Now we're stuck in Caernarvon. We're stuck here for good, and my father doesn't even seem to care.

Hᴡᴇʟ shuffles to the steading door. For a moment I'm wroth, Dafydd sending his cousin to ply me with more fruit- less talk of marriage. But Hywel looks hagridden, his eyes red and his face blotchy. He's been weeping.

"All of them," he whispers.

He loves them like children. He names them and weaves crowns of flowers for their horns.

Step away from the fire. "You had them up high. How could they have caught it?"

Hywel shrugs, scrubs a wrist over his eyes. "I know not. They're all dead. Sweating and staggering. Yours. Mine. Every beast in the vale."

They're all dead. Cattle. Goats. Sheep. The murrain leaves nothing on the hoof untouched. No meat. No milk. No butter. No cheese.

No food left but what's doled out in Crown measures for ten times its worth.

"Forgive me," Hywel whispers, as if it's his fault. Tears slide down his cheeks, winding through bristly beard-fuzz. "They all had to burn."

Beckon him in. Give him some mead. He refuses half an oatcake. Cannot eat, he mutters.

Best eat now. Soon enough we'll all be too hungry to care about the morrow.

A thrash. The stumble of feet. Something being dragged.

Awake. Instantly. The door-curtain wicks back to reveal a square of deep night-blue and a harsh silver wash of moonlight.

They've come. As they did for Dafydd. Cudgels and thatch everywhere.

On my feet, grappling for something heavy.

"Gwen, it's me!" Gruffydd's voice is strained, as if he's winded or bearing something heavy. "Help me. Right now."

Cannot move. Can barely breathe. The cooking pot slides out of my hand.

From the dark comes gasping. Harsh bursts of sound a man would make were he drowning.

Or hanging from an English rope.

"Gwenhwyfar!"

Kneel to stir up the coals. By the raft of sickly orange light, I can make out Gruffydd on his knees. Covered in blood.

Sweet. Merciful. Christ.

"Hssst! No fire! They'll be looking for light!"

Swipe up Mam's water and douse the struggling coals. A great billow of smoke rises with a hiss of steam and the stench of burn.

"No." Whisper is choked. "Oh, Christ, no."

"It's not my blood, Gwen. Please. He's dying. Help me."

For a long moment, all I can do is tremble.

Not his blood.

Then I feel my way across the steading, moving toward Gruffydd's voice. The disembodied gasps dry up as I near.

"What happened?" Even as the words come out, I bite my lip. The less I know, the better for all. "To him, I mean."

"Cut," Gruffydd replies tersely. "And never mind. He's gone. God rest his soul."

Bump into Gruffydd and kneel at his side. Press my shoulder against his.

"They got Cadwgan and Rhodri ap Tudur. Naught we could do. Bastards will hang them on the morrow. God *damn* those English sons of whores!"

Stickiness spreading over my shoulder, soaking in. Not Gruffydd's blood.

Reckoning the fire now. Lackwitted of me to cast water on the coals. Somehow I'll have to get the fire started again ere I leave for the brat's.

"Someone will have to tell their wives. And their mother."

This is why. Because I cannot bear to lose them both.

Gruffydd beside me still draws his breath unsteadily.

One day, a shadow will come to my door. He will push his hood back and scuff the dirt with one heel, and he will tell me to go to the market common should I want to say farewell ere the hangman does his work. Or that my brother died well in some anonymous way, calling down the only kind of justice the likes of us have recourse to.

Then I will have naught left to lose.

1294

SAINT JOHN'S DAY

TO

MICHAELMAS EVE

MMALINE'S father is accused of murder.

I'm not supposed to know a word of it, of course, but it's impossible to get a moment of marketing done without absorbing who's with child by whom or who's fighting with her mother-in-law or whose baby has rump rash bad enough to blister.

As near as I can figure out, Sir John de Coucy was out on his endowed cropland and caught a Welshman foraging in the stubble. Apparently there was a struggle and Sir John slew the Welshman with his falchion.

My father keeps combing a hand through his hair and muttering that it could have been him, it could have been him.

Murder is the Crown's jurisdiction, not the borough's, and the royal justice itinerant will be coming from Conwy to hear the case.

The Coucys' mousy servant appears on our doorstep with the message that the lady de Coucy will not expect me this Monday, nor on any Monday until further notice. My father says that no man can blame her, even though the look about him suggests that he's a man who could. I merely glance up from my embroidery frame with my good-girl smile *that says whatever the lady de Coucy thinks is best* and all that rot.

And I spend Monday peaceably for a change, outlining the city walls of Caernarvon with a strand of purple-gray thread that seems made for the purpose.

It's high summer, and that means there isn't much hired work to do around the townhouse. I explain to my father that Gwinny is worried about her brother, who's finding it hard to get a job of work, and I ask if there's something that needs doing at one of the mills.

My father has some sort of merry wine-tinted exchange at the Boar's Head with the provisioner of the castle garrison and learns that one of the timber gangs is a man short. If Griffith wants the work, he's to report to a man with the rather unsavory name of Snagnose John at the Newdale site on the morrow at dawn.

One of the Glover lads is dispatched to inform Griffith of the offer, and I dance toward the kitchen to tell Gwinny what I've done, but I pull up short the instant I step into the rearyard.

She'll think it's a trick. And she'll tell him not to go.

I hesitate in the doorway for a long moment.

Then I take myself to my workroom and plant my backside before my frame.

I know he takes the work, though. I know because

Gwinny comes in one day smiling in a way that makes her every step light as she sweeps and tidies.

Gwinny is rather pretty when she smiles. I wonder why I never noticed ere this.

Emmaline de Coucy turns up on my doorstep unbidden and unannounced. She's robed in servants' linsey and her eyes are red.

"Mother doesn't know I'm here," she whispers. "Won't you please let me in ere someone sees me?"

I bite back the choice words I have for the lady de Coucy and show Emmaline into the hall. I pour her a mug of new cider and steer her to the hearthbench, away from Salvo's pallet.

"Forgive me breaking your peace." Emmaline's voice quavers. "I couldn't bear to be alone. I'm so worried about my father. What if the royal justice finds against him? They hang felons! Just like those two poor Welshmen, God rest them!"

I pour myself some cider and take a long drink. It could very well have been my father who drew steel on a trespasser, and me weeping secretly at Emmaline's hearth.

If the lady de Coucy allowed it.

"Do you think the king would truly hang your father?" I make my tone reasonable. "Sir John de Coucy? Burgess and *honesti* of Caernarvon?"

"Yes! His Grace the king is adamant that this province

be governed by statute and his law applied evenhandedly regardless of blood." Emmaline wipes her eyes. "If the mayor himself were found guilty, he would be hanged."

"His Grace the king is rather generous," I reply. "Mayhap he has never been here and met the Welsh."

Emmaline chokes on a giggle. "The king knows the Welsh very well. He would have them as subjects, so he must trust his officials here to govern as he bids. And he must trust us to treat the Welsh as neighbors."

"Neighbors," I echo. Neighbors who pay all the taxes. Neighbors who rob one another at the market out of hunger. Neighbors who cannot get a decent job of work without the intervention of a burgess.

"Oh, Cecily, my father had no murder in his heart!" Emmaline toys with a loosening stitch of her handkerchief. "It was all misadventure, but out there in county court there will be Welshmen on the jury. They'll want vengeance, not justice."

Out there. Without the walls. I pat her shoulder as she sniffles into her handkerchief. "All will be well. Truly. His Grace the king would not suffer a man to be punished wrongfully. Especially a man like your father. There will be justice. You must believe that."

Emmaline worries the stitching on her handkerchief. She doesn't believe it. The king might want Caernarvon ruled by statute, but it's hard to insist on it when he's so far away.

* * *

It's not even Tierce and it's sweltering. The market is dusty and the basket is heavy and I'm thirstier than a year's worth of Augusts. Mistress Tipley bustles ahead. I sway behind her, heaving the basket because this task is rightfully mine.

At the bakery, Mistress Tipley hands over the five wads of bread dough. The baker pulls out five loaves and pushes them across the counter.

"Are you not supposed to keep one?" I ask him. "To feed the castle garrison?"

The baker shakes his head. "Don't need it now. The garrison is being thinned since the order to muster came down."

"What order?"

"Every man of military age in the Principality is summoned to fight for his Grace the king in Gascony and— Demoiselle, what ails you?"

No.

Not him, too.

I tear out of the bakery, leaving Mistress Tipley and the market basket behind. Past shoulders and around carts and over puddles and he's a trial and a goose but the king cannot make him go to Gascony, he just cannot!

I burst in, slam the door, stumble down the corridor. My father is in the hall buckling on his wrist braces. I fling myself at him and hold on hard.

"Don't go! You cannot go!"

My father peels me off gently and steers me toward a bench. "What's all this, sweeting? Where can I not go?" He sits on the other bench, forearms on knees, all wrinkled brow and downturned mustache and gray at his temples.

"Gascony! The baker said that all the men here must fight for the king in Gascony!"

"Sweeting, that summons isn't for the burgesses. His Grace is summoning the Welshmen of the Principality to his standard. They're the ones who must fight abroad."

I lift my head, scrub my eyes. "The Welshmen? Not you?"

"No, sweeting. I owe for my burgage twelvepence a year. I owe no military service abroad. I owe no service in England, either. All I must do is defend the king's interests in the Principality. Remember?"

My father is not going to Gascony.

I let out a long, shuddering breath.

"Now, your uncle Roger," my father says with a smile, "is responsible for equipping two and a third serjeants for service in Gascony, if he does not go himself."

I giggle. Two and a third serjeants. I wonder what good a third of a serjeant would be to the king.

My uncle Roger owes service for Edgeley. He must pay taxes like lastage and passage and a fifteenth of his movable goods when the king requests it. He must trade on market day.

We don't have any such restrictions. Here in Caernarvon, we're friends of the king.

"That's my girl." My father embraces me and rises. "I'm

off. The mayor is expecting a report on the state of the mills. Have you seen my counter-roll of fines?"

"In the coffer. Where it always is."

"Good girl."

And he's out the door with a tromp of boots and a whuffle of wood.

Thank Christ. Thank Christ and all the saints for our friendship with the king.

Gwinny stands before the hearth, clinging to the broom. She looks like a corpse, bloodless and stiff.

"Oh, Gwinny, your brother!" I press a hand to my mouth. "Your brother will have to go."

She sinks to the floor and runs both hands over her hair. The broom clatters behind her. She looks greensick.

"He's all I've got," she whispers.

Gwinny looks so small crumpled like a dishrag in the hearth corner that I sift for something to say that will make her feel better.

Someone else might try, "Mayhap it'll be a good thing. His Grace the king pays wages, you know." Or, "Griffith will be fine. He'll come back with a purse full of silver and tales of heroics in Gascony. And September is a long time from now."

But I keep my mouth shut.

Because if anyone had said those things to me an Ave ago, I might have clawed her eyes out.

TAKING. They're always taking. Da. Pencoed. Coin. Beasts.

Now they want my brother.

Hands out, rattle parchment, cry it down in grating, rusty English.

Those who do not give freely lose all.

Know not where I first hear the name. It rises from the dusty ground, from the powdered ash of charcoal bones that once were live and lowing and keeping us from hunger.

Madog.

It's breathed like prayer from the very soul of the Welshry, wreathed round the horns of distrained cattle peaceably browsing Watched burgess land. It's in the Crown measures, the market pennies, the chalk.

Madog ap Llywelyn ap Maredydd ap Llywelyn ap Maredydd ap Cynan ab Owain Gwynedd. Disinherited son of a slighted line, trembling with quiet rage in some forgotten corner of this land.

Know not if he's even real, and if he is, know not what to make of the mutters men pair with his name.

They are the mutters of sharpened staves. Of spears hidden in the rafters. Murdered fathers and seized estates. *Con-*

tra pacem, they said. Da had taken up arms against the king, *their* king, a man he never swore for, so they took all.

Madog. Breathe it like prayer. Madog ap Llywelyn ap Maredydd ap Llywelyn ap Maredydd ap Cynan ab Owain Gwynedd.

Please God let him be real. We are all becoming men with blackened faces, even with the gallows in plain view.

POTTAGE AGAIN. Miserable, misbegotten refuse better suited for filling gaps in the wall slats.

I cheerily serve a plate of it to my father. "Look at the delicious pottage, Papa. How much I love eating it day after day. So delightful that we may eat it for breakfast and dinner, too. And such flavor! Not at all like the mud pasties that the Glover children serve one another."

"Sit down and eat it," my father growls. "Not even the mayor has a haunch of meat."

I do, but now I'm thinking of wall plaster and every bite goes down that much harder for it.

Thank all the saints that my father thought to stockpile the oats and barley given him by the millers of Caernarvon as part of his office. Even if he does stand over Mistress Tipley like a mastiff and see that she measures out shares for all four of us for breakfast and supper. If he hadn't thought to keep that grain back, we'd be down at the market paying the price of ten horses for half a quartermeasure of crawling rye.

Or going without.

I'm terribly glad that I can use the workroom again. In winter, we were packed into the hall because every other room was so cold that our breath came out in puffs. There are precious few times I can bear my father's feeble attempts at humor and smile politely at his tales of millers attempting to get out of castellaria or Welshmen who hid their handmills to avoid the fine.

"The sacks were in the byre, if you'll believe it! A little, er, *persuading* and he came out with them." Or, "Thought he could hide the handmill in the dunghill, but that fool surely didn't think I'd throw him in to find it!" And so on. It's tiresome.

But now it's summer and he's hardly ever here. If he's not officering the mills, he's in and out of *honesti* houses or meeting with castle men or putting himself forward for extra turns at Watch and Ward.

Gwinny enters the workroom and stands quietly till I look up from my embroidery frame.

"Mistress Tipley says to come to supper."

"Very well." I flex my fingers. They ache like penance, but Saint Joseph is finished and the Holy Child outlined. I stow my needle and stretch.

Gwinny regards me as if I'm on sale at the market but she's not sure of my teeth. Then she brings something out from behind her back and holds it toward me.

It's pink. A most familiar rose pink.

I let the small folded packet fall open. Sure enough, it's the rose wool from my Michaelmas gown, but it's been carefully trimmed into a square and stitched around the edges with tiny, precise stitches to stop the fraying.

A handkerchief. From one of the scraps.

Gwinny lifts her chin. "Taking all of it makes me no better than you."

I hold the handkerchief close to my chest. At length I whisper, "I'm sorry, too," but Gwinny has already gone.

Saints keep me, the constable of Caernarvon and the justiciar of North Wales are coming to our little house! They will be here for supper and the kitchen is in an absolute uproar, eel sizzling and pots bubbling and fingers flying and Mistress Tipley shrilling.

My father pulls me aside. "Now, sweeting, I need not tell you how important these men are. I'd send a child to her chamber to keep her out of the way, but you are old enough to serve us at table. I know you'll make me proud."

Not only will I make him proud, I'll prove that I've learned *honesti*craft like the paternoster and therefore never need suffer the goodwill of the lady de Coucy again.

"And it'll give you a chance to be seen." My father winks. "Both of these men have sons who need wives."

High-ranking borough officials will expect naught less of a man with ambitions toward *honesti*hood, and my father would have himself seen by these men just as much as he would me.

When the guests arrive at Vespers, the hearth is blazing with fragrant pine. The constable of the castle is called Adam de Whetenhale, and he has the reddest hair of anyone I've ever seen. I already know the justiciar's name, and, very well, I'm glad I know to curtsey.

They sit on either side of my father at the trestle, and he has both men laughing within moments.

I walk like a fine borough lady. I pour wine from the right and cast my gaze down and smile when one of them makes a jest, but not too much because of my crooked teeth. Emmaline could not have done it better.

But they're not even looking at me. They're talking about Sir John de Coucy's *problem,* as they call it.

"We cannot ignore it," my father warns. "Not with the king's Gascony edict atop the famine and *taxatores* on their way. The Welshry is demanding justice. And the whor—men with blackened faces will see that they get it one way or another."

The justiciar grins. "They'll get the justice that's coming to them. But Coucy will be tried by a jury of his peers. And that's why we're here."

Mistress Tipley appears in the rear storage chamber with a tray of fried eel that demolished our savings. I glide over to take it from her, but it's hard to remember to keep my eyes down and not trip over my hem and keep the tray level all at once.

"We need you for Coucy's jury," the justiciar says to my father. "A fortnight's time. The bailiff's clerk will come for you."

My father frowns. "I owe no suit at county court."

"County court, mayhap," the constable replies, "but not a county jury. God forbid."

I slide the tray onto the trestle where all three can reach, then step back, hands clasped and head bowed. Surely one of them will tell my father what a charming and lovely daughter he has. They will say what a fine borough lady she is, and how any man would be fortunate to have her to wife.

But they don't. Three daggers spear slices of eel and the men tear in like beasts, swigging wine and spitting out stray bones.

They don't even notice me.

"Coucy is a burgess of Caernarvon, and he'll be tried by his *peers*." The justiciar smiles like a sated cat. "He could cut down half the Welshry and that right would still be his. Matters little *where* Coucy sits for judgment, for I have every confidence that you lads will hear the oathgivers and come to the right conclusion."

My father squints thoughtfully for a moment, then grins big as market day. He clasps wrists with both visitors and agrees to serve as a juror. Then the three of them attack their meal once again with relish.

I stand in the hearth corner trembling with rage. I did everything I was taught. Everything, just as an *honesti* lady might. And it gained me naught.

HE was tried by his peers. Fellow burgesses. English-men all.

This is justice, they tell us. English justice.

Out in county court, away from stone and mortar, he should be judged by a jury of Welshmen.

But the Crown looks away.

English returns to Caernarvon in smug horseback tri-umph. He killed a man in cold blood and the verdict is Not Proven. Twelve of his peers see to it.

1294

MICHAELMAS

TO

CHRISTMAS EVE

MICHAELMAS dawns clear and blue, the kind of fierce autumn sky that promises endless summer. I lean on my window frame, shutters thrown wide, and breathe the thick, briny wind.

Today is the fair. Today is jugglers and trained marmosets and pasties hot from carts and ribbons and carole-dancing in the street. It's Michaelmas!

As I reach for the shutters, I smell something strange. A dark haze is rising over Anglesey, smearing the blue.

It's almost like smoke.

First the crop failure, now a fire. Anglesey must have done something to anger the Almighty. God willing, next year will be better.

My father is much more sober this Michaelmas. He eats his porridge in measured mouthfuls while staring at the hearth. There are fresh scars on his forearms. He's still on his first mug of ale.

"Papa," I purr, sliding into my place at his right hand. "May I go to the fair?"

"If you stay within the walls, sweeting. Take Gwinny and be careful. The countryside is still hot."

"Could I have fivepence to spend?"

He makes a show of choking on his ale. "Fivepence? Surely. Let me just pull that out of my purple and ermine tunic!"

I fold my arms and huff big. Good old pinchpenny Papa. "How about three?"

"Two, you little spendthrift," he says, tugging my plait. "Honestly, you'll have to marry an earl. Only blooded men will be able to keep you."

"Give me his hand and point us toward the church door," I reply, and my father laughs aloud. He pulls out his purse and hands me the pennies. I kiss my father's bristly cheek, then Gwinny and I are out the door and into the whistling, singing, stomping, and shouting.

This fair seems smaller than last year's. Not nearly as many sheep on tethers, or skeins of wool. The prices are higher, too. A stall in front of the Glovers' wants a half a penny for a single honey cake!

Surely there are better prices. I have but twopence and I want to stretch them. With Gwinny in tow, I thread through Shire Hall Street and move down High.

Someone screams.

Man or woman, I cannot tell. It came from the gates, though, and I strain on tiptoe for a glimpse. Betimes the Watch will hack off a cutpurse's ear while the wronged man watches, or they'll thrash a minstrel for singing in the street.

No such fortune. All I can see are hooded heads, bobbing and plodding and swaying.

I tug Gwinny's sleeve. "Come, let's go see what the excitement is!"

Gwinny stands like a sighted hare.

"It'll be fun!" I hop and crane, but I can see naught. "We surely don't want to miss out."

"Madog," she whispers.

A boy flashes past me. At least I think it's a boy. He was running too fast to be certain. Then another boy, then a woman dragging a child by the wrist, then men.

There's a rumble like thunder far away, yet the sky is so blue it hurts the eye.

And there's screaming and shouting and the shing-shing of metal and the dull thud of blades in flesh, like a hallful of people eating meat with daggers in both hands.

I turn.

High Street is rushing toward me in a massive wave. Men, women, children, dogs, goats. They thrash and tumble and scrabble away from—

Welshmen. Welshmen who chase them like animals, cut them down with sword and spear and falchion and dagger, leap over the corpses and hack at whatever's moving.

They're running past me, men and women and boys and dogs bumping me shoulder and elbow, and I cannot move.

Gwinny will help me. She'll intercede with the butchers,

tell them I'm to be spared, that I gave her a gown and kept her fed and found her brother a job of work.

But Gwinny is not at my elbow. Or up the street. Or anywhere.

A Welshman shoulders in a door not an armslength from me. He plows inside with several fellows on his heels. Things crash and there's screaming. And then sobbing. And then silence.

I must get home. My father will protect me. He has a big sword and a falchion and he'll hold the door against them.

I fly up High Street, straight through the gutter. Already it's full of blood.

A Welshmen startles as I wick past and he stabs his spear at me. Two brutes peel off and pursue me at a dogtrot.

Christ, no.

I stumble over a limp arm and hit the gutter face first. I come up mired with mud and blood and it reeks and purple stars dazzle my eyes and my mouth waters and I vomit my porridge and cream.

Footfalls behind me. I heave myself up, retching, swiping at the mess gobbeting my gown. The arm I fell over hangs limply in the gutter.

It belongs to one of the Glover lads. His belly is cut open and his guts are sliding out.

And I'm off, away from feet crunching mud and rock, away from the Glover boy, and crossing myself with every other step, falling over my hem and gagging at the smell of myself and dodging bodies and getting home so my father can pet my hair and keep me safe.

The racket is hellish and everything smells like burning. I round the corner of Shire Hall. Smoke pours from the windows of the Tutburys' house on the corner. The screaming comes from everywhere at once like the sound of some unholy choir. Ahead I can see our house, and I pray to every saint who's listening that it's not afire.

It's not. God is merciful to sinners.

I try the door, weeping and weak in the legs, but it doesn't budge. Not a margin. And the two brutes are rounding the gate and four more are following, all of them ragged and raw-eyed and brandishing blood-smeared weapons and looking right at me.

"Papaaaaaaaa!"

I screech and pound and kick the oaken slab and they're going to cut me up for the pigs and it's forever ere the door opens a crack and a slice of my father's face floats beyond. His eyes are wild. I throw my shoulder into the crack, trying to cram inside, but a massive palm slams into the door a handswidth from my ear. The door flies open and my father staggers back from the force of the blow. Welshmen crowd through, one after another, pushing me ahead of them.

I hit the wall hard. Black pain over my eyes, then I'm blinking and the wall is holding me up.

My father is in the middle of a crowd of Welshmen, all elbows and fists and knees, flailing like a drowning man.

They're going to kill him. They're going to beat him to pulp right before my eyes.

Even in my own house, I can still hear the screaming.

"Papa!" They're killing my father. And I'm standing here.

"Get out!" His voice is raspy, as if he's swallowed ground glass.

I cannot move.

Gwinny appears from the rear chamber and points through the hall, jabbering in Welsh. Men troop past with grain sacks from our shed on their shoulders, and she directs them to the door with stabs of her finger.

The Welshmen are dragging my father toward the stairs, but he's fighting them knuckle and jab, tooth and backhand. He's bleeding from nose and mouth, and clumps of his hair are missing.

I stagger across the room and fall into Gwinny. "He's going to die! They're going to kill my father!"

She snorts. "Aye. They are."

"Stop them!"

Gwinny shrugs. "I couldn't even if I wanted to. He's been digging his own grave with every fistful of barley, every handmill fine, every door kicked in, every word in the bailiffs' ears."

They've got him halfway up the stairs. All I can see of my father are his boots, catching winks of hearthfire as he kicks and struggles. Another Welshman follows with a length of rope.

I'm weeping at Gwinny's feet and clutching her hem and I can still hear the screaming above my own shuddering breath.

"Help me, Gwinny," I sob, "please, for the love of God. They'll come for me next. Help me. Do something."

The hem jerks from my hands and swishes away. I look up at Gwinny, up and up and into her bird-black eyes.

"Justice," she hisses, "for those who deserve it."

Then Gwinny swings a quartermeasure sack over her shoulder and follows the men out the gaping front door.

There's no more scuffle abovestairs, no thumping or scraping or dragging. Only cheering and hooting.

Get out, he said. He cannot mean alone.

I stand up. My legs are watery. Heavy footfalls drum on the stairs. Toward me.

I stumble through the storage chamber and out the rear door. The rearyard is a shambles. The henhouse is tipped over and kicked in. The pig and goat are missing. The rain barrel has a foot-shaped hole in the side.

I totter through the wreckage and peek through the kitchen door. No sign of Mistress Tipley. Pots and kettles and spoons and paddles lie scattered like driftwood. The shelves are bare.

I slip through the greenway toward the street. This time I do not run. Running draws their attention. Welshmen heave past, toting lengths of wool and quartermeasure sacks.

They storm along Shire Hall bloody to the knees with blades drawn. The screaming is louder here. The whole town is screaming for mercy.

In front of my house, I search the street for someone to help me. Anyone. Master Glover. Sir John de Coucy. Even Edward Mercer. But there are only Welshmen, smoke, and blood.

Something creaks. Something behind me, in what's left of my house.

It's my father. Hanging from his chamber window. Stripped naked. A handmill dangling from his neck, strung on the cord of his bedrobe. Neck awry, eyes bulging, blank.

I'm running. The ground flashes past my feet in smears of brown and green. My stomach is hot and stabby and I land in dirt as I retch and retch but nothing comes up.

My garden. I'm in my garden. I'm crushing tansy and borage.

The shed door has been torn off. I grapple my way inside and sink into the corner nearest the door, pull knees to chin, and weep.

I'm little. Not more than three or four summers, because I'm small enough that my father can throw me high in the air in Edgeley's sunny yard. He catches me in strong, sure arms and I crow *again again again* because I know he will never let me fall. A wooden top with a red plaited pull-string skitters over Edgeley's trestle and clatters to a stop and I squeal and my father smiles and pets my hair and oh Christ he's gone he cannot be gone because I was going to buy him some gingerbread with one of the pennies because I did not think to tell him farewell.

Get out, he said. Ere a handful of whooping devils put a rope round his neck and pushed him out his chamber window.

I heave myself up. The screaming is muffled here, but somehow that's worse. If I go through the streets, they'll see me. I'll have to follow the walls through rearyards till I get to the gate.

I check my rearyard. Empty. So I make myself walk. Running draws their attention and they're in the houses, tipping coffers and seizing garments by the handful. They'll see me through shutterless windows and sweep down.

Near the fence, I step on something furry. It's Salvo, lying peacefully on his side as if he's asleep on his gorse bed. But he's not. His throat has been cut. A collar of shiny red from ear to ear. Bleeding a scarlet fan into the mud.

I cross myself and keep walking.

Next door's rearyard is torn up like a byre. My shoe sucks into the mud. Then the other. So I leave them. The mud squishes cold and gritty around my ankles.

At the corner, I peer down High Street. What's left of the Michaelmas fair is strewn and thrashed. Broken carts and dead sheep and ragged scraps of bunting still clinging to smoldering buildings. And Welshmen bearing plunder, sacks and crates and bundles. Welshmen with torches, setting town-houses afire. Welshmen everywhere, armed and wroth as demons loosed from Hell.

It's about a stone's throw across High Street to Church. And I must cross High in plain view of these butchers.

I'll never make it. They'll descend on me like a pack of dogs.

I take a deep breath and step into the road. Chin up, eyes forward. The walk that earned me penance from the lady de Coucy.

Over my shoulder is the castle's gray profile. The cross of Saint George does not fly above the Eagle Tower, nor the arms of the constable. There's another banner, one I don't recognize. A red and gold banner, quartered.

The Welsh have taken the castle.

All dead. The castle garrison. The porters at the city gate. No one's left. They'll spare none of us.

Cannot stop. Welshmen everywhere. One foot before the other, slipping in blood.

An apron drifts across the Sandyses' greenway. A shift, too. Three adjoining townhouses are ablaze, smoke pouring from the windows. A baby cries somewhere in a pathetic, straggling wail.

If I survive this I will confess my sins like an anchoress, for if Hell is anything like the fall of Caernarvon, I want to be perfectly certain of my soul.

* * *

Follow the wall. Drag my hand against it. Don't look too closely at limp shapes in corners or furtive movement behind sheds. Stand still as a hare when Welshmen pour out of town-houses, smearing sooty handprints on doorframes. Count towers till I reach the Penny Tower, then the city gate.

At the gate, Welshmen stream in and out weighed down with plunder, making a great din with their shouting, singing, roaring. Somehow I must get through that gate. It's the only way out of Caernarvon.

I lean against a shed. Suck in trembling breaths. My feet are raw. My legs are like cooked parsnips and I cannot go on. Not another step. Not through that gate.

Get out, he said to his only living child, the light of his otherwise meaningless life.

Grip my muddy gown. Let out a shuddery breath. Then I plunge around the shed corner and plow through the alley toward the city gates.

One gate has been torn from the hinges and trampled to splinters. I fix my eyes on the bridge that spans the river beyond the dark arch. Welshmen stagger and storm through the gate-hole. I look through them as I pass. They do not exist.

There are scrape marks on the ground where the toll trestle stood. Not even a splinter remains.

Outside the gate, I choke on acrid smoke. The wharves are burning. Every last boat sends diagonal flames to the heavens and the canals are crammed with charred flotsam.

Chin up, stride even. Running draws their attention. I

pray to every saint who's listening to surround me with angels bearing swords.

Something snares my plait.

The saints are elsewhere today.

I reel backward and twist, but whatever has me jerks my hair downward and slings me hard against the bridgehouse. The whole world is naught but purple stars and agony from scalp to backside.

Then a Welshman appears before me and pins me by the neck to the bridgehouse with one big hand. His other hand pushes my gown up in scrabbly grips and grabs. He's grinning. He's missing teeth.

The sky behind him is glowing blue while all the world burns.

No one is coming to help me. They're all dead.

The Welshman gets my gown over my knee and I kick. I kick as hard as I can between his legs and he roars as if I've killed him. I hope I have. He falls away bellowing like a poorly stuck pig and that's all I see because I run for the bridge, attention be damned.

There's a clamor of harsh noise behind me but I don't look back. I fly across the bridge through a crowd of Welshmen fighting over plunder and getting drunk off tuns of wine that must have come from those burning ships.

Mayhap they chase me. Mayhap they don't. They don't catch me. I stop running only when I'm deep in the greenwood gasping for breath and there's not a soul around save birds and insects and quiet, ancient trees.

No more screaming. No more smoke. Only riversong and the chirring of birds, the wet, woody smell of earth.

My legs give way. I collapse in the brush. Take breath after breath. My skin burns. My neck. My legs, where his damp eager hands dragged upward.

Caernarvon stands on its plain while a curtain of black smoke rises as if the Adversary himself has come to claim it.

I'm out.

I'm alone.

It'll be dark soon. Were there any bells left, they'd be ringing Nones.

My gown crackles, a stiff sheet of blood and muck and vomit. It reeks like a midden in August. My feet are laced with cuts and blistered from sun-baked ground, stinging as if full of pins.

Water murmurs somewhere nearby. As on the outing with Emmaline and her kin all those months ago. When angry Welshmen pelted William with rubbish because he was a *taxator*.

And I was wroth because of my ruined gown.

We'd regret it, the poor wretch swore, sweltering at borough court as serjeants hauled him away. Every last act of it.

I crawl beneath a tree. Curl up. And tremble.

They murdered my father. They hold Caernarvon, seat of his Grace the king's government in the Principality of North Wales. My house will soon be char and timber if it isn't already. I am without the walls with naught in the world but the clothes on my back.

And it'll be dark soon.

Someone's coming. There's no time to hide, so I huddle as small as I can, a cat in January. No tromp of boots, so it's a Welshman.

Go past. You don't see me.

But he does. And his face darkens.

It's Griffith.

He's smudgy with soot and his tunic is torn. He squares up like a boar and looks me up and down, as if I'm something to scrape off a shoe.

Tremble and whimper and my breath comes in tiny gasps as if I'm pulling air through a reed.

Griffith snorts, shakes his head, and starts toward the ford, disappearing in margins over the hill.

Swipe at my wet cheeks again and again.

Then he stops. For a long moment he does naught, and I will him on his way with every bit of will I have.

But Griffith comes back up the rise, piece by piece, face, shoulders, torn tunic, till he's standing over me like an idol.

Get out, he said, ere they killed him in cold blood. He did not mean like this.

"No. It won't do." Griffith sounds weary, as if he is a thousand years old. "The worst is coming. Here."

He holds out a hand.

If whatever's coming is worse than the sack of Caernarvon, Hell must be opening its great maw.

"Go away." I try to stand. If he knows I cannot fight back, I'm done for. But I cannot even climb to my knees.

Without fanfare, Griffith hauls me up like a wet pallet, looses me roughly, and leaves me swaying like a sapling on legs that won't make it ten steps.

"Wh-where are we going?" I whisper.

He makes no reply, merely fixes me with a look that shuts my gob very quickly and jerks his chin at the greenwood. So I make myself stumble behind him on colt-legs and feet burning like sulfur.

Mayhap it'll be quick. Please, God, let it be quick.

We walk. The sun sinks. One foot before the other. Days and se'ennights and years we walk.

Just when I cannot go another step, we come to the bottom of a wooded hill.

And I collapse.

So Griffith drags me step after staggering step toward a sagging hovel decaying amid thick brush. He shoulders the curtain aside and lowers me before a ring of embers. Next to me is a pile of moth-eaten blankets outlined faintly in orange light. He hangs the quartermeasure sack from a hook in the rafters, then approaches me.

Flinch. And flinch. Dear God, this is it.

But Griffith only kneels to build up the struggling fire. He's close enough that I can smell him, smoke and sweat and soot, but he does not so much as look at me. The coals glow like stars. At length, flame licks up the tinder and begins to crackle.

I can see better now. There are wattled walls, patched and repatched. Dirt floor, damp at the edges. The whole place smells of mold and rot with the faint whiff of goat.

When the fire is busy, Griffith goes to the sack hanging from the rafters. He withdraws a hand-sized wedge of cheese and a loaf of bread. The bread is bloody on one heel, but he cuts a slab from the other end and sets it in a shallow vessel.

He has not cut my throat, raised a hand, pushed me down. He does not seem to even want to.

Behind me, someone screams as if cornered by a haunt.

Gwinny's in the doorway. She's wearing three cloaks dangling with silver cloak-pins and brooches and armor-buckles. About her waist is a man's belt stuffed with two daggers and a length of silk, and she clutches quartermeasure sacks in her fist like a wilting bouquet.

And she looks like the Adversary's Hellspawn daughter as she storms across the room, raving in Welsh.

THE brat is in my house. *The brat is in my house!*

I storm across the room to serve her with the back of my hand what I served the other English of Caernarvon, but Gruffydd catches me in a tight embrace. "Gwenhwyfar, thank Christ! You weren't . . . I didn't . . ."

My little brother is hugging me as he hasn't since we were small. I hold him close for more long moments than I can count, and I'm the one who pulls away first.

"Jesu, lass, you look . . ." By the look of him, Gruffydd is casting about for the word *vengeful,* but seems unwilling to say it aloud. "Were you trapped there? Did any man hurt you?"

I take off the cloaks one at a time and they jingle to the floor. Then I toss down my quartermeasure sacks and slide out of the belt. I take off the too-big felt shoes and dump coin from both. I look at him in triumph.

"I'll be damned," he murmurs, and he cannot keep the admiration from his voice.

"I'm perfectly sound. I was not trapped anywhere. Not today." I prime a mighty slap and turn toward the brat, but Gruffydd catches my hand and holds it fast.

"Leave her be."

"I'll not suffer her in my house." With my free hand, I fling a shoe at the brat. It bounces off her back and she squawks like a wrung-neck chicken. "English at their best are still bloody well English. But now I'm rid of them all. I'm free."

Gruffydd tightens his grip. "We're not rid of them, and we're certes not free."

I hiss and wrench toward the brat, ready to pummel, but my little brother pulls me up cold.

"I said leave her be."

I snort. "If you're not man enough to give her the justice she deserves, be assured that I will."

"Vengeance," Gruffydd says in a low, dangerous voice, "is not justice."

The brat looks up. She knows we're speaking of her, though she cannot understand a word of Welsh. It is Justice Court, then, and I am justiciar, bailiff, and hangman. I am handing down a sentence in a foreign tongue and carrying it out with the rope.

I narrow my eyes. "You of all men can say such a thing?"

"No. Yes." Gruffydd runs a hand through his hair. "I cannot, but I must. She . . . tried to make it right."

"By taking the boot off your neck? How charitable."

"How do you think the likes of me got on that timber gang?" Gruffydd jabs a finger at the brat.

I flinch. "It was never! You're mad!"

"Her father has the ear of the *honesti* now. She leaned on

him, and the castle provisioner passed over all the lackeys who bribed him for months and what do you know? Gruffydd ap Peredur with his tainted malcontent blood has a place on the most sought-after work gang in the Principality."

I press my lips together. Study the brat crumpled before the fire, tattery and pale and small.

"I know not why she did it," Gruffydd says. "I only know that she did it knowingly, with intent."

"You're as much a fool as Dafydd." I fold my arms. "We must get rid of them. Every man, woman, and child. Every brat and dog."

I say it in English so she'll tremble and cower.

"Is that what you think this rising is about?" Gruffydd shakes his head as if I'm a child. "Destroying the English? Pushing them out of Gwynedd?"

"We took the seat of royal government. I watched Madog ap Llywelyn wipe his arse with the town charter while the whole Exchequer burned."

Gruffydd smiles faintly. "Gwen, the English king will come with a massive army and put the rebels down. But then he will want to know why he had to. Have you any idea how much it cost to raise that monstrosity in stone and mortar? Do you really think he'll just let Caernarvon go?"

I toe my pile of goods. There's blood beneath my fingernails.

"When the rising is all over," Gruffydd says, "the rebels crushed and Madog ap Llywelyn hanged from Caernarvon's walls, the burgesses will come back. They'll rebuild Caernarvon, but they'll remember what happened here. As will the English king. The burgesses have learned what happens when Welshmen are pushed to the wall, and they will not push so hard again."

Da went out, but Caernarvon happened anyway. Ten years he's been dust, and English have learned naught.

Gruffydd nods at the brat. "This girl has learned it better than most. And now she's the sole holder of her father's burgage. She'll bring her husband into the privileges of Caernarvon and tell him exactly what to think of us. That's who we'll live under. Those who remember the aftermath."

Not if she doesn't survive the aftermath. Not if I turn her out, let the men with blackened faces take care of her.

Sharp pain shoots up my arm and Gruffydd's breath rushes past my ear. "I see it in your face, Gwenhwyfar. And believe me, I'm sorely tempted to let you, but by God, we are not animals, no matter how many times they say as much."

I pull free, glare down at her.

"She stays," Gruffydd says in a ragged voice. "Come what may, we will not harm her or allow harm to come to her."

The brat is trembling now. Hard. Ripping at a loose thread on her cuff as if it's biting her.

Like as not she thinks she's escaped a terrible fate, but she'll come to envy those who fell in Caernarvon.

She is without the walls now.

* * *

For the first time in as long as I can remember, I don't get up at bare dawn. I lie abed till the whole sky is pink, stretch like a hearthcat, and smile up at the thatch.

Then I rise and spend a long, delicious moment deciding what I'm going to do next.

Sometime in the night, the brat moved. She's huddled near the door even though it's the coldest place in the house. She's staring hard at the floor, and there are stark lines down her cheeks where tears have carved runnels through the grime.

I ignore the brat, stir the fire to life, tend to Mam. Gruffydd comes in with a bucket of water and she flinches hard, even though he thumps right past her without a look.

Gruffydd and I are eating bread and cheese when we hear a shuffle, and there she is before us. She's trembling so badly she can barely keep her footing, but she stands chin up, shoulders back, as if she's priming for hemp about her neck.

The brat swallows several times, then chokes out, what will become of me?

Gruffydd glances my way, but I fold my arms and shrug. "She's here because of you," I tell him in Welsh. "You deal with her."

He glares at me, then fixes the brat with a cool stare. That depends, he says in English. Have you anyone that will come for you?

Yes! She jumps on it, clings to it. My cousin. Nicholas of Coventry. He's a squire for Sir Reginald de Tibetot. You'll find him at Wallingford. He'll come. I know he will.

Gruffydd nods and tells her, we'll ask the priest's boy to fetch him here. Should you value your life, you'll not stir from this house till your cousin arrives. Those men out there are not to be trifled with.

"And until then," I say in Welsh, "you work." I pick up the empty bucket and shove it into her arms. "Go fetch water."

What did you say, she asks, and I grab her wrist and rough her toward the door.

"Water! Go. Fetch. Water."

The brat frowns at me in utter bewilderment as she clutches the bucket. Her clawed-up fingers stand out white and stark.

"Best hope you're a fast learner." I smirk and narrow my eyes. "Some of us learned English beneath the rod."

She blinks rapidly, then squares up like a cornered beast.

You're savages, cries the brat, the lot of you are savages who killed my father!

"And many other swine besides," I reply. "The master was decent enough, but the Officer of the Town Mills deserved worse than the nice clean hanging he got."

Her grip tightens on the bucket rim. She isn't moving.

"Do what you're told or it'll go hard for you." I point to

the door and she follows my finger with the round eyes of prey. "I can make things go *very* hard for you."

The brat swallows. She gets ten steps into the yard ere she asks, where is the water?

I stare her down from my doorway. She is within *my* walls now. I will show her what it is to be mistress.

All at once she falls, shoulders and back, scowl and teeth, and she shrinks like a helpless child. Then she shuffles around, stumbles downhill, and disappears in the brush.

When I return to the fire, I take the bread Gruffydd offers and say firmly, "No harm."

Gruffydd smiles. "God's honest truth? I enjoyed every moment of that."

The brat does not return till well past midday. Brambles in her hair and gown soaking wet, a gash across her forearm and muddy to the knees. But the bucket is full and she drops it at the fireside, jaw clenched, gallows-defiant.

I wait till she collapses by the fire and pries a crust of burned oatbread from the bakestone. Then I pour the water into the cooking pot and hand the bucket back.

"Go fetch water," I tell her in Welsh.

The brat trembles to her feet. Staying upright is costing her, but every line of her is mutinous, furious.

She is coming undone slowly. First her arms, then her hands, then her eyes.

She would strike me.

Do it. I've been waiting for this moment longer than you know.

But she masters it. She closes her eyes and bites it back. Hard through the arms, stiff like a fence-rail. The brat throws the crust down, takes the bucket, and sweeps out the door.

This will not last. She will break. And I will laugh till I weep while the brat nurses bruises and a split lip with naught to look forward to but more of the same. Day in and day out. Because the vale will give her ten times worse just for being English.

Because I'm her only hope.

And she knows it.

The brat sleeps heavy, like sodden wool. Day after day, I kick her awake and work her. From bleak not-dawn till long past sunset, she fetches and carries. Cuts firewood. Bears water. Tends Mam. Dirties her hands with pitch and shit and ash and mud. Day after day.

There's no spinning. No embroidery or hemming.

The brat does not break.

She looks bad, though. Her skin is gray. Even her lips. She keeps wrapping her hair behind her ears as if her fingers need busying.

One day I catch her idle in the clearing, the bucket at her side, staring at the soot-smudged walls and crumbling towers of what was once the king's borough of Caernarvon. There's no fear about her, though. No anger. It's more as though she would reach down and embrace it, gather it together and rebuild it as a child might a castle of stones.

Her father still hangs from the window. Like Da once, from the walls.

The next day, I find the priest's boy and send him for the brat's kin.

SHE CALLS me lazy. At least I think she does. What she doesn't know is that I cannot sleep with my cheek against dirt and I cannot close my eyes without fire and blood and smoke and the red-raw terror of his last moments of life.

Nicholas is coming.

I don't sleep, exactly. Betimes I close my eyes, then blink awake to Gwinny shoving the leather bucket into my hands and barking something in Welsh. The hempen handle digs into my palms so hard that I don't think about how the rope must have roughed up his neck as they shoved him toward the window. I close my eyes and picture the market on a bright blue day. I'm meeting Mistress Sandys at the well, letting her lanky half-grown son draw my water. Trading Mistress Glover a handful of thyme for a length of thread.

I'll startle awake when Gwinny piles my hands with slimy privy rags and growls more commands I cannot understand. When I'm wringing the rags out in water so cold it reddens my knuckles, I don't think about crisp autumn air against his bare flesh, the terrible weightless instant ere the drop. I'm walking home from Mass in my best kirtle, holding one of Nessy Glover's hands while Emmaline holds the other, and betimes we swing her, squealing, high in the air.

Nicholas will come. I know he will.

Gwinny piles on task after task, then watches me like she might a limping horse. Or mayhap a colt in the breaking pasture, mouthing the bit.

But every bucket of water I haul is one less whiff of soot, one less flash of steel to wake me gasping. Every armload of wood I gather is one less reason for Gwinny to put me out of her house and leave me at the mercy of men who will not be trifled with.

That's a lesson I've no need to study.

Get out, he said.

This is the only way out.

I'M in the yard picking tiny rocks out of a bucket of barley when there's a crunch of brush and Dafydd angles out of the greenwood. Gruffydd slings the leather tunic he's working over his shoulder and nods a greeting.

"Give me another day or two," Gruffydd says, holding up a corner of the garment. "They're heading east, so they should be easy to find."

Dafydd shakes his head. "I came to tell you to go ahead of me. I've some things I must do ere I join Madog's lads."

My mouth falls open. "You? Joining the revolt?"

"If this is the only way to get the king's attention, so be it." Dafydd must mark my disbelief, for he smiles and adds, "I'm not afraid to fight, Gwenhwyfar. It just has to be the right fight."

There's a tiny flicker of motion just inside the doorway. The brat, disappearing into the shadows. She's still convinced I'm going to beat her senseless or Gruffydd's going to have his way with her. She regards us as if we're capable of anything.

"Who's that?" Dafydd asks.

"She's the heiress to your townhouse." I smile, blade-sharp. "It would be a shame should anything befall her. Shall I turn my back?"

Dafydd shrugs. "Should anything befall her, they'll just give the house to another Englishman. This doesn't work if we profit at their expense. It only works if we're granted what they already have—and the Crown enforces it."

Gruffydd busies himself with his tunic, the coward, so I face Dafydd steady on and reply, "I want no part of what they have."

"I do," he says. "I would be a subject. Not one of a subject people."

This is why, Dafydd. Because you're so damn sure it's even possible.

"And you believe that rising in revolt against their king is the way to gain that?"

"The king will be wroth, true enough," Dafydd replies, "but not just at us. He'll demand a reckoning from Havering and Whetenhale and it'll all come out. How they weren't governing according to the king's laws, but for their own profit. How their abuses were what turned us to such extremes. Once the king learns all this, he'll be forced to act."

I swallow. "And how do you know that the result won't be ten times worse than it was ere this?"

Dafydd smiles sadly. "I don't. One way or another, though, Caernarvon will never be the same."

"And given all this, you'd still see us married?"

"Tomorrow. If not sooner."

"Why?" I fling a hand. "It would change nothing!"

Dafydd meets my eyes and whispers, "It would change *everything*."

I don't reply. And don't reply. And don't dare look at him again.

Know not when Dafydd leaves. Too blurry. Only know when I look beyond the bucket and his feet are no longer there.

A FAINT LIGHT filters through the doorway. It's not yet dawn but the curtain is pulled back. Gwinny and Griffith stand in the doorway, murmuring intensely in Welsh. Griffith wears one of Gwinny's plundered cloaks and shoulders a weathered spear.

He's leaving. I catch enough words in Welsh to realize Griffith is going somewhere. Somewhere dangerous.

I catch words in Welsh.

They embrace, fiercely. Then Griffith pulls away and disappears. Gwinny snaps the curtain shut and slumps against the wall. In the stillness, her tiny sobs fill every corner.

It's blood and fire and they're all dead and I cannot keep the tears down.

Gwinny turns on me like a Fury and snaps in English, "Shut up! Don't you dare weep or by God I'll put you out of my house this moment!"

I picture Anglesey out my window, the silky band of green held at arm's length by the shimmering strait busy with boats. I'm in my chamber and the gulls are crying and daylight is just beginning to seep in and it's going to be a lovely brisk day.

At length I master myself, steady my breathing. Gwinny's

shoulders relax bit by bit, but she still glares damnation at me. "You will not weep for my brother. I will not have it."

I don't tell her I wasn't weeping for him. There's no way those words will come out properly.

"You've no right to even *think* his name. Should you be so bold as to utter it, I'll douse you in blood ere I turn you out."

I don't remind her that Griffith told me that I could stay, that I shouldn't try to leave if I valued my life. He's not here to say her nay. He's not here to seize her hand.

He's gone somewhere dangerous, and he's all she's got.

I lick my lips and say, "I know that . . ."

Gwinny fixes me with a venomous look.

"I thought to . . ." That's when I hold my tongue, for Gwinny's jaw is grinding like a millwheel and what I thought to do cannot erase what I did.

"Is it true?" Her voice is gravelly. "About the timber gang?"

Mayhap she's trying to trap me, but I haven't the strength to lie. "Yes. It's true."

Gwinny grunts. "Had I known, I would have told you where you could shove your pity."

"Not pity. Justice."

Gwinny draws back as if I've struck her. She repeats the word in English as though she's never heard it ere this. And she regards me so intently that I swipe up the water bucket and hurry toward the stream, trembling every step of the way.

THEY come at night. I tell them that Gruffydd has already gone, and I give them the knives I plundered from Caernarvon in memory of Peredur ap Goronwy, who once stood with men like them.

They don't loot the house. Out of respect, they say. I bid them Godspeed and they disappear into a vale that's bracing for the worst.

I return to the fire, sit with Mam. She does not move. Her flesh is still warm. Her chest still rises. But she takes only tiny mouthfuls of breath. She drinks less every day.

Once they've been gone for some time, the brat creeps out of the byre where she had the good sense to hide. She's panting like a lathered hound as she edges toward the fire.

I thought they were going to kill you, she says. Right in your own house.

"The rebels are only ravaging," I reply. "There's not much to take, so we'll be rid of them soon."

The brat blinks rapidly, whispers, r-rebels?

"The rebels, fool. The men of Gwynedd who follow Madog ap Llywelyn to finish what they started at Caernarvon." I even out my voice. "Men like my brother."

The brat gapes like a fish.

I say it in English so there'll be no mistake. Rebellion.

Welshmen have taken and trampled your worthless borough and even now reduce it to rubble. They'll take their spears and blades to the Perfeddwlad, where they'll run roughshod over your worthless king and with God's help send him to Hell where he belongs.

Whether any of it is true beyond the sack of Caernarvon I have no notion, but it puts such a panic on the brat that I press down.

More men gather every day. Ere long, all Wales will be in revolt and not a single English man, woman, or child will be safe. We'll be rid of you ere Christmas. Every last damn one of you. And then we'll take apart your castles and boroughs brick by cursed brick until the very land forgets you were ever here.

Rebellion, echoes the brat. But that means that Nicholas . . . mayhap he won't . . .

I smile all teeth. "Well then, best pray hard for my continuing good health."

He'll come, she whispers. I know he will.

The brat speaks clear and sure, a voice that does not match her slumped shoulders, her clenched jaw, her hard stare at the fire.

The same voice I use to say that Gruffydd will return alive. Clear and sure, the way Mam once spoke of Da.

Fanwra's baby is stillborn. I wrap half a plundered cheese and bid the brat ready herself. The brat watches the cheese disappear beneath cloth. Hunger is not a ghost she knew within the walls.

I ready Mam. Firewood, linen, a rag soaked in liquid porridge. Then I pet her hair and nod to the brat.

The brat gestures to Mam and asks, what of your mother? Who'll care for her?

"The saints. Come."

She follows me outside while saying, any manner of man or creature could come through that flimsy curtain. How can you leave her?

"Where shall I start? The part where your lot dictates what jobs of work lads like Gruffydd can do for how much coin, or the part where they tax us so heavily that girls like me have to take up work to keep breath in body?"

The brat rakes her hair behind her ears thrice, glances over her shoulder toward what's left of Caernarvon. At length she says, I'll stay with her.

"You'll not. You'll come see the piteous creature my neighbor bore."

The brat looks as if she'll protest, then wisely closes her mouth and nods. As we walk through the greenwood, she flakes the biggest chunks of filth from her ratty gown. The stains remain. They will never wash clean.

THERE'S A SWEET, burny smell. Just ahead is a wide patch of blackened earth scattered with what look like tangled branches till I get closer and realize they're bones. Scorched and melted and left to bleach.

Animal bones. Cows and sheep and goats. A twinkly star fallen to a black landscape. Ones and dozens and hundreds.

That's bad enough. Then I see the bodies.

Three of them, two men and a woman, hanging from a tree not far from the path Gwinny forges. Purple faces. Crooked necks. Pecked-out holes where eyes once were.

The woman is Mistress Sandys.

I'm on my knees in mud and gasping and choking and they're all dead and all I want is my father back even if he does his fool dancing before every window in Christendom.

A hand on my shoulder, and Gwinny is hauling me up by one arm. "Don't look. Take my hand. Face ahead."

I do as she tells me. My gown is heavy with clinging mud. We're a hundred breaths away when she says, "It'll get better. Not for a while, but it will."

I want to ask Gwinny why. Why the Welsh of the countryside attacked Caernarvon with such sudden violence. Why they hanged and cut down the innocent. Why they tore up the market and looted the wharves and reduced the toll trestle to a pile of splinters.

I don't, though. I think I already know.

F ANWRA'S steading is damp and airless. There's no fire. The brat hovers in the doorway and I jerk her in, stumbling. She does not twitch or gag as I expected. She bears up straight, despite her bloodless face.

I kneel at Fanwra's head and smooth her sweaty hair. Then I tuck the cheese into her hands. I do not ask how she fares.

A bundle lies beside the door. The creature within is colorless and smooth, oddly calm. Like statuary, or a figure cast in wax.

I shove the bundle into the brat's arms. She shudders and scrambles to hand it back.

"You'll hold it," I tell her. "You did this. So have a good look at what you wrought."

Her eyes widen and she says, I did not do this.

I pinch the warm pink flesh of her upper arm. "This is hunger's work."

The brat rubs the reddening patch and says, your poor neighbor. Who will look after her? Where is her husband?

"Husband?" I snort. "She should be so lucky. I reckon you believe I gave Edward Mercer justice merely for your benefit."

The brat swallows hard. She looks greensick. She whispers words in English I do not recognize.

Fanwra eats the cheese as if it will disappear.

Ave Maria gratia plena, whispers the brat, and she holds the bundle close as if it's a live, breathing child.

The walk is the same as before, same tree-stump hillsides and stolen fields, but now I stride through those fields that by right should be Gruffydd's. The Watchers have been scattered, the cattle loosed, the struggling barley thrice trampled. I grind my heel into the parched, prickly roots. Give me salt enough and I would sow every handswidth.

The market trestle is splinters, scattered like kindling. Even the walls don't seem as high. The market common is torn up, littered with rubbish. No bodies, though. No bodies anywhere.

There are no more gates, only hinges clinging to the walls like broken spiders. I can look all the way up High Street to where it curves like a spine, obscuring the Water Gate and the strait beyond. Men on what's left of the towers watch me enter the gravetown, blades shouldered, careful.

They must be Madog's men, guarding their prize. As if there's an English soul within a day's ride who still breathed God's air.

Already they're taking Caernarvon down. Brick by brick, timber by timber, plank by miserable plank. By the time the English king arrives, this place will not be worth fighting for.

Farther up High, I pass men bearing long rolls of canvas slung between them. Little wonder there are no bodies. Madog's men are disposing of them.

They must plan to be here for a while.

The master still hangs from the window, sightless, gray, withered. I pass beneath him and into the house, into the brat's old demesne.

Not a stick of furniture remains. Not trestle nor coffer nor wall-cloth. There are only bare, battered floors and sooty walls. I put it to memory. I will tell her every spill and scorch, every last absence.

I will enjoy watching it hurt.

Something is wadded in the corner. It's head-sized, washwater-colored and lumpy like vomit. I toe it and it becomes linen. A ray of glowing blue turns over. I kneel, peel apart the folds.

The castle appears first. The castle and a walled town. It's unmistakably Caernarvon, notched and purple-banded in tiny tight stitches high in the corner. Then Saint Joseph, his cloak a field of backstitches and his curly hair spilling over his collar while the Holy Child sits serenely on his arm, haloed. The Virgin is unfinished, an outline cast in blue and scarlet.

The castle appears first. Even she has built it.

Caernarvon, in stitches and thread.

I jab the tip of my plundered knife beneath the stitches

and twist. Thread catches, strains, and I gouge hard. More thread falls, tiny worms of purple and gray. I rip and stab Caernarvon from the linen even as Madog's men pull down walls and townhouses.

Finally there's no more thread. I've cut myself twice and my blood stains the frayed edge.

But Caernarvon is not gone. There's a faint outline on the linen where the stitches were, tiny holes suggesting towers, walls, gates, rooftops. Ghosts of color where thread rubbed cloth. Caernarvon still presides over the Holy Family, present even without substance.

And I look out the half-shuttered window at the castle just clipping the sky, dark as rain. My throat tightens and I grip the brat's linen in both hands because Gruffydd is right, curse him, and it's all for naught.

The extents and rolls may be ash, the town charter may be naught but privy rag, but none of these acts can undo Caernarvon. Brick and plank have stood. Kings have blessed. Men have seen. Girls have stitched. We could pull it down again and again. They'll come back. They'll always come back.

Outside, I ask one of the labor gangs carrying corpses to cut down the master and bury him. I wait till the crow-pecked body is wrapped in canvas and laid in a grave ere I fold the brat's linen into a tight packet and head home, dirtying my feet through once-Watched fields.

E VERYTHING," Gwinny says, and she smiles as if the Adversary himself did the wrecking.

"Everything," I whisper.

"Every trunk and chest and wooden spoon," she prods, still smiling. "Not a splinter or scrap remains."

"Did you see Mistress Tipley or Mistress Pole?" I ask. "Emmaline de Coucy? I would give much to know they're sound."

Gwinny draws back and eyes me. "Naught remains in your house. Everything you have in the world has been kicked in or made off with. Your precious embroidery frame. Your colored threads. Your mother's gown."

I swallow. "What of the Glovers next door? There are so many little ones, and Mistress Glover bore her baby not long ago. Surely they wouldn't have slaughtered children. Would they?"

"Madog's men garrison the town," Gwinny says stonily. "Should any English remain, God help them."

"They must have fled." I nod, fierce and sure. "They must have."

Gwinny narrows her eyes. "Fled home, you mean. Back to England. Where they belong."

"Emmaline has no memory of England. All she knows is Caernarvon. That's her home."

"It's not her home. It's not *your* home."

I square up and look Gwinny in the eye. "I would that were true. But it's not. My home isn't mine any longer. He took it, and I must make shift with what's left me. Caernarvon is my home now."

Gwinny flinches, blinks, turns away.

Horseback English, a decree from their king, and the new lord of Pencoed rode right up to the hall door and kicked it in and that's all I saw because Mam threw the blanket over Gruffydd and me and there was screaming and clatter and ere long we found ourselves in a ditch tangled in that blanket a stone's throw from the hall and Mam next to us was weeping quietly and there was nowhere to go but into the greenwood, away from that timbered hall that the prince himself granted Da, where I was just old enough to kneel before the prince during his final days on God's own earth.

IF I close my eyes I can see it still, the new chimney, the dovecote, the endless rolling yardlands of barley and oats and rye.

But it's his now. It'll never be mine, and even if I go back, I'll be at their mercy. My thieving uncle Roger and his wretchedly fertile girl-wife and their little pink baby. I'll have to pretend to like the howling brat who stole Edgeley from me and mayhap even play nursemaid to it.

Gwinny said everything I had in the world was kicked in or made off with, but that's not true. I have what's left of a townhouse on a plot of ground sixty feet by eighty on Shire Hall Street in the king's borough of Caernarvon. Out of one window you can see Anglesey, green atop green like layers of infidel silk. Out the other, houses and roads and the walls curving around it all like a great embrace. On one side the Glovers, on the other, the Poles. The church downstreet, the castle up, the middle alive with dogs and children and neighbors.

I'll find a way to have what's mine. What my father made mine because he'd have more for me than the lot of a steward's daughter on an estate, hers by right, that she could never have.

Get out, he said.

He did not mean forever.

I'M pounding barley between two stones when Dafydd appears in the doorway. He's dressed for weather even though the sky is holding blue well past the time it should have hunkered down for winter. He leans on the frame, flashes that damn carefree grin.

"I've come to ply you ere I go to war," he says cheerfully. "I've ten reasons why you should agree to be my wife, and I'll not leave till you hear every one."

There's a swish and a grunt, and the brat lurches past Dafydd into the steading, slanting beneath the water bucket. She greets us in English as she sways toward the hearth with a long and purposeful stride. She does not seem to notice that her hem is caked with mud or her hair is streaming from its plait like a halo of snakes.

She looks nothing like a borough lady.

Daughter Shrewcy would be in pieces by now, weeping for her veil and her blistered hands. But this girl looks as though she doesn't even care.

The brat would care.

"Reason number one is—"

"I will." My voice is low and steady. I thought I'd want my words back right away, but I don't.

Dafydd closes his mouth. "You . . . what?"

Now that I've said it, I cannot take my eyes off him. "If we both survive, that is."

"I'd hate to think you were mocking me," Dafydd says in slow, measured words. "I've never once played you false."

"I'm not. I mean it. I'll marry you should we both survive this."

"You'll pardon the question, but I'll not have you unconsidered." His voice wavers. "What's happened?"

The brat wipes muddy hands on her gown, steps around the leaky place in the thatch, heads for the door with the water bucket. Dafydd steps inside to let her pass, then watches her stumble down the hill.

"Ah," he says quietly. "The crack. Caernarvon just wants one."

Dafydd kneels before me till I look up from my grinding, then takes the stones out of my hands and lays them aside. He pulls me gently to my feet and draws me into an embrace so deep it feels as if he's been saving it up, as if he'd never let go should the choice be his.

I curl beneath his arm and let him hold me, my cheek against his shoulder, and all at once I'm back in his bed, snug beneath the woolens and listening to the muffled beating of his heart, ere he single-handedly took on the task of undoing the English stranglehold on Caernarvon's privileges with the simple act of requesting a burgage. All these months, and he's still warm and solid, like city walls. He's still flippant, maddening, and irresistible.

He'd still have me.

After this is over, everything will change. One way or another, Caernarvon will never be the same again.

Rain is pelting the steading as if we're under Heaven's eaves. The roof is leaking in no less than a dozen places, and the smell of moldy thatch is stronger than usual.

Gwinny is sharpening her meat-knife, sliding the whetstone down the blade in lengthy, irritable shings. She's in a foul mood because it took me too long to figure out she wanted me to patch the wall wattle, which I'm doing now, coated to the elbows in mud.

"When you're done," Gwinny says in Welsh, "something something roof and fix the something something."

I almost glare at her. She cannot be serious. Assuming I could get on the roof *and* had half a notion what to do, the rain would wash me away like all the sinners in the Flood.

"I hope your cousin never comes," she taunts in English. "I'm growing quite used to having a servant. How idle and dissolute I've become. Almost like a fine lady of the borough."

"He'll come." I slap some mud on the wall hard enough to spatter my face. "I know he will."

"You *hope* he will," she drawls. "Wallingford's a long way from here. Anything could happen to the priest's boy. Imagine a lad that young trying to cross a countryside in revolt, to say naught of him finding one knight among hundreds. It's already been what, a fortnight? A month?"

I want to tell her to shut her mouth, but instead I picture the sun streaming through my workroom windows and spread some mud on her wretched walls.

Nicholas is coming.

He has to be.

"And what if your king calls him and his lord to the royal standard?" Gwinny presses a hand to her cheek in mock-horror. "Surely he could not say your king nay. And you'd have to stay here. Unless I put you out. I could always do that. How far do you think you'd get? Do you even know which way to go?"

If she's going to put me out, I would she'd just get on with it. I cannot contain a glare, and she's on me like a ratter.

"Don't you look at me like that! You'll be in the ditch ere you turn around!"

Picture the market. Picture the hall, the table set with broadcloth and pewter.

But all I feel is cold on my skin, raw terror in every direction.

Gwinny is smiling.

"You'd best hope it's the wolves that find you," she purrs. "They'll merely kill you."

"Stop it!" I fist up both hands and brandish the mud spreader like a dagger. "Do you take pleasure in this? Why are you doing this to me?"

And I freeze. Lower the mud spreader.

Justice for those who deserve it.

Gwinny rises slow, draws shallow breaths as if she's run to London and back.

"I'm done," I whisper. "I'm done playing games."

And I turn back to my task because there is naught like justice well served. Mud up my arms, over my face. No one can even see my cuffs anymore.

I've studied my lessons, but now it's too late.

After a while, there's a shuffling behind me. Gwinny crosses the small room, takes up a second mud spreader, and wordlessly begins to patch the walls alongside me.

ENGLISH collapses into sleep within moments of gobbling her corner of bread. Without the walls, labor is a ghost she has come to know painfully well.

Those first few se'ennights are the hardest, English. Ere calluses roughen everything on you and in you. Barely a month bereft, you're still pink and raw.

You'll have to harden, though. Even if you weep as it happens.

At least it's just you. You've no one who wept for trapped hares and maidens in nursery tales, pushed beyond your protection then and now and forever.

The steading is still. I withdraw English's length of linen from my apron and unfold it.

The linen is cleaner from several washings, but the shadow of a ruined Caernarvon still towers over the Holy Family. Saint Joseph and the Christ Child, faded but finished, all but leap off the wrinkled gray cloth.

Da went out. Gruffydd went out. Should I ever bear a son, he will go out. He will meet the same fate. He will die for this realm already twice lost.

English whimpers in her sleep. Her cheeks are wet.

The burgesses will come back and she will be among

them. She will bring her husband into the privileges and tell him what to think of us.

I have not harmed her. I have not allowed harm to come to her. It's more than her lot has ever offered me, and English has seen what befalls them when they press the boot on our necks. She has survived the wages of justice through luck, mettle, and wit enough to open her eyes.

English finally sees.

If I'm to be ruled, may it be by those who see.

GWINNY AND I eat the last of the plundered bread. The loaf-end has deep finger-holes, one of which is bloody. I cannot look at the bread while I eat it, but nor will I stop eating.

The pile of blankets near the fire begins to quake and gasp like a rusty bellows. Gwinny drops her bread and flies to her mother's side.

The old woman's eyes roll back in her head and her tiny frame shudders as if throttled. Gwinny holds her mother down at the shoulders and kneels on the blankets to still her legs. The poor dame's face is bloodless and her blue lips stand out like leeches.

"Fetch the priest," Gwinny snaps as she wrestles a piece of wood between her mother's clattering teeth.

I can barely find the stream. I shrug helplessly.

Gwinny groans like a wounded beast. "Then you hold her!"

The old woman looks like a corpse, all waxen and pale, but I kneel and gingerly lean my hands on her shoulders as much as I dare. Her shoulderbones poke like peg hangers.

"Hold her steady," Gwinny says, and out the curtain she races.

Gwinny's mother jerks like a puppet on strings and there's a fresh privy stench. She must have loosed her bowels.

I gag and retch but I don't let go. She's gasping low and harsh at the back of her throat and I beg her not to die till Gwinny comes with the priest, till she can be shriven and have her own daughter holding her head as she goes.

Her struggles are fading. I'm losing her.

I pray. I pray, clinging to the old woman's shoulders as I might a paternoster. I pray with my every fiber that she not die, not yet, not like this.

Something tugs at my collar. It's Gwinny, with a cold-eyed priest hovering over her shoulder. I let go. I stumble away and they both kneel at the old woman's side, blocking her from view. I'm in the corner again, overlooked and passed by.

Rattly gasping drowns out Extreme Unction and the viaticum. Gwinny's profile stands out against the dark wall like a new-stamped coin. Tears slide down her cheeks and my face is wet and I'm in the corner praying and we're the same, Gwinny and I, we're the same.

I BURY my mother. All those who knew her gather at the grave and commend her to God.

English comes, too. She stands at my elbow and wipes away tears as four graybeards lower Mam's body into the frozen earth.

She's brave to show her face at this burial. My neighbors glare at her sidelong and mutter, but she does not look away from the grave. Her lips are moving. Her fingers, too, as if they're sliding over beads on a paternoster.

I should be weeping for my mother. I should be tearing my hair and smearing my face with soot. Or at least drying tears, as does English, who barely knew her.

Instead I feel light. As if I could float away on the wind, somewhere far from here.

Ashes to ashes. Mam is buried. My neighbors cluster, pushing English aside.

Your mother is with God now, they say. Her suffering is over. Beyond the cares of the world.

It's like saying the sky is blue or the Pope is Christian.

I lag behind till they strip away and head for their own hearths to what's left of their children and beasts. Soon it's just English and I, heaving uphill toward the steading that's mine now. Empty and mine.

And English says, even when you know it's coming, it still hurts. She squeezes my hand and whispers, I'm sorry . . . Gwennaver.

She's filthy and tattered and hungry, waiting on a cousin who may never arrive. Her hands are blistered raw and her cheeks windburned, but she looks me in the eye and she hasn't broken and she's sorry.

Now mayhap time can do its work.

Nicholas arrives when the wind off the strait is flinging angry snow against the steading. He lurches up the hill on a half-dead horse and leaps from the saddle as if it's afire. His face is mottled red and his hands are like leather, but I throw my arms about him and hold on hard.

"Thank Christ," he whispers into my hair. "Oh, Cecily, I never thought I'd see you again in this world."

It's Nicholas. Lop-eared, gingerfool Nicholas. My eyes sting.

"I had a look at Caernarvon as I passed," he growls. "They will pay for what they've done, mark me. His Grace the king is even now massing forces at Chester."

"What they've done," I echo, in the shadow of hungry crofts and churchyard graves and toll-table splinters.

"Come, we ride for Chester," Nicholas says. "Father will meet you there and take you back to Coventry."

He's tugging me toward his horse, but I pull away. "First I must bid farewell."

"To whom?"

She puts the bucket down as I near the steading door. We regard each other for a long moment. She's a lot thinner than the girl who came with my house, but she stands just the same. Chin up, shoulders squared, steady as the Adversary's throwing arm.

But I understand why.

"*Pob llwyddiant*," Gwennaver says. "*Hwyl.*"

"*Di-diolch yn . . . er, fawr,*" I stumble, and I mean every word. I need every bit of good fortune I can get, and although a simple thank-you seems inadequate, it's the best I can do with my new words.

I turn away, but Gwennaver catches my sleeve and presses a folded packet into my hands. Ere I can respond, Nicholas manhandles me atop the rickety horse and leads it away.

I look over my shoulder, but she has already disappeared.

"Barbarous," Nicholas mutters. "I cannot believe Henry thinks to return once these beasts are put down."

"What else is he to do?" I ask, and Nicholas grunts.

What else am I to do?

Swaying on Nicholas's horse, I unfold the packet Gwennaver gave me. Saint Joseph and the Christ Child wait while the Virgin, still merely an outline, prays at the roadside. Caernarvon has been torn away, but its outline remains. It will not be hard to restitch.

I fold the linen and stow it close to my heart.

I wish Gwennaver health and Griffith safety, for both will need it for what's coming. Then I pray for my father's soul.

From this far, Caernarvon looks just as it did upon our arrival. Gray and weathered and solid as Jerusalem, and it's only because I know to look that I see the makeshift gate and crumbled tower-tops.

The king will have it back. The burgesses will return. They will all remember what happened here, and why.

My cousin Henry will be among them. He will need a chatelaine to run his house and preside over his kitchen. Someone who knows the market and the countryside, someone who knows the Welsh and how to treat with them. Someone with a townhouse two streets over, held in trust till her marriage, when she will become its lady. Someone who'll not dishonor her father's memory and give up her new birthright as if it's worthless.

I know just the girl for the job. She will walk her cousin's townhouse amid a faint jingle of keys while a wolfhound puppy follows at her heels.

HISTORICAL NOTE

Caernarvon in 1294 was a great place to live—as long as you were English. A decade earlier, after two hundred years of near-constant conflict, the English brought about the final collapse of native government in Wales with the battlefield killing of Llywelyn ap Gruffydd and the execution of his brother Dafydd, the last Welsh Princes of Wales. Although the fall of Wales was not his precise intention, Edward I, king of England, quickly consolidated the old princely lands into what became known as the Principality of North Wales.

Once Edward held Wales, he wanted to ensure that it never troubled England again. To that end, he instigated an extensive—and expensive—castle-building, urban development, and settlement program to maintain control of the land and its inhabitants. A critical aspect of this project was a series of walled towns like Caernarvon, intended to attract English settlers to support the castle garrisons and help develop the local economy.

These towns were very much on the frontier, surrounded by a hostile, newly subjugated Welsh population—people like Gruffydd and Gwenhwyfar—who were still becoming accustomed to English government. Cecily's concern that she would be murdered was not entirely unfounded. Wales had a fierce reputation in the thirteenth century, so Edward had to offer settlers an array of privileges to entice them to take burgages, mostly in the form of tax breaks and subsidized farmland. One of the few requirements was residence, and one of the only burdens was a modest yearly rent. In the Middle Ages, this kind of offer was almost unheard of.

But Caernarvon was not the best place to be if you were Welsh. The same conditions that attracted English settlers to the Principality made life very difficult for the Welsh, who had until recently been governed by a familiar and long-standing set of laws and customs. Gwenhwyfar would have been raised on stories of Welsh princes who resisted encroaching English domination with diplomacy when they could and with the sword when they had to. It was not an easy transition for the Welsh, and Gwenhwyfar's resentment toward her new English masters had ten years to simmer.

On the surface, the introduction of English rule to Wales was surprisingly lenient. There were no wholesale executions of Welsh nobility, and only a few, like Gwenhwyfar's father, who died fighting the English, lost their lands. Edward made no attempt to ban the Welsh language or any other type of cultural expression. In many places, Welsh civil law remained in effect, and it was only for criminal cases that English law was imposed. Although he enacted a number of underhanded, semilegal measures to protect the castles and new walled towns, Edward went out of his way to ensure as peaceful a transfer of power as possible, mainly because he was more concerned with events on the Continent than with those in Wales.

Since Edward's attention was elsewhere, he placed a number

of officials in charge of Wales with express instructions to govern according to the Statute of Rhuddlan, a document issued by the king in 1284. But the burgesses in the walled towns had different ideas. They were nervous already, outnumbered fifty to one by a disgruntled populace, and they harbored a certain sense of entitlement due to their presence on the front lines of a hostile frontier. Some of them had lost loved ones in the two wars leading up to the fall of Welsh native government. All of them saw the opportunity to profit from a demoralized and marginalized population that was in no position, legal or otherwise, to fight back. It wasn't long before corruption set in, and Edward's officials either looked the other way or benefited right alongside the burgesses at the expense of the Welsh.

The first hint of trouble was a famine that swept through Wales and England in 1290. Famine was not uncommon in the Middle Ages, but in the subsequent year, 1291, Edward called for a tax that amounted to a fifteenth of the movable goods of all of his subjects—including, for the first time, his Welsh subjects. Welsh landholders didn't object on principle to being taxed, but medieval taxation was assessed and collected in such a way that the burden per capita fell more heavily on the Welsh because of their lower population, and also because the burgesses in the walled towns were not subject to this type of taxation.

By 1294, Wales had been suffering under four successive years of famine and three years of a tax many Welsh landholders saw as unreasonable and dangerous in its precedent. In the summer, when the king proclaimed that Welshmen of military age like Gruffydd and Dafydd would be compelled to serve overseas under the royal standard in Gascony, it became clear to the Welsh that things in the Principality had to change.

By all accounts, the English were taken completely by surprise by the events of Michaelmas 1294—not just the sack of Caernarvon, but the simultaneous attacks on castles across Wales, nearly all of which were successful. It was Christmas before Edward could divert enough troops from his campaign in Gascony to deal with the rebels. The rebellion was put down conclusively by the summer of 1295, but there were no mass executions or crippling legal retributions. The royal inquiry into mismanagement that Dafydd predicted did in fact come about, and the outcome told Edward all he needed to know about how to secure peace in the Principality. Wales was not taxed to any significant degree until well into the fourteenth century, and the next time he needed fighting men for his army, Edward did not attempt to conscript the Welsh. Instead, he invited them into the army at full pay, the same as English foot soldiers, and they volunteered by the thousands.

When the burgesses returned to Caernarvon after the revolt, they were forgiven the payment of their rents for ten years to help them recover. Although the rebellion stirred up a lot of English mistrust and hostility against the Welsh, it wasn't long before all the boroughs in North Wales recovered from the physical damage and experienced a social and demographic shift. By the middle of the fourteenth century, every walled town in the Principality had some Welsh burgesses, a few of whom had made their way into civil government. This social shift was a result of interactions very much like those among Cecily, Gwenhwyfar, and Gruffydd. Each community had to come to terms with this new world, and such exchanges set the precedent for cooperation, even if it was initially reluctant.

As the frontier became less volatile, and indeed stopped being a frontier at all, local government became more diverse and the culture of the walled towns began to better reflect the communities that shared the space. These changes took time, but the cracks that began in Caernarvon shaped Wales well into the future.

In chronological order, my sincere thanks go to . . .

My mother, for reading to me every night till I was nearly twelve. And for patiently fueling my teenage research interests with a never-ending stream of interlibrary loan materials.

My father, for buying the first book-length manuscript produced by thirteen-year-old me, thereby ensuring I kept writing through a very dark time. It's quite possibly the best ten dollars he ever spent.

Kelly Stromberg and Dean Rieken, two AP English teachers who tolerated my teenage hubris, doused my writing in red ink, and held up a mirror at all the right times.

The staff and librarians at too many research libraries to count, but particularly those at Bryn Mawr College, the University of Pennsylvania, and the University of Washington.

My husband and son, for their love, encouragement, and most of all, patience. Living with a writer is no easy thing.

Mary Pleiss and Sara Polsky, my beta readers. Without their time, insights, and raw honesty, this book would not exist. Thanks also to Mary Cummings for her valuable comments on an early draft.

My agent, Ammi-Joan Paquette, for her excellent advice and tireless work on my behalf. I'm very fortunate to have her in my corner.

Reka Simonsen, my editor, for her wisdom and enthusiasm. I couldn't ask for a better hand on the tiller.

The Body in the Basement

Phyllis G Humphrey
1994

KATHERINE HALL PAGE

The Body in the Basement

St. Martin's Press   New York

I would like to acknowledge Barbara Brackman, quilt detective extraordinaire, and her excellent guide to identifying and dating antique quilts, *The Clues in the Calico*, EPM Publications, Inc. Thanks, as always, to Ruth Cavin, my editor, and Faith Hamlin, my agent, for their insight, advice, and above all, friendship.

THE BODY IN THE BASEMENT. Copyright © 1994 by Katherine Hall Page. All rights reserved. Printed in the United States of America. No part of this book may be used or reproduced in any manner whatsoever without written permission except in the case of brief quotations embodied in critical articles or reviews. For information, address St. Martin's Press, 175 Fifth Avenue, New York, N.Y. 10010.

Illustrations by Phyllis G. Humphrey

Library of Congress Cataloging-in-Publication Data

Page, Katherine Hall.
    The body in the basement / Katherine Hall Page.
        p.   cm.
    "A Thomas Dunne book"
    ISBN 0-312-11470-2
    1. Fairchild, Faith Sibley (Fictitious character)—Fiction.
2. Caterers and catering—Maine—Fiction.   3. Women detectives—Maine—Fiction.   I. Title.
    PS3566.A334B63   1994
    813'.54—dc20   94-25764
                                                            CIP

First edition: October 1994

10 9 8 7 6 5 4 3 2 1

Editor's Note

The Body in the Basement includes, at the end of the story, six full recipes from Faith Fairchild's (fictional) cookbook, *Have Faith in Your Kitchen*, as well as a number of descriptions in the text of the way Faith and Pix make some of the delectable New England dishes featured in the action.

In praise of aunts, and uncles, this book is dedicated to:
Ruth and Charles Samenfeld
and all my dear cousins

Two residents are standing on the post office steps in a small Maine coastal village observing the increased traffic on Memorial Day weekend.

"Well, this time of year always brings two things: the summer people and the black flies," says one.

The other nods. "Yup, but you can kill the black flies."

—Anonymous

The Body in the Basement

Chapter I

There were days when Pix Miller was forced to agree with her husband, Sam's, observation that "Don't worry, Pix will do it" would be the epitaph carved on her tombstone in the family plot in Maine.

She was at the plot on Sanpere Island now, thinning the potentilla that grew on her father's grave. The sky was slightly overcast and the woods that surrounded the cemetery were dark and dense. She preferred to be there on sunny days, when the white birch trunks shimmered and the stately emerald evergreens looked as if they had been and would be there forever. The dead were not dead on those days, but came alive in memory as she walked past stones with familiar names to their own bit of earth, the ground covered with wildflowers until Freeman Hamilton came with his scythe.

Today as Pix looked down at her father's grave, she had no trouble remembering that first shock, the first grief, although he had been gone for a dozen years. She put down her clippers and stretched out on the green, very green, grass. "Pix will do it." Apt, extremely apt.

She sat up, feeling a bit foolish at the picture she presented—spread-eagled on her forebears. If there was anything Pix Miller was not, it was foolish, however much she tried. She plucked a piece of grass from the ground, slit it with her thumbnail, and put it to her lips. The ensuing high-pitched whistle was gratifying. She still knew how. She'd taught her children the trick, just as she'd taught them all the other things she'd learned on the island when she was young: how to sail, canoe, and swim; where to find the best clams, best blueberries, best shells; to leave nests undisturbed and to walk silently through the forest; to get every last morsel from a boiled lobster and to wake up in anticipation each morning.

That was how she had awakened this morning. It had taken about thirty seconds for her to realize she was not in her bed in Aleford, Massachusetts, but tucked under the eaves in her bed in Maine. Pix didn't waste any time getting to Sanpere for the summer, and this year was no exception. Yesterday at exactly twelve noon, she'd picked up seventeen-year-old Samantha at the high school, then swung by the middle school for twelve-year-old Danny and turned the Land Rover, packed to the gunnels, due north. She had already driven her oldest, nineteen-year-old Mark, to Logan Airport in time for the early shuttle to Washington, D.C., where he was spending the summer as an intern in their local congressman's office. Mark had protested the ungodliness of the hour all the way to Boston, but Pix was too busy running through her mental lists, making sure she hadn't forgotten anything, to pay him much mind.

At the airport, he had given her an affectionate bear hug and said, "It's okay, Mom. I know you can't help yourself. The old Siren call of Sanpere, and probably they'll be a few moments this summer when I'll wish I was there, too. When it's a hundred degrees in the shade in D.C."

Pix had had a sudden hope. This was the first summer the

whole family wouldn't all be together for at least part of the time. "It's not too late to change your mind, sweetie. We could swing by the house and get some of your more rugged clothes." Mark was dressing for success these days.

"Mom, I said, moments, 'a few moments.' Sure, life on Sanpere is gripping: 'Mrs. Walton will be entertaining her daughter and family from Bangor for the weekend' and 'Sonny Prescott has a new lobster boat, which he has named the *Miss Steak.*' Health-care reform and balancing the budget are going to seem pretty tame." Mark had rolled his eyes. "Time to let one of us fly."

"But you'll come up Labor Day weekend?" Pix was trying to hold on to the end of the string.

Mark said something that could have been a yes or a no, the string snapped, and he was gobbled up by the crowd of morning travelers just beyond the terminal's automatic doors.

Still absentmindedly picking at the grass, Pix realized this was going to be a summer of women, not an altogether-bad thing, of course, but different. On the way up last night, she'd dropped Danny off at his beloved Camp Chewonki near Brunswick for a virtually whole-summer stay, and Sam probably wouldn't be able to get away until the Fourth of July, and then only for a few days until his August vacation.

Samantha had picked up on her mother's mood the night before as they drove through the darkness, bent on getting to their cottage no matter what the hour. "We'll have fun—and think how easy the housework is going to be, and the cooking." Pix had brightened considerably at this prospect. She didn't mind the housework, but unlike her friend, next-door neighbor, and now employer, Faith Fairchild, food preparation as a pleasant activity was up there with lighted matches under the fingernails. If Pix had not been endowed with a superabundance of Puritan guilt, it would have been Hamburger Helper every night—instead of merely some nights.

Faith was the Faith of Have Faith, an extremely successful

3

Manhattan catering company that Faith had recently reopened in Aleford. She'd moved to the village following her marriage to the Reverend Thomas Fairchild. Pix's responsibilities at the catering company didn't involve cooking. Keeping the books, counting forks, and other organizational feats were the areas where Pix excelled.

Over the years, Pix Miller had developed a reputation for getting things done. And having earned it once, she kept on earning it. She was the townwide coordinator for the Girl Scout cookie drive, although Samantha hadn't been in uniform for years. Then there was the United Way appeal, Town Meeting, the library board of trustees, and so forth. She'd ceased being a room mother now that her children were out of elementary school, but she still held her seat on the PTA Council. And she did all this along with chauffeuring these children to soccer, ballet, French horn lessons, ski team, swim team, as well as making their Halloween and school-play costumes. Some Alefordians called Pix a superwoman, but she didn't feel like one. She'd talked about it once with her friend Faith in a sudden burst of self-examination: "I'm not working, so I feel I can't say no, and everyone always calls me. I don't want to disappoint them—or my kids—but sometimes I wonder how the heck I got in so deep."

Faith had taken a dim view of the whole thing, especially the notion that Pix wasn't working. As a minister's wife, Faith lived in fear that she would end up in charge of the Christmas pageant or fund-raising for a new roof. Fortunately, Pix had taken this job. "You *have* to start saying no. You know the slogan, 'Just Say No'. All this is not so different from doing drugs, Pix. I think you've gotten to the point where your system needs it and you have to go cold turkey. Besides, now you are gainfully employed and you have a perfect excuse."

It was hard for Pix to face the fact that Faith might be right—that Mrs. Miller had a reputation to uphold and had grown dependent on the praise she got from all these unpaid

4

jobs. But then again, often no one knew she did them—except Pix herself—so she supposed it was the same thing. That night, more confused than ever, she'd talked about it with Sam. He'd been slightly exasperated with Faith, not an unusual occurrence. "Pix, you like to help out. You're good at it. There's nothing wrong with any of that. Except, you take on too much and don't have enough time for us—or yourself. Pure and simple. Samantha's driving now and Danny's the only one who really needs you. You can start getting out of some of these other things—like the cookies." Sam was always annoyed at how much room the boxes took up in the garage. He had to park his precious sports car outside for the duration.

Pix had stopped listening after the phrase "Danny's the only one who really needs you." Where had all these years gone? It was like shrubs. You put them in and they looked so tiny and inadequate, then before you knew it they had outgrown the space and you had to get a backhoe to yank them out. Maybe Danny would go to college nearby. With all the colleges and universities in the Boston area, Mark had to pick one in Colorado and Samantha was considering Reed in Oregon.

Her mind drifted back to the present. A summer of women—three generations of women, to be precise. Pix's eighty-year-old mother, Mrs. Arnold Lyman Rowe, Ursula, was already in residence at The Pines, the immense "cottage" Ursula's father had built for his family by the shore in the late 1890s.

In those days, the rusticators' journey was not a five-hour drive from Boston, but one stretching out over two days, starting with the embarkation from the Eastern Steamship pier on Atlantic Avenue—complete with steamer trunks, portmanteaus, wicker lunch hampers, hatboxes, and all the other bulky accoutrements necessary for a back-to-nature summer. Ursula Rowe reflected ruefully on the soft-sided nylon luggage that sufficed for her now and told her daughter there would never be a better way to travel than those long-ago voyages.

Mother. Pix blew another shrill note on a blade of grass. Just as she was bewailing the departure of her fledglings, she was wondering how to clip Ursula's wings a bit, and once they were clipped, what would Pix do with her? Ursula resisted every effort to change her way of life and Pix was plagued with anxiety about all the things that could happen to her mother, still living alone both in Aleford and on Sanpere, rattling around The Pines with only Gert Prescott coming in a few times a week to do for her. Yet, where else would Mother go? Mother and daughter got along very well, but Pix was not sure how it would be if they were ever under the same roof. She had the strong feeling any roof Mother was under would soon become Mother's roof, and while Pix as a dutiful and loving child might be able to cope with this herself, Sam would not like it. At all. As it was, when everyone was on vacation on the island at once, away from work and school, ready for leisure activities specifically with Pix, she felt as if she were slowly being stretched to fit Procrustes's bed—pulled in opposite directions by her loved ones. She could navigate the road between her own cottage and The Pines blindfolded.

But something was going to have to be done about Mother. She even refused to wear one of the Medic Alert medallions supplied by Blue Hill Hospital. "There are so many people going in and out of my house every day that if anything ever happened to me on this island, you'd know before I did," she'd told Pix. There was some truth to this. Sanpere was a close-knit community; some might even call it too close-kit. But still Pix worried. Mother was so stubborn.

Just like Samantha. Pix had unfortunately assumed any adolescent turmoil on her daughter's part would be over at age seventeen. Recently, it seemed Samantha was making up for lost time, a late bloomer—not that she stayed out until daybreak or had pierced her nose. But "Oh, Mother" punctuated their conversations with alarming frequency. Lately, Samantha hadn't seemed very interested in completing her collection of island mosses, last summer's all-consuming passion, *and* she was letting her hair grow, abandoning the style Pix favored for what she feared might be "big hair."

Pix looked around. It was a typical Maine day, which meant the sky was perfectly blue, the air clear, the sun pleasantly warm. If she was at the shore, the water would be a slightly darker blue, with an occasional whitecap. She took a deep breath. For Christmas one year, her brother had given her a can of Maine air, the kind they sold to tourists up at Bar Harbor. She'd laughed along with everyone else, then late that night she'd gotten out a can opener and opened it, closing her eyes and burying her nose inside before it could mix with the Massachusetts molecules. She didn't think it was her imagination. There was a hint of balsam and a crispness, then it was gone. She opened her eyes to look into an empty can that she quickly threw away before anyone could tease her.

Arnold Rowe, her brother, an orthopedic surgeon, was thirty-nine, six years younger than Pix, and there were just the two of them. He and his wife, Claire, lived in New Mexico. Arnie was attentive to Ursula—from a distance—and of course reaped all sorts of glory merely by showing up. He was the fair-haired son, and if Pix hadn't loved him so much, she might have resented all the attention he got, arriving in Sanpere on vacation or for fleeting holiday visits in Aleford when he would not be called on to drive Mother to doctor's appointments, Symphony on Fridays, tea with her friends, the flower show, the . . .

Arnie and Claire would be arriving sometime in July. Mother had had his boat taken out of storage and all was in readiness for his return. Gert would leave Arnie's favorite, a strawberry-rhubarb pie, for the first night's dinner, and then they'd see very little of the two Rowes, what with sailing, golf, tennis, cocktails, and dinners at their innumerable friends' houses on the island and mainland. They wouldn't see them,

7

but the house would still be in a whirlwind as they dashed from place to place. He'd leave with regret: "Where did the time go? We'll take that sail to Vinalhaven next year, I promise." Things would settle down, and Pix would find herself missing the clutter of Arnie's tennis things and golf clubs in the hall.

All this reminded Pix: she had taken Mother's supply of sheets down to Aleford for the winter to wash and repair. "You can't get percale like this anymore," Ursula asserted, and Pix agreed. The linens were like silk. She'd have to unearth them, or her brother and his wife would be sleeping on mattress ticking. She laughed at herself and felt better. Sure Arnie and Claire were a little self-centered, but they were also fun to be with and very generous to their nephews and niece. With no children of their own, they encouraged visits; Mark had once spent a whole vacation with them, exploring cliff dwellings and learning about the Anasazi.

Pix stood up and stretched. The first day with one foot still in Aleford was always a little difficult. It would take some time to get into her island rhythm—maybe another hour or two.

After returning home, she spent the rest of the afternoon unpacking. Samantha had left her a note saying she'd taken her bike over to Arlene Prescott's house but would be back by five o'clock, in plenty of time to go to Granny's. Ursula had invited them for dinner this first night. Arlene was Samantha's best friend on the island. They'd known each other all their lives and each year picked up where the last had ended. They had been faithful pen pals when younger. More recently, the correspondence had degenerated to a few postcards. Presumably, teenage life on Sanpere was just as time-consuming as it was in Aleford—even with the closest mall sixty miles away.

Pix unpacked her clothes. It didn't take long. She smiled to herself at what Faith would say about her choice of raiment.

On Sanpere, Pix lived in jeans, shorts, and turtlenecks or polo shirts, depending on the weather. Tonight, though, she'd change into a skirt. Mother had worn pants all her life, but she didn't like to see them at dinner. Pix donned a white wrap-around skirt and, with a nod to Faith, paired it with a bold black-and-white-striped Liz Claiborne shirt. She slipped on some red espadrilles, washed her face and hands, combed her hair, and was ready. When Samantha came home, she eyed her mother approvingly. "You look nice, except you forgot your lipstick."

"No I didn't," Pix replied. "I'm on vacation."

"Oh, Mother." Samantha went off to get ready, a process that took considerably longer than her mother's titivations.

She emerged in what Pix knew was the latest fashion, but it still looked like something she'd give to the thrift shop: a long flowered-print housedress with a crocheted vest on top. To complete the ensemble, Samantha was wearing a pair of heavy-soled black boots that managed to suggest the military and orthopedics at the same time. Sam's hair was at that in-between stage where everyone either comments, "Are you growing your hair?" or says, "You need a haircut." Pix chose the latter.

"Your hair is so cute when it's short, and think how easy it is for the summer." They'd had this conversation before.

Samantha explained patiently, "I want it to look good when I go back to school. Up here, it doesn't matter what I look like and please, Mom, for the last time, I don't want to look cute. That's not the idea."

"Well, attractive, then." Pix knew she should shut up, but old habits die hard.

Her daughter nobly chose to ignore the remark. "Why don't we go to Granny's? You know how much she hates it if we're late."

"We're never late!" Pix protested.

"There's always a first time." Samantha smiled sweetly. "Why don't I drive?"

Pix sat in the passenger's side, wondering when the reins had slipped from her grip.

Ursula Rowe greeted her daughter and granddaughter. "Don't you both look lovely."

"You're looking pretty spiffy yourself, Granny," Samantha said as she gave her a kiss.

Gathered in the hallway, the three generations bore a general resemblance to one another, most blurred oddly enough in Pix, not Samantha. They were all tall and had good posture. Ursula, in her ninth decade, carried herself as proudly as she had at Miss Porter's in her second. Ursula's high cheekbones were softened in her daughter's face, only to emerge sharply again in Samantha's. All three had the same thick hair. Pix and Samantha's was the dark chestnut color that Ursula's had been before it turned snowy white. Pix's was cropped close to her head. Her mother's was almost as short but curled slightly, whether by nature or art, she did not reveal. Samantha's eyes were a deeper brown than her mother's and grandmother's. Her father's genes had turned almond into chocolate.

"Shall we go in?" Ursula linked one arm through Samantha's, the other through Pix's. Pix felt a sudden rush of wellbeing. It was going to be a good summer. She'd tend her garden, put up a lot of preserves, spend time with her mother and her daughter, and maybe clean out the attic at The Pines, a herculean task that had been put off for twenty years of summers. And she'd make Arnie take her over to Vinalhaven.

Over the creamed haddock Gert had left, they talked about the summer. Ursula had been on the island since Memorial Day. Unencumbered by school-age children, she spent May to October on Sanpere. Pix was dying to ask her the latest gossip, but their custom of not discussing such things in front of the children, even when said children weren't children anymore, was too strong, so they stuck to safe topics.

"When do you start working, Samantha? Have some more beans, Pix dear. They're the last of last year's."

"Monday. The campers arrive tomorrow, but Mr. Atherton said he won't need me until then. I'll be there in the mornings to teach the younger children sailing, stay to help with lunch, then I'm through for the day. I promised the Fairchilds that I'd be able to take care of Ben and Amy when they come up in August, so that will be in the afternoons."

"Phew, that's quite a schedule."

"Yes." Samantha laughed. "But think how rich I'll be!"

"Are you going to have any time for fun?" Her grandmother looked concerned.

"It's all fun! Besides, Arlene is working at the camp, too—full-time, so I wouldn't be seeing her, anyway. And I don't work weekends."

"It's nice that Jim Atherton keeps the camp going. It must have been the early thirties when his parents started it. He certainly doesn't need the money." Ursula exchanged a sharp glance with Pix hinting good gossip to come.

"A labor of love," Pix remarked. "I can't imagine Jim without the camp, and Valerie seems to enjoy it, too, although it's not really her thing."

"What do you mean, Mom?" Samantha asked.

"Well, Valerie Atherton is some kind of interior decorator. I think she likes having the camp around to keep Jim busy while she goes antiquing."

"It's funny. We're so close to the camp if you go by water, but we don't really know them. I guess it's because none of us ever went there. I haven't even met Mrs. Atherton. My interview was with him."

"I think you'll like her," Ursula said. "She's not as flashy as she looks."

Samantha brightened, "This is going to be interesting."

"You know she has a son about your age from her first marriage."

"Yeah." Samantha made a face. "Arlene says he's a real dork."

"It couldn't have been easy for him, moving to the island, especially after losing his father the way he did," her grandmother commented, correctly translating Samantha's opinion. "Now, why don't you clear the table. We can have our dessert on the porch. Gert left your favorite—lemon meringue pie!"

"What a sweetheart! Please thank her for me." Sam jumped up from her chair and began to clear the old, large, round dining room table with alacrity.

"I'll make some coffee," Pix offered, wondering how she could drop a gentle hint to Gert Prescott that Pix's own personal favorite was black walnut. Gert probably figured Pix made her own pies, but she figured wrong.

After consuming two pieces of pie, Samantha went down to the shore to poke around and watch the sunset. Her mother and grandmother stayed on the porch in the fading light.

"More coffee, Mother?"

"No thank you. I want to sleep tonight."

Ursula was a notoriously sound sleeper, and Pix laughed.

"You could drink the whole pot and not worry."

"So *you* say. Nobody knows how much I toss and turn. Now, when is Samuel coming?"

"Not until the Fourth. Maybe the weekend before, if he can get away. He's preparing a big case and it goes to trial soon. It all depends how long the jury takes. We could get lucky." As Pix spoke, she realized how much she was going to miss her husband. It happened every summer. She didn't want to leave him, but she really wanted to go—and it was wonderful for the kids.

"Now, tell me what's been going on since you've been here," she said to her mother.

"Not much. You know how quiet things are in June. It's

heavenly. And the lupine was the most spectacular I've ever seen."

Ursula said this every year. Pix had come for a long weekend one June especially to see the fields of tall purple, blue, and pink spiked flowers. She had no doubt that every year would be better than the last, because no memory could equal the impact of that palette stretching out—in some parts of the island, as far as the eye could see.

"No scandals? Come on, Mother, you're slipping," Pix chided.

"Let me think. You heard that the manager of the IGA is keeping company with his ex-wife's sister? And the two sisters have, of course, stopped talking to each other and the ex-wife has to drive clear off island now every time she needs a quart of milk.

"And what else? Oh, I know. It will probably be in the paper this week, but Gert told me about it this morning. They had a real scare at the nursing home. When Karen Sanford went to open up the common room, she found glass all over the place, and she'd left it spick-and-span the night before. Obviously vandalism. So she called Earl to come investigate. Turns out the vandals were a Yoo-Hoo bottle that had exploded and knocked over a tray of dishes!"

"It will definitely make 'Police Brief,'" Pix said when she finished laughing. What a change from reading the news at home, she thought to herself. Sgt. Earl Dickinson was the one and only law-enforcement official on the island—and so far, the only one needed. It reminded her.

"Do you think Earl and Jill are going to get married?" Jill Merriwether was the proprietress of a gift shop in Sanpere Village.

"It's certainly about time, but they seem to be content the way they are and so long as they both feel the same, it's fine."

"I know what you mean. If one or the other starts getting itchy for the altar, then there could be a problem. Still, I don't know why they don't. It's nice being married." Pix had no regrets.

"Then, as you might imagine"—her mother continued to catch her up—"there's a lot of talk about the Athertons. I didn't want to say too much in front of Samantha, but their house is finally finished and everyone's calling it 'the Million-Dollar Mansion,' which is quite likely close to the truth. I don't think there's a person on Sanpere who doesn't know they have six bathrooms, three with bidets."

"The bidets may have taken some explaining."

"True, but the gold-plated faucets didn't."

"Where did Jim get all his money? The fees at the sailing camp have always been pretty steep, yet nothing that would produce an income like this."

"His mother's father invented scouring pads or some such thing and money made money. Keeps on making it, if the house and those boats of Jim's are any indication."

"So they really intend to live on the island year-round. I'm not so sure I'd want to be here all winter. It gets pretty quiet." Pix thought of her constant round of activity in Aleford and realized with a start that she'd miss it if she moved.

"Your father and I considered living in The Pines when he retired, but when it came down to it, there were too many things and people we didn't want to leave."

The two women paused in their conversation and looked out across the water at the sunset. They could see Samantha silhouetted against the horizon. The Pines had been built to take advantage of "the view." There was a large front porch and one extending off the second-floor bedrooms. It was an ark of a house, with rooms added to the rear as needed. By modern standards, it was dark. The windows were small and the interior pine paneling old-fashioned. The only remodeling that had been done since it was built was to the indoor plumbing and the addition of a gas stove and other modern appliances in the kitchen. The old woodstove was still used for heat and Gert kept it blackened, its chrome sparkling. Pix had seen a similar one for sale in an antiques shop for five hundred dollars. Her mother had been stunned.

The sun was a ball of fire, descending rapidly into the sea, leaving streaks of purple, pink, and orange as it fell that would have seemed garish in any other context. Flashy. It brought Pix back to the Athertons. It wasn't that Valerie dressed in gaudy colors or was dripping with rhinestones. Her jewels were real, especially the large diamond solitaire Jim had given her as an engagement ring. It was that she *dressed*. She wore *outfits*. Blouses matched shirts and pants. Sweaters matched both. Her shoes matched her scarves, as did the polish on her perfectly manicured nails. Pix's nails, clipped short, tended to suggest activities like weeding and clamming. Valerie's indicated pursuits like sunbathing and page turning.

"Let's see, the Athertons have been married for about three years, right? And they used to spend the winters in Virginia, where Valerie lived?"

"Yes, we all thought Jim was a confirmed bachelor. He met Valerie when he was sailing someplace in the Bahamas. It was just after her husband died so tragically."

Pix had heard the story. Valerie, Duncan, and Bernard Cowley were sailing when a sudden tropical storm hit, almost destroying the boat and sweeping Bernard overboard. Valerie had developed an understandable aversion to boats of any size or shape amounting to a phobia and refused to set foot on one. That her new husband ran a sailing camp was definitely ironic.

Pix looked over at her mother. She'd been widowed a long time. It was a prospect Pix kept firmly shoved way in the back of her mind. She sincerely hoped she and Sam would go at exactly the same moment.

"And what are you going to do with yourself while Samantha's busy making all this money?" Ursula asked.

"The usual—and maybe this year we'll tackle the attic.

Then remember, I'm overseeing the Fairchilds' new cottage."

"I'd almost forgotten about that. Seth Marshall is building it, isn't he?"

"Yes, and tomorrow I want to go over and see how much he's done since Memorial Day."

Faith and Tom were building a modest house on a point of land not far from the Millers. The Fairchilds had hired Seth Marshall as the architect and contractor after seeing his work. It was a very simple plan, yet Faith had still wanted Pix to keep an eye on the progress. Pix had steadfastly refused to accept any money for the job, insisting that having the Fairchilds as neighbors on Sanpere as well as in Aleford was reward enough. Besides, Pix argued, she was the one who had lured them to Sanpere in the first place, with somewhat startling results. But Faith had pressed hard. She knew the amount of time Pix would devote to the project, so finally they'd compromised on an amount. Pix grudgingly agreed, especially when Faith threatened to bar her from the site if she wouldn't take the money.

It was the kind of thing Pix loved doing, and being paid for it seemed wrong. There was nothing more exciting than watching a new house go up. She loved all the smells—from the fresh concrete of the foundation to the fragrant fir of the framing. She'd miss out on the concrete. Seth would have poured the foundation long ago. They'd seen the gaping hole in May.

"It will be nice to have the Fairchilds on the island," her mother remarked. "I'm not surprised they decided to settle here. Sanpere has a way of getting into one's blood."

"Just think. This is your eightieth summer on the island. We should make a banner to carry in the Fourth of July parade."

Her mother sighed. "I've lived a very long time. Maybe even too long."

Pix was used to this sort of remark, but her heart never failed to tighten. "Don't be silly."

"Oh, I'm not silly. I'll tell you what the funny thing is, though. Eighty years old and I still feel twenty inside. It's all gone so fast."

Pix stood up and called Samantha to come in.

Too fast. Much too fast.

The next morning proved to be another typical Maine day and Pix proposed to Samantha that they pack sandwiches and walk out to the Point to check what progress had been made at the Fairchilds' cottage. Her daughter agreed wholeheartedly. She was curious about the house, too.

"Show me the plans before we go, and let's take the dogs."

Pix had assumed any walk they took would automatically include the golden retrievers that she regarded as canine offshoots of the Miller line: Dusty, Artie, and Henry.

"Of course we'll take the dogs." She leaned down to stroke Dusty. "Do you think you can keep up with us, old lady?" Dusty's muzzle was turning white and she no longer raced into the mud at low tide when one of the children threw a stick, her former favorite and extremely messy pastime.

It was close to ten o'clock by the time they set off, feeling vaguely wicked about skipping church.

"We'll start next week," Pix vowed. "Most people don't even know we're here yet."

"Granny does," Samantha reminded her.

"True, but look at this sky. Surely this is a day that the Lord hath made, and I'm sure both the Lord and His representative on earth would be glad we're enjoying it."

"Hey, Mom, I don't even like going to church here. It's so boring compared to Reverend Fairchild's service. You don't have to convince me."

Through a quirk of faith, and through Faith's quirks, the Fairchilds had managed to buy the entire forty-acre parcel of land known locally as the Point, a long finger of land stretching out toward the open sea. It had one of the only white, sandy beaches on Sanpere and was a popular spot for swimming and picnicking. The Fairchilds had given most of the land to the Island Heritage Trust, saving a few acres for themselves at the very end. An old road had been improved and they had been able to get the power and the telephone companies to string lines out to the site—no mean accomplishment, Pix had informed them. Faith had been surprised. "How could we possibly be out there without power or a phone?" She was even more surprised when Pix had told her that the Millers hadn't had a phone at their cottage, by choice, until the kids had started to go to sleep-away camps off-island and Pix's nerves couldn't take it. "It was wonderful. A real vacation when no one can call you." Faith had privately thought this New England eccentricity in the extreme. No phone!

Today, Samantha and Pix were following the road straight down the spine of the Point. They'd take the shore way back, clambering over the rocks when the tide was lower. The road went through the woods, but there were openings that cut down to the sea. Judging from the number of sailboats out, local pews were pretty empty this Sunday morning. The sun sparkled on the surface of the water and the clouds in the sky were as white and billowy as the sails beneath them. Pix thought how much of their lives on Sanpere was governed by the sea. Their days were planned around the tides. When it was high, they swam. When it was low, they dug clams, gathered mussels, or simply combed the beaches for shells, peering into the jewel-like tidal pools at the starfish, sea anemones, tiny crabs, and trailing seaweed. The Millers' cottage was not on deep water, unlike The Pines. First-time visitors were always shocked at the broad expanse of pure mud revealed where a few hours before the ocean deep had beckoned. Pix had grown to prefer the change, charting the summer by the time of the tides.

She remembered suddenly what the tide had revealed to her friend Faith several summers earlier and shuddered. She stepped determinedly along and almost bumped into Samantha, who was crouched down on the shady path leading from the road to the construction site.

"What are you looking at?"

"Someone dropped a key," Samantha answered. "It looks like an old one. Isn't it pretty?" The cut work on the top of the key was done in intricate swirls.

"Hold on to it and I'll ask Seth next time I see him if anyone has lost it. I'd take it, but these pockets have holes in them, I'm ashamed to say."

"If that's all you've got to be ashamed about, Mom, you're in good shape." Samantha shoved the key in her jeans pocket. If no one claimed it, she'd wear it on a ribbon around her neck.

Pix was debating whether to follow up Samantha's comment with a veiled inquiry as to what Samantha might be ashamed of that would lead her to make a comment like this. She stepped into the sunlight; news that Samantha was running a lunch-money extortion ring at school would have been welcome compared with the news that greeted her eyes.

Seth Marshall hadn't done a thing since Memorial Day. No, she quickly took it back. An ancient cement mixer had been brought in and there were empty cans of soda and other potables on the ground, nestled next to Twinkies wrappers and squashed Mother Goose potato chip bags.

"Mom! Didn't you say they would be framing the house by now?"

Pix was speechless. She nodded dismally. The Fairchilds hoped to move in at the end of the summer. They'd be lucky if the roof was on before bad weather struck.

Her anger mounted, and she found her vocal chords worked after all. "Wait until I get hold of Seth! This is totally inexcusable!" Pix's voice, which at times like these assumed the strident tones of a sideshow barker by way of the Winsor School and Pembroke, rang out indignantly in the crisp Maine morning air. She strode to the edge of the hole where the basement was supposed to be, the dogs following at her heels. "I know he's not dead or injured. It would have been in *The Island Crier.*" The Millers subscribed to the Sanpere weekly paper year-round. Next to *Organic Gardening*, it was Pix's favorite reading material. "He'd better have a pretty darn good excuse!"

"Look over here," Samantha called. She was behind a stand of birches the Fairchilds had specified be left. "Aren't these the things they use to stiffen the concrete? It must mean they're going to do it soon. They wouldn't leave them here to rust."

Pix went over to get a closer look.

"You're right. These *are* reinforcing rods, and here are some anchor bolts. But even if they pour tomorrow, we're still weeks behind schedule. And in any case, they couldn't pour any concrete without putting in the footing forms, and I don't see any sign of them."

Samantha tried to cheer her mother up. "Come on, let's go down to the shore and eat our sandwiches. It's not like it's your fault. Mrs. Fairchild will understand." Samantha correctly zeroed in on the thing Pix was dreading—telling Faith.

"I know, but I'm so mad at Seth, I could scream. Promises, promises. I should have known better and called him every day."

"Well, scream if you want to. It will make you feel better. Tiffany Morrison says her therapist told her to, and it's awesome."

"Why is Tiffany seeing a therapist?" Pix was suddenly sidetracked. The Morrisons owned a real estate agency in Aleford and had always seemed like the perfect apple-pie family. Maybe that was the trouble.

"Oh, you know, the eating thing. She won't eat anything, then she eats like crazy. I think she first started doing it to get her parents' attention. They're always so busy. Then it kind of got out of hand. She tells us about it in gym, and it's totally gross. But she's doing okay now. I guess the screams worked."

They both laughed, then Pix said, "Really, an eating disorder is no laughing matter."

"That's not what we're laughing at," Samantha pointed out sensibly. Sometimes she thought the term *guilt trip* had been coined for her mother.

Pix felt much better. She'd call Seth as soon as she got home. Then once she pinned him down to a firm date—and she would tell him she would be there watching—she'd phone the Fairchilds and might providentially get Tom.

She called to the dogs. Dusty and Henry came running from the woods, barking happy doggy greetings as if they had been crossing the country for months, desperately trying to find their people. But the third dog did not emerge from the greenery.

"Artie! Artie! Arthur Miller! Come now! Do you see him, Samantha?"

"No, but he can't be far. He never strays from the others."

Pix found him immediately. "Oh, naughty, naughty dog!"

Artie was down in the cellar hole, digging furiously. He glanced up at the sound of his mistress's voice, then went back to his work.

"What is he doing? He must have found an animal bone."

Pix jumped in, landing on the soft earth. She went over to the dog and grabbed his collar. "Stop it this instant!" As she pulled the dog away, she noticed that what he had unearthed was not a bone, but a piece of fabric.

"Samantha, look what Artie's found. I think it's part of an old quilt."

"I'll get something to dig with."

"It's probably in tatters. Remember the beautiful Dresden Plate quilt I saw in the back of Sonny Prescott's pickup? He was using it to pile logs on, to keep the truck clean!"

"Here's a stick. It was all I could find."

Pix took it from her and scraped away the dirt. So far, the quilt seemed to be in good shape.

"It looks like a nice one. I love the red-and-white quilts," Sam said excitedly.

"Me, too." Pix crouched down and tugged at the cloth. "It's Drunkard's Path. I've always meant to do one, but sewing all those curves seems much harder than straight lines."

"Artie, sit!" The dog had come to her side, about to resume his labors. The other two were looking over the edge of the excavation, puzzled expressions on their faces. At least this was how Pix interpreted them, and she prided herself on knowing her dogs' moods.

"Look at Dusty and Henry. They're all confused. People aren't supposed to dig like this." Dirt was flying out behind her as she dug deeper. "You pull while I dig."

Samantha gave a yank and a large chunk of earth flew up, revealing more of the quilt. And as it unfolded, something else was exposed.

That something else was a human hand.

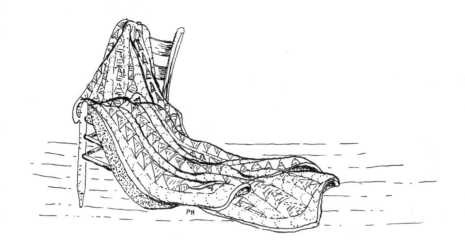

Chapter 2

At first, Pix thought it was one of those plastic joke hands that had been all the rage in Maine the previous summer—sticking out of someone's trunk or trash can. The first time she'd seen one, she'd laughed. After a while, it got boring—and ghoulish.

This hand wasn't plastic.

Pix and Samantha looked at each other, aghast. Samantha was the first to speak.

"It's a dead body, isn't it?" she whispered. Her face looked pale and sickly.

Pix gently lifted the hand with the stick. It was flaccid and curiously heavy. The cuff of a blue denim work shirt was revealed. Pix assumed there was an arm attached, leading to all the other parts wrapped in the quilt in the shallow grave. She nodded and stood up. Her legs were shaking.

"I'll stay here and you go to the Hamiltons' for help. They're the closest. Take the dogs."

"No, Mom. Keep the dogs with you."

"All right," Pix agreed. The dogs could slow Samantha down if they decided to chase a squirrel or even a leaf blowing across the path. She felt immeasurably comforted to have them stay.

The two women climbed out of the hole in the ground at the lower end, opposite the spot where the body had been buried. As they walked across the level dirt, Pix gave a thought to the footprints they were obliterating, but there was nothing they could do about it now. From the moment the dog had jumped in, the murder scene had been messed up.

Murder scene. Murder. There couldn't be any doubt. This was not the way loved ones were laid to rest.

Samantha paused briefly to give her mother a hard hug. "Is this really happening?"

Pix held her close. "I'm afraid so, but I can't believe it, either. You'd better go," she said, holding her tighter.

Samantha broke away and ran off toward the road. She was a fine athlete, and as her mother watched her graceful long-legged stride, the horrible discovery they had just made was forgotten for an instant—but only an instant.

The first thing Pix did was to tie the dogs to one of the trees. She didn't want Artie or the others to continue the exhumation. She sat down on a granite boulder, a massive one disgorged by the inexorable progress of the glacier, and tried to think.

But the horror of their discovery was making rational thought impossible. At least she'd been able to send Samantha for help. What was filling her mind now was the picture of that hand lying there on the ground, disembodied. It was growing larger and larger in her imagination. She hadn't even noticed whether it was the right or left, and what did that matter, anyway? What mattered was that it was a person, someone who had been alive perhaps only a day or two ago. She took a tissue from her shirt pocket, blew her nose, and swallowed hard. She sat up straighter. So far, she'd done what she was supposed to; now she had to force herself to think of something besides that hand.

For instance, whose it might be? She hadn't heard anyone was missing on the island, and her mother would certainly have mentioned it the night before. If it wasn't someone local, the police were going to have a difficult time identifying the remains. The end of the Point was a lonely, sheltered spot. A boat from anywhere along the Maine coast—or the Eastern Seaboard, for that matter—could easily land and dispose of a body without anyone knowing.

But . . . Her thoughts were sliding back into their old, familiar logical patterns. The killer had to be someone who knew about the construction, someone who knew the foundation hadn't been poured yet. It was too unlikely that an individual looking to get rid of a dead body would just happen upon an excavation site. No, the whole thing did not point toward chance. It pointed toward someone well acquainted with what was happening on Sanpere. Roughly 95 percent of the population.

The initial shock and disbelief were beginning to wear off and Pix was drawn to the edge of the basement, above the body. She looked down. The hand was dead white against the dark soil, just as she'd left it. She hadn't imagined the whole thing and naturally nothing had moved. She jumped into the hole again, being careful to land on the same spot and retrace her steps. Somehow, Pix couldn't continue to sit on a rock with a corpse lying a few feet away and not investigate further.

She didn't disturb anything; she simply stared at what had already been revealed and noticed several things she had missed before. There was a noticeable but small X sewn in blue thread near the border of the quilt where people sometimes put a name and date. Roman numerals? The beginning of a date? X was ten. She remembered that much from her years of Latin.

The hand looked like a man's—or that of a hirsute woman who worked with her hands. The nails were short, uneven, and one was blackened—the way a nail gets if you close it in a door or hit it with a hammer. It was the left hand, but there was no ring on the ring finger, although that didn't mean whoever it was wasn't married. Few of the men around here wore wedding bands, except to please their wives when they dressed up. The kind of work they did was not kind to jewelry.

The final thing she noticed sent her quickly up aboveground. The quilt was indeed a red-and-white one, but there were two reds, one a slightly rusty one—dried blood. It had been a violent death.

Back on the rock with the dogs stretched out next to her, she realized she could be here a long time. It would take Samantha at least a half hour to get to the Hamiltons' house at the beginning of the Point. Nan would be in church and probably not home yet. It was Sunday, so Freeman Hamilton wouldn't be out pulling his lobster pots, and Pix hoped he was puttering around the house and not off someplace. He wouldn't go too far, though, and risk being late for his Sunday dinner.

Freeman wasn't a churchgoer. Said he liked to talk to God directly. She remembered what he'd told her once when she was a girl and he and Nan were a young married couple. He'd come by with some lobsters for her grandfather, pointed to the view of their cove, with islands that seemed to stretch beyond the horizon across the wide expanse of deep blue water, and said, "You know, if you want to speak to God, it's a local call from here."

Pix thought a few words with the Almighty were most certainly in order now, but her mind was teeming with so many questions, such as how long the body had been there, that she settled for a few devout entreaties for the peaceful repose of whoever the unfortunate soul might be and a Godspeed for Samantha.

Pix realized that she felt oddly distanced from the event. Was she in shock? Or was it because the hand still seemed like plastic and without a fully identified being, the death wasn't a reality yet? Nothing had been personalized, except their reactions to the idea of murder.

She must be in shock, she thought, to be thinking this way and to be thinking about what she was thinking so consciously. She was going in circles, but she wasn't frightened. Whoever had brought the body here was long gone. She tried to imagine what might have happened. An unknown man (presumably) was stabbed to death by person or persons unknown, wrapped in a quilt (why a quilt?), taken to this out-of-the-way spot either by boat or car, and buried. It would have had to have been at night. It would have been risky to come during the day, when there was a chance the construction workers might be around. She saw the scene vividly: the body wrapped in the quilt to keep the blood from leaving any telltale signs, carried from the car or boat, and placed in the basement; the digging of the grave by the dim light of a flashlight beam—make haste; make haste—finally leaving the corpse and slipping back into the role or roles played everyday, with no hint of the night's work crossing a face. Her breath was almost taken away at the audacity of it all. If Pix hadn't brought the dogs, the concrete basement floor would have covered the grave and no one would have been the wiser. The Fairchilds would be living above a crime and never know it.

But wouldn't the dead person have been missed eventually? What kind of person has no one asking his whereabouts?

Pix stood up and walked farther away from the house. Sketching the scene in her mind had removed some of the distance—or the shock was wearing off. She began to feel queasy and afraid. Where was Samantha?

Think about something else. There's nothing you can do. Why had she stayed behind? They both could have gone for help. But it had seemed wrong to leave that hand so exposed, untended. The sky was filled with the shrill cries of gulls and terns. She shuddered at the notion of their beaks pecking at the hand, unearthing more of the body in the basement.

She threw her head back and gazed up at the circling birds: herring gulls; laughing gulls; two cormorants, portentous black creatures, necks bent like shepherds' crooks as they landed on the rocks; arctic terns, streamlined and elegant, swooping gracefully among their gull cousins. She watched as one lone tern hovered over the water, then suddenly plunged headfirst after a fish. A hundred years ago, this tern would have been prey, not predator. Pix's mother invariably mentioned it at least once a season when watching the birds dart and dive. Thousands at a time were killed in their summer nesting grounds and island women were hired to skin them, preparing them for the New York feather market to grace a hat or trim a dress. The terns were saved from extinction just in the nick of time by the first Audubon Societies and legislation controlling the plumage trade.

The terns were summer people. They were from "away" and had nested on the islands at their own peril. The corpse lying here under the sky, was it someone from away, as well? Someone unknown and unfamiliar to the island who could vanish without a trace? Vanish as the terns nearly had?

Samantha must surely be at the Hamiltons' house by now.

Think of other things.

It was almost July, but the long hard winter buffeting the island with snow and heavy rains until late April had delayed the already-short growing season even further. And now it was dry. There wouldn't be the traditional fresh peas to go with salmon for the Fourth of July. No one had been able to sow much of anything Memorial Day weekend because the weather had been so bad. Pix imagined what her garden would look like in August: green tomatoes that she'd have to bring back to Aleford to ripen between sheets of newspaper; lettuce; too many zucchini; the eggplant was doubtful— Her pessimistic reverie was interrupted by a loud shout.

"What the hell are you doing here!"

She hadn't heard anyone approach, and it was obviously not Freeman Hamilton, Samantha, or Sergeant Dickinson.

She jumped to her feet and ran in the direction of the shore, with some notion of trying to attract attention from a passing sailboat.

The tethered dogs were barking their heads off. As she raced down the slope toward the beach, her heart pounding with fear and from the exertion, she glanced back at the animals and caught sight of the intruder. It was Seth Marshall, glowering. His long dark hair, heavy mustache, and the anger in his eyes made him look like a pirate from a children's book illustration.

Pix stopped abruptly and turned around. Her own anger of an hour ago returned full force, fueled in addition by the fright he had given her.

"What do you mean what am *I* doing here? How about what the hell *you* were supposed to be doing here? I thought you were building a house. The foundation isn't even poured!"

Her voice was booming and she was almost face-to-face with him before she collected herself. Seth Marshall knew when and where the concrete foundation was going to be poured. Seth Marshall had a handy pickup filled with shovels and all sorts of other digging equipment. Seth Marshall's mother was a quilter.

"I didn't know it was you." He was almost apologizing. "Don't want people messing around out here."

"When were you here last?" She wanted some information before she broke the news.

"Look, Pix, I can't afford to turn work down. I told the Fairchilds that when they hired me. I've got to make enough in the spring and summer to last me all year. The Athertons needed some repairs at the camp before they could open and I've been over there the last few weeks. And I've been finishing a cottage for some people on the reach road. But we'll be here every daylight hour from now on. The soil is good and dry. We'll be able to get everything done, even the floor, by the end of the week. The Fairchilds will have their place before Labor Day. That's a promise."

Pix heard him with only half an ear, although that half did cause an internal comment of promises, promises, before zeroing in on the matter at hand—literally. She'd have to watch out. Her mind was running amok. So, Seth claimed not to have been at the site for several weeks. The police could probably tell how long the soda cans and other debris had been around. Without carbon dating, it would be impossible to say when the venerable cement mixer had been set in place.

There was no point in delaying further. She had to tell him. He'd spot it the moment he walked over to the excavation, and he was moving that way.

"There's a dead body buried in the cellar hole. My dog started to dig it up."

"What!"

Seth's bushy eyebrows rose clear out of sight, disappearing somewhere into his mane of hair.

Pix was patient. It was a lot to take in. "The dog was digging at something and when we went to see what it was, it turned out to be somebody's hand. There's a very dead person over there. Wrapped in a quilt."

"A quilt?" Seth seized on the word, the only one suggestive of normalcy.

"Yes, a patchwork quilt."

"I don't believe it!"

Pix knew he wasn't referring to the quilt. "Come and see for yourself." He followed her over to the edge of the pit he and his crew had dug in the spring. There hadn't been anything other than rocks in the ground then.

"Holy shit! It's a hand!"

Pix nodded. It was the third time she'd approached. The hand was beginning to look familiar.

"We've got to get Earl out here!"

"Samantha was with me and she went to the Hamiltons' for help. They should be here soon."

"I've got a shovel and a pickax in the truck. You sit out of the way and I'll dig him up. It could be pretty nasty."

Pix figured Seth would want to take action. Most men usually did, however she'd been close enough to her friend Faith's sleuthing activities to know that they should leave well enough alone. Not that she had exactly, but digging the body up would definitely be regarded by the police as tampering with evidence, and she told Seth so.

Without something to do, he seemed visibly shaken and went to the truck for a beer.

"Want one?"

Pix did, but somehow the picture she might present to her daughter, Sergeant Dickinson, and Freeman Hamilton, who would surely not stay home once he learned there was a body on the Point, was a bit unseemly. Not to mention that it would be all over the island that she had been drinking with Seth Marshall while someone lay stone cold only a few feet away. Not by any stretch of the imagination could this be called a wake. At a wake, it was customary at least to know the name of the deceased.

"Do you have anybody new working for you this summer? Anybody who's been missing for a while?"

Seth came and sat down next to Pix on her boulder. The dogs had long since quieted down and were snoring peacefully in the afternoon sun.

"You're trying to figure out who it is, right? Well, I haven't. It's the same crew as last summer, and some from the summer before. The Atherton kid was helping us on the camp work, but I told his folks I couldn't afford to hire him for other work. They were paying him for what he did there. Or didn't do is more like it."

"Have you heard of anyone missing? Here or on the mainland?"

Seth shook his head. "Of course, we don't know how long the body's been here, but I haven't heard anything at all, and you know the way news gets around."

Pix continued to pursue her line of questioning.

"I assume the whole island knew you were working out here and had dug the hole for the foundation."

"Yup, it wasn't a secret."

"But who knew you hadn't poured yet?"

"Probably all the same people, since I've been at the other places instead of here for some time now. But I was planning to pour this week. Not too many people would have known that."

They were getting somewhere.

"Who would have known?"

"Okay now, let me see. I was ordering the lumber for the footings at Barton's and I may have mentioned it then. I told my mother, because she said you would be here soon and if I didn't get going, you'd have my hide, which is true." Seth smiled and the pirate was replaced by a mischievous little boy—little boy, despite his thirty-odd years. He'd been one of the island's footloose and fancy-free young bachelors for so long, it was hard to think of his ever settling down—or getting any older. He lived with his parents in Granville, the larger of the island's two main towns, Sanpere Village being the other. His mother, Serena, was a member of the Ladies' Sewing Circle with Pix's own mother. The Sewing Circle. That tore it. If Serena knew, it might as well have been listed under "Coming Events" in *The Island Crier*.

Small-town life made criminal investigation nearly impossible. There were rarely any skeletons in anyone's closet, because at one time or another, some friend or neighbor had opened it "by mistake," ostensibly looking for something else. "How's your uncle Enoch doing?" asked in the right tone of voice would be enough to elicit the information that he was drying out up to Bangor and how the hell did you know, anyway?

All this was running through Pix's mind, along with the inevitable conclusion that she couldn't figure anything out, island mores or no, until she had found out who the corpse had been for a start. She abandoned her previous line of inquiry.

"So, this is definite? You're going to start work tomorrow?"

"If Earl will let me," Seth replied.

They sat in companionable silence for a while. There was a slight breeze and the leaves in the aspen grove behind them rustled softly. Seth took a pull on his bottle of beer, then asked, "Did it seem like it was attached?"

Pix knew what he meant. "I think so."

"Could be part of him is here, part someplace else."

"I hope not," Pix said, her queasiness returning at the idea of dismembered body parts turning up at construction sites from Kittery to Calais.

They were quiet again, subdued by the grisly suggestion, but Seth couldn't stay still for long.

He smacked his forehead dramatically. "I must be losing my mind. I've got a CB in the truck. I can call Earl myself and find out what's keeping him." He walked rapidly toward the pickup and soon Pix heard the crackle of static and Seth's muffled words. He was back within minutes.

"He's already on his way. But I bet Freeman beats him."

Scarcely were the words out of his mouth when Freeman's truck pulled in and screeched to a halt, sending gravel flying in all directions and starting the dogs barking again. Samantha flew out her door and was at her mother's side before Freeman had even opened his. When he stepped out, Pix could see he had his Sunday clothes on, which meant several less layers than usual. His fisherman's tan—forearms, face, and neck—was a deep mahogany color, contrasting with his thick mat of light gray-white hair.

Samantha spoke, her voice full of concern: "Mom, the police will be here right away. Are you okay?"

Considering the only danger had been from her own overactive mind, Pix was able to answer, "I'm fine. How about you?"

Freeman answered for her, "She was a little wobbly when she first got to me, but she's calmed down some. Nan came home and that helped." He did not seem surprised to see Seth and nodded to him. "Hello, Seth. Where's this body of yours now? Lucky I decided to fix Nan's washer today instead of going fishing with Charlie Porter."

"It's over here, in the foundation. And it's *not* mine," Seth added snappishly.

The two men went over to the edge of the excavation. Pix decided she'd seen enough of the hand to last her a lifetime and returned to her perch on the rock, making room for Samantha and holding her near. Her daughter still looked very pale and seemed to be shivering in her jeans and T-shirt despite the warmth of the sun.

"Gorry," they heard Freeman exclaim. "Think someone cut him up in pieces?"

Seth's speculation and Freeman's further reaction were cut short by Sgt. Earl Dickinson's arrival. Uniformed, tall, and ramrod-straight, he looked very official. And with his closely cropped light brown hair and deep blue eyes, he looked very handsome. He addressed Pix and Samantha first. "Show me where you found it and how you got down and up."

Earl Dickinson was a man who always went straight to the point. When it became apparent that the earth had been disturbed by both of them, as well as Artie, the sergeant jumped in the hole himself, inspected the evidence, and climbed back out. "No one else been in there?"

Pix answered for them: "No."

"All right, then, stay out of it. I've got to call in to report, then we can talk. The state police are sending a unit."

He was back in a few minutes with his notebook out and pen clicked. They sat on and around Pix's boulder, at his feet like so many schoolchildren. First he wanted to know exactly when the Millers had arrived and how the body had been par-

34

tially unearthed, then he asked all the questions Pix had. Did Seth have anyone new working for him? When had Seth been at the site last?

After he was finished, he closed his notebook with a sharp snap and buttoned it into his pocket, along with the pen. "Not a whole lot you folks can do here, so I suggest you go home and keep your mouths shut as much as is humanly possible when everyone on this island will be asking you what's going on. Until we dig him out, we don't have anything to go on, except that somebody appears to have used a perfectly good quilt as a shroud."

The sergeant's vocabulary was taking on a new richness, Pix noted. Maybe it was Jill's influence. But he had hit upon the thing bothering her, too. Yankee thrift being what it was, why not wrap the body in an old tarp or burlap? She wanted to tell him about the mark she'd found on the quilt, yet heeding his caution, she decided to wait until they were alone. Not that she didn't trust Freeman and Seth, especially Freeman.

"Then Samantha and I will be going. I'd like to get her home." And into her nice secure little bed with a cup of chamomile tea, she thought.

"I'll take you," Freeman offered. Seth looked a bit lost and said he'd stick around to keep Earl company until the staties showed up.

"No, you go along, too. We know how to get a hold of you if we need you," Earl said. Effectively dismissed, Seth mumbled what could have been a good-bye and roared off in the pickup.

"Needs a new muffler," Freeman commented.

Earl nodded and Pix half-expected him to take out his notebook and make an entry, but most of the pickups on the island needed new mufflers. It wasn't considered a citable offense, unless you were caught drag racing on the old cemetery road in Granville, a road so blackened by burned rubber that locally it was called "the speedway."

So they went their separate paths to spend the afternoon

trying not to think about what was uppermost in their thoughts: Who was the body in the Fairchilds' basement—and who had put it there?

The dead man turned out to be Mitchell Pierce. While not exactly an island resident, he was not unknown on Sanpere, having spent time living there off and on while he was working at his purported craft: the restoration of old houses. But Mitchell also lived all along the coast from Camden past Bar Harbor, depending on where he was working. And to complicate matters still further, he was known to disappear for months at a time, purportedly (again) to the Pacific Northwest. *Purport*, in various forms, was a word that turned up often in conversations about Mitch. In addition to his restoration work, he dabbled in antiques, buying and selling. In fact, he bought and sold almost anything from Mercedes coupes to odd lots of canned goods. He was a man who lived by his wits and it was a well-known fact that these wits often took him close to the law. *Provenance* was something that Mitch defined broadly, as it suited his own needs. An exquisite piece of folk art could have been made in 1890 or 1990. What mattered, Mitch was quick to point out to his detractors, was that it was exquisite.

In another era, Mitch might have sold snake oil, and the pitch he made to new purchasers of old houses was not unlike the slippery patter of his antecedents. His charm was hard to resist and levelheaded Boston businessmen found themselves uncharacteristically turning their houses and charge accounts at Barton's Lumber over to Mitch so he might bring the dwelling back to its pristine glory. Mitch got free rent and free rein. Sometimes the customers were satisfied. Mitch *did* know what he was doing. And sometimes they returned in the spring to find hide nor hair of him, their pipes burst, and an astronomical bill waiting at Barton's. Still, he kept getting jobs.

It wasn't that he was particularly good-looking. Short, with a wide widow's peak, the adjacent bald patches threatening to spread back across the dome of his head, he'd developed a paunch at thirty; now at forty, it could be described less kindly. He had an impish grin, an infectious laugh, took no one, including himself, seriously, and was wonderful company.

He'd done some work on The Pines a few years ago and Ursula stood over him the whole time. He'd expected nothing less and they parted friends, but Pix hadn't fallen under his sway. She didn't trust him—not on her tintype, and especially not on his.

It was Mother who called to reveal who the dead man was, of course.

Ursula was miffed that Pix hadn't informed her immediately about her grisly find, but Pix had always been a good little girl. So when Earl told her to keep her mouth shut, she took it as a sacred trust.

"But certainly you could have said something to your own mother!"

"I didn't even tell Sam. Now, of course, I can, since everyone seems to know even more than I do and I found him." Pix often found being good didn't shower one with the rewards implicitly promised.

"Why don't you come over here for tea and we'll talk about it. How is Samantha?"

"She slept when we came back and seems fine now. Arlene and her boyfriend asked her to go to the movies in Ellsworth and that should take her mind off it. And it will help when she knows who it was. I doubt she ever met him. If it had been someone she knew, that would have been worse."

"All right, then. When she leaves, you come on over."

Pix agreed and hung up. She really ought to call Sam now and most certainly should call the Fairchilds. Tom was probably out on parish business. Maybe it would be better if they were both together and she could tell Sam at the same time, because the first thing he'd do after hanging up would be to run next door. Besides, her mother might have picked up some more things and Pix would have further information for them. She'd wait until she came back.

Feeling like the abject coward she knew herself to be, she waved good-bye to Samantha, whose color was back, and set off for tea and maybe sympathy.

The tea tray was on the front porch and her mother was waiting. The family took as many meals outside as the weather and time of day permitted. None of the Rowes liked to be indoors when they could be enjoying the view and the air up close.

"It must have been terribly upsetting for you, darling," Ursula said, taking Pix's hand in both of her own.

"It was." Pix sat down in one of the wicker chairs that they had never thought to cushion. The latticework that appeared on the back of one's legs when one was wearing shorts was a kind of badge of authenticity. "I was mostly worried about Samantha. But she seems to be all right, even a little excited. None of her friends have ever found a body," Pix added with a slight grimace.

"A dubious distinction at best, but I'm glad she is not upset. The whole thing is puzzling, though. Who on earth would want to kill Mitchell? He was always a complete gentleman when he was here, although I know others have not been so fortunate in their dealings with him. He did a beautiful job removing all that dry rot in the back addition. I'd hoped he would be able to repair the latticework on the porches this summer. I suppose it's too late now."

"Much too late, Mother. The man is dead."

"I know, dear. I told *you*, remember."

Pix did.

"I hope the Fairchilds weren't too disturbed by all this. It's not the way one likes to start a new house."

"I haven't reached them yet." Pix skirted the truth. "But I don't think they'll be too upset. It just happened to be their basement. It could have been anybody's—and they didn't know him."

"This business of wrapping him in a quilt . . . such an odd thing to do. What was the pattern?"

Pix was amazed there was something her mother didn't know.

"It was a red-and-white Drunkard's Path—very nicely done, tiny hand stitching. It looked old. Although, I couldn't see much of it." And there were those bloodstains obscuring the work. Pix gagged on her tea and her mother had to pound her vigorously on the back before she stopped coughing.

"Well, whoever did kill him must be an exceptionally nasty person."

"I think we can assume that," Pix said.

"No, besides being evil. Drunkard's Path—it's just plain nasty to call attention to Mitchell's drinking problem. He's been fighting it for years."

Ursula must have grown very close to Mitchell over the dry rot, Pix speculated. There didn't appear to be much she didn't know about the man. No reason not to take advantage of Mother's winning ways.

"Did he have a family? I never heard that he was married."

"No, he never married. I don't think he was really very interested in women—or men. Just things. He definitely liked things, especially beautiful and valuable things. Of course he must have had a mother and father, but he never spoke of them—or any brothers or sisters. He did mention that he grew up in Rhode Island, though."

"We should tell Earl that. It might be a lead."

"I will, or you can tell him. Mitchell knew a great many people on the island, but not many people knew him. He minded his own business."

And probably for very good reasons as far as Mitchell was concerned, Pix thought.

"Seth knew him best, I'd say."

"Seth!"

"Yes, when he was a teenager, he worked for Mitchell. I've often heard Seth say he learned everything he knows about building and restoring houses from Mitch. They were very close for a time. You know the way boys that age look up to someone a little older who seems to know everything. I think Mitchell even lived with the Marshalls one winter. Maybe Seth can repair the latticework. I hadn't thought of him."

"Not until he finishes the Fairchilds' house," Pix said firmly. "The latticework has needed repair for several years and it can hold out a little longer."

She took another cup of tea, turned down her mother's offer of sherry as sunset drew nigh, and set off for home to make her phone calls.

The Pines was across a causeway connecting Sanpere and Little Sanpere. It was a short road, but it twisted and turned precariously above the rocky shoreline. It was another favorite place for the local kids to drag and had witnessed several tragedies over the years. There were no guardrails. Large rocks had been set on either side and this year they were painted with bright white luminous paint to help keep drivers on track. It wasn't a road she liked to think of Samantha negotiating at night.

She passed through Sanpere Village with its lovely old ship captains' houses, some with widow's walks, facing the sea. Her friends Elliot and Louise Frazier lived in one, and Louise was planting geraniums in a huge old blue-and-white stoneware crock in the fading daylight. Pix waved and continued on. The Fraziers belonged to the same group that Pix fancied her family did—people not orginally from Sanpere who either now lived here year-round or had been coming in the summer for so long that the line between native-born and "summer person" had blurred. They weren't islanders, but they were close to it. Elliot Frazier had been the postmaster for years and both he and Louise had served on many of the town's boards. They were even further across the line than the Millers and Rowes, although if there had been an honorary islander award, Pix's mother would have won it years ago. Being admitted to the Sewing Circle amounted to the same thing.

As Pix drove across the island on one of the three roads that connected the loop Route 17 made around the circumference, she thought about all these distinctions and wondered why people always found it so necessary to put other people in neat little categories, and why indeed she prided herself so much on her own label.

Many of the summer people actively fought the moniker—buying their clothes at the fishermen's supply, driving beat-up old trucks, and studiously avoiding the vacation community on the island. These same people tended to count how often they received the traditional island road greeting—a few fingers casually raised from the top of the steering wheel and maybe a slight nod as vehicles passed.

The rusticators, families who had been coming for generations, had always hired local people to work for them as caretakers, and cooks and they didn't pretend—or in some cases want—to blend in. Their ways had been set by a grandmother or grandfather in '02 and successive generations found no reason for change. They sailed. They took vigorous walks. They picnicked—with the same immense wicker hampers outfitted with thermos bottles, china, utensils, a rug to spread on the ground, and a folding camp stool if required by an elderly member. They wore squashed salt-encrusted, white canvas sun hats that did not prevent their faces from turning a ruddy bronze, complete with peeling nose, by August.

Where did Mitchell Pierce fit into the social scheme? Pix wondered. He wasn't a summer person, but he was from away. He was more intimate with the native population of Sanpere, since he'd boarded in various island homes at times. These people generally spoke approvingly of him, even after some major disaster when a foundation he had finished crumbled because there was too much sand in the concrete. He loved to listen to the old-timers' stories and could recount the history of the island better than most who had grown up here. He played the mandolin passably and was a popular addition for musical evenings, where he was sure to be asked for "Rainbow" and "The Girl I Left Behind Me." Yet his last series of misadventures had left an unpleasant taste even in the mouths of these supporters.

He'd been working on a large Victorian mansion originally constructed by a shipyard owner in Sanpere Village. The current owners, wealthy summer people, lived in Chicago during the winter. Mitch had charged not only building supplies at Barton's but also food at the IGA and bread and other baked goods at Louella Prescott's. Louella ran a small bakery from her kitchen and had learned the same delectable recipes from her mother that her sister, Gert, had. Both women were noted especially for their pies, and in Louella's case, the best anadama bread in Maine, or perhaps anywhere.

Mitch had disappeared midwinter and was sighted up in Northeast Harbor with a booth at an antiques show. He told someone there that he planned to return to Sanpere to finish the job and settle his accounts, but he never again crossed the bridge to anyone's knowledge—and there were plenty of people looking for him. Barton's was a big outfit, and in any case, the owners of the house he was working on would be forced to cover the bill, since they'd given Mitch carte blanche. But Louella, and Vincent at the IGA, had trouble absorbing the loss. Mitch had run up quite a tab. His habit of turning up on your doorstep with a pie in one hand and a few pints of the expensive ice cream Vince stocked as a luxury item didn't seem the generous and kindhearted gesture it once had. Local opinion was that Mitch should come back and face the music.

Pix could almost hear what people were no doubt saying now. Well, old Mitchell is back, but the only music he's facing is harp music, and that might be doubtful.

She added another category for people like Mitch.

The Fairchilds were clearly going to be summer people, arriving for a vacation, pure and simple, leaving only their footsteps behind.

Samantha's employers were a blend, since Jim's family had been coming for such a long time, plus they were now living here year-round. But Valerie's southern accent alone would keep them at arm's length as outsiders for years.

Jill Merriwether drove past Pix on the opposite side of the road. They'd reached the two steep up and down hills that were so much fun to drive, like a roller coaster. Jill gave more than the laconic salute—a big smile and a wave. Had she heard about Mitch?

Pix suddenly remembered that Jill had added antiques to her shop. She'd talked about it during the Memorial Day weekend and mentioned that Mitch was one of her suppliers, so she must have known how to get in touch with him. Pix made a note to herself to talk to Jill and try to find out where Mitch had been living.

Jill's shop was close to the Sanpere Inn, lovingly restored six years ago by its new owners and saved from certain ruin. Mitch had worked on that, too, she recalled. The inn sat next to the millpond, facing the harbor across another small causeway. In a short time, it had become well known for its picturesque location and fine cuisine. Jill had quickly noted that its clientele was more interested in nineteenth-century marine paintings and pine chests than in mugs decorated with lobsters or jars of blueberry jam. She'd been excited about getting into the antiques business and had told Pix she was reading everything she could get her hands on. Pix reminded her not to overlook finds at the dump. A previous enterprise in Sanpere had obtained most of its stock that way when various local people traded up for a matching living room set from Sears, complete with his and her recliners, leaving the old rickety stuff off to one side by the household trash.

Pix turned down the long dirt road to their house. No matter how often she did this, she always felt an immediate sense of well-being. The first cove she passed had been posted for red tide this summer and no clamming or worming was allowed. But the cove at the foot of the meadow by their house had always tested out fine. It was illegal to cross private property to get to the shore, though anyone could come by boat and did. She'd see them bent over the mud with their short-handled rakes. Clamming and worming were backbreaking work. Digging in the mud for sea worms and bloodworms, freshwater bait, wasn't any better. Eking out a living on Sanpere had never been easy, but it was especially hard during the current recession. Men and women had to be Jacks and Jills of all trades. And that brought her back to Mitch again.

Which of his enterprises had led to the grave in the basement? Who had wanted him dead? Someone left with a half-finished or botched job? But they'd be more likely to sue or at least try to get him to complete the work, wouldn't they? She also couldn't see Louella working herself up to a murderous frenzy over unpaid bills for baked goods. But then there were people on the island who might get pretty steamed on her behalf, particularly after a night filled with too many beers.

Someone had had a reason. When they could figure that out, they'd have the murderer. This was the way she understood it usually worked in books. Look for a motive. Who inherits? Who had been scorned? Some event in his past? Something to do with his family? Maybe the whole thing was totally divorced from his shady occupations.

The newspapers played up random craziness, serial killers selecting victims at whim. But altogether too much thought had gone into the planning of Mitchell Pierce's death—the location, the timing, maybe even the quilt, Drunkard's Path. Had he been killed because he drank too much? Maybe it was insanity, some crazed temperance fanatic?

She pulled the car to the side of her house. The simple Cape wasn't an old one, but the seasons had worn the cedar shingles so that it looked as if it had been in place for centuries. Pix's garden added to the image. It was filled with old-fashioned flowers: delphinium, cosmos, phlox, oxeye daisies, and coreopsis. A combination of fragrances from the old varieties of peonies and the rosa rugosa bushes welcomed her home.

Inside, the cottage had been furnished with castoffs from The Pines, yard-sale finds, and a gem or two from local auctions. These embellished the myth that it was an old house, as did the Boston rocker needing some new paint and the gently faded chintz slipcovers on the down-cushioned sofa. The braided rugs scattered across the pine floorboards had been made by Pix's grandmother in shades of muted rose, blue, and green. Field guides, knitting projects, sailing charts, and Samantha's tennis shoes were strewn around the living room.

Other than the shoes, there was no sign of Samantha. She was still at the movies. Pix decided it was now or never. She *had* to call Faith. Having refused Ursula's sherry, she felt justified in pouring herself a scotch, dropped an ice cube in it, and dialed Sam.

He answered on the fourth ring.

"Hi, honey, I was going to call you two tonight. I was just out in the backyard in the hammock. You wouldn't believe how hot it is here!"

"That's nice," Pix said, then realized the inappropriateness of her remark. "I mean, that must be terrible."

"All right, what's wrong?"

"Samantha and I walked out to the end of the Point today to check on how the house was coming along. . . ."

"Is Seth doing a good job?"

"He hasn't done much of any job so far, but that's—"

Sam was as indignant as Pix had been earlier and she decided to let him have his say before finally interrupting. "Darling, we found a dead body on the site. In the excavation, actually."

"What!"

Pix told him the whole story. It was turning out to be a much-needed dress rehearsal for her star turn with the Fairchilds. Sam agreed to give her fifteen minutes before he went over.

"I know they're both home. I just saw Tom pull in and Faith has been in the yard with the kids all afternoon. They went inside about an hour ago.

Baths, supper, stories, Faith would be pretty busy.

But not too busy to answer the phone.

"Pix! This is great. I didn't think we'd get a report so soon."

Pix took a deep breath and a large mouthful of scotch.

"Is Tom around?"

"Yes, he's reading to the kids in the living room. Why do you ask? Don't tell me. They've screwed something up. Put something in upside down or left us with no doors!" Faith was attempting to speak lightly.

"Samantha and I went over this morning to see how things were progressing and one of the dogs dug up a dead body in your basement—or rather, the hand. The police uncovered the rest."

"I can't believe it!" Faith turned away from the phone, "Tom, get on the extension. Quick!"

"We had trouble believing it ourselves, but . . ."

"This is going to put us terribly behind schedule," Faith wailed.

From the extension, Tom asked, "What is?"

"Pix found a body buried in our future basement, and I know how the police work. It will be weeks before they'll let us continue. We may have to get all sorts of new permits and getting the ones we have was like something out of Dickens."

Pix graciously decided Faith must be in shock. She also decided she needed to get back into the conversation.

"The man who was killed was Mitchell Pierce. I don't think your paths ever crossed. He never had a permanent place on the island." Until now, she added silently. "He restored old houses, sold antiques, and tended to move around a lot."

"Isn't he the one who left Louella Prescott holding the bag?" Faith had become friendly with the baker.

"Yes, that was Mitch."

"I can't see Louella committing murder over a few crullers, though."

This time, Tom interrupted.

"How are you and Samantha? It must have been terrifying for you."

Pix felt a warm glow, a combination of Tom and Johnnie Walker.

"It was at first, but we're all right now. Fortunately, the dog only unearthed a hand."

"Oh, Pix"—now it was Faith's turn—"I've been such a jerk, thinking of my own petty concerns when you and Samantha have been through a horrendous day. What can we do? Should I come up?"

"No," Pix and Tom said in unison, Pix adding, "There really isn't anything you could do, and I know how busy you are getting ready for all those Fourth of July parties."

The Fairchilds' doorbell rang audibly in the background.

"That's probably Sam," Pix told them.

"Why don't you get it, sweetheart," Faith said.

Tom said good-bye and hung up the phone.

"Now, Pix," Faith said sternly, "I know you've seen me get involved in a number of murder cases, but it's not something I recommend, and I think you should stay out of all this as much as possible."

Pix found herself feeling somewhat annoyed. Who had located Penny Bartlett missing in Boston last year? It hadn't been Faith, but none other than her faithful friend and neighbor. Surely this same friend and neighbor should be able to ferret out a few salient details about Mitchell Pierce's death here on Sanpere, where she knew not only the names and characteristics of all the flora and fauna but the two-legged inhabitants and their habits and habitats, as well.

47

"Please, Pix, listen to me. It could be dangerous. I'm sure it's a total coincidence that someone picked our particular cellar hole, but you can't be too careful."

It was all Pix could do to refrain from comment, something referring to Faith's possible reactions upon hearing these same words. But Faith had become her dearest friend, and if she was a bit insensitive, a bit self-absorbed, a bit like a steam roller, other sterling qualities more than made up for it.

So she said, "Yes, Faith" as meekly as she could muster and hung up with promises to stay in touch with everyone on the hour every hour if necessary. Sam had picked up the extension and both he and Tom were exhorting her along the same lines Faith had.

She hung up, drained her glass, and then remembered: She had totally forgotten to tell Faith that Seth hadn't done any work since Memorial Day.

It would just have to wait.

Chapter 3

No one claimed the body.

After the medical examiner finished the autopsy and established that the cause of death was most certainly due to multiple stab wounds, the state police let it be known that whoever wanted to was free to take Mitchell and hold whatever last rites deemed fitting and proper. The remains were transported to the back room of Durgen's Funeral Home in Granville, pending the wishes of the near and dear.

Those wishes were still pending at the end of the week, by which time Donald Durgen had sensibly opted for cremation. Aside from the obvious reason, Donald told his brother and partner, Marvin, "We don't know how long we're going to have Mitch's company. Could be quite a while, and you know we need the space." He conscientiously labeled the cardboard box and placed it next to their tax receipts from 1980 to 1985. If someone wanted to come along and pay for an urn, why

49

then they'd be only too happy, but for the moment, Mitch would stay filed.

That Mitchell Pierce had been stabbed to death with a hunting knife did not make the investigation any easier. On Sanpere, hunting was not merely a sport but a passion, and in many cases, a necessity. Finding a household without a hunting knife would be as surprising as the use to which this particular one had been put. Far in advance of opening day, knives and guns were honed and oiled, stories told and stretched. The winners of the state moose lottery, those fortunate individuals who got the chance to track a really big creature, were targets of envy for weeks.

But the fact remained: No one seemed to be in a hurry to claim any kinship with Mitch. He seemed destined to remain at Durgen's, not even perched by the one window in the room where his spirit would have had an unobstructed bird's-eye view across the harbor to the old granite quarries on Crandall Island and straight out to Isle au Haut, rising from the sea in the distance—with its Mount Champlain resembling some sort of Down East version of Bali Hai. Durgen's was one of the best vantage points in Granville.

Pix was expressing her surprise at Mitchell's lack of earthly ties to Louise Frazier who had called to remind the Millers about the Frazier's annual Independence Day clambake on Sunday.

"The police have tried to track down a relative or even a close friend, but so far no luck. There's *got* to be somebody. It's really very sad. I told Sam we ought to bury him and hold a small service. There's plenty of room in the plot, and I don't imagine mother would mind. I can't stand thinking of him on some shelf at Durgen's for eternity, but Sam is sure someone will turn up. He told me to wait."

He'd also told her that there was no way Ursula was going to let a nonfamily member eavesdrop on their conversations in the next life, particularly when they had been careful to avoid revealing more than where to replace a two-by-four in this. Pix was sure her mother would be more accepting, but Sam convinced her to let things lie for the moment.

"It is odd," Louise agreed, "but Mitchell was a loner. He seemed to know everybody—and he certainly knew a lot about everybody; he was a wonderful gossip—but I can't ever remember his having a good friend. Nobody lived with him whenever he was on the island, although he lived with plenty of people."

It sounded illogical, but Pix knew what Louise meant.

"He was certainly adept at mooching a place to stay when he needed one, but when he was working on a house and living on the premises, you're right: He was always alone. He lived with other people only when he couldn't live in the house. The time he was restoring that barn in Little Harbor, he lived with one of the Prescotts."

"And didn't he board with John Eggleston once?"

"Very briefly. I don't think he was there a week before they quarreled and John threw him out. I'd forgotten that." Pix made a mental note to talk to John. A former Episcopal priest, now a wood sculptor, he might have evoked some revelations of a confessional nature from Mitch before things went awry. It would be interesting to discover what had happened to cause the heave ho, although it would no doubt turn out to have been something like Mitch's using John's towel or drinking milk from the carton. In Pix's experience, this was usually why roommates parted ways—nothing dramatic, just irritating little everyday things that piled up to actionable proportions.

Pix continued: "Jill told me that Earl told her the state police have been trying to find out about Mitch's past from his tax returns and Social Security. It seems everybody has a paper trail. He was born in Rhode Island, but his parents are dead and there were no siblings. His permanent address was a post office box in Camden. They got all excited when they went over the court records—you know, he's been sued a number of times. They found a lawyer's name and got in touch with him, but he says Mitch never told him anything personal, just hired him by the case. Never, apparently, made a will, either—at least not with this guy. Now they're going over his bank records, seeing whom he may have written checks to and if he had a safety-deposit box anywhere. The last place he was living was a rented room in a house in Sullivan, and there wasn't much in it except a few clothes and a whole lot of paperback mysteries."

"It does seem amazing to us. We're so embedded in our families, our relationships, and yes, our legal affairs." Louise laughed. "What I'm saying is, people like us don't often think of people like Mitch—someone with no roots."

Louise came from a large South Carolinian family, bringing with her to Maine softened speech, a penchant for drinking iced tea all year long, and an endless supply of stories about various family members. She had a tendency to talk of the living and the dead in the same tense, so Pix was never sure whether Aunt Sister, who dressed all in white and spent fifteen minutes every day of her life with slightly dampened bags—which she fashioned herself from silk and rose petals—on her closed eyes, was still alive or had passed on. Surely, however, Cousin Fancy, who saved the sterling from the Yankees by burying it in the family plot, moving Grandaddy's stone to mark the spot—merely for the duration, you understand—was no longer rustling along the sidewalks of Charleston in her hoop skirts.

Pix accepted Louise's invitation, hoping that Sam would be able to be there with her. He liked to help Elliot prepare the pit. It was an old-fashioned clambake always held in Sylvester Cove, with half the island in attendance. She offered to bring her usual vat of fish chowder, her grandmother's cherished, but not particularly closely guarded, recipe—unlike some she could name, she told Louise, both women having tried unsuccessfully for years to get Adelaide Bainbridge's recipe for sherry-nutmeg cake. Pix had tried not so much because she wanted to make it, but because of the principle of the thing, and besides, her mother would like it. Louise wanted it because it was a favorite of Elliot's.

Pix always thought of the Fraziers as ospreys, the large fish hawks that were once more returning to the islands, building their enormous nests on rocky ledges, high atop spruce trees, and occasionally even balanced on a channel marker. Ospreys were birds who mated for life. She'd told her theory to Sam, who agreed, commenting that Elliot was actually beginning to look a little beaky as he got older. Whatever the name or the comparison, the Fraziers were a devoted couple.

Louise accepted Pix's offer of the chowder gratefully. "Timing at clambakes is so unpredictable, and people always get hungry before we uncover the pit."

After she hung up, Pix thought she'd better put in a quick call to Faith before Sunday to ask her advice about making a large quantity of chowder. Usually, she simply quadrupled or quintupled the recipe, but working at the catering company had heightened her sensibilities. Maybe there was some special proportion known only to dedicated cooks or foodies. She wished the Fairchilds could come up for the Fourth of July festivities on Sanpere, which actually started the weekend before. The day itself would begin with a parade in Sanpere Village, followed by children's games in the elementary school playground, before moving to Granville for first the Odd Fellows Lobster Picnic, then later the Fish and Fritter Fry run by the Fishermen's Wives Association on the wharf. The day ended back in Sanpere Village, with fireworks over the harbor at nightfall. But Faith was catering four different functions and couldn't get away.

Pix would miss the Fairchilds, but it might be best if they weren't around until the whole business with Mitchell Pierce was cleared up. She reminded herself to call Earl and see when Seth could start work again. She presumed they'd been over the site with magnifying glasses, tweezers, fingerprint powder, and whatever else it was they used to find clues. They'd taken both her and Samantha's sneakers away on Sunday, so examining footprints was one activity, although it had been so dry that the slightest breeze would have long since blown away any traces in a cloud of dust.

All right, she told herself briskly. Call Earl, call Faith, get out chowder recipe, make shopping list, pick up Mother at the Bainbridge's, where she is lunching, stake tomato plants, set out beer-filled tuna cans to kill slugs, pick up Samantha at work . . . She got a pencil and made a list. Pix had lists everywhere—in her purse, in her pockets, on the wall, on the fridge, tucked into books. She'd told a friend once, "My life is one long list," and the friend had replied, "I know—and the list is never done." It had depressed Pix at the time and it depressed her now. She decided to take the dogs outside and do the tomatoes first.

The exercise and the fresh air lifted her spirits immediately and she stood up and stretched. It was a long one. Pix was not her given name, but an abbreviation of the childhood nickname "Pixie," bestowed by her doting parents when she was a wee mite of two. At four, she had shot up to the size of a six-year-old, but the name persisted. And as she grew older, she was thankful to whatever fate had been responsible for that brief petite moment. As a name, Pix was vastly preferrable to what was on her birth certificate, Myrtle—for her father's favorite aunt and her horticulturist mother's favorite ground cover. In retrospect, Pix was grateful Mother hadn't opted for the Latin and chosen Vinca Minor instead of little Myrtle. When Aunt Myrtle died, she left her namesake a cameo, a diamond brooch, and some nice coupons to clip. Everything but the cameo had long since been converted into a hot-water heater, braces for the kids, and, one particularly tight winter, antibiotics for the dogs, the cost of which had led Pix seriously close to fraud as she considered listing them under their given names of Dustin, Arthur, and Henry Miller on the family's health insurance.

After all, what was in a name? Pix, like most people, seldom remembered she even had another one, unless she received a notice for jury duty or her mother was particularly annoyed with her. Her mother! She dropped her tools, ran into the house, hastily washed, and dashed out to pick Ursula up. It wouldn't do to be late.

Samantha, on another part of the island, stopped for a moment to look about. It was bright and sunny—a little too warm for Maine. They still hadn't had any rain. She'd been working for several days and was beginning to get the lay of the land.

Maine Sail Camp consisted of a number of small rustic wooden cabins plus a large dining hall that doubled as a recreation center scattered over a sloping hill ending at the shore with a large dock and boathouse. When not actually on the water, campers could still see it and the sailboats that were the focus of each encampment. In addition to the sailing lessons, campers were instructed in nature lore, swimming, and the all important crafts of lariat making and pot-holder weaving. The oldest campers were thirteen; the youngest, seven. An invisible but impenetrable wall ran down the middle of the hill separating the boys' from the girls' cabins. There were campers whose parents and even grandparents had attended Main Sail. Reunions were nostalgic affairs and camp spirit was actively encouraged. A tear in the eye when singing "O Thou Maine Sail of My Life" was not viewed amiss. Jim Atherton, the director, was the embodiment of a Maine Sail camper. He lived, breathed, and now ran Maine Sail.

He had told Samantha her first day the camp wasn't just a camp but a state of mind. Kids returned year after year, not simply for the sailing and all the rest but for the "experience." Samantha had noted that he seemed to be too choked up to put it into words. Finally, he'd told her, "You'll have to feel it for yourself."

Mostly what Samantha was feeling was tired. She was responsible for teaching ten of the youngest children beginning sailing, which was going to involve everything from knot tying, to reading the water, and finally to putting a tiny hand to the tiller. Then she had to race up to the kitchen and help serve lunch, cleaning up afterward. She'd thought it would be fun to work with Arlene, but so far, they were much too rushed to do more than exchange a quick greeting in passing. Arlene stayed on with the crew to prepare dinner and clean the cabins. She told Samantha that if last year was anything to go on, the counselors would be much worse pigs than the kids. The kids had to keep their own bunks tidy. There were no such rules for the staff.

Today was as busy as the earlier part of the week had been. Samantha raced up the hill to the dining hall, swinging open the screen door, then letting it close behind her with a bang when she saw the kitchen crew surrounding Jim, all talking at once.

"Now, now, let's not get hysterical," he said, "There are mice all over the place. You know that. We'll put out some more traps."

Mabel Hamilton, Freeman's sister-in-law and the cook at the camp for so many years that local people thought of Maine Sail as "Mabel's Place," spoke above the din. Everyone quieted down.

"We've all had mice in our kitchens. I found one poor little fellow suffocated in a sack of flour once, but what we have not had until now are three mice with their heads cut off laid out on the counter along side a carving knife."

Samantha had moved next to Arlene. "Did you see them?" she whispered.

"Yeah, it is so gross."

"I think we should call Earl." Dot Prescott's voice was firm. Everyone nodded. Dot was in charge of housekeeping and, like Mabel, had been at the camp forever.

Jim tried a jocular approach. "The police! Over a few dead rodents!" He laughed. It didn't work. A sea of tightly shut lips faced him. Mabel and Dot stood directly in front of him, feet

56

planted solidly on the worn pine floorboards, arms folded tightly across their ample bosoms.

"All right, all right, I'll tell Earl. Now, can we clean the mess up and feed the hoard of hungry kids who will be streaming through that door in less than thirty minutes?"

Everyone returned to the kitchen. Mabel scrubbed the counter, muttering angrily to herself. "I don't like it. Not one little bit. Have half a mind to . . ." No one learned what Mabel was going to do with half of her mind, although all hoped it wouldn't be the lobe with the recipe file. She was far and away the best cook on the island. She suddenly stopped and addressed them in a louder and determinedly cheerful voice. "Let's forget about this now. It doesn't do any good to think about such foolishness. Probably a prank somebody thought would be funny."

Samantha wasn't sure. She also didn't think it should have been cleared away until Earl had had a chance to look at it, but no one was asking her, and she didn't feel she knew anyone except Arlene well enough to offer an unsolicited opinion. Besides, she was a kid and they were mostly grown-ups.

She had been unable to keep herself from looking at the gruesome sight. The tiny creatures were neatly laid side by side in a row, with their gory heads tidily set above each carcass. Samantha had seen dead mice before, even a mouse who had met its demise in a trap, but this precise carnage was worse than all the rest put together.

She watched as Mabel scoured the carving knife. Mitchell Pierce had been killed with a hunting knife. Carving knifes. Hunting knives. It suddenly seemed that there were an awful lot of knives in the news on Sanpere. She felt a bit dizzy and shook her head.

"Sam, are you okay?" Arlene was loading bread into baskets. The diet at Maine Sail leaned toward a carbohydrate overload. Today's entrée was macaroni and cheese. Dessert was bread pudding. There was a salad, though, lemon Jell-O with shredded carrots and mayonnaise dressing on an iceberg lettuce leaf.

Samantha nodded. "I'm fine. It's just creepy, especially after Sunday."

Arlene nodded knowingly and put an arm around Sam's shoulder. Since she'd started going steady, she'd begun to adopt a kind of big-sister attitude that Sam wasn't sure she totally liked.

"It is creepy, but I know who did it, and he's a harmless creep, believe me."

"You know who did it!"

"Well, I'm almost positive. It's got to be Duncan, of course. He's like stuck in the third grade or something, and I bet he thought this would be a really great joke on us and Jim. He hates it here. Maybe he thinks if he does enough weird stuff, they'll send him away. They should send him away all right—to the loony bin. It would serve him right."

Samantha hadn't given much thought to Duncan Cowley, whom she had yet to meet. Given everything she'd heard, though, Arlene's theory made sense. Samantha was willing to bet this had occurred to her employer, too. It certainly would explain why he wanted to make light of the incident.

She was about to ask Arlene to tell her some more about Duncan when one of the doors to the kitchen opened and a woman walked in. It wasn't the way her mother walked, Sam immediately observed—those purposeful strides meant to get you someplace. This walk was more like a glide. A dancer's walk. A beautiful walk.

The woman had very short, very fair hair that hugged her head in a silken helmet. Her eyes, or her contact lenses, were turquoise blue.

"It's Valerie," Arlene said in a low voice, "She's so awesome. Dunc had to have been switched at birth. He just can't be her son."

Valerie Atherton was speaking to Mabel Hamilton, then came over to the counter where the two girls were working.

"You must be Samantha Miller. I'm Valerie Atherton." Her voice was as smooth as the sea on an dead-calm day when you sat in the boat anxiously watching the drooping sail for a hint of tautness. Nothing was taut about Valerie, except her trim body and unlined face, shadowed by a large straw hat with a big red poppy pinned to the brim. Sam's mother had three hats: a floppy white sun hat with something that was paint or rust on it, a black hat for funerals, and a yellow rubber rain hat that made her look like the old salt on the package of Gorton's fish sticks.

"Hi." Samantha, star of the debate team, lead in the junior class play, searched for some other words, something that would make an impression on this witty and urbane woman, a woman Arlene worshiped. Sam had heard so much about Mrs. Atherton, she felt she already knew her—her clothes, her car, her cat, Rhett Butler. Valerie hailed from the South and what was a hint in Louise Frazier's speech was a full-blown answer in Valerie's.

"Hi," Samantha said again, now ready with a remark. "I'm Samantha Miller."

She met Arlene's eyes and turned scarlet with embarrassment. Someone else might have said, "I know. I said that, stupid," but Valerie appeared to find it new and delightful.

"I just adore your grandmother and your parents. It's lovely of you to be helping us out this summer. I hope you'll come by the house real soon. We can't show it off enough. It was in such bad taste to build such a big place and we have no excuse, except we all seem to take up so much space and if the house was any smaller, Jim and I would probably end up getting a divorce, so really we're helping to change those terrible statistics about failed marriages."

Mabel Hamilton, who'd been beaming since Valerie came into the kitchen, burst out laughing, "I have to remember this. Maybe if I tell Wilbur it's to save our marriage and set a good example for folks, he will finally winterize the porch so I can have my sewing room."

Samantha's cheeks were back to their normal color. She didn't know anyone who blushed as much as she did; it was annoying, so immature. She realized Valerie had entirely changed the mood of the kitchen and gotten everyone thinking of something else in a very short time.

Valerie perched on one of the stools and asked Mabel if she could have a bowl of the macaroni and cheese. "It's my ultimate comfort food." She was looking at Samantha, so Sam nodded and finally found some words. "Mine, too, along with chocolate pudding and whipped cream."

"And warm applesauce," Arlene suggested. Soon everyone was listing their favorites—mashed potatoes, cinnamon toast, tapioca—until Mabel brought the reverie to a halt with her own candidate—sardine sandwiches.

"Ugh! That's more like bait, Mabel," Dot said. She was about to elaborate when they heard the trample of little feet, many little feet. Samantha and Arlene jumped up to take the huge trays of steaming food out to the tables, where the kids helped themselves family-style. But first Jim asked for quiet. Samantha expected some reference to the mouse incident: "If anyone has any information"—the old "Put your heads down on your desks and I won't tell who raises a hand" kind of thing. Yet he didn't mention it. Instead, he recited from Tennyson's "Crossing the Bar," his voice growing slightly husky at "Sunset and evening star/And one clear call for me!" Jim started every meal with some inspirational nautical quotation. The man must have spent years memorizing them all. Sam was curious to see whether he recycled them each session or whether there would be a new one every day. Irreverently, she wondered whether he had picked today's quote as a tribute to the mice.

She stood near the wall on one side of the dining room, ready to refill platters and the pitchers of milk and water that were set in the middle of each table. She took the opportunity to study Jim. He didn't seem to be Valerie's type. He dressed invariably in L. L. Bean khakis, the camp T-shirt, and, of course, Top-Siders. He was handsome. Days on the water had bleached out his light brown hair and given him a good tan. His eyes were clear and blue. He always looked as if he'd had a good night's sleep. But there was nothing exotic about him, nothing special. He didn't have any style. Samantha found herself searching for the exact words that would sum up her employer. Jim Atherton was . . . well, he was just so straight.

As she'd groped for the definition, Jim's antithesis appeared at the dining room door: black/white, ying/yang, right/ wrong, you say *either*—all rolled up into one. It had to be Duncan. A nudge and a whisper from Arlene confirmed it. Samantha watched as Jim Atherton's gaze, which had been sweeping steadily across the room at regular intervals like the beam from the old Eagle Island lighthouse, rested on his stepson. There was no mistaking Jim's look of dismay. He concealed it hastily and walked toward the young man.

"Duncan. Hello. Are you hungry? Take a seat. We're still on the macaroni and cheese." Jim made the mistake of resting his hand on the boy's shoulder. Duncan shook it off with disdain. Arlene whispered, "Cooties" in Samantha's ear. Sam had to bite her lip to keep from laughing. Duncan *had* looked childish.

Duncan Cowley inhabited that curious limbo between childhood and adulthood, called, depending on the speaker, "the best years of your life," "the process of self-actualization," or "teen hell." To stake out his own particular territory in this strange land, Duncan had chosen to dress all in black. Today he wore a Metallica concert T-shirt under an unbuttoned black denim shirt, black jeans, and black high-top L.A. Lites, untied and without socks. A black leather bracelet complete with lethal metal spikes completed the ensemble.

"His parents should make him smell his shoes for punishment," Samantha said, adding, "I thought only elementary school kids wore those shoes that light up. You're right. What a loser."

Without a word to his stepfather, Duncan made his way to

the kitchen, his shoes indeed flashing tiny red spots of light as he walked. The girls turned to the wall. It was the kind of thing that could send them into uncontrollable fits of the giggles.

"And he stinks, too! What is that smell?" Samantha gasped.

"Musk and B.O."

"Poor Valerie." Samantha was in total sympathy with his mother, something that would have astonished some of her Aleford friends. But then, she wasn't in Aleford, and besides, Valerie wasn't like a regular parent.

At dinner that night, Samantha couldn't stop talking about the Athertons. She and her mother had taken big bowls of chili down to the deck by their own boathouse. Life with Samantha was turning out to be very relaxed, Pix thought as she reached for a tortilla chip straight from the bag. She hadn't even bothered with a bowl and she pushed thoughts of what Mother—and Faith—would say far from her mind. Instead, she concentrated on a cold Dos Equis—Faith would at least approve of the beer—and on what Samantha was saying. Obviously, the girl was in love.

Had Pix's own besotted crush on their neighbor, Priscilla Graham, been as boring, and even slightly irritating to Ursula? Pix sighed. If she was going to have to listen to paens to Valerie every night, she'd better lay in some more booze. What made it worse was that Valerie was a pretty fascinating creature and Pix liked her. She also knew, though, that in terms of types of women, she, Pix, was somewhere in Julia Ward Howedom, while Valerie inhabited the realms of Carole Lombard and Claudette Colbert, women who could and did wear satin.

"You have got to see him, Mom. He wears an earring, but not one like normal people—it's a notebook ring. I don't even want to think about how he got it through!"

It was an unappetizing thought, Pix agreed. Her mind swerved to the current fashion that bestowed normalcy on male earrings and she laughed aloud. She liked the freedom today's kids had to dress the way they did, although she still wished Samantha would cut her hair. In Pix's day, the most outré thing one dared do was wear one's Pandora cardigan buttoned up the back instead of the front.

"What are you laughing at?"

"Nothing in particular. I was just thinking about how differently teenagers dress now compared with when I was growing up."

"Your kilts and kneesocks? Your Weejuns? Your circle pin?" Samantha teased her.

"Someone told me circle pins were coming back. I always used to get so confused about which side to wear it on that I never wore mine much—one side meant you were a 'nice' girl and one meant the opposite. The middle meant something, too, but I can't remember what."

Now Samantha laughed. "Where would you have put it?"

"None of your business." Pix was not the type of parent who believed in revealing all to her children, especially before they had passed through the particular stage.

"Do you really think Duncan put the dead mice on the counter?" Pix was ready to move on to another topic. This had been the first thing Samantha had blurted out to her mother when Pix picked her up. Pix knew there could be no possible connection with Mitchell Pierce's murder, but it was another unsettling event in a place usually devoid of such things.

"I don't know. It's no secret he hates Jim, hates the camp, maybe even hates his mother for bringing him here. Arlene says he only has a couple of loser friends, mostly younger kids who are together not because they particularly want to be, but because nobody else likes them. They all wear a lot of black and listen to mope rock, that kind of stuff."

"Mope rock?" This was a new one, but Pix had grown to expect unrelenting novelty after raising one adolescent. The temps and mores changed at roughly the speed of light.

"Yeah, The Cure, New Order. I mean, I like them sometimes, except it gets a little much—tormented souls, desperate love. It's depressing."

"I think these were the kids who used to write poetry and try to get their parents to let them take the train down to Greenwich Village in an earlier day."

"Beatniks! I read about them in my American history book."

Sometimes children could make you feel very, very old with merely a few well-chosen words.

"I've read about them, too," Pix countered. She picked up her empty bowl and glass—she had taken the trouble to pour the beer from the bottle—and stood up. It was still light and she hated to go indoors, but she told Samantha, "I really have to call Faith. The kids should be asleep by now."

"I can't wait until they come. I miss seeing Ben and Amy. By August, they're going to be all different. Amy probably won't even remember me." Samantha had gone straight from passionate involvement with horses to small children, and now, it appeared, to soignée thirtysomething women, as well.

"I'm sure the Fairchilds can't wait to see you, either," Pix assured her, silently adding, Especially Faith.

"So what's going on? No more bodies I trust." Faith felt she could be flippant. If another corpse had turned up, in their well, say, surely Pix would have called her at once. Besides, she knew every nuance of her friend's speech. From the moment Pix had said hello on Sunday, Faith had known something was disastrously wrong on Sanpere. Tonight's greeting had been cheerful, everyday Pix.

"No, not human ones, anyway." Pix hadn't intended to start the conversation by telling Faith about the mice, but here it was.

Faith's reaction was similar to Pix's. "It seems unlikely that the two events have anything to do with each other, except proximity in time, and the use of knives. But why three mice? Were they blind?"

"I imagine they weren't taking in any movies," Pix said. "I've tried to think of a connection with the rhyme, but Valerie Atherton isn't a farmer's wife, nor are you, and there aren't any other wives involved."

"That we know of," Faith reminded her.

"That we know of. Besides, if it was meant to illustrate the nursery rhyme, their tails, not their heads, would have been cut off."

"Maybe the person has a bad memory and thought it was 'cut off their *heads* with a carving knife.' "

This actually made sense. Pix often misremembered childhood ditties, much to her mother's dismay. Her mother was supposed to be in the time of life when one's gray matter retreated into the shadows. Ursula's was a veritable Costa del Sol.

"What kind of mice were they?" Faith asked.

"Common field mice, I suppose. They're all over the island, you know."

Faith did not know and wasn't sure she was grateful for this new information.

"Not white mice, the kind kids keep as pets?"

"Samantha didn't say, but I don't think they were; otherwise, she would have mentioned it."

"Well, it is odd. Let me know if anything of a nursery-rhyme nature occurs again. There isn't anything in Mother Goose about a body in the basement, is there?"

"Probably. Some of the rhymes were pretty violent. I'll ask Mother."

"Speaking of violence, what's happening with the investigation?"

Pix told her everything she knew, including Mitchell Pierce's present whereabouts.

"I agree with you. It is sad. And it certainly gives new meaning to the phrase 'on the shelf.' If no one has claimed him by August, he should be interred someplace on the island. Tom can do the service," Faith said, cavalierly offering her spouse. "If relatives or friends haven't turned up by then, they would be unlikely to later."

"As soon as they calculate his estate, they're going to advertise—not the amount, of course, although Mitch couldn't have had much—just that you could hear something to your interest. If this doesn't bring someone forward, nothing will—or there's no one to be brought. I'm not saying it well."

"You're saying it wonderfully. Why, I don't know, but the whole thing reminds me of the time I went in the backyard and saw this man scattering ashes on the rosebushes. It must be the ashes," Faith added parenthetically.

"You never told me about this!" Pix exclaimed, surprised at the incident and even more at the fact that she hadn't known about it.

"It was shortly after we were married, and I didn't know you as well then as I do now. I probably thought you'd be scandalized, because I was furious with him. I mean those were our roses! He could at least have had the decency to ring at the front door and ask permission. It turned out that he was a former parishioner who was passing through and just happened to have his aunt Tilly in the car and thought she'd like literally to be pushing up roses."

"Her name wasn't really Tilly."

"Possibly not. I don't remember. Of course I ended up feeling sorry for him. He finished his sprinkling and I gave him something to eat. I think it was some leftover blueberry tarte."* Faith's food memory was flawless.

"I want that recipe, remember. We're going to have a bumper crop this year and the wild strawberries in the meadow are already ripe. I should have plenty for jam."

*See recipe on page 287.

"Don't make me jealous. I wish I hadn't accepted all these jobs for the Fourth. I'll never do it again."

Pix got her chowder advice; it wasn't complicated, simply good old multiplication. Faith suggested she might like to sprinkle fresh dill on top, but Pix told her this was a chowder purist crowd, eschewing even oyster crackers.

Faith then asked Pix's advice on how to stay sane while Amy was determinedly learning to walk, reeling around the house on feet that looked too tiny to support any kind of movement, let alone something as complicated as standing erect unaided.

"I want to give her knee and elbow pads, plus a helmet. Ben never went through this self-destructive phase. Sure he pulled himself up on things a lot, but he basically just sat, then started walking when he was about fourteen months."

"You just don't remember. It's a merciful forgetting. All that falling down."

They talked and laughed about the kids some more. Pix had yet to receive one of the stack of self-addressed stamped postcards she had sent off to camp with Danny. She had wanted to do the same with Mark but dared not. She'd have to pray for collect calls. She told Faith about Samantha's Valerie worship, was reassured—and realized she needed it—by Faith's own loyal remarks as to Pix's superiority, despite her lack of a subscription to *Vogue*.

"It wouldn't hurt to put on a little lipstick occasionally, though. I know what happens to you in Maine. Squeaky-clean is not all that intriguing. And leave a fashion magazine or two around the house with your cow-manure manuals or whatever you're reading these days."

"I'd rather have manure on my roses than what's on yours," Pix retorted.

"That was years ago. Besides, they've bloomed like crazy ever since."

It was very difficult to get the last word with Faith. Pix said good-bye and went to bed but not to sleep. They were showing movies at the old Opera House in Granville again and Samantha had gone with a group of friends.

As she lay listening for the sound of a car door, she thought about putting up another trellis in the garden for morning glories, across from the one that now sported a lush purple clematis. Building. House building. Earl wasn't sure when Seth could get back to work again.

Bang. Samantha was home. Pix turned out her light and was almost startled into wakefulness by remembering.

She'd forgotten to tell Faith what she still didn't know—that Seth hadn't done anything at all since May. Forgotten to tell her *again*.

The Sanpere Stitchers, which was what the Sewing Circle had decided to call itself about twenty-five years before, was meeting at The Pines this month. Many island routines were disturbed by this sacrosanct meeting. Louella closed the bakery for the afternoon; Mabel Hamilton left a cold dinner for the camp; and Dot Prescott's daughter went over to fill in for her mother. Anyone in residence at Adelaide and Rebecca Bainbridge's bed-and-breakfast would find the doors locked. A note affixed to the shiny brass front knocker announced their return at five and suggested a long walk or drive to Granville until then.

When the ladies convened at her mother's house, Pix's life was not her own for about twenty-four hours. She wasn't a member of the group, although they graciously allowed her to sit in when it was at Ursula's. Membership was a closely guarded affair, bestowed infrequently and only to women of a certain age and level of skill. The Sanpere Stitchers were very proud of their handiwork, and their annual sale in August to raise money for the Island Food Pantry was sold out by ten o'clock.

Pix's role began the night before with a call from Mother.

"You remember, dear, that tomorrow is Sewing Circle at my house, don't you?"

Since Ursula had managed in subtle and not-so-subtle ways to work this into the conversation every day since last Friday, Pix did indeed remember. It was written down on several lists.

"Yes, of course, and I'll be there early to help. I know you want my big coffee urn. Is there anything else you need?"

"Not really. Gert has things under control. She's been baking since Tuesday and cleaning since *last* Tuesday. But it occurred to me that you might bring some savories—a cheese spread, some crackers, you know the kind of thing. Perhaps arranged on a nice plate with some grapes, for those who don't want just sweets."

Pix developed a bowline in the pit of her stomach. Mother wasn't talking about a Wispride spread or Cheez Whiz. Her reputation was at stake.

"I'll see what I can do," she promised, vowing to call Faith as soon as Ursula hung up. This was an emergency.

Faith, knowing Pix's culinary expertise, gave her two very simple recipes* and told her to go to the foreign-food section, one shelf, at the IGA and pick up some Carr's water biscuits and Bremer wafers.

"Basically, these are cream-cheese spreads. For the first, blend some of the goat cheese from the farmers' market with an equal amount of cream cheese. That goat cheese by itself is too crumbly. If you don't have any, it's Mrs. Cousins who makes it, and you can go to her house. Try to get the kind she puts herbs in. For the other spread, take some of the green-tomato chutney you put up last year—you must have some left; you made vats of it—and mix it into the cream cheese. Don't make it too gooshy; taste it as you go along. Then put each in a pretty little bowl and decorate the top with a nasturtium or some other nonlethal posy from your garden. Put them on a platter and arrange the crackers and grapes around the bowls with more flowers."

The next morning, Pix stepped back from her creation and

*See recipes on page 285.

was tempted to take a picture for Faith. The platter looked beautiful—and tasty. Julia Child, watch out. She decided to go early to mother's and show off.

"Isn't that lovely!" her mother exclaimed. One of the nice things about Ursula was that she expressed her appreciation, even if it was for something she herself could have done with one hand tied behind her back, especially in earlier years. This was a woman who still gathered her grandchildren and their friends together at Easter to make the sugar eggs with the frosting scenes inside from scratch. "Gert, come see what a good job Pix has done."

Pix usually felt about twelve years old on Sewing Circle days. Today it might be ten.

The ladies started arriving promptly at one o'clock, bearing work bags and projects, some to display; some to complete. Pix scurried around fetching chairs and even a footstool or two for those who needed them—like Adelaide Bainbridge. She was an immense woman and said the blood ran better in her legs if her feet were up. She took up two spaces on the couch, further claiming territory as she spread out her work. There was a tiny corner left to sit in and she called over to her sister-in-law, seated in one of the multitude of Boston and Bar Harbor rockers, "Rebecca, there's plenty of room here and I need you to thread my needles. My eyes aren't what they used to be," Addie explained to the group. Rebecca obligingly gathered her things together and squeezed into the space. Fortunately, she was spare and lean, with elbows exposed in the warm weather that looked as sharp as the needle she was now threading. She had brought Ursula an old-fashioned, beribboned nosegay—pale pink sweetheart roses mixed with dried sea lavender surrounded by lily of the valley leaves. It graced the table now in a small white pitcher Pix had found, perfect for a tea party.

Louise Frazier had been voted into the group some years ago and after giving Pix a warm hug sat down on the other large couch next to Mabel Hamilton and pulled out a child's

70

sweater with brightly colored crayons worked on the front. "I have just got to finish this today," she said, needles clicking away. "The sale is only six weeks away and I have two more to do!"

After appropriate praise was given for various articles, the talk turned to how many raffle tickets each member had sold for Adelaide's quilt.

"It's so good of you to give it, Addie. The summer people are buying chances like crazy and now that the inn is displaying the quilt, even more people will want tickets," Dot said.

Adelaide Bainbridge was one of the island's celebrities. Fame had come late in her life. She now admitted to seventy-nine and friends politely ignored the fact that this admission had been made several years ago, as well. She'd started quilting as a child, taught by her mother to while away their time on one of the small islands off Sanpere. Adelaide's father had been a lighthouse keeper in the days before automation replaced the families who faithfully tended the beam. Pix always pictured Addie as one of those lighthouse keeper's daughters in old storybooks, battling through the storm to keep the light burning while Papa lay tossing with fever at her feet. If her childhood had been lonely on the island with only her parents for company, she never said anything. She seemed to have learned how to do an enormous number of things well from her mother—the art of housekeeping, reading and ciphering, and sewing.

Her quilts had become collector's items, depicting elaborately appliquéd scenes from her childhood and island life. A few of the recent ones were more abstract—colorful shapes suggestive of trees, waves, birds, and fish. Some of the quilts were in the permanent collections of museums. No shrinking violet—her appearance alone claimed center stage—Adelaide enjoyed being the Grandma Moses of the quilting world. Just when people thought her head couldn't get any bigger—an entire article in the *Ellsworth American*—"Good Morning America" included her in a special about Maine.

She lived with Rebecca, or rather Rebecca lived with her, moving into the large white nineteenth-century farmhouse after her brother James, Adelaide's husband, died. That was thirty years ago. Rebecca was the perfect handmaiden, basking in Adelaide's glory. No mean quilter herself, Rebecca had already contributed two quilts to the sale, a Double Wedding Ring and a Log Cabin. Now she was turning out an endless number of counted cross-stitch Christmas ornaments, hunched over her work, looking even smaller than she was next to Adelaide's bulk. The two were the island's own odd couple. Adelaide ran the household and was totally down-to-earth and practical, despite the fits of fancy her quilts represented. Rebecca drifted through the day with her head in the clouds—and occasionally her purse in the refrigerator or the garden implement she'd last been using set on the table in place of a fork.

Pix knew what she was supposed to do at these gatherings and announced that the coffee was ready. People filled their plates and she was gratified to see the cheese spreads disappearing. They put their handwork aside and sat back. Pix and Gert passed around more goodies.

"My word, but these are tempting, Ursula, how did you find the time to do all this?" Mabel asked.

Credit where credit was due. "Oh, Gert and Pix did most of it." Her self-deprecating smile hinted at the possibility that she might have sliced a lemon or two and put out the milk.

The talk drifted away from the sale to what was uppermost on every islander's mind these days—Mitchell Pierce. Most people were regarding it as an isolated incident, so it wasn't stirring up anyone's fears. Talk about it tended to the matter-of-fact.

"And the police don't have any leads? You'd think someone would have seen something." Adelaide Bainbridge declared emphatically after consuming one of Gert's cream puffs in two bites.

No one seemed prepared to respond. All eyes turned to

Pix. She was certain that they knew as much as she did but supposed her discovery of the body conferred some sort of mantle of expertise.

"I'm sure the police have leads that we don't know about. Mitchell hadn't been seen on the island for some time, so they're concentrating around Camden and Bar Harbor. As for seeing something, anyone could have landed on the Point at night—or even driven out there without being noticed. There were no signs of a struggle, so they are probably assuming the murder occurred someplace else. If you were lucky and no one was picnicking, you could even get away with bringing in a body in broad daylight."

"And Seth hadn't started working out there yet," Gert added.

"I know." Pix still found it hard to keep the irritation from her voice whenever she thought about it. If Seth had stuck to his promised schedule, or what Pix had assumed was promised, the foundation and basement would have been poured and the murderer would have had to find someplace else for the body. Yet with Seth's mother sitting across from her, hard at work on a smocked baby's dress, Pix couldn't give vent to her true emotions.

"Poor Mitchell, he was a likable soul," Louella said.

"But he swindled you out of all that money!" Pix's emotions found an outlet.

"I know, I know, still I'm going to miss him." It was the first real expression of mourning Pix had heard. "It hasn't been easy to make up the loss, but he intended to pay me back, I'm sure. He simply didn't have it."

"Well, he'd have it now if he could've taken it with him," Ursula commented dryly, "Seems like there's quite a fortune in his bank account in Bar Harbor—close to half a million dollars."

This was news, and for an instant the ladies were too amazed to comment, then everyone spoke at once.

Mother has been holding out on me again, Pix thought, and

after I slaved away all morning concocting gourmet cheese spreads for her party!

Ursula's voice cut through the fray. "I found out just as you were all arriving and haven't had a chance to tell anyone." She gave her daughter an apologetic look. "Nan Hamilton called to say she'd be late and told me Freeman had heard it from Sonny, who picked it up on the police band."

This was an impeccable source, and the obvious question was voiced by one of the Sanfords, "Where in this world would Mitchell Pierce get all that money?"

It was what Pix was asking herself. Less than a year ago, he was skipping town to avoid his debts and now he was on easy street—or would be if alive. Either he'd been restoring houses at breakneck speed up the coast or he'd been branching out into some other lines of business. The multitude of coves and inlets on the coast brought to mind several illegal possibilities.

Jill offered a suggestion. She was younger than the other members, but she had come so often with her aunt, who had raised her, in days gone by that when the aunt died, it seemed only right to ask Jill to take her place. "He did sell a lot of antiques and maybe he came across something really valuable."

"That's possible," Pix agreed, "but the police would have discovered that by now."

"How do we know they haven't?" Jill asked.

"Well, if you don't know, no one on this island does," Dot teased her, and Jill obliged by turning red.

"Has anybody claimed him yet?" Serena Marshall asked. "Because when they do, you march right down, Louella, and get your money back." Serena was partial to Court TV. Cable had changed the landscape of the minds of islanders forever. "They have to settle his debts from the estate."

Everyone nodded and they moved away from the topic of Mitch to the consideration of a new member.

"She hasn't lived here that long, but she does beautiful work and they are year-round now."

Pix assumed they were talking about Valerie Atherton. She said Samantha was enjoying her work at the camp.

"Oh no, not Valerie"—Mabel laughed—"though she'd liven things up. I don't believe that girl has ever even threaded a needle in her life. We're talking about Joan down to the inn." Joan Randall and her husband, George, owned the Sanpere Inn. Smiles of the "silly old Pix" variety crossed some lips and Pix lowered her age to five. She loved these women— but one at a time.

"I don't see why we shouldn't have her," Louise said. "There's a space open." Everyone grew silent for a moment as they remembered their friend who'd died the year before. "Joan's eager to join and she's a gifted quilter, although a bit shy about her talents. I've seen her quilts. In some of them, she's taken the traditional patterns and given them a new twist by using contemporary fabrics. She has a wonderful sense of color."

It was agreed that Joan would be the newest Sanpere Stitcher and informed of this signal honor as soon as possible so she could contribute to the sale.

The afternoon drifted on. A lot of coffee was drunk, some gossip conveyed, and a surprising amount of work accomplished. The only note of discord had been struck when Adelaide misplaced her scissors and, finding that her sister-in-law was sitting on them, chewed Rebecca out in no uncertain terms, "I do believe you are getting scattier by the minute, Rebecca! You know you put cream that had turned in the gravy last week." Rebecca appeared not to hear her and just went on working. It was something she'd grown adept at over the years. The other women ignored Addie, too. They'd also heard it all before.

After the last woman left, Ursula looked about at the wreckage of half-filled cups and crumb-laden plates and said, "Don't you wish we could leave all this until tomorrow?" Unfortunately, Gert had had to leave, as it was her evening to do for the Bainbridges. Besides Ursula, Gert seemed to do for most of Sanpere.

"Why don't we? Come to my house for supper and leave everything," Pix suggested. She had no problem with it, yet she was sure what her mother's response would be.

"Getting up and seeing a pile of dirty dishes in my living room would be worse than seeing a . . . well, let's just say would be unpleasant."

Pix knew what her mother had intended, but she didn't agree. Seeing a body would be far worse. And she, Pix, should know.

It didn't take as long as they thought to clean up. Ursula turned down Pix's offer of supper. "Maybe it's the noise, but all I ever want on Sewing Circle days is a boiled egg and early bed."

Pix kissed her mother good-bye and headed home. She felt like talking to Sam and hoped her husband would be around. She'd always thought it was one of life's little inequities that when a man was left on his own, he was showered with dinner invitations—the poor thing. When Sam was out of town, kids home or not, no one so much as offered her a casserole.

Samantha was in the living room reading. Pix was glad to see it was Alice Hoffman and not Martha Stewart—this after Samantha's remark the other evening that their soup bowls didn't match. It had never come to her attention before, and the bowls had been around as long as she had. She'd be tying ribbons around their napkins next.

"How was your day, sweetheart?"

"I like the teaching part, but it's boring standing around while they eat, then it's a big rush to clean up. The kids are great, except it's kind of sad."

"What do you mean?"

"Well, some of them really don't want to be there, although I think they kind of like me."

"They're probably just homesick. Most kids are that way at camp in the beginning."

"I know. I remember Danny sending you all those cards to come get him, then when you finally broke down and went, he wanted to know what you were doing there."

Pix remembered the incident well. Danny, or their unexpected little dividend, as she and Sam called him in private, was predictably unpredictable in all things.

"But these kids have been sent to camp for years, even though they're so young. It's like their parents want to get rid of them," Samantha continued.

"Maybe their parents need to have a program for them. If both are working, a child can't simply stay home."

"I know and I think that's true in some cases, but there's one little girl, Susannah, who's so sweet, and I know her mother isn't working. She said so. And then there's this boy I'm kind of worried about. He's really mad at his parents for what he calls "dumping" him at camp while they're on vacation."

"It's hard to know what's going on in other people's families." With that understatement, Pix went to make some supper for the two of them, after which she had a delightful and foolish talk with her husband, reminiscent of all the talks of all the other summers.

"Dad thinks he will be up on Sunday," Pix happily told Samantha. "And he can stay on through the Fourth."

"I'd better make myself scarce," her daughter teased her. "I know what you two are like."

Pix was still not used to the idea that her older children knew their parents had and enjoyed sex. "Oh, Samantha, don't be silly. Daddy wants to spend as much time as possible with you, too."

And it was true. Sam was taking the thought of his daughter's leaving for college in the not-too-distant future even harder than Pix.

The phone rang and Samantha grabbed it, but this time it was for her mother.

"Pix? It's Jill. What are you doing tomorrow? Valerie and I

are going to go antiquing over in Searsport and toward Belfast if there's time. Could you join us? Valerie says prices are especially low because of the economy, and since it's still early in the season, things haven't been picked over. We'll leave after breakfast. I have someone to cover the store then."

"I'd love to. I have to be home in the afternoon to make chowder for the Frazier's clambake, so the morning is perfect for me," Pix answered. "I'm looking for a night table to go in the guest room at home, and in any case, it's always fun to poke around."

"Plus, Valerie knows so much about everything. Whenever I go with her, I always learn new things—and she's very good at dickering. I can never find the nerve."

Pix had always been amazed that Jill had found the nerve to open and run her store. She was extremely quiet and shy. Both Pix and Faith thought Jill was beautiful—what was called in another day a "pocket Venus"—tiny but perfect, with thick, silky dark brown straight hair falling to her shoulders. Her attire betrayed the fact that she spent winters off-island working in Portland. The outfit she'd worn today at the Sewing Circle—a hand-painted turquoise tunic over a gauzy white accordion-pleated skirt—hadn't come from the Granville Emporium, where it was still possible to find printed shirtwaist dresses circa 1955. Tom and Sam both said "attractive" was as far as they would go in describing Jill, thereby confirming Faith's oft-stated notion that men knew nothing about female pulchritude.

The next day, Valerie met them at Jill's. Pix had offered to drive, but Valerie had a van and there was always the possibility they might be carting home something big. Jill hoped to get some things for the store—small folk art items and thirties jewelry had proved especially popular.

"Hop in," Valerie called out cheerfully. She was wearing work clothes—jeans, turtleneck, sneakers, each discreetly emblazoned by Lauren.

The first place they stopped was a barn. The sign outside promised TRASH AND TREASURES. Jill had found some alphabet plates at a procurable price there earlier and wanted to look in again. Pix walked through the door feeling the tingle of excitement she always did at an auction, a yard sale, any place that offered not just a bargain but a find.

Jill started sifting through boxes of costume jewelry and Valerie was climbing over dressers and bedsteads to examine an oak dining room set. Pix strolled through the musty barn. There was a pile of *Look* magazines next to a windup Victrola. Tables were filled with a mixture of fine cut glass and gas station giveaways. She was slightly taken aback to see the kind of tin sand pail and shovel from her childhood behind locked doors with other toys of various vintages. Maybe hers was still in the attic at The Pines. At the end of the aisle, there was a heap of linens, and her heart began to beat faster when she saw there were some quilts in the pile. She started to sort through them. Motes of dust floated in the strong light from an adjacent window.

Some of the quilts had suffered a great deal of damage, but one was remarkably well preserved. Left in a trunk or used only for company, it was the Flying Geese pattern, done in shades of brown and gold. The triangular "geese" were several different prints—some striped, some flowered. The setting strips were muslin and elaborately quilted. It was a real scrap quilt and Pix fell in love with it. There were occasional touches of bright red, perhaps flannel, and the handwork was exquisite. She took it and two of the damaged ones that she thought could be repaired to the front of the barn.

"How much for all three?" she asked the owner. "Some of them are very badly worn."

"Came out of a house over near Sullivan. Nothing that went in ever left until the party that owned it departed in a pine box." He seemed to find this very funny. Pix had heard about these untouched houses before.

"What's your price?"

"Two hundred dollars," he said firmly.

Pix almost gasped. The man obviously didn't know what quilts were bringing. She held on to her senses and countered, "A hundred and fifty."

"We'll split the difference, deah. How about one seventy-five—plus tax."

Pix agreed. She wasn't about to lose her quilts. She paid him and ran over to Jill, who had a fistful of Bakelite bracelets.

"Look what I got!" Pix kept her voice down, but it was hard.

"Quilts! How wonderful. I'll pay for these and then let's go where I can see them properly."

They called to Valerie that they'd be outside, then spread the quilts on the grass by the van. The Flying Geese quilt looked even better in the sunlight against the green grass.

"Pix, it's gorgeous," Jill enthused.

Pix was elated and bent down to look at the stitching again. That's when she saw it. Close to the border, just like the other one. Two crossed blue threads.

Two crossed blue threads just like the ones on the quilt that had served as Mitchell Pierce's winding-sheet.

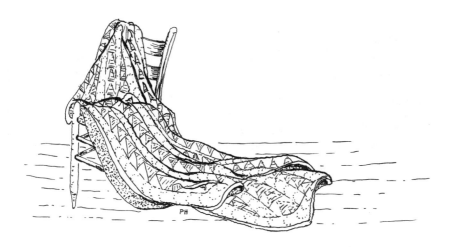

Chapter 4

Pix was so startled that she grabbed Jill's arm.

"It's the—"

She started to speak, then stopped abruptly. She hadn't told anyone except Earl about the mark, a mark that had come to represent a hex in her mind. He hadn't seemed very interested. Pix quickly decided to change course.

"It's the best quilt I've ever found. What a treasure!"

Jill did not appear to find Pix's overt enthusiasm odd. Quilters were known for their passion.

"It *is* beautiful. You are so lucky. I could probably get three or four hundred dollars for it, maybe more." She sounded wistful. "What about the other quilts, what are they like?"

Pix was suddenly eager to examine them for more marks. They spread them out in a row.

"What a shame! This quilt is almost perfect, only some wear in the corner. But that could be repaired. What's the pattern?"

"I'm not sure. Some variation of Pinwheel. This one is Irish Chain, though, and it will take some work, but I think I can replace the parts where the fabric has disintegrated."

Pix wanted to go back to the pile of linens to examine them further. For all she knew, the blue cross-stitches could be a kind of laundry mark, but it was strange to find them in exactly the same place on both quilts.

"Shall we see what else we can turn up? Valerie seems to be engaged in mortal combat with the owner over that dining room set, so we might as well look around some more."

Jill commented, "Mortal combat with velvet gloves. When I was leaving, I heard her tell him, 'My, what lovely things you've got here. I have so many people asking me to find antiques for them, I just *know* I'm going to be coming here all the time.' "

Pix had to laugh at her imitation of Valerie's accent— Down East meets Down South. It was a curious encounter.

Happily, Jill wanted to look at the linens, and Pix led her to that corner of the barn. They sorted through the stack of mismatched napkins, huck hand towels, and tablecloths, turning up the two badly tattered quilts Pix had previously spotted. Pix shook out each one thoroughly, ostensibly looking for holes. There wasn't a blue mark to be seen. Jill decided to take some of the monogrammed guest towels.

"People don't care whose initials they are so long as they have them. It adds a touch of class to one's powder room."

"I'll have to remember that if I ever have one," Pix remarked. The downstairs half bath off the kitchen in the Miller household always seemed to be filled with the kid's overflow from the bath the three shared upstairs. In the past, it was dinosaur toothbrush holders and whatever toothpaste manufacturers had dreamed up to entice kids to brush—sparkles, stars, exotic flavors. Now it was hair gel and hot combs. The towels, while not actually on the floor, were always in disarray, except for the first five minutes after she put out clean ones.

With her mind torn between a vision of what a home inhabited by two reasonably tidy adults would look like and how dreadful it would be not to find mud-covered cleats in the living room anymore, she wandered toward the big open barn door.

At the front of the store, Valerie was writing a check and arranging to come back later for the dining room set. She didn't want to stand around and wait while he unearthed it all. When the owner's back was turned, she shot Pix a triumphant glance and winked.

Outside as she looked at the quilts, she softly crowed, "Golden oak, never restored—perfect condition and everything my client wants, even the lion's paw feet on the table. It's not my taste, but at the moment it's delicious. He said he was happy to get rid of it, wants the room!" She picked up the corner of the Flying Geese quilt to examine the stitching. "It looks like you made a steal, too, Pix. This is gorgeous. You sure you want to keep it? I have just the place for it. I wouldn't sell this one."

"And neither would I, thank you," Pix said gleefully. Somehow it added to the sweetness of the coup to have a professional's approval—and envy.

"Ladies, the morning is young. Let's get going!"

By lunchtime, they were ready to quit. The shops had begun to merge together into one antique haze. Valerie had picked up some yellowware bowls and pitchers. "These used to go for a song, but now that everyone has a country kitchen, or a modern one that has to be accented with a few old pieces, the prices are up. Still these were good buys." Pix did not find her night table. What she did find was an elaborate Victorian wire plant stand perfect for the second-floor landing in her house in Aleford. She might even bow to convention and put a Boston fern in it.

Jill had found several more small items, including an old doll made from a clay pipe that she knew would appeal to someone. Also a cigar box full of old hat pins. Her find for the day was an elaborately carved picture frame, a sailor's valentine. The picture was gone, but the wood was in perfect shape.

"Who do you suppose looked out from here," Valerie mused, "his sweetheart, his mama? We'll never know."

"Maybe his dog," Pix suggested. That would have been her choice. She'd see what price Jill put on the frame. Dusty's face would look perfect surrounded by the intricately carved wood, the same golden honey color as her fur.

They decided to stop for lunch at Country View, a stand on the way back to the island that overlooked a large cow pasture and blueberry fields. The view changed with the seasons, green and yellow now with a few contented Swiss Browns in clover, their tails swinging like pendulums at the flies. Pix had a sudden image of a chirpy cuckoo emerging from a yawning pink mouth on the hour.

Happily munching fish sandwiches—and the fish was so fresh—Pix realized she'd be up to her elbows in haddock and cod for much of the afternoon. She wasn't going to get any gardening done, but at least the chowder was foolproof. No anxiety there. She'd made it dozens of times before.* And it had to be made the day before so the flavors could blend. If she put it off until the morning, it would still taste delicious, but at the first bite Ursula would go into her old "Can you look me straight in the eye and say that?" routine, asking, "When did you make this chowder?" She might even call her Myrtle. It had happened before.

Over their coffee and thick wedges of the pie made at the stand, apple today, Jill brought up the subject of Mitchell Pierce.

"Did you know Mitch, Valerie? It's funny. I hadn't thought about missing him until someone mentioned it at the Sewing Circle yesterday. But he was a part of life here—both his good and bad sides. And, of course, the whole thing is so disturbing." Jill did seem to be extremely disturbed. She was picking

*See recipe page 283.

84

at the handle of the paper coffee cup, reducing it to shreds. And several of her cuticles were ragged. Pix had never seen her display any nervous gestures. Jill was normally as imperturable as a china doll—and just about as easy to read.

"I've met him," Valerie replied, "but I didn't know him. I saw him at a few shows and bought things from him once or twice. He sold me that sweet little collection of fans I had framed to hang in my bedroom. We'd planned on having him down to the house sometime. Jim says he was quite the storyteller. The two of them were friends, but we've been so busy with the move and the house, there hasn't been much time for anyone."

Pix was tempted to tell them about the cross on the quilts and see whether they had any idea what it could mean. Valerie, especially, might know if this was a common mark on antique quilts. But again, she decided to do as Earl had advised and keep quiet.

"I hate to break up the party. It's been so nice to get away— and with grown-ups, too—but if I don't make the chowder, I really will break up a party. Louise is counting on it."

"I'm taking some of Louella's pies. I don't dare try to cook any of my southern specialities for Louise."

"Well, I'm bringing festive plates and napkins from the store," Jill said. "Louise knows the size of my kitchen—and the extent of my culinary expertise. Dinner guests are lucky to get a hamburger. I need Faith to give me a few lessons."

This was encouragingly domestic, and Pix longed to give Jill a little more of a nudge altarward. "There's a wonderful house for sale on the crossroad. The last owners put in a new kitchen and the back has an orchard that slopes down to one of the long inlets from Little Harbor." She could picture Jill, rosy-cheeked and smiling, hanging up her wash near the old apple trees, a pie keeping warm on the stove for Earl's return. "And Faith likes nothing better than teaching people how to cook. Dismal failure though she's been with me, she keeps trying."

But Jill wasn't biting. "How could I afford a big house like that? Besides, it's so convenient living over the store."

Pix sighed. Maybe another time.

The first thing Pix did when she got home was spread out the quilt in the living room. It had not diminished in effect, yet she found herself with a definite feeling of unease as she stood looking at it. The blue threads—but what else was nagging at her? It was too cheap. Why had the dealer let it go for so little?

She thought about it all the way over to Sonny Prescott's lobster pound. Sonny dealt in all kinds of marine life, besides those succulent crustaceans. Pix had already ordered the cod and haddock for the chowder. The mixture of the two fish, as well as the use of slab bacon instead of salt pork gave the Rowe family chowder a distinctive flavor. They also put in more onions than most recipes called for.

Hearing the car, Sonny stuck his head out the bait shed doorway and yelled, "I'm over here." Pix followed him in. He'd been close to the only other murder investigation on Sanpere in recent memory and Pix wondered what his thoughts might be on Mitchell Pierce's death. Among others, Mitch had boarded at Sonny's one winter, so he knew Mitch better than most.

"I've come for my fish," Pix said. The smell of the bait, decomposed herring, was overwhelming, but it didn't bother her. It was one of those smells you got used to in childhood and never noticed again. She vastly preferred it to all those perfume samples magazines and catalogs were including in their glossy pages with increasing eye-watering and nose-itching frequency.

"Be right there, deah. Got to get this ready for Jeb Sanford." Sonny supplied fishermen with bait, fuel, and whatever else was needed. In turn, they sold their catches exclusively to him.

While she was waiting, Pix left the shed and sat at the end of the pier, dangling her legs over the side. She'd known

Sonny since they were both teenagers and had occasionally "borrowed" a dinghy from the yacht club to row out into Sylvester Cove to watch the sparkling phosphorescence magically drip from the oars, a mirror image of the mass of brilliant stars shining overhead. What else Pix and Sonny might or might not have done in the way of canoodling was between the two of them, but they always had a special smile for each other. Sonny came and sat down next to her, the huge package of fish fresh from the boats tied up and set behind him.

"I cleaned it for you. Save you some time. It's for chowder, right? The Fraziers' clambake?" Sonny probably knew the social plans of every inhabitant on the island for the holiday just from the orders that had been placed.

"Yes, and I'll be peeling potatoes until midnight. I've been dreading cleaning all this fish. You are truly a godsend. What would I ever do without you?"

Sonny grinned. "Let's not find out." They sat for a while looking at the boats moored in the cove. There were some beautiful yachts from farther down the coast. From behind Barred Island in the distance, one of the windjammers sailed into view.

"Is it the *Victory Chimes?*" Pix asked.

Sonny nodded. "Funny to think these were workboats, hauled lumber, whatever else was traded. Now they're hauling rich tourists who want to experience the good old days—cramped sleeping quarters and plenty of hard work to sail the things. Me, I'd like to take one of those cruises Kathie Lee advertises. That would be some good time."

Pix laughed and asked if he'd heard what the weather was going to be for the next couple of days.

"Same as it's been. Good for vacations and good for me; not so good for the crops or fires. Heard they had a big one up to Baxter State Park," Sonny observed.

"My garden is going to shrivel up and die." There was that word. Pix had used it on purpose. "Like Mitchell Pierce."

They looked at each other.

"If you hadn't have gone out there, no one would ever have found him. Seth was fixing to pour this week."

"I know. It's scary. Who do you think wanted Mitch out of the way so badly?"

Sonny had to have a theory. He did about most things and he did about Mitch.

"I figure he must have gotten in over his head somehow with the antiques or maybe the cars. He was a trusting soul for a crook and not a real good judge of character. This time, he put his faith in the wrong man."

"Crook!"

"Come on, Myrtle," Sonny was virtually the only person who used her name in everyday conversation. "The man was running scams up and down the East Coast. Where do you think he got all those fancy cars?"

Mitch had a fondness for vintage sports cars.

"Saved up?"

"Touch one of those fenders and like as not you'd burn your fingers."

This was food for thought: a stolen-car ring.

"Lot of talk about a car wash place in Belfast that really laundered the vehicles. Mitch was a regular."

"And the antiques?"

"Fakes. Don't look so surprised. Just because he could tell a good story and did a nice job for your mother doesn't make him a member of the choir. People are not always all of a piece like you."

Pix wasn't sure whether this was a compliment or not. She suspected something in between. Oh, for a bit more intricacy.

"Not that I'm suggesting you change. I like you just the way you are—especially those long legs of yours." Sonny stood up and eyed them, exposed to full advantage in Pix's denim shorts. For an instant, they were teenagers again, ready to take off for a picnic on Strawberry Island, a little knoll off Prescott's Point. Pix was suddenly acutely aware that Sonny was divorced and her own husband was almost three hundred miles away. She paid for her fish and left with a pleasant sense of having been tempting and tempted. The fact that she was absolutely and totally in love—and loyal—to her husband made it all the more enjoyable.

At home, she began the mammoth task of cutting and chopping, running what Sonny had said about Mitch through her mind as she alternately was drenched in tears from the onions and splattered fat from the sizzling bacon.

Maybe there would be a chance to talk to Earl in private at the clambake tomorrow. Jill said he was coming, although he'd probably be called away just as they were uncovering the lobsters. There were going to be about fifty people of all ages at the party, and Pix found large gatherings often offered more opportunities for intimate conversation than small ones. Two people strolling off to gather driftwood for the bonfire were much less likely to attract anyone's notice than say two people disappearing from a group of eight at a dinner party.

She decided to call Faith and have her give Sam a book that Pix had about identifying quilts, so that he could bring it up. Sam would never find it himself, and Faith wouldn't stop until she did. Pix was absolutely sure it was in the stack of books by her bed, in with the cookbooks in the kitchen, or down in the basement in a carton waiting for more book-shelves. The quilt looked authentic, yet it was possible that it was a fake. Using the book, she could date it. Which would mean what? That she had been swindled? The man hadn't said it was an old quilt. Maybe the quilt on Mitchell Pierce's body wasn't old either, but what would that matter? It did some-how, though. She was sure. She took her cleaver and whacked the head off an enormous cod Sonny had missed when he cleaned the fish. She thought of the mice. She thought of Mitch. The cod stared at her, glassy-eyed. She came to her senses. Chowder, rich, fragrant fish chowder. She tossed the head into a pot for stock and beheaded the other cod she found with aplomb. These were fish, not French aristocrats, and she was definitely not a murderess.

"Anything I can do to help?" Samantha's voice was a welcome alternative to the sound of tumbrels.

"Perfect timing. Could you peel these potatoes?"

"Mother! There are mountains of them," Samantha shrieked.

"Well, just do as many as you can and I'll help when I get the onions done and the rest of the fish cut up."

Samantha had spent the morning at The Pines. She often bicycled over to see her grandmother. They had a very special relationship. Pix wondered what they found to talk about, but they shared a love of the outdoors and it was Ursula who had started Samantha on the first of her many collections—seashells at age three.

"Granny's helping me with the mosses," Sam told her mother.

"I thought you'd given the project up."

"Of course not, after all that work last summer!"

"This wouldn't have anything to do with the fact that Arlene is otherwise occupied, would it?" Pix was curious to know how Samantha was taking Arlene's defection.

"Not really. Besides, she and Fred aren't married. She is allowed to go places without him." Samantha cut the sarcasm in her voice and admitted to her mother, "It's true, I miss her, but with her job, we wouldn't see each other that much, and she does like to spend time with her boyfriend. Otherwise, why bother having one?"

Pix decided to change the subject.

"I bought some beautiful quilts this morning antiquing with Jill and Valerie. One is especially lovely. It's on the couch. Take a break and go look at it."

"You didn't tell me Valerie was going. I thought it was just Jill! What did she buy?"

Correctly surmising Samantha meant Valerie and not Jill, Pix gave an account of the morning.

"She has got such perfect taste. We should hire her to do our house."

"But our house is done."

Samantha raised an eyebrow, clearly indicating that a decorating scheme that had evolved simply because that was where things had happened to land did not represent interior design in her opinion.

"How about my room, then? We could send her pictures. I'm sure she'd have some great ideas."

"Some expensive ideas,"

Pix heard it inside her head before it was said: "Oh, Mother!"

Samantha, happy for an excuse to leave the potatoes, went to look at the quilts.

"The one with the triangles is really beautiful, Mom. We should hang it on a wall here or at home."

"That's what I was thinking." Pix went into the other room and the two of them held the quilt out.

"What's that blue cross on the bottom?" Samantha moved her thumb to indicate the threads.

"I have no idea," Pix replied truthfully, but something in her voice betrayed her.

Samantha looked her straight in the eye—and where she had picked up this trick, Pix didn't like to think. "Come on, Mom. What aren't you telling me? You are such a bad liar."

"And you're a good one?"

"Don't try to change the subject."

Pix realized that the proximity in which they were spending the summer would make keeping secrets difficult. "I don't know what it means. Probably nothing. It's just that there was a cross like this one on the quilt out on the Point, too."

"Nothing! It could be a major clue!" Samantha was excited, yet after they discussed it some more while finishing the chowder preparations, both women were forced to agree that if it was a clue, they were without one.

The chowder was simmering and Samantha had gone off to the dance at the Legion Hall. It was an island institution, a mixture of ages, groups, and most especially music—everything from "Like a Virgin" to the Virginia reel, with a stop at "a one and a two and a three" in between.

She'd called Faith, who had then called back to say she'd located the book and placed it in Sam's car just before he left. That was at six o'clock. He'd arrive, like Samantha, before midnight. Pix told Faith about the discovery of the quilt and the second mark.

"Perhaps both quilts belonged to the same family," Faith suggested.

"Sullivan!" Pix was annoyed she hadn't made the connection before. "The man said the linens had come from Sullivan and that was where Mitch was living before he was killed."

"It does seem like more than a coincidence. What you need to do is figure out if your quilt is authentic and talk to Earl."

Pix was tempted to say she'd already planned this very course of action, but instead she thanked Faith for getting the book and told her she'd be in touch soon.

"I know," her friend said before she hung up.

Pix never minded being in the cottage alone. It was so familiar and felt so safe that she thought of it as a kind of shell. Now she curled up inside, actually in one of the big overstuffed armchairs in the living room, with a mug of Sleepytime tea and the latest issue of *Quilter's Newsletter Magazine*.

The first car door slam was her husband's. She'd dozed off but awoke instantly at the welcome sound and was at the door. He dropped his suitcase and held her tightly.

"I wish I could have come up right away. It has to have been a hellish time for you both."

After a moment, she leaned away and told him, "It honestly hasn't been too bad. Everyone is more puzzled than alarmed, and it's easier because none of us was really very close to Mitch."

"He was an interesting son of a gun, though. Remember the night he came and played the mandolin at the Hamiltons and he and Freeman got to trading stories. I don't think I've ever laughed so hard in my life."

"That was a great night." It had been many years ago, before Danny was born. That reminded her. "Did you stop at Chewonki and see Danny?"

"No, I did not." Seeing the look on her face, Sam took both his wife's hands. "First off, it was late and I would have interrupted the evening program, thereby embarrassing him for the remainder of his summer, and second, he likes, even loves, his old man, but at home. Chewonki is his turf, a parent-free zone for Danny. Don't worry, sweetheart, he'll be back before you know it and expecting you to do everything for him just as usual." It was not entirely a frivolous observation and they'd had this conversation before—many times before, inserting Mark or Samantha for Danny.

"Are you hungry?" Pix asked, hoping Sam would want only a drink and maybe some crackers and cheese. She had some of the chutney spread still left from Friday's Sewing Circle.

Sam saw the look on her face. He had not stopped to eat, but he couldn't do it to her.

"Not very, how about a drink and maybe a few crackers or whatever you have around."

Pix beamed. Why wouldn't Jill—or Earl—want to get married?

In bed, Pix found having someone to keep her company while she listened for Samantha to come home did a great deal to diminish the anxiety. Also, they were busy telling each other all the things that had happened in their respective worlds since they'd last been together. Atypically, more had been going on in Pix's than Sam's.

He did not seem to think the quilt marks meant much. "It was probably a common way to mark where something else was going to go—the name and date, as you suggested. Or maybe it was part of the basting that didn't get removed." Sam had watched his wife complete several quilts and was quite knowledgeable about how they went together. Sam was the type of man who liked to know the way things worked. This had led him to medical school, but the discovery that he fainted with great regularity at the sight of an abundance of blood curtailed his career, although not his interest. He still read *The New England Journal of Medicine* and the *Harvard Health Newsletter* in between briefs.

Slam—music to the ears of parents of teenagers, just as the cessation of noise was for the parents of toddlers. Samantha was home safe and sound.

Pix reached up to turn out the light.

"No, I want to say hello. I'll be right back." Sam threw on his robe, a well-worn Black Watch plaid flannel one he kept hanging on the back of the door, and went downstairs. He had missed his daughter and wanted to tell her so. He also wanted to tell her that a quarter after midnight was the thin end of the wedge on a twelve o'clock curfew. Pix had enough to cope with this summer without Samantha's coming in just a little bit later every Saturday night.

The weather continued unbroken and the Millers awoke to gorgeous blue skies and almost balmy weather. Too balmy, Pix thought as she got dressed. It wasn't supposed to be this hot on the coast of Maine.

Sam was already gone, having offered as usual to help Elliot get the clambake ready, no small task and one Pix suspected the men relished for its complexity and the opportunity to dig in the sand. After constructing a pit unpleasantly reminiscent of what she and Samantha had stumbled across the previous week, they would line it with rocks and pile driftwood, plus anything else that would burn—charcoal if there wasn't enough wood—on top. The fire had to heat the rocks for at least five hours. Otherwise, when they threw the wet seaweed on, there wouldn't be enough steam to cook the lobsters, clams, corn, chicken, and sausage that would be layered on top. The Fraziers' clambake was famous for its authenticity and had become a Fourth of July tradition. They always seemed to be able to find room for more guests and it had grown each year from humble beginnings to the kind of quintessential red-white-and-blue photo opportunity that politicians running for office dream about.

Pix and Samantha were going to church. After last Sunday, Pix was not about to skip it, even though she relished the clambake preparations as much as her husband did. She was not a superstitious person, yet something told her she'd enjoy the day a whole lot more if she'd bent a knee in a pew rather than hauling rocks.

Sam returned before they left. He wanted to get more wood from their cove.

"We'll be back at noon to change," Pix told him, "and then I promised Louise I'd help her bring things to the beach, so I'll see you there." She kissed her husband good-bye. He returned it somewhat absentmindedly and she knew his thoughts were on hot rocks and rockweed, the "snap, crackle, and pop" seaweed, the kids called it, because of the sound it made beneath your toes and when squeezed between your fingers.

"I'll get rid of this load of wood, then change cars with you, so take both sets of keys." It wasn't that he didn't like her driving his Porsche—he allowed it because he knew he should. It was that he didn't want coleslaw, chowder, and whatever else was going to the clambake to be stowed on his particular leather-covered backseats.

"Don't worry, Daddy, we'll take good care of your baby," Samantha teased him. "Can I drive?"

"Don't even joke," her father replied.

Pix enjoyed the short trip across the island to the small

white clapboard church where they worshiped. It was nice to drive a sleek, jazzy machine that sped forward instantly at the slightest pressure on the gas. Maybe she should trade her Land Rover in. It was such a symbol—Pix, the trucker, the transporter of men, women, children, animals, and all their worldly possessions. It would certainly be nice to have an excuse: "Sorry, I can't pick up twenty watermelons for the school picnic. They won't fit in the car," and so on.

"Mom, what are you thinking about? You have the funniest expression on your face."

"Do I? I was thinking maybe I ought to get a new car, something smaller."

Samantha shook her head. "Your car is always loaded now. If it was any smaller, you'd have to get a trailer. Make Daddy let you drive his more. I wish *I* could. It must be a blast," she added longingly.

They stopped outside the church and hurried in, sliding next to Ursula just as the bell in the steeple began to toll.

"Such a perfect day for the clambake," Ursula whispered. "I figured Sam would be with Elliot, but I was beginning to wonder where you two were."

At one o'clock, Pix was helping Louise set up. Sam had started a smaller fire, let it burn down, and placed a grill on top for the huge pot of chowder Pix had made. They lugged it over and gingerly set it in place. Sam took off the cover and inhaled. "Sweeter than all the perfumes of Araby. I believe this is going to be the best ever. Why don't I get a cup and give it a try?"

"You say the same thing every year!"

"That's not true. I don't remember ever comparing your chowder to perfume before."

"Possibly, but the rest. Anyway, by all means get a cup. You know me—a bottomless sink for reassurance when it comes to cooking."

Sam got a cup and ladled some out. He took a heaping spoonful. "It's . . . well, how can I describe it?"

"Good or bad?"

"Superlative."

Pix heaved a sigh of relief. He always said *superlative*, too, but it was comforting to hear. The perfume simile was new, though: "All the perfumes of Araby." Wasn't it "Arabia"? *Macbeth*. Lady Macbeth scrubbing at her hands. She wished he'd picked something else.

It was impossible to forget that only a week ago on such a day as this, a corpse had turned up. As people began to arrive, struggling with food, sports equipment, and small children, she wondered whether the guilty one walked among them. She had to put it out of her head. Sonny Prescott had provided the most logical answer. Mitch had gotten in with the wrong business partners.

"Pix, Pix, could you help set these out?" Louise always became mildly flustered at the start of the clambake. She was nervous that the food wouldn't cook until it was too dark to eat, although the rare years when Elliot had miscalculated and they did eat late, nobody had minded a bit. Eyeing what Louise had provided and others were bringing, Pix thought the problem would be finding room to eat anything else when the tarp was taken off and the fragrant layers of food exposed.

"There's enough to feed an army here!" she said, gesturing to the tables they'd constructed from planks and sawhorses, then covered with red-checked oilcloth.

"Good," a voice behind her commented, reaching for a deviled egg—Louise's great-aunt Lily Sue's prized recipe.

It was Earl, and Jill was by his side, Pix noted happily. They were carrying paper plates, napkins, and other necessary objects. For the next hour, Pix was busy ladling out her chowder, which was disappearing fast. The party was in full swing. The volleyball net had been set up and there was a ferocious game of over forties versus unders going on. The younger

97

children were exploring the shore, climbing over the rocks, oblivious of the sharp barnacles and other hazards that threatened their bare feet. Samantha and some of her friends were with them. Arlene and her boyfriend had put in an appearance, politely tasted the chowder, then left for the Prescott clambake. There were time-honored functions occurring all over the island and the problem was not having enough time, or room in one's stomach, to visit them all.

The actual day of the Fourth was so crammed full of activities that years ago, islanders had started celebrating early with their family picnics, usually clambakes.

Seth Marshall had also dropped by with his parents. He didn't partake of any of Pix's chowder. Maybe he was saving room for the next clambake. And maybe he was avoiding her. The crime site was still sealed off by the police, so this was unlikely. But when she waved him over to ask him how quickly he could start once the police gave the word, he was so engrossed in conversation with Jill that he appeared not to see Pix's gestures. Overseeing the Fairchilds' cottage could be more work than she had envisioned. The first, almost overwhelming task was proving to be getting it started.

Pix reached up to mop her brow. Her T-shirt was beginning to stick to her back. It was getting unpleasantly hot, especially standing over the chowder. She was glad she'd worn her bathing suit under her clothes. The cove was on deep water, which explained why the yacht club had selected the spot roughly eighty years ago—a yacht club that consisted of a venerable equipment shack, some moorings, and a few life buoys with SANPERE YACHT CLUB stenciled on them. Some people were already in the water, and Pix was amused to see friends who expressed amazement at the Millers' tolerance, even enjoyment, of the cold temperature, bobbing about and calling others to join them.

The Athertons had arrived laden with pies and Valerie and Jim promptly joined the volleyball game—on opposite sides of the net, Pix noted. She glanced around. Duncan, who she recognized from Samantha's description, was at the other end of the beach. It was hard to see him. He was sitting high up on a granite ledge at the point where it met the woods. His somber attire blended into the shadows of the trees. A figure of melancholy, a figure of gloom. Of doom? A mouse killer. Pix firmly shoved back all the morbid thoughts that persisted in crowding into her conscious mind and joined the volleyball game—on the over-forty side. Away from the chowder fire, she felt ten degrees cooler, and giving a good hard thwack to the volleyball felt terrific.

During a break, Sam brought her a cold beer. "Who's that guy with the Bainbridges?"

Pix turned to look. Adelaide was settled into a monstrous lawn chair with all sorts of cushions, rugs, and satchels strewn about her. Rebecca was pressing sunblock on her. "You know how you burn, Addie."

"Oh, can't you let a body be? I'm fine. You'd think I was a two-year-old." This last comment was made to the man Sam had wondered about.

"I think he's staying at their bed-and-breakfast. I've seen him in the post office. But it would be odd for them to bring one of their guests to the Fraziers' clambake. I'll ask Louise."

Pix walked over to her hostess, keeping the unknown visitor in view. He was very slim, attractive, with dark closely cropped curls and a small neatly trimmed beard but no mustache. His clothes were appropriate and looked expensive. His jeans were pressed. Faith would be able to tell the brands and how much he'd paid instantly, but all Pix could determine was that his shirt might be silk. He'd knotted a raspberry-colored cotton sweater about his neck and there wasn't a drop of perspiration evident anywhere on his body. Pix's own damp hair told her what she looked like. After her swim, she'd get the fresh shirt she'd left in the car and put it on. Looking at this guy was having this kind of effect on her. He was tan and the only jewelry he wore was a watch. Maybe if she got closer, she could see what kind. Faith always said that you could tell almost everything about a person by his or her watch and shoes. Pix looked down. He was barefoot. Her own feet were clad in serviceable white Keds.

Louise was drinking a glass of white wine, not a good sign. "I don't know when we'll be ready to eat," she announced. "I've decided not to let it bother me, though." Her tone belied her words.

"Good, you shouldn't worry about a thing," Pix reassured her emphatically. "Everyone is having a marvelous time. And besides, what have we been doing since we got here? No one would leave hungry, even without the lobsters and clams. But they'll be ready soon, so we won't have to find out."

"You're right. Some years it just takes longer than others." She put down her glass and picked up one of Aunt Lily Sue's eggs from a carefully shaded area on the table. "Don't you just love the Fourth of July celebrations? It's my favorite holiday. When I was a little girl, we'd have big picnics like this. Of course we didn't bury our food in the sand."

It must have been something more than mystifying when Louise met Elliot and first heard about a Down East clambake.

"By the way, do you know that man who came with Addie and Rebecca?" Pix asked.

"Haven't you met Norman? He's been here for two weeks now. That's Addie's beau." Louise smiled.

"Beau!"

"Well, perhaps not strictly speaking, but he does dance attendance on her—and on Rebecca, too. He's an antiques dealer from New York City and he's taking a working vacation, he told them. They're to keep his room available for a month and he comes and goes."

New York City—that explained the clothes and the good haircut. Pix was trying very hard in what she hoped was the second half of her life—and look at Mother, so it was not impossible—to cultivate a more open mind about certain things, one of them being New York City. She now had a dear friend in Faith, who had actually been born and raised there. In fact, truth be told, she might even prefer it to Aleford and Boston, although Pix was always careful never to ask outright. She didn't want to know for sure. Try as she might, the name New York City did not suggest the Statue of Liberty or the Empire State Building, but fast living and danger. Whenever she was there—and they dutifully took the children, as well as making one or two adult forays—she felt like a rube who would leap at the chance to buy the Brooklyn Bridge before she knew what she was doing.

She looked over at the Bainbridge group, appraising Norman in light of this new information.

He certainly seemed to be enjoying himself. Whatever Addie had just said had sent him into peals of laughter. He'd been sitting on a blanket literally at her feet and got up now, walking toward the table with the drinks.

"Addie says he told her she's the most interesting woman he's met in years. Every time he goes off-island, he brings something back for them."

"I'll bet he just wants to get her quilts cheap," Pix said skeptically.

"No, he doesn't sell anything made after 1900. He told her he liked her work, but they're not his 'thing.' "

"Then, what do you suppose he sees in her?"

"We all take Addie for granted because we know her, but she *is* a great storyteller. Elliot thinks Norman is writing a book. Most people are. And Addie is a great source."

The afternoon wore on. Pix took a swim, which felt heavenly while she was in the water, but without a shower to wash off the salt, increasingly itchy later, even under her clean dry shirt. She sat down with her back against a log cast up on the shore by one of the winter storms and glanced around to check on her family, a reflex. Ursula was in deep conversation with John Eggleston, whose bright red beard and hair blended well with the shade his face had taken on during the day. What on earth could they be discussing? Was Mother going to take up wood sculpture? Pix would not be surprised. Sam was poking at the mound with Elliot. They might have been considering a Viking tomb, given the intensity of their expressions. And Samantha was . . . walking toward her.

Samantha sat next to her mother, leaned back, and stretched her long legs, almost as long as Pix's, out, wriggling her toes in the sand. The two considered the view for a moment before speaking. This one from Sylvester Cove was every bit as good as the one from The Pines, or the Millers' cottage, or just about anywhere else on the island Pix could name. Today there were dozens of sailboats, crisp white triangles against the dense green outer islands and the deep blue sea.

"I love the Fraziers' clambakes," Samantha said, "but not when the weather is like this. We might as well be home, it's so hot."

Pix nodded. She considered another beer, then decided to wait. Others had not waited and the laughter and talk was noticeably louder than it had been earlier. Some of the children were getting whiny. It was definitely time to eat. A sudden onslaught of sand fleas sent Pix and Samantha flying from their seats.

"At least it's not blackfly season," Pix said. Nothing came close to that. They'd all worn beekeeper's hats when they'd tended the graves on Memorial Day. It had been a strange sight.

A possible discussion of "annoying insects I have known" was sharply curtailed by the noise of a loud disturbance farther down the beach. It was moving toward them.

"It's that jerk Duncan!" Samantha said as she moved closer. Pix followed, out of curiosity and to get away from the fleas.

"I'm speaking to you, young man! Don't you walk away from me!" It was Valerie. Her face was red, and as she'd been wearing a fetching sun hat since she arrived, it wasn't from a burn. She was absolutely furious.

"Fuck you!" Duncan answered, and kept walking.

"I saw that beer can in your hand! Don't you lie to me!"

Duncan stopped and turned to face his mother. "So what? Only grown-ups can get wasted?" He said this last in the jeering singsong tones of a small child. Pix marveled at Valerie's self-control. Sure, she was yelling, but had Duncan been Pix's son, she would have had him by the arm by now and marched him straight to the car.

Jim appeared. He'd been swimming and was dripping wet. It magnified his rage—a bull from the sea.

He stood next to his wife.

"Don't you *ever* talk that way to your mother again! Where do you get off using words like that? Now, I've had just about all I'm going to take from you. Get in the car. You're going home."

"Home?" Duncan screamed. "You call that 'home'? Your home maybe, not mine!"

Valerie stepped forward and put her hand on his arm. "Now Duncan, let's calm down. . . ."

He pushed her away rudely and she went sprawling in the sand. Everyone on the beach froze for an instant, including Duncan. He stared at his mother and seemed about to reach for her before noticing Jim virtually foaming at the mouth.

Duncan took off, the tiny red lights of his sneakers blinking frantically in the late-afternoon light.

"Let him go," Valerie said to her husband. "He needs to be alone." She brushed the sand from her white pants, adjusted her hat, and said to everyone with a big smile, "I apologize for my son. In his case, adolescence really is a disease. I only wish there were shots for it."

People laughed and Jim let out what seemed like the breath he'd been holding since confronting his stepson. He hugged Valerie and echoed her sentiments. "My parents always said someday I'd get mine the way they got theirs from me, and boy, were they right!"

"I don't believe it." Samantha said. She and Pix were on the fringes of the group.

"About Jim, you mean?"

"Yeah, I don't believe he was ever the way Duncan is. And he's definitely not the type who got in trouble when he was a kid. More the kind other parents wanted their kids to be like."

Pix was not unduly surprised at her daughter's analysis. Samantha was a good judge of character.

"I agree. Plus, I happen to know for a fact Jim was an Eagle Scout. But I think you're being a little hard on Duncan. He may feel like the odd person out in that big house. And he must miss his father terribly. Then, the move couldn't have been easy."

"I guess it's because I like the Athertons so much. I wasn't thinking of it from his point of view. It's hard to be sympathetic, but you're right. What if Daddy died and you got married again and made me move from Aleford, although coming to Sanpere wouldn't be so bad." Samantha was working out a whole scenario. "Except no matter who you picked, it wouldn't be Daddy."

"Who wouldn't be Daddy?" Sam appeared at his daughter's side.

"Mom's next husband—that is, if something happened to you and she remarried," Samantha added hastily, seeing her father's startled look.

"I thought you were going to be faithful to my memory," Sam said to his wife. "Now I find out you're getting hitched when I'm barely cold in the ground."

Whether it was the heat, the sand fleas, the scene with the Athertons, or something altogether different, Pix suddenly felt a sense of deep despair. She didn't want to joke about Sam's demise. She didn't want to talk about death at all.

"Samantha, why don't you and your friends see if you can find Duncan. He may want someone to talk to." Pix had not liked the look of fear and anxiety on the boys's face as he'd run off. "He's probably up in the ledges at the other end of the beach. I saw him sitting there before."

"You're right, Mom, but I think he'd be more apt to talk to one person than a bunch of us. I'll go."

She ran off. Sam looked at Pix. "What's going on?"

"I don't know. I wish I did. It's probably just me. I got tired all of a sudden."

At that moment, Elliot began to bang on the lid of Pix's now-empty chowder pot with the ladle.

"Hear ye, hear ye! Gather round!"

Elliot, normally a reticent and mild-mannered man in his late sixties, assumed an entirely different persona at the clambake. He wore an apron that proclaimed him "The Clam King," a gift from a partygoer some years ago and now indispensable garb, as was his broad-brimmed straw hat decorated with small plastic clams, lobsters, and various seashells bearing absolutely no resemblance to reality.

People crowded near to the pit, knowing that before they would get their hands on a lobster or an ear of corn, they'd have to listen to Elliot's traditional clambake speech.

"Some of you have heard this all before," he started.

"Many times before," a friend called out, and everyone groaned.

Elliot continued undaunted.

"When my friend Sam and I dug the pit and lined it with rocks this morning, getting everything ready for you sleepyheads who were still snoring away, we were continuing a tradition that goes back to the first summer people to come to Sanpere—the Abenaki Indians. Along with all the other useful things Indians taught the early colonists, they showed them how to cook in the sand this way. I always like to remember them—we could be eating at the site of one of their clambakes—and say thank you before we tuck in."

"Thanks, Abenakis," a little girl shouted, and everyone laughed. She buried her head in her mother's skirt in embarrassment.

"Now, I'm not quite done yet. At the risk of being accused of being sentimental—"

"Risk it, Elliot." This, much to Pix's surprise, came from her own mother.

"Thank you, Ursula, I will. I'd like to make a toast to all of you good people, who mean so much to Louise and me, and also, as always, to absent friends. Finally, in the words of Sean O'Casey, 'May the very best of the past—be the worst of the future!'" He took a swig of beer, handed the bottle to his wife, took the first stone anchoring down the tarp covering the steaming pit, removed it, and flung it into the sea. It resounded appropriately with a loud splash. Everyone cheered and rushed to help uncover the steaming food, packed in cheesecloth parcels.

Pix stayed close to Sam. "I love Elliot's toasts." Things were beginning to be all right again.

"And I love you," he said, kissing the tip of her nose. "Now let's eat." Definitely all right.

Perhaps because they had been waiting so long for the food or because the various potables that had been imbibed created an atmosphere of heightened enjoyment, one and all declared the food the best ever. Pix knew she was a mess. She'd dripped melted butter down her chin as she'd consumed her lobster and clams. Her fingers were sticky from the chicken—Louise always charcoal-broiled it a bit first—and corn. Above all, she was full—and there was still dessert. She and Sam were sitting on the blanket she'd brought when Earl and Jill strolled past laden with lobster carcasses and clam shells.

"Come and join us," Pix called.

"Just as soon as we dump this stuff," Earl answered.

She'd have to go see Earl down in Granville at the combined post office, town hall, and office of the law to get him alone and talk about the blue quilt marks. Although her appearance at the tiny hole-in-the-wall that served the needs of justice on the island would immediately cause talk. She'd better call him. Now she might just try to steer the conversation to antiques, quilts in particular, perhaps, and fakes. She was feeling comfortably sated and the demons disturbing her earlier were gone. She didn't want to waste the opportunity. Earl was right here and she hadn't made much progress in her investigation so far. Faith would no doubt have had the whole thing sewn up by now—but maybe not. Pix sat in the growing darkness waiting for Jill and Earl's return. Elliot had lighted his huge bonfire and a few people were playing guitars. It was a lovely scene. She was content to wait.

Samantha had not been able to find Duncan at first. He wasn't in plain sight and she walked deeper and deeper into the woods before she found him, curled up in a fetal position on a bed of pine needles.

"Duncan, it's me, Samantha Miller. I'm a friend of Arlene Prescott."

He didn't move for a second, then slowly sat up and eyed her warily.

"You work at the camp. I've seen you. Did they send you to get me?" He spat the words out.

Assuming he meant Valerie and Jim, Samantha answered, "No, I just thought maybe you'd like to talk to somebody. You seemed pretty upset." He was so antagonistic that she'd begun to wish she hadn't been the good little Samaritan her mother expected and had stayed down on the beach.

"I'm not going back."

"It's a long walk." She almost said *home*, then quickly changed it to *the house*.

"So what." He leaned against a tree and put his arms behind his head. He was pathetically skinny and short for his age. Samantha hoped for his sake that he would grow a few inches this summer and maybe start to work out. It would certainly make life easier if he looked a little more attractive.

She decided to give it a try. "I know a kid whose mother

died last year—cancer. It was really terrible. Anyway, I wanted to say I'm sorry about your dad. I know how my friend feels, and she didn't have to move."

Duncan looked as if he was going to cry. His face got all screwed up, then he opened his eyes wide and shook his head. The ring in his ear wobbled. Samantha noticed that the hole was red and angry, obviously infected. Now completely grossed out, she decided she'd done her duty and turned around to return to the party.

"Hey, are you leaving?"

"My parents might be wondering where I am," she lied, "and besides, the food is almost ready and I love lobster cooked this way. You ought to try it."

"I don't eat fish—or meat," he added.

Definitely not getting enough protein, Samantha thought. She sat down beside him. He was so pathetic. "There's lots of corn. It's steamed in the husk. My dad brought it up from Boston, since there's no corn here yet. Come back and you can eat with us." It was worth a try.

"Why are you being so nice to me?"

She didn't have an answer ready.

"I don't know. I guess I feel sorry for you."

He nodded. She assumed he felt sorry for himself, too.

"Life sucks. Especially in this rinky-dink place."

"It must seem small after living in Richmond. That was where you were, right?"

"Yeah. Richmond was okay. The best place was where we lived before my real father died. Outside the city."

"There are a lot of good kids here, though. I've been coming every summer since I was born and I know everybody. You could come to the movies with us next week if you want." Samantha had no idea why she proposed this. Arlene would kill her.

"I don't need your friends. I've got plenty of my own." She should have saved her breath.

"Well, that's great. Now I'm going to go get something to eat before I starve." Enough was enough.

"Plenty of friends. We even have our own club."

"Club? That sounds like fun," Samantha commented perfunctorily. She was picturing a steaming red-hot lobster.

"Maybe you'd like to join." Duncan's tone was mocking.

Samantha resented the implication—that she was too good for his little club, or whatever.

"Maybe I would—and maybe I wouldn't," she said in as even a voice as she could manage. He really was irritating. She stood up to go. Duncan got up, too. He seemed to have sprouted during the conversation and stood only a few inches from her face. He had a sour smell and the skin on his face was oily. She took a step backward. He followed.

"Naaah, I don't think you could get in."

Suddenly, she had to know.

"So what do you have to do to be a member of your club?" she said slowly, moving away from him.

"You have to kill something."

Chapter 5

Jill and Earl had joined the Millers, bringing cups of fresh-brewed coffee for everyone. As soon as the sun had gone down, the air had assumed some of its more characteristic Maine snap and the sight of the steaming cups was a welcome one.

"You take yours with milk and Sam doesn't take anything, right?" Jill had an amazing memory. Pix could barely recall the preferences of her immediate family, let alone friends. This was why she made lists. But then, Jill might get lost on the intricate carpool routes Pix routinely negotiated without a second thought.

"Thanks," Sam said, "When I find the energy—which could be sometime next week—I'll make a pie run."

They talked about the summer. Jill bemoaned the economy; Earl bemoaned the increase in the island population—it doubled during these months—and Sam bemoaned the fact that he wouldn't be back again until August. It took a while for Pix to steer the conversation around to antiques.

"We had a good time with Valerie the other day exploring the antique stores in Searsport. She has a wonderful eye. Plus, having an expert along was insurance against getting duped by fakes. Have you heard much about antique fraud along the coast?" She addressed Earl directly, evidently striking a nerve.

"Have we! It's big business. I went to some seminars last winter in Augusta on this very subject. The Sheriff's Department has a special unit that does nothing else but deal with these scams."

"What kinds of things are being faked?" Pix asked in as idle a way as she could muster, aware that her mother had joined them, slipping quietly next to Sam.

"You name it. Toys are big." Earl started to warm to his subject. He must have been a star pupil. "One way is to make them from scratch, putting celluloid or bisque into molds from originals to imitate things that are popular collectibles, like Mickey Mouse figures. The modern ones are easy to spot once you know how—different colors, obvious brushstrokes, but even dealers get fooled. Especially if they're made by joining a new toy with an old one, it's called 'marrying.'"

"What do you mean?" Pix was glad to hear the word introduced, yet this sort seemed more likely to be headed for divorce.

"Well, you might have a part missing from an original and you substitute a fake, but often these two never left the factory together. Like Mickey in a car becomes Minnie at the controls. That sort of thing. Then they even forge Steiff buttons and insert them in the ears of new stuffed bears or other animals that have been made to look worn. Another thing we learned is that both fake and genuine toys are put into 'original' boxes printed by color laser to increase the values. The boxes are the easiest to detect. You just need a good magnifying glass, my dear Watsons. You should see dots, not the parallel lines the laser produces."

Pix remembered that Valerie had a whole battery of devices tucked into her jaunty Pierre Deux bag when they had gone off yesterday: a fancy kind of flashlight, a Swiss army knife with more than an extra blade and toothpick, plus a magnifying glass.

"This is amazing," Ursula commented. "I had no idea things were so sophisticated. Tell us more."

Pix looked at her mother. Ursula's face showed nothing other than sincere interest, but it was almost as if she was in on the plot. Whatever the motive, Pix silently thanked her for keeping the conversation going.

"Oh, I could talk all night about this," Earl said jovially, "There's nothing I hate more than a fraud, and these crooks are accomplished ones."

Jill, oddly enough, since antiques were a current and growing interest, did not seem as fascinated. "I'm sure we all do, but I think Louise is cutting the pies."

"Oh, she's barely started, and I can't eat anything yet, anyway," Pix said quickly. "Do tell us some more, Earl."

"Part of the problem is that some people pay such fool prices for things that even legitimate dealers get itchy. Take a painting, for instance. You might think it's old, but you get tempted to sweeten the pot a little by rubbing some dirt and grime on it, tucking it under the cobwebs you don't sweep away in the back of your shop for some tourist to 'discover.' A real con man—or woman—takes what he or she knows is a new painting, maybe even painted it him or herself, and does the same thing. Just now, the unit is getting a lot of calls about paintings—and photographs, fake tintypes and ambrotypes."

"What's an ambrotype?" Sam asked. "Is that anything like a daguerreotype?"

"Yup, daguerreotypes are older and they were more expensive. Ambrotypes used a glass plate to capture an image. And tintypes were obviously on metal. They were the most common, relatively cheap compared with the other two. The thing is that now all three methods can be duplicated using the old cameras or even doctoring a modern image with the right emulsions. So you get a friend to dress up as an Indian chief or a Civil War soldier—this is what people want—and lo and behold, in a few months you've made enough for that condo in Florida."

"I had no idea you were learning so much at those seminars," Jill remarked a bit tartly. "Do you think it has much relevance for law and order on the island?"

Earl frowned. Her tone was decidedly un-Jill-like.

"Maybe not, although what with everyone and his uncle putting some thundermugs in the shed and calling it an antiques store, it will probably pay off one of these days."

"Are you by chance referring to my decision to carry antiques?"

Pix was not happy with the turn the conversation was taking. Not only were they veering from the topic but it seemed that Jill and Earl were heading for a quarrel and about to topple off the top of the cake.

"Of course he isn't!" she said in what she hoped was a light-hearted tone. "We're just gossiping. It's fun to hear about how other people get fooled, so long as you're not one of them."

"Exactly." Ursula came to the rescue again. "Like the Pilgrim chair hoax."

"What was that?" Earl asked eagerly, slipping his arm around Jill in an attempt to make up—for what, he knew not. She sat stiffly but didn't shrug him off.

"This all happened about twenty years ago and it was big news. Our forefathers and mothers didn't have dining sets,— they were lucky to have a crude trestle table and a few stools, however there were exceptions. These few people, men, of course, had imposing thronelike chairs with elaborately turned spindles at the back and below the rush seat. You can see the one said to have belonged to Elder William Brewster at the Pilgrim Hall down in Plymouth. Sometimes the chairs are called 'Brewster chairs,' and nobody had to remind you to sit up straight in one. It must have been pure torture for them, and perhaps why they always have such sour expressions in the paintings. Now, where was I? Oh yes, in the 1970s, a Rhode Island furniture restorer concocted one of these chairs and aged it by, among other things, putting it in a steel drum with a smoky fire to get the right patina, if that's the right word, on the wood. He then allowed the chair to surface on a porch here in Maine."

"I *do* remember this story," Earl exclaimed, "Some museum bought it for a bundle, right? And now they have it on display as a fake next to one of the real ones."

"Yes." Ursula nodded. "The hoax worked and the restorer always claimed it was not his intent to make money, merely to point out how easy it was to fool even the experts, and you can believe him or not." Ursula's stern expression made her own prejudice clear. "It's in the Ford Museum in Michigan. I don't know if it's next to a real one, but they do have it on display with a note telling the real story—that it was still a tree in 1969."

Earl was off and running again. "Furniture can become an antique over night—a little ink spilled in a drawer or table and chair legs rubbed with a brick on the bottoms to simulate wear. Old furniture isn't that difficult to duplicate for a master furniture builder. You can age wood by just throwing it into the woods for a winter, and period nails are available— people collect those, too! But legitimate reproductions are marked as such, and they command a lot of money!"

"Yet not as much as originals," Sam said.

"There are still bargains to be had," Jill asserted emphatically.

"I know"—Sam laughed—"just look at what my wife carts home!"

Before they got back on the question of pie again—Pix had noticed Sam's eye turning in that direction—she squeezed in her last question. "Who's doing the faking mostly, and what kind of crime is it?"

"To answer your first question, we'd like to find out. Some of the rings have been broken up and they've included dealers, but it's also people who know nothing about antiques, except for the ones they're duplicating. It's a business to them, just not a legal one. Which answers the next part: Selling fakes is larceny. Transporting them across state lines is not a federal offense, however a phone call to set up the transport is—fraud by wire—and we got some guys that way. I guess I get pretty worked up about the whole business, because people come to Maine trusting that they'll find some nice old things here and instead they get burned by a few selfish, crooked individuals. And we haven't even talked about all the traffic in stolen antiques!"

"But we have talked enough about this business for one night. I for one want dessert." Jill jumped up and headed for the table with a seeming determination for pie that brooked no opposition.

"Sure, honey, I want pie, too." Earl joined her and Pix could hear him asking, "Now what's going on? What did I . . ." The rest of his remarks were inaudible, as was Jill's reply, but what all could see was that this time she did shake his arm away.

Pix and her mother looked at each other. Ursula raised one eyebrow. Even Sam, normally oblivious to the ins and outs of the relationships about him—his own was enough to keep track of—noticed and said, "I thought those two were an item. They don't seem very chummy tonight."

"A lovers' quarrel—or more like a spat," Ursula said. "I expect they'll iron things out. You and Pix do."

"Oh, come on, Mother, Sam and I never fight."

"Then you probably should."

It was hard to get around Mother.

With one accord, they all started walking toward the dessert table, discreetly waiting for Jill and Earl to get theirs and disappear in the darkness. At least, Pix thought Jill got a piece of pie. In the dim light, it was hard to see.

"Did I hear you talking about antiques as I passed a while ago?" asked a voice at Pix's elbow. It was the Bainbridge's guest, Norman, and he was returning for seconds, or maybe thirds, judging from the crumbs that lingered on what Pix assumed was his normally impeccable mouth.

"I'm Norman Osgood, by the way. I came with Adelaide and Rebecca Bainbridge."

The Millers introduced themselves in turn and while doing so, Pix reflected that it was never Rebecca and Adelaide, always the other way around. Was it Pix and Sam Miller? Or Sam and Pix? She thought they were getting roughly equal time.

"We were talking about antiques, or rather, fake antiques."

"Fakes. So unpleasant when one has been burned. I'm in the antique business myself and have been totally tricked on several occasions—once by a nice Russian lady from New Jersey who one would have sworn was directly related to the Romanovs, but in fact, all her trinkets might as well have been prizes from a penny arcade. Has one of you come across such artifice lately?"

Pix wondered whether it was her imagination at work again, but his query seemed to be couched in a rather probing tone. Why was he so interested? Merely because it was his business?

"No—at least not to our knowledge," she added. "But all of us are interested in antiques and we like to know what to guard against."

"Stick to reputable dealers and beware of bargains, that's my advice," Norman said.

Pix thought of her quilt with a twinge. It was too gorgeous. It *had* to be real. The pile had been in a dusty corner with more than a few cobwebs, but the whole barn had been like that.

"Of course, one does sometimes come across a steal. But that's pretty rare these days."

"What kind of antiques do you sell?" Pix asked.

"Early American furniture, some European; paintings before 1900; and clocks. I adore clocks."

"My mother was just telling us about the Pilgrim chair hoax. You must have heard about it."

"Oh, indeed. Such a scandal. Now I must rejoin my lovely hostesses. I believe Adelaide is getting tired. It's been quite a day."

Pix watched his elegant back retreat into the darkness. Up close, she could see some extremely attractive muscles of the rippling variety under his thin silk shirt. The man kept himself in good shape. It was hard to say whether he knew the story of the hoax or not. A real dealer would, no doubt. And he was a real dealer, wasn't he?

"It has been quite a day," Sam said contentedly, tucking into an enormous slab of strawberry-rhubarb pie. "I wouldn't miss this clambake for the world. Thank goodness we had a sensible jury."

"Obviously, since they found in favor of your client."

"That's what sensible means—and they did it quickly."

Pix looked at her own pie. She really wasn't hungry, but she began to eat it in a mechanical fashion that became less so as her taste buds awoke. It *had* been quite a day, and night. There had been that scene with the Athertons, then the talk with Earl and his tiff with Jill. She looked about the beach at the shadowy figures. Then there were all the things that might have gone on at the party that she didn't even know about.

"Let's get Samantha and start packing up ourselves. I want to check on the dogs." Dusty, Artie, and Henry tended to run amok at gatherings like this and so had regretfully been left at home. "I don't know why having this much fun should be so tiring, but it is," she added.

Sam nodded. "Something about the combination of sand, sun, and beer, I think. Where is Samantha, by the way?"

"I saw her with a group of kids by the bonfire a while ago. She was eating her lobster. I think I can still make her out. They're all singing old Everly Brothers songs with John Eggleston. That man has talents we've never suspected."

"I'll make them sing 'A Real Nice Clambake.' Louise always likes that. I think that *Carousel* was the sum total of her knowledge about Maine before she arrived here. It must have been a shock to find out that bait smelled and people didn't dance on the wharf."

Sam went off down the beach in the direction of the fire and Pix started to assemble the stuff they'd brought. She knew the Fraziers hired some of the local kids to help clean up each year, so she didn't feel she had to stay any longer. Ursula called out to her as she was making the first trip to the car.

"Pix, are you leaving? May I beg a ride? Then I won't have to trouble the Moores."

"Of course you can have a ride. I was planning to look for you. Sam is getting Samantha and they'll start back in his car." As she spoke, husband and daughter came up the path with the rest of the Millers' belongings. Sam's song suggestion had been successful and he was singing along from afar: "The vittles we et were good, you bet! The company was the same." His energetic performance contrasted with his daughter's lagging footsteps. She wasn't joining in, not even at her favorite part: "Fitten fer an angel's choir!" Pix was immediately concerned.

"Samantha, are you all right? You look a little wan. I hope you haven't picked up something from one of the campers, all those small children just loaded with germs."

Samantha was quick to squelch any notions her mother might have of bed rest and herb tea.

"Mother! I'm fine. There's absolutely nothing wrong. No bugs, no microbes of any sort whatsoever."

But she wasn't fine. Duncan's words continued to haunt her. She hadn't seen him come back to the beach and would be happy never to see him again. She needed to talk to Arlene.

If she wasn't home, she might be at Fred's house. The last thing Samantha wanted was her mother's eagle eye on her. She'd made plans for the evening while she sat staring into the flames of the bonfire, listening to everybody sing. Samantha didn't want to be watched at all.

Ursula came straight to the point as usual. "What are you up to, darling? All those questions to Earl about phony antiques. *And* Mitch sold antiques, among his other trades. You're trying to find the answer to his murder, aren't you?"

It was the time-honored parental ploy for asking questions—trapping one's offspring in the car. Short of turning the wheel over to her mother and walking home, there was no way for Pix to escape.

"Don't be ridiculous," she lied. "I'm just interested in the antiques business. You yourself said it was all 'amazing,' if I recall correctly."

"Hmmmm," her mother replied, which left the conversation hanging until Pix could stand it no longer and started talking again—another trick, and one Pix herself had used occasionally to her advantage with her own children.

"Anyway, I don't see how asking a few questions that may or may not relate to Mitchell Pierce's death can hurt anything."

"But it can hurt something—you, or dear Samantha, or Sam. We have all assumed the person who did this left the island after the terrible deed, yet it may not be so. I think you need to exercise some caution."

"Stop worrying, Mother. I'm not going to do anything foolish."

"I believe I've heard that before."

Mother could, in fact, be very irritating. Pix saw her into the house, kissed her good night, and then took great pleasure in driving as fast as she dared up and down the hills across the island to her own cottage.

Sam was groggily reading the latest issue of *The Island Crier* by an unlighted hearth.

"Honey," Pix asked immediately, "why don't you go up to bed? And where's Samantha? In her room?"

"Arlene and that pimply-faced boyfriend of hers came to get her for some kind of bonfire at his parents' camp. You know, where the Ames' are—down near the bridge. Bert Ames is taking everyone in turns in his outboard to look at the underneath of the bridge by moonlight, all very safe and sound. I said yes and reminded her when curfew rang."

Sam was feeling mellow and happy. Pix hated to destroy his mood. She ventured a tentative, "But Samantha did seem tired . . ."

"So she'll go to bed early tomorrow night or the night after. Besides, my little chickadee, this gives us a few precious moments alone, a rare thing, you may recall, these last twenty-plus years."

There was something to what the man said. Samantha was young and healthy. And so were her parents.

An hour later, Pix was stretched out next to her sleeping husband. The only sounds she could hear were his heavy breathing, the soft wind in the trees, a far-off bullfrog, and her own heart pounding insistently in her ears as she lay in bed wide awake.

Samantha Miller was not at Fred Ames's parents' camp. Neither was Arlene or Fred himself. They had put in a brief appearance for appearance's sake—not long enough for a boat ride, to Samantha's regret. She loved seeing the long arch spanning the Reach from all vantage points, especially gliding underneath through the water, looking straight up. The bridge—Sanpere's connection to the mainland. To the outside world. There were still some people on the island who wished it had never been built and blamed it for everything from teenage rowdiness to the increase in traffic on Route 17.

"I can't believe he actually said that!" Arlene was nestled

close to Fred in the front of his pickup. Like his father, Fred planned to be a fisherman as soon as he graduated from high school next June. Also like his father, he planned to marry his high school sweetheart shortly thereafter. Things looked good. He and Arlene had been king and queen of the junior prom, which virtually ensured a long and happy life together, Fred believed. If she still wanted to go to college, fine. He didn't care—just so long as she went as Mrs. Fred Ames.

Samantha was feeling a lot less frightened now that she'd told Arlene and Fred about the scene with Duncan. Sitting by the fire at the clambake, she'd decided she had to find out what he was up to. It could be nothing—or it could explain a lot of what had been happening lately. She had a feeling that after the fight with his parents, he wouldn't go home, but would gather his "club" together and do something. Arlene and Fred agreed. Fred had an idea where Duncan might be.

"There's an old cabin in the woods behind the camp that used to be a place counselors went on their days off in the olden times before Jim was the director and figured out it was the perfect place to screw. Maybe used it himself." Fred laughed. Arlene made a face.

"It's gross enough to think of adults doing it, without having to think of Jim Atherton as a teenager."

Samantha agreed and asked, "What about the cabin? Do you really think Duncan hangs out there? It's pretty near the camp. Wouldn't he want to get farther away?"

"That's what I've heard. Besides, the kid isn't old enough to drive. How far can he go? Though some of his loser friends are older and have cars. But I think he'd pick his own spot, something close to hand, and chances are he'll be there tonight. After what you described, he'd be nuts to go home. Doesn't spend much time in the mansion, anyway. My cousin worked on it and said Duncan's room was pretty cheesy compared to the rest of the place. Small and no Jacuzzi in the bath."

"Well, no wonder the boy's disturbed," mocked Arlene,

and they all laughed. It occurred to Samantha that she'd never heard Fred talk so much, and what he said made sense. Maybe Arlene knew what she was about.

"We can park on the road and go in the back way. I'm pretty sure I can find it."

"You sound awfully familiar with the cabin yourself, Frederick Ames," Arlene said.

"So, maybe we took some brews there once or twice on a cold winter's day," he admitted, "but we never hurt anything. The place was pretty well trashed before we ever found it."

He stopped the truck, got a flashlight from the glove compartment, and they started to walk silently through the woods. Samantha wasn't sure what she thought she would find, yet it seemed like a good idea at the time, and if she'd stayed at home doing nothing, she would have gone out of her mind. If nothing else, she'd provided Fred with some excitement for the night. He was as keyed up as if he was stalking a stag.

They almost missed the tumbled-down cabin. Evergreen boughs and fallen trees had been piled around it in an attempt at camouflage. In the dark, it was quite effective.

"Probably doesn't want his stepfather to notice it's still here when he's leading one of his hikes," Arlene whispered.

"Sssh." Fred put his hand over her mouth, expecting a kiss. The abruptness with which he pulled away told Samantha he got something else. Arlene was not easily shushed.

They crept up to the front of the cabin and could make out the door. It was closed and no light shone beneath it, nor at any of the windows.

"It doesn't look like he's here," Samantha said. She was disappointed.

Fred switched on the flashlight and they went up the steps. A board was missing from one and Samantha's foot almost went through. She grabbed at the rickety railing.

"Be careful. This place is liable to fall apart like Lincoln Logs," Fred warned.

They peered in the window, glass surprisingly still intact, unless Duncan had replaced it. It was pitch-dark and they couldn't see a thing. Fred shone the flashlight in and they could make out a heavy-metal calendar and a King Diamond poster on the far wall.

"What did you expect? Joey Lawrence? Come on, let's go in," Arlene said.

The door was open. It appeared the cabin had never been wired for electricity. There were lots of candles around, especially on a low shelf just above a small footlocker. A table with an ashtray filled with cigarette butts, a couple of dilapidated chairs, and a mattress with a sleeping bag on top completed the decor. There were more posters on the walls: Kiss, AC/DC, and one with a winged skull. Fred walked over to the ashtray and sniffed at the contents. "Marlboros, nothing else. If he's got a stash, it's someplace else. Like in that trunk over there."

The trunk had drawn Samantha's eye, too. So far, the room indicated perhaps a borderline unhealthy fascination with the occult and satanic music, yet nothing like upside-down crosses or inverted pentagrams to indicate the need for an emergency exorcist. Duncan seemed to spend his leisure time reading—not Proust or even *Catcher in the Rye*, but comic books. There was a stack of them next to the mattress. Arlene picked up a couple. "Look at this. The kid is really totally weird. I mean he's got *Ghost Rider* and *X-Men* mixed in with *Archies*. He doesn't know if he's six or sixteen."

Fred had flipped the two catches and was fiddling around with the center lock on the footlocker. It looked like the kind you took to camp, and maybe Duncan had, some summer in his past life. Samantha found it hard to imagine him as a normal kid in shorts playing capture the flag in a camp T-shirt.

"These things are pretty easy to open." Fred took out his knife.

"What's that sticking out from the side?" Samantha asked.

Fred pulled at it. "I dunno. Some kind of black cloth.

Maybe he has orgies or something here and they dress up."
He inserted the knife into the lock and began to twist it open.

Samantha had a funny feeling about all this. It was one thing to walk through an open door but another to open someone's private property, even if that someone was Duncan Cowley. She was also not sure she wanted to know what was inside.

"He's coming! Let's get out of here!" Arlene had been watching at the window. "I can see his shoes! Come on, run!"

They flew down the front stairs and into the woods. Samantha could see Duncan's shoes blinking in the dark. He wasn't far behind them and he'd realized someone had been at the cabin.

"You bastard!" he screamed, "Come back here. I know who you are. You can't get away from me."

They ran until they reached the pickup and then were back on the main road in a few moments.

"That was close," Fred said.

They drove in silence for a while. The feeling of the dark cabin and what it might contain seemed to have invaded the thoughts of all three teenagers. Now that she was away, Samantha perversely felt she had to find out what Duncan was up to—even if it meant breaking into the footlocker. She reached over and grabbed Arlene's hand. It was as cold as her own.

"It was great of you guys to come with me, but I've got to get home or my mother will have a fit."

"Mine, too," Arlene said.

They pulled into the drive in front of the Millers' cottage and Samantha got out. "Tomorrow night?" Fred asked. In the beams of his headlights, Samantha nodded solemnly. Tomorrow night.

The phone rang early the next morning. Sam was asleep and Samantha had already left for work, taking her bike. Pix was drinking a cup of coffee, still in her nightclothes, out on the back deck. She dashed inside. Her hello was a little breathless. It had been the fourth ring; islanders were known to hang up after less, assuming no one was home or didn't want to be bothered.

"Mom!" It was Samantha and she was breathless, too. "Get over here right away! It's the sails! They're covered with blood and all these dead bats are lying around in the hulls!"

"Blood! Bats! My God, what's happened?" Pix could scarcely believe Samantha's words. "Samantha! Samantha!" The line appeared to have gone dead.

"That was Arlene." Samantha was back on the phone and her voice was marginally calmer. "It's not blood. It's paint, red paint. And the bats are plastic. But it *looked* like blood when the sails were raised and the bats were totally gross with red stuff coming out of them, so we all ran back here. I could have sworn it was real!"

"Darling, how dreadful!"

"Just come, okay?"

"I'll be there as soon as I can." Pix was already unbuttoning her pajamas. After she hung up, she raced upstairs.

"Sam, Sam, wake up! There's some trouble over at the camp. Someone painted the sails with red paint and they all thought it was blood, because there were bats in the boats that they thought were dead. But they turned out to be fake too." Pix was struggling for lucidity.

"Bats? What kind of bats? Baseball bats? Paint? Blood?" Sam sat up, rubbing his eyes. "What the hell is going on over there? Wait while I throw something on."

When the Millers pulled into the parking lot at Maine Sail Camp, they could see that Sergeant Dickinson had beaten them. They hurried down to the waterfront, where the entire camp was gathered. Samantha was in the center of a group of the youngest campers. Two were literally clinging to her. Pix was proud of the way her daughter was handling the crisis. Stroking one head while patting another, Samantha was saying, "It's just someone's idea of a stupid joke. A very, very bad joke and that's all. We'll get the extra sails and be out on the water in no time."

One of the children, a little girl, looked up at Samantha with absolute certainty that she would get an honest answer from this goddess. "Are you sure? So many spooky things have been happening—the mice and those other tricks."

Sam turned to Pix. "Mice?" he asked softly, not wanting to upset the scene further.

"I'll tell you later," Pix replied. "Another nasty prank." She wanted to listen. What was this about "other tricks"?

Jim strode over to them, obviously pleased at their presence.

"Sam, Pix. Good of you to come. Earl is down on the beach now and then he wants to search all the cabins. Clayton Dickinson is working here as handyman this summer. He's Earl's cousin, I believe, and is going to help him. The kids are understandably upset. Do you think you could give us a hand? We're going to gather in the dining hall and sing some songs. Mabel is getting together some cookies and milk. The counselors have been terrific, but the kids need some more adult reassurance."

"No problem," Sam replied, abandoning his morning sail with only a slight trace of regret. "Before you start your hootenanny though, I think you'd better talk about what's happened. There's the possibility that someone may have some information, but mostly you want to keep it all out in the open or you're going to have them jumping ship in droves."

"Don't I know it. One kid has already demanded to leave. His parents are on a barge in Burgundy, pretty unreachable, as he well knows, but he's stirring up the others."

"Is this one of Samantha's group? She said there was a boy who was pretty annoyed at his mother and father."

Jim nodded. "Geoff Baxter. He may have been too immature for such a long sleep-away session."

Pix went over to Samantha and began to help her move the

kids into the dining room. Sam went to another group. "Hootenanny?" Had her husband been listening to his old Pete Seeger records while the family was away?

The clingers were still clinging and Pix gently pried the little girl away from Samantha. Pix had the distinct impression that the campers around Samantha, and especially those who had commandeered each of her daughter's hands, were not so much scared as excited, despite appearances to the contrary. There was definitely something in the air. She made a mental note to talk to Samantha about it later—and also ask her how she liked being the object of such devotion. The crushes at Maine Sail were beginning to resemble some sort of food chain—beginning with Samantha's on Valerie.

"Now, listen to Samantha. She's right. It's just a rotten trick. What's your name?" The girl gulped, took a tissue Pit offered, and blew her nose. "It's Susannah." Obviously the effort was too much and she began to cry, adding the tearful protest, "I didn't do it. I don't know who did it!"

"Shut up, Susannah, and stop showing off." It was one of the boys in the group. "Nobody thinks you did it. Besides, you would never have the guts."

Pix was inclined to agree with him. Whoever had done it would have had to have nerve and some to spare. The sails had been fine the day before, Samantha said, so the deed involved getting up in the dead of night, raising the sails, painting them without leaving a trace of the evidence on one's person, then making everything shipshape before going back to bed.

It would have been very difficult for any of the campers— or counselors—to do without someone detecting his or her absence.

That left . . . Arlene supplied the name uppermost in everyone's minds, whispering to Pix as she swept by, several charges in tow, "It's just creepy Duncan again. If this doesn't get him sent away, I don't know what will." She was smiling.

In the cavernous dining room, the commotion was deafening and it took Jim several minutes to get everyone quieted down. During that time, Pix saw Valerie and Duncan slip in through the side door. Valerie looked furious. Duncan's mouth was set in a tight line. He looked as if he hadn't slept—or changed his clothes—for a few weeks. When Pix tried to read the expression in his eyes, all she could come up with was fear. If there was red paint on his body, it wasn't anywhere that showed.

"Campers, staff, I know how upset everyone is, and believe me, I feel it just as much as you do—more. Right now, what we need is to stay calm and do everything we can to help Sergeant Dickinson figure out who did this. While the kitchen crew gives us a little snack, we'll have a few songs and practice for the parade. I'm going to be in my office in case any of you wants to come to talk to me. If you want to bring a friend, fine. I'm prepared to treat this as a very bad joke—something that maybe seemed like a fun idea at midnight, to scare your friends the next morning. But I *will* find out who did it."

Jim Atherton was definitely displaying the nonpussycat side of his camp-director role this morning. Nobody but nobody messed with Maine Sail.

Samantha joined her parents. Pix took the opportunity to ask her a few questions as the group began to sing "There Was a Tree," volume increasing as they went along, until it sounded like any other camp group. All they needed was to be on a bus or tramping through the woods

"What did the kids mean by the other tricks?"

"Oh, those were just the normal things that go on in a place like this—salt in the sugar bowls, short-sheeting the counselors' beds—the ones who don't have sleeping bags—and cowpats in people's shoes."

Pix nodded. These were the typical perils of camp existence. "Nothing else? Nothing like the mice?"

"Not that I know of, though the kids have been saying they hear creepy noises at night—scary music, rustling in the bushes—but I'm pretty sure it's one or two kids wanting to get the others worked up."

"Now what is this about the mice?" Sam demanded. He really wanted to be sailing. It was a gorgeous day and through the window he could see luckier folk skimming the surface of the water just beyond the vandalized boats moored in the camp harbor. They did look pretty dreadful and reminded him of an ancient Greek myth, only those sails had been black. He shuddered slightly and put any and all implications firmly out of his mind.

They filled him in on the mice and he commented, "The sole connection I can see is blood and gore. Kids this age love it, but I'm damned if I can figure out how a kid could have done it."

"The Athertons were at the clambake all afternoon; someone could have snuck away then," Pix proposed.

"Except the whole camp was here practicing for the Fourth of July parade. The counselors have planned an elaborate routine where the campers flip cards as they march and sing, like at sports events. If someone was missing, it would have been spotted right away. You couldn't do that much damage in the time it might have taken to go the bathroom."

"Samantha's right, which leaves an outsider."

Samantha elaborated. "Which leaves Duncan. We know he had a wicked big fight with his parents. What better way to get even than try to get the camp closed down? If Jim can't keep this hushed up, there are a lot of parents who'll want their kids out of here. You know, 'Kid's Camp Cult Target'— that sort of thing.

"Duncan had plenty of time to do it while the rest of us were eating lobster—or he could have done it later after everyone was asleep." Or, she said to herself silently, he could have been coming from his painting party just in time to surprise us at the cabin.

"Well," Sam said, rubbing his hands together, "I don't see

that there's too much more we can do here." The group was lustily singing "One Hundred Bottles of Beer on the Wall" and it was time to leave—tide or no tide. "Why don't we go talk to Jim, see if anything more has turned up, and skedaddle." Skedaddle? Pix thought. What was happening to her husband's vocabulary. He definitely needed to be around his family more.

"I'll come, too. Are you staying, darling?"

"Mother! Of course! It's my job. Besides, I want to." Samantha went back to her post. The worshippers were waiting.

"It seems odd that little Susannah would have felt it necessary to protest her innocence," Pix remarked to her husband as they started across the ground, so heavily carpeted with years of fallen pine needles that their every footfall released a strong scent of balsam as they crunched along.

"Maybe she's the salt/sugar culprit. She has the perfect face for it—those big baby blues and that sunshine-from-behind-the-clouds smile."

Pix looked at Sam admiringly. "You would have made a good detective."

"Thank you, Mrs. Holmes. Now let's say good-bye and not waste any more of this beautiful day."

Outside the office, they could hear voices, raised voices.

"I tell you, young man, one more incident and you'll go. This is not a threat; it's a promise. You are not hiding behind your mother's skirts anymore. Of all the idiotic things to do, frightening some of the younger children half to death!"

"I didn't do it, I tell you!" Duncan screeched. "And I'm not going to any fucking military academy. Go ahead and send me. But you can't make me stay there."

"Duncan, Duncan, what choice do we have? Your behavior has been so odd lately." It was Valerie and she sounded as if she had been crying. "At least won't you see the counselor again?"

"I'm not the one who needs a shrink; you are! And this has

nothing to do with Daddy. Why can't you just leave me alone!"

"Fine." Valerie's voice was resolute, the voice of a woman who has come to the end of some sort of tether. "We will leave you alone—and you leave us alone. One more of these incidents and you'll be sent off. Maybe your grandparents will keep you for the rest of the summer."

"That's a laugh." Duncan sneered. "Don't forget what they said to you the last time we were there."

"That will be enough, young man, I will not have you address your mother in that tone of voice." The Millers were unable to move from their spot right outside the door—in Pix's case from outright curiosity; in Sam's because he was mortified they might be heard leaving.

"Don't you touch me!" Duncan's voice was frantic and what sounded like a chair falling over was followed by the more recognizable noise made when a sharp slap connects with flesh on some part of the body.

Head lowered, Duncan plunged out the door, past the Millers, oblivious to their presence. Pix could see two things: He was crying and an angry red handprint streaked across the left side of his face.

They waited a few seconds before Pix called out, "Jim, are you there? We have to be going."

"Come in; come in." Nothing was out of place.

"We've just had another scene with Duncan," Valerie admitted to them. "The last psychologist we took him to said it was all an extended grief reaction, but I'm beginning to think Duncan is milking it. At the moment, he is simply a pain-in-the-ass teenager, no ifs, ands, or buts about it." She laughed at her pun. "Excuse me. This has been a pretty awful morning."

Pix patted Valerie's shoulder. "I know—and if there's anything more we can do, give us a call."

"Thank you both for coming." Jim was a bit stiff. Pix knew he must be wondering how much they had heard—and seen.

"It will all sort itself out," Sam assured him. "Maine Sail

has one of the finest reputations of any summer camp in the country. Parents know this."

"I hope so," Jim said dismally. "I also hope I can keep it out of the papers."

As the Millers were on the point of leaving, Earl walked into the office. Pix sat down.

"You can let the kids back into their bunks. Nothing, not so much as a drop of red paint on anything. The only thing we've found with any paint on it is a rubber glove—the kind you use for dishwashing. It had washed up on the shore and its mate, the paint, and brush will probably float in, too. After being in the water for this amount of time, there's no way we can get any prints off it. We'll just have to hope there is a guilty conscience—or more than one—out there. I'm assuming the paint was down in the boathouse. There's a space between two cans of white primer."

"We use red paint for the waterlines and the names, so if you didn't find another can of it, that's where it came from," Jim said, then put out his hand for a hearty masculine shake. "Thanks, Earl, for all your work. I'm pretty convinced it was my stepson. We've been having a lot of trouble with him. You know that."

Earl nodded and gave them a sympathetic look. The first week in June, Duncan had been picked up for driving his mother's car without a license. He'd only made it down to the end of the Athertons' road when he had the bad luck to encounter Earl. Rather than get bogged down in the juvenile-court system, Earl had placed him on a kind of supervised probation of his own. Now when the boy saw the policeman coming, he tended to walk in the other direction, but not before giving Earl a look that spoke volumes—pretty unprintable ones.

"If you find out anything more, give me a call. I'll write it up, plus it will have to go in *The Island Crier*. Let's hope none of the eager beavers in the national press are reading 'Police Brief' these days."

"Thanks."

Pix knew what Earl meant. There had been a spate of quaint column fillers reprinting items from local Maine papers—examples of life Down East. The latest had a Sanpere dateline and purported to quote an island schoolboy's report on George Washington in its entirety: "George Washington was born off-island." True, that said it all, but the image of the life it represented was as faded as one of those daguerreotypes Earl had been mentioning—just yesterday?

"We have to be going." Ever so gently, Sam pulled his wife to an upright position. "See you."

They spent the afternoon sailing, and despite her every intention to forget the events of the morning for the time being, Pix kept seeing gobs of red dripping down the smooth white sails they passed.

Ursula Rowe sat on the front porch of The Pines trying to decide whether she should walk down to the beach or stay where she was and finish the book she was reading about Alice James. A few years ago, there would have been no question. She would have leapt up, taken her walk, and returned to read—or even taken the book with her. Now she eyed the ascent. First there were the porch stairs, then the sloping grass, and finally a line of low rocks that separated the beach from the dirt road leading to the dock. She sighed. It was too much, especially with no one around at the moment. It was all well and good to assert her independence when people were near, but she knew she was slowing down and there were things she just shouldn't attempt anymore. It was profoundly depressing.

It had all started with the car. She'd resisted the calls of common sense for several months, then when she'd backed over one of the lilacs her mother had planted for her when she first moved into the Aleford house, she'd called Pix and told her to come get the keys. For the first few days, she felt not only trapped but angrily dependent. Gradually, she'd become used to relying on friends, taxis—and Pix. Fortunately, the house wasn't far from the center of Aleford. The day Ursula couldn't walk to the library would be the day she took to her bed for good, she'd told herself dramatically. Now she knew she'd hang on to every bit of mobility she had, from house to garden, from bedroom to bath, as her world diminished.

The unchanging scene before her lifted her spirits. For all the waves knew, she could still be that little girl in braids chasing the foam as it swept down the wet sand. Yet this summer had not been a typical one. The murder of Mitchell Pierce hung suspended in the air, accompanied by whispered rumors, hints, accusations. She wished Pix would stay out of it, but knew she wouldn't. Children were so influenced by their friends. Pix was taking a leaf from Faith's book. But then Pix wasn't a child anymore and she, Ursula, wasn't really a mother—some other category. The magazines talked about role reversal and children becoming parents. Ursula hated that notion. Only it was true. She wasn't walking to the beach anymore without Pix to watch her. Retired mother? Perhaps, but when she thought about Pix and Arnold, named for his father, the fierce pangs of maternal love were not retiring in the least.

It would be good to see Arnold and his wife. What was the old saying? "Your son is your son until he takes a wife. Your daughter's your daughter for the rest of your life." Or was it "her life"? Some daughterly element in one's makeup that just kept on going along, even when the mother was gone? Had she felt this way about her own mother? She didn't think so. Her older sisters had assigned themselves caretaker roles early on and there wasn't much left for Ursula to do save visit from time to time—like Arnold and Claire. He was her son. She was proud of him, but it was a good thing she had Pix.

She thought about her conversation with John Eggleston at the clambake. "It's no loss to anyone I know or can imagine." She'd been surprised at the uncharitableness of the remark. She ought to tell Pix about it. The clambake had seemed like a kind of play. Perhaps it was because she knew that at eighty, she wouldn't be at too many more of them. She had tended to regard the day as several acts and many scenes one after another. Addie Bainbridge had been watching, too. Or maybe holding court was a better description. Ursula resolved to invite Addie and Rebecca for tea later in the week, after the Fourth of July festivities. Give Rebecca a break. Addie was inclined to ride roughshod over her. What could Adelaide's childhood have actually been like out at the lighthouse? It sounded idyllic, and reflecting on her own upbringing, one of seven, in a well-appointed but unavoidably crowded town house on Boston's Beacon Hill, Ursula thought how lovely it would have been not to have so many people to talk to all the time. That was what had always made The Pines so special. You could be alone.

She could still be alone. Except now she didn't want to be.

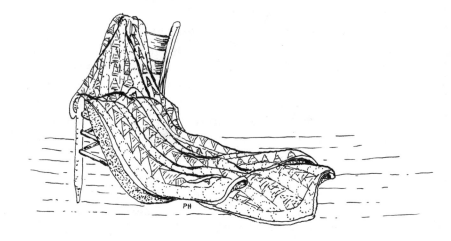

Chapter 6

A midnight curfew was a definite disadvantage to detective work, Samantha decided as once more she entered the woods behind Maine Sail Camp with Fred and Arlene. Fred had no curfew, of course, and Arlene's was a great deal more elastic than Samantha's own. Whatever Duncan and his friends were up to, Sam was willing to bet, things didn't get rolling until the wee hours.

This time, there were lights flickering in the windows of the cabin, just visible through Duncan's elaborate camouflage.

"Should we try to look through the back window?" Arlene whispered.

"Let's wait a while and see what they do," Fred suggested. "They may go someplace else. The cabin is pretty small."

They retreated behind a row of tamaracks and took turns watching.

"More kids are coming," Samantha reported. True to Fred's prediction, soon a group of about eleven teenagers came out of the cabin and headed straight for the tamaracks. Samantha froze in position after crouching close to the rough trunk, the sharp-needled boughs pricking her bare arms. Why hadn't she thought to wear a sweatshirt? The weather was still peculiar for Maine, up into the high eighties every day. She'd been shedding clothes, not adding them.

The group passed by without noticing anything. Samantha, Fred, and Arlene waited a minute before following. Once again, Fred was full of ideas. "There're only two places where they could be headed, the quaking bog and the old settlement quarry—unless they're planning to dispose of something or someone, which would mean the bog—I'll bet they're on their way to the quarry."

"What do you mean?" Samantha had never been to the bog, deterred all these years by reports of mosquitoes as large as robins and giant Venus's-flytraps.

"The suction—you put your foot down wrong and it takes two men to help you twist it and pull yourself out. People used to junk cars there before Earl came. And there's always talk, especially on Halloween, of what may be lying under the surface from years past."

"You know that's all nonsense," Arlene whispered angrily, "except about the cars. That's true. Stop trying to psych us out Fred. I'm nervous enough as it is."

Samantha had to agree with her and was glad the bog had been eliminated as the probable gathering place for the club.

Fred put out his arm to stop them. "See, they're turning left. That leads to the top of the quarry." The flashlights the group ahead of them was carrying did go left, darting like so many fireflies through the dark woods.

Samantha had been to the quarry. It was one of her favorite places—also her mother's and grandmother's. They picked blackberries there and then, later in the season, tiny tart mountain cranberries that appeared as conserve at the Millers' Thanksgiving table.

The view from the top of the quarry was spectacular—

straight out to sea across vast expanses of granite carved in huge blocks, like Brobdingnagian steps. During the day, you had to be careful not to walk into one of the crevasses where the charges had been set to blast the stone. At night, it would be treacherous. Was Duncan's club an elaborate game of chicken? Fred stopped suddenly and led them up a granite ledge until they were directly above the group below. A fire had been lighted and everyone was drinking beer. Duncan was nowhere to be seen. It looked like any other gathering of kids from Maine to California, eager to put themselves at a distance from adult supervision. A few were smoking. One of the cigarettes was being passed from person to person—obviously not tobacco.

"So, what's the big deal? They're partying," Arlene said. "Let's go home."

Samantha wanted to wait until Duncan came, and Fred agreed. It was at least fifteen minutes before they heard the music and saw him leap suddenly into the midst of his friends, dangerously close to the fire. He was wearing a black robe—it looked left over from someone's graduation—unfastened. They could see that he was stripped to the waist underneath and had covered his body with symbols and lines done in red marker—at least Samantha assumed it was marker. He didn't seem to be oozing blood, but the effect was dramatic and she felt instantly nauseated. Everyone grew quiet and the words of an old Black Sabbath song filled the stillness from the tape deck he set down.

When the music stopped, Duncan began to chant "We are everybody and everybody is nobody" over and over. The group picked it up, some laughing a little—maybe because of the beers and the pot. A few of the guys stripped off their shirts and pranced unsteadily around the fire.

Duncan took out a chicken that looked like a roaster from the IGA and made a great show of slitting its throat—or rather, the place where the throat would have been if the head was still attached. Blood flowed; he must have stuck a sack of red-colored liquid inside.

"The asshole!" Fred whispered, "He couldn't even get a live chicken."

Samantha wasn't finding the scene humorous. Duncan's intent was the same as if the chicken had been alive—or if it had been something other than a chicken. She shuddered and gripped the granite hard with her hand to remind herself that this wasn't a movie. She wondered what would happen next. The kids below her looked so normal. She stared at one girl in particular: short dark hair, a striped tube top, and cutoffs—a typical teenager on a summer night. Maybe she wore a little too much makeup, especially the exaggerated black mascara around her eyes. But she wasn't typical. The whole gathering wasn't typical at all, and Samantha began to feel frightened. Duncan had somehow managed to tap into an unhealthy fascination shared by this group, and it was a vein better left unopened—and it might well have been if he hadn't come here to live.

The kids passed the chicken around. Solemn now, each smeared some of the "blood" on their foreheads. One girl almost broke the mood by declaring she was not going to touch something so gross, but the boy next to her did it for her, loudly declaring she was a wuss. The dark-haired girl fiercely told them to shut up. "You're spoiling it!" There was no question about her own dedication.

Throughout, Duncan watched intently. If the scene had not been filled with such potentially evil symbolism, Samantha began to think, it would have been pathetic. Duncan was pitifully thin and his chest concave. All the kids seemed to have spent more time indoors than out; and if they were robust, they were overly so—tending in one boy's case to obesity.

"Do you know everybody?" Samantha whispered to Arlene.

"Yeah, I'll tell you later. It's what we've been saying—loser kids. But sometimes it's not their fault, like Karen over there.

Her old man beats her pretty badly. Everybody knows it." It was the girl with the dark hair.

Now Samantha did want to leave and she poked Fred. They started to back away from the ledge.

"Let the games begin!" Duncan threw off his robe and turned on the music again, louder. He grabbed a beer, chugged it down, threw the empty can high into the air, and stripped off his pants. The beer can clattered down the rock and rolled off into the darkness.

"We are all and all is in us. Join with the darkness. Cast off your garments." He'd definitely been reading more than comics, Samantha thought. His language was getting positively gothic.

"Nobody wants to see your dick, Duncan," one of the girls said. "And besides, I'm not allowed to take my clothes off. My mother says so."

Duncan looked at her with scorn. "You are not a true sister of blood."

"I'm not a sister of anybody here. If you're going to get foolish, I'm leaving."

A few others stirred and Duncan appeared to weigh losing his audience against maintaining his noble position. He decided to go for the numbers and pulled his jeans back on. "All right. Let's go climbing instead." This appeared to find more favor. Armed with beers and smokes, they set off, teetering dangerously close to the edge of the quarry precipice.

"Someone's going to get killed!" Samantha started forward.

"No, come on. We'll make an anonymous call to Earl from the CB in my pickup. They're not going to stop because we tell them to," Fred advised.

The three climbed down to the woods below and went back to the truck as fast as they could.

"Assholes," Fred was muttering. "And Duncan's the worst. After we call, I want to see what's in that trunk of his.

Obviously, the black stuff was the thing he was wearing. He is really into it."

Sensibly, Arlene pointed out that as soon as Earl got the news, he'd be up at the quarry and they'd come running back to the cabin.

"Another time, then," Fred said.

Samantha wasn't so sure. The day had been filled with images of blood—intended images: the gory sails that greeted them in the clear light of the morning and the streaked faces around the flames in the dark of night. Another time? She'd have to think about it.

The next morning Pix was putting away her chowder pot. She must have been more fatigued than she'd thought to have left it on the beach. Louise had dropped it off. As Pix was pushing it up onto the top shelf in the pantry, the lid fell, clattering to the floor and narrowly missing the side of her head. As she put the pot down and bent to retrieve the lid, she discovered a large Tupperware bowl had inadvertently been placed inside. She opened it up and found a few cookie crumbs. A piece of masking tape clearly marked BAINBRIDGE was on the bottom. The two women had brought a number of desserts to the clambake and this must have been an offering Pix had missed. The crumbs smelled delicious. She washed the bowl out and decided to go to the village to drop it off. Norman might be around and she could pick up some more information about fake antiques. She'd also like to get him alone to ask him about Mitchell Pierce. Mitch dealt with museums, and presumably a New York dealer in the know would be familiar with Mitch's name, even if there hadn't been any business transacted between them. She'd try him on Mother's Brewster chair story again, too.

Pix could not shake the feeling there was something that didn't quite ring true about Norman. She was trying hard to be objective about him and knew that a good part of her mistrust had to do with his Big Apple shine. Then too there were few strangers on the island. There were tourists and people who rented cottages for a week or so, but Norman—someone from away—had managed to insinuate himself into everyday island life to an alarming degree. Why, he'd even been at the Frazier's clambake! Things, especially socially, moved slowly on Sanpere and people waited a decent interval, say ten years, before expecting invitations.

Why was Norman here? She knew what was purported. There was that word again. It reminded her of Mitch. "Purported" activities. Norman and Mitch. Dealers in antiques. Norman had arrived on the island well before the murder. Where was he at the time?

There was a lot to work into a conversation.

Driving down Route 17 past the turnoff for Little Harbor, she wished Faith were around and resolved to call her later to talk about these misgivings. Pix turned into the Bainbridge's drive, stopped the car, and got out. The property had once included many acres to the rear and on both sides, but the land had been sold long ago, leaving the farmhouse and barn. The first thing to greet her was the sound of hammering. Curious, she followed the noise and discovered Seth Marshall and someone obviously working for him inside the barn, replacing a beam.

"Seth!" He dropped his hammer in surprise.

"Now, Pix, I have to keep busy. The police won't let me out there yet."

"But it could be tomorrow. Well, not the Fourth, but maybe the next day, and you'll be all tied up here!" She was livid. The Fairchild house was becoming a dream one, literally.

"I told Aunt Addie I would have to stop once I got the go-ahead on another project. Don't worry." Seth spoke soothingly and tried flashing an ingratiating grin. It made him look more like Peck's Bad Boy than ever and Pix was not mollified.

"I'll give Earl a call and see if we can get some idea of how much longer they need. Goodness knows, they should be finished by now. I think you had better plan to start Thursday at the latest."

"Which means working here tomorrow," the other man muttered angrily, stopping the rest of his complaint after a glance from the boss.

"Thursday will be fine. Now, please, remember I want to get started as much as you do."

Pix certainly hoped so, said as much and good-bye, then walked out into the sunshine and over to the house. "Aunt Addie" indeed, although she could really be his aunt, or more likely, great-aunt. The whole island was connected by ties of varying degrees of kinship.

Rebecca answered the door—the back door, of course. A bed of ferns had grown up over the front steps and Pix thought it unlikely that the door with its shiny brass knocker in the shape of an anchor had been opened since James Bainbridge had been carried out in his coffin. It would never have done to take him the back way through the kitchen.

"Who is it?" a querulous voice called out. "Don't just leave whoever it is standing with their chin hanging out! Invite them in!"

Rebecca ignored Addie's remarks and reached for the Tupperware bowl.

"Oh, Pix, am I glad to see this. I couldn't remember where I had mislaid it, but I knew I had it at the clambake, because I'd filled it with butterscotch shortbread* that morning."

She *had* missed something good, Pix thought, stepping into the room. The Bainbridge's shortbread was another of those secret family recipes.

"I'm glad I found it. It was in my chowder pot and I might have put it away without opening it until next year, but the top fell off the pot when I was putting it on the shelf."

"The Lord works in mysterious ways," Rebecca said confi-

*See recipe page 286.

dently, then led Pix to the front parlor, where Addie was somehow managing to keep herself poised on the slippery horsehair Bainbridge fainting couch. Pix knew that it was a fainting couch because Adelaide had told her once, adding, perhaps unnecessarily, "not that it has ever been used as one." Oddly enough, today she did seem a bit under the weather. She wore a housecoat that made her look like a large pink-and-orange-flowered tea cozy. Her legs were stretched out and she apologized for wearing her bedroom slippers.

"The heat is some terrible for my circulation; I can't even get my shoes on this morning. I told Rebecca to order the next-biggest size, but she forgot and got the same as always."

"We could send them back. It wouldn't be any trouble."

"Well, it would be for me. What will I do for footwear while they're gone, I'd like to know?" She kept right on going: "And there must have been something I et at the clambake that didn't sit right—not that I think for a moment it was your chowder, deah," she added, looking Pix straight in the eye. The intent was clear. Now was the moment for Pix to confess to buying suspect fish and last year's potatoes. Pix stared right back. Nobody else had suffered from the chowder in the slightest and Addie's indisposition was more than likely a case of overindulgence. Addie was starting to catalog her major symptoms, such as severe diarrhea and stomach cramps, rather graphically when Rebecca tactfully broke in.

"Pix brought our Tupperware bowl back, the one we thought was lost at the clambake. It was in her chowder pot."

Adelaide beamed as if she'd recovered the family jewels instead of an airtight storage container. "It's hard to get good Tupperware nowadays and I won that at one of Dot Prescott's parties when she was selling Tupperware. I don't know who's doing it now."

Pix tried to steer the conversation away from plastics to antiques and Norman.

"It must be interesting having an antiques dealer like Norman Osgood as a guest." The Bainbridges always called their bed-and-breakfast customers "guests."

"Oh my, yes, he's been a treat. The stories that man can tell. We sit and laugh for hours."

Rebecca didn't look quite so merry, and Pix wondered whether she was included in these funfests.

"Is he around now? I had a question I wanted to ask him."

"No, he's off on one of his jaunts today. Be back in time for the parade tomorrow, he said. What's your question? I'll ask him for you."

Pix had been afraid Addie would say this and was now thankful she'd prepared a mythical inquiry about the best way to take care of an old Sheraton dresser her mother was giving her.

"Just keep it clean with a dust cloth," Rebecca advised, "if the wood is not too dry and the finish still good."

"And what do you know about the care of valuable antiques, Rebecca Bainbridge? I don't recall too many down in that shack you grew up in. No, Pix. I swear by Olde English and plenty of it. You can't go wrong there."

Faith could smell it had been put to good use in the parlor. She looked anxiously at Rebecca. It might have been that Addie had gone too far.

"Your own husband was raised in that 'shack,' Addie, and you're lying on Grandmother's couch this very moment. I guess we had just as many nice things as you did out at the lighthouse."

Pix was glad to hear Rebecca answering back. It didn't happen very often.

"You couldn't have had many, then," Addie one-upped her. "I slept on a cot in the kitchen and there wasn't a decent piece of furniture in the place. The only thing worth any money at all was the light, and that belonged to the government. Now where are my regular glasses? You've gone and fetched the wrong ones, as usual! Can't see a thing with these."

"Those are the right ones. Remember, you put a piece a tape on the frame so we wouldn't get mixed up. There it is, plain as the nose on your face."

Addie pulled her glasses off. "Can't see a danged thing. You must have put tape on both."

Before the fur could fly any faster, Pix made her farewells with promises to sit together at the parade the next day. The Bainbridge's lawn sloped agreeably down to Main Street and was a perfect viewing stand.

"And don't forget your mother!" Addie called after her.

As if I would—or could, Pix thought.

After leaving the Bainbridges, she felt a little betwixt and between. Sam was on a long cruise to Swans Island with a sailing buddy and Samantha was still at work. She thought she might pop in to Jill's store and pick up a baby sweater made by one of the women on the island that The Blueberry Patch stocked. One of Pix's cousin's children was having a baby, which would make Ursula a great-great-aunt and make Pix a what, a cousin some number of times removed?

Removed. She realized Mitchell Pierce's death had removed her from her normal embedded island feelings. She had the constant sense that she was on the outside looking in, not because she was from away but because there were things going on she couldn't quite make out. She had the illusion that if she could only squint hard enough, she'd be able to make out the shapes.

Jill was at the register. The store was empty.

"Hi, Pix," she said. She had been working on her accounts evidently and now shoved a large ledger under the counter. The cash register was an antique—and not for sale. It had been a fixture in the previous store to occupy the space, a cobbler's shop owned by Jill's grandfather.

"My cousin's daughter is having a baby soon and I want to send a sweater."

"Do they know what they are having? I always think that sounds so odd, but you know what I mean?"

"Yes, I do, and they don't, so the sweater had better be white or yellow."

After taking a pleasurable amount of time, Pix took her purchase to the front of the shop. It was always fun to buy baby gifts. A few years earlier, she used to toy with the idea of another bundle of joy herself, then remembered all the home-work supervision that would entail and opted to wait for grandchildren—a wait she fervently prayed would be a long one.

Earl had come in while she'd been in the back and was buy-ing a paper.

"How are you, Pix?" he asked, "Quite a business yesterday at the camp. Samantha was great with the kids. Really kept them calmed down."

"Fine, thank you, and thank you for saying that about Samantha. I'll tell her. She's always wanted to go into science, marine biology, but she's so good with people."

"Maybe she'll figure out a way to combine the two. Now I've got to go pick up something to eat at the IGA or I'll start to get malnutriated."

Earl looked anything but. Pix smiled. Jill didn't. Hadn't they patched things up yet?

The next exchange made it clear they hadn't.

"So, I'll see you about eight?" Earl asked.

"I'm afraid I can't make it tonight. Maybe another time," Jill answered. The time, from her expression and tone, could possibly be well into the new century.

"Okay." Earl flushed and left quickly.

Pix was tempted to ask what was going on, but Jill did not look as if she'd welcome inquiries into her personal life at the moment. She rang up the purchase and Pix was soon out on the walk planning a dinner party with a few friends, mainly Earl and Jill—soon.

She got into her car and noticed Earl was parked next to her. It was the perfect time to tell him about the mark on the quilt, if he was not too distracted by his own affairs of the heart. But Pix doubted it. Work was work. The notebook would be out in no time, just the way it had the day before at the camp. When they'd arrived, it was the first thing she had noticed. There was Earl standing before the bloody red sails, calmly writing down each and every word.

He was at his car soon, carrying what she knew to be one of the IGA's Italian sandwiches—bologna, salami, and cheese on some sort of large hot dog roll. It also had green peppers and onions if those were to hand and a drizzle of Italian dressing, hence the appellation.

"Earl, have you got a minute? There's something I've been meaning to tell you. It's probably nothing, yet I thought you should know."

The notebook came out. He clicked his pen.

Mercifully, they were parked behind the post office. They might be news, but not big news, particularly if she spoke fast. She explained about finding the mark on the quilt she'd bought—a mark identical to the one on the red-and-white quilt.

"I know you told me. It's a blue cross, right? Like this?" He drew one on the pad.

"Yes, maybe a bit smaller. I wouldn't have noticed it on the one around the body if the quilt had had more colors. Then in the one I bought, it just seemed to jump out at me."

"Do you have any idea what it could stand for?"

"It could be some kind of family laundry mark. Both quilts may have come from Sullivan. I mean, that's where the antiques dealer said the quilt was from, and Mitch was living in Sullivan when he died. The red-and-white one may have been taken from his room."

Earl agreed. "That makes sense. Although I'm not sure

what kind of link there could be. He hadn't been in his room for some days before he was killed, according to his landlady, but she admitted he could have been there one of the times she was out doing errands."

"There's another possibility. Much as it pains me to realize I may have been duped, I think the quilt I bought could be a fake. The price was suspiciously low. I have a book about dating quilts and I'm going to go through it to try to establish when mine was made. If it's a modern one, as I suspect, the mark could be a way whoever was faking the quilts kept track of which were real and which weren't."

Earl looked at Pix admiringly. "Good thinking. Obviously, we don't want it spread around, but we're pretty sure Mitch was involved with one or more of the antique scams. Unfortunately, he was also involved in some other tricky businesses, so the field is pretty broad." His face fell a bit.

He continued: "So that's why you were asking all those questions on Sunday."

"Yes," Pix admitted.

"Look, I'd like to photograph the mark and see how it matches with the one that was wrapped around Pierce's body. I've got my camera in the trunk. All right if I come over and take a picture now? I'll be able to send it to Augusta right away. They may also have something in their files about it."

"Sure," Pix agreed. She was excited. They were beginning to get somewhere. Maybe.

As Earl got into his car, he called over to her, "By the way, since you're turning out to be so interested in detective work, how about finding out why my girl is giving me the cold shoulder?"

Pix was sorry to disappoint him. "I'll try, but I'm sure it's nothing much. You two have been together a long time."

" 'Nothing much,' " Earl was uncharacteristically sarcastic. "Do you think the fact that she had dinner with Seth Marshall last night might mean something? The entire island and half the mainland saw them down at the inn."

Pix did not have an answer.

Nor did she have an answer shortly thereafter when she spread out the new quilt on her living room floor.

"Where is this mark?"

She looked. Then looked again.

It was gone.

"I felt like a fool. Fortunately, I thought to get one of Samantha's magnifying glasses and I showed him where the holes were. There had definitely been something sewn there."

The first thing Pix had done after the police car had pulled away from the house was call Faith. She was at work.

"But this proves that the marks mean something." Faith was excited. "Why am I stuck down here making blueberry pies and coleslaw, not to mention a cake in the shape of an eagle some patriotic soul has ordered, while you're having all the fun!"

Pix thought of Mitch and the incidents at the camp. It wasn't exactly what she'd call fun, but Faith tended to view life a bit differently.

"I wish you were here, too. Sam has to leave after the parade. He's got a client coming in early Thursday morning. It must be someone important, because it's not like Sam to miss the fireworks. Since he's been here, I've realized how nice it is to have another adult around. Samantha is wonderful company, but she's at work or off with her friends. In fact, I think she's doing too much. She looked terrible at breakfast—as if she hadn't slept a wink, but she says she's fine."

"Well, what did you used to tell your mother? Speaking of whom, she certainly qualifies as an adult. Why don't you get her to come over for a while? No, that's not right. That's not what you need."

Faith knew her so well, Pix thought. Much as she loved her mother, it would not provide the ease she was seeking.

"Even before we got here, I asked her to come until my brother arrives. I don't like to think of her alone in that big house, but she wants to be on her own, and when we're her age, we'll be exactly the same."

"I should hope so. Now, back to the quilt. Obviously, nothing else in the cottage was disturbed or you would have said so."

"Right, and yes, I did leave the door unlocked as usual. There's nothing of value here, and it's such a nuisance for Samantha to carry a key. I have one with my car keys, but I can't remember the last time I used it."

These New Englanders, Faith thought to herself. The unlocked door represented their trust in humankind and belief in a certain way of life: "Come in; it's off the latch." And she knew Pix would still keep her doors unlocked even now. What would it take? Faith hoped Pix would never find out.

"I've been doing some detective work for you in between shucking corn for corn pudding and the like. There was an article on quilt making in the paper. You remember that controversy about the Smithsonian's decision to reproduce some of the quilts in their collection using overseas labor? That's what it's about mainly, however it started me thinking. These new quilts could be made to look old, particularly if they are unmarked. I think the Smithsonian ones have an indelible tag on the back, but a lot of mail-order companies and department stores offer quilts. I doubt they're all labeled so conscientiously. Anyway, I mailed the article to you and you should get it by Thursday."

"It's pretty easy to spot some of the reproduction quilts, even if they are made by hand, because the stitching is uneven and there are fewer stitches to the inch. Handmade quilts, like the one I got in Pennsylvania last year, have ten to twelve stitches."

"What about this one? How many does it have?"

"Ten in most places, more in a few others."

"But it could still be a new one made to look old."

"Yes, and that's what I have to do now—figure out for sure if it's a fake. Then I can tell Earl to have an expert look at the

one the police have. I also thought I might do some more antiquing and see if I turn up any more marked quilts."

"So what else is going on up there—or I should say down
there?"

Pix had patiently explained to Faith her first summer on the
island what Down East meant. The term dated from the days
when the coastal towns of Maine were part of an active exchange of goods with the port of Boston. Timber, quarried
stone, and of course fish were sold to purchase manufactured
goods from Massachusetts. Since the coast curves eastward as
it heads north to Nova Scotia and since the prevailing winds
from Boston to Maine are southerly, a sloop sailing before the
wind, downwind, from Boston to Bangor was headed down
east. Pix made Faith learn it until she was letter-perfect, but
although she was sure she had the words right, it had never
made a whole lot of sense to Faith. Up was north and down
was south. And Maine was north.

"The clambake was great, but the weather's been much too
hot."

"It's the same here. Thank goodness this place is air-condi-
tioned. It's a relief to come to work. The parsonage may self-
ignite, it's so stuffy—even with fans going. Tom's afraid the
window frames are too fragile for an air conditioner, but if the
heat keeps up, I will personally pay to have the old ones
ripped out and new ones put in, never mind the blasphemy. I
know God allows New Englanders to be very cold in the winter and very hot in the summer because they prefer to suffer
in this way, but I'm tired of taking the kids to work or to a
movie when I want them to cool off!"

Pix felt a twinge of guilt. She was on the Parish Buildings
and Grounds Committee, which, among other things, saw
to the upkeep of the parsonage. No one had ever raised the
notion of air conditioning. The Millers had never had it,
and Faith was no doubt right—some of Pix's fellow committee members would definitely classify it as wickedly self-
indulgent.

They talked a bit more, then Faith let out a shriek. "Got to go! Amy's at the pies!"

With a vivid picture of a toddler smeared from head to toe with blueberry pie, gleefully licking her hands, Pix hung up. She was on her own.

She spread the quilt out on the floor and opened her book, *Clues in the Calico* by Barbara Brackman. It had been bedtime reading the last few nights. She leafed through it, then set to work. First, she considered the fabric: lots of small-figured calicos, some shirting material. The abundance of brown-colored triangles indicated a pre-1900 quilt, a time when this was a very popular color. It wasn't used much again until the 1960s and was still favored. She took her scissors and turned the quilt over, snipping a piece of thread, then pulling out a few stitches. With a fine needle, she unraveled it and looked at the strands through Samantha's magnifying glass—Six-ply. That meant post-1860. She was narrowing the date down. Maybe the quilt was genuine after all and she had scored a terrific coup. She teased a bit of the batting from between the top and backing and rubbed the fibers between her fingers.

Her heart sank. It was very cleverly done. The thickness of the batting mimicked what would have been used earlier. But they did not have polyester in the late 1800s. It could be an old top newly quilted. With that optimistic thought, she turned the quilt over and spread it out again. On hands and knees she looked at each and every triangle and at one fabric design in particular. It appealed to her, as it had when she bought a yard of it herself last year.

Pix closed the book and carefully folded up her quilt, laying it across the back of the couch. She stroked the fabric. No question, no question at all: The whole thing was as phony as a three-dollar bill.

The Miller family was quiet at dinner that night. Pix had set the table, rather than eat on the deck, in honor of her husband's presence and also as a nod to the gracious living à la

Valerie Atherton that Samantha continued to espouse. They had cold blueberry soup, a big salad with fresh crabmeat, rice, sweet red peppers, and plenty of lettuce. There were some of Luella Prescott's rolls and ice cream for dessert. Nothing was even remotely connected with Pix's having to turn on her stove.

"This is good, Mom. Did you make it?" Samantha asked, tilting her bowl to get the last of the soup.

Pix was tempted to reply, "No, the fairies left it on my doorstep," but chagrin at her culinary reputation and the soft glow of the candles she'd put on the table tempered her reply. "Yes, I did." She paused. "Faith gave me the recipe."

Sam and his daughter both laughed and Sam said, "The important thing is that you made it and we're eating it. You have many other talents."

Which were? Pix waited for him to go on. When he didn't, she got up to get the salad. Samantha followed with the soup bowls—the unmatched ones.

"I was at the Atherton's house today. Jim asked me to take some mail over to Valerie that had come to the camp by mistake. You should see it. It's like something from a magazine."

Jim and Valerie, it had come to this.

Oblivious to her mother's lack of interest, Samantha prattled on and on about the house: the two-story fieldstone fireplace—"And Valerie selected every rock herself"—the artwork, the Italian leather couch, apparently large enough to accommodate Michelangelo's *David*—if he could sit, of course. Pix felt increasing giddy as she listened to her daughter repeat the tour Valerie Atherton had given her. Simpler to put it on video.

"Salad's ready. Get the plates, will you?"

Samantha placed the three plain white ironstone plates on the table. One had a tiny chip.

"Get another one, Samantha, and put that one aside, please," Pix said grandly. She'd stick it back in the pile when Samantha was otherwise occupied.

                              * * *

The Fourth of July was supposed to be sunny and it was. The
sky was supposed to be blue and it was. The Millers were supposed to be sitting on lawn chairs brought from home, waiting for the parade to start at 10:00 A.M., and they were. The
only thing that felt odd to Pix was that she didn't have any
children to remind not to run into the street or get over-
heated. Samantha was lined up with the camp at the far end of
Main Street, waiting to march, and of course her other two
were far, far away. Not even a postcard or a call yet. Such was
a mother's fate.

Her own mother was on one side, Sam on the other. Various friends and relatives of the Bainbridges, as well as the B
and B guests were strung out in a line. Pix waved to Elliot
Frazier, who was perched with the other judges in chairs set
up on the porch roof of the old Masonic Hall. It was the ultimate viewing platform. Louise was down on the ground next
to Ursula.

"I think Elliot agrees to judge every year just so he can go
up on the roof," Louise said. "The view must be magnificent."

"Where's Adelaide?" Ursula asked Rebecca, who was
coming down the lawn carrying a big pitcher of cold lemonade and some cups. It was already hot and she was greeted
enthusiastically.

"She'll be along. She's feeling a little poorly this morning.
Must be the humidity."

Pix didn't wonder Adelaide was suffering. With all the
extra weight she carried, this weather must be brutal.

John Eggleston appeared, chairless, and plopped down at
Pix's feet.

"Am I in your way?"

"Not at all. It's good to see you."

Pix had always liked John, despite his being odd, even for a
place that tolerated a wide range of differences in human nature. It wasn't merely his appearance, his shoulder-length

wiry red hair and bushy red beard made him unique, especially since there was usually sawdust, and occasionally wood shavings, in both. Nor was it his reluctance to discuss his past life, although Pix knew that as a priest he had served a large church somewhere in the South. She'd also learned something about why he left, but not from him—rather, from Faith. There were lots of people who came to Maine to start fresh, leaving certain doors firmly closed. In his present incarnation as wood sculptor, John's talent was enormous and widely recognized. He received orders for carvings from all over the world and specialized in religious objects. The last time she'd been in his studio, he was working on a huge menorah. "I did not lose my faith," he'd told her once, "just my head."

But what made him unusual was his unpredictability. You never knew what kind of mood he would be in. Pix had seen towering rage and quiet gentleness. The kids on the island flocked to him for advice and it was only with them that he seemed able to maintain his equilibrium. Pix thought of these younger people as his new parish. Arlene had told the Millers many stories about the help John had quietly given to one or another child. Today he seemed mellow and gave Ursula a big smile. She was a favorite.

"What's the theme this year?" he asked her.

"I believe it's storybook characters, but I think it's being interpreted rather loosely in some cases. I know the Fishermen's Wives Association has constructed a lobster boat, and I can't think of a book to go with that."

Ursula was managing to look completely cool in a crisp white blouse and navy skirt. She'd tied a red silk scarf around her neck in honor of the day. A sunshade was clipped to the side of her chair and its resemblance to a parasol lent Mrs. Rowe a timeless air.

"It's a new book, Mother, based on a true story. Two twenty-pound lobsters got caught in a dragger's net and ended up way down in Rhode Island. They were sold to a seafood dealer and eventually went on display in some fish store in Philadelphia. Somewhere along the line, someone named them Bob and Shirley. Anyway, people got upset seeing them in the tank and wanted the owner to set them free. They were flown back up here and released!"

Ursula was laughing. "I want to read that book! Of course, if they'd been caught in a trap, they would have had to be released right away, since they were oversized. But this way, they got to do some traveling."

"It's starting!" someone called out. The crowd along the parade route had grown considerably. The high school band was playing "It's a Grand Old Flag" and another Sanpere Fourth of July was marching along its invariable course. First came the kids on their decorated bikes. Pix remembered how excited she'd been as a child to thread crepe-paper streamers through the spokes of her Schwinn, then ride grandly with the others at the head of the parade. Except for the color scheme and crepe paper, today's bikes looked radically different, although two or three were relics obviously handed down by a previous generation. After the bikes came the school band.

"Isn't that Arlene's boyfriend?" Sam asked.

Pix nodded. Fred had been completely transformed by his drum major's uniform, gold braid dripping from his shoulders and sparkling in the sun as he solemnly raised and lowered the baton. It was a very important position. Fred was class president, too.

"Nice kid," John commented. "I guess he'll be the fourth generation to lobster from Ames Cove, although things have certainly changed since his great-great-grandfather used to go out with nothing more than his traps, buoys, a compass, a watch, and a hank of rope with a weight on it to tell him how deep the water was around the ledges."

"It's simpler now," Sam said, "and safer, yet some of the romance is gone. I think it every time I see the plastic buoys, instead of the old wooden ones they carved, and the new traps."

"The new traps weigh less, same with the buoys, and both don't require the kind of upkeep as the old ones. But I'm with you, aesthetically—maybe even practically. Sonny Prescott told me the other day he's not so sure all the new computers are helping the industry. Makes it too easy, and God knows these waters are being overfished enough." John seemed to be off and running on a favorite topic and Sam was ready to join him, but Pix didn't feel like hearing about the demise of the island's fishing economy today. She wanted to enjoy her lobster at the noon Odd Fellows Lobster Picnic without worrying about the cost of bait and later at the Fish and Fritter Fry she didn't want to think about the growing scarcity of clams. As her friend Faith Fairchild was wont to say, "Denial ain't just a river in Egypt."

"Look at the children. Imagine making all those lobster costumes! Aren't they precious!" The lobster-boat float had to be a major contender for Most Original. The boat itself was a miracle of construction, papier-mâché over chicken wire, and the red-clad children gleefully wriggled about its hull snapping their "claws" at the parade viewers.

Barton's lumberyard sponsored a huge float with Mother Goose figures and the cannery had opted for Alice in Wonderland. Sonny Prescott drew a big round of applause as Robert McCloskey's Burt Dow, Deep-Water Man, dragging his double-ender, *The Tidely-Idley*, complete with rainbow stripes, set on wheels behind him.

"He must be roasting in all that foul-weather gear; they'll probably give him Most Foolish for that alone," Sam commented.

"More lemonade, Pix?" asked Rebecca.

"Yes, thank you, but let me help you." Suddenly, Pix realized she'd been so intent on the parade, she'd forgotten about Rebecca, who was dispensing lemonade and now cookies in the hot sun. "Does Addie feel any better?"

Before Rebecca could answer, Norman Osgood, coming toward them from the house, beat her to it. "She says she's fine.

158

Just wants to be left in peace—that's a direct quote—and she'll see everybody later." He took the pitcher from Rebecca's hands and started pouring. "I brought your hat," he said, and plunked an old leghorn—her grandmother's?—on Rebecca's head. Handy man to have around, Pix thought. He was beginning to seem more like a member of the family and less like a guest all the time.

"Oh, Norman, thank you," Rebecca gushed. "This is so much better." She turned to Pix. "It's my gardening hat; actually, it was Mother's. The straw makes it light."

Pix was off by one generation, yet, who knew where Rebecca's mother had picked it up. Rebecca's garden was one of the showplaces of the island. She did put in some vegetables, at Addie's insistence, but they were behind the house. In front and on the sides were Rebecca's borders, plus an old-fashioned cutting garden. Her roses never suffered from Japanese beetles and her delphinium, in intense blues and lavenders, had been known to stop traffic during the tourist season.

"Look, it's Samantha! Samantha!" Pix called, and was rewarded with a brief acknowledgment. The campers, singing lustily, dressed in immaculate Maine Sail Camp T-shirts and crisp pine tree green shorts marched in perfect synchrony, stopping opposite the judge's platform to flip their cards to form a perfect replica of Old Glory. They then crouched down so the crowd could see and flipped the cards again, displaying for all the message: HAPPY FUCK OF JULY, SANPERE ISLAND! written on the hull of a sloop with yet another flag for its sail. The prankster had struck again. A gasp went up from the crowd and the judges all stood up simultaneously like puppets on strings, peering down from the roof. The children knew something was wrong, and predictably, Samantha's adorers moved in her direction. Jim, attired like his charges in the camp uniform, except with long pants, was shouting, "Put the cards down! Put the cards down!" Ranks broke and the campers raced for the bank parking lot, parade's end, to the

strains of "Anchors Aweigh" as the band played valiantly on.
"I can't believe Duncan would do this. Not after what happened on Monday!"

"Why do you assume Duncan did it?" John asked. Pix was struck by the protective tone in his voice.

"Well," she wavered, "he seems to be very angry at his parents and there have been a number of incidents at the camp, unpleasant things happening."

"Yes, I know," John said impatiently, "but that doesn't necessarily mean it's Duncan. Lots of kids fight with their parents and don't chop the heads off mice."

"Whoever did it, it was a horrible thing to do. They've been working on the parade routine for days!"

The old fire engine, bells ringing and crank-operated siren blaring, was bringing up the rear of the parade. It effectively put an end to any conversation, and Pix, for one, was glad.

She stood up and stretched, trying to recapture the mood of the day. "Anybody going to the children's games? Why don't we walk up and leave the car here," she added to her husband.

"Darling." He kissed her earlobe, "You don't have any children in the games anymore. We don't have to go and watch our progeny dissolve in tears when the egg rolls off the spoon or the balloon breaks when they try to catch it and they get soaking wet. There are other things we can do. Things at home. Grown up things."

Pix blushed. She couldn't help herself. Mother was here.

"I know, sweetheart, but the camp will be there. I'm sure everyone is quite upset, and Samantha may need help."

"All right, we can check in, however I doubt Samantha needs or wants us. She's doing a fine job on her own, and remember, I have to leave straight from the picnic."

Pix remembered. She went to thank Rebecca and say goodbye to everyone. Ursula was going to the picnic with the Fraziers.

"Go home with your husband and help him pack, Pix," her mother said with a very amused look in her eye.

Saying good-bye to Sam had been hard. He would try to get up again for a long weekend, but the likelihood was that they wouldn't see each other until August. She didn't want to think about it. They'd checked in with Samantha at the games and the kids were not as upset as Pix had feared, especially since the judges had awarded them the prize for Best Walking Group. Everyone was studiously ignoring the incident, except for some of the younger campers who were still giggling. Samantha's sidekicks, Susannah and Geoff, were among the worst. They would get in control, glance at each other, and burst out laughing again. Pix watched in amusement herself at her daughter's struggles to be firm with the two. Samantha had told her that their initial homesickness had quickly given way to a friendship based mainly on a mutual love of corny "Knock, Knock" jokes and mischief.

Jim and Valerie were overseeing the three-legged races, laughing just the right amount as they partnered unlikely combinations—fifteen-year-olds with five-year-olds. Everyone seemed to be having fun. Duncan was nowhere in sight. Samantha's camp duties ended after the Odd Fellows Lobster Picnic and she told her mother not to worry, which Pix correctly interpreted as meaning mother would not see daughter until midnight. She was tempted to extend Samantha's curfew—it *was* a holiday—yet the girl was still looking pale, quite unlike her usual hale and hearty self. Pix wondered whether anything was wrong—unrelated to health. Samantha had seemed preoccupied for the last few days. Of course with everything that was happening, this was a reasonable response. But Pix's motherly intuition was picking up more, her antennae were twitching. She'd try to talk to her daughter later. Maybe the two of them would drive to Ellsworth for dinner and a movie tomorrow night. She needed to get her in the car for a good long drive.

Pix spread her blanket out on a choice spot on the library hill overlooking Sanpere Harbor and waited to see who would join her for the fireworks. They were due to start at 9:00 P.M. and it was 8:30 now. You had to arrive early to grab a good place. Her mother had decided to forgo the fireworks this year, as she had for the last two years. The first summer she'd declared she was going to bed early and had seen enough fireworks to last the rest of her life had Pix ready to check her mother into Blue Hill Hospital for a thorough examination. Ursula loved fireworks—or so she had always claimed. "It's the beginning of the end," Pix had told Sam mournfully. "First fireworks, then she'll stop going out of the house altogether." Sam had reacted less dramatically. "Just because your mother doesn't want to sit on the damp ground with hundreds of people chanting *ooh* and *aah* while they get cricks in their necks plus kids running around throwing firecrackers, waving sparklers in everyone's faces, doesn't mean she's cashing in her chips." And of course he'd been right. But Pix didn't like things to change.

Well, her mother had made it both to the Lobster Picnic and the Fish and Fritter Fry. Few Rowes would miss the chance to eat lobster, dripping melted butter and lobster juice all over themselves and their neighbors at the picnic tables the Odd Fellows erected especially for the occasion in the ball field each year. Some of the older people always reminisced about the days when lobster was so cheap and plentiful that they would beg for something else. Ken Layton, Sanpere's resident historian, would remind everyone that around the time of the Civil War, lobsters, regardless of weight, were two cents apiece—and they pulled in bigger lobsters then. It had all happened again this year and Sam had managed to eat two lobsters, since he was going to miss the Fish and Fritter Fry, but Pix had stopped at one to save room.

She lay back on the rough wool blanket, an old army blanket of her father's, and gazed up at the dark sky. You never saw so many stars in Aleford and certainly not even a quarter in Boston! She felt as if she were peering into a big overturned bowl and the milky white constellations were tumbling out above her. The fireworks would have some competition. It was even a full moon.

Just as she was beginning to feel a bit sorry for herself, no kith nor kin by her side, Jill came and sat down.

"Do you have enough room for me?"

"I have enough room for ten or twelve of you," Pix said, sitting up. "Sam had to go back early and Samantha's off with her friends."

"What a day! Business hasn't been this good in years." Jill was clearly excited. "People stuck around after the parade and I even sold the lobster-pot lamp that one of the Sanfords made. It's been sitting in the store for years."

Pix knew the lamp well. She had threatened to give it to Faith more than once and vice versa. Not only had the resourceful craftsman wired the pot buoy but he had attached netting, cork floats, and, as the pièce de résistance, a whole lobster that glowed when the lamp was turned on. The plain white shade had been lavishly painted with yet more bright red crustaceans.

"That's great, especially about the lamp." Pix laughed.

"Don't worry," Jill said, "you can still have one. He's bringing another one up tomorrow! If I'd known, I might have been able to sell them as a pair!"

"I doubt it. When you buy such an object, you like to think it's one of a kind."

"The only thing about being so busy was that I didn't close for lunch or dinner. I missed the picnic and the fry." Jill sounded very disappointed.

"I think I ate enough for both of us," Pix said. "And everyone at the parade and in your shop must have gone down to Granville for both. I've never seen so many people! Mabel

Hamilton told me they went through three hundred pounds of potatoes, a hundred and sixty pounds of fish, twelve gallons of clams, fifty pounds of onions, and goodness knows how much else for the fry!"

"That's wonderful. All the profits go to the scholarship fund for kids from fishing families, which really helps the island. Those women are amazing. Think of all that peeling."

But Pix was not thinking of peeling potatoes or any other vegetables. She was thinking of what Earl would say. Seth Marshall was standing next to them, obviously waiting for an invitation. Jill gave it.

"You said there was room, didn't you, Pix? Why don't you sit down, Seth." The woman actually patted the blanket. It wasn't that Pix disliked Seth. It was just not the way things were supposed to be. And come to think of it, Seth wasn't exactly flavor of the month.

He appeared to realize this and eyed his hostess a bit warily as he sat down.

"You do know we're pouring tomorrow," Seth said.

"Yes, Earl told me this morning. I'll be there at seven. That about right?"

"You don't really need to be, unless of course you want to," Seth added hastily.

With the start in sight, Pix was feeling generous. "Don't worry, I'm not going to hang around all the time. I just want to see the foundation go in and call Faith." It was the least she could do.

"No problem," Seth replied.

Pix sighed. She had the feeling she'd be hearing this phrase often in the weeks to come. And Seth was also sitting awfully close to Jill. In the moonlight, his resemblance to to one of Captain Kidd's mates was even more pronounced. Maybe Jill found him romantic. Pix thought him hirsute—and suspect. She started to think what he could possibly gain from Mitchell Pierce's demise—she'd never been happy with Seth's explanation for being at the site—when a long shadow fell across the blanket.

"May I join your party?" Norman Osgood asked. Pix was delighted. She might have the chance to work in some of her questions, although with Jill and Seth around, it might be hard to steer the conversation toward Mitchell Pierce. Jill had made it plain that she didn't want to hear anything at all about the subject whenever Pix had referred to the event.

"Are Addie and Rebecca watching from their lawn?" Pix asked.

"No, Addie is still not feeling well and she needs Rebecca. I suggested they go over to the Medical Center or at least call a doctor, but Addie won't hear of it."

"According to my mother, neither lady has ever had any contact with the medical profession," Seth said.

"That's amazing." Norman was astonished. "At their ages. Not even tonsils?"

"If they did have them out, the doctor did it in the kitchen, and since that meant a boat trip in Addie's case, it might never have been done."

Norman was still shaking his head when the first rocket went up and they all said "Aah."

A huge golden chrysanthemum shape filled the sky and the petals dropped slowly toward the sea, leaving trails of golden sand. The show was spectacular. The finale was positively orgasmic and the cries of the crowd grew louder and louder as bursts of color and sound exploded overhead. Then suddenly, it was finished and only smoke hung in the air like dense fog.

Norman sighed happily. "That was wonderful. I love fireworks, especially over the water. I was in a boat on the Hudson for the Statue of Liberty display in 1986. Sublime, but this came close."

"Have you lived in New York City all your life?" Pix asked as a way of starting her inquisition.

"No, my dear, I haven't, however you'll have to wait for the tale, which is a lengthy and enthralling one. I told the Bainbridges I'd be back as soon as the show was over, and I am a little concerned about Adelaide. She hasn't been eating, and you know how she enjoys her table."

Something must be wrong indeed, Pix thought. "Please call me if there's anything I can do. Maybe my mother could convince her to call a doctor."

"I doubt that the Almighty Himself could convince Mrs. Bainbridge to do anything she didn't want to do, but if I think otherwise, I'll call. Thank you."

Pix had the peculiar feeling that Norman had become closer to the Bainbridges than she was—two people she'd known all her life.

Seth picked up on it, too. "Who do you think is adopting who?"

"I'm not sure," Pix said. "Maybe it's mutual."

Jill jumped up and said she was exhausted after her busy day. "All I want to do is collapse." Pix said good-bye to them both and slowly began to fold up her blanket as she watched the crowd disperse—as she watched Jill and Seth go into The Blueberry Patch together.

Duncan Cowley was lying on the mattress in his secret cabin, staring up at the rafters. Long-ago inhabitants had carved their names and various epitaphs into the wood. He'd painted over the ones on the walls in disgust at such sentiments as "Maine Sail Camp. I pine for yew." He was disgusted tonight, as well—and angry. What a bunch of pussies. They knew how important the full moon was and still his friends had deserted him for some stupid fireworks.

The cabin glowed with the candles he'd lighted. He looked at his watch. It was still too early. He closed his eyes yet knew he wouldn't sleep. Restless, he got up and went over to the trunk.

He'd just have to do it alone.

It was a long wait until midnight. Pix had been tempted to call Faith but didn't want to bother her. If she was home, she'd be weary after working the holiday. She hadn't had a chance to tell Faith about the blood red sails at the camp. Amy had diverted her mother's attention just as Pix had remembered she hadn't mentioned the incident to Faith. She'd call tomorrow. Telling Faith what was going on was making things clearer, or, if not clearer, making Pix feel better.

She did call Sam, to make sure he'd gotten home all right. She missed him more than ever when she hung up. Finally, she got into bed with the latest issue of *Organic Gardening* and tried to get interested in mulch. When Samantha did get home, just before the stroke of twelve, Pix called out to her daughter to come say good night.

"Weren't the fireworks awesome? The best ever." Samantha had clearly had a good night. Pix felt less worried.

"Truly awesome," she agreed. "Whom were you with?"

"Oh, the usual people—Fred, Arlene, their friends. How about you?" Samantha sounded slightly anxious.

Oh no, Pix thought, don't tell me Samantha is starting to worry about poor old Mom. The way I do, a still-deeper voice whispered.

"We had quite a crowd on the blanket. I was by the library. Jill, the antiques dealer who's at the Bainbridges, some others." Pix didn't care to get more specific. Samantha was hoping to be a junior bridesmaid at Jill and Earl's wedding.

"That's nice, Mother." Her daughter actually patted her hand. "Now I see you've got your usual exciting bedtime reading, so I won't keep you from it a minute longer."

"Don't you patronize me. And where's my kiss!" Pix grabbed Samantha for a hug. Sam had given them all magazine subscriptions last Christmas: *Organic Gardening* renewed for his wife, *Sassy* for his daughter, and the *Atlantic Monthly* for his mother-in-law. There they were in a nutshell.

Pix drifted off to sleep. Maybe this was a new way to categorize people. She'd have to talk about it with Faith—*The New Yorker*, obviously. And who else? Valerie Atherton, *House Beautiful*, without question, and Jim, *Boys' Life*. Jill? Not *Modern Bride*, not yet anyway.

She thought she was still thinking about magazines, then realized that dawn was streaking across the sky outside in shades of burnt orange and magenta. The phone was ringing. She grabbed the receiver in a panic. Nobody called this early. It was just over the edge of night.

"Pix, Pix, are you awake?"

It was Mother.

"What's wrong? What's happened? Are you all right?" Pix ignored the obvious question. Of course she was awake.

"I want you to get over to the Bainbridges as fast as you can. Addie's dead."

Pix was momentarily relieved. "Oh dear, Mother, what sad news, yet I suppose with this weather, her age and all that weight, it—"

"Rebecca found her on the floor of her bedroom with an old quilt Rebecca's never seen before wrapped around her—a red-and-white quilt."

"I'll be there as soon as I can."

Chapter 7

Once when Mark Miller had been about nine years old, he had inveigled his mother into trying out the new tire swing at the school playground. Somehow, Pix had gotten her feet caught in the rim and for what seemed like a giddy, reeling eternity was unable to stop or get off. The world whirled around. She was almost sick and momentarily terrified. As she pulled into the Bainbridge's drive and opened her car door, she felt as if she was back on that swing.

Rebecca opened the door before Pix could knock. The sight of the grief-stricken old lady, pathetic in a worn flannel robe, her gray hair untidily sticking out in clumps around her face, brought Pix soundly back to earth. She put her arms around the woman and hugged her hard. "I'm sure there's some explanation for all this. Maybe Addie had a quilt you didn't know about, felt cold, and got up to get it." It didn't sound especially plausible, but it was something to say.

Rebecca shook her head. Tears had been filling the soft

wrinkles of her cheeks ever since Pix had arrived and obviously for a long time before that.

Pix looked around the kitchen. Ever since she'd driven up, she'd had a sense something was wrong besides what was so obviously wrong, and now she knew what it was: No one was around. Where was Earl? Where were the B and B guests? The Bainbridges had countless relatives all over the island. Where were they?

Rebecca followed her glance. "Your mother thought I should call Earl, but I just couldn't, so she said she'd do it. I couldn't call anybody except her."

Ladies like Rebecca and Adelaide did not get involved with the police. Well, they were involved now. Pix wondered when Rebecca had discovered the body. But first things first. Rebecca appeared to be in shock.

"Let me make you some tea. Are you warm enough?"

It was already stifling hot again, but Rebecca was shivering. Pix took a jacket from one of the pegs inside the door and put it around Rebecca's thin shoulders. From the size, it must have been Addie's.

"Tea." She managed only the one word and Pix took it as a yes. After a moment, Rebecca finished the thought. "I was on my way to make our morning cups when I went in to check on Addie. She's been poorly lately and I wasn't sure she was awake or, if she was, whether she'd want any." Rebecca sighed heavily. Pix could imagine what would have ensued if her sister-in-law had awakened Addie or brought her a cup of unwanted tea. Yet Addie had been Rebecca's main job in life for so many years, now what was she going to do?

"And there she was, all wrapped up like some kind of parcel. I went over and pulled that strange quilt down. It was her feet first. Then I found her head and she wasn't breathing." Rebecca broke down completely and sobbed noisily. What was taking Earl so long? Pix wondered frantically. She wanted to get Rebecca over to Mother's. Ursula had obviously called her daughter first so someone would be there to take care of

Rebecca, but the best thing of all would be to get her with her old friend. Pix debated waking Norman. He had become so close to the two old ladies. She decided to let Earl handle things and put a mug of tea with lots of sugar in Rebecca's hand. The warmth of the liquid seemed to steady her. She stopped crying to take a few sips.

"Why don't you go up and say good-bye? They'll all be here soon and you won't have a chance."

It was exactly what Pix wanted to do, except she hadn't wanted to leave Rebecca, and it wasn't really to say good-bye.

"Are you sure you'll be all right?"

Rebecca nodded and patted Pix on the hand. There seemed to be a lot of that happening lately. "You're a good girl. Now run up quick. I'll be fine here."

Adelaide's bedroom was a large one in the front of the house. Pix darted up the stairs, glad the rag runner was there to muffle her steps. She wasn't sure how many of the rooms were filled and she didn't want anyone waking up right now.

She turned the old glass doorknob slowly—Rebecca had already obscured any prints—and went in. At first, the room looked empty. The big old four-poster that had been in the family for generations had obviously been slept in, but no one was there now.

Then she saw the quilt. Rebecca had covered the body again. It was so close to the bed as to be almost underneath. Dark red patches in a spiral pattern stood out sharply against the white muslin background, which, as she bent down, she realized was not completely white. There was a second spiral, the material white, with the tiniest of red dots. Dots like pinpricks.

But there was no sign of any blue thread—in a cross or not.

Pix stood up to steel herself. She looked around the room. There was no sign of a struggle. Addie's comb and brush, along with several bottles of scent, Evening in Paris vintage, were arranged neatly on the embroidered dresser scarf gracing the top of the painted Victorian dresser that matched the rest of the furniture in the room. Her quilting frame and the quilt she'd been working on were in one corner, next to a chest filled with sewing supplies. When Pix was a child, Addie had let her play with the button box kept there. Pix suddenly realized she *did* want to say good-bye. She'd been forgetting this was Addie, her friend. She got down close to the body and pulled back the quilt—at the end she'd have expected the feet to be, after Rebecca's description.

It was horrible, and a more lengthy good-bye would have to wait for the funeral service. Rebecca must have assumed Pix wouldn't uncover the body. Adelaide Bainbridge had died in great agony. Her face was contorted in pain and there was a foul smell of vomit. Pix jumped up and headed for the door. This was definitely a police matter.

She almost collided with Earl on the stairs. He put a finger to his lips, so it was obvious he didn't want the whole house roused yet. He also made it plain from a look of annoyance she'd never seen directed at her before that he wasn't pleased with her presence at the scene—or upstairs, at any rate. She passed him quickly.

"What will they do now?" Rebecca asked tremulously as Pix reentered the kitchen.

Pix took the mug for a refill and decided to make herself some tea, as well. Her legs were trembling and it was all she could do to answer Rebecca.

"I'm sure Earl called the state police. They'll probably be here soon. They'll take pictures of everything and ask everyone who's here a lot of questions." She tried to keep her voice steady. It was going to be a bitch was what it was, but she couldn't say that to Rebecca Bainbridge with her companion of many years—and the object of the investigation—lying dead upstairs.

"I hope we can have the funeral tomorrow. Reverend Thompson will do a beautiful service, I know, and Addie liked him so much better than Reverend McClintock, although I never minded him myself. It was the candles on the altar that did it. Addie stopped attending after that until he left." Rebecca was speaking calmly, even affectionately. Pix decided to try to keep her going on the same track. Now was not the time to suggest that a funeral tomorrow was extremely unlikely.

It was the calm before the storm. The state police and the coroner arrived in two cars and the guests were roused. Pix was kept busy making tea and coffee. Norman Osgood seemed to be in almost as bad shape as Rebecca. Besides Norman, there was a couple from Pennsylvania and a young woman from California. The Californian was in the small downstairs room off the parlor the Bainbridges used when they were crowded. She was excited by the drama of it all, she told them breathlessly, bemoaning the fact she was such a heavy sleeper that she had missed everything. Pix was a bit puzzled by this last remark, then realized the woman believed if she had only managed to wake up, she could have caught the perpetrator single-handedly. The perpetrator. The whole thing was insane. Someone going around killing people and then wrapping the bodies in quilts? A lunatic? A serial killer? Who could possibly want to get rid of Adelaide Bainbridge? Pix needed to get to a phone. She had to call Faith.

It was going to be quite a while before she would be able to chat with anyone except the police, she soon realized. First, they questioned Rebecca. Earl thought it might be a good idea for Pix to come with them, since Rebecca was unable to let go of Pix's hand and had sent an imploring look his way. The older woman had been bewildered by all the activity and had sat in a rocker in the kitchen, shrinking away at the arrival of every new stranger.

Adelaide had been sick for a couple of days, she told them, and was no better or worse the night before when she, Rebecca, had looked in on her before going to bed at about ten o'clock. The noise of the fireworks had kept them up a bit later than usual, Rebecca explained, and Addie had been a bit put out. Addie had first felt ill Sunday night after the clambake. They had both assumed it was something she ate, then when it didn't go away, just a touch of summer sickness.

"Summer sickness?" Earl stopped writing for a moment. It was a new one to him.

"You know, the heat and some kind of bug. There's a lot going around." Rebecca seemed surprised that she'd had to explain.

"And she didn't go to the Medical Center?" he asked.

"No, Addie didn't hold much with doctors. Said they'd only send her up to Blue Hill for a lot of expensive tests or tell her to lose some weight, which she already knew she needed to do and wasn't going to." She seemed to be repeating the words verbatim.

"And you didn't hear anything during the night?"

Rebecca shook her head and started to cry. "If only . . ." She couldn't finish. They waited for her to compose herself, which she did, finishing her sentence with "I had" and adding, "There was a bathroom off her room, so even if she was up in the night, I wouldn't have heard her in the back where I am. Sometimes I hear the guests, but after they all came in from the fireworks, I didn't hear a thing until this morning."

"And what was that?"

"Oh, the first birds and a cricket or two. It was still dark. Addie and I have always been early risers."

Pix knew this to be true, but she hadn't known just how early. It made the Rowes, who carried some sort of puritanical gene that made sleeping beyond seven o'clock physically impossible, look like layabouts.

"When you opened the bedroom door, what did you see?"

"Nothing."

"Nothing?" Rebecca was getting flightier as the questions went on, what with birds, crickets, and now this.

"There was no one in the bed or in the room. I thought she was in the bathroom and so I went in to call to her. I didn't want to wake the others, of course. They do like their sleep.

Why, we had a couple here last summer who didn't get up until noon every single day!"

Earl tried to lead her back to the matter at hand.

"You didn't see her, so you called to her at the bathroom door?"

"Oh no, I didn't get that far. Why, you couldn't miss seeing that quilt, and I had no idea Addie was in it until I pulled it off and then it was her feet first and I knew right away she had passed, because they were so still." The tears were running down her cheeks again.

"And you're sure this wasn't one of her own quilts or a quilt that's been in the house."

"Oh no, not a red-and-white one. Addie didn't like them. Said they looked too plain. Hers had lots of colors," Rebecca added admiringly.

"But isn't it possible the quilt was one someone else made and it's been in a drawer or trunk for a while?" Pix gave Earl credit. He knew the ways things happened in these entrenched families. She was sure there were things in the trunks in the attic at The Pines that neither she nor Mother had ever laid eyes on.

"No," Rebecca said firmly. "We cleaned out everything last fall and there isn't a trunk or drawer in the house and barn we didn't go through. Got rid of a lot of rubbish. Made some money from it, too. What people will pay for worthless junk never fails to astonish me."

And that appeared to be that. Earl took Rebecca back to the kitchen and left her under Norman's care. Another state police officer was chatting with the guests. Her grandparents had come from the western Pennsylvania town where the couple had lived all their lives and they were having a grand time playing "What A Coincidence!" and "Do You Know?"

After Rebecca was settled, Earl returned and said to Pix, "So your mother called you first?"

"Yes, I think she wanted someone to be with Rebecca as

soon as possible and I'm not that far away. I'd like to take Rebecca over to Mother's when you're finished. It must be very painful for her to be here."

Earl was shaking his head. "First, Rebecca doesn't call me, then your mother waits God knows how long." He was taking it altogether much too personally.

"They're old ladies. Even a policeman they know as well as you is frightening at a time like this. I'm sure nothing was hurt by the slight delay."

The state police officer looked tired.

"We understand you went upstairs after you arrived." His tone indicated it wasn't clear whether she'd be indicted or not.

"Yes. I wanted to say good-bye." Pix had the grace to lower her eyes.

Earl was getting impatient. "Look, we have to talk to the rest of the people. Pix, what do you make of all this business with the quilts? Beats me how there can be any connection between Mitchell Pierce and the Bainbridges. I doubt he ever did any work for them. Addie wouldn't have trusted him."

"I didn't see any mark on this quilt. Of course I wasn't in the room long and most of it is wrapped around the body. But I agree. I can't see a connection. Although"—she was thinking out loud—"Rebecca just said they sold a lot of things from the barn and attic. Maybe they sold some of it to Mitchell, except I don't know what that tells us."

"Good thinking." Earl was scribbling hurriedly.

"Isn't it possible that a woman her age might forget about a quilt or two?" the officer asked. "There seem to be enough quilts in this house to cover half the beds in the county."

Pix had thought of this, too—and Rebecca was definitely absentminded—but the fact that the quilts around both bodies were the same colors had to be more than a coincidence.

"It's possible—maybe even more than possible. I don't see any reason why you shouldn't take her to your mother's after we ask her about who they sold the stuff to. We'll go over there if we need her for anything. And where are you going to be?"

Pix was glad Earl wanted to stay in touch. She was sure he'd tell her if there was a cross on the quilt and maybe what had killed Addie when he knew. It was hard to believe from the expression on the woman's face that the death had been a natural one.

"After I leave mother's, I want to go over to the camp and tell Samantha what has happened. She's probably wondering where I was this morning and I don't want her to hear the news from someone else. Then I'll go home."

"Okay, but no details at the moment. I know you know how to keep your mouth shut."

Pix thought Earl intended this as a compliment. It also meant she was forgiven for going upstairs. The state policeman was not so cordial. He didn't even look up as she left the room.

Rebecca was still in her night things, but it didn't take her long to change. She seemed relieved to be going to Ursula's. Pix had phoned her mother while Rebecca was getting ready to say they were on their way and admonished her to keep quiet about what had happened.

"It's a little late for that, dear. Half the island has seen the police cars in the drive. Gert told me that when she got here an hour ago and of course I had to tell her Addie was dead. I didn't mention the quilt, but it will get out soon enough. These things always do."

So much for shielding Samantha, Pix thought, but she resolved to stop by the camp, anyway.

Driving Rebecca over to Mother's, Pix was struck by the normalcy of the day going on all around her. Vacationing families were beachcombing alongside the causeway. Someone was taking advantage of the influx of holiday visitors and having a yard sale. The UPS delivery truck barreled past in the opposite direction and old Mr. Marshall sat on his front porch overlooking the brightly painted Smurfs, flamingos, posteriors of fat ladies in bloomers, and other tasteful lawn ornaments that he made for sale in his woodworking shop out back.

"Mother says you're to stay as long as you want," Pix said.

"I know, it's very kind of her, but I don't like to be away from my garden. In this weather, I have to water twice a day. Addie always loved my roses." She was breaking down again. "Now I'll be putting them on her grave."

There was a lot Pix wanted to ask Rebecca. She'd said there hadn't been any strangers around this summer—except for the guests, whom of course they didn't know until they'd been there a while—when Earl had asked her. But Pix wanted to ask about Norman and also whether the Bainbridges had sold anything to Mitch. This last, she was able to work in. Rebecca had quieted down again by the time they turned off the main road. The Pines was at the tip of a small peninsula and often there was water on either side of them. The view of Eggemoggin Reach was spectacular at this point. Today it was filled with sailboats, moving slowly. There wasn't much more wind offshore than on. Pix had a sudden desire to be on one, cruising gently toward the Camden Hills, watching the granite shore meander along below the tall evergreens. Sailing always bordered on voyeurism: a house at the end of a private road exposed for all to see, occupants of that special beach no one else had ever discovered forced to share the secret.

Rebecca was looking with an appraising eye out the window at the postmistress's flower garden.

"So, you and Addie had a real turnout last fall. I'm hoping to do the same with Mother at The Pines this summer. We have no idea what's up in the attic."

"Not in the heat, deah," Rebecca said anxiously. You won't make your mother go up there now."

"Of course not. Only if it cools down." And besides, Pix added to herself, I've never been able to *make* Mother do much of anything.

"We may find there are things we want to get rid of, too," she continued, "Who did you get to take yours?" Surely this was subtle and gentle enough. Pix felt a little guilty probing someone in the extremes of grief.

"It was Addie's idea." Typically, Rebecca was answering some other question. "She had a horror that after she was gone, people would be going through her things. You know what it's like at those auctions."

Pix did. She'd been to plenty of estate sales where Grandmother's letters to Grandfather were heaped in a box lot with the odd buttonhook and mismatched cups and saucers, but it had never struck her until now how awful this would be if you'd known the people. She resolved to winnow out her own mementos ruthlessly.

"But Addie wasn't planning on having an auction." Pix tried to keep Rebecca going.

"Mitchell Pierce was interested, you can imagine. Addie met him in the IGA and told him she would sell him some things if he wanted."

It worked.

"What kind of things did he buy?"

"Rubbish. Addie got a good price. Do you know he gave us one hundred dollars for an old yellow painted shelf that's been in the barn ever since I can remember? It was fly-spotted and even had a chip out of the top!"

Pix recalled an article in the paper about the skyrocketing value of country antiques, particularly those with their original paint. It sounded as if the Bainbridges had been well and truly snookered.

Rebecca's next remark confirmed the impression. "He took all the junk. There were some dirty old blanket chests. One even had the top off. And he wasn't even interested in our Wallace Nuttings. I was beginning to think *we* knew more about antiques than he did."

Pix pulled the car alongside the dock into the grassy area

that served as their parking area. "Well, I'm glad to know all this and that you were able to make some money out of it. Did you do anything special with it?"

The last question popped out from she knew not where—and it was none of her business.

Rebecca didn't seem to mind, answering directly for once. "Oh nothing special. Addie just liked having money. 'A heavy purse makes a light heart,' she used to say."

Along with several thousand others, Pix thought.

Ursula and Gert were waiting on the porch and as soon as they saw the car arrive, Gert ran down the steps to help Rebecca into the house. She was in good hands and Pix left soon after. She decided to head straight for the camp, although the fact that she had rushed out of the house so fast that she hadn't brushed her teeth or properly dressed—she'd thrown on a sweatshirt of Sam's with the sleeves cut off and a pair of shorts over her underwear and was glad she'd remembered this much—was beginning to bother her.

It was lunchtime and she walked into the dining room, where she soon spied Samantha pouring milk for a table of younger campers. She caught her eye and Samantha came straight over.

"Oh Mom, it's so sad! What will Rebecca do now? She'll be so lonely."

"Why don't we go outside for a minute. I'm sure it will be all right."

Samantha nodded and they walked toward the waterfront. The sails were sparkling white again—the extra sets. The red paint had turned out to be latex and those were being cleaned, so there was no great loss. Apparently it hadn't been the marine paint they used for the waterlines. Pix was sure that Jim was relieved. It wasn't the money so much as the waste. She put her arm around her daughter's shoulders and they sat down on the dock. Samantha seemed extremely shaken by the news.

"How did you hear?"

"Gert called Dot and she told us. Is it true that the police are there and there's something funny about the way she died?"

"The police are there, but it's not altogether clear whether anything's wrong. She was not in the best shape, avoided getting medical advice, and probably had a million things wrong with her that she didn't know about. You know how short of breath she was. She could barely walk down and back to her own mailbox."

"I know. It's just . . . well, after the other thing, everyone's saying there's a killer loose on the island."

Pix drew her daughter close. "We can't leap to conclusions like that. There doesn't seem to be anything to connect the two events at the moment, except that both people died."

And the quilts. But she didn't want to burden Samantha with that knowledge yet; besides, she was supposed to keep her mouth shut. A word to Samantha meant a word to Arlene, another Prescott, and it would be simpler to print up announcements and drop them from a plane over the entire island.

"It's not only Mrs. Bainbridge. Everything's still going crazy at camp. There was a dead seagull on the dining room porch this morning when the breakfast crew arrived. None of the kids saw it, thank goodness. Arlene said it was horrible."

"But these things happen—probably an injured bird who just happened to end up there."

"With its throat cut?"

Now Pix was shivering. Knives. Too many knives.

"Are you sure?"

"Yes, and Arlene thinks it's Duncan again. I mean after what we saw—" Samantha stopped abruptly.

"After you saw what?" Pix had to know. This was obviously what Samantha had been keeping from her.

"Mom, I promise I'll tell you, but I can't now. I have to get back. The kids are very jumpy. They swear there's a ghost around, although I think that's some of the older campers trying to scare the little ones."

"How are your two imps?"

"Not exactly happy campers. Kids are so weird, Mom. One minute everything is fine, the next they're imagining all sorts of gruesome things, especially these two. I think maybe they *are* too young to be here. Anyway, all this is going to affect them for a long time. Susannah leaps a foot in the air if someone startles her, and she and Geoff are always off by themselves. At the moment they're feeding each other's fears. I can't even get them to tell their stupid jokes."

Kids are so weird. The understatement echoed through the long tunnel of maternal memory. You never know, until you're there, Pix thought. Samantha was arriving sooner than her mother had.

"It's Parents' Weekend soon, isn't it? Maybe we should bring them to our house for a day, since they won't have visitors."

"That would be really great, Mom. They need to be with the dogs."

Pix understood. There was nothing more therapeutic than a good roll in the grass with an overly affectionate golden retriever.

"I've got to go, and I'm sure you want to get home and change." Samantha clearly did not approve of her mother's choice of outfits.

"Honey, I was in a rush. I just grabbed what was on the chair."

"That's all right. I understand." To avoid more hand patting, Pix grasped her daughter's paw firmly in her own and pulled her to her feet. They walked back toward the car together and were saying good-bye when, as luck would have it, Valerie came out of the director's office, a vision in a short Adrienne Vittadini brightly patterned sheath with a matching scarf tied carelessly around a broad-brimmed chapeau.

"Pix! I just heard about Adelaide Bainbridge. Come over to the house and tell me what happened. What a tragedy!"

Pix hesitated. She was curious about the fabled abode, but she wasn't really dressed, or even combed sufficiently, and she wanted to get home to call Faith. She hadn't reckoned on Samantha's reaction. Samantha clearly regarded an invitation to the Atherton's "Million Dollar Mansion" as a command performance for those fortunate enough to be asked. She actually poked her mother in the back.

"Well, perhaps for a minute. I have to get home. Mother may be calling. Rebecca is over at her house."

Valerie smiled brightly. "You come, too, Samantha, unless you are needed here."

Crestfallen, Samantha admitted she should be inside helping with lunch.

"Another time." Valerie turned to Pix and said just loud enough for Samantha to hear and swoon, "You have the most precious thing for a daughter I ever did see." Valerie occasionally lapsed into the Kappa Kappa Gammanese expressions of her college and deb days in the real South.

"Thank you. We like her," Pix replied, then realized it sounded a little snippy and added, "We're going to miss her terribly when she goes off to college."

"You're so lucky having a daughter," Valerie commented wistfully as they went down the path connecting the Atherton's house to the camp. "But then, you have sons, too." Her voice was full of commiseration. Pix was tempted to say they had never put them through the kind of hell Duncan seemed to be inflicting on his parents, yet it seemed inappropriate to gloat, and Danny was still young. Pix was loath to make any predictions—or say anything out loud—that might jinx things.

Valerie led her into the huge living room with teak-paneled walls soaring to a cathedral ceiling. The shape of the room—it swept forward, following the lines of the bluff on which it was situated—and all the wood made Pix feel as if she was in a boat, a very spectacular boat, and that must have been the architect's intent. She admitted inwardly that she was indeed envious. The house *was* gorgeous. Every plate-glass window framed a spectacular view. One set looked straight out to sea, another to the cove. Jim's boats, including the souped-up lobster boat he'd recently purchased, were picturesquely moored there. It looked like July on a Maine-coast calendar. The fireplace was as stunning as Samantha had described. Pix noticed a large photo on the mantel of a handsome smiling man with his arm around a much younger, and happier, Duncan. Valerie followed her gaze. "My first husband, Bernard Cowley. Duncan looks a bit like his father. I wish he could act like him. Buddy was a saint. I don't think I'll ever stop missing that man. Of course," she added quickly, "Jim is just about the nicest thing on two feet I've ever met, but you never get over something like this, and Jim understands."

"It must have been a terrible time for you and your son."

"It was—and if I hadn't met Jim, I don't know how I would have survived. Coming here was just what I needed and I know Duncan will settle down." Valerie did seem genuinely happy, more so than Pix had noted recently. Maybe things were going better with her son. Certainly it would be hard to be depressed in these surroundings. Most of the furniture in this room was modern, with a few well-chosen antiques: a softly burnished cherry card table, a child's Shaker chair, and an enormous grandfather clock, the sun and the moon slowly changing places above a stately schooner on the face. Scattered about in what Pix was sure was not a haphazard fashion were old brass navigational devices, a collection of Battersea enameled boxes, and other conversation pieces.

"Now tell me about poor Adelaide while I make coffee. I think there are two of those devastating muffins from that bakery in Blue Hill left. I swear Jim and Duncan devour whatever goodies I bring into this house like a swarm of locusts."

Pix begged off. The locusts could feast on her devastating

muffin. She really had to get home, so she quickly gave a brief account of Adelaide's death.

"I didn't actually know them well, but Jim and his family had," Valerie said. "Poor old lady. She did kind of let herself go, if you know what I mean."

Pix looked at the svelte figure gracefully draped across the leather couch before her and did indeed. Valerie Cowley Atherton would never let herself go. Pix saw her twenty years hence with face as smooth as plastic surgery could make it, body as trim as aerobics and a diet of lettuce and Perrier would supply.

She left and promised to return for a full tour of the house.

"It's beautiful, Valerie, and everything you've done is perfect."

"Thank you." Her hostess flashed a well-satisfied smile. "I've always wanted to live in a modern house. Buddy's family, bless their hearts, would have a conniption over this place. The Cowleys are an old family and they never let anyone forget it. You can't imagine the inconvenience they put up with in order to stay authentic!"

Pix laughed. She had often heard Faith on the same subject with regard to New Englanders. She hoped the heat was breaking in Aleford, although it wasn't here. She still felt guilty about the question of air conditioning at the parsonage.

"I can imagine. I'm afraid in my family, we may tend in this direction ourselves. Thank you for showing me the house. I'll take a rain check on the coffee."

"Bring Sam. We'll make it something else and all go into the hot tub," Valerie called after her. Pix waved good-bye. You'd have to put a gun to Sam's head to get him to disport in that kind of revelry.

A hot tub sounded particularly unappetizing at the moment. A cold shower would be more like it. The temperature was up over ninety again. No one could remember such a long stretch of searing hot days.

But everything, including bodily comfort, took a backseat

to her most important task; she was rewarded by Faith's answer on the second ring. What was more, Ben was at a friend's house and Amy was napping.

Faith was shocked at the news. "I know who Addie Bainbridge is. She's the fat one who runs the bed-and-breakfast and makes those incredible quilts, right? Her sister—what's her name again? She lives with her."

"Yes, except it's her sister-in-law. She's a Bainbridge, too, Rebecca. They've lived together for over thirty years."

"Oh, the poor thing. What will she do now?"

"Her main worry at the moment, besides getting Adelaide buried, is keeping her garden watered, so I think she'll be all right. She's got something to focus on. Then, too, she may not really be taking it all in. Rebecca's always been a bit scatterbrained and it's become more pronounced recently."

"Totally gaga?"

"I wouldn't go that far, definitely bordering on eccentricity though."

"Well, so are most of the people I know, including you. There's nothing wrong with that, but what is going on up there? I think I'll pack up the kids and come this weekend. There has to be a connection between the two quilts. Let me know as soon as you find out whether there's a mark on the latest one and what killed her."

"I will—and it would be lovely to have you here." At least Pix thought it would be, wouldn't it? A tiny voice was whispering that these were *her* murders, but she valiantly ignored it.

"The only problem is, we promised to go to Tom's sister's for a big family picnic, since everyone couldn't get together on the Fourth, and you know how they are about these things."

Pix did know, having listened to Faith lo these many years. Fairchild gatherings were sacrosanct, as well as invariable. They were a family that celebrated—birthdays, major holidays, and then their own specific South Shore rituals: First

Spring Sunday Raft Races on the North River, All-Family Autumn Touch-Football Saturday, and so forth. Faith's own family had tended toward less strenuous fetes, such as taking the children to the tree at the Metropolitan Museum of Art or shopping for Easter dresses at Altman's, followed by lunch in the store's Charleston Gardens restaurant. Pix wasn't sure what her own family did all those years, because they were much too busy.

"Maybe you can come up the following weekend." Things should certainly be sewn up by then, which brought her back to the quilts.

"I told you the quilt I bought is a fake, right?"

"No, but I know you've suspected as much. Have you heard about the one found with Mitchell Pierce's body?"

"No, Earl hasn't said anything. They'll probably send the one around Addie to Augusta for testing, too. By the way, the Bainbridges sold Mitch a lot of antiques, things they thought were worthless, although I'm sure they were anything but. Maybe Addie discovered that she had been swindled, but that would mean she'd be angry at Mitch, not somebody at her. But she might have had a reason for wanting him dead, except I can't imagine her killing him. In fact, it would have been a physical impossibility for her to transport his body, let alone dispose of him in the first place."

"Could the sister-in-law have helped?"

Pix was stunned. "Rebecca! God, no. I don't think she even swats flies."

"I think what you need to do is sit down and make some of your lists. You're so good at that. You know the kind they do in all those British detective stories. There's got to be some link you're missing."

Pix had been thinking all morning that she hadn't exactly been bringing the organizational skills that propelled her to the fore of every cause in Aleford to bear on this situation. It wasn't just making some lists, although that might help. She planned to sit her daughter down as soon as she came home and find out what she knew. And the same with Mother. It wasn't going to be easy, but somebody had to do it.

"I'm going antiquing again," she told Faith, full of plans and energy now. "Maybe Jill will come along. I want to find out if there are any more of those quilts around. Perhaps the police can trace them. We'll go up toward Bar Harbor—and Sullivan."

"That's where Mitch was living, right?"

"Yes. Maybe I should talk to his landlady. I could pretend I was looking for a place for a friend to stay."

Pix was learning fast, Faith realized with a twinge. If she wanted to be any part of this, she'd have to get up to Sanpere as soon as possible. Damn the Fairchild fun and games, she thought guiltily.

Looking out the window over her struggling squash vines to the imperturbable line of firs beyond, Pix wished life on Sanpere would return to normal. She told Faith about the paint on the sails, adding, "And don't say a word about red sails in the sunset."

"It never crossed my mind," Faith lied. "It's more red and white, though."

Pix hadn't thought of that. Things were becoming more complicated by the minute.

Amy was waking up. Faith heard soft little coos that would soon become bellows of rage. She told Pix, who remembered the scenario all too well.

"Call me as soon as you find out anything more."

"I will," Pix promised. "Oh, one last thing." She couldn't hear the baby yet, so Faith had a few seconds more. "Jill and Earl have apparently split up and Jill has been going around with Seth Marshall."

"That's a surprise. Seth is all right, but he's not what I would call husband material. Who left whom?"

"Jill, according to Earl, and he's as puzzled about it as I am. Jill is very touchy this summer. I haven't felt that I could ask her what's going on."

"*Definitely* invite her to go on your little jaunt."

Pix laughed and suddenly perversely wished Faith were on Sanpere.

"Talk to you soon."

"Bye-bye."

As soon as she put the phone back in the cradle—it was an old black dial phone that no one wanted replaced—she remembered she had completely forgotten to tell Faith that Seth had planned to pour the foundation today. Maybe she'd go over there with Samantha before dinner. At the moment, she wanted to get to work. She felt more like her old self now that she had a plan. The tire swing was receding into past memory.

She couldn't talk to Mother so long as Rebecca was there, but she should call to check in. Gert answered. Her mother was napping and Rebecca was sleeping, too. Earl had sent Dr. Harvey from the Medical Center over and he had given her a mild tranquilizer. The police had roped off the Bainbridge's house and the guests had moved on, leaving addresses, except for Norman, who was now staying at the inn. Norman. It occurred to Pix that he probably would have given his eyeteeth for some of the rubbish the Bainbridges had disposed of so blithely last fall. She wondered why Addie had gotten it into her mind to clear things out then—intimations of mortality, or simply wanting a heavier purse? And for what? She made quite a bit of money with her quilts and it wasn't as if she was a lavish spender. If she'd traveled as far as Ellsworth in the last ten years, Pix would be surprised, so Paris or cruises to the Caribbean were not the incentive.

The last thing Gert told her was that Addie's body had been taken away for the autopsy and the police hoped to be able to release it for a funeral by Saturday or Monday at the latest.

It was horrible to think about. Pix went into the kitchen and made herself a tuna-fish sandwich, taking the time to toast the bread. She grabbed a pad of paper, poured some milk, and went out on the deck to get to work.

Samantha came home just as she got to the fourth heading

for the columns she'd neatly folded: "Suspects." The others were "Who Benefits?"; "Causes of Death"; and "Quilts."

"I'm out here on the deck," Pix called. "Come join me. There's tuna fish if you want a sandwich."

Samantha came directly.

"Well, wasn't it fabulous?"

Pix was tempted to tease her daughter and ask what was fabulous, but obviously the subject was too important.

"*Fabulous* is exactly the right word," she told her, "and I was even a little jealous. The view is spectacular and the house is in exactly the right spot."

"'A little jealous,' the view! Oh, Mother, what about the fireplace, the furniture, and that rug! Valerie had it woven to order when she couldn't find one the right size with the colors she wanted."

Pix remembered the rug. It went from dark to light blue, with every possibility in between. It looked like the sea and the sky in every conceivable light. But what she wanted to do now was talk to her daughter about what she wasn't telling dear old Mom, not discuss Grecian versus Roman shades or any of the other fine points of interior decorating. She decided to be direct; besides, she couldn't think of another way.

"You started to say something about Duncan at the camp and told me you'd explain later. It's later now."

Samantha saw the look in her mother's eye and knew she meant business. Any attempt at avoidance would mean being nagged for days. It was best to get it over with. She plopped down in one of the canvas sling chairs from the fifties that her grandmother had happily donated and told her mother everything about Duncan, starting with the conversation in the woods during the clambake.

Pix was aghast. "The boy is clearly disturbed. He needs help. We have got to tell his parents."

"Mom, Arlene says they've taken him to a million shrinks. I'm sure they know he's got problems. I mean, look at the way he treats them."

"But I doubt they're aware of his 'club.' " Pix was torn. She really didn't know what to do. Jim Atherton's response had been so harsh. She hated to think she might be responsible for the boy's being struck again—or sent to the military school, which appeared to be the next course of action. And she really wasn't acquainted well enough with Valerie to gauge her reaction. John Eggelston had come to Duncan's defense. Maybe the best thing would be to talk to him.

Samantha was speaking. "It's like I feel sorry for him and hate him at the same time. I don't want to get him in trouble, but maybe you're right."

"Don't say *like*," Pix said automatically. "Why don't I tell all this to John? He knows Duncan and he also seems to know a lot about teenagers."

Samantha brightened. "That's a great idea. Maybe he can talk to all three of them together. He's done that for some other kids who are having problems at home here."

Duncan Cowley disposed of, Samantha wanted an update on what was going on at the Bainbridges. Pix gave her the PG-13 version and soon Samantha headed for her room to write letters to Aleford friends. There was a lot to tell.

Pix went to the phone to call John. She was more disturbed about Duncan's behavior than she wanted Samantha to know and the sooner someone talked to the Athertons, the better. As she dialed, she realized Duncan had to be added to the list of suspects. He was clearly drug-involved and might have graduated from mice and poultry to larger game.

John answered immediately. He sounded cheerful. "Hello, Pix. I just sent off a large piece to a congregation in Australia."

"Congratulations."

"And I accept them. I've been working on this altarpiece for several months. Now, what can I do for you?" John was not one for idle chitchat.

He was completely quiet as Pix related what Samantha had told her.

"And I don't know whether I should talk to Valerie and Jim, try to talk with the boy first, or what. You know him better than we do and I thought you'd have an idea about what would be best to do."

"Poor Duncan. He has never been allowed to grieve properly for his father. He feels responsible, you know. They were caught in a terrific storm and had all been taking turns at the helm—or rather, Bernard and Valerie were. Duncan was sitting up with his father to help him stay awake while his mother got some rest. The child became exhausted himself and agreed when his mother suggested he sleep for a while. That's when Bernard Cowley was washed overboard."

"How horrible!"

"I knew Duncan was fascinated with certain aspects of the occult. It's a way to make himself feel powerful, but I didn't think it had gone this far."

"The whole thing is terribly sad. I'm sure his parents will understand."

"Maybe and maybe not. Jim is a pretty straight arrow and I'm sure any suggestion of witchcraft will have him on the phone to that school he's always threatening Duncan with. Not that I blame Jim. He walked into a pretty hopeless situation. There was no way Duncan would ever have accepted him."

"But we can't simply ignore this and hope it goes away. Some night, one of the kids is going to get hurt or worse up in the quarry."

"I agree. I'm not suggesting we ignore the matter. Let me handle it. I'll talk to Valerie in private without getting too specific. This worked after Duncan took her car earlier in the summer. The main thing I'll do is start seeing more of Duncan. I've been so involved in this commission that I haven't had time for him these last months. He likes to come to the workshop. I'll go see if I can round him up right now. I have the feeling it won't take much to start him talking. We've talked a great deal about the supernatural before. I've lent him some books, so he won't think it odd if I bring it up."

Pix felt relieved, although she would have thought the Hardy Boys or, since the boy was interested in other worlds, perhaps Tolkien, more appropriate for John to have suggested.

"Thank you so much, John. And let me know how things go."

"Thank you for telling me." He'd been speaking in a serious tone of voice and now it took on almost a warning note. "You've had a pretty full plate and I'm sure it hasn't been pleasant. And then there's this business with the Bainbridges. I hope you're not getting too involved."

"Involved?"

"Like that friend of yours—Faith. There are things about the island better left alone. I know you summer people think it's paradise, but paradise had a dark side, too, remember."

Pix was stung by his remark: "summer people." She'd thought they were better friends, and even his closing words did not mollify her.

"I just don't want anything to happen to you. I care about all the Millers deeply. You know that. Bow out, Pix. Bow out."

"Don't worry. Nothing is going to happen. I'll let Samantha know about what we're doing and if either of us finds out anything more, we'll let you know."

She hung up feeling much less satisfied than she had earlier in the conversation. She walked back out to the deck and picked up her list. How well did she know John, anyway? Loaning books about the occult and supernatural to Duncan? John was a very colorful, at times charismatic figure. He had a great deal of influence over the youth of the island, most especially Duncan Cowley, it seemed. Maybe too much? And what kind was it exactly? Mitchell Pierce had stayed with

John. She had to find out why Mitch left. She put it on the "To Do" list.

With Samantha occupied with her own writing tasks, Pix got out the folded paper and started to fill in the columns. Under "Suspects," she decided to list everyone, no matter how far-fetched, starting with Mitchell's death. There weren't many. Duncan Cowley, the knife wounds were suggestive of some sort of ritual slaying. Seth Marshall, just because he had access to the spot and could pour the foundation when he pleased. John Eggleston, because he might have nurtured some sort of grudge since Mitchell had lived with him or because Mitchell had found something out about John during that time. Norman Osgood. These *were* far-fetched, but she had to put something down. Osgood might have had some kind of falling-out with Mitch over antiques. Last, she wrote down Sonny Prescott's suggestion: unknown partners in crime. Of course, others could be known ones, yet as she jotted down this final possibility, she was forced to admit it made the most sense.

Now Adelaide—If, in fact, she had been murdered. The only thing pointing toward foul play was the quilt. She went over to the "Who Benefits?" column. Adelaide may have left at least part of her estate to her nieces and nephews. Seth Marshall was a nephew. She wrote him down. Who else? Norman Osgood again? Although if he was hoping to do a book with her, that wouldn't make sense. But he was there. Maybe Addie had found out something about him. She wasn't known for her reticence. Pix considered the other bed-and-breakfast guests and reluctantly ruled them out. Unless they were seriously deranged people, which the police were no doubt checking, she couldn't come up with any motives.

She listed Seth under "Who Benefits?" with the initials A.B. after his name. She couldn't think of any way he would benefit from Mitch's death, unless Mitch was blackmailing him. Mitch a blackmailer: It was a thought. He had been charming and eminently likable, but if desperate for money, he might have done anything. He certainly hadn't shied away from other crimes. Except he hadn't been desperate for money. He'd had a huge bank account and it was the result of what? As Jill suggested he might have made a killing—strike that phrase—a huge profit from the sale of something. Then again, he might also have been blackmailing someone, or more than one person. Pix sighed. She wasn't getting anyplace. Maybe you had to be in a large English country house staring out the window at the hedgerows. But at least she had a list. She'd get Mother to find out about Addie's will. Rebecca surely must know.

"Causes of Death." Mitch was stabbed and Addie's was unknown at the moment. She'd like to call Earl, yet she had a feeling she'd do better to wait. It was certainly too soon to know anything and she thought he probably wouldn't take kindly to being hounded right now. She remembered the look on Adelaide's face and the stench. The woman had obviously been violently sick and the police might have found further signs in the bathroom—all of which pointed to poison of some kind. Addie had been sick for days and Pix recalled the graphic account of her symptoms. What did one have to do with the other? Was her illness merely a coincidence? Poison. This made absolutely no sense. Things like this didn't happen on Sanpere.

Then there were the quilts, two red-and-white quilts. Three quilts, including Pix's purchase with the disappearing mark. She *would* call Earl later to find out whether there was a cross on Adelaide's. It would be impossible to sleep otherwise. She also wrote down *sails*. As Faith had pointed out, they were red and white, too. Sails were made of cloth, so were quilts. Quilts and sails. Sails and quilts. Mitch had been wrapped in Drunkard's Path. Could there be some connection between the name of the quilt pattern on Addie's and her death? Pix closed her eyes and concentrated on remembering the spirals she'd seen that morning. She drew a square at the bottom of the page and filled it in as best she remembered: two pinwheel shapes, the tiny dotted fabric alternating with the red. She'd go through her quilt pattern books after supper and try to find the name.

It wasn't much of a list, not up to her usual standards. But it was a beginning. She went to the bottom of the stairs and called to Samantha to come for a walk with the dogs. They all needed to get out.

For once, Samantha was staying home. After an early supper of toasted cheese sandwiches and tomato soup, one of the Miller family's favorite repasts, the phone rang. During the course of a lengthy conversation, Pix heard Samantha tell Arlene she was tired and ask her how about the following night. The phone rang again as Pix was getting out her quilting books. It was Ursula. Rebecca had agreed to stay the night, since Earl had promised to water the garden. So that's where he was, Pix thought. She'd been trying to reach him.

She started to ask her mother about Adelaide's will and how big the estate might be, but Ursula cut her off, obliquely indicating Rebecca had attached herself limpetlike and was at Mrs. Rowe's side every waking moment.

"I understand completely. Poor Rebecca! I know you can't say anything, but could you find out if she has any further thoughts about where that quilt might have come from? And perhaps see if she knows what the provisions of Adelaide's will are?"

Even though her mother would not be able to comment at length, Pix had expected a note of disapprobation to sound in her reply—Pix was prying—but Ursula said in an even tone, "Good idea, dear. I'll do that."

It amounted to approval. Addie's death had changed things and it might just be that Mother was on the trail, as well.

It was much too hot for a fire in the fireplace, but they sat in front of it, anyway, Pix with her quilting books and Samantha curled up on the couch with E. B. White. She was rereading *Charlotte's Web*, as she did every summer.

Charlotte had finished saving Wilbur's life the first time and Samantha stood up and stretched. She really was tired, yet that was not why she'd put Arlene off until tomorrow. Fred wanted to go back to Duncan's and check out the trunk. He was convinced Duncan was responsible for what was going on at the camp, including the dead gull. Arlene also hinted that Fred thought Duncan might be responsible for the other bizarre things happening on the island. "Fred's good and steamed," she'd told Samantha. Samantha was afraid he might be right and she, too, thought they'd better look around the cabin some more, but she just couldn't handle it after everything that had happened today. She'd known the Bainbridges all her life and Addie had always been nice to her. At the moment, all Samantha wanted to do was read about Charlotte, Wilbur, and Fern until she fell obliviously asleep.

Pix found the pattern shortly after midnight. It had become an obsession. Samantha had long since gone to bed. Pix, though, remained wide awake and when the design jumped off the page at her, she was jolted into even-greater consciousness. Her mother's earlier words regarding Mitchell Pierce's killer came immediately to mind. Whoever was responsible was not simply evil, but nasty.

The name of the pattern was End of Day.

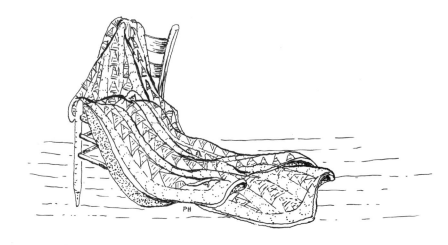

Chapter 8

The next morning Samantha left for work after a big breakfast of sour-cream pancakes and fresh strawberries. Pix had picked the first ones in the garden, thankful the heat hadn't ruined what looked to be a bumper crop.

As soon as her daughter was out the door, Pix piled the dishes in the sink and went to the phone. As she dialed, it struck her that she was spending an inordinate amount of time on this instrument—especially for Sanpere. Other summers when it did ring, it was usually for one of the kids, and she seldom made many calls herself.

Earl was in his office, as she had hoped. He'd recovered from whatever feelings of pique her actions at the Bainbridge's had engendered and said he didn't see any harm in telling her no cross of any color had been found on the quilt surrounding the corpse.

"Now whether the quilt's an old one or not, I can't tell you, because I don't know. The other one wasn't, though."

Pix was grateful for this confirmation of her suspicions.

"I thought I might do some more antiquing," she told him. "Maybe head up toward Bar Harbor. I'm hoping Jill will come along." Pix had thought of asking Valerie, too, but decided that a third person would provide a further excuse for Jill to avoid talking about her love life.

"Well, say hi from me, that is if she remembers who I am."

Pix returned to what was obviously a more cheerful topic. "Do you have the results of the autopsy yet?"

"So far, all I've heard is heart failure."

"Then it may not involve any foul play?"

Pix was finding comfort in phrases like this. The alternatives were overly specific.

"Not necessarily. Could be something was given to her to cause the heart attack. But could also be she was due."

Pix hung up, feeling better than she had for days. No mark on the quilt and the possibility that death was from natural causes. Addie's weight and eating habits—she disgustedly referred to salads and the like as "rabbit food"—definitely put her at risk. And as for the quilt, it was no doubt one Rebecca had simply forgotten about.

Next she called Jill.

"Oh Pix, I *would* like to go. It's so horrible about Addie. I can't think about anything else, and if I don't get out of the shop today, I think I'll go insane."

Pix was surprised at the intensity of Jill's reaction. She hadn't realized the two women were so close. Maybe Jill was some kind of niece, too.

"But I don't have anybody to cover for me. I can't afford to just close up. There are still so many tourists in town. Would you mind waiting while I try to find someone?"

"Of course not. Too bad Samantha's working at Maine Sail, but she does get through after lunch. We could go then if you don't find anyone sooner."

"That would be great. I'll call you in an hour if not before to let you know what's happening."

Pix was not in the mood to sit by the phone. "If you don't get an answer here, call me at The Pines. I want to see how Rebecca is." And maybe get a few words with Mother, she added to herself. She also wanted to drive out to the Point on the way and inspect the foundation. There hadn't been any time yesterday to make sure Seth was doing as he had promised.

Seth and his crew were taking a break when Pix drove up. Nobody jumped up to greet her, but she didn't care. The sight before her eyes was greeting enough. The foundation and basement floor for the Fairchild's house had been poured and the tart smell of fresh concrete filled the air. It was more fragrant to Pix than any number Chanel.

Seth did come over to her as she walked the perimeter of the house, inspecting the job intently.

"It'll be smooth as a baby's bottom. Don't worry," he said.

"I'm not. It looks fine." Pix believed in credit where credit was due.

"We're working on the stairs to the beach today. If the weather holds, we should be able to strip the forms and start framing the floor by Thursday, maybe even Wednesday. The wood's already cut and Barton's is holding everything for me—nice number-two Douglas fir."

Pix nodded. Maybe this wasn't going to be Mr. Blandings' dream house after all. Maybe Seth would come through.

"The family is some upset about Aunt Addie. Don't understand why Earl had to get all hot and bothered. There was no need to get Augusta involved. Gorry, we'll be lucky to have the funeral by Labor Day." Seth sounded extremely annoyed.

Pix's recent well-being vanished.

"He *had* to call the state police. Rebecca never saw the quilt before—and it was a red-and-white one, just like the one here." She had been consciously trying not to recall what had recently lain beneath the surface of the ground now covered by the gray concrete.

"Rebecca doesn't know the color of the blanket on her

own bed once she's out of it. No, Earl had no right to ship Addie off for them to cut up. He's been watching too much TV. This is Sanpere, not New York City."

Seth had bent down and picked up a stick. He was poking the ground ferociously with it as they walked. Pix made sure to keep well to one side.

She could understand why Adelaide Bainbridge's relatives might be upset, but surely they wanted to find out what had happened. She made a mental note to ask Ursula what she'd heard about their reactions through the island grapevine.

Pix tactfully changed the subject. "It's going to be lonely for Rebecca in the house now, but I suppose she'll keep running the bed-and-breakfast."

"Well, she may not be there for long," Seth stopped stirring up the dust with the stick and gave it one final shove, driving it into the soil. "She has life tenancy under Addie's will, unless she's found unable to be left on her own, and that seems pretty certain."

"Where will she go and who will get the house then?" If you didn't ask, you didn't find out.

Seth did not seem too concerned about Rebecca's future and Pix realized that of course Addie was the relation and Rebecca merely a distant in-law to some one of Seth's parents or grandparents.

"Probably a nursing home on the mainland or maybe one of the Bainbridges in Granville will have her. The house will be sold and the whole kit and caboodle gets divided in equal shares."

Given what Addie's quilts sold for plus the value of the lovely old house and barn, it would add up to quite a caboodle, Pix figured.

She had the answer to one question at least.

Seth Marshall, unaware that his name had just been starred under two columns, called to his crew to get back to work.

"I'd love to chat with you some more, but I wouldn't want you to think we were wasting time." He smiled warmly to soften his sarcasm. It almost worked. He really was attractive, particularly at the moment, stripped to the waist because of the heat, his skin glistening slightly with sweat. Maybe Jill was tired of good old Earl and wanted a fling with bad old Seth.

"I have to get going, anyway," she said. "If Jill can find someone to cover the store, we're going to drive up to Bar Harbor." She decided not to get too specific about what she intended to do. She needn't have bothered to be circumspect.

"Yup, so I hear. Going antiquing, right?"

Pix's mouth dropped. He laughed. "Heard it on the CB just before you drove up. Jill's got one of the Ames kids. I heard her asking her dad if she could do it."

"There are no secrets on this island," Pix remarked.

"Oh, I don't know about that," Seth said as he walked toward his crew, the sound of their hammers ricocheting in the still air. "I'd say there were plenty."

Doris Ames was sitting at the register reading the latest issue of the *National Inquirer*, and from the speed at which she was chewing her gum, Pix suspected the story was more racy than some of the fare: MOM SELLS KIDNEY TO BUY FURNITURE or SPACE ALIEN BABY FOUND ON MOUNT EVEREST MEDICAL DR. SAYS NOT HUMAN.

"Oh, hi, Mrs. Miller. Jill has been trying to get a hold of you. She's upstairs."

"I'll go on up, then. How's everything with you this summer?"

"I can't complain. Making good money and don't have to work days." Pix remembered that one of the Ames girls was waitressing at the inn, which was only open for dinner, and it must be Doris.

"I hear the food is even better than last year."

Doris made a face. "It's too fancy for me. I like to recognize what's on my plate. I eat at home before I start."

Pix laughed. "Well, maybe some of it is an acquired taste."

She decided to take Ursula and Samantha to the inn soon, all three of them having acquired a taste for any and all good food.

Jill had a snug little apartment over the store. Pix walked up the outside stairs and knocked at the door. Hearing no reply, she pushed it open, stepping inside. She could hear water running and Jill had obviously decided to take a quick shower while waiting for Pix.

"Jill," she called loudly, not wanting to startle her when she emerged, "It's me, Pix."

"Oh great," Jill replied above the noise of the spray. "I'll be out in a minute. I just had to cool off."

The apartment was divided into two large rooms plus bath. The front room was Jill's bedroom and the larger back room served as living room, dining room, kitchen, and storage for the overflow from the store. There were several large boxes in the corner by the door, but this wasn't what caught Pix's eye. She was struck by the change in the room's decor since she'd been there last summer. Jill had been buying a great many antiques over the course of the year and the Goodwill finds spruced up with paint and fabric that had previously filled the room were mostly gone. An Early American cupboard with open shelves on top stood against one wall, behind a trestle table and chairs from the same period. Pix walked over to take a closer look. She wondered whether Jill had gotten the things from Mitch. Spying a pumpkin pine stand that would make a perfect bedside table, she also wondered whether these things were for sale. She tripped on one of the uneven floorboards and her hip bumped into the corner of the cupboard. Jill's apartment had originally been used for storage by the cobbler's shop below and the floor had never been finished off. One of the cupboard doors flew open. Pix bent down to close it, rubbing her hipbone, which, with little cushioning, smarted sharply.

She didn't close the door; rather, opened it wider. The shelves were filled with various items: some wonderful folk art carvings, especially one who looked like one of the prophets; miniature furniture—the kind that used to be carried around as samples; and several patchwork quilts. The shower was still running. Pix was sure Jill wouldn't mind if she looked at the quilts. At least that's what she told herself. Her self also wondered what they were doing up here instead of down in the store, where they would certainly attract buyers. For that matter, all the things in the cupboard would. Perhaps Jill was saving these things for herself.

Pix careful removed the top quilt and opened it up. It was an appliqué sampler quilt, every square a different wreath or bouquet and intricately quilted. The quiltmaker had used red, green, yellow, and white. It was museum-quality. The shower stopped and Pix started to call out her appreciation, but her words froze in her throat as her eyes moved down to the lower corner. Moved down to a tiny, barely perceptible blue cross.

She folded the quilt up and quickly put it back, latching the cupboard securely. When Jill came out, she found Pix sitting in a low rocker by the window reading this week's *Island Crier*.

"The parade pictures are wonderful. Sonny is going to love the shot of him as Burt Dow," she said brightly—too brightly.

Driving across the bridge to the mainland with Jill at her side, Pix was in a quandary. Should she come right out and ask Jill about the quilt and the other antiques? She probably should have done so immediately, but she wanted to take time to reflect. What could it possibly mean? That Jill had unwittingly bought a fake quilt—or wittingly? It was the latter possibility that was keeping Pix's tongue securely tied. Was Jill somehow connected to an antiques scam? At this point, Pix was certain it had been one of Mitchell Pierce's activities. Had they been in it together? She had certainly gotten antiques from him. This would explain Jill's recent attitude toward Earl, and perhaps her new alliance with Seth. Supposedly, Seth had learned everything he knew from Mitch. Did that include how to construct old from new?

The blue crosses were no laundry mark, as she'd speculated to Earl. They must be an indication to those who knew that these quilts were not the real McCoy. Had Jill seen the mark on Pix's quilt when it was spread out on the ground and later come into the house and removed it?

Jill was talking and Pix realized with a start that she hadn't heard a word the woman had been saying. She forced herself to concentrate. Jill was suggesting where they might go.

"There's that barn right outside Blue Hill as you head up the hill toward the fairgrounds. I found a wonderful bamboo easel at a very reasonable price last spring. Why don't we stop there first, then go farther up the coast?"

"Sounds fine to me," Pix answered. Anything was fine at this point, when her main worry was how she was going to get through this trip without coming unglued.

The barn door was firmly shut and they didn't have much luck in Ellsworth, either: no quilts to examine and nothing else tempting. Pix knew why nothing appealed to her, but Jill seemed just as restless and disinterested. Maybe she had simply needed to get away because of Addie's death and the antiquing was an excuse. Whatever it was, neither had bought anything by eleven and Pix suggested they drive straight to Beal's in Southwest Harbor for an early lunch. A big bowl of their chowder consumed at the pier while looking across the water at Acadia's Mount Cadillac was exactly what she needed to soothe her troubled mind, and perhaps it would do something for Jill's too. Pix had noticed that whenever Jill wasn't speaking, her fingers were finding their way to her mouth and her cuticles looked red and sore.

Many of the tables at Beal's were already full. In tacit assent, they took their food to the one farthest away from the groups noisily cracking open the lobsters they had picked out of the tank.

A cool breeze was coming off the harbor and for a while they sat in silence consuming the delicious chowder thick with clams. Pix was in no hurry to get back into the car. Eating gave her something to do and think about other than what was pressing most on her mind.

"Coffee and pie?" Jill asked. Beal's was known for their blueberry pie.

"Sure, we came all this way. We can't leave without pie."

More silent enjoyment followed, or rather, Pix thought, more silence. The pie was as good as ever, yet it was beginning to turn to ashes in her mouth. She had to say something to Jill—Jill, who had been a friend for years.

"Maybe—no, probably—it's none of my business, but you know how much we care about you, both of you. Do you want to talk about what's gone wrong with Earl?" Pix decided to start with this trial balloon to gauge Jill's reaction before attempting to discuss such matters as antiques fraud and breaking and entering, although Jill had always been free to walk into the Miller's unlocked house whenever she pleased.

Jill frowned. "I don't know why everyone thinks something's wrong between us. Goodness, if you don't happen to be climbing all over someone every minute of the day, the whole island assumes you've broken up, and of course it's not true. No one's bothered to remember we both have jobs. I've been busy and Earl's been even busier with all that's happened. We haven't had time to see each other."

She jammed a large forkful of pie into her mouth. Some of the juice dripped onto the front of her gauzy white blouse.

"Damn," she said, rubbing at it with a paper napkin, which only made it worse. She seemed close to tears. It didn't seem the moment to mention Earl's remarks or the fact that Pix had been there herself when Jill had turned her swain down the day after she was spotted dining with another. Nor was Pix inclined to raise anything else. They finished eating quickly, paid, and got into the car.

"Are you game for some more or do you want to head back?" Pix asked, hoping Jill, like she, had had enough.

"Let's keep going. Doris can stay until she has to go to work at the inn." Jill's chin jutted out. "Besides, I haven't had any luck yet."

Nor have I, Pix thought dismally.

They retraced their steps and went into a large antiques shop in Trenton. It was one Pix had frequented before, but Jill said she had never been there. They walked in and the owner greeted Pix warmly. The shop was free of cobwebs and dust. Everything was shown to its best advantage. It was quite a contrast and at the moment a welcome one. When Pix asked about nightstands, he said he thought he had the very thing and led them into another room. There were several customers browsing and one turned at the sound of their voices to greet them. "Pix, Jill! I never expected to see you two playing hooky again so soon." It was Valerie, and contrary to her earlier impulses, Pix was delighted to have a third wheel. This day out with Jill had begun to seem like a week.

"It was a spur-of-the-moment thing. I'm still looking for a table for my guest room and Jill was able to come along."

Not wanting to keep the owner waiting, Pix followed him to what was in fact "the very thing," except not the very price. Even with some friendly dickering, she knew it would be way out of her range. Valerie and Jill joined them. Pix said she liked it but would have to wait for something less expensive.

"It *is* a lovely piece," Valerie commented, "Are you sure you're not going to take it?"

"Yes. Saying no to this price tag, besides saving my marriage, gives me something to keep looking for this summer."

Valerie was on her hands and knees, examining the chest from all angles.

"Take your time, ladies," the owner said, "I'll be in the front of the store."

"Do you have any quilts?" Pix asked before he left.

"I have a crib quilt and a nice quilt top from the thirties but nothing else at the moment. Good ones are getting harder and harder to come by. The market in general has been hurt by the foreign imports that look old—and also by the fakes."

What it her imagination or did Jill give a sudden start?

"I'm a quilter and very interested in all this," Pix told him. "How do you spot the fakes?" It was too much to hope that he would say they were marked with a little blue cross, but she might learn something.

"It's very difficult, especially now that the fabric companies make so many reproduction fabrics. I look at the stitching, examine the material, and mostly consider the source. I get pretty suspicious when someone comes in with an armload of quilts they just happened to find in an old trunk that hasn't been opened since goodness knows when in Grandmother's attic."

"They aren't marked in any way, then?" Pix felt her investigation was going nowhere and she had to ask.

He laughed. "That would make it easy, now wouldn't it? No, they aren't marked. Do you want to see what little I have?"

Pix did and so did the others.

"I think I'll take the stand, if you're absolutely sure you don't want it," Valerie said.

"Absolutely sure. I can visit it at your house."

"Anytime."

The crib quilt was precious, Valerie declared, and that was the word for the price, too, Pix thought. She wasn't really interested in crib quilts—not for a long time to come—but she did like the quilt top with its bright 1930s prints. It wasn't particularly unusual. Someone had simply machine-pieced the rectangles together, yet it was someone who had had a good eye for color. Pix figured she could tie it rather than quilt it and have an attractive cover for Samantha's bed in Sanpere. If Samantha didn't want it, Pix would keep it for her own room. The price was reasonable and her spirits lifted.

"Do you have time to head up to Sullivan?" she asked Jill. "And can you come with us?" she added to Valerie.

"That's going to be a little far," Jill said. "I can't cut it too close with Doris or she may not want to help me out again."

"Why don't you ride back with me?" Valerie suggested. "There's only one place I want to check in Surry and it won't take long."

"Thanks," Jill said. "Then I won't feel like I'm spoiling Pix's fun."

Pix felt a major stab of guilt. How could she suspect such a nice person? And instead of talking to her about Addie and Jill's feelings about the death, Pix had pried into her private life, upsetting her further. Certainly she did not look any better for the outing. If anything, she seemed more perturbed. Pix was tempted to call it a day herself and drive Jill home.

But at this point, she was compelled to keep going, even though she didn't have the slightest idea where Mitchell Pierce had lived in Sullivan. A quick stop at the post office should take care of that. Mitchell Pierce—it had all started with him, Mitch and antiques. Antiques—and antiques dealers—were cropping up regularly.

She paid for her quilt top and impulsively asked the owner, "Did you ever have any dealings with Mitchell Pierce?"

"Everybody in this business had dealings with Mitch and most of us wish we hadn't, however I don't want to speak ill of the dead. You do know about that, don't you?"

"Yes, yes, I know," Pix said. But not enough.

She waved good-bye to Jill and Valerie and drove north to Sullivan. Without Jill, her mind raced from subject to subject, trying to figure out a way to link Mitchell, Addie, Jill, Seth, Duncan, and John, plus God knew who else, together in one pat solution. As she pulled up in front of the Sullivan post office, she was sure of only one thing: She needed to talk to Faith.

She had prepared what she hoped was a plausible story on the drive. It was hard enough to pry information from taciturn Mainiacs without the complications of whatever oaths postal employees swore. Not that this ever seemed to bother the ones in Aleford, who considered return addresses and what was written on a postcard public information.

"Hi," she said in as self-confident a voice as she could muster, and it wasn't half-bad. "I'm looking for someone named Mitchell Pierce. I understand he lives here."

"Lived" was the laconic reply from the other side of the counter.

"You mean he's moved?"

"You might say."

Pix waited, then, when that appeared to be the full extent of the reply, asked, "Do you have a forwarding address for him?"

"I have my ideas, but I'd rather not say."

Just as she was beginning to wonder whether she was dealing with yet another would-be "Bert and I," the recording of classic Down East humor, her informant turned inquisitor.

"Why are you so interested in Mitchell Pierce?"

The story came out smooth as a new dory down the slip into the water. "Mr. Pierce took some old things my mother wanted to get rid of on consignment. He told her they might be worth something, especially the quilts." Pix planned to mention quilts whenever possible. "He gave her a receipt and his phone number and said he'd be in touch, but that was over a month ago and she hasn't heard a thing. The number must have been wrong, because a recording says it's no longer in service."

Maybe it was the word *mother* or the tale itself, but it unleashed a veritable fountain of information.

"He's dead. Guess if you want to find out what happened to your stuff, you'd better talk to the police."

"Police?"

"Mitchell got himself planted in somebody's cellar hole down to Sanpere. It's a police matter. And I wouldn't hold out any great hopes of finding your things."

"Oh dear, what am I going to tell my mother?" This last bit was genuine enough. "Isn't it possible that they could still be in his house?"

"I doubt it. He boarded with the Hardings just up the road. Didn't have a place of his own."

"Well, I'm glad I came. At least we know now why we didn't hear from him. Thank you for all your help."

He nodded in acknowledgment.

It was nice to find some humor in all this, Pix thought as she started the Land Rover. Faith was going to love the post office story.

The Hardings had thoughtfully painted their name in white on their mailbox, which jutted out into the main road. It was a neat little house, the upper story painted bright yellow, the bottom dark brown, the shutters white. The yard was filled with machinery in various states of repair, several pot buoys, and broken traps. Whatever Mr. Harding did, it wasn't fishing. She knocked on the back door, noting the bright pink and purple petunias that grew profusely in the planters made from old tires on either side.

An elderly woman in a flowered housedress with a bib apron covering most of it answered.

"Yes?"

"Are you Mrs. Harding? I got your name at the post office."

This appeared to be vetting enough.

"Yes, I am. Why don't you come in, deah, and sit down? It is too hot for man or beast today. I told Virgil—that's my husband—that he was to stay in the shade as much as possible and keep his hat on. He's bald, you know, and bald people have to be very careful not to get burned. He won't let me put any of that cream I got from Marge Thomas. She sells Avon. Anyway, Virgil says he doesn't want to smell like a perfume factory, but it has no smell I can make out. Those summer people work him to death, cutting the grass, weeding the garden. He caretakes now, you know."

This, Pix thought, profoundly grateful, was going to be a piece of cake.

She told her story again—or rather, tried to. Mrs. Harding—"Call me Bessie, deah. Everybody does, even the grandkids"—tended to use Pix's every word as a jumping-off point for one of her own tangents. But after hearing about the priceless antique garnets—necklace, bracelet, earrings, *and* ring— Mr. Harding's mother had owned and which were promised to her, Bessie, but just because Mother had lived in their house, Mr. Harding's brother's wife, "who was no relation at all" claimed everything and she, Bessie, did not get so much as a button of her own mother-in-law's who also happened to be a second cousin, Pix was able to get on with her story.

Once Mitchell Pierce's name was mentioned, Pix didn't have to do anything else.

"I know he was no better than he should have been, but I liked the man. Always paid his rent on time and sometimes he'd come down here to the parlor—that's where we watch TV—and sit with us. Played that mandolin of his. A couple of times, he'd bring a bottle of something, not that Mr. Harding and I are drinkers, though we do enjoy a nip of something now and then. I don't know what he was doing down on Sanpere in a basement, but the whole thing is very sad and we miss him. That man could make you laugh from here to Christmas."

"Do you think it's possible he may have left some of Mother's things here in his room or maybe someplace else in the house? Mother is particularly concerned about her quilts. He said they might be valuable."

It was the longest remark she'd been able to make so far.

Bessie shook her head. "He never did keep much here. Told me once that he put his wares—that's what he called them—over to Ellsworth in one of those storage places people rent. Why on earth, I can't imagine. If you don't have room for what you've got, then you've got too much, is what I say.

Somebody else is in his room now, a real nice man who's working at Acadia this summer. We don't see too much of him, though, and of course he can't tell a story the way Mitch could. I think he's from New Jersey or one of those places." Pix made one last try. "So you never saw any quilts—or other antiques—that Mitch might have taken on consignment or bought?"

"No, deah, and I'm real sorry for your mother. The only quilt Mitch ever brought into this house was the one he gave me last year for my birthday. I was some surprised. Don't know how he knew, but he come into the kitchen right after breakfast—I always gave him breakfast when he was here— and gave me the most lovely quilt. It's too nice to use, so I keep it on a rack in the parlor. Do you want to see it?" Bessie had a sudden thought. "You don't think it could be one of your mother's? I mean, with this talk about Mitch being a little crooked and all."

"Oh no," Pix hastened to reassure her, speaking with the conviction the absolute truth gives. "It couldn't be. It's only been a little over two months that he's had ours."

She followed Bessie into the parlor and stood to one side as the woman spread the quilt out for her to admire. Pix made all the right comments—and once again she was speaking the truth. The quilt was beautiful, intricately worked, the colors lovely. And Pix ought to know. She'd bought the twin of it a week ago—the twin, even down to the tiny blue cross at the edge.

It was difficult to get away from Bessie Harding, but after drinking two glasses of iced tea and promising to drop in again if she was ever up that way, Pix got in her car, waved good-bye, and backed out of the drive. Bessie watched her go, then ran to the mailbox calling after the car, "I never did get your name, deah! What was it again?" Pix turned onto the main road and headed south. The car windows were rolled down, but she missed Bessie's last words.

213

* * *

The sight of the bridge from the mainland to Sanpere always gave Pix a feeling of well-being. A welcome-home feeling. She drove up the steep incline and looked at the sky overhead. She felt inches away from the heavens on the top of the bridge. As a teenager, she and Sonny had climbed to the uppermost crossbar of the bridge a few times before their parents heard about it and forbade them to ever do such a crazy thing again. Still it had been wonderful, swinging your legs into nothingness and seeing all of Penobscot Bay at your feet. She let the car coast down the other side and reminded herself to mention, as she did each summer to her children, that the top of the bridge was strictly off limits.

She was eager to talk to Faith but decided to stop at The Pines before going home. She had spoken with her mother earlier to tell her about the planned excursion and see whether she needed anything in Ellsworth, it standing in relation to Sanpere roughly as, say, Paris to a French village on the Atlantic Coast. Mother had wanted for nothing and told Pix that Rebecca was fine, sitting by Ursula's side as she spoke and sipping a cup of tea.

Tea, or rather, iced tea again, sounded good. It was a long drive from Sullivan to Sanpere and Pix was tired. She needed to recharge before calling Faith and trying to figure everything out.

She walked into the living room, surprised not to see her mother and Rebecca on the porch.

"Hello," she called. "Mother, where are you?" She walked through to the kitchen and saw the two women in the garden vigorously attacking anything that wasn't supposed to be there.

"You have to keep at it every day," Rebecca was saying, "They really do grow up over night."

Ursula was about to reply when she saw Pix. "Will you excuse me for a moment, Rebecca? I have to talk to my daughter." Pix liked neither the expression on her mother's face nor the tone of voice in which she had said "my daughter." What have I done? she wondered.

She wasn't in the dark for long. Mother pulled her unceremoniously up the back stairs into the kitchen and plunked her down on a chair.

"Myrtle Rowe Miller! What have you been doing? What could you be thinking of going up to Sullivan like that!"

Mother was definitely clairvoyant. The word *witch* did not even occur to Pix.

She was stunned. "How did you know where I was?"

"Earl called. The Sullivan post office thought they should report to the state police that someone was asking about Mitchell Pierce. They called Earl, who knew, of course, from the description it was you. There was no answer at your house, so he called here to see if I knew whether you were off-island. It was quite embarrassing."

"I'm sorry," Pix mumbled, "It seemed like a good idea at the time." And still does, she thought defiantly. She was sorry she had upset her mother, but some prices had to be paid.

"You're to call Earl immediately. Now, you must be exhausted, all that driving. Would you like a cup of tea?"

She was forgiven.

"After I call Earl." Sometimes virtue was its own reward, and besides, she might get a cookie.

She went upstairs to call, since Rebecca might run out of weeds and Pix didn't want her activities known by any more people than she could help.

He answered on the first ring. "Now before you get mad at me, let me tell you what I found out," she said, hoping to distract him, which she did.

"We knew he had the storage place. It was clean as a whistle, but this business with the quilts seems to prove he was involved in antiques fraud."

"Does this mean you'll have to take Bessie's quilt?" The

woman had been so proud, Pix was sorry to be responsible for having it impounded or whatever they called it when they seized evidence.

"Yes, but she'll get it back. It's her property, unless at the end of this mess we find out differently."

"No one has stepped forward to claim the estate yet, right?"

This would have been big news on Sanpere.

"Not so far, but it hasn't been very long."

It just seemed long.

Pix was about to hang up, grateful that she had avoided a talking-to, when she remembered Jill's protest. "Oh, by the way, according to Ms. Merriwether, any problems between the two of you are a figment of the public's imagination. She and you have simply been too busy to see much of each other lately."

"Oh, is that it? Better than nothing, I suppose." From the way he spoke, it sounded much better.

Rebecca and Ursula were sitting in the living room. "It's too hot on the front porch. The sun has been beating down on it all day," her mother explained.

"If you don't mind, I think I'll lie down for a while. I can't understand why I'm so tired all the time," Rebecca said.

"I'm sure you'll feel better soon," Pix reassured her.

"Thank you, deah, but I know one thing. I'm not going to feel any better until we can have a proper Christian burial for Addie." Her voice broke. "It's not fair to do this to her."

Pix went upstairs with Rebecca and spread the afghan she requested over her, despite the warmth of the room, tucked up under the eaves as it was.

"I like to lie here and look out the window at the water," she told Pix drowsily. "I could never see it from my bedroom in the back, but Addie could."

The woman was almost asleep. Pix left, closing the door. When she went back downstairs, her mother was in the kitchen pouring iced tea, adding sprigs of mint she must have just cut in the garden.

"In all this commotion, I forgot to tell you Faith called. It seemed every call was someone looking for you. She said for you to call her back as soon as you could."

"I wonder what she wants?"

"I have no idea. She didn't mention anything to me." Mrs. Rowe smiled. Let the girls have their secrets was its implication.

Pix didn't feel like going back upstairs and so called from the kitchen. She got the answering machine and left a message.

"Still too hot for the porch?" she asked her mother.

"Yes, but not the backyard. Let's sit there."

They took their glasses and a plate of sugar cookies out back. There were chairs and a small table set out under a large black oak surrounded by a bed of lilies of the valley. They weren't in bloom now, but the columbines that had sprung up among them, managing to get just enough sunlight, were lovely.

"It's because I worry about you," Ursula said. "That's why I was angry."

"I know, but I wouldn't put myself in any danger." Pix suddenly thought of all the things she was responsible for, starting with her family. Well, she certainly hadn't been in peril. Half the state of Maine knew where she was every minute.

"It's just this terrific need to know what happened—maybe because I found the body. I can't not try to find out whatever I can," she told her mother.

"I understand. An enormous wrong has been done, two wrongs if, as we suspect, Adelaide was killed, too."

"You don't think she died of natural causes? A heart attack?"

"It may have been a heart attack, but I don't think it was natural. However, I could be wrong. I hope I'm wrong."

"Did Earl say anything more about the autopsy?" Pix realized she'd forgotten to ask him.

"He said they're not finished doing their tests. Rebecca wants very much to go home, although she's happy enough here. But the house is still sealed."

"This whole thing has been terribly hard on her."

"Yes, I suppose it has."

Pix told her mother what Seth had said about Addie's will.

"I haven't felt right about asking Rebecca so soon, but I'm not surprised. The whole show was always Addie's and James's, her husband. You wouldn't really remember him. Besides, he was sick at the end of his life. But he and Addie were well matched—two very strong-minded people. He was First Selectman for years. His people hadn't farmed for a long time, so he fished, yet buying the house in town set them apart from some of the others. Rebecca had lived in the house, taking care of her parents until they died, then moved out when James inherited it. She lived in Granville and worked at the Emporium until Addie asked her to move back in to help take care of James. After he died, she just stayed. But it was always James and Addie's house, even though Rebecca had lived there for most of her life."

"I hope she can stay at least for a little while. I get the feeling she'd like to move into Addie's big front bedroom with the view."

Her mother nodded. "I'm sure she would."

"What about the quilt? Has Rebecca said anything more about it?"

"I did ask her that, only she insists she's never seen it before and that if it had been in the house, she would have known about it. I suggested maybe the antiques dealer staying there had purchased it and left it for Addie to look at, but she said it wasn't the kind of thing he bought."

"That's true. Remember, he told us he was interested in clocks and furniture at the clambake." An image of Ursula deep in conversation with John Eggleston earlier that same day came into Pix's mind and she remembered she wanted to ask her mother some questions about him.

"Which reminds me, what were you and John talking about so earnestly over your lobsters?"

If her mother wondered at the abrupt change in subject, she did not show it. She was working on a pair of mittens with sailboats on the back for the Sanpere Stitchers Fair and her needles continued to click rapidly. Pix had worn similar mittens in her youth, ones with kittens, ice skates, and once her flower namesake done in purple on green. Pix was a fair knitter herself, but her mittens tended to be utilitarian solid colors, as the Miller children scattered them all over Aleford while sledding, making snow forts, and skating on the old reservoir.

"We were talking about changing one's occupation in midlife. He was expressing some amazement, and contentment, with the way the Lord had worked things out for him."

There didn't seem anything untoward here.

"What about Mitchell Pierce? Did John mention him to you or have you heard why Mitchell moved out?"

"It was foolish to think those two could ever have lived together. They were both much too stubborn, but that wasn't what happened. John caught Mitch using his tools without permission and went through the roof. It seems he's very, very particular about them—the same way an artist would be about his brushes, I imagine."

"What was Mitchell making?"

"That, I cannot tell you. You'll have to ask John. I do know he was very upset, because Mitch had waited until John was asleep, then went out to the woodworking shed. It may have been the subterfuge that bothered John most."

Woodworking in the dead of night, a fake quilt for his landlady: It all sounded very much as if Mitch had been in the business of making and selling forged antiques. But had John realized this, too?

Or had Mitch found something in John's shed? Something John didn't want him to know about?

Pix wanted to go home, make herself a drink, and stretch

out in the hammock. There was a pizza in the freezer and she could make a salad for their dinner. It was the utmost effort she could envision, and she knew Samantha wouldn't mind.

As it turned out, she didn't even have to do that much. Samantha called as she was about to leave to tell her she was going out with Arlene. Fred was helping some relative move and he'd let his girlfriend have his car. Samantha and Arlene were looking forward to Girls' Night Out: dinner and a movie in Granville. Pix gave her consent, said good-bye to her mother, and went home.

She poured herself a drink, put the pizza in the oven, and tried to decide whether she had enough energy to wash some lettuce for a salad. She didn't. She grabbed a handful of carrot and celery sticks to munch on instead and prepared to head for the hammock until the pizza was ready.

They kept only a small portion of the lawn mowed, so the kids could play croquet and badminton. The rest they left to its own devices, watching the cycle of wildflowers and grasses change over the course of the summer. Now the meadow was filled with white daisies, purple vetch, and hawkweed, yellow and dark red against the green. Pix stretched out in the hammock and looked up into the sky. The air was cooler as dusk approached. She gave herself a swing with her foot and balanced her glass on her chest. The phone rang.

She leapt from the hammock, setting the drink down on the grass, and sprinted for the house. Fortunately, Faith did not hang up.

"I figured you'd be out doing something energetic in the garden or digging clams at the shore. Whatever."

"Actually, I was lying in the hammock."

This did not sound like the Pix Miller she knew, Faith thought. When her Pix Miller indulged in contemplation, it was usually paired with something else—taking the dogs for a run or a ten-mile hike with Danny's Boy Scout troop. Things must be seriously out of kilter on Sanpere.

"What I have to tell you may help put some of the pieces together—or confuse things further. I'm not sure."

"Tell me. Tell me!"

"A few days ago, I called a friend of mine who has an antiques shop on Madison Avenue. She knows everybody in the antiques world, nationally and internationally. Anyway, right off the bat, she hadn't heard of Norman Osgood, which was pretty surprising. But she said she'd check her professional directories and ask around. She called me back today, and the man does not exist. She didn't even find him in the Manhattan phone book!"

"Faith, this is amazing. What made you think about checking on Norman?"

"You kept saying something wasn't quite right about him, and I trust your impressions absolutely."

"I'll let Earl know right away. Obviously Norman Osgood is an alias. If they can find out who he really is, we may have found the link between the two murders." And the murderer. She couldn't bring herself to say it out loud, even to Faith. The murderer? He'd been sitting on her blanket watching fireworks two nights ago.

"So, you actually think Adelaide was murdered?" Faith asked.

"Yes, and what's more, so does Mother."

"No question, then." Faith sighed. She knew how Pix and the whole Miller-Rowe clan felt about Sanpere Island, and now it would never again be the unsullied Eden it had been.

Pix told Faith about her trip to Sullivan and what she'd found at Jill's.

"I can't see Jill being involved in this—fake antiques, murder. Besides, she was close to the Bainbridges, wasn't she? And isn't she in that sewing group of your mother's? I believe it's an unwritten law in these societies that one lady does not bump another off."

221

"It does seem improbable, but I saw the quilt with my own eyes, and she *has* been behaving strangely this summer."

"True, if you're engaged in any sort of criminal activity, the last person you want for a fiancé is a cop."

They talked a bit more, particularly about the possibility that Mitch and Norman, or whoever he was, had been in business together.

"All those buying trips Norman made off the island—maybe he was meeting Mitch. And staying with the Bainbridges—that could have been to swindle them out of more things. Addie must have found out something. Oh dear, it's too dreadful to think about."

"Forget the Fairchilds and their traditions! I'm coming up this weekend!" Faith felt she belonged with her friend—and besides, things were heating up.

"No, you go. Plan to come up the following one. Arnie and Claire will be here by then and I'm giving a party for them."

Faith correctly sensed that Pix was more thrown by the idea of cooking for the party than solving any multitude of crimes.

"If you change your mind, call. We won't be leaving the house until ten."

"I will—and have fun."

"*Fun* is not the word we're looking for here, but I'll have something. Mosquito bites and sunburn maybe."

They laughed and said good-bye.

Pix had to cut some burned edges off the pizza and it was pretty crusty. She'd completely forgotten about it while talking to Faith. It tasted fine with the scotch she'd retrieved from the lawn, only one small ant having invaded the alcohol. She might not be hitting all the food groups, but it was exactly the kind of supper she wanted.

Afterward, she cleaned up, taking a mere merciful three minutes, and called Earl. He wasn't around, so she left a short message for him on the office machine to call her back, which he did an hour later. He did not seem unduly surprised at the news she had uncovered about Norman. Maybe he was getting used to having her for a partner, she thought somewhat smugly. Well, Faith had John Dunne, a detective lieutenant with the Massachusetts State Police.

She went to bed early and tried to read while she waited for Samantha. So, Norman Osgood wasn't an antiques dealer and might not be Norman Osgood, either. Who and what was he?

Samantha and Arlene had gone to the early movie and at nine o'clock found themselves in a booth at the new pizza restaurant near the cannery, consuming a large pie with everything on it but anchovies.

"Who eats those things? Why do they even bother putting them on the menu?" Arlene asked.

"My father loves them," Samantha said, making an appropriate face. "He says our tastes are not as refined as his."

"Yuck!" Arlene popped a stray piece of pepperoni in her mouth. It had taken her a few years to work up a taste for that. "What do you want to do? When do you have to get the car back to Fred?"

"I'm supposed to pick him up at his cousin's around ten-thirty. He's going to be ready to leave, I'm sure. They've been working since early afternoon."

The girls gave their full attention to the food before them for a moment. It was disappearing fast.

"It's great having a place where you can get real pizza on the island. Gives us somewhere to go, too."

The restaurant was jammed and the crowd at the door was eyeing their booth longingly—and in some cases, aggressively.

"Let's go," Samantha said after catching one particularly beady eye.

"Yeah, I'll take the rest for Fred in case he's hungry, although his aunt and mother sent over enough food for an army."

They got in the car and Arlene started the engine.

"Are you thinking what I'm thinking?" she said to Samantha.

"Will Fred be mad if we go without him?"

"No, I told him we might. He just wants to know what's in the trunk. He doesn't care if he's there or not. I don't think he likes to go into the cabin, anyway. He told me if he sees the stuff Duncan has around again, he might be tempted to smash it to pieces."

"Maybe it's better he doesn't come, then."

Arlene turned the car down Main Street and drove up the steep hill by the old Opera House, where the movies were shown now. In an earlier era when Granville had been a boomtown because of the granite quarries and fishing industry, Nellie Melba and other stars had tread the boards.

They parked the car by the side of the road again and made their way to the cabin with no difficulty. It was dark. Fred had left his flashlight in the glove compartment. With it to guide them, they went back up the tumbled-down stairs and pushed open the door. It was much as before—the bed mussed, some dirty clothes in the corner, the candles placed about. Samantha had come armed with several bobby pins.

"I'll try to open it and you stand guard."

She directed the beam of light on the lock and wiggled the bobby pin around, trying to press down on the catch. The first pin snapped and she tried another with greater success.

"It's open!"

Arlene came quickly to her side and they raised the lid slowly.

A heavy smell of incense made Samantha sneeze. The black robe was on top and they lifted it away apprehensively. Underneath were some books, magazines, and several large photograph albums. There were also more clothes.

"This is really weird. Why would he keep his clothes locked up?"

Samantha thought she knew why and she found she had a lump in her throat.

"These aren't his clothes. They're his father's. Look at this Nautica sailing jacket. It would be huge on Duncan."

At the bottom of the trunk was a box with a man's watch, some cuff links, and a bunch of birthday cards—all from Duncan to Dad.

"And the albums are probably full of pictures of him," Arlene said. "I can't believe it, but I'm actually feeling sorry for the creep."

The albums did have pictures, starting with Duncan as a baby and his young parents, smiling and looking straight into the camera with the confidence they would all live forever that a moment like this brings.

"Let's put it back. It's too sad."

"Sssh," Arlene said, and grabbed the flashlight, clicking it off.

Samantha heard it, too. Someone had jumped off the porch and was running into the woods.

They went to the window, but all they could see were some tiny red flashing lights disappearing into the darkness.

"Let's get out of here before he comes back!"

They hastily put the things into the trunk, trying to remember exactly where everything had been. Some of the books were about the supernatural, but the magazines were mostly back issues of *Hustler*. As Arlene refolded what must have been Mr. Cowley's gown from some graduation, something fell from the pocket and onto the floor with a clunk. Samantha trained the light on it.

It was a hunting knife.

"Should we give it to Earl?"

"Let's ask Fred. But I'll tell you one thing, I'm not leaving it here." Arlene took off the tank top she was wearing over her shirt and wrapped the knife in it.

They closed the trunk and returned to the car through the woods, much faster than they had come.

It was almost 10:30. They had been at the cabin much longer than they had thought.

"Look, just drop me at the end of my road and go get Fred."

"Are you sure?"

"So long as I have the flashlight, I'll be fine. I'd probably be fine without it, I've walked this road so many times."

"All right, but I'm calling your house in a little while. I want to be sure."

"That's very sweet, but be real. What's going to happen to me?"

"Do you want to take the knife?"

Samantha shuddered. "No thank you. And tell Fred that I think we should give it to Earl as soon as possible. Tonight. I think I should tell my mom about it, too."

"Yeah. I'm sure he'll agree. Why do you suppose Duncan didn't come in and blast us for being there? The last time, he yelled his head off."

"Maybe he planned to come back with his friends and ambush us. Or maybe he didn't know who or how many we were."

This first alternative left Samantha feeling distinctly shaky.

They were at the end of the Miller's road. Arlene stopped the car.

"Good-bye. I hate to do this, except I'm late already—"

Samantha cut her off. "Don't be silly. Go! It was my idea. If Fred is nice enough to let us have the car, the least we can do is get it back to him on time. He's probably imagining all kinds of things, from crumpled fenders to dropped transmissions."

Arlene laughed. "Talk to you later."

The moon was waning yet still quite full and bright. Samantha switched the flashlight off and decided to jog home. It was beautiful and the familiar sight of the dark trees on the opposite shore as she passed the first inlet comforted her. But who would comfort Duncan? The trunk and the candles above it were a virtual shrine to his dead father. She imagined him slipping his skinny arms into the sleeves of that familiar jacket, trying to recapture some of the warmth and security those other arms had provided. She thought about her own father and what would evoke him most. His handkerchiefs, she decided. Big white squares of the finest cotton. When she was sick with a cold, her nose raw from Kleenex, she used those. They smelled slightly of the drawer where he kept them—a drawer filled with years of Old Spice soap on a rope sets given to him by his kids. She felt tears pricking at her eyes and stopped to speak to herself sternly. "Your father's not dead, Miss Samantha Miller. Get a grip, girl." She laughed when she realized she'd said it out loud. She started jogging again, her mood elevated as she brought her knees up and down. She was almost home.

She was almost home before she realized that she wasn't the only runner out that night. Someone dressed in black streaked by her and knocked her to the ground. She screamed, felt a sharp pain on the back of her head, and had time for just one impression before losing consciousness.

Lights. Small, red twinkling lights.

Chapter 9

The phone was ringing. Pix swung her legs over the side of the bed, shoved her feet into her slippers, and ran downstairs. It must be Samantha needing a ride home.

"Hi, Mrs. Miller," Arlene said cheerily. "I know it's a little late, but can I speak to Samantha?"

"Isn't she with you?" Pix's chest tightened and her heart began to pound.

"You mean she's not home yet! I left her off at the end of your road about half an hour ago."

Pix dropped the phone and raced up to Samantha's room, calling her daughter's name. She had to be there. Pix hadn't heard her come in. Obviously, Samantha hadn't wanted to bother her and had gone straight to bed. Even as Pix opened the door, she knew none of this was true. The room was dark and the bed still neatly made.

Pausing only to grab her keys from the kitchen counter, she picked up the phone and told Arlene to call the police—and the ambulance corps. Then she got in the car and started slowly down the road, searching on either side for Samantha. The moon was bright; if it hadn't been, she would have missed her. Samantha was lying under a tree, partially concealed by a stand of large ferns. A few feet farther on, the ground dropped off to a ledge of jagged granite rocks, now nearly covered by the incoming tide.

She ran to her, calling, "Samantha! Samantha!" But there was no answer. She was sobbing as she reached her daughter, carefully putting her arms about her. She was warm and Pix could feel her soft breath on her mother's cheek. She was alive.

"Samantha! Oh dear God, please help us!" Pix had no idea what her child's injuries might be, so she dared not move her, but knelt next to her, cradling her, burying her face in her daughter's sweet-smelling hair. The night air was warm, yet Pix had never felt so cold.

She held her daughter's hand and felt for her pulse. It was steady. Samantha's eyelids fluttered.

"Samantha? Can you hear me?"

"Where am I, Mom? What's going on?" Samantha's voice started as a whisper, then got stronger. She looked about her in agitation. "My head hurts. It was Duncan. His shoes. I saw his shoes. Duncan hit me." She reached her hand to the back of her head and pulled it quickly away.

"Mom, I'm bleeding! I'm scared! Do something!" She began to cry.

"The ambulance will be here soon. Try to stay still." Pix had not seen the blood. She lay down next to her daughter, with her arm over Samantha's body to keep her calm. Where was the ambulance! With her other hand, she grasped Samantha's hand, wet with her own blood, tightly.

"Sssh, honey, don't worry. Everything's going to be all right."

But it wasn't.

After what seemed like several hours, she heard the ambulance siren and tears streamed down her face in relief. Earl was right behind them. He ran toward them.

"What happened?" he asked as the rescue workers rapidly assessed Samantha's injuries.

"I don't know! Arlene Prescott called and said she'd dropped Samantha off at the end of the road. When Samantha wasn't in the house, I came to look for her. She said it was Duncan. She saw his shoes!" The rescue workers were wrapping Samantha in a blanket and moving her onto a stretcher.

"She's had a concussion; we're treating her for shock," one of the squad said. "And she has a scalp wound that's going to need some sutures, but nothing seems to be broken. You want to ride with her?"

Pix climbed in the back of the ambulance for the drive over the bridge to the mainland. Samantha seemed to be sleeping. Pix was on one side, a corps member, bless him, on the other.

Duncan Cowley had attacked her daughter. Intending what?

At the hospital, Samantha was taken away before Pix could get out of the ambulance. Earl had been following and gave her a hand.

"I've been in touch with the state police and they're going down to the island to question the boy and his parents. You know she's going to get the best care possible here. I know how hard it is, but she's young and healthy. Everything's going to be fine, Pix."

Pix did not trust herself to do more than nod and let him lead her into the waiting room, where a nurse promptly put a cup of coffee loaded with sugar into her hand. Arlene and Fred were already there. For a moment, Pix was in the peculiar position of having to comfort Arlene when what she was feeling was anger. Why hadn't she driven Samantha to the door!

"I shouldn't have let her walk home," Arlene wailed.

Fred looked at Pix and told his girlfriend to be quiet. "No

one's blaming you. Now stop bothering Mrs. Miller." Arlene took a mighty gulp and calmed down.

Then they waited.

Someone at the nurse's station offered them more coffee, but Pix didn't want any. The cup she had drunk was making her feel jangly. She had called Sam soon after they'd arrived and he was waiting by the phone. She wanted him by her side. Hospital waiting rooms. She thought of all the hours she had spent in them: her father's last illness, a friend's mastectomy, Sam's ulcer, Danny's broken arm. No one talked except in occasional hushed voices. Each was totally absorbed in the thoughts being directed toward the room you weren't allowed to be in.

She knew, as Earl had said, that Samantha was going to be okay, but the nature of the attack—and all that blood—was taking her down these dark corridors in her mind.

Then, as it happened in hospitals, the time stretched out beyond anxiety into boredom, and finally numb fatigue.

Arlene suddenly got up. "The knife! I forgot all about the knife. It's in the car."

"What knife?" Fred asked.

"The one in Duncan's trunk. Thank God he didn't have it with him."

Earl tuned into the conversation. He'd been off with Jill on the long white sandy beach out at the Point.

He came over to them and said, "You better tell me all about it—and keep your voices down. We don't want to worry Mrs. Miller."

If Pix noticed that Earl and Fred left soon after, it didn't really register, nor did Fred's return alone. Earl walked in later. What did capture her immediate attention was the entry of a man in a white coat.

"Mrs. Miller?" Pix jumped up, for once unaware of the picture she presented. It was an odd one in these wee hours of the morning—she was in her pajamas, with Earl's jacket over them.

It was a young doctor, as most of them seemed to be these days. "Your daughter would like to see you." He was smiling.

"She's going to be all right?" Her tears flowed freely. Earl, Arlene, and Fred gathered close.

"Yes, though she's going to have a very large lump on her head and we had to do a little embroidery on her scalp—not much. The ambulance crew said from the way she was lying, she struck a tree root or a rock when she fell, which knocked her out cold. Samantha says someone pushed her and it must have been with some force. We also did a CAT scan and I don't see anything to be concerned about. We do want to keep her over night to be sure, but she's a very healthy specimen and should be just fine."

The news was overwhelming.

"When can I have a few words with her, Doctor?" Earl asked. "There seems to be an assault involved and we need all the information she can give us."

"If you keep it very brief, I don't see why you can't do it now. But"—he looked back at Arlene and Fred—"that's all. The best thing for her now is rest. She was pretty shaken up."

They nodded solemnly.

"Tell her . . . well, tell her I'm sorry and give her my love. And I'll be here as soon as she can have visitors."

Pix gave Arlene a hug, her recent anger totally vanished. Samantha had been dropped off at the end of the road, as had all of them day and night, hundreds of times.

The sight of her daughter in a hospital bed threatened to unhinge her, but Pix took a firm hold of herself—and Samantha.

"I have to call Daddy right away. He's waiting. Then I'll be right back. Earl wants to talk to you about what happened. Do you feel up to it?"

"They gave me something to make my head stop hurting

and I feel a little dopey, but I can tell him what happened. It was so quick, Mom." Samantha gave a little sob. "Duncan must really hate me!"

"Don't think about it, sweetheart. He's a very, very troubled boy."

As Pix was leaving to get Earl, the nurse came in. "You have a phone call, Mrs. Miller. You can take it out here."

Pix followed her and soon heard her husband's familiar voice. She told him what the doctor had said. "I just wish you were here, even though she's fine."

"Well, I will be in about three and a half hours tops."

"What!"

"I couldn't simply sit home. I'm a little south of Portland and will be at the hospital as soon as I can. Nobody's too concerned about speed limits at this time of night. If I do get stopped, I'll have them call Earl."

"Please be careful, darling." Pix was thrilled that he was on his way, but one Miller in the hospital was more than enough.

"Don't worry, I will."

She hung up and went back to Samantha's room, where she intended to spend the night.

Earl had finished questioning her.

"We'll let you know what happens with the Athertons. Duncan must have been upset that they were in his cabin and he blamed Samantha. But why he didn't confront her, I don't know. Usually, he just yells. I never expected violence." Earl's lips were tight. "He's been trouble since he arrived and we've been too soft with him. Not this time."

"In his cabin?" Pix had missed the story so far.

"I'll let Samantha tell you. The doctor told me I had five minutes and they're up. Take care of yourself, Pix. I'll be by in the morning." He gave her a quick hug and left. Before the door closed, she ran over and told him, "Sam is on his way." Earl nodded. "I'm sorry this happened. Samantha's a terrific kid. Now you get some rest, too."

Samantha was barely conscious, but for different reasons than earlier. She had heard the last part of their conversation, though.

"Daddy's coming?"

"Yes, he'll be here in a couple of hours."

"Good. I bet he wants to beat the shit out of Duncan."

Pix did not deny it. She wanted to do it herself.

The next morning, things were not so clear. Duncan Cowley had been at the nine o'clock movie that did not get out until past eleven. Two friends swore to it and Wendell Marshall, who manned the ticket booth, distinctly remembered selling him a ticket.

"It's hard to forget a kid with a hoop in his ear and green hair," he'd told Earl. Duncan had apparently streaked his locks with some sort of dye for the evening out. Now in the hard light of day, it looked pretty pathetic as he sat in Earl's office uneasily flanked by his parents. The state police had come to the house the night before and Jim had still not shaken off his indignation at his stepson for being the cause of their visit.

"In all my years on Sanpere Island, the police have never had to come to my house for any reason whatsoever. Now we want some answers here and we want them fast."

Earl thought this was his line, but he let it lie.

"Duncan," he said to the boy in a milder tone. The kid looked like he'd been through the mill. "We just want to know what happened. No one's accusing you of anything."

"Be real," the boy shouted. "You're never going to believe a fucking word I say, so why don't you go ahead and lock me up!" Earl wondered where Duncan had found the energy. Since he'd come in with Valerie and Jim, he'd sat slumped over in the chair, dressed as usual in black and smelling of stale beer and cigarettes. He was probably hungover from the night before. When the police had not found him at home, they'd driven around the island, turning their flashlight beams into a number of cars and soon locating Duncan in the backseat of one, trying to hide a six-pack under his scrawny frame.

Earl was pretty tired, too. This was the second time he'd talked with the Athertons and the boy himself. Duncan's denial and alibi had left Earl in a dilemma. He'd been asking around. There were only a few other kids who had the same shoes, mostly summer people. Those things cost a fortune. But in light of Duncan's alibi, he'd have to track down every pair and owner. As alibis went, it was a pretty good one. Patrons who got up in the middle of the film, obscuring the sight of those behind them, did not go unnoticed or unremarked on Sanpere. The only possibility was that Duncan had bought a ticket from Wendell and then immediately went out by another door. Could he have been so furious at Samantha that he'd plotted the attack ahead of time, even providing himself with an alibi? Of course his friends would lie through their teeth for him. At the moment, Earl was trying to find others, less loyal, who might have seen him in the audience. The whole thing was complicated by the group's penchant for the same style and color of dress. He'd have to hope Duncan was the only one with the nifty hairdo.

The boy claimed that he had not even known Samantha and Arlene had been in his cabin. He seemed pretty upset about it. Until Jim told him to shut his mouth and keep it shut, Duncan had tried to turn the tables, inveighing against the two girls. "They're the ones you should get. Trespassing. B and E. That's private property!"

Earl didn't say anything about the knife the girls had taken away. The night before, he'd taken it to the police station in Blue Hill for the state police to pick up. He hadn't heard anything since.

After a further wearying hour, Earl sent Duncan home with Jim and Valerie to what he was sure would be house arrest. Duncan cast an odd look back at the sergeant and Earl had the distinct impression that Duncan would have favored the one and only cell down the hall from the office—mostly used to store stationery supplies for the town hall.

Valerie had sat tight-lipped and grim throughout the ordeal. She seemed to have erected a wall between herself and the rest of the world. She was dressed in a simple blue-checked skirt and white blouse, no hat, no makeup. At one point, Duncan turned to her and said, "Why would I want to do anything to Samantha Miller? I don't even know her." Valerie just shook her head in utter defeat.

Earl walked out with them to their car. "Thank you for coming in."

"A rotten business," Jim said, "a sorry mess. Samantha's one of the best sailing instructors we've ever had at Maine Sail." He glared at Duncan.

An old pickup came roaring down the street—it needed a new muffler—and screeched to a halt next to them. John Eggleston, his hair a mess of disheveled fiery locks, leapt out and ran toward them.

"I just heard. Please, let's sit down and talk about what happened before anyone goes off the deep end."

During the long wait the night before, Pix had filled Earl in on everything Samantha had told her and had also mentioned her conversation with John. And John had, in fact, been in touch with Earl, asking him to keep an eye on the old quarry. Earl had touched on some of this with Duncan and the Athertons.

"You've done enough harm here! All your little talks! We know about the kinds of 'literature' you've been recommending and you may be hearing from my lawyer." Jim had apparently already dived in.

John stood for a moment, openmouthed. "Too late," he muttered, "too late."

He stood with Earl, watching the family drive away.

"I was hoping they'd let the boy stay with me for a while until things cool down."

"I doubt there's much hope of that. One way or another, Duncan Cowley is going off this island."

It was almost dark when Pix woke up. She lay still for a moment. Sam had thrown a light blanket over her. The heat was finally breaking. She looked out the window at the familiar line of pines pointing to the boathouse and shore. The outcroppings of pink granite were faintly visible, or maybe it was because she knew they were there that she could see them. She could hear Sam and Samantha talking in her room down the hall. Pix felt warm and safe. She stood up and draped the blanket around her shoulders, trailing it like a queen's mantle as she went in to see her daughter and husband.

"Mom, Daddy's cheating!" Samantha laughed. They were playing Uno.

"That's nice," said Pix. "What do you want for supper?"

Samantha was still in a good mood three days later, but was beginning to get restless. She had been showered with attention in both tangible and intangible forms. The campers had all made cards for her. Susannah and Geoff had created three gushing ones each. The Fairchilds had sent a basket of yellow roses, baby's breath, and daisies—not the kind the Millers gathered in big bunches from the meadow to weave into crowns or set about the house in a variety of containers, but perfect daisies with huge yolk yellow centers and every creamy white petal perfect. No tiny holes as evidence that some creature had rested there. Gert Prescott left two lemon meringue pies. Ursula brought a beautiful conch shell Samantha had long coveted.

Valerie dropped by to leave a tiny porcelain box with the words FORGET ME NOT surrounded by the flowers on the lid. She tried to say how sorry they were to Pix, but Pix, feeling very uncomfortable, cut her off, thanking her and adding,

"Samantha is fine, thank God, and maybe Duncan will get the help he needs now."

That you all need, she finished silently.

Sam had stayed until Monday night and he and Pix had spent a great deal of time talking together and with Earl about what to do. In the end, with Samantha's approval, they decided not to press charges. It wasn't because of lack of evidence but, rather, because they felt that Duncan might only become more withdrawn and disturbed if caught up in the juvie system. Both Pix and Sam had been very moved by Samantha's description of what the boy kept in his trunk. Earl spoke to the Athertons and they were going to find an appropriate residential school with a summer program—not the military one—for their son as soon as possible. Depending on how he did and what those working with him said, they'd decide whether he would return home in the fall or stay.

Sam had left reluctantly, trying up to the last minute to get his wife and his daughter to go back with him, but neither woman wanted to budge.

"I'm not going to let her out of my sight," Pix told her husband, "especially at night. Earl doesn't think she's in any danger. Duncan will be leaving soon, and we can't run away."

Sam agreed intellectually, yet his gut told him otherwise. "I'll be back Friday night." Pix wasn't going to argue with that.

Adelaide Bainbridge's funeral was Tuesday morning.

Pix and Samantha had driven out to The Pines to get Ursula. Rebecca had been picked up earlier by a contingent of Bainbridge cousins feeling pangs of familial obligation: "Poor old Becky."

Samantha had had plenty of company since she'd returned home from the hospital Saturday morning, none more constant than her grandmother's. Pix knew her mother would be terribly shaken by what had happened and she was right.

Today, Ursula opened the door to Samantha, who was running up the steps, the only evidence of the attack and her slight concussion hidden by her hair. To all intents and purposes, she was fully recovered, but the pain in the older woman's eyes was fresh. Pix was struck anew by how much her mother seemed to have aged since Saturday. There were dark shadows and lines that Pix had never seen on Ursula's face before. When she spoke, it was not in her usual timbre. The volume had been turned down and the treble increased.

"Mother, are you sure you want to go?" Pix asked. "They'll be so many people at the service, no one will miss us."

"Of course I want to go—and Rebecca would notice, for one. Besides, I couldn't miss Addie's funeral. I've known her for so many years."

Pix thought her mother would say this and she resolved to get her away as soon as possible after the graveside service.

As they drove across the causeway back toward Sanpere Village, Pix again noted the happy vacationers on the beach and out in their boats, enjoying the typical Maine day. The heat spell had broken and normal July weather was back. There was a good stiff breeze on the water, turning up small whitecaps. The sun shone just enough for comfort and a few hardy souls were swimming.

"I'm glad it's not so hot today. The idea of sitting through the service wondering who was going to pass out, maybe even me, is distinctly unappealing."

Samantha laughed. The idea of her mother passing out in any situation seemed pretty far-fetched—but then, she had been in no shape to judge on Friday night.

"Addie could never take the heat, even when she was thin."

"*Addie was thin?*" In Pix's memory, Adelaide had always been a substantial woman.

"Oh yes, she was thin—and very pretty—when she was young. She could have had her pick of any number of the boys. My brother, Tom, used to talk about the beautiful lighthousekeeper's daughter. She'd come over for dances and such, but even then she tended to be outspoken. He thought she'd probably boss a man to death.''

It hit Pix that they were on their way to a funeral. So much had been going on that she'd been viewing the morning's activity as a kind of respite, especially since the medical examiner had ruled the death due to heart failure, plain and simple; nothing to do with quilts, crosses—or knives. Samantha had told her about the knife they'd found. She would have to ask Earl about it.

"Rebecca must have been mistaken about the quilt,'' she said to her mother, who was sitting up straight in the seat next to her, holding her purse in gloved hands. "I hope it's not a sign that she's beginning to deteriorate.''

"I don't think Rebecca Bainbridge's going downhill any faster than the rest of us—but she may have made a mistake with the quilt.''

Pix looked over to exchange a smile with her mother about the downhill remark, but her mother's face was shut up tight.

The whole island was crowded into the simple white church that sat high on a hill facing out to Penobscot Bay where Addie had worshiped, off and on—mostly on, of late.

The Sanpere Stitchers all sat in one pew, immediately behind Rebecca and the rest of the family. Pix reached for Samantha's hand and gave it a squeeze. She had told her daughter she didn't need to come but had been happy when Samantha wanted to be there. Pix was still not ready to be separated from her, even for an hour or two. She looked around the church, flooded with sunshine from the clear long, glass windows that framed the bay above the plain altar and that on the sides offered a view of the woods on the left, the cemetery on the right. Soon Adelaide would join her husband, James, there. The stone with both their names had been in place for many years, merely waiting for this last date to be carved on its polished granite surface.

Pix looked down the row of faces in her pew: Nan Marshall; Gert, Dot, and Louella Prescott; Mabel Hamilton; Louise Frazier; Jill Merriwether; Serena Marshall; and others. These island women held the community together in so many ways, a root system like the evergreens and ground covers that kept the thin layer of earth on top of this inhabited rock from washing off into the sea. The women were all subdued but showed no outward signs of grief. It was Addie's time. And she had had a long life, not like some: Louella's grandson, lost diving for urchins; Mabel's daughter, killed in a car accident. Pix saw Jill bow her head suddenly. In silent prayer? What—or whom—was she thinking about? Ursula's head was unbowed and her face appeared swept clean of all expression, except to one who knew her as well as her daughter did. Something was troubling Mother. The slight lowering of her eyebrows, the barely perceptible tightening of her lips. Pix looked at her mother's lap. Her hands were clenched together, thumbs locked over each other. Not in prayer. She had been upset about the attack on Samantha and the death of her old friend, of course, but was there something else? Mother was remarkably good at keeping things from people. Pix resolved to find out what was bothering her, even if it took the rest of the summer.

She gave a surreptitious glance over her shoulder as they stood for a hymn. The church was indeed packed. Norman Osgood was in one of the rear pews, solemn-faced. Seth was also in the rear. He seemed perfectly at ease in his unaccustomed formal garb, a well-cut dark suit. Pix wondered why he wasn't up with the rest of the family. Had to get back to work quickly?

They sat down and the minister began his eulogy. Rebecca began to cry audibly. She was going home today, she'd told Ursula. She'd been able to go back ever since the final report from the state medical examiner's office, but at Ursula Rowe's urging, Rebecca had decided to stay at The Pines until after the funeral. Would she move to the front bedroom right away? Pix wondered. Or would she stay in the small one in back until a decent period of mourning had passed? And what would the family do? Surely not turn her out immediately. Pix hoped the force of island opinion, mainly the formidable force of the Sewing Circle, would prevent that from happening.

She realized she had barely listened to the service. She was agitated, too. The world was topsy-turvy and the sooner she could get her feet firmly planted on the ground, the better. One death was resolved, but the other was not.

They all filed out of the church in silence as the organist played Adelaide's favorite hymn, "Abide with Me." Then they buried her.

"Mother, you cannot keep me locked up like some princess in a tower! I want to get back to work. They need me! And nothing could be safer. I'm surrounded by hordes of little munchkins every minute I'm there. You can drive me over and pick me up. I won't even go to the bathroom by myself, I promise. But you've got to let me leave. I'm starting to go nuts here."

The argument had begun the night before and had not been resolved by bedtime. Now, the next morning, Samantha was up bright and early, perched at the foot of her mother's bed, picking up where she had left off. Pix hadn't slept well. She knew Samantha would have to resume her schedule sometime, but why did it have to be today? She'd hoped to keep her close to home for another week at least to make sure she was all right.

"I'm fine," Samantha argued. "The doctor said I could go back to work when I felt up to it, and I feel great. This is *your* problem, not mine. Would it make you feel any better to follow me around the whole morning?"

"Yes," Pix answered immediately, "it would."

"Oh, Mother!" was Samantha's annoyed reply as she noisily stomped off to her room.

Pix knew she was beaten and she also knew that she had to let her daughter go. Much as she wished to, she could not keep Samantha wrapped in cotton wool for the rest of the summer—or the rest of her life. She followed her down the hall.

"All right. But I drive you there and back. Plus, if you get tired or feel anything out of the ordinary at all, you call immediately. I'll be here all morning." Sitting by the phone.

Samantha flung herself at her mother and gave her a big kiss. "I love you, Mom. Now we'd better hurry. I don't want to be late."

Well, at least it was Mom again.

Samantha felt like a bird let free from its cage. She darted into the kitchen to say hello to everyone before meeting her group down by the waterfront.

"It's great to have you back, Sam. I didn't think your mom would let you out so soon," Arlene said after giving her friend a big hug.

"Desperate situations call for desperate measures. I had to get tough. Would you believe at the last minute she wanted me to bring the dogs? Like they would really protect me. And can you imagine how nuts the kids would be!"

They laughed and Samantha went down to the waterfront, where she was greeted with enthusiasm, Susannah dramatically throwing her skinny little body straight into Samantha's arms. "You're okay! I thought I'd never see you again!"

Susannah could be headed for a career on the stage, and living in Manhattan as she did, this might come to pass, Samantha thought. The little girl seemed constantly to be playing some sort of role. Geoff was hovering nearby. Samantha quickly got her group together and they started for the boats. The kids had been quick learners and she was taking them out on the water two at a time while the others practiced knot tying and studied the sailing manual. She'd allowed them to pick their own partners, figuring they'd work best with someone they liked. Geoff and Susannah had chosen each other and were the fourth pair to go with Samantha. She kept quiet and let them set sail. They started off fine, but soon the sail was luffing and the boat almost at a standstill.

"All right now, what do we do?" Samantha asked.

"We did it on purpose, Samantha," Geoff said. "We have something to tell you." His voice was firm and serious.

Susanna had less control, or more theatrics. "It's our fault that you got hurt."

"What!" Samantha said in amazement.

"Well, not exactly our fault," Geoff explained, "but we kind of feel that maybe if we'd told you what we'd been doing sooner, then it might not have happened."

"What *have* you been doing?" Samantha asked sternly.

"Your getting hurt was like a punishment to us." Susannah was off and running. Geoff interrupted her.

"Let's just tell her." He turned toward Samantha. "It started because Susannah and I were really pissed off at coming here. Maybe we kind of hoped we'd get caught and be kicked out."

Samantha got a sinking feeling in the pit of her stomach. The mice. She looked at the two cherubic faces in front of her.

"You're not telling me you put those dead mice in the kitchen are you?" she gasped.

"Yuck! No Way!" said Susannah. "Although it did make things more fun."

Geoff continued patiently. "We did all the other stuff—the short sheeting, the spoiled milk, the salt in the sugar . . ."

"Not the paint!" Again Samantha leapt to the worst.

"No, not the paint. We like sailing. But," he had the grace to lower his head slightly, "we did screw up the parade."

"And God punished us," Susannah declared solemnly. "He let you get hurt and you're the most decent thing here. Besides you, Geoff," she hastened to add.

"God doesn't work that way, but we'll talk about that some

other time. What we have to do now is tell Mr. Atherton what's been going on."

Geoff and Susannah's expressions clearly indicated they would rather face their Maker.

"Do you think he'll send us home?" Geoff asked.

"I thought that's what you wanted?"

"Only at first, then doing stuff was fun because everybody was getting so crazed at everything else that was going on. This is the best camp I've ever been to."

Susannah nodded agreement.

The idiots, Samantha thought as she headed the boat back to shore and proceeded to give them a talking-to that would have made her mother proud.

The rest of the group was waiting for them on the dock with puzzled expressions on their faces.

"What was taking you guys so long? There's a good wind today. Why couldn't you come about?" one of them asked. "We're going to be late for lunch."

"You all run along and I'll put everything away. Tell Mr. Atherton that Geoff and Susannah are helping me. We'll be there as soon as we can."

As they stowed the gear, the two children chattered happily like the reprieved felons they were. Samantha, the godess, didn't hate them. She had barely yelled.

Samantha was preoccupied. So it hadn't been Duncan who had spoiled the parade.

But that still left everything else.

After lunch, Samantha called home with the news. Her mother had been surprised, amused, and ultimately sympathetic.

"So, I'm going to take them to Jim now and then I'd really like to spend the afternoon here. The counselors can use my help and I hate to leave the kids like this. I won't stay any later than five and you can pick me up at the Athertons' house, where I will stay absolutely put. I left without my paycheck

Friday, Jim told me. I didn't know I would be getting one so soon and it's at the office over there."

"As long as you're not too tired, but swear that you'll get someone to walk you over."

"All right, but I'm only doing this to make you happy."

"Could there be a better reason?"

"Mother! I've got to go."

Jim reacted to Susannah and Geoff's confession almost absentmindedly. Samantha could only assume that his problems with Duncan overshadowed everything else, even the sabotage of the Fourth of July parade, one of Jim's favorite camp events. "The jewel in the crown of summer," he called the fancy formations they dreamed up each year.

Chastised and chastened, the two children were released to their counselors. They would have to apologize to the whole camp. Jim would also inform their parents and he was firm. He didn't think he could accept them as campers again. Still, he told them they could write and plead their case this winter.

"He was really fair," Samantha told Arlene at the end of the day as her duenna escorted her through the woods to the "Million Dollar Mansion." "Maybe if he treated Duncan the way he treats the campers, things wouldn't have gotten so messed up."

"Dream on! The guy is wacko. He's responsible for those stitches in your head, remember."

"I know." Samantha stopped in the middle of the path. "But something has to make someone like that."

"You are too good. Remind me to call Mother Teresa and tell her to move over. Duncan is pond scum, pure and simple."

Samantha had to laugh at Arlene's choice of imagery, from Mother Teresa to pond scum.

"All right, I agree."

Arlene waved good-bye as Samantha knocked at the front door. Valerie opened it immediately. She was expecting her.

246

"Come in. How are you feeling? Are you sure you should be back at work so soon?"

"You sound like my mother," Samantha said. "I'm fine and I was beginning to get stir-crazy."

"Come on upstairs. Your check is in my office."

Samantha followed her up the spiral staircase, made by one of the last practitioners of this art in the state.

The only thing that distinguished the thoroughly feminine boudoir Valerie ushered Samantha into as an office was the Macintosh on a pale green-and-white sponge-painted table underneath one of the windows. Beside it was a daybed covered by a billowy white spread and piled high with pillows. Samantha imagined how lovely it would feel to lean back into that down sea of rose chintzes and white eyelet. The rug was covered by more roses, woven against a dark green background. In contrast to the rest of the house, the walls were not painted off-white, but papered in a sage stripe with a Victorian frieze of lilacs above. Two wicker chairs with plump cushions—you wouldn't have marks on the back of your legs from these—sat on either side of the French doors leading to a small secluded balcony overlooking the cove.

"I like to sunbathe there," Valerie said, following Samantha's eye. "I let myself go in here. I do spent quite a bit of time in this room. Jim hates it. Too much froufrou, he says," and she laughed.

"Well, I love it. I'd give anything for one like it!" Samantha enthused, forgetting her insistence two years earlier that Pix get rid of any and all vestiges of flowers, dotted swiss, and ribbon from Samantha's bedroom.

Valerie was rummaging around on the table, pulling open the drawer in the middle.

"Your check must be in Jim's study. Why don't you admire the view. I'll be back in a minute."

Samantha dutifully sat in one of the chairs. It was as comfortable as it looked. The phone on Valerie's desk rang, then stopped. She must have answered it downstairs. Samantha stood up and walked around the room, admiring the primitive still lifes that hung on the walls. Next to a plant stand with an arrangement of wax fruit and flowers never seasonal mates in nature, under a large glass dome, there was a closet door. Feeling slightly guilty, Samantha decided to open it after first listening carefully to make sure Valerie wasn't coming up the stairs. She just had to see what kind of leisure wear Valerie kept here—Victoria's Secret or Laura Ashley? She giggled and wished Arlene was with her. She'd die when Samantha told her.

She quietly turned the intricately embossed brass doorknob.

The closet was huge, but instead of the negligees, tea gowns, and whatever that Samantha had expected, there was nothing except a large antique armoire. It had an ornate lock but no key. The closet smelled strongly of potpourri and Samantha sneezed. She reached into her jeans pocket for a tissue. She didn't have one. Yet, there was something else there. Down at the bottom was the key she'd found over two weeks ago, that sunny day when she and Mom had taken the dogs for a walk to see how the Fairchild's new house was coming along—a sunny day that seemed to have had its start in another life.

All of a sudden, she felt nervous. She held the key in her hand. It had been so warm, she hadn't been wearing jeans much. This was the first time since that long-ago Sunday she'd had this pair on.

It was an ornate key, like the lock.

Before she could change her mind, she put it in, turned, and heard the click as the doors opened. When she saw what was inside, she laughed in relief. A whole shelf of plastic Mickey Mouse figures, old ones. There were also some folk art carvings of animals and one of a figure that looked like someone from the Bible. On other shelves were piles of quilts. This was obviously where Valerie kept her finds.

Samantha closed one of the doors and bent down to make sure the quilts didn't get in the way. She reached under a bunch to ease them farther into the chest and immediately pulled back, as if she'd put her hand into a blazing fire instead of a stack of linens. She closed the other door, pocketed the key, shut the closet door fast, and sat back down, looking straight out to sea. Her heart was pounding, her cheeks blazing.

There had been a neat little blue cross stitched on the binding of each of the quilts. They lined up like little soldiers. The crosses again. There had been one on Mitchell Pierce's quilt. There had been one on the quilt her mother had bought, a quilt her mother had told her was a fake. Should she tell Valerie? What should she do? She put her hands up to her cheeks to try to cool them down. They felt ice-cold against her blushes. She took a deep breath. Valerie was coming.

"The view is really something. I could stay here forever," she said in as normal a tone as she could.

"I hope you don't have to, dear." Valerie's tone wasn't normal at all. Samantha twisted around in the chair.

Valerie might have brought the paycheck, but she had also brought an extremely lethal-looking gun, which she was handling with ease, pointing it directly between her employee's big brown eyes.

"I have to run. I'm already a bit late picking Samantha up, but she's waiting for me at the Athertons' house, and it's certainly no punishment for her to revel in Valerie's company amid Valerie's perfect taste. If anything, she'll probably 'Oh, Mother' me for getting there too soon."

Faith laughed—while she still could. Amy, happily playing next to her adored Mommy on a water-filled mat, complete with floating spongy fish, would no doubt put her through this sometime in the future, as well.

"All right. I just wanted to check in and hear about the funeral, though this one sounds pretty tame." Faith and Pix had attended a more dramatic service on the island several summers ago—one that people were still talking about.

"Yes, poor Addie. Poor Rebecca. But I suppose their lives have been happy ones, if not bursting with excitement. And Adelaide really did make a name for herself in the quilt world."

"Hmmm," Faith was ready to move on back to the living, especially her own life. "If Tom can get away early, we'll be up Friday night. Do you think Seth will have started the framing by then?"

"He said he would, and even though it's been cooler, we haven't had any rain, so the foundation should be dry soon."

"I can't wait to see it—and you, and Samantha."

"Likewise, I'm sure."

The two women hung up. Faith reached for Amy. "Your first trip of many to Sanpere Island," she told her child, who listened intently and replied with a string of appropriate nonsense syllables. Was it just because she was a mother that Faith thought she could discern the words *wanna go, wanna go?* Well, I want to go, too, Faith reflected. With the amount she was spending calling Pix, it might have been cheaper, and more sensible, to have shut down the company and gone up in July in the first place. Besides, although things seemed to have settled down on the island, she knew she wouldn't feel easy until she saw Pix and especially Samantha for herself.

"You'll like it there." She continued to hold a one-sided conversation with her child, a situation she'd eventually gotten used to with Ben. In his early days, she'd felt as if she was talking to a cat or some other domesticated pet. "It has icy cold water, lots of bugs, no place to eat, no place to shop, nothing much to do." And they were building a house in this Shangri-la.

Pix knocked loudly at the Athertons' front door and, receiving no reply, knocked again. Perhaps they were on the deck in the front of the house. She walked around, didn't see anyone, and went back to the door. She knocked yet again, then did what she normally did in Sanpere: walked in. She could hear Valerie's voice coming from upstairs.

"It's me, Pix," she called from the bottom of the spiral. Taking the silence for an invitation, she went on up. She was curious to see more of the house. At the top of the stairs, she saw an open door and through it Valerie's back. She entered the room. "Sorry I'm a bit late . . ." Her apology was cut short first by her initial impression of the decor—it was fit for a little princess, or an aging romance writer—then by the gun.

"What's going on! Samantha, are you all right?"

"Shut up and sit down in the other chair."

Pix was so stunned that for a moment she couldn't move. It was simply too much to take in all at once. Valerie?

"Move!"

She moved.

Samantha had been similarly turned to stone. She had hardly moved a muscle since Valerie had entered the room; even Pix's arrival did not cause more than a flutter of an eyelash. Every thought she had directed her to keep still and stay alive. Her mother reached for her hand and she grabbed it, but did not shift her gaze or open her mouth.

Valerie, however, was talking to herself nonstop. Tapping her foot in annoyance yet maintaining a steady aim, she sat down on the daybed, incongruously surrounded by lace.

"Everything was perfect! Mitch was out of the way. We'd heard Seth tell his crew that they would be pouring the foundation after they finished the work at the camp. Perfect!" She was fuming. "Mitch, the old lush. Couldn't keep his mouth shut *and* he thought he should get more money. For what? I ask you." Pix correctly assumed this was a purely rhetorical question, especially since Valerie did not even pause before continuing her tirade. "So he could make things look old. Big deal. There are plenty of people to take his place—or who could have taken his place." If looks could indeed kill, Pix would have been effectively demolished and the gun superfluous. "But *you* had to start playing Nancy Drew. Still, that didn't get anywhere, and I was home free. I had even gotten rid of Duncan, so life around here could be a little more peaceful. I thought we were all going to have a lot of fun together. You haven't been a good friend at all!" She was pouting now.

The woman must be absolutely mad, Pix thought. She was talking as if Pix had done her out of an invitation to the Magnolia Ball or some such thing at the same time as she was confessing to murder! What else could the references to Mitch being "out of the way" and "pouring the foundation" mean?

The initial shock had passed and Pix was never one to sit meekly by.

"Valerie, put that gun down before someone gets hurt. I have no idea what you're talking about and you're upsetting Samantha—and me." Pix grasped for an out. "Did you think she was an intruder?" It was pretty feeble and she quickly followed it with some soothing words in as warm a voice as she could manage, "And what's this nonsense about our not being friends? You know that's not true."

If Samantha was surprised at her mother's sudden gift for bold-faced lying, she didn't show it.

"Now, Pix"—Valerie shook the gun like a chiding finger— "friends help friends, and you haven't helped me one little bit. I was all ready to settle down in my beautiful house for the rest of my life, but that's all spoiled. And you're to blame. Now, I have to think what to do."

Pix offered a suggestion. "Why don't we just forget that any of this happened and we'll go home."

"I said I was thinking! Shush!"

Samantha squeezed her mother's hand and Pix obeyed. She felt a sudden bleak stab of despair.

The spiral staircase did not muffle footsteps. Pix listened with a lifting of her heart as the sounds continued, mounting quickly to the second floor. Jim threw open the door.

"I don't have much time. I have to be back for my nature group after dinner."

So much for any hope of rescue. The Athertons were definitely a team.

"Her mother just barged in. Came to pick her up. As I said on the phone, I saw her go into the closet on the monitor in your den. Somehow she had a key to the armoire." Valerie looked away from Jim, to Samantha. "And where did you get that key, young lady? How many other times have you been snooping around our things!"

Samantha opened her mouth, but words did not come out. She thought she might be sick.

"Answer me!"

"In the woods. I found it in the woods out by the Fairchilds' new house," she whispered.

"Mitch must have had it in his pocket and it dropped out when we were carrying him," Jim said meditatively. He might have been mulling over the answer to a crossword-puzzle clue.

Meanwhile, Pix was trying to piece it all together. Samantha must have stumbled across something incriminating in the closet, something no one was meant to see. Pix had heard that along with their gold faucets and bidets, the Athertons had a state-of-the-art surveillance system. Yet it was the innocent caught by the guilty in this case.

"Jim, Samantha merely came over to get her check. I'm sure she didn't mean to pry into anything, but you know how teenagers are." She was sure her daughter would forgive her. "There doesn't seem to be any harm done, so why don't we simply stop this. I'd like to go home."

"And I wish I could let you go, but we can't." Jim sounded genuinely sorry. "You may not understand all that is happening now—I know you wouldn't lie to us; you're too good a friend—however you'll figure it out later and have to tell Earl. Then where will Valerie and I be? No, I'm afraid it's too late."

There it was again. The friendship thing. Well, friends didn't aim guns at friends in Pix's book. She couldn't think of anything to say and decided to keep quiet and concentrate on how she and her daughter were going to get away from these two lunatics. She was trying to replace all her fear with anger and it was working.

"It doesn't matter if we make a mess in here, because we're going to have to leave the house in any case." Valerie was speaking matter-of-factly. "So, why don't we kill them both now and get rid of the bodies after dark?"

"What!" Pix couldn't help herself.

Jim seemed a bit taken aback also.

"Honey, I'm not so sure. I mean, I've known Pix for simply ages, my whole life, in fact."

"So what? You knew Mitch—and Buddy, for that matter."

Buddy? Bernard Cowley! They had killed him, too!

"But not closely. I only met Buddy once or twice, remember, and of course he really did drown, albeit with a bit of help from you. Pix is another matter. Our parents used to play bridge together."

"Oh, well then, that changes everything." Valerie spoke with heavy sarcasm. "Why *don't* we let them go, then?"

Jim put his arm around his wife's shoulder in a gesture of affection. "Now, don't go getting all huffy, sweetcakes. I know we can't let them go, but I don't like the idea of having their deaths on *my* hands. We'll figure something out, don't you worry."

Pix had the feeling she was watching a strange combination of Ozzie and Harriet and Bonnie and Clyde.

"Look," he continued, "we'll tie them up and you can keep on eye on them. We can't go anywhere until after dark, anyway. And now I really *do* have to get back. The kids will be waiting. We're going to look at slides of seabirds."

The camp, Jim's beloved camp.

"Jim," Pix asked, "how can you give up Maine Sail? It's been a part of your family all these years. You love it. It's in your blood. Do you want to say good-bye to it forever?" Pix thought if she talked like Jim, she'd have a better chance of getting through to him.

He did indeed look downcast. "I know. There's always been the sad possibility we'd have to cut and run. That's why I got the new boat, biggest diesel engine Caterpillar makes. I was going to enter the lobster-boat races next month." He nodded his head toward the cove, where it bobbed in the water not far from the sloop. "Maine Sail was the most important thing in my life until I met Valerie, and you're right, I will miss it. But, Pix dear, there are other places and I'll have another camp. Of that, I'm sure. Don't you worry. Now, why don't you come with me? I think we'll have to separate you." This last was in a sterner, "caught talking after lights out" voice.

Separation—it was what Pix was afraid of, Samantha, too.

"Mom!"

"No." Pix stood up and pulled Samantha into her arms. "I'm not leaving my daughter's side." She hoped Jim's parents had been lucky at cards.

He sighed. "Oh all right, you can stay together. Give me the gun, honey, and get some rope from the basement. Here's a thought. Maybe we should lock them in the wine cellar? It would be quicker."

"Yes, and why don't we give them some of the Baccarat so they can enjoy a glass or two." Valerie was still bitter.

"I doubt they would wish to imbibe now, Val. Besides, Samantha is underage. No, we best leave them here. They might break one of the bottles."

Nuts, completely nuts. The words echoed in Pix's head as she waited for Valerie's return. When Jim had mentioned the wine cellar, she'd had a thought. There was always the possibility that someone delivering something—the handyman at work, or maybe Gert Prescott coming to clean—would see the odd procession through the huge plate-glass windows, but they couldn't court even this slim chance.

"All right. That should do it."

Valerie dumped enough hemp to tie up the *Queen Mary* at her husband's feet and took the gun firmly in her own hand.

"Good, good," Jim said as he started to wind the coils around Pix, finishing with what she knew must be very efficient knots. After all, the man taught the art.

"Oh, by the way, my love, I almost forgot." He gave a sharp yank to tighten the rope around Pix's wrists. It dug painfully into her skin and she winced. "Sorry, Pix," he said, then continued to address his wife. "As I was saying, Samantha was very clever and got two campers to confess to some of the pranks that have been occurring. Apparently, they were angry at being here and wanted to get sent home or that's how it started anyway. It actually is rather funny. *They* were responsible for the parade! Here we thought it was Duncan all this time."

Valerie did laugh. "That *is* one on us, but it helped to tarnish his reputation. I probably didn't need to paint those sails—the mice and maybe the bird would have been enough with the parade. I ruined a perfectly good pair of pants for nothing."

"I do wish you had consulted me before that one." The change in Jim's voice was a grim reminder of the way he behaved when pushed to anger. "What if it hadn't come off? Those sails are custom-made for us."

"If you had known, you wouldn't have been so convincing, sugar. Now I thought you were in a hurry."

"What can I be thinking of?" He hastened to bind Samantha.

The job done, complete with handkerchiefs over their mouths, he kissed his wife good-bye and ran down the stairs, but first he took Pix's car keys from her purse, apologizing. "We mustn't leave the car parked out front. Sorry."

Jim gone, Valerie had clearly had enough of the Millers' company and told them, "Now remember, my parents didn't play games with yours and I'm in no mood for any games with you. I can see everything that goes on in here, so don't try anything." She closed the door hard.

Trussed up like the proverbial Thanksgiving bird, Pix thought this virtually impossible, nor was she planning on giving any indication like rolling over and futilely trying to cut the rope by rubbing it on the slick paint of the desk leg. Valerie alone was as dangerous as a well full of copperheads. Pix could hear her now: "Oops, sugar, the gun just kind of went off." Her well manicured hands seemed able to support any number of deaths.

At least she was lying close to Samantha. Now she inched still nearer. Her daughter had tears in her eyes and Pix could almost smell the fear coming from her body. Every maternal nerve ached to comfort Samantha. She clenched her teeth, unclenched, and miraculously the handkerchief loosened. She tried it again. And again. Soon she was able to talk.

"Clench and unclench your jaw. I've been able to loosen the gag," she whispered.

Samantha went through similar contortions and after a while was able to whisper back, "What are we going to do? Are we going to die?"

"No. Don't even think of it." Pix wanted to distract Samantha. "Now tell me what happened? What's in the closet?"

"Oh, Mom, there are stacks of those quilts. The ones with the blue X's—and more shelves full of a lot of other antiques."

"What kinds?"

"Toys mostly—plastic Mickey Mouse figurines. Also some wooden carvings of animals. Oh, and one of a figure. It looked like John the Baptist or someone like that from the Bible."

Mickey Mouses. Pix could hear Earl's voice explaining just how they were faked. And the folk art, folk art similar to what was at Jill's.

Mitch and the Athertons' business partners in marketing fake antiques—deadly partners for Mitch. They had killed him and used one of the phony quilts to bury him in. She'd been right. The marks indicated which were real and which were copies. They'd gotten sloppy about removing them. And Samantha had opened the door.

"But what did she mean about Duncan? And Mom, she killed her own husband!"

"I know, darling, it's beyond belief. Poor Duncan. All this time he's felt responsible, and really his mother was just waiting for him to go to sleep so she could push Bernard overboard." Pix shuddered. It was getting cooler as the sun dropped steadily toward the horizon. Obviously, it hadn't been only Jim who couldn't stand the sight of Duncan. Valerie wanted him out of their lives, too, yet didn't want public opinion against them. Hence, Duncan the incorrigible. Duncan may have attacked Samantha, perhaps pushing her harder than he intended. Pix was ready to give him the benefit of the doubt, considering his parents. But the rest had been manufactured by them out of the boy's own unhappiness and depression. What a thing to do to a child!

She wouldn't have to bother asking Jim why he did it, though. She thought of his wine cellar, the boats, all the expensive video toys, this whole "Million Dollar Mansion." He may have been partly motivated by the love of a bad woman, but the real answer was the old tried and true "for the money." What he had inherited and what he made from the camp had evidently not been enough. The Athertons were all set to live the good life—until the Millers happened along.

Pix looked around the room. Even if she could get free of her bonds, there was nothing even remotely resembling a weapon, unless you were up for a pillow fight.

They'd have to untie them enough to walk—that is if they were going to move them, and Pix was afraid they were. Left in the house, they might be found too soon and raise the alarm.

"Mom, can you think of anything? What would Faith do?"

Pix was stung. So far as she knew, Faith had never been

bound and gagged. She'd probably do exactly what Pix was doing–try to keep her circulation going. She decided to ignore her daughter's remark.

After a while, Samantha asked timidly, "What time do you think they'll come back?"

"They said at dark. The sun set at eight-nineteen last night." Pix did know some things. She continued to parade her expertise. "I'd say they'll come back around nine. They're obviously planning to leave by boat and they'll want to get a good start. This is deep water, so they don't have to consider the tide."

"Which gives us less than three hours."

"I'm afraid so."

"And no one to miss us. Arlene was leaving for Ellsworth straight from work with Fred. They knew you wouldn't let me go. How about Granny?"

"I spoke to her this afternoon, so she wouldn't expect to hear from me again. I asked her to come over tonight, but she said she was tired and wanted an early night."

"If Daddy calls, he'll think we went somewhere for dinner."

"And I talked to Faith just before coming over. That's what kept me."

Pix gasped, but Samantha quickly reassured her. "Even if you'd been on time, it would have been too late. She didn't have the check upstairs. The one thing that would have saved us was if the phone hadn't rung. Then I wouldn't have done such a stupid thing and opened the closet door. She must have been talking to Jim."

"Earl would have no reason to think it odd if we weren't home." Pix continued the litany with decreasing hope.

"And there's no one else."

"Only us."

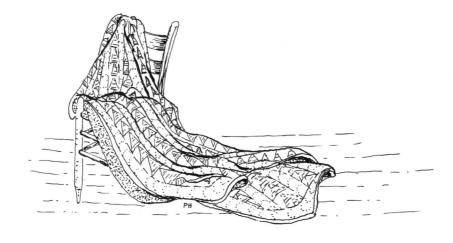

Chapter 10

The Athertons came back at 9:30.

When Valerie had first left the room, Pix had not been anxious for their return, but as dusk fell, her muscles and her nerves were crying out for some sort of change. And what that might be was something she had been speculating about for hours—silently. Samantha was calmer and had even dozed off at one point. Pix had felt drowsy herself, yet she dared not shut her eyes. She heard them before she saw them, rapid footsteps on the stairs.

The door opened and with a flick, light flooded the room, blinding Pix temporarily with its abrupt brightness. She could see how frightened Samantha was now. Her eyes were wide open, pupils dilated, like a fawn teetering about on the road, caught in the beams of a car's headlights.

"I still say we should take the silver service," Valerie was whining.

"We'll buy another. It's not that special and it weighs too

much. We'll be lucky to make any speed at all with everything you've packed." He bent down and untied Pix's ankles. The pain was intense but bearable. She knew she could walk. The question was, could she run? He helped them to their feet and said, "Get going—slowly in front of us, and don't try anything. Any noise and I'll shoot you both."

So much for Pix's plan to scream her head off the moment she was outside. They didn't know the gag was loose. With the way sound travels over water, the whole island would have been alerted. Only no one would be able to get there in time.

She started to head for the spiral staircase.

"No, the other way."

They filed down the hall past doors to rooms whose decor Pix could merely imagine. She had no doubt that had Jim not been around, Valerie would pull the trigger in a moment just because she was having to leave her fabulous house. And given her treatment of husband number one, Jim ought to be looking around a great deal, Pix thought ruefully. Her hands were tied behind her back and she gave a little wave to Samantha. Jim didn't want to leave two bodies behind. Pix was convinced they would remain alive, she told herself fervently. The question was, where?

They marched through the kitchen and out the back door. It was very dark. The moon had not risen yet and Pix stumbled on the stairs. If she broke a leg, would they shoot her?

"Down to the dock," Jim ordered.

As they left the house, lighted up like a Christmas tree to indicate occupancy, Pix wondered what they had done with her car. Another thought struck her. What had they done with Duncan? He was still on the island as far as she knew.

They reached the dock. Jim's Boston Whaler was pulled up.

"We're all going to take a little boat ride," he said. "Honey, you get in first." Pix was pretty sure he didn't mean either of them. Valerie slid by them awkwardly. She was struggling with a heavy canvas bag that she must have picked up on their way out. She was dressed for the voyage: heavy pants, jacket, and a kerchief tied over her hair. Pix gasped in surprise. Not at Valerie's outfit, but at what she was wearing on her feet—running shoes with twinkling red lights that flickered on and off as she got into the boat.

It hadn't been Duncan at all.

Why hadn't Pix tripped her, pushed her body straight over the side—this monstrous woman who had knocked Samantha to the ground, leaving her injured, with no more compunction than she would have felt swatting a mosquito? It was all Pix could do not to yell out every filthy name she had ever heard. But even if they didn't kill her, they would surely tighten the gag, and if she had sent Valerie sprawling into the sea, Pix herself might have followed her.

No, there was absolutely nothing she could do.

They got in the boat. If she had been in the mood, Pix would have been amused at the sight of a large wicker picnic basket—a few bottles of the bubbly and other assorted goodies for a midnight feast on the bounding main? Valerie set her bag next to it with a defiant look at her husband. The silver after all?

"We should be in Nova Scotia before dawn," Jim said with obvious pleasure, anticipating the trip. He was where he was happiest—on the water.

"Duncan won't be back until late—if he comes here at all. He'll probably sleep in his moldy old cabin as usual."

"I liked that 'good mother' touch." Jim chuckled. "How he wouldn't be seeing his friends for a while and you wanted to treat them all to pizza and the movies. Here, you steer. I've got to change my shoes."

Valerie took over. She was in a boat, steering a boat. The phobia, like everything else, had been fake.

Jim sat beside Pix companionably. They could see Valerie at the helm, shifting her feet every once in a while, causing the lights in her shoes to flash. Jim chuckled. "Technology. What next? Shoes that talk or sing? Sorry about Samantha, incidentally. Valerie must have pushed her a bit harder than she'd planned. We had merely intended to give you a scare so you'd stop sticking your nose into things. We hoped Samantha would see the lights and assume it was Dunc. It all worked out perfectly."

Depending on one's viewpoint. Pix was reaching the boiling point.

She saw they were headed for a small island that she knew belonged to the camp. It was a long way from shore. They used it for overnights, teaching the kids survival skills. Now it appeared it would test Pix's own. Valerie cut the motor and eased the boat into shallow water. Jim jumped out, pulling them farther onto the beach. The hull scraped along the rough sand, then all was quiet. The only sound was that of the waves gently breaking to either side.

"Last stop," Jim said heartily. He reached in the boat and picked Pix up, depositing her more or less upright on the sand. Samantha was next.

Pix had never noticed how strong he was. She'd never noticed a lot of things about Jim.

"Toss me the rope, Val. I won't be a minute." He pulled a gun from his pocket. "Okay, up the path."

Pix couldn't imagine where he was taking them, and although the night was still warm, she felt a cold sweat break out. Was it really going to be the last stop? Behind her, Samantha moaned.

They walked to a clearing in the middle of the island. Some summer's campers had built a lean-to and it was this that was apparently their destination.

"Get in and lie down. Let's not make things hard. I do so wish you two had not become involved. Believe me, I hate doing this," Jim said as he began to expertly bind Samantha's feet together again.

Pix thought about trying to kick the gun from his hand. She could do it easily, though with her hands behind her back, it would gain her nothing. Every plan she had devised had come to nothing. She had failed miserably. But she would not cry, she told herself angrily. She would not let the bastard see her cry.

He finished with Samantha and went to work on Pix. In a moment, he was standing up.

"Well, good-bye, I guess. There's really nothing else to say."

A few minutes later, they heard the boat start up again. Mother and daughter started talking at once. "Mom, they're gone!" "Are you all right?"

They were almost giddy with relief. They were alive. But, Pix soon realized, taking stock of the situation, not in good shape.

The island was uninhabited, and tied securely the way they were, there was no way they could attract attention tomorrow morning from a passing boat. When the Athertons didn't turn up at the camp and it became apparent that Pix and Samantha were also missing, a search would be made, yet it was unlikely that anyone would think to come here. There were countless islands of varying size dotted throughout Penobscot Bay. It could be days or even weeks before they were found.

Jim wasn't going to be directly responsible for their deaths. Obviously, he'd come up with a plan that effectively kept them out of the way while the Athertons headed for the Canadian border and still kept his hands clean. Pix could almost hear him explaining it to "sweetcakes," "That's all we need, a few hours. If they're found, fine. If not . . ."

If not . . .

"Samantha, we *have* to try to cut these ropes with something. Can you stand up?"

"I don't know." She strained to bend her knees and get into a sitting position. "It's no use. He's tied our hands and feet together."

"Maybe I can untie the knot. My fingers are free."

Pix rolled over to Samantha and began to pick at the knot at her ankles. Her fingers soon began to ache and she wished she hadn't kept her nails so short. Manicures didn't last long gardening.

"At least one of us has to get down to the shore and start yelling. There's always the chance that a boat could have pulled into the cove for the night. Distract me. Sing. Anything." The pain and frustration were intense.

"All right. What shall I sing?" Samantha mind's was suddenly blank. She and Mom had rather different tastes in music. The latest from the Indigo Girls would not do much to speed the process. "I know—what you and Daddy used to sing to me when I couldn't get to sleep." Her voice started out shakily and got stronger, "Hush, little baby, don't say a word. Papa's gonna buy you a mockingbird."

By the time Papa had purchased the sixth horse and cart, Pix had undone the knot and Samantha's feet and hands were no longer tied together. She stood up.

"Look and see if there are any nails in the wall or anything sharp you could use to try to undo mine." Pix did not want her daughter to suffer the way she had; she knew her fingers were bleeding from the rough rope.

Samantha hopped around the lean-to. The moon had risen. It was past eleven o'clock.

"Here's a bunch of nails. They must have hung stuff on them. I'll try to get one with my teeth."

"Be careful!" All those years of orthodontics, fluoride treatments, sealants. She watched Samantha hop back toward her with a rusty nail in her mouth and kneel by her side. Samantha dropped the nail to the floor and deftly picked it up, starting in on the knot, looking over her shoulder the same way her mother had.

"Boy, are we going to be stiff in the morning."

"Yes," Pix agreed, stiff, but not stiffs.

"All right, it's your turn."

Pix started to sing. This time Mama bought.

After what seemed like hours, Pix was somewhat freed also and they gingerly made their way down to the shore. Coming through the trees, the ocean with the moon streaking across it like a beacon was a welcome sight. Pix had almost fallen in the woods and now she fell on purpose, rolling over and over toward the shoreline, well away from the ledges. She closed her eyes as the hard rocks pressed into her body, then opened them when she reached the smoother sand. Samantha followed her and they began to call, "Help! Help! Please, someone help us!"

They decided to take turns, then figured they might as well wait until morning. No one was within earshot. Pix once more lay as close as she could to her daughter. The wind was picking up. It was getting colder. Even if they could free themselves, it was too far to swim to the mainland through the frigid waters. Pix reassured Samantha. It offered a measure of comfort for herself, too, despite the disbelief of a quick rescue steadily rising like the tide.

"Don't worry, everything will be all right in the morning. Why don't you close your eyes."

"I don't think I can sleep."

"Hush, little baby . . ."

Before she could get very far into the lullaby, Pix thought she heard the sound of an oar or a paddle. She lifted her head. Wishful thinking. Then the sound came again, more distinctly.

"Yoo hoo! Pix? Samantha? Where are you?"

It was Mother.

* * *

The three women and Duncan made a somewhat outlandish grouping as they sat on the deck of the Athertons' house waiting for Earl. Neither Pix nor Samantha had wanted to go inside, so Duncan had fetched blankets for them to wrap around themselves and a bottle of brandy and glasses at Mrs. Rowe's suggestion. Pix was drinking from the Baccarat after all. The teenagers had Cokes and were steadily devouring a bag of potato chips. Although hungry, Pix herself did not feel like eating anything from this particular larder.

Warm, the brandy seeping into her weary bones and bloodstream, Pix wanted her mother to tell the story again—and again—just as a child with a favorite book. Like most other parents she knew, she had more quotations from Doctor Seuss and Margaret Wise Brown to hand than Shakespeare.

"You actually have Duncan here to thank more than me," Ursula said.

"I know," Pix answered, and gave the boy yet another hug. Since her mother had climbed out of the canoe and deftly cut their ropes with the Swiss army knife she always carried, Pix had been doing a great deal of hugging.

"I knew something was weird. They had been treating me like shit—excuse me." Duncan flushed and looked at Ursula. "I mean, they had been yelling at me and saying I was never coming back here, then suddenly Mom gives me some money and tells me to take all my friends out." He shook his head. "She's been real jittery all summer and it's been worse lately. I thought because of what was happening at camp, and"—he lowered his voice—"because of what they thought I was doing."

Pix was indignant. "We owe you an enormous apology!"

"Don't worry about it. I probably would have thought it was me, too. Like who would have thought Mom would go out and buy the same shoes? They're for kids."

Pix pulled the blanket closer around her. The wind was picking up and it seemed they might finally get the rain they'd been waiting for all these weeks. It could come. The Fairchild's foundation was dry. Even if Seth couldn't work for a few days, the ground was so parched, it would be worth it.

The deck they were sitting on seemed another island and time was suspended, making it difficult for her to decide to move. Behind them the house was still illuminated, a gaudy backdrop to the dark landscape on either side. The waning moon shone across the water and the stars were out, mixing with clouds moving across the sky in an ever-increasing number. The air was fresh. Tilting her head back, Pix drank it in gratefully.

She realized she hadn't been listening to the conversation, and Duncan, uncharacteristically, was continuing to talk.

"So I go to my friends, 'Let's blow the pizza, get snacks, and see the early movie.' I wanted to check out what was happening. I came back here alone. All the lights were on, but no one was home. They weren't in the office at camp, either, and all the campers and staff were in their cabins. Mom's car was in the driveway and when I looked in the garage, Jim's was there, but yours was, too. It didn't make any sense. You couldn't have all gone somewhere together, unless someone else had picked you up, but you didn't seem to be that kind of friends, anyway. I decided to call your house. I was going to hang up when you answered so you wouldn't think I was a jerk. When you didn't answer, I began to get this funny feeling. I couldn't call Earl. We aren't exactly buddies. So I thought of your grandmother. She seemed okay."

Ursula took up the tale. "I couldn't imagine who was calling me at such an hour. Duncan wanted to know if you were there and of course you weren't. I told him I'd be right over." What Ursula did not say was that she knew immediately something was very very wrong. It was a summer out of sync and the disappearance of her daughter and granddaughter had to be serious. She stopped at their house to make sure and found it dark, completely empty.

"It's amazing what we can do when our adrenaline gets

going," Pix marveled, thanking God that she had not know at the time her octogenarian mother, who had not driven for years, was racing from The Pines across the causeway to the Athertons in the dead of night in her venerable "Woody"—a 1949 Plymouth Suburban wagon.

"Fortunate that I had just had the car serviced for Arnie and Claire to use while they're here. Anyway, Duncan had been doing some investigating of his own while I was on my way. When I arrived, he told me there were many things missing from the house—valuable things—and the lobster boat was gone; the Whaler was at the mooring. I called the police, then decided to take the canoe out. Duncan had found some rope and your purse on the floor in one of the rooms upstairs and we were both convinced that you'd been taken someplace under duress."

Pix liked her mother's choice of words—a quaint way to describe the terror that she and Samantha had just suffered.

She looked at the group. It was very late and they were all in one stage or another of extreme exhaustion.

"I think we'd better go home, especially because it seems a storm is on the way. I know Earl was coming here, but surely the state police have been in touch with him and told him we're all right. He'll know we went home—and all of us are sticking together for the rest of this night, anyway."

When Duncan had reached Earl, the sergeant had immediately launched a search of the area around the camp, including the quarry, calling back to tell the boy to stay put with the Millers if they turned up at the house.

There was one more thing Duncan wanted to say. Everyone was being so nice and he felt guilty. "I didn't think Mrs. Rowe should go out in the canoe like that, but I don't know how to paddle one, and she was pretty insistent."

Mother had won the Women's Singles Canoe Trophy at various events on the Concord River for more years than Pix could remember and had been paddling the Penobscot since she was a child. And "pretty insistent" was definitely a euphemism.

"She's very good at it, in fact, she'll teach you." Samantha thought it was time Duncan had some new interests and she fully intended to take her rescuer under her wing, if he would let her.

"That would be great," he said, then mumbled, "except I don't know if I'll be here."

Pix had studiously been avoiding any reference to Duncan's parents. It did not seem the moment to break it to the boy that his mother was a murderer, including of his natural father, and that both Jim and Valerie were involved in larceny up to their shirt-pocket emblems. Seeing him on the dock, as soon as they were within shouting distance, they'd called to him to phone the state police and get the Coast Guard to stop Jim's boat. Other than this, all mention of their captors had been moot.

"But Granny, why did you go to the island?" Samantha asked the one question that had not yet been answered. Pix felt foolish not to have thought of it. Why indeed?

"It was the only place that made sense. Their boat was gone. If you were still alive, and I believed you were, they had to put you someplace, but it couldn't be close to the camp. So, I simply started paddling along the shore, then out toward sea. Plus, I heard you shouting."

Sgt. Earl Dickinson was surprised and happy to see a group of laughing, obviously healthy friends as he drove up. Someone had been in time.

"Start throwing things overboard!" Jim shouted to his wife.

"What?" She couldn't hear him above the gale-force winds and rain that had greeted them farther out to sea.

He motioned with his hands and spoke louder, "Get rid of some of this stuff. We're too heavy."

"Are you crazy?"

He left the cabin, went to the back of the boat, and started tossing bags into the water. Valerie fell upon him, screeching, "My boxes! My collection of Battersea boxes! What are you doing!"

He slapped her hard across the face. "Shut up! I'm going to try to make for shore. We can't ride it out and we're not exactly in a position to radio for help."

She began to cry. "I'm scared, Jim."

"So am I. Now, do what I said and come back under cover." They were both soaking wet.

She threw the wicker hamper over the side and then the silver. We can always buy more, she told herself. We can always buy more.

At the wheel, Jim reached for a handkerchief to dry his face and found Pix's car keys in his pocket. She won't be needing these, he thought, and lobbed them in a long arc into the churning water. Then he turned the boat toward land, looking for a safe harbor.

The raging storm hampered the Coast Guard's search for the next few days. It was not until the sun broke out on Saturday that some children found a life buoy with the name VAL 'N JIM washed up on the shore—along with an empty wicker picnic basket.

"It's a great party," Faith Fairchild said to her friend, Pix. They were sitting side by side on the back steps of the Millers' house, watching a variety of activities. A large convivial group—with Pix's brother, Arnie, at the center—continued to consume lobsters at the large picnic table. "Frankly, at my age I'd rather have a talking frog" was obviously the punch line to a very funny joke. They all burst into laughter. Sam, who had once again made a mad dash for his loved ones, arriving early Thursday morning, started to tell one of his.

"He never gets this one right," Pix told Faith, "but he laughs so much while he's telling it that everybody laughs with him, anyway." Faith nodded. As far as she was concerned, the world was divided into people who could tell jokes and people who couldn't. Totally unable to remember even the most sidesplitting gem, she didn't even try, and kept to strictly off-the-cuff.

Another group was playing croquet. Pix watched her mother tap some poor person's ball miles off course, recalling that even when they were children, Ursula had played to win. "Otherwise, you won't learn," she'd explained with triumphant sweetness. Claire, Arnie's wife, had obviously drunk from the same well. Her ball hurtled through a hoop, smashed into another, which she briskly sent into the tall grass. Claire had been out for a long bicycle ride and still wore her black Lycra biking shorts with a bright periwinkle blue oversized linen shirt. She was one of those petite, nicely-put-together women who always made Pix feel much taller and much clumsier than she actually was—like Alice after eating the first cakes. Pix never knew what to do with her hands and feet when someone like Claire was around. Pix had assumed that in middle age you'd stop caring about what other people thought of you. Supposedly, it was one of the perks. She was still waiting.

The children were all over the place. Samantha and Arlene had immediately taken command of the Fairchild offspring, to Faith's unabashed delight. They seemed to be playing a game that involved a great deal of running and screeching, with little Amy riding piggyback and the dogs racing at their heels, barking happily. Duncan was with them. There had been no sudden transformation. He still wore a black concert T-shirt and black jeans, but his hair was clean and he and Fred were joining the game with every appearance of friendship.

There had been no word about the Athertons, other than the finding of the life buoy, and they were assumed lost. Duncan's paternal grandparents had been notified and were only too happy to have him come live with them. Pix did have a passing thought as to when they'd seen him last, but it seemed that they had always disliked Valerie intensely, especially after their son's death, when she'd contested his will, seeking to prevent certain bequests, among them a trust fund for Duncan. The Cowleys had told her they didn't care to see her anymore and she had retaliated by keeping Duncan from them, never allowing the boy to visit. He was living with John Eggelston at the moment and John was going to take him south the following week. John had been the one to break the news of his mother's probable death to Duncan. He'd told Pix the boy had pretended indifference at first, saying he'd never really loved her, since she'd never loved him. Then he'd sobbed for hours. Looking at him now playing like the child he still was in part, Pix hoped he would find what he needed from his grandparents. At any rate, it would certainly be an improvement.

"It *is* a good party, if I do say so myself," Pix said tritely and complacently. "What could be easier than lobster, especially when my guests brought almost everything else?"

Ever since Faith and family had arrived on Thursday, leaving Aleford as soon as they heard of Pix and Samantha's ordeal, Faith found she was happiest right by her friend's side. First, of course, she had to hear about it all. Then she realized she simply wanted the reassurance of physical presence.

"Do you think people are ready for dessert?" Faith had made a tableful of blueberry tartes with the succulent wild Maine blueberries now in season.

"Not yet. Arnie's still oozing butter and charm." Pix looked at her brother fondly. He'd been sticking to her side, too. He was reaching for a thick wedge of the corn bread* Louise Frazier had brought. She insisted that this treasured family recipe from the Deep South went perfectly with Down East fare. And she was right.

"Now that the rain has stopped, we can get a better look at the house. Do you want to drive out after everyone leaves?" Pix remarked. "It should also be a beautiful sunset." The Fair-

*See recipe on page 284.

childs had bravely faced the storm yesterday, but after driving out to the Point, they didn't even attempt to get out of the car. "These weren't drops; these were tidal waves," Faith had told Pix. "Wonderful climate."

"It is." Pix had stoutly defended what she thought of as her native clime. "Think how hot it is in Boston. I'd rather have rain, and especially fog, any day." Maine without its occasional soft, dense gray fogs molding land and sea alike into new shapes was unthinkable.

"I'd like to go out, especially for the sunset, and you can tell us what it's all going to look like."

Pix was a bit shamefaced. "I do feel that I should have been after Seth sooner. You might even have had the roof by now."

"Pix! No grades, remember? Did I tell you or did you tell me that life is not a final exam? Except maybe finally. Never mind. How you can possibly think this is your fault is totally absurd. Next, you'll be taking responsibility for what the crazy Athertons did!"

"Absolutely not!"

"Absolutely not what?" It was Jill—arm in arm with Earl, Pix noted with pleasure.

"Too complicated to explain," Faith said.

"Speaking of which . . ." Earl gave Jill a surprisingly piercing look.

She drew the word out, "Yes, I suppose now is as good a time as any. I do need to talk to you, Pix."

Faith stood up. "I'll leave you to it, then, and rescue the long-suffering teenagers from my adoring progeny." She didn't really mean it, and fortunately Jill said, "Oh you don't have to leave, Faith. It's not exactly a secret." Faith resumed her place, aware that good manners often paid off.

Jill sat down on the lawn. Earl stretched out next to her. She was finding it hard to begin, pulling at tufts of grass beside her until Pix began to worry seriously she'd have to reseed.

"You know I started carrying antiques at the end of last

season and stocked even more this year. They've been doing very well and I've made more money at the store than ever before."

"That's wonderful," Faith said. Pix had told her about Jill's cupboard, not exactly Old Mother Hubbard's, and she wanted to keep the young woman's turgid flow of conversation moving.

"Not really. You see, almost all the antiques I bought from Mitch were fakes—and these were the bulk of my stock."

No one said anything.

"I didn't know it when I bought them, of course. I should have been suspicious, since they weren't as expensive as similar things I'd priced at other dealers', but I thought he was giving me a good deal because he liked me. Then there began to be all this talk about phony antiques after his death. I got scared. If he was involved in something, I might be charged as a receiver. And I'd sold a good many. I had to be sure what I had were fakes for sure, so I began to go up to the library in Bangor and read whatever I could. I also talked on the way up and back to some dealers, without saying why or giving my name."

"And here we were spouting off about it at the clambake." Pix was sympathetic.

"Yes. I know it was wrong. I should have told Earl in the first place, but . . . well, I just didn't. Maybe I didn't want him to know what I'd done. No, make that definitely—I didn't want him to know what a fool he had for a girlfriend."

Earl put his arm around Jill. She didn't shrug it off and she continued speaking as she leaned toward him, "Once I was certain, I took everything from Mitch out of the store and put it all upstairs."

Faith gave Pix's hand a knowing squeeze.

"Despite Mitch's giving me a break, I was still out a lot of money and I couldn't afford the loss. I simply didn't know what to do, so I decided to talk to Seth."

"Why Seth?" Faith asked. Earl looked a little grim.

275

"I've known Seth all my life and I knew I could trust him. He was a good friend of Mitch's, plus he hears things." Faith finished her sentence silently for her: Things an officer of the law might not.

"And I thought he might know where the fakes had come from and maybe I could get some or all of my money back. I knew Mitch couldn't be making quilts, though he probably was manufacturing the furniture and the wood carvings. Seth was furious. If Mitch hadn't already been dead, Seth would have gone after him himself. He told me he'd do a little investigating on his own."

"What did he turn up?" Faith had assumed the role of chief interrogator. It was fun—so long as you were sitting in the afternoon sun at a backyard Maine lobster fest.

"Nothing much. We both suspected Norman Osgood, the antiques dealer who was staying at Addie and Rebecca's. Seth followed him when he went off-island a couple of times, but all he did was go in and out of antique shops, just as he said he was. We couldn't have been more wrong." She looked at Earl, who was grinning broadly.

"Norman Osgood is an undercover agent investigating antiques fraud. He's tickled pink that you, Pix, your mother, and Samantha somehow managed to crack a ring he's been following up and down the entire East Coast for a couple of years. The Athertons fortunately did not think to erase their computer files and Norman has been having a field day."

"I was right!" Faith exclaimed, "He wasn't a dealer!"

It was Jill's turn again. "I finally told Seth I'd have to tell Earl, what with the whole island talking about us, and besides, I missed him. That's when Seth had the idea that I could sell the fakes, just not as antiques. He helped me label every piece as a reproduction—indelible ink on the quilts, marks burned into the wooden pieces. They're very good copies and I have a big sign—'Genuine Fakes, Guaranteed to Fool Your Friends.' People think it's some more Maine humor, like the sign Wally Sanford has had outside his store for years—'Clams

Dressed and Undressed.' It's true, and so is mine. I've already sold two quilts and one of the carvings since I put them out yesterday."

Such being the joys of confession, Jill went with Earl to join the croquet game, an almost-noticeable weight lifted from her lovely shoulders.

"Is there anything left?" Faith asked.

"What do you mean?"

"Are all the loose ends tied up? Anybody not accounted for? Clues left dangling? Red herrings?"

Pix realized her friend was indeed much more adept at all this than she was.

"I think so." She leaned back against the gray shingles of the house.

She thought about her list. The columns with "Suspects"; "Causes of Death"; "Who Benefits?"; and "Quilts." Duncan, Seth, John, Norman—all eliminated. Sonny Prescott had been right all along: unknown partners in crime. Except they had known them, especially Jim.

"It's pretty clear that Valerie was not overly maternal—or wifely. But what an actress! I can hear her now speaking about Duncan's father—he was 'a saint' and so forth. She wished Duncan could be more like him. Maybe Duncan was like him and she hated them both. You should have seen her horror at the sails and the bloody bats! As soon as I heard it was latex paint, I should have known it was one of them. But Jim—an Eagle Scout! And the camp, it was like his child, wife, everything all in one."

"Until he met Valerie, my dear Watson."

"Now, don't be so patronizing. Just because you want to be Holmes, I don't have to be the poor dense doctor."

"My point is, don't underestimate the power of good old sex," Faith said.

"And in this case, the seduction of good old money."

"I'm sorry about the Watson crack," Faith apologized.

Appeased, Pix said, "Jill's cleared up the last question I

had. It must have been Valerie who came in and clipped off the X from my quilt. Which just about does it, I'd say."

"They never did find the weapon that killed Mitch?"

"No. Earl thought it might have been the knife the kids found in Duncan's trunk, but that turned out to be a special limited edition one belonging to Bernard Cowley. The knife had never been used for anything. And now, how about dessert?"

"Yes, but it's so hard to move. I could sit here in the sun for the rest of the day. Look at the kids. They are having a ball. Fred seems very nice, and I'm sure he and Arlene will be model parents, unlike some of the rest of us." Fred was showing Ben how to climb the apple tree.

"Look, Arlene is wearing bell-bottoms! I should have saved all those clothes I wore in the sixties," Pix commented.

Faith disagreed. "You did the right thing. Trust me."

Pix was cutting the tartes and Faith was putting everything on another table that had been set up out of the sun. Earlier, Samantha had picked a large bouquet of wildflowers and put them in an old white ironstone pitcher filled with water. Faith added a few roses from Pix's garden and several stalks of delphinium. She placed it on the dessert table now with the tartes and several large bowls of fresh strawberries. Pix had provided whipped cream and sugar, although preferring her berries straight. These were so full of flavor, they didn't need anything, even the crème de cassis Faith favored when she got tired of them plain. This never happened to Pix.

Arnie and Claire had apparently cleaned out Louella Prescott's entire stock of cookies—chocolate chip, oatmeal, and hermits—and surprisingly the Bainbridge's butterscotch shortbread. Apparently, Rebecca was not the one who hoarded the secret recipes. There was hope of sherry-nutmeg cake yet.

Pix was arranging the cookies on a large blue willow platter.

Ursula had come in to get a sun hat and see whether her daughter needed help.

"These are the most delicious cookies. I hope Rebecca will give me the recipe, too," Pix said, eating one that had conveniently broken in the box.

"I'm sure she will, dear." Her mother gave her a quick kiss, something that had become a habit of late.

Her daughter and grandaughter safe and sound, her beloved son in residence, Ursula should have been in clover, and she was—almost. But Pix thought she could still detect a wrong note in her mother's voice. She started to ask her about it when Faith came in with the empty tray to get the rest of the things.

"Everyone's already at the desserts. Tom says it's Maine air. Gives him an appetite. And this from a man who has consumed two lobsters, coleslaw, and untold pieces of corn bread all in the recent past!"

As soon as she left, Pix said to her mother bluntly, "Tell me what's bothering you." When he mother did not reply at once, Pix suddenly realized it was always when the Bainbridges' name came up that Ursula seemed perturbed. Could her mother miss Adelaide to such an extent? They had been close but not the best of friends. Addie. Faith had been talking about putting the last pieces in place. Surely the picture was complete. The card table could be cleared for another puzzle or tucked in a hall closet to make room for other activities. Wasn't it time to put everything away?

"Does it have to do with Addie? Are you worried about Rebecca? Oh, Mother, surely you don't think the Athertons killed Addie, too? I always thought the quilt was too much of a coincidence! She must have discovered what they were doing!"

Her mother sat down on a stool by the kitchen window. The voices outside were clearly audible. Arnie was teasing his wife about the size of the piece of blueberry tarte she'd taken.

When Ursula spoke, Pix had trouble hearing—and believing—what her mother said.

"The Athertons didn't kill Adelaide, but the quilt was not a coincidence. I know she'll tell one of us soon. I've been waiting and waiting. Perhaps me, maybe Earl, or maybe you. She's a good woman, though very disturbed in mind, and is probably home thinking about it right this very minute."

"You can't mean Rebecca!"

"Addie was very difficult to live with, especially these last years," Ursula said slowly, "and Rebecca did long for a room with a view."

Myrtle Rowe Miller, better known as Pix, lay flat on her back in the cemetery. The bright blue sky seemed very close, almost brushing the tip of the long piece of grass she was chewing on. She'd slipped out from Arnie and Claire's going-away party at The Pines, ostensibly to see how the plot had fared in the heat and subsequent rains. She doubted she'd be missed.

The last two weeks had been filled with picnics and excursions of one sort or another. Arnie had, in fact, taken her to Vinalhaven, a lovely long, lazy sail.

Samantha had not remained jobless for long; the camp having obviously shut down, much to the loudly expressed sorrow of Susannah and Geoff, who had begged Samantha to take over. Now Arlene and Samantha were working for Louella, rising early to help bake, then tending the register while Louella kept cooking.

And Seth seemed to be accomplishing miracles of construction at the Fairchilds'. Pix went every day, watching the house rising from its foundation before her eyes.

Everything had turned out all right after all—except two people on the island were dead who should still be alive.

She rolled over and propped herself up on one elbow, looking at the stone that marked her father's grave. What was the line from Edna St. Vincent Millay? "I am not resigned to the shutting away/of loving hearts in the hard ground"? That was it. And Pix was not resigned. Not for her father, nor Mitch, nor Addie.

Rebecca had told Earl, the same day as the party Pix gave for her brother. Possibly while the Millers and Fairchilds were gazing at a magnificent pink-and-purple sunset from a spot on the Point where all hoped a deck would be by Labor Day.

Lilies of the valley—they grew in dense clusters on the edges of the cemetery. A British friend of Pix's had once told her it used to be considered very bad luck in her country to plant a bed of lilies of the valley, that the person who did would be the next to die.

But it was not the person who sowed who perished. Rebecca had given Addie the plant poison in every way imaginable. She'd brewed her sister-in-law's tea from the deadly roots and added the water in which she'd placed the cut leaves to Addie's juice. She'd even, she confessed to Earl, pushed Addie's tiny quilting needles into the berries, hoping she might mortally prick herself. One or all had worked.

And the quilt was no coincidence: End of Day. Rebecca had made it herself years ago, hiding it away when Addie had criticized the handiwork—hidden away, but not forgotten.

Had she wanted to be caught? If she hadn't wrapped Addie in the quilt to try to link her crime with the other, no autopsy would have been done on someone Addie's age. And the autopsy, like so many others, had not been able to pick up this natural poison. It mimicked heart failure. A failure of the heart—Addie's. Rebecca's.

Pix lay back down again. It felt good. Peaceful. The only noise was the raucous cries of the gulls and, if she listened very hard, the sound of her own blood pulsing. Slow, steady—reliable. She sighed. Another epitaph? But the reliable part wasn't so bad. They were reliable women: her mother, her daughter, and Pix herself. So different—and so alike. She was looking forward to spending the rest of the summer in their company.

Maybe she'd get to the attic.

Maybe not.

Have Faith in Your Kitchen

by Faith Sibley Fairchild and Friends

A WORK IN PROGRESS

PIX ROWE MILLER'S FAMILY FISH CHOWDER

*6-7 slices of bacon, 1/4"
thick
3 cups diced yellow onions
5-6 medium potatoes, peeled
1 lb. haddock
1 lb. cod*

*2 cans (3 cups) evaporated
milk
1 cup whole milk
salt
freshly ground pepper*

Fry the bacon, remove from the pan, and place on a paper towel. Sauté the onions in the bacon fat and set the pan aside.

Cut the potatoes in half the long way, then into 1/4" slices. Put them in a nonreactive pot large enough for the chowder. Cover the potatoes with water and boil until tender. Be careful not to put in too much water or the chowder will be soupy. While the potatoes are cooking, cut the fish into generous bite-sized pieces. When the potatoes are ready, add the fish to the pot, cover and simmer until the fish flakes.

When the fish is done, crumble the bacon and add it to the pot along with the onions and any grease in the pan, the evaporated and whole milks. Bring the mixture to a boil, cover, and turn the heat down. Simmer for five minutes and add salt and pepper to taste.

Chowder invariably tastes better when made a day ahead.

The word "chowder" comes from the French, "la chaudière," a very large copper pot. Several centuries ago, French coastal villages would celebrate the safe return of their fishing fleets with a feast. The main course was a fish stew made in la chaudière into which each fisherman would toss part of his catch. "Chaudière" became "chowder" as the tradition made its way across the Atlantic to Canada and Down East. Chowders have continued to be just as idiosyncratic as these long ago concoctions. Pix does not even want to hear about the Manhattan version, but others of us are more open. The Rowe recipe may be happily modified in all sorts of ways.

The chowder is still quite delectable with olive oil instead of bacon fat. You may also use salt pork. Two kinds of fish make for a more interesting chowder, but these can be any combination of the following: haddock, cod, pollack, monkfish, and hake. Finally there is the question of garnishes: dill, chopped parsley, oyster crackers, butter are all good. And Faith and Pix's friend on Sanpere, Jane Weiss, swears by her chowder to which she adds curry spices!

LOUISE FRAZIER'S SOUTHERN CORN BREAD

1 1/2 cups stone ground corn meal	1/2 tsp. salt
	1/2 tsp. baking soda
3 tbsps. flour	1 cup buttermilk
2 tbsps. sugar	2 eggs, well beaten
3 tsps. baking powder	4 tbsps. dripping

Preheat the oven to 350°. Combine the dry ingredients and stir in the wet. Pour the mixture into a lightly buttered 8" square pan and bake for 40 minutes, checking after 30. This is a dense, chewy cornbread and serves 6-8. Again, substitutions can be made: skim buttermilk, Egg Beaters, and butter substitutes for the dripping and to grease the pan. Do try to find stone ground cornmeal, though. It gives the cornbread a wonderful flavor and texture. The batter may also be fried in a large pan on top of the stove, flipping it over so both sides are crunchy.

FAITH'S EMERGENCY SEWING CIRCLE SPREADS: CHUTNEY CHEESE AND CHÈVRE WITH HERBS

Chutney Cheese:
8 ounces plain cream cheese, room temperature
1 cup chutney

Cream the chutney and cheese together by hand. Do not use a food processor or blender otherwise you end up with cheese sauce. Pix used her own green tomato chutney, which is a spicy combination of the tomatoes, onions, raisins, and walnuts. All and any varieties of chutney work well.

Chèvre with Herbs:
4 ounces plain cream cheese, room temperature
4-5 ounces chèvre (100% goat's milk cheese)
Herbs to taste

Herbed chèvre is readily available in most markets and cheese shops. Pix likes to keep things simple and buys the herbed variety. Combine the cheeses by hand. The cream cheese makes the combination easier to spread. If you are using your own herbs, rosemary, tarragon, and summer savory are good choices, alone or in combination.

*   *   *

Use both spreads to stuff snow or sugar snap peas, spread on cucumber or zucchini rounds, sweetmeal biscuits, water biscuits, or slightly toasted miniature bagels. The chutney spread makes a tasty sandwich when combined with smoked turkey or Virginia ham or by itself on date and nut or buckwheat walnut bread.

BAINBRIDGE BUTTERSCOTCH SHORTBREAD

1 cup unsalted butter
1/2 cup dark brown sugar
2 cups flour
1/2 tsp. baking powder

1/4 tsp. salt
1 cup finely chopped
    walnuts or pecans

Sift the flour, salt, and baking powder together and set aside. Cream the butter until soft and gradually add the sugar. Add the flour mixture a little at a time and mix well. Refrigerate for one hour.

Divide the dough in half and keep one portion in the refrigerator while rolling out the other to approximately 1/4" thickness. (The dough gets soft quickly.) Sprinkle the dough with the nuts and gently press them in with the rolling pin. Cut into 1 1/2" squares. Pix uses a paper pattern as she is hopeless at estimating things like this, unlike Faith. Prick with a fork and place the squares on an ungreased cookie sheet. Repeat with the rest of the dough.

Bake until golden brown, approximately 15 minutes in a preheated 350° oven. Makes 6 dozen squares. This is a devastatingly rich, crumbly cookie.

FAITH FAIRCHILD'S MAINE BLUEBERRY TARTE

Pastry:

1 1/2 cups flour

1 tbsp. sugar

a pinch of salt

12 tbsps. unsalted butter

3 tbsps. ice water

Filling:

3 cups blueberries

4 tbsps. sugar

2 tbsps. flour

1 tbsp. lemon juice

Put the flour, sugar, and salt in the bowl of a food processor. Pulse once. Cut the butter into pieces and add to the dry ingredients. Pulse again until the mixture resembles coarsely ground cornmeal. (You may also cut the butter into the flour mixture with two knives or a pastry cutter.)

Add the ice water through the feeder tube with the motor running and briefly process until a ball is formed. Wrap the dough in wax paper and refrigerate for 1/2 hour. Faith makes ice water by adding a few cubes to a glass of water before she starts making the dough.

Roll out the dough on a lightly floured surface and line a 10" fluted tarte pan—the kind with the bottom that comes out. Prick the bottom of the dough-lined pan with a fork.

Combine 2 tbsps. of flour with 2 tbsps. of sugar and dust the bottom.

Add the lemon juice to the fruit and spread evenly over the dough. Sprinkle 2 tbsps. of sugar on the top and place on a baking sheet. Bake in the middle of a preheated 375° oven for 40 minutes, or until the edges turn slightly brown. Let cool for ten minutes and remove from the pan to a serving plate.

Tastes best warm or at room temperature. Serves 10. This recipe is also delicious with other summer fruits. Caution: do not use frozen blueberries or you will have a soggy mess. Pix knows.

Author's Note

There are cooks—and cooks. Pix represents one school; Faith another. I fall somewhere in between. As with the recipes in *The Body in the Cast*, these can be made successfully by cooks of all natures. Substitutions have been suggested in some cases and certainly feel free to experiment. I'm told I make great chili, but since I put different things in each time depending on what's to hand, I may never develop a recipe for it.

A relative once told me that anyone who could read could cook, a notion I heartily endorse. Cookbooks are always in the stack of books next to my bed (along with mysteries). Crime and food go together well. Occasionally a passion for one will lead to the other—as in Faith's and my case. There's nothing we enjoy more than sitting in the backyard with a plate of Bainbridge Shortbread and a cup of tea . . . or a glass of wine and a stack of crackers and Chutney Cheese or . . . being transported to whatever world a favorite mystery author has chosen this time. I hope you will join us.

"You'll get bitten and love it."

—Rachel Caine, *New York Times* bestselling author

Night School

"An action-packed story with appealing characters, dark humor, and a new spin on both the worlds of the undead and the fae. Though primarily targeted to a YA audience, this novel will appeal to adult fans of *Buffy the Vampire Slayer* as well as the Harry Potter series and the Twilight novels."

—*Library Journal*

"Another thrilling installment to Rayne and Sunny's story!"

—*Romance Reviews Today*

"Fifth of the Blood Coven Vampire series takes a darker turn . . . [an] engaging young adult urban fantasy. It is entertaining watching the twins mature through this fast-paced series that packs enough twists and humor to hold readers' attention to the last page."   —*Monsters and Critics*

"This book has it all! Vampires, vampire slayers, and faeries, what more could you ask for? . . . A fast-paced book from start to finish. I can't wait to read more about Sunny and Rayne's adventures. This is a must-read for anyone who enjoys paranormal fiction and a good story."

—*Night Owl Reviews*

continued . . .

Bad Blood

"A vampire book so worth reading, with dark humor, distinctive voice, and a protagonist clever enough to get herself out of trouble . . . A great ride."

—Ellen Hopkins,
New York Times bestselling author

"Mancusi writes with a wicked sense of humor and keeps readers turning the pages, eager for more."

—*Novel Reads*

Girls That Growl

"An amusing teenage vampire tale starring a fascinating high school student . . . Young adults will enjoy growling alongside this vampire slayer who has no time left for homework."

—*Midwest Book Review*

"A fast-paced and entertaining read."   —*LoveVampires*

"A refreshing new vampire story, *Girls That Growl* is different from all of those other vampire stories . . . a very original plot."

—*Flamingnet*

Stake That

"A fast-paced story line . . . both humorous and hip . . . A top read!"   —*Love Vampires*

"Rayne is a fascinating protagonist . . . readers will want to stake out Mari Mancusi's fun homage to Buffy."

—*The Best Reviews*

Boys That Bite

"A wonderfully original blend of vampire/love/adventure drama which teens will find refreshingly different."

—*Midwest Book Review*

"Liberal doses of humor keep things interesting . . . and the surprise ending will leave readers bloodthirsty for the next installment of the twins' misadventures with the undead. A ghoulishly fun read."   —*School Library Journal*

"A tongue-in-cheek young teen tale starring two distinct, likable twins, the vampire between them, and a coven of terrific support characters who bring humor and suspense to the mix . . . Filled with humor and action . . . insightfully fun."

—*The Best Reviews*

SOUL BOUND

MARI MANCUSI

BERKLEY BOOKS, NEW YORK

THE BERKLEY PUBLISHING GROUP
Published by the Penguin Group
Penguin Group (USA) Inc.
375 Hudson Street, New York, New York 10014, USA

Penguin Group (Canada), 90 Eglinton Avenue East, Suite 700, Toronto, Ontario M4P 2Y3, Canada (a division of Pearson Penguin Canada Inc.) • Penguin Books Ltd., 80 Strand, London WC2R 0RL, England • Penguin Group Ireland, 25 St. Stephen's Green, Dublin 2, Ireland (a division of Penguin Books Ltd.) • Penguin Group (Australia), 250 Camberwell Road, Camberwell, Victoria 3124, Australia (a division of Pearson Australia Group Pty. Ltd.) • Penguin Books India Pvt. Ltd., 11 Community Centre, Panchsheel Park, New Delhi—110 017, India • Penguin Group (NZ), 67 Apollo Drive, Rosedale, Auckland 0632, New Zealand (a division of Pearson New Zealand Ltd.) • Penguin Books (South Africa) (Pty.) Ltd., 24 Sturdee Avenue, Rosebank, Johannesburg 2196, South Africa

Penguin Books Ltd., Registered Offices: 80 Strand, London WC2R 0RL, England

This book is an original publication of The Berkley Publishing Group.

This is a work of fiction. Names, characters, places, and incidents either are the product of the author's imagination or are used fictitiously, and any resemblance to actual persons, living or dead, business establishments, events, or locales is entirely coincidental. The publisher does not have any control over and does not assume any responsibility for author or third-party websites or their content.

PUBLISHING HISTORY
Berkley trade paperback edition / March 2012

Library of Congress Cataloging-in-Publication Data

Mancusi, Marianne.
Soul bound / Mari Mancusi. — Berkley trade pbk. ed.
p. cm. — (A blood coven vampire novel ; 7)
Summary: When Rayne is chosen to track down her twin sister, Sunny, and Sunny's vampire boyfriend, Magnus, for what will mean certain death at the hands of the Vampire Consortium, she and her boyfriend, Jareth, go deep beneath New York City and through the Gates of the Underworld in hopes of saving them.
ISBN 978-0-425-24547-7 (pbk.)
[1. Vampires—Fiction.   2. Twins—Fiction.   3. Sisters—Fiction.   4. Hell—Fiction.   5. New York (N.Y.)—Fiction.]   I. Title.
PZ7.M312178Sou 2012
[Fic]—dc23   2011045746

PRINTED IN THE UNITED STATES OF AMERICA

10   9   8   7   6   5   4   3   2   1

Rayne McDonald
Las Vegas, Nevada

Queen Shrinking Violet
Cinderella's Castle
Light Court, Fairyland
Tir na nÓg, Ireland

Dear Mom,

How's Fairyland these days? I'm guessing it's pretty sweet—
you being queen and all. I mean, it has to beat the whole
nine-to-five gig you had back in Massachusetts, right? And
let's just say the replica of Cinderella's castle that you now
call home completely trumps our old three-bedroom, one-
and-a-half bath. BTW, I totally call dibs on the tower bedroom when I come to visit this summer, k?

So . . . not to get all mushy or anything, but I miss you
tons. I mean, staying at our stepmom Heather's place in
Vegas is fine, I guess. She bought the condo next to hers and
did a little renovation so we all have our own bedrooms
now. And I love being able to teach Stormy everything there
is to know about video games. Seriously, my half sister is so
smart. Guess we know who she takes after, right?

Anyway, you're probably wondering why I'm writing
you this letter, especially since we just signed off of Skype a
few minutes ago. Well, Mom, I think it's time to come clean.
There's still so much you don't know about what happened

to Sunny and me in the last year and it's my New Year's resolution to be more honest with people. I'm sorry we kept you in the dark for so long, but let's face it—if you had known what we were up to, you'd have totally flipped, right? Though, um, now that we know what you've been keeping in the fairy ancestry closet all these years, I don't think you're one to talk.

So here goes nothing. And please, I beg of you as your firstborn daughter (by seven minutes—woo-hoo!) read all the way through and spare us any judgment, okay? We always claimed you were the "cool mom" to all our friends, so try to live up to your rep.

It all started back in the spring. When I met these really cool vampires at the local underage dance place, Club Fang, and they recruited me into their vampire-in-training program. I know, I know—you're not happy with me becoming a vampire. But, Mom, it's my life, right? And think about it for a moment: eternal life, riches beyond belief, a hot blood mate to call your own. There really aren't a lot of downsides to the gig.

In any case, I started my training—taking courses, achieving my certification, getting on the waiting list for my very own blood mate. (It's a very complicated process, you see, involving DNA matching and blood testing for ultimate compatibility.) I was on the road to becoming a creature of the night—and totally psyched.

But then something terrible happened. On the night I was meant to be bitten by my new blood mate, the stupid vampire (Magnus) accidentally bit Sunny instead. I know, right? I suppose it was an honest mistake. I mean, even you can't tell us apart sometimes and you gave birth to us. So how could we expect some random vampire to make out the differences in the dark?

Sunny was so not happy, as you can imagine. She hadn't even heard of vampires up until then. (She always was the Goody Two-shoes of the family!) And now she finds out she's going to be morphing into one a week before prom! Needless to say, I got the brunt of the blame, even though, I'd like to—again—point out it was Magnus who made the actual mistake.

Luckily for everyone involved, Magnus was able to make it all work out. The two of them located the only thing able to cure new vampires—the Holy Grail—and bang, boom—Sunny's human again, just in time for prom. (Okay, it was a little more complicated than that, but you get the picture.) In addition, she's suddenly head over heels for Magnus, the Master of the Blood Coven, and they start the interspecies dating thing.

Things didn't go so fairy tale for me. At least at first. Not only did I lose my chance to become a vampire, but our drama teacher, Mr. Teifert, suddenly informs me that I'm destined to become the next vampire slayer. Yes, the girl voted most likely to go vamp has now been charged with slaying them for a living. Bleh!

Luckily, as you know, Slayer Inc. is usually a pretty upstanding organization. They only ask us to slay the bad *vamps, not the upstanding ones who play by the Vampire Consortium rules. For my first assignment, I teamed up with Jareth, the Blood Coven general, to infiltrate a seedy blood bar and stop its owner from spreading a nasty blood virus. Jareth wasn't so happy at first to be teamed up with a slayer— after all, his whole family was killed by slayers back in the day. But in the end, he came around. We saved the day and fell in love. And I finally got my wish, too! Remember that day last spring when I was completely dying of a mysterious illness? And remember how I was miraculously cured? Well, wonder no more. That was the day I became a vampire! And thanks to a weird mutation due to the blood virus in my veins, I became one of the very few vampires not allergic to the sun. Which is useful in carrying out my Slayer Inc. duties.*

Anyway, you pretty much know the rest. How you and Dad sprung the news that we're not mortals at all, but actually fairy princesses and how we had to hide out at Riverdale Academy, a school for slayers, while the two of you went off to talk the Light Court into letting us live "normal" lives. (Ha-ha! If only you knew!)

Unfortunately, Riverdale had some deadly secrets of its own—namely, a fringe group of slayers called the Alphas, who were determined to take over the world. They captured me and planned to drain my fairy/vampire blood to create a powerful hybrid army of "vamshees" (their word, not mine). If it wasn't for Sunny's bravery during a showdown in Tokyo, I'm pretty sure I'd be dead—and they'd be in charge. You'd be proud of her, Mom. Really proud.

4

Sadly, not everyone shares the sentiment. The power-hungry leader of the Vampire Consortium, Pyrus, was furious at Sunny and Magnus for going against his orders and infiltrating the Alphas without permission. (He wanted war, not a peaceful solution, so he could reinforce the Consortium's dominance over the world.) Now he's given orders to have them "brought to justice"—which I think is a fancy way of saying executed for treason. Sunny and Magnus had to escape in the dead of the night and I have no idea where they went.

I'm worried about them, Mom. Really worried. Please let me know if you hear anything. . .

With love, your daughter,
Rayne

1

Charles Teifert looks like your typical high school drama teacher. He's got wild black hair, thick glasses, and appears to have the inability to button his shirts correctly. (And don't even get me started on his wacky ties.) He walks around life with a slightly frazzled look on his often unshaven face. To the common passerby, he appears to have nothing more on his mind then how his students will perform on the opening night of the senior class production of *Camelot*.

Certainly no one meeting Charles Teifert for the first time would ever guess that beneath that carefully structured, stereotypical, nutty drama teacher facade lies one of the top protectors of our generation. But indeed Charles Teifert is that and more; he serves as vice president of Slayer Inc., an international conglomerate with a mission to keep the world safe from vampires, fairies, werewolves, and other supernatural beings. (Including, but not limited to, leprechauns, Sasquatch, and even jolly old Saint Nick, should he ever decide to start dropping bombs instead presents down his constituents' chimneys.)

Charles Teifert is also my boss. He's the one who first told me I was destined to become a vampire slayer last spring when his former star slayer, Bertha, had to retire to fat camp due to her inability to stop supersizing her McDonald's French fries. I didn't exactly welcome the guy with open arms at first, but somehow he managed to wear down my resistance and train me to use a stake to kick vampire (and other supernatural creature) ass. Since then we've had our ups and downs—can't say I've always been an A+ pupil. (Heck, I'm lucky if half the time I deserve a C-!) But over time we've managed to develop a sort of grudging respect for one another.

In any case, today I'm meeting him at the back room of the L.A. Sports Club in Vegas. He promised me a little sparring before he heads back to Massachusetts, where he lives and teaches. But when I push open the door to the small yoga studio he told me to meet him at, I realize he's not wearing his workout sweats, but rather a stiff, three-piece suit.

"Dude, what's with the outfit?" I ask. "Doesn't look like something you'd want to get blood on when I kick your butt!"

He doesn't laugh at my joke. Instead, he motions to a set of nearby chairs. "Sit," he instructs, without even saying hello.

Worry worms through my insides as I follow his instructions. "What's going on?"

He pulls out a manila envelope from his briefcase. "The

Consortium has sent out a request to Slayer Inc., an official commission from Pyrus himself."

I make a face at the House Speaker's name. "What does Mr. Tall, Dark, and Slimy want this time?" I query.

Again Teifert doesn't laugh. "They've got a rogue vampire on the loose and are asking that Slayer Inc. track him down and deliver him for trial," he explains. "And they're offering a great deal of money to the slayer who does the job."

"Money?" My eyes light up. "Are you saying I'll actually get paid for this gig?" Usually I'm required to do Slayer Inc.'s dirty work all in the name of "destiny" instead of cold, hard cash. Could I really score an actual paycheck this time?

"If you were to bring in this vampire and his companion," Teifert says carefully, "you'd get ten percent of the commission." He looks down at his clipboard. "A sum of one million dollars."

My eyes widen in excitement. One million dollars? Under the table? No taxes required? "Dude, I'll take it!" I cry, grabbing for the envelope. But Teifert's fingers lock on and refuse to let go. For an old guy, he's still got a killer grip. "What?" I ask, making a face. "Don't bogart my newfound fortune, man."

"Maybe you should take a closer look before you start racking up any credit card bills," he suggests in a strange voice that hints that he knows something I don't.

"What?" I ask indignantly. "Don't think I can handle the big bad this time? Come on, Teif, you know by now I'm super slayer. Able to stake evil vampires in a single bound." I try again for the envelope.

Teifert raises it out of my reach. "Trust me when I say I would never doubt your abilities, my dear," he says slowly. "I simply think you ought to look before you stake."

I sigh loudly. "Well I'd be simply overjoyed to look, if you would let me see the envelope in question. . . ."

He nods, finally tossing it in my direction. I grab it eagerly and rip it open. Two black-and-white photos fall into my lap.

"Okay, let's see which naughty little vampires need a talking to this time arou—"

The words die in my throat as I pick up the first photo. I look over at Teifert in horror, my gut wrenching.

"But . . . there's got to be some mistake!" I cry.

"No." He purses his lips. "No mistake."

"But . . . but . . ." I pick up the other photo and a mirror image of my own face stares back at me. "They want me to slay *my own sister*?"

2

Teifert gives me a grim look. "The official commission," he corrects, "simply asks that you track down your sister and Magnus and extradite them back to the Consortium for justice. So that the two of them can face the charges that have been brought against them and be judged by a jury of their peers."

"Right." I roll my eyes. "In other words, Pyrus doesn't want *me* to slay them. Because he wants to have all the fun of killing them himself."

My mentor doesn't answer. Instead, he slowly rises from his seat and walks over to the yoga-studio door. He turns the lock, then heads over to a small radio sitting by the mats, cranking up the volume to eleven. My ears are suddenly assaulted by Justin Bieber.

"Um, Teif?" I try to shout over the noise. "Though I truly,

completely respect the fact that you're secure enough in your masculinity to rock out to the Biebs, I really don't think it's the time or place to—"

"Lower your voice!" he admonishes, returning to his seat.

I reluctantly clamp my mouth shut, staring at him expectantly.

He glances around the room with nervous eyes, as if to make sure it's empty save the two of us. Then he turns back to me. "Pyrus has spies everywhere," he informs me in a hushed voice. "You need to be completely careful of what you say from this point out."

Right. I swallow hard, nodding my head, now taking my own inadvertent glance around the room. I knew the vamp was bad news. I just had no idea he had such a far reach.

But at least Teifert seems to be aware of it. "So you know then," I whisper back, once satisfied the room is empty. "You know what a tyrant he is. And what he's reduced the Consortium to."

Teifert nods. "We've been investigating his leadership for some time now. We know that under his command the Consortium is more dictatorship than democracy. We have reports of the other coven masters living in fear, only going along with the leader's mandates in order to protect their own covens."

"'Cause if they speak up, they'll end up like Magnus," I add eagerly. "Facing their own so-called trial for treason."

"Normally we at Slayer Inc. don't get involved in vampire politics," Teifert admits, "unless we come to believe their policies may cause harm to humanity. We now feel Pyrus's lust for power may have reached that point. And we are considering the need to step in."

"Perfect!" I cry. "Can I be the one to take him out then?" Man, it would be so satisfying to stake that jerk through the heart once and for all. And then my sister and Magnus could come home and we could all live happily ever after and—

"Not so fast," Teifert says. "We need to build a case first. And solicit support from the other coven leaders without Pyrus knowing it. If we act too soon and without support from the organization, it could be seen as act of war."

"Right," I say, a little disappointed. "I guess that makes sense. But where does that leave me? Even if I did know where Sunny was I couldn't hand her over to them. After all, she did what she did to save my life. And I'm so not going to enable Pyrus to end hers because of it."

Teifert gives me a sympathetic look. "I know it's a tough position to be in. But unfortunately, you don't have much of a choice. Pyrus knows about the nanocapsules in your bloodstream. If he feels you are not doing your duty, he can petition that we activate them and . . . terminate your employment."

I scowl. Terminate my employment indeed. That's just the fancy way of saying they can stake me from the inside out, thanks to that stupid virus they injected into my bloodstream at birth. It used to be something they did to all potential slayers, back in the day, to keep them in line. A barbaric practice now completely abolished by the kinder and gentler Slayer Inc. of today. Not that it does me any good . . .

"But why does he want me?" I ask. "I mean, *hello conflict*

of interest! It's my sister we're talking about here. Why would I turn her in?"

"Because of all the slayers in the organization, you have the strongest connection to her and the rest of the Blood Coven," Teifert reminds me. "Pyrus sees you as in insider. Someone who could find out things that he can't." He shrugs. "And he believes that like the other coven masters, you will do what he says—in order to save your own skin." He throws me a wry smile.

"Yeah, well, he's got another thing coming," I mutter. "Even if I did have some kind of freaking connection with my sister— which I don't. That whole 'Wonder Twin Powers Activate' crap is just for Saturday-morning cartoons. Sunny and I never had a secret twin language or any hint of ESP. Hell, the guy behind the counter at Burger King has as much chance of knowing where she is right now as I do."

"And that's the way we'd like to keep it," Teifert concludes.

I stare at him for a moment before the admittedly slow lightbulb goes off over my head. So that's what he's getting at. "So you want me to *pretend* to look for Sunny . . ."

". . . but have no luck in finding her." He nods. "Exactly. After all, it's not your fault, right? You've been doing your slayer duty—scouring the globe, racking up the frequent flier miles, following up on every lead under the sun. It's not your fault your evil sister and her boyfriend are so elusive!"

"And by the time he starts getting suspicious of my loyalties," I conclude, "you and your team at Slayer Inc. will have gathered enough evidence to bring the bastard down!"

"Now you're thinking like a true slayer," Teifert says with a grin. Then his expression turns serious. "But you can't mess around with this, Rayne. It's too dangerous. If Pyrus discovers you've been stalling before we can build the case, we will not be able to protect you. If he demands we terminate your employment, we must oblige."

I shiver at his words, not liking what he's saying one bit. But at the same time, what choice do I really have?

I square my shoulders. "You can count on me," I tell him, my voice strong and determined. "I'd do anything in this world to save my sister's life."

"I know you will, Rayne," Teifert says, patting me on the back. "Let's just hope it doesn't come down to ending your own."

3

"I need to see Jareth. Now!"

Marcia, Jareth's secretary (who used to work for Magnus and is decidedly the most annoying vampire in the known universe) looks up at me over horn-rimmed glasses. (I assume she wears them in an effort to give off that whole "sexy secretary" vibe, seeing as even the most nearsighted human gets twenty-twenty vision once they become a vampire.) She frowns.

"The Master has asked not to be disturbed," she announces snottily before turning back to her romance novel.

"Oh, he means by other people, I'm sure," I say quickly. "Not me. He'll be happy to see me, I promise."

Marcia makes a big show of looking up from her book again, as if I'm some pesky fly she can't manage to shoo away.

"Ecstatic as any mortal or vampire might be at the announcement of your illustrious arrival, the fact remains, I was told not to disturb him. And, I can assure you, there were no 'except that weirdo Goth chick I'm hooking up with' caveats to that order."

I roll my eyes. She is *so* ridiculous. Is this what poor Sunny had to go through every time she wanted to meet up with Magnus? Well, sadly for Marcia here, I'm not my sweet little sister, respectful of authority and proper procedure and all the rest.

I start toward the office exit. Then I make a big show of looking down the hallway to my right. "Oh wow. I didn't realize Race Jameson was coming in today," I remark casually.

"Wait, what? Race Jameson?" Marcia stammers, her face turning beet red at the name of everyone's favorite vampire rock star. She scrambles from her seat to take a look for herself.

It's all the opportunity I need—dashing past her desk and pushing open the door that leads to Jareth's office. Behind me, I can hear the secretary screaming bloody murder as she realizes she fell for the oldest trick in the book. Seriously, they should probably start administering IQ tests before turning people into vampires.

"I'm sorry, Master!" she cries, bursting into the room behind me. "I tried to tell her—"

But Jareth waves her off. "It's okay. Thank you Marcia."

"You want me to drag her out on her ass?" the secretary asks hopefully.

Jareth chuckles. "I don't think that will be necessary. But I appreciate the offer."

Marcia scowls. I shoot her a big smile. "Can you get me a glass of O-negative?" I ask sweetly. "Extra sugar? I'm *sooo* parched!"

The secretary glowers at me and slams the door behind her. I plop down into the chair across from Jareth's desk. He gives me an amused look. "She'll probably spit in it, you know," he says.

I shrug. "That's okay. I'm not thirsty anyway. Just wanted to make sure she felt useful and valued in her current position."

"As always, Rayne, your thoughtfulness to the well-being of others simply astounds." Jareth replies drolly. Then he turns serious. "So to what do I owe this visit? Not that I don't love seeing you, but I am a bit busy this evening." He sighs, looking down at the mounds of paperwork on his desk. "Sadly, being Coven Master isn't as glamorous a job as it might seem."

"I bet," I say sympathetically. "And this isn't going to make your night any better, I'm afraid." I toss the envelope with my assignment down onto his desk. He picks it up and pulls out the paperwork, his pale face growing pinker and pinker as he reads.

"Those bastards," he growls, crumpling the paper in his hands and tossing it across the room. "I should have suspected something like this." He groans loudly, then looks at me. "You turned down the assignment, of course."

"Well, not exactly . . ." I hedge. "It's complicated."

He raises an eyebrow. "Turning down an assignment to slay your own sister is complicated?"

"Well, kind of. I mean, look, I know you're not a fan of Slayer Inc., but . . ."

"Not a fan?" Jareth repeats incredulously. I wince, realizing my bad choice of words. "Not a fan? Rayne, they murdered my whole family in cold blood." He scowls. "Or did you happen to conveniently forget that little trivial fact about your precious employer?"

I sigh. Here we go again. God, at this point I can't even count on both hands the number of times we've had this argument. In his mind Slayer Inc. is evil incarnate, out to destroy the world. And maybe they were, once upon a time. Hundreds of years ago under completely different management. (Unlike vampire political organizations, which have no term limits and whose rulers can live a thousand years or more, mortal Slayer Inc. officials tend to take the cushy retirement plan when they hit sixty-five.)

But how can you argue semantics with someone whose own sister and brother were targeted for annihilation for no reason at all, except for the unfortunate fact that they'd been turned into vampires as children. (The vampire who turned them had only wanted to save them from the deadly plague that had consumed much of Europe. But to Slayer Inc., child vampirism was—and is—an abomination.)

"I'll never forget that day," Jareth says, staring down at his desk, looking miserable. "The day we were asked to vote on whether or not to let Slayer Inc. in as an official police force for the vampire community . . ."

He trails off, but it doesn't matter. He's told me the story a thousand times before. How the vote was split right down the middle. How he was forced to become the tie-breaker. How his vote effectively established Slayer Inc. into the role they still hold today.

Of course he could have never known the consequences of his actions . . .

"It didn't take them long to come after us," he says in a hoarse whisper and I wonder suddenly if he even remembers I'm still in the room. "We held out for days in our family's castle—trying to outlast the siege. But the blood ran out and our hunger overtook our good senses. We tried to fight our way out. But they were too strong."

I walk around his desk, trying to put a hand on his arm—in an effort to comfort him. But he shakes it off, rising to his feet, his body seething with anger.

"I will never forget the look on my sister's face as that damned slayer struck her in the heart with his stake." His voice cracks. "She looked straight into my eyes, condemning me for what I had done—blaming me for her death."

He stands silent for a moment, fists clenched at his sides, in such agony I can't bear it any longer. I grab him, holding him tight against me, fighting his attempts to shake me away. Finally, his body slumps, as if in defeat, crumbling against my own, soaking in the strength I so willingly try to give him.

"I'm sorry," I whisper. "I can't imagine what that would have been like."

Half of me still wants to argue my case. That the Slayer Inc. of today has introduced so much good into the world—keeping the peace and saving so many lives. With their donor program, for example—which allows humans to be compensated for donating blood to vampires, rather than be murdered as twisted cattle to satisfy the beastly hunger we vampires share.

But I know in my heart Jareth cares little for the thousands of mortal lives saved by my employer. He thinks only of those lives they ended. His sister's and brother's—for a crime they didn't commit. His parents—for trying their best to protect them. I guess I can't really blame him for feeling as he does.

He looks down at me with bloodstained eyes. "And now they want to take away your sister," he says slowly. "Just as they once took mine." His face twists with rage and he shakes free of my grasp. "I won't let them do that. I won't be responsible for another innocent death!"

I squeeze my eyes shut in frustration, then open them again, entreating him. "But Jareth, you don't understand," I try. "Things are different now. Slayer Inc. doesn't want to slay Sunny. Or Magnus, for that matter. They know Pyrus is a tyrant and they want to bring him down as much as we do. They're on our side this time."

"I will never, ever be on the side of Slayer Inc."

I give up, walking around and slumping back into my chair. How can I argue with a vampire who holds a 700-year-old grudge?

"Look, I'm not asking you to sit around the campfire with them, singing 'Kumbaya,'" I remind him. "Just let me work with them for now. Let Pyrus think I'm on the job. And in the meantime, Slayer Inc. can work to build their own case against him and his reign of terror. I mean, imagine if they were successful! We could get rid of him forever. Magnus and Sunny could come back home. The Consortium could return to a democracy. These are all things I know you want, Jareth. And Slayer Inc. is the only one right now that can give them to us."

My boyfriend rakes a hand through his blond hair. Considering vampires never age, he's suddenly looking kind of old. I guess stress can do that to you.

"I see what you're saying," he says at last. "I can't make a move against Pyrus while still running the Blood Coven. If he suspected disloyalty, he'd have me removed from power—leaving the vampires in my protection in danger."

"Exactly," I say, rising from my chair, excited he's finally seeing the point. "So why not let Slayer Inc. do the dirty work instead? After all, that's what you hired them for in the beginning, right?" I hold my breath, waiting for his reply.

"Right," he says at last. "But I still don't like the idea of you involved in any of it. It's dangerous. And don't think for a moment Slayer Inc. won't throw you under a bus if it allows them to keep their cover. Are you prepared to deal with that possibility?"

I nod my head resolutely. "Absolutely. If it means saving my sister and Magnus—not to mention the Blood Coven."

He stares at me for a moment and I stare back, my shoulders squared and my chin held high. Sure, I'm scared as hell, but he doesn't need to know that right now. He needs to see my dedication to the mission ahead. He needs to know I'll do whatever it takes to save my family. Just as he once tried to save his own.

And then he's on me in a movement so quick I can scarcely track it, pulling me into a hot embrace, burying his face into the top of my head. I find myself melting into his arms, rejoicing in the feel of his strong body, pressed against mine. God, I love this vampire so much, it hurts sometimes.

"You're so brave," he whispers in my ear, stroking my hair with trembling hands. "So fierce. I wish I were more like you. Maybe then I would have been able to save my family, too."

I open my mouth to protest, but he places a finger to my lips. "I don't want to talk any more about the past," he whispers. "I just want you to listen to me now."

I nod slowly, meeting his beautiful eyes with my own.

"I love you," he says. "And I trust you more than anyone in the world. If you say Slayer Inc. can help us—well, then I will respect your judgment and not interfere."

"Thank you," I whisper, knowing how hard it must be for him to make such a promise.

"And I will do anything I can—within my limited capacity— to help you keep your sister safe." He pauses, then adds, "No matter what it takes."

A chill trips down my spine at his words and I throw my arms around him, not wanting to let go. "I love you, Jareth," I murmur as I cover his face with kisses before finding his lips with my own. "And I won't let you down."

4

"Take that, you putrid jumble-gutted zombie!" I cry, mashing my PS3 button as fast as I can, letting loose a stream of deadly bullets from my AK-47 and splattering zombie brains, blood, and other assorted bodily fluids all over my bedroom television screen. The game dings as I beat my own high score once again and I lean back in my chair, feeling oh-so-satisfied. *Yeah, baby!* No one's better at Vampires vs. Zombies than me. I should enter a tournament. I'd blast all those wannabe zombie slaying nerds out there from here to kingdom come without even trying.

I'm about to start the bonus round when there's a knock on my door.

"Come in!" I call, hoping it's my half sister, Stormy. She's the only one who can come even close to beating me at the game and I'd love another chance to kick her ten-year-old video game–addicted butt.

Sure enough, the door opens and Stormy pokes a blond head into my room. "Hey, Rayne," she says. "There's some girl here to see you."

"A girl?" My mind races for possibilities but comes up blank. I've never really been good with making girlfriends in general, and I'm almost positive I haven't given my home address to any mortal ones here in Vegas. (Unlike my much more social twin, Sunny, who made like ten friends in two days just by breathing the air at Las Vegas High School.) And, of course, no self-respecting vampire would be swinging by for a chat on a Saturday afternoon while the sun is still high in the sky. "Who?"

Stormy shrugs. "I've never seen her before," she confesses. "Though she looks a lot like the girl from *Resident Evil.*"

"Video game or movie?"

"The movie. Definitely the movie."

Hmm. I'm pretty sure I'd remember making friends and influencing people who looked like Milla Jovovich. . . .

"Well, send her in, I guess," I tell my sister. What the heck, right?

Stormy nods and disappears. While I'm waiting I go and save my game. It's a little embarrassing to see the game clock pop up and realize how many hours I've been sitting in front of a television set. *But it's for a good cause,* I remind myself. After all, if Pyrus received reports of me hitting the slot machines or dancing up a storm in downtown Vegas he might decide I'm not taking my whole mission to bring down my sister and her boyfriend as seriously as he'd like. Out of sight, out of mind, that's what I say. As far as he knows, I'm scouring the world, one step away from my bounty.

I hear the door creak open and turn around to greet my strange visitor. Stormy isn't wrong—the girl does bear a remarkable resemblance to the famed zombie-slaughtering film star. Not only does she kind of look like her, but she dresses like her, too. I mean, it's not every day you see someone sporting a tight white tank top under a green army vest, tucked into little black shorts with garters that cling to ripped thigh-high stockings— even in Vegas. (Unless, of course, Taylor Momsen's in town . . .) The girl tops off the outfit with an amazing pair of knee-high, stack-heeled, black leather boots and two matching black leather holsters strapped to her perfectly toned and tanned thighs.

But unlike the zombie killer of the 3-D silver screen, these holsters aren't slotted with guns. They contain stakes.

A vampire slayer. I let out a low whistle, wondering where on Earth she scored an outfit like that. Is there some kind of secret online Slayer Inc. uniform shop that no one told me about? I mean, I'm not all about the army vest. But those boots, man! I'd pretty much sell my soul to slip my feet into those beauties—if I hadn't already given it away when I first became a vampire.

Of course, I'm not entirely sure my current not-so-tanned, not-so-perfectly sculptured thighs could carry the rest of the outfit as well she does. After all, I'm still recovering from all those high-calorie blood milkshakes they force-feed you at the vampire rehab I was made to attend after having an eensy-weensy little blood-drinking issue. . . .

"Rayne?" the girl asks, looking down at me and removing her mirrored aviator shades. She wears a slightly disdainful look on her otherwise flawless face and I suddenly get a weird feeling I've seen her somewhere before, though for the life of me, I can't figure out where that could possibly be. "Rayne McDonald?"

"That's my name, don't wear it out," I reply automatically, feeling a little defensive. After all, she showed up at my house out of nowhere, giving me dirty looks like that. Even if she is the hottest thing known to slayerkind and I'm three days over-due for a shower and wearing vampire bunny slippers instead of kick-ass boots.

She purses her obviously collagen-injected, over-glossed lips, looking at me with clear disapproval in her purple contact–covered eyes.

"Um, did you want something?" I ask, suddenly eager to get rid of her and go back to my game. After all, those brain-hungry zombies won't explode themselves, you know.

She sighs loudly, as if she's carrying the weight of the world on her perfectly sculpted shoulders. "My name is Bertha," she says at last.

"Bertha?!" I burst out laughing. I'm sorry—I can't help it! This über hottie's name is Bertha? For realz? I had always as-sumed there was some kind of law against hot chicks being named Bertha. A name like Bertha should be reserved for girls who look like that crazy ex-vampire slayer from back home who—

Oh crap. So that's why she looks familiar. . . .

"Bertha?" I cry, scrambling to my feet, trying to hide my shock. "Bertha the Vampire Slayer? Bertha the Vampire Slayer from Oakridge High School?"

Bertha had been the number one slayer in my neck of the woods, back in the day. She had some pretty major kills to her name, too. She'd even bagged Lucifent, the former leader of the Blood Coven. Unfortunately, her career had stalled out due to her inability to ever meet a drive-thru she didn't want to go through twice. Those pesky blood pressure issues can really put a damper on one's vampire slayer career.

But um, wow. I guess she kicked that problem.

"I probably look a little different then when you saw me last," she says, preening a little. I catch her glancing at her own reflection in the bedroom mirror.

I nod. I mean, holy understatement of the century, Batman! This chick did not merely get her stomach stapled. She'd had a complete Heidi Montag makeover. Her once-pockmarked face is now porcelain-doll smooth. Her old stringy hair now flows down her back in silky waves. Her nose is at least three inches shorter and her breasts would make even Katy Perry cry.

"Wow, Bertha," I say. "You look great. Really great." And I mean it, too. Not that I'm into girls or anything. But if I was, she'd totally be first on my list.

She sniffs and I realize she's moved away from the mirror and is now giving me a critical once-over. It's then that I remember I'm currently dressed in *Nightmare Before Christmas* flannel pajamas, wearing no makeup, and haven't brushed my hair since Tuesday. At this point, I'd be dead last on pretty much anyone's list—male or female.

But still, there's no need for the judgment here. I mean, it's not like she gave me any heads-up of her impending arrival so I could apply some mascara.

"So to what do I owe the pleasure of this visit?" I ask curiously. "I'm sure you didn't fly more than halfway across the country to show off your extreme total makeover." Though, to be honest, if I looked like her, I'd pretty much make that my full-time job from here on out. Tracking down all those boys who once rejected me, showing off my curves . . .

"I'm your new partner."

. . . finding even hotter boys and stealing them away from their cheerleader girlfriends, only to dump them after—

Wait, what?

I stare at her. "My partner?" I repeat. If my heart was still beating, it'd be slamming against my chest right about now. What the hell is she talking about?

She nods. "The powers that be felt you might need some . . . motivation . . . in tracking down your sister. So they flew me out here to assist you."

"Motivation?" I cry indignantly. "They think I have a motivation problem?" I give a loud, barking laugh at the ridiculousness of it all. A laugh that cuts short as I realize she's staring smugly at the video game behind me. Particularly the game clock that's still flashing on the screen.

"Oh, that!" I wave my hand dismissively. "That's just practice. After all, you never know when you might meet up with a zombie while out on a Slayer Inc. mission. But don't worry, Berth, my girl. Can I call you Berth? I am unsurpassed at perfect head shots. Seriously, brains start splattering all over the place at the mere the sight of my mighty BOOMstick."

She raises an eyebrow. "That's very . . . reassuring."

I grab the remote and quickly shut off the TV. "But enough about me. Let's talk about you! What have you been up to? Are you enjoying Vegas so far? Done any gambling? You have so got to try the Krave Lounge on Fridays. Amazing Goth scene. They've got the hottest—"

"Rayne!" Bertha interrupts. "We don't have time for *clubbing*," she says, spitting out the word as if it were poison. "We're on assignment to track down your sister and Magnus. Or perhaps you forgot?" she adds, giving the television set another look of condemnation.

I frown. Am I missing something? After all, Teifert made my mission perfectly clear. As in, this is all basically a cover-up to buy them time. So why would they assign me back-up? Back-up who, I might add, seems awfully eager to get the job done . . . Could Jareth have been right? Could Slayer Inc.'s mission not be as heroic as I argued it to be?

No. I'd trust Teifert with my life. There's got to be something else going on here.

"Who put you on this so-called assignment?" I ask, narrowing my eyes. "Not Slayer Inc. They would have told me."

"That's for me to know and you to find out," Bertha sneers.

Evidently she can play third grader as well as me. She plops down onto my bed. "Now, let's talk strategy. Do you have any leads? Any idea where your sister and her boyfriend might have gone?"

I shake my head. Luckily, I can give her an honest answer on that one. Don't ask, don't tell. That's my policy. "Sorry, she hasn't updated her Foursquare lately. In fact, I think she even lost her mayorship at the local Olive Garden."

Bertha rolls her eyes. "Trust me, I already checked her Facebook. Even her MySpace. But you're her twin. Can't you . . . sense . . . where she is or something?"

"Please. The only thing I can sense is a super-annoying presence currently residing in my bedroom," I retort, irritated at the whole "Twenty Questions" routine. Who is she working for? Someone else at Slayer Inc.? Pyrus himself? Does Teifert know any of this is going on?

She frowns. "Go ahead, be a bitch. You're not going to scare me away." She shakes her head. "This is the new and improved Bertha. And she doesn't take crap from anyone." She rises to her feet, staring directly into the mirror. "I'm back. I'm hot as hell, and I'm not going to take it anymore!"

She raises a fist in triumph then looks at me expectantly. As if she's hoping I'll cheer on her newfound sense of self-esteem.

"Um, yay?" I try. "Go on with your bad self, you hot mama you?"

She glares at me. "Laugh all you want," she growls. "But you won't be laughing once I have your sister and her stupid boyfriend in handcuffs."

That's it! I leap from my bed, grabbing her by her vest. "We'll see about that!"

She smirks and I realize I've walked right into her trap. "Oh, I'm sorry," she says with wide innocent eyes. "For some reason I thought you were supposed to be on my team. You know, the team that hired you for the job? The one that has the ability to wipe you off the face of the earth by activating the nano virus inside of you if you don't obey their rules?"

Argh. It takes everything I have inside to let her go. But of course she's right. I can't let on that I'm more interested in protecting my sister than doing my Slayer Inc. duty—at least until I figure out who she's really working for. After all, if I'm killed then who will protect Sunny?

Better to bide my time. Pretend to play by her rules for now. And figure out a way to beat Bertha at her own game.

"Of course," I say brightly, gritting my teeth and wishing I could bite through that juicy little neck of hers and suck her dry. "I just meant, as a superior slayer, I'm sure to get there first."

Her lips curl into a nasty grin. "Oh right," she says. "Of course you did." She chuckles. "But, you see, that's not going to happen either. I've been given a second chance. And I'm going to use that chance to prove I'm the best slayer on Earth—no matter what I have to do." She smiles triumphantly. "Even if that means going above and beyond—and staking your sweet little sister through the heart."

5

"The Master asked that he not be disturb—"

"Suck it," I interrupt, pushing past Marcia as I head toward Jareth's office. Thanks to Bertha, I no longer have time to play her little reindeer games. I walk through the door and turn, shoving her backward so I can close it behind me.

Jareth rises from his seat, taking in my face with a look of alarm. "What's wrong?" he demands, coming around from his desk. He gives me a quick hug, then ushers me over to his black leather office couch, sitting down beside me, holding my cold hands in his own. He searches my face anxiously. "You look like you've seen a ghost."

"You're not half wrong," I mutter, going through the highlights of Bertha's recent visit. (Or should I say lowlights?) "You should have heard her," I finish with a moan. "She's like, on this crazy vendetta to bring my sister and Magnus down. All to prove she's worthy of returning to Slayer Inc.'s good graces. She obviously has no idea of Slayer Inc.'s real mission to stall Pryus until they can make their case against him."

Jareth gives me a sharp look. "You didn't tell her, did you?"

I shake my head. "No, of course not. I didn't know if I could trust her with the truth. Not after seeing that cruel look in her eyes."

"Right." Jareth lets go of my hands and starts shuffling through the magazines on his coffee table. "Well, that's something at least." He grabs an issue of *Afterlife and Style*—the one with Race Jameson and his band on the cover—and starts flipping through.

"Am I boring you or something?" I demand. "I mean, hello, we've got a crazy slayer on the loose. Doesn't seem to be the appropriate time for *Vamps: Just Like Us?*"

Jareth doesn't respond at first. Instead he drops the opened magazine into my lap. "Is that her?" he asks.

I squint at the photo. "Um, no that's the girl from *1,600 and Pregnant*—that new reality show that follows vampire moms and—"

"Not her," he corrects. "Her." He points to the photo on the adjoining page.

"Oh my God!" I cry, staring down in disbelief. Sure, it's a fuzzy photo—your typical night-shift vamperazzi, but the image is unmistakable. Bertha, getting out of a limo . . .

. . . with none other than Pryus himself, holding her hand.

"What the hell?" I look up at Jareth. He shrugs.

"If you believe the tabloids, the two of them have been hooking up for the last month or so," he informs me grimly.

"Well, that explains it," I realize. "When I called Teifert to find out what the hell was going on, he told me he knew nothing about her being on the case."

Jareth frowns. "That means Pyrus must already be suspicious of your true intentions, meaning you could be in danger."

I glare at Bertha's photo. "Well, Slayer Inc. isn't even close to being ready to make a charge against Pyrus. I mean, they're working on it, but they're going to need more time." I look up at Jareth worriedly. "What if Bertha is able to track them down beforehand? What if she really goes and slays my sister?"

Jareth shakes his head. "I don't know, Rayne. I just don't know." He pulls me into a hug but I find I can't relax in his arms this time. I try to close my eyes, but all I can see are visions of Sunny's pale, frightened face. Of Bertha, chasing her with a stake.

The door bursts open and we reluctantly break apart. I turn around to see Marcia standing smugly in the doorway.

"So sorry to interrupt," she says in a voice that tells me she's totally not. "I just wanted to deliver the dry cleaning."

I sink back down onto the couch as Jareth takes the bags from her and starts hanging them in his closet. She looks at me, a patronizing smile on her face. "Oh, Raynie," she coos. "Trouble in slayerland?"

I halfheartedly flick her off, but my mind stays on Sunny. This is all my fault. If I hadn't gotten involved with vampires last spring, none of this would be happening. We'd be living normal, everyday lives. Sunny could be starring in the latest school play, my friend Spider and I could have reached level eighty on World of Warcraft. The whole point of our parents running away from Fairyland long ago was to give us a chance to live safe, carefree, mortal lives.

But what do I do instead? Oh well, I choose to seek out the most dangerous creatures around and actually sign up to become one of then, putting not only my own life—but also my innocent sister's at risk. Let's face it—from that very first night at Club Fang, my decision to become a vampire nearly cost Sunny her mortality. Not exactly the stuff Sister of the Year trophies are made of.

And that was only the beginning. Time after time in the last year, the vampire world has placed her in danger. In Vegas, in England, in Japan. Hell, the only reason Sunny went against the Consortium's orders to begin with was to save me from the Alphas. If I hadn't put her in that position—by stupidly getting myself kidnapped—she'd be here with me now. And her biggest fear would be Mom finding out about the C she scored on her math test.

Instead, she's out there, somewhere, unprotected and vulnerable, with a crazy, deadly vampire slayer with something to prove determined to hunt her down. Ready to actually kill her—if she gets half the chance.

I cannot let that happen.

"We have to warn her," I say as Jareth escorts Marcia out and closes the door behind her. "Her and Magnus. We have to let them know there's a vengeful slayer on the loose."

Jareth turns back to me, biting at his lower lip, looking worried. "I'm not sure that's a good idea," he says at last.

"Why not?" I demand. "We can't just sit around and do nothing."

"Well, for one thing, we don't know yet if Bertha's truly a danger," he reminds me. "Just because she wants to go after Sunny and Magnus doesn't mean she knows where to look. And if we make an overt move to find them—and get caught— well, we've already talked about the consequences of something like that."

Right. He loses the Blood Coven forever and I get nano'ed. Not good. But still . . .

"Can't we. . . I don't know, call them or something?" I ask. "I mean, you've got to know where they are, right?"

Jareth sighs. "I do have some idea," he confesses. "But they've gone deep underground. Under the streets of New York, where there is no Internet, no cell service, no connection to the outside world. It would be impossible to reach them unless we traveled there ourselves and gained admittance to the secret world below."

"Well, we need to be ready to do that," I reply. "If push comes to shove."

"I don't know Rayne. Like I said . . . if we get caught . . ."

"Fine. You don't have to come," I reply quickly. "But don't expect me to stay home and sit around, wondering if my sister has been butchered by the winning contestant of *Bridalplasty*."

"Of course not," he mutters. "That just wouldn't be you."

I can't help a small grin at that. "You know me very well."

He shakes his head. "Fine," he says at last. "I'll have a chartered jet standing by. We can't use the Blood Coven ones—it'll arouse too much suspicion." He reaches into his drawer and hands me a small metal device. "In the meantime, take this," he says. "It's a bug," he adds, at my confused look. "I want you to leave it somewhere in Bertha's room where she won't find it. This way we can listen in on her conversations. Try to determine whether or not she knows anything about their whereabouts."

I take the bug and put it in my pocket, throwing my arms around Jareth and hugging him to me, relief washing over in me in waves. "Thank you!" I murmur over and over again. "Thank you so much. I promise you we'll make this work. We'll keep them safe and no one will be any the wiser."

"I hope you're right," he says, pulling away from the hug and staring down at the photo of Bertha and Pyrus again. "Because if we fail, there will be hell to pay."

6

It takes a lot of calling around—let's just say Vegas has a LOT of hotel rooms—but eventually I figure out where Bertha is currently residing. Turns out Pyrus hooked her up big time—putting her up in the Bellagio itself. I guess we can't add cheap bastard to his list of evil qualities, though we could add "not too bright," considering he didn't put her under an assumed name. And it only takes a teensy bit of vampire scenting to seduce the drooling front desk clerk to hand over her room number.

Sometimes I love being a vampire.

I head up to the tenth floor and down the hall to her room. I knock on the door, nervously fingering the bug Jareth gave me, in my pocket. He suggested I put it under the toilet, saying it's sensitive enough to pick up conversations in the next room, and this way it'll be out of sight, out of mind. So all I have to do is get Bertha to let me pee in peace and I'll be golden.

I am so the female James Bond.

There's no answer, so I knock again. A few minutes later, I'm about ready to go back down to my desk clerk friend and convince him to give me a key when the door finally slips open. Bertha has stripped from her former *Resident Evil* costume and is now wearing a Bellagio Egyptian cotton robe and slippers, her hair piled high above her head. I worry for a second she might be entertaining company—namely a certain politically connected vampire we both know and love. But a quick peek into the room behind her tells me she's alone.

"What do you want?" she demands, squinting her eyes at me.

"Can I come in?"

"Why would you want to come in?"

I suck in a breath. Here goes nothing. "I want to talk. I think we got off on the wrong foot earlier. After all, we're both working for the same people, right? We both have the same mission? I was thinking maybe we should start working together or something." It's all I can do not to gag at the words. But I need her to let me in.

For a moment I'm positive she's going to slam the door in my face. But instead, she widens it, allowing me entrance. Which makes sense, I guess. After all, she's still relying on me to tell her where Sunny is hiding out. She's probably relieved I've come to my senses at last.

I step inside the hotel room, past the closed bathroom door, and take a quick look around. Though the place is beyond gorgeous—draped in gold and crimson—with an amazing 180-degree view of the famous fountain outside below—there's something that seems . . . off. Wrong. Though I can't, for the life of me, figure out what it could be.

I mean, it's certainly not messy by any stretch of the imagination. In fact, it's oddly . . . clean. And really orderly, too. The stakes on her nightstand are lined up in perfect rows. Each queen-sized bed is made within an inch of its life. Even her makeup sits on a nearby table in perfect order—lipsticks lined up, blushes and eye shadows in careful stacks. Heck, I wouldn't be at all surprised if the pile of fashion magazines she's carefully placed on the bed are in alphabetical order.

"Wow, your maid's working overtime, huh?" I remark, plopping down on one of the beds. "Hope you left her a good tip."

I catch Bertha's cringe as I wrinkle the bedspread. "Be care—" she starts, then stops, and I can see her hard swallow. I reach over and switch on another lamp, allowing light to flood the darkened room. Only then do I get a good look at her face. Her hollow eyes, her smudged makeup. And is that a bruise on her cheek?

"Are you okay?" I ask against my better judgment. After all, she is the enemy, out to destroy my sister. But she doesn't look very evil at the moment. If anything, I'd say she looks a bit scared.

"Yeah, I'm fine," she says, recovering quickly. She sits down in nearby chair, straightening her robe. "Now, how about you tell me about Sunny and Magnus."

"Look, before we get into all of that, do you mind if I use the bathroom?" I ask, bouncing up from my spot on the bed. Might as well get that part over with right away in case she goes and kicks me out. Not to mention it'll give my stupid hands a reason to stop shaking. I start stumbling to the room in question, not waiting for her obligatory yes.

To my surprise, Bertha leaps from her seat and throws herself into my path, blocking the way to the bathroom, an utterly panicked look on her face.

"What?" I ask, worry knotting my stomach at her extreme reaction to my seemingly innocent move. There's no way she can expect me to have a bug, is there?

"Um, nothing. It's just . . . the bathroom's dirty. I don't think you want to use it," she stammers.

Oh-kay. My spidey senses start to work overtime. Is she hiding something in there? Or worse . . . someONE? Could Pyrus himself be lurking behind door number one, waiting for me to implicate myself somehow?

No, that's impossible. It's morning. Her blinds are wide open. Any vampire worth his salt would be deep asleep at home right now, not lying unprotected in a Vegas bathroom. Too easy for some random slayer to come by and stake him through the heart.

"I really have to go!" I cry, trying to dodge her and reach the door. But she remains an unmovable force. I'd be impressed by her reflexes if I weren't so annoyed at them foiling my supposedly no-big-deal spy plan.

"I bet they have one down in the lobby," she suggests, her face white with panic now. What happened to the cocky, confident slayer who waltzed into my bedroom the day before? "I'll wait for you here, okay?"

I don't think so. "Sorry, I won't make it that far," I moan, clutching at my crotch. A little crude, I know. But it works for two-year-old boys . . . "If I don't go now I'm going to piss my pants!" I do a little pee-pee dance to hopefully better prove my point. She stares at me, then at her perfectly pristine room, in horror.

"Okay, okay!" she cries. "Go ahead. But don't say I didn't warn you!" She steps out of my path, biting her fingernails. What the heck is behind this door? Do I even want to know? So help me if she's hiding a bunch of severed heads or something . . .

I wrap my hand around the doorknob, praying for something not gross. Even Pyrus himself would be a better alternative than blood, carnage and . . .

. . . pepperoni pizza?

The large bathroom is filled practically waist-high with room service trays. Plates, bowls, and silverware fill the bathtub, covered in half-eaten food. I stagger backward, the myriad of smells assaulting my senses.

What the hell? I turn back to Bertha. She slumps down on her chair, staring at her hands, her face flaming red.

Wow. I guess you could say she isn't quite as recovered from her eating disorder as I first assumed. Abandoning my mission for the moment, I walk over and sit across from her, peering at her with worried eyes. I try to remind myself once again she's the bad guy. But the pity I feel won't go away. I must be getting soft in my old age.

"Have you talked to anyone about this?" I ask. "I mean, I know it's scary. But—"

She looks up, glaring at me with eyes full of hate. "How do you know anything?" she demands. "Little Miss Perfect!"

I raise my eyebrows. "Perfect?" I look around the room, making sure she's not talking about someone else. "Um, are you talking about me?"

"Duh," she spits out. "Everyone loves you. You're beautiful. You ace every mission you're given. Your Teifert's little golden girl—able to do no wrong."

Wow, if I'm Teifert's golden girl, I'd hate to see who gets the bronze. Most of the time he's too busy yelling at me or calling me a complete screw up to even consider singing my praises. In fact, up until now, I would have bet my life he wouldn't know a praiseful tune with my name on it if it smacked him upside the head.

"You don't know what it's been like," Bertha continues, all her haughty poise forgotten at my discovery of her dirty secret. "All my life I've been told I'm too ugly, too fat, too stupid." She scrunches up her face. "And then, when I finally *do* find something I'm good at? Being a vampire slayer? It all gets ripped away—because Slayer Inc. wants someone more *attractive* on the payroll. So they can get more positive media attention, like they did when Buffy was on the air. They didn't care one bit that I was the best there was when it came to slaying actual vampires. They just knew you looked good in a leather pantsuit."

While I have to admit I do look damn fine in a leather pantsuit, her words make me cringe all the same. Was she telling the truth? Was that really why they retired her and brought me on in the first place? It would make sense, I suppose, judging from the extreme measures she's taken to achieve external perfection— at the expense of sanity and health.

"I'm sorry," I say, reaching out to touch her hand, in what I hope appears to be a comforting gesture. "I had no idea."

"Of course you didn't," she growls. "You were too busy living the perfect life."

I snort at that. "Oh yeah, my life is so perfect," I reply. "My father was murdered by evil fairies. My mother currently lives in an alternate dimension. And my twin sister is running for her life—and I'm the one who's supposed to track her down—or else I get dusted, too."

Bertha scowls, staring down at her hands, picking at a hangnail. I draw in a breath. I really don't want to get into any of this—especially not with her. But at the same time, I realize she needs serious help. And I'm the only one, it appears, willing to give it to her.

Here goes nothing.

"Look, Bertha, I understand what you're going through more than you know," I start cautiously. "I had an eating disorder, too. Well, a drinking disorder, if you want to be technical.

I had denied myself real blood for so long—feeling as if that gave me some kind of control over what was happening to my body as a vampire." I cringe, remembering the hunger I felt at Riverdale Academy. How the bloodlust raged inside of me as I slowly starved to death.

"But it was all an illusion," I continue. "And I ended up losing control big time—causing someone I cared about to lose his life because of my weakness." My mind flashes to Corbin's anguished face. The pain, the betrayal in his eyes, all because of me.

"So . . . what happened?" Bertha asks softly, as if against her better judgment.

"I got help," I tell her. "I sucked it up—pardon the pun—and went to vampire rehab. I learned healthy drinking habits and how to control my bloodlust. It wasn't easy. In fact, it was damned hard. It still is. But I feel so much better now, I can't even tell you." I pause, trying to meet her eyes with my own. "You could feel better, too, you know," I tell her. "You can kick this addiction for good."

She looks up at me with tear-stained eyes. "I was doing so good," she says. "But then he dumped me!" She bursts into tears.

"Who? Who dumped you? Pryus?" My body hums with excitement. Is she serious? This could be very good news indeed.

She nods. "He told me he loved me," she says. "He told me he was going to turn me into a vampire—so I could finally achieve perfection and never have to worry about being fat again. But then I caught him making out with this blond bimbo vampire. I freaked out, screaming at him. Of course he just laughed at me and called me a fool."

I give her a sympathetic look. Poor girl. Even if she is an idiot to have ever trusted someone like Pyrus. We've all been there, done stupid things for love.

She bites her lower lip. "I got on my knees, Rayne. I begged him not to leave me. To turn me into a vampire as he promised." Tears well in her eyes. "I'm so embarrassed to even think of it now." She pauses, then adds, "Finally he got fed up with me and he . . . well, he hit me." She reached up and involuntarily touches her bruised face. "I guess I should be lucky he didn't shatter my cheekbone."

I squeeze my fists in anger. "That bastard," I swear. I know I'm supposed to pretend to be on his side, but at the moment I can't help it. How dare he hit a human? Especially one as emotionally fragile as Bertha.

"I was so upset. I got back here and . . . well . . ." She gestures to the bathroom. "And now I don't know what to do. I can't even sleep—thinking about that food being there. Rotting away, waiting for someone to discover it."

My heart aches at her obvious pain. "Why don't we take it outside?" I suggest. "Let housekeeping come and take it away."

She looks up at me in panic. "No! Then they'll all know. They'll all know I ate all of . . ." she trails off, a horrified look on her face.

Right. I think for a moment. Then I smile. "I've got an idea," I tell her. "We'll take it out, tray by tray and place each one in front of someone else's door. Then they'll assume everyone had one room service meal. No big deal."

Bertha looks up at me with extreme gratitude on her face. "You'd do that for me?" she asks.

"Absolutely."

And so we start piling up the trays, sneaking quietly into the hallway, surreptitiously placing each tray in front of another door. There are so many, we eventually have to hit the next floor. But in the end, the bathroom is clear and it's already beginning to smell a whole heck of a lot better.

"Oh, Rayne, thank you!" Bertha says, collapsing onto her bed once we're finished. "I didn't know what I was going to do. How can I repay you?"

"By getting yourself help," I tell her. "Find a meeting or something. Or a doctor."

"You're so nice," she says. "I had no idea. I thought you'd be totally stuck-up. After the way Teifert talked about you . . ."

I give her a regretful smile. "I have my moments," I tell her. "But what you're going through? That's something I understand. And I would have given anything when I was going through it myself to have someone help me."

"I want to help you, too," Bertha says, looking bashful. "But I don't know how."

I hold my breath, wondering if should dare. Do I trust her?

I decide to go for it. "You can tell me what Pyrus knows about my sister and Magnus's whereabouts," I tell her. "That would really help."

She cringes. "I almost forgot about your sister," she admits.

"You must be really worried about her." She hangs her head. "I'm sorry I told you I'd slay her. I was just so mad. I wanted to prove myself to Pyrus. That I was worthy to be turned into a vampire. Not that it did any good."

"Right." I give her a pitying look.

"That blond bimbo I was telling you about? She's one of his spies. Before I walked in on them, I heard her telling him something about Sunny and Magnus hiding out in New York City, in some underground place or something. I assume he was going to send me there to find them—before I freaked out on him. But now I don't know what he's planning . . ." She looks up at me and shrugs. "I just know it can't be good."

I swallow hard. "Thanks," I tell her, rising from my seat. "I appreciate you telling me, more than you know." I start toward the door, anxious to get to Jareth and tell him what I've learned.

"Where are you going?" Bertha asks, scrambling to her feet, looking anxious.

"To find my sister and Magnus before Pyrus can."

"Right." She squares her shoulders. "Good luck, Rayne. I hope you find them."

I head out the door, closing it behind me. It's only then that I realize I never placed the bug in her bathroom. Though I guess there's no need now. We know Pyrus or his men will soon be on the move, and we know they know exactly where to go.

I just hope we can get there before they do.

7

Slipping the black hood over my head, I scan the airfield, making sure the coast is clear. Then I make a run for it, my combat boots pounding against the pavement. Once I reach the plane, I make a dash up the stairs, bursting into the main cabin. My eyes fall on Jareth, already sitting there, in one of the reclining leather seats. I take one look and burst out laughing.

"What?" he demands. Then a light of recognition sparkles in his eyes. "Oh." He yanks the fake handlebar mustache from his upper lip and removes the floppy wig on top of his head. He throws me a sheepish grin. "I forgot about my little disguise."

"What were you going for? One of the Village People?" I tease, settling down on his lap and kissing him thoroughly on his now hair-free mouth. "One of Ke$ha's bearded boyfriends?"

"You know, there was a time when mustaches were quite

the gentlemanly accoutrement," he reminds me when I come up for air. "For at least a century I had to wear a fake one, to fit in with the locals."

"Poor baby," I coo, running a finger over his smooth upper lip. "I don't know what I'd find worse: life without penicillin and the Internet or the ridiculous fashions. I mean, however did you survive the seventies?"

His smile fades and I immediately regret my bad joke. To Jareth, who lived through the Black Plague that consumed Europe, there was nothing funny about the medicine that could have saved all his family and friends. The magical cure made from simple mold that could have allowed them all to live normal, human lives, instead of being forced to turn into monsters.

"I'm sorry," I say. "I'm an idiot."

"It's okay," he assures me, attempting a smile, though I can tell he's still a bit shaken. "It's just . . . all this talk about Slayer Inc. and your sister has brought back some painful memories." He shrugs uneasily. "It's hard to believe how much I still miss them," he says, staring down at his lap. "I mean, it's been centuries!"

"Yeah, I always figured that whole 'time heals all wounds' thing was a bit suspect," I commiserate.

"I wish you could have met my sister. The two of you would have gotten on like a house on fire," he says. "She was so spirited. So full of life—even after she was technically dead." His voice cracks on the last sentence and my heart melts for him. I curl my body into his own, stroking the back of his head.

"I would have been honored to meet her," I whisper in his

ear. After all, I know how hard it must be for him to speak of his sister—he who likes to keep everything emotional buried deep inside, like I do. And I want desperately for him to know how much it means to me that he's willing to open up and share. "I bet she was amazing."

For a moment he surrenders, allowing me to cuddle him, to soothe his trembling body. Then he stiffens under my touch. "Excuse me," he says abruptly, removing me from his lap and rising from his seat. "I'm going to check with the pilot. See if he's ready to go."

I sigh, curling up in the soft leather seat, watching him practically run in his emotional retreat. I know half the reason the past is so hard for him to face is the fact that he still hasn't forgiven himself for what happened to his family. And, to be honest, I'm not sure he ever will.

Not that I blame him. If something were to happen to Sunny—if I fell down in my duty and allowed a monster like Pyrus to take her life—I don't think I could forgive myself either. Which is why we're on this plane to begin with.

"We'll be taking off in a minute," Jareth says, all business-like as he returns to the cabin. "Buckle your seatbelt." He sits down in the seat beside me and straps in, even though it's ridiculous to do so. Not like a vampire can die from turbulence.

"We'll land in approximately five hours," he informs me. "Just before dawn. And then we'll head straight to the tunnels. Hopefully we'll be able to get to them before Pyrus does."

"Do you think he'll go himself?" I ask. "I mean, now that Bertha's no longer doing his bidding?"

Jareth shakes his head. "That's not his style," he tells me. "He wants to appear above it all, that he's only asking that the two of them are brought back to face trial with a jury of their peers. If he went himself, it would raise too many questions."

"I suppose that makes sense. He gets them back and coerces the other coven leaders to convict them—and then he can do whatever he wants."

"Pyrus is a very patient vampire," Jareth adds, as the plane starts rising into the air. "He didn't get where he is today by being impulsive." He pauses, staring out the window at the Vegas strip. "I wonder what he's got up his sleeve."

"Well, at least Bertha's now on our side," I remind him. "That definitely helps."

Jareth turns and gives me a sharp look. "Don't be too sure," he says. "You don't know she was telling the truth. Which reminds me, I need to check the recordings from the bug you placed in her bathroom."

Er . . . Ugh. "Um, about that . . ."

Jareth looks at me questioningly.

"I may have . . . forgotten to actually put the bug in. I mean with everything else going on." I feel my face flaming with embarrassment. "But I swear, she was done with Pyrus. I mean, the guy hit her. He told her to get lost. I'm sure there's no way . . ." I trail off. I am so fired from James Bond duty.

Jareth lets out a long sigh. "Well, I guess we'll have to see for ourselves," he says at last. "And hope we're not too late."

8

"So do you think there are rats down here?" I ask worriedly as I watch Jareth pry open a large metal grate embedded in the pavement with his crowbar. It groans as it slides from its decades-old resting point, revealing a slime-covered rusty ladder leading down into the darkness. I stifle a shiver as I stare down into the black pit we're about to descend. *Really, Sunny? Would it have been so hard for you and Magnus to hole up in the Four Seasons with a room service menu and downloadable movies while on the lam?*

We flew all night long and arrived in New York City a few hours before the sunup. I really did try to get some rest, but let's face it—it's not easy to sleep when your sister's life is on the line. By the time they opened the cabin doors and allowed us to exit the plane, I was so tired I could barely see straight. And Jareth didn't seem much better. Not surprising—from what I could tell, he spent the night torn apart by nightmares—tossing and turning and moaning his sister's name. I feel bad for him and wish there was some way to help relieve his guilt. But at the same time, I really hope it doesn't distract him from our mission.

"At this point, rats are the least of our problems," Jareth replies, hooking the crowbar to his belt and scanning the small park for any wandering early morning police patrols. From the airport, we took a cab downtown to the Financial District, where Jareth hit a hardware store for supplies and I hit a butcher shop for a pound of raw hamburger, which I had already devoured on the way here. Due to the undercover nature of our mission, we couldn't bring blood donors with us. And the little bit of synthetic Jareth did manage to stash away in the jet isn't doing the job of quenching my thirst. I don't know how I ever lived on it for so long.

"Least or not, they're still creepy," I remind him. "Those beady eyes, those bald tails . . . I mean, why the heck are their tails bald, anyway? It doesn't make any sense." My stomach releases a loud growl, evidently not caring about the grossness of the vermin in question. Hopefully the vampire coven Sunny and Magnus are staying at will be able to hook us up with some real cocktails. The last thing I need is to get too hungry—and fall off the wagon—after spending so much time learning good blood-drinking habits in vampire rehab.

"Well, I'm sure they think you're creepy, too," Jareth says. "Considering you don't even have a tail at all. Now go! Before someone sees us!"

"Right." After one more scan of the park, I scramble down the ladder and into the awaiting sewer. Jareth follows me, using his vampire strength to drag the grate back over the hole—and cover our tracks—so our little trespassing adventure won't be spotted by the NYPD or other concerned citizens. Last thing we need is to be mistaken for terrorists in some kind of "See Something, Say Something" public service campaign gone wrong.

As I jump from the ladder onto the slick concrete floor, the grate crashes shut with an echoing boom, stealing away the predawn light and leaving us in complete darkness. I squint, trying to get my eyes to adjust, wishing I'd eaten more carrots while I was still alive. Normal vampires, as I mentioned before, have perfect twenty-twenty vision, but mine is still a bit suspect—due to the blood virus—especially when I haven't had a decent drink in a while, which weakens my vampire powers. I'm more than a little thankful when Jareth hands me a small flashlight, though at first I'm scared to click it on, wondering what I might see. Especially if he's right about rats being the least of our worries down here.

Eventually curiosity and practicality win out over my fears and I flick on the flashlight, turning the device toward the sound of rushing water—praying it is, indeed, water and not some kind of human sewage or radioactive slime. (Hey, it happened in *Friday the 13th Part 8: Jason Takes Manhattan*.) The beam of light illuminates a small concrete waterfall, where (thankfully) relatively clean-looking water rushes from one drainage pipe to another. I let out a sigh of relief.

"Back in the day there used to be an aboveground waterway flowing through what we now know as Canal Street," Jareth, my tour guide, explains, joining me on the ground. "They paved it over around 1812 and it became New York's first underground sewer." He motions upstream—to the dank, low-ceilinged concrete passageway the water is gushing out from. "Let's go."

"In there?" I ask, biting my lower lip, nervous all over again. "Through the water?" I mean yes, at least it's not radioactive slime, but still!

Jareth looks down, consulting his map. "It's not the most direct route," he confesses. "Or the most pleasant. But at least we'll avoid being seen by construction workers or MTA employees walking the subway tracks." He throws me a grimace. "Getting arrested isn't going to help us save your sister."

Unfortunately his words make a lot of sense, so I suck in a breath and prepare to dive in. Sunny better be damned grateful for this rescue attempt, that's all I can say. Like, "letting me borrow her Tiffany heart necklace for at least three special occasions" grateful. Especially since my brand-new, not-so-waterproof Doc Martens boots are never going to be the same after this little spelunking mission. (Yes, I know, I know, one should never buy and wear new boots when embarking on an undercover mission through the sewers of New York City. But you didn't see Bertha's hot slayer outfit and experience the pains of wardrobe inferiority.)

Of course now, I'm just experiencing the pains of foot blisters, so what do I know?

Doing my best to sidestep the waterfall, I plunge into the narrow, squared-off tunnel, crouching as to not hit the low ceiling. The freezing water splashes over my ankles as I press forward, dodging slimy purple plant tentacles that drip down from the occasional metal grates above. Radioactive or not, the water smells foul and I try not to breathe in too much as I hug the tunnel's left side, dodging rusty, mold-covered pipes sticking out from the concrete.

After about a hundred feet, the square tunnel widens out and the concrete gives way to a rounded archway of brick and stone. It'd be kind of pretty, if it wasn't so smelly.

"This is the older part of the sewer," Jareth explains. "It's going to split off in a bit and we're going to take the right fork. It should be a little easier going from there. Or dryer, at the very least."

"Sounds good to me." I pick up the pace and soon come to the split he mentioned and take a right. The good news? Not only is it dryer, but the ceiling is higher, allowing me a chance to straighten up and give my aching back a break. The bad news? The absence of rushing water allows my ears to pick up not-so-distant squeaking noises. I try to push them out of my mind and press onward through a twisty tunnel that dead-ends at a wooden barricade. Jareth pulls out the crowbar again and rips the wooden planks away, revealing an entrance into what appears to be a subway tunnel.

I step through the gap, peering up and down the tracks. "Um, we're not going to get run over by a train, are we?"

Jareth chuckles. "Don't worry," he assures me, tapping on one of the rails with his crowbar. "These particular tracks are no longer used." And sure enough, upon closer examination, I can see heavy rust caked on the rails. No train has been through here in years. Okay, well, that's something at least.

Less comforting? The wooden log ceiling that shakes violently every time a car drives by on the surface roads above. As we head down the tunnel, I shine my light on the extremely rotted-out support beams with growing concern. I mean, is that really all that's keeping the heavy New York City traffic from crashing down into this underground world? I try to remind myself that these tunnels have been here for more than a hundred years—no need to think they'd pick today of all days to suddenly give way and collapse. But the thought isn't as reassuring as it should be, especially after another car drives by and crumbling dirt rains down on my head.

We walk in silence, our journey sound tracked by an occasional dripping sound and a host of squeaking in the distance that I do my best to ignore. But though the tunnel is mostly dead empty, there are some strange signs of life poking out here and there. At one point we even pass a little bricked-in room just off the tracks, with a table and chairs and a couple of cobwebbed milk crates serving as furniture and a pile of ratty blankets made up as a bed. Fascinated, I abandon the tracks for a closer look, finding a notepad wedged between two stones.

Someone's diary? I try to imagine what it would be like to live down here in the darkness day in and day out, with only the rats to keep me company. The thought makes me sad, as does the diary entry I randomly flip to.

"I sink beneath the skin of the street with each step, walking closer and closer to my final death . . ."

"Put it down," Jareth instructs, popping his head into the room. "We need to keep moving."

Reluctantly, I set down the diary and follow Jareth farther down the subway tunnel, trying to imagine the person who would write such lyrical lines while trying to survive underneath the "skin" of the world. How did they get here? Why did they stay? Are they still living down here, somewhere? Are they happy or scared or a combination of both? I get so caught up in this fanciful idea of my homeless poet, I scarcely notice at first when we emerge from the dark tunnel into a large, arched underground subway station, the end of the line.

Like the rest of this secret world below, it's crumbling and abandoned, but at the same time, it's gorgeous beyond belief. A work of art, painted with colorful tiles, delicate stonework, and breathtaking sloping arches. Of course now the tiles are spray-painted with graffiti and dirty needles lie scattered by the stone benches on the platform. But I try my best to block out the modern ugliness and imagine the station as it once was— bustling with busy New York businessmen and fine ladies in fur coats and smart hats.

Jareth hops up onto the platform, then leans back down, hand outstretched, in order to give me a boost. I take his hand

and scramble up, rubbing my aching thighs. We've been walking half the morning and after that bad night's sleep and lack of blood, I'm worn out. Collapsing onto a nearby bench, I let out a contended sigh. Across the platform, my eyes catch sight of a large graffiti sign.

In December 1995, the forgotten men of the tunnel received city housing. They've just begun to move.

"There used to be whole communities of people who lived down here in these abandoned tunnels," Jareth explains. "But with new construction in the last twenty years, most of them were kicked out and their little makeshift shacks were destroyed."

So my poet is probably gone for good. Leaving his or her journal behind. The thought makes me oddly sad.

"But not the vampires?" I query, remembering our mission.

"They're a little harder to exterminate," Jareth says with a wry grin, sitting down beside me. He consults his map for a moment, then nods. "I think our entry point may be up ahead," he says. "Stay here and rest a moment. I'll go check it out."

"Um, you sure you don't want company?" I ask, torn over the proposition. I mean, I'm thrilled to be able to rest for a minute or two, but I don't relish the idea of hanging out with the squeaky creatures that live down here and might be thinking of vampire for lunch.

"Rayne, are you still seriously scared over a few little rats?" Jareth clucks. "What kind of vampire slayer are you anyway?"

"Yeah, yeah," I mutter, rolling my eyes, realizing I do sound like kind of a wimp. After all, technically *I'm* the monster down in the sewer. They should be more scared of me than I am of them.

"Don't worry. I'll be back before you know it. Rest for a moment. You deserve it." He leans over and kisses the top of my head.

"Okay," I agree, rubbing my sore legs. I have to admit, it does feel nice to sit down. As he heads toward the edge of the platform, I pull out my phone. A quick game of the mobile version of Vampires vs. Zombies should cure any residual rat phobia. As I load up the game, I watch Jareth hop down onto the tracks and continue his journey, disappearing into the darkness, his heavy footsteps quickly fading into the distance.

I turn back to my game, trying not to think about where I am and what we're doing. But the creepy noises seem to rise in volume, echoing through the station with relentless beats. Clanging, clunking, dripping, squeaking—every sound has me half-jumping out of my skin, and I pray Jareth won't be gone much longer.

Suddenly, the other noises seem to vanish as my ears catch a low growl in the darkness, followed by a distinct scratching sound—like the skittering of claws on metal, but way too loud to be coming from your typical everyday, non-mutated rat.

What the hell . . . ?

Sucking in a breath, I slip my phone into my pocket and grab my stake as the noise grows louder and louder, closer and closer. I look down at the stupid piece of wood in my hand and wonder what exactly it is that I plan to do.

Oh why, oh why didn't I bring a knife? Or a gun? Or some kind of other deadly weapon good for more than taking out vampires? And speaking of vampires, why on earth did I let my vampire boyfriend leave me here all alone in the first place? I mean, sure, I'm a kick-ass slayer chick who doesn't need a man to protect me from harm. But, come on, it's never a bad thing to have a partner in crime on the scene, in case of trouble, right?

"Jareth?" I hiss hopefully into the darkness, though in my heart I realize there's a better chance of it being Freddy Krueger, sliding his nail glove against a pipe than my boyfriend. Especially since the sound's coming from the opposite end of the tunnel. Fear pounds inside me as I rise from my bench, creeping to the edge of the platform, holding my stake in one hand and my flashlight in another. Half of me wonders if I should turn off the light—better hide myself from whatever's coming around the corner. But the other half is too scared not to at least get a glimpse of what's probably going to eat me for lunch.

I guide my flashlight along the tracks with a shaky hand, a lump the size of Texas in my throat. Where are you, creature of the subway? And what are you going to do?

After a few moments of searching, I take a step backward, trying to still my trembling body. Probably nothing, I tell myself. Just a rat. Or one of those alligators people flush down the toilet. Scary, but not deadly.

Finally steadying my breath, I turn around to head back to my bench . . .

. . . and find myself face to face with a pair of glowing red eyes.

9

I stagger backward, nearly falling off the edge of the subway platform in shock. The flashlight falls from my hand and clatters to the ground, bulb breaking and light extinguishing. Before I'm abandoned to total darkness, I'm treated to a flash-frame image of a nightmare, standing before me: four feet of dark, matted fur, dripping fangs, and razor-sharp claws.

I suddenly no longer give the slightest crap about rats.

"Stay back!" I cry, waving my hands blindly in front of my face, praying my eyes will adjust to the cave darkness. I try to remind myself that I'm a vampire—I'm really tough to kill—but, to be honest, the mantra doesn't make me feel much better. After all, the creature might not have a wooden stake to drive through my heart, but it's going to be pretty much impossible to regenerate if I'm chewed up and eaten alive—which, let's face it, seems the most likely scenario in this case.

The creature snarls and snaps its teeth, its large ruby-red eyes the only clue to its exact whereabouts on the platform—which, currently, is way too close for comfort. Should I make a run for it? How far will I get with no light? After all, if I cracked my ankle or snagged it on a subway track I'll be worse off than I am now.

So instead I tighten my grip on my stake. Better to stand my ground. Maybe I can at least hold it off until Jareth gets back.

"Good monster," I whisper through the darkness, side-stepping away from the platform edge. "Just chill out. I'm not here to hurt you." If only I'd brought a cookie.

Unfortunately it appears that the monster in question fails to have a strong grip on the English language. Or maybe it just doesn't like the way I smell. Or does like it—'cause let's be honest, I did eat raw hamburger for breakfast. It lunges at me, knocking me backward with the force of a speeding train. I crumble to the ground, trying to wrestle it off my body as it snaps at my neck. In addition to mangy fur, the creature seems to have a row of sharp quills on its back and I accidentally stab my hand on one of them, cool blood flowing down my arm. Damn it!

The creature freezes, sniffing the air. I use my momentary advantage to flip it over—accidentally dropping my stake in the process. After diving on top of the creature and pinning it down with my thighs, I try to keep it prostrate with one hand as I search the ground for my only weapon. My eyes are now adjusted enough to see the beast's mouth seeking and finding my bleeding hand, its fangs sinking into my flesh.

Well, what do you know? It's a blood drinker . . .

I suck in a breath as the pain shoots through me—hard and unyielding—and it's all I can do not to rip my arm away. Instead, I force myself to stay still—to let the creature drink, as I search for the stake with my free hand.

Finally, my fingers close around the wood and I make my move. Bringing my arm up in the air, ready to stab the beast through the heart and end this fight—

"Enough!"

I stop, milliseconds before driving the stake through. Who said that? I try to search the darkness for the source of the voice.

"Fluffy! Release her. Come!"

To my shock and extreme awe, the bloodsucking beast—Fluffy?!—immediately unlocks its grip on my hand and scurries off into the darkness.

I scramble to my feet, holding my hand to my side, trying to put pressure on the wound. "Who's there?" I cry. "Show yourself."

A light flickers and a moment later the glow of a lamp shines through the darkness. I gasp as a tall, dark figure, dressed in a long, black cape steps into view. His skin is as white as snow. His hair as dark as night. His lips are as red as blood. Meaning he's either some kind of cross-dressing Snow White . . .

. . . or a vampire.

"Oh my God," I cry, relief flooding over me like a tidal wave. "Thank you so much!" I attempt a step forward toward the elderly vampire, but Fluffy—now standing by her master's side—snarls, bearing her fangs—which, I might add, are still dripping with my blood. I stop, holding up my hands in surrender. "What is that thing?" I ask.

The vampire smiles, revealing a set of gleaming white fangs under the flickering lamplight. "Chupacabra," he says, reaching down to scratch the creature's mangy head. Fluffy looks up at him and pants happily.

Chupacabra. I draw in a breath, remembering my studies at Riverdale Academy. Chupacabra are legendary bloodsucking creatures, hailing from Mexico and the southwestern United States. Their name literally means "goat sucker"—with goats and other livestock being their favorite menu items.

So what was this one doing up here in New York City—which, let's face it, is not exactly the biggest farm community around . . . And . . . I glance around nervously . . . are there more of her kind lurking the darkness?

"Who are you?" the vampire asks, his deep voice echoing through the dark chamber. "And what brings you to the tunnels?"

"Oh! Sorry—my bad! My name is Rayne McDonald," I say, deciding to keep my distance from Fluffy this time, hoping the guy will ignore my rudeness in not shaking his hand. "I'm a member of the Blood Coven and my boyfriend, Jareth, and I are searching for my sister and her boyfriend, Magnus. They're supposedly hiding out down here with a group of anti-Consortium vampires." I pause, then add hopefully, "You don't happen to know where they are, do you?"

The elder vampire is silent for a moment, considering my words without addressing my question. At last he speaks. "Most vampires I know don't go around wielding wooden stakes."

I look down at the weapon I'm still clutching in my hands and I feel my face heat. "Oh that," I say. "Well, I sort of free-lance for Slayer Inc. as well. It's a long story." I strain my ears to hear if Jareth might be coming back soon—surely he must have heard all the commotion. But all that greets me is silence. I hope he's okay. . . .

"So you're telling me you're a vampire who works as a vampire slayer," the elder says, raising a wooly eyebrow.

I shrug. "That and a fairy princess," I add. "And a cheerleader, too. Though they've probably kicked me off the team by now. It's been a while since I've been home." For some reason the thought makes me a little sad. "In any case, you don't need to worry. I only take out the bad vampires, not the good ones."

"I see . . . And who, may I ask, makes that call?"

I cock my head in question. "Excuse me?"

"What I mean is . . ." He clears his throat. "Who decides which vampires are good . . . and which are evil?"

"Oh right." I scramble. "You know, to be perfectly honest, that's actually become a bit of a muddy question these days." Way to go, Rayne. After all, according to someone like Pyrus, these vampires are anti-Consortium—and therefore totally stakeable. "In any case, I'm not looking to stake any vampires right now. I'm on a mission to find my sister, as I told you. Are she and Magnus hiding out with you by any chance?" I cross my fingers for an affirmative.

"Maybe they are, maybe they aren't. But if they were, surely they would not wish to be found."

"Yeah, I know, I know," I reply quickly. This guy is going to be harder to get through than Jareth's secretary, isn't he? And I can't trick him with Race Jameson sightings down here—even if he is a fan, which seems unlikely anyway. "But they need to hear what I've got to say. Pyrus, the leader of the Consortium, has discovered where they are and he's probably sending a team right now to come and find them. If they're caught, they'll be tried for treason." I scowl, thinking of the Consortium speaker. "And if they're found guilty, they'll be killed. I can't let that happen."

The elder vampire rubs his chin thoughtfully. "A member of Slayer Inc. who claims to fight against the Consortium," he ponders aloud, more to himself than anything. "Very interesting."

"Yeah, yeah, I know. It's fascinating." His slow talking is driving me crazy. I mean, let's get on with it here—time is running out! "And if we had more time, I'd totally explain all the ways. But we don't. So please, will you take me to my sister and Magnus before it's too late?" I dare take another step forward. Fluffy growls, snapping her teeth. The elder vampire holds out a hand.

"And how am I supposed to know this is not some kind of trick?" he asks. "That you are not here on a mission to do exactly what you claim you wish to prevent?"

"Because Sunny is my sister! Family doesn't do that to one another."

"Really." The vampire chuckles softly. "Are you sure about that?"

"I'm sure that I would never harm a hair on my sister's head!" I vow. "That I would protect her with every bone in my body."

He rubs his chin again. I have to say, it's really weird to be looking at such an old vampire. Most every other vampire I've come across was turned undead while still in their prime—and, thus, given the gift of eternal youth. This poor guy should at least consider investing in a little Botox or maybe some fillers . . .

"You certainly do seem like you're telling the truth," he says at last. "Or at least a truth you believe. I'm sorry, however, that in this case I cannot be of assistance."

"What?" I cry, my heart sinking in my chest. "Why not?" Does he really expect me to believe he doesn't know where my sister is?

"I once made a vow to protect those who entered my coven," he says. "Promising that only those who speak the ancient password of peace will be allowed entrance. Since you do not seem to know this password, I can only assume you come here uninvited. Therefore it would be a disservice to my people to let you in." He smiles patronizingly at me. "Now why don't you come with me and I'll escort you back up onto the city streets? I'll help you find a lovely hotel with a hot shower where you can wash the stink off your clothes before returning home and rejoining your cheerleading friends."

"No!" I cry, furious at his trying to dismiss me like that. "Hell no! I'll never leave without my sister!" I step forward, ignoring Fluffy's warning growl. Screw her—I'm not going to let some mythical beast and old guy vampire tell me to go take a bubble bath. Not when Sunny's life is in danger! I grip my stake tightly in my hands. "Now you tell me where Sunny is or I'll—"

A voice breaks out from the darkness. "What's going on here?"

I whirl around, happy beyond belief to see Jareth step out from the shadows. Thank goodness. And just in time, too. After all, I'm pretty sure I wouldn't be able to rightly stake this guy—and what if he decided to call my bluff?

"Jareth!" I cry, rushing over to my boyfriend. "This guy knows where Sunny and Magnus are, but he won't tell us unless we know some sort of stupid password. Let him know that we're here to—"

Jareth sidesteps me and heads straight to the elderly vampire, giving him a low bow. *"Pax tecum,"* he says.

The elder grins. "Now why didn't you say so in the first place?"

"Say what? What did you say? You knew there was a password?" I demand. "Why didn't you tell me there was a freaking password?"

Jareth gives me a sympathetic look. "Sorry," he says. "I didn't think you'd run into them before me. The vampire underground railroad has always used the same password over the millennia. *Pax tecum—Peace be with you.* I learned it long ago when I sought protection after Slayer Inc. killed my family. They helped me reinvent myself and rejoin society as a new vampire—to absolve me of my crimes against Slayer Inc."

I give a low whistle, completely sobered by his words. "Wow. I had no idea." Poor Jareth. I assumed once he'd escaped from Slayer Inc.'s siege, he was free and clear. But I guess it makes sense. After all, if he'd taken out some of their agents in the big fight, they might end up holding a bit of a grudge.

"The Consortium has been around a long time," Jareth adds. "But there are many vampires who have been around a lot longer." He nods his head respectfully in the elder's direction. The elder gives him a small smile.

"Well, all righty there," I interject, a renewed sense of hope surging through me. Maybe this will work out after all. "What are we waiting for? Let's go get Sunny and Magnus."

10

The elderly vampire—who introduces himself as Drake—unlocks an ancient-looking door at the far end of the platform with a golden key tied around his neck and ushers us into a narrow passageway, leading off into, yes, more darkness. Luckily, he goes first, illuminating the path with his lantern, his trusty Chupacabra, Fluffy, sticking to his side. The creature wags her tail as she scampers along with her master—she's so freaking cute, it's hard to believe she tried to eat me ten minutes before.

We walk for what seems like forever, through a twisted maze of passages lined with booby traps, which Drake helpfully points out as we go. I realize there is no way on earth Jareth and I could have discovered this place on our own—never mind survived all the traps. Guess Magnus knew what he was doing when he picked this place over the Four Seasons when choosing his and Sunny's hideaway. Maybe I shouldn't have been so worried about Pyrus tracking them down after all.

Still, it can't hurt to give them a head's up. And I'll be thrilled at the chance to see my sister again after so much time apart. I finger the box in my pocket, wrapped in black-and-gold paper. The Christmas present I never got to give her until now.

Suddenly, Drake stops. I look up. The passageway ends abruptly at a large stone wall. Confused, I search the area for some kind of side exit, but see nothing. Are we lost? Did Drake take a wrong turn?

"Here we are," he says instead. "The entrance to our lair."

I squint at him, then at the solid rock wall ahead. "Um, entrance? I don't see no stinking entrance."

He smiles. "Down here, my little slayer, things are not always as they appear." He whistles for Fluffy, who runs up to him, tongue lolling from her mouth. He nods at her and claps his hands once. I watch in amazement as Fluffy turns and dives at the wall, without hesitation—bracing myself for a loud crack as her head slams into solid stone. After all, I'd much prefer to be able to say that no animals were harmed in the making of this rescue.

But to my surprise—the creature does not hit her head. Instead, the head in question completely disappears into the rock, followed by her furry body.

"Holy crap!" I cry, reaching out to touch the rock wall with my own hand. Sure enough, my fingers slide easily through the optical illusion. "I want one of these for my bedroom door."

Drake chuckles, then his expression turns serious. "We have many vampires among us who do not wish to be found under any circumstances," he tells us. "It is best to be overly protective in all cases." He gives me a small bow. "After you, my dear."

Right. I suck in a breath and take a determined step up to the rock. As I move forward, I'm still half sure I'm going to whack my head against solid stone. But instead I slide right on through—enveloping myself in a slick curtain of mist—before reappearing on the other side. A moment later I'm joined by Jareth and Drake.

"That is too cool," I mutter. "You are so going to have to give me that secret."

Jareth reaches out and squeezes my hand, giving me a small smile. "We made it," he whispers.

I look up, taking in my surroundings. My brows furrow as I scan the wide, high-ceilinged, rock-walled cavern around us. I guess I wasn't sure what to expect here, but I can tell you for sure I didn't expect to see such heartbreaking poverty. I mean, practically every vampire I've ever met is super rich, possessing luxury and amenities beyond compare—or at least a decent middle-class income. This place is like the opposite: a shantytown of cardboard box homes and half-rotted tents. Hammered tin, shattered glass, bones strewn about. The camp centers around a large fire pit, the heavy smoke stinging my eyes. I glance over at Jareth, trying to shoot him a look of dismay without Drake seeing. This is where my sister has been living all this time?

He gives me a grim smile. "Welcome to life for vampires outside the Consortium's embrace."

I swallow hard. Wow. When he said the Blood Coven would suffer if they were kicked from the Consortium, I guess I figured they might be stuck with Top Ramen once in a while. Not living in ultimate squalor. No wonder the other vampire masters in the Consortium are so scared to go against Pyrus's orders. I wouldn't want this for my people either!

Drake gestures for us to follow him toward the center of the camp. All around us I can feel the stares of vampires hiding behind closed doors or cloth tents. Here and there I catch sight of some movement behind an oily glass window—but as soon as it comes, it's gone.

"My apologies," Drake says, ushering us over to the bonfire and inviting us to take seats on the rotted wooden logs placed around it. "My people are quite shy. They do not meet many outsiders. And many still fear being tracked down by Consortium agents and made to suffer for their alleged crimes."

I grimace as I take my seat beside Jareth, trying to imagine what it would be like to be stuck down here in eternal darkness, never able to leave. It's not like with vampires you can even outlive the current regime. Unless someone stops Pyrus, his reign is likely to be eternal.

"Would you like something to drink?" Drake asks, peering at us from across the fire. "You must be very parched from your trip. And you, slayer, have lost quite a bit of blood."

My mouth waters and I glance down at my hand, which has barely scabbed over by this point. My powers of regeneration suck when I haven't had a good drink. Still, I can't just chill with a cocktail when we've got more important matters to deal with.

"First I need to see Sunny," I tell Drake. "And Magnus."

He nods and picks up a bell from the ground and lets it ring. A moment later, a small dark-haired, pale-skinned girl who appears to be about fourteen years old but is probably more like 1,400, steps up to the fire.

"Cinder," Drake addresses her. "Please have someone track down Sunshine McDonald. And then fetch our visitors some blood."

The girl nods and disappears. A few moments later she returns with two plastic 7-Eleven Big Gulp cups filled with red liquid. She hands one to me and one to Jareth. "Sunshine is down by the canal," she informs us. "I had Aleisha go and get her."

"Thanks," I tell her gratefully, putting the cup to my lips. Good thing I no longer have an aversion to real blood. Otherwise this might be a bit awkward. I take big gulp and—

—totally gag! Ew! This is the grossest blood I've ever tasted!

"Sorry," Drake says, evidently catching my look of disgust. "Cinder, these are our honored guests," he scolds the girl. "Get them something fresh . . . and human." He turns back to Jareth and me. "I apologize. You're probably not used to rat blood. Unfortunately, it's one of our main sources of sustenance down here."

I open my mouth to reply, but Jareth shoots me a warning look. So instead, I force myself to take another tiny sip, swallowing it down without puking—but let me tell you, it is no easy task.

"Tastes like chicken," I manage to spit out.

Drake laughs appreciatively. "Oh I'm sure," he replies, reaching over and taking my cup and setting it on the ground.

"So what's the deal?" I ask, wishing I had something to get the oh-so-nasty taste out of my mouth. "I thought vampires couldn't survive for the long haul with anything but human. Not enough vitamins or something."

"It's true," Drake agrees solemnly. "And if you look at the vampires around the camp, you'll see the aftereffects of using animal blood as a substitute. They're scrawny, fragile. Unable to regenerate if wounded. That's one of the reasons we keep Chupacabra around as guard dogs. The vampires themselves are too weak to put up a good fight." He shrugs. "But without access to the Consortium's bank accounts, we're not able to hire proper blood donors. And my people, though outcasts, aren't barbaric enough to hunt humans as the vampires of old. Once in a while we're able to come up with enough money to bribe a blood bank for some bags. But it's definitely a special treat."

I look around the camp in wonder. They're starving—literally—and yet they still retain respect for human life. How are they considered the bad guys, the ones unworthy of joining the Consortium's ranks?

"Man, your vampire government really sucks," I mutter to Jareth. "No pun intended."

He gives me a sad smile. "It's true," he says. "And seeing places like this makes me realize how badly we need a new leader. Someone who will provide justice and protection and resources to all vampires—not only a precious few."

At that moment Cinder returns with our drinks, this time in crystal wine goblets that gleam in the firelight. "You're very beautiful," she murmurs, reaching out to touch a strand of my hair, after handing me my drink, an awed look on her sallow face. "Like your sister."

"Uh, thanks," I reply, feeling my face heat. It's so unfair that I've had all the advantages and vampires like her have had none. "You're really pretty, too." And she is—though her skin is so pale it's nearly translucent. And her eyes are shadowed with dark circles.

"Here," I say, handing her back the goblet, mind made up. "You drink this. I actually quite dig the other stuff." With great effort I force myself to grab the rat gunk by my feet and slurp it down with big mouthfuls. *Tastes like chicken. Tastes like chicken.* Somehow I manage to drain my glass without throwing up.

Cinder glances over at Drake with nervous eyes, but he gives her a succinct nod. She breaks into a huge smile and I realize she's missing one of her fangs. "*Gracias!*" she cries. "Thank you so much!" She gulps down the Homo sapiens cocktail as if she hasn't eaten for a week. Sadly, I'm guessing that's not far off the mark.

"So did you guys always live outside the jurisdiction of the

Consortium?" I ask when she's finished. I'm curious how this all came down.

Drake shakes his head. "I was once one of the top leaders of the organization," he tells me. "That is, until my protégé and I had an argument."

"Your protégé?"

"Pyrus," he says flatly. "Once upon a time, I was his sire. I turned him into a vampire and helped him rise to his current position as house speaker. Little did I know of his true intentions. Not to better the world—but to take over. When I saw how power hungry he was becoming, I tried to step in—to knock him down a peg or two, remind him it was a democracy, not a dictatorship." He sighs. "Pyrus didn't care for my intervention. He cast me and my coven out of the Consortium, forcing us to flee like dogs. We finally settled here, deep underground, and started a mission to help other vampires who were cast away. It's not a glamorous life, as you can see, but it's the only one many of my people know."

I cringe, looking at the camp, thinking of some of the other covens I've visited. All the luxury, the riches, the gallons of blood to drink from waiting donors.

"That doesn't seem fair."

"It's not fair," Cinder speaks up, her dark eyes flashing fire. "But at least here we are free."

The elder smiles at her. "That is true, my dear," he agrees. "By living outside the Consortium, we are not bound by their rules. We are not caught up in their endless wars and politics.

We are allowed to bring in stray vampires and rehabilitate them into coven lifestyle. We can offer a safe haven to child vampires—who would otherwise be sentenced to death by Slayer Inc."

I open my mouth to speak, but suddenly I'm interrupted by a high-pitched squeal of delight.

"Rayne! You're here! You're really here!"

11

"Rayne!" Sunny cries, throwing her arms around me. "You came! You really came! I can't believe you're here."

I squeeze her back, not bothering to check the bloody tears streaming down my cheeks. I guess I didn't realize up until now how much I'd missed her. My Sunny. My sister. My better half. The McDonald twins—united again at long last.

"Thank goodness you're all right," I murmur before we part from our embrace.

"What are you guys doing here?" she asks. "Did you get kicked out of the Consortium, too? Did Pyrus figure out you're not on his side? Is the Blood Coven okay?"

I hold up my hands in protest. "Whoa! One question at a time. Sit down and I'll give you the scoop."

She plops down on the log. I notice she's a lot skinnier than

when I last saw her. I guess blood isn't the only scarce food supply down here in the vampire refugee camp. I wish I'd saved
some of that hamburger. Not that Miss Vegetarian would probably eat any of it.

"Come on, Rayne. Don't keep me in suspense here."

"Oh, right." I shake my head to clear it, then give her the
CliffsNotes version of the last few days. When I'm finished, she
gives a low whistle.

"Wow, Bertha the Vampire Slayer," she says. "I never thought
we'd run into her again."

"Yeah, well, to be honest, I think she's the least of our problems at this point. Pyrus knows where you are, and who knows
what he's going to do with that information. I mean, the guy's
really out for blood, if you know what I mean. We need to get
you and Magnus out of here," I tell her. "So hurry up. Go pack
your things. Or don't even bother—we can buy you more once
we get you away," I add, remembering all the baggage she tried
to drag with her when we made our escape attempt from Riverdale. I rise to my feet, putting out a hand. "Come on. There's no
time to lose."

Sunny looks at my hand, but doesn't take it. "Rayne, I can't
just leave," she says. "I mean, what about Magnus? He's out
hunting with the others. He won't be back for a few hours,
at least."

I frown. This is so like Sunny. To completely dismiss my self-
less, death-defying rescue attempt because she's more interested
in her boyfriend's whereabouts than her own safety. She makes
it tough, let me tell you.

"Sun, Jareth will stay here and wait for Magnus," I tell her. "They're vampires—they can take care of themselves. But in the meantime, we've got to get you somewhere safe."

Sunny's eyes narrow. "Because I can't take care of *my*self?"

I groan. In her extended absence I guess I'd conveniently forgotten how sensitive Sunny is about the whole *she's more weak and vulnerable than a vampire* thing. I'm guessing any second now she's going to start going off about how she's a fairy princess and perfectly able to take care of herself.

"I'm not some helpless mortal, you know! I'm a fairy princess! I can take care of myself! So don't even start on this whole 'Sunny is sweet and innocent and helpless and needs to be rescued' crap. In fact, last I remember, *I'm* the one who saved *your* butt."

I grit my teeth. "Exactly! And I let you, right? So how about you let me return the favor?"

"You only let me because you were half-dead and poisoned," Sunny points out. "And don't even think of trying to tell me you would have taken off with me and left Jareth behind if he was in danger, too."

"I would too have!" I protest. I catch Jareth's raised eyebrow. "Sorry, babe," I say, "but only because I respect your vampire prowess and know you don't need me to get out of a tight situation."

Sunny rolls her eyes. "Rayne McDonald, you don't fool me one bit. Now sit down, drink your damn blood, and wait with me for Magnus to come back."

I sigh, resigning myself to plopping down on the log. "Since when you did you become the pigheaded, annoying twin?" I ask. "I thought that was my job description."

Sunny smirks then softens. "Look, Rayne, it's not that I don't appreciate you coming here to rescue me. I think it's really sweet. In fact, I couldn't ask for a more loyal and devoted twin. But you know I couldn't live with myself if something happened to Magnus. I love him. I've sacrificed everything to be with him up until now. I can't abandon him."

"I know." I sling an arm around her shoulder and pull her close. "You're a good girlfriend. Magnus is lucky to have you."

"And I'm lucky to have you."

As she rests her head on my shoulder happily, I try to quiet the worry whirling through my brain. So we have to wait an hour or two. No big deal. I mean, this place is more heavily guarded than Fort Knox. Booby traps, secret passageways, Latin passwords, optical illusions, and a Chupacabra army. Even if Pyrus did have an inkling as to where the two of them were hiding out, it's not like he could just waltz in here with no difficulty. Surely we're safe for at least another few hours.

"So where are you taking us, anyway?" Sunny asks. "I mean, what place could be safer than this?"

Huh. Good question. In all my determination to rescue, I actually didn't really consider our next move. I glance over at Jareth, hoping he's done a bit more preplanning.

"There's another vampire refugee camp deep in the heart of Mexico," my boyfriend says. "Down at the bottom of a 1,200-foot pit."

Wow, that sounds about as appealing as having all my teeth

pulled at the dentist. But I guess vampires have different out-
looks on vacation destinations. After all, if a 1,200-foot-deep
pit doesn't shield them from sunshine, nothing will.

Suddenly Cinder reappears before us, her eyes shining with
excitement. "Lord Magnus and the hunting party are back!"
she exclaims.

I let out a sigh of relief. Thank goodness. Now we can get
this show on the road.

Sunny bounces from the log as her boyfriend approaches
the fire pit. He's dirty and drained and skinny, his already chis-
eled cheekbones looking even more gaunt than usual, comple-
menting the dark circles under his eyes.

"Mag!" Sunny cries, throwing her arms around him as if she
hadn't seen him for weeks. "Look who's here! Jareth and Rayne!"

Even from here, I can see Magnus's startle at the news. He
breaks from Sunny's hug and approaches the two of us, a string
of dead rats in his hands. (I try not to remember that's what I
just finished drinking.)

"Jareth," he says, addressing my boyfriend in a stern voice.
"What is the meaning of this?"

I can see Jareth's face pale as he rises stiffly to greet his co-
master and friend. I wince. In my excitement to rescue Sunny
and Magnus, I kind of forgot about the fact that Jareth is technically going against his friend's wishes by coming here.

"My lord," Jareth says, bowing low. "There has been a
threat against your life. Pyrus has learned where you are and is,
even now, sending out a team to oust you. We must get you and
Sunshine to safety as quickly as possible."

Magnus does not seem surprised by the news. Instead, he looks angry. "You broke your promise," he growls. "You abandoned the coven. How many times did I tell you, I'd rather die than have my people suffer." He gestures to the shantytown around us. "Do you not see what could happen if Pyrus doubts your loyalty and kicks our vampires from the Consortium? Would you really want this for our people?"

I cringe. I see what he's saying, of course. But damn—Jareth was only trying to help him! "Look," I interject. "You need to chill. No one's going to take the Blood Coven away. Pyrus has no idea that we're here. We took all the precautions—private plane, assumed names and fake IDs, disguises—the works! So why don't you cut Jareth a little slack here and maybe thank him for coming all this way to save your sorry ass?"

But Magnus refuses to look in my direction or acknowledge my words. Instead, his green eyes pierce through Jareth. "Perhaps," he says, "you are unaware of Pyrus's propensity for trackers then."

Wait, what?

Even from here, I can see Jareth's hard swallow. "Trackers?"

"Micro GPS. Usually sewn into a piece of clothing. Who has had access to your clothing in the last twenty-four hours?"

Jareth shrugs. "No one," he says. "I mean, just the dry cleaners."

"And you picked up the dry cleaning yourself?"

"Well, no. I had Marcia . . ." Jareth trails off, his face rife with horror. "You don't think . . ."

Drake steps up, holding a finger to his lips. He whistles once and a moment later Fluffy and a few of her Chupacabra friends approach. He speaks to them in a language I don't understand and a moment later they're on Jareth, sniffing him to an inch of his life.

Jareth scowls. "I am sure, Magnus, I would be aware if—"

Fluffy lets out a howl, pawing Jareth's left pant leg. Then she opens her mouth and rips at the fabric. Sure enough, a tiny piece of metal—the size of a pin, clatters to the stone floor. You know that saying about it being so quiet you can hear a pin drop? Well, there you go. Drake steps forward, grinding the piece of metal with his foot.

"Oh God," I whisper, staring at Jareth. He looks at me, his face stark white, then at Magnus.

A loud braying cuts through the silence of the camp. Followed by the sound of a hundred stampeding footsteps.

Sunny looks at me in horror, then at Magnus. "Oh, Rayne," she whispers. "What have you done?"

12

The camp erupts in activity, with Cinder leading the charge. Gone is the innocent girl with hollow eyes—now she's like a warrior princess as she barks orders to the camp. The vampires emerge from their tents armed with sticks and rocks and metal bars—and a few rusty knives here and there. At their feet, the Chupacabra swarm—teeth bared and claws on the ready. Cinder yells something in Spanish, raising her own staff above her head and the Chupacabra break into a sprint, racing down the dark passageways to meet the threat head-on. Meanwhile the vampires scurry to stand together, ready for the inevitable onslaught. To be honest, they look quite a sad and sorry bunch—undernourished and sickly—but they wear fierce determination on their hollow faces—making me half believe they may stand a chance.

Someone grabs my shoulder and I whirl around, heart in my throat. It's Magnus, looking down at me with wild eyes. "Rayne, there's a secret passageway through the purple tent at the back of the camp. It leads back out into the sewers."

I stare at him, uncomprehending. "Are you kidding? I can fight! I can help!" I hold up my stake in my hand.

"I know you can. But I don't want Sunny in danger," he explains. "I'd take her myself, but it's my fault these vampires are being attacked. I must do what I can to save them. But in order to do that, I have to know that Sunny's safe." He pauses as the roar of beasts grows closer. "Go now!" he commands. "Before they get here!"

I nod, giving him a small salute before taking off to go find my sister. After some searching I locate her at Cinder's side, fairy wings fully furled and a dagger in her hand.

"Come on!" I cry, grabbing her by the arm. "I know a way out."

She turns to me, looking at me as if I asked her to skin a baby puppy for its fur coat and then eat the remains for breakfast. "Are you kidding? I told you before, I'm not leaving without Magnus."

"He's the one who asked me to get you out of here!"

Sunny frowns. "Yeah, well, too bad. I'm not going anywhere. And you know you'd do the same thing if you were me."

She's got me there. But then again, I'm the foolish, rash, crazy twin. She's supposed to be the one with more common sense. "Sunny, don't be an idiot!" I scold her. "You know Magnus won't be able to fight if he thinks you're in danger. Which means you being here endangers the entire coven."

A loud roar cuts through Sunny's protest. I look over, my jaw dropping as I see a horde of what appear to be werewolves stampeding toward us with lightning speed. Pyrus must have hired these mercenaries to do his dirty work once he realized he couldn't rely on Slayer Inc. The wolves tear through the poor Chupacabra, chomping down on them with jaws of steel then tossing their broken bodies away as they advance on the trembling vampire front lines.

"Come on!" I cry, grabbing Sunny's arm again. "For Magnus's sake if not mine!"

"Fine!" Sunny breaks her stance and turns to follow me. Together we rush through the camp until we find the purple tent. Diving in and digging through the ratty blankets and pillows, I discover the trap door, embedded in the ground. Ripping it open, I motion for Sunny to go through, praying her claustrophobia won't pick now to rear its ugly head. Luckily, Sunny doesn't object, dropping down into the hole without question. I follow, pulling the trap door shut behind me.

We find ourselves in a damp, narrow crawl space slick with some kind of lime-green moldy moisture. I shove Sunny through, then suck in a breath and follow, praying the tunnel won't collapse on top of us, burying us under a thousand tons of dirt and rock. Especially since, as a vampire, I wouldn't actually die from this kind of horrific experience. I'd just be spending eternity trying to claw my way out. After the first hundred years, I'm guessing I'd go at least a little bit insane.

I push at Sunny's butt in front of me. "Hurry!" I hiss. She doesn't reply but picks up the pace.

After what seems an eternity, we finally emerge from the crawl space into a wide subway tunnel that is illuminated by large ceiling grates. Guess it must be mid afternoon by now. Above us I can see the shadows of cars—commuters going about their days without a care in the world. With no idea of the immortal battle being fought below.

Sunny tosses me a worried look, then glances back to the crawl space. She doesn't have to speak for me to know what she's thinking.

"He'll be okay," I try to assure her, though in my heart I'm not so sure. After all, there were so many of them. And those refugees were not exactly healthy vampire soldiers trained in combat. Do Jareth and Magnus and the rest even have a chance? And if they are overpowered, will they be killed outright? Or dragged home for Pyrus to do the dirty deed himself?

"I'm not thinking about Magnus," Sunny corrects, glancing at the crawl space again. "I mean, of course I am. But . . . did you hear something?"

I freeze in my tracks, training my vampire-enhanced ears to listen for noises coming from the tunnel. Maybe it's just the corridor collapsing behind us. Or an echo from the battlefield. Or one of the Chupacabra . . .

. . . I hope.

"Let's keep moving," I say, urging my sister to pick up the pace. But the sound only grows louder as we rush down the tracks. And as we hit a collapsed section of tunnel ahead, blocking our path, a familiar female voice cuts through the darkness.

"Rayne and Sunshine McDonald! Show yourselves!"

Oh God. We slowly turn around, coming face to face with pretty much my worst nightmare.

"Bertha," I whisper.

The slayer is back in her full *Resident Evil* attire, her long brown hair pulled back from her sneering face and a razor-sharp stake in her hand. She smiles slowly, a greedy look in her beady eyes.

"Um, what are you doing here?" I ask. As if I hadn't already pretty much figured it out. One soppy phone call from her asshole ex-boyfriend and she was back on the payroll. Did all my wise advice mean nothing to her?

"You stupid, stupid girl," she spits, taking a slow step toward us. "Falling for my ridiculous trap. You know, I totally laughed at Pyrus when he first suggested it. I told him there was no way on earth you'd believe that this beautiful body of mine was carved from some eating disorder. That I, Bertha the Vampire Slayer, was nothing more than a weak, lovelorn teen, craving food to make up for her ongoing self-esteem issues like some bad teen novel."

She's lying. I know she is. There's no way she could have been faking her panic when I discovered her ugly secret in the hotel bathroom. Unfortunately I'm not sure this knowledge is going to do me any good now.

But I have to try. "Bertha, you have a problem," I say, taking a cautious step forward. "You need help. Why don't you come with us? We can help you get away from Pyrus. And then, once you're safe, we can deal with your food issues."

"I have no food issues," she growls, her eyes narrowing into furious slits. "It's all diet and exercise, bitch." She raises her stake.

"Bertha . . ." I want to tell her overcoming denial is the first step, but I'm worried it will only make her angrier. "Look, I know what you're going through. I know it's hard. But—"

"Please. You don't know anything," Bertha cuts me off, her voice thick with scorn. "You're just a total idiot who fell for my trap. All I had to do was hint that Pyrus knew about Sunny's whereabouts and you were on the next plane—in some moronic attempt to save her. Then we simply had to follow our noses—or, more technically, the bug our loyal Consortium member Marcia placed on Jareth's dry-cleaning. And BINGO— the two of you led us straight to our prize." She smirks. "Way to go, slayer. You've done your job and then some! Sunny, Magnus, and some other vampires in the refugee camp whom we've been after for centuries—what a bounty! Feel free to head back home. I can take it from here."

"Come on," I try, switching tactics. "You know you don't want to do this. Sunny and Magnus have been wrongfully accused. They're innocent. Sunny only did what she had to, to save my life."

"Keep on defending her," Bertha replies smugly. "It'll be

fun to report back to Slayer Inc. about how you not only denied your commission but also purposely set out to obstruct justice."

I have to bite my tongue to stop myself from informing her that actually I'm following Slayer Inc.'s directives to the letter. Don't want her to go back to Pyrus and tell him he's been played like a fool this whole time—and that the organization would much rather dust HIM than my sister's boyfriend. That would ruin everything.

"What commission?" Sunny demands. Uh-oh.

Bertha turns to her smugly. "Oh, didn't you know? Your sister was assigned to bring you back to justice. And if she doesn't follow through, her employment—and also her pathetic little life—will be terminated, permanently."

I cringe as Sunny's eyes widen in horror. Great. For the millionth time, I wish the two of us had telepathic powers—so I could let her know the real deal without spilling the beans to Bertha.

"Rayne!" Sunny cries, grabbing my arm. "Let her arrest me. It's not worth you getting nano-ed over."

I try to shake her off. "Sorry, sis, but that's not going to happen. I refuse to stand here and let this Barbie-doll bitch take you away for a crime you didn't commit 'cause she's trying to please her sicko, abusive boyfriend."

"Well, I refuse to let you die for simply defending me."

Argh, she is so impossible. "Well I refuse to—"

Bertha makes an exaggerated yawn. "Can you two let me

know when you're done bickering so I can get on with arresting Sunny already? I don't want to miss *American Idol*."

"I hope you set your TiVo," I tell her. "Because while there is breath in my body, you will never take my sister away."

"I don't own a TiVo. So I suggest *you* prepare yourself for a fight!"

Now when most people use the word *prepare*, that means they're planning to give you time to get ready for the upcoming event in question. Not Bertha. The moment the words leave her mouth, she's diving at me, screaming like some freaking banshee from Hell. It's all I can do to leap to the side, a split second before she nearly stakes me through the heart. As she whirls around, I shove her as hard as I can, now wishing I'd taken Cinder up on the human blood—to shore up my admittedly pathetic vampire strength.

Bertha stumbles for a second then regains her balance, waving her stake in my direction, ready to spar.

"Sunny, run!" I yell at my sister as I dance at my enemy, attempting to get a punch in while avoiding her stake. It really sucks that she can end my life in a second with her weapon and I can only give her glorified splinters with my own. Of course I can do some serious damage with my teeth, if only I can get close enough.

Time to make my move. A roundhouse kick takes out her stake; it goes skittering across the room. Then I follow up with a one-two punch to the stomach, attempting to knock her back. She blocks my second punch, then makes a right jab at my head, her fist slamming into my temple. The world spins, and I stumble backward, trying to see through the blood that rains down my face—cut by one of her razor-sharp rings. Bertha takes advantage of my momentary blindness and slams a fist into my stomach, causing me to double over in pain.

She grabs me by the shoulders, slamming me against the rock wall over and over again until I think my back's about to break. It takes all my might to smash my boot down on her foot, then kick her to the stomach. As she falls backward, I throw myself on top of her, wiping the blood from my eyes and then finding her throat with my two hands and squeezing with all my might.

Her eyes bulge from her head as I tighten my grip. From behind me I can hear Sunny screaming—begging me not to kill her—to think of the consequences. But the rage inside of me is too great, and the sudden bloodlust washes over me in a tidal wave. All the kinder, gentler vampire training flees as my anger takes control, pure fury spilling over at this girl who thinks she can hurt my family and get away with it. My fangs descend from my gums and I sink them into her now-bloated jugular, ready to steal away her life as she tried to steal my sister's and my own.

"Rayne! Stop it!" Sunny's cries are dim and muted under the bloodlust rushing through my ears. "Don't kill her! Don't sink to her level! Remember what you learned in rehab. Remember what happened to Corbin!"

It takes all my strength and willpower, but somehow I manage to pull away, ripping my fangs from her flesh and staring down at her blotchy face, full of broken blood vessels. Is she dead? Did I kill her? Oh God. I'm supposed to be the good guy here. And the good guys arrest the bad guys and bring them to justice. They don't eat them.

"Bertha?" I venture after a hard swallow. "Um, are you okay?"

Suddenly her eyes shoot open and she flips me around. With one movement, the tables are turned and I'm the one on my back. Pinning me between her strong thighs, she reaches for her stake, managing to grasp it in her fingers.

"Now we see who's the real vampire slayer," she snarls, her face beet red and her mouth dripping blood. She pulls back, ready to stake me through the heart. I squirm, desperately trying to get away. But she's too strong. She's got me down. This is the end. My final swan song.

"Please, Bertha!" I cry. "Please don't—"

I squeeze my eyes shut, not wanting to watch myself poof into dust. What will it feel like to die? Where do I go afterward? I sold my soul a long time ago to become a vampire. Does that mean this is it? The end of me? Or the beginning of a life of eternal suffering?

Suddenly Bertha screams. My eyes fly open. Sunny has her by the hair, dragging her off of me. "No one stakes my sister, you bitch!" she cries in a voice I've never heard her use before. She smacks the stake out of Bertha's hands.

I try to scramble to my feet, to help my sister. But I'm woozy and stunned and stumble backward instead. Bertha yanks free from Sunny's grasp—leaving my sister with nothing more than a handful of hair extensions. (I should have known that gorgeous head of hair was nothing more than a weave!) Then, as I watch in horror, she pulls something else from her pocket.

A knife made of iron.

No! I dive at Bertha, using everything left inside of me to get to her before she can touch my fairy sister and poison her with her blade. As a vampire/fairy combo, I have some resistance to iron—it won't kill me, but it'll make me pretty damn sick. But Sunny—one touch and . . .

I leap onto Bertha, trying to wrestle the knife away. I manage to knock it from her grasp and yank her backward. This time there will be no mercy. She's gone too far. I rip out her throat with my teeth and let the blood spill onto the floor without any interest in drinking. She's too repulsive for that.

A moan interrupts me and I drop Bertha to the ground and run to my sister. Oh God! My eyes widen as I realize that my efforts were too late. Sunny falls to the ground, blood seeping from a small cut in her arm. But it's enough. The poison is already swimming through her veins.

"Rayne!" she cries, her eyes going glassy and her legs and arms flopping uselessly.

"No!" This isn't happening. It can't be happening! I fall to the floor, grabbing her arm, trying to suck out the poison best I can. I suck and I suck until I puke, but it doesn't seem to be doing any good. Her body convulses and her eyes roll to the back of her head.

"I'm cold, Rayne," she sobs as I pull her into my arms, rocking her close as bloody tears stream down my cheeks. "So cold."

"It's going to be okay," I try. But I know in my heart it won't be. The poison will take her, just as it stole our dad away.

And it's all my fault.

"Rayne . . ." she tries to speak, but I can see it's an effort to do so. "Rayne . . ."

"Shhh . . ." I try to shush her. "Be still."

"You're the best sister a girl could ever have. I love you." Sunny whispers before closing her eyes. I watch in horror as her breath dies in her throat and her body goes limp.

"No!" I cry, trying to shake her awake. "Sunny! Stay with me!" But even as I scream and pound at her, I know it will do no good.

My sister. My beautiful, innocent, sweet twin sister is dead. Forever. And there's nothing I can do to bring her back.

13

I can't tell you how long I sat there in the cold, dank, dark abandoned subway tunnel underneath the skin of New York City, my sister's lifeless body resting silently in my lap. I can tell you that I didn't cry much at first. Not that I didn't want to, but for some reason the sobs refused to break free from my frozen body. Instead, I mostly stared into space, into the darkness, numb with overwhelming grief and filled with wild wonderings of when the hell I was going to wake up and realize this was all some terrible nightmare. That my sister wasn't actually dead.

Because she couldn't be dead. That's not how this story was supposed to go. I was supposed to rescue her and we were supposed to live happily ever after. I mean, who would ever want to read a story or see a film where the heroine dies a bloody, nasty death for a crime she didn't commit? Hollywood doesn't work like that.

Unfortunately, real life, I realize with a sickening thought, often does.

Eventually I manage to haul myself to my feet, dimly aware that, though at the moment, nothing else seems to matter, in truth something does. Jareth and Magnus—did they survive the attack? Are they worried sick—wondering where we are? I need to get back to them. I need to tell them what happened. If they're even there to tell. My stomach heaves and I lean over to empty the rat blood I drank a mere hour ago, mixed with Bertha's vile bodily fluids. It's insane how one hour can change the rest of your life.

I want to take Sunny. I don't want to leave her lifeless body sprawled out on the tracks, a gourmet meal for some lucky subway rats. But try as I might, I can't manage to carry her dead weight in my arms. Especially not through the tiny crawl space we came from. You know that old sixties song "He ain't heavy, he's my brother"? Well, either that dude had some seriously anorexic brother—or he spent way more hours than me in his local gym. Finally I give up, deciding to drag her to the collapsed section of the tunnel and cover her body as much as I can with stones and debris. The best burial I can do under the circumstances.

"Dear God," I murmur when I'm finished, kneeling down in front of the pile. I'm not a very religious person by any means, and let's face it, God probably isn't all that into vampires either.

But for Sunny's sake I try. "Please take care of my sister," I whisper, the tears now falling unchecked from my eyes. I place her birthday present—still unwrapped—into her hands. "She didn't deserve this."

I find I can't say any more. The lump in my throat is too big. I rise to my feet and slowly head back down the tunnel from where we came. As I crawl through, no longer really caring whether the ceiling collapses on me or not, all I can think, all I can beg for in my muddled, grief-stricken brain, is that Jareth is there, waiting for me on the other end. Because otherwise I seriously don't know how I'm going to deal.

Soon, I arrive at the trap door, pushing it open and standing up into the purple tent, which, I quickly realize, has been torn to shreds. In fact, the entire camp is pretty much in shambles. The aftereffects of what appears to be a massacre. Vampires scurry past me, blood bags in their arms, rushing to and fro to attend to the wounded who lie scattered everywhere, their mournful cries sound tracking the air.

"We need more blood over here!" cries a blond vamp nearby.

"This is the last bag!' calls another from across the camp.

I want to puke all over again. It's hard enough to believe these vampires have survived as long as they have drinking mostly rodent blood. And they're going to need a serious surplus of the human stuff if they expect to heal these types of wounds. All around me I see torn limbs, slashed-open stomachs, and massive head wounds. The kind of injuries that, without human blood transfusions, may take decades to heal on their own. The wolves came in and did their worst. It would have almost been kinder of the Consortium to send in a hundred slayers armed with stakes. At least that way death would have come quickly and painlessly.

But Pyrus, I realize, has never been one for kindness.

My eyes search the camp, frantically looking for a familiar face. At last I see Cinder carrying two buckets of blood over to a large group of wounded. She's scraped up pretty bad but looks damn healthy compared to the rest of them. That human blood I let her drink before the attack probably saved her immortal life.

"Where's Magnus? Where's Jareth?" I ask, rushing over to her and grabbing her by the arm, not one hundred percent sure I want to know the answer to either question. *Please don't let them be dead. Please don't let them be dead.*

Cinder turns to me, a solemn look on her face. "Lord Magnus surrendered to the wolves," she says. "He let them take him away."

"What?" I cry. They took Magnus? So everything we tried to do was for nothing? "Why would he do something like that?"

She gives me a hard look. The look of someone who has seen far too much pain in her life. "To save the rest of the camp," she says flatly. "Now, if you'll excuse me, I must get this blood distributed." She tries to push past me, but I stand my ground.

"What about . . . what about . . . Jareth," I manage to finally spit out, though I have no idea how I'm going to take the news that something happened to him.

"He's over in one of the remaining tents," she says, giving

me wan smile. "Some of the vampires . . . well, they believe he brought the wolves upon us. I felt that it was best he remain out of plain sight."

"So he's . . . alive." My heart surges with hope.

She nods. "He's doing much better than most. But then, he started out healthier to begin with." She looks around the camp, dismay in her eyes. I rest a hand on her arm.

"I'm sorry," I whisper.

"No more than I am," she replies, then rushes away to deliver the blood to those who need it.

I draw in a long breath, then start toward the tent where Jareth hides, my stomach feeling as if it's going to flip inside out as I step over dismembered limbs and bloody entrails. How could Pyrus get away with something like this? Was it simply because the other Consortium members have no idea what's really going on? I force myself to pull my iPhone from my pocket, wincing as I click it on and see the wallpaper photo of Sunny and me making funny faces at the camera. Somehow I manage to find the photo app and start taking pictures. The others must know what went on here today.

"Get out of here!" cries a redheaded vampire in a ratty woolen dress, kneeling over a bloody child. "Don't you have any respect for the dead?"

Guiltily, I stuff my camera back in my pocket. "I'm sorry," I reply. "I didn't mean . . . I mean, my sister died, too," I tell her, my voice cracking as I relive the scene all over again.

Her face softens, and she rises to her feet, placing a comforting hand on my arm. "I'm sorry," she murmurs. "It's all so terrible. I thought when I came here I left all the atrocities from home behind. That I finally had a chance to make a fresh start. But even here, deep in this pit, it seems we are still not able to shrink from the Consortium's grip."

I don't know what to tell her. Words seem so meaningless. I mean, sure they can try to rebuild. But now their secret world has been breached. They'll probably have to abandon their home and find somewhere else to hide. To try to make a new life for themselves, somewhere.

"I promise you," I vow, anger rising within me, "someday, somehow, I will make this right. Pyrus will pay for what he's done to you."

She gives me a sad smile. I know she doesn't believe what I say. But it doesn't matter. I believe it. And I'm not going to rest until justice has been served. Until my sister—and all of these innocent vampires—have been avenged.

I say my good-byes and continue to the tent, pretty sure the only thing keeping my legs from collapsing out from under me is the knowledge that Jareth is inside, alive and well and waiting for me. That in a moment I can throw myself into his arms and stop being brave. That I can scream and cry and mourn and he'll be there to pull me close and kiss away my tears.

"Jareth!" I cry, stumbling into the tent.

At first glance I think I have the wrong place—I don't see him anywhere. Then my eyes fall upon a crumpled, trembling heap in the far corner. I rush to his side, hurling my arms around him. "Oh, Jareth," I cry. "Thank God you're okay!"

I wait for him to lift his head. To pull me into a strong embrace. Instead, he cringes at my touch, burrowing farther into the canvas wall of the tent.

"Go away," he growls in a low, menacing voice.

I back away, staring down at him in shock. "What?" I whisper. "What did you say?"

"You heard me. Go away."

Okay, obviously he's suffering from some kind of post-traumatic shock. "Jareth, it's me! Rayne! I'm back. I'm okay." I decide not to mention Sunny just yet. I don't want to make things worse. I try to put my arm around him again, but he shrugs it away.

"Please, just leave me alone," he begs.

"Absolutely not!" I cry. "Jareth, look at me." My voice cracks as I try desperately to reach him. But it's as if he's built a tall stone wall around himself and refuses to let anyone through.

"Go home, Rayne," he whispers.

"I'm not going anywhere without you."

"Well, I'm not going back."

"What? What are you talking about? You have to go back!"

Suddenly, Jareth turns, his bloodshot eyes drilling into me like knives. "And why is that?" he demands in a raw, angry voice. "What is there to go back to? Because of me, the Blood Coven will be kicked out of the Consortium. Magnus will be staked through the heart. Your sister—"

I burst into tears. He gives me a grim look.

"She's already dead, isn't she?" he asks flatly. Somehow I

manage a nod. He shakes his head slowly. "Once again my actions—my bad decisions—have doomed all those around me. Just like long ago with my own family. Magnus, your sister, the Blood Coven. All these vampires here at the camp. It would have been better if I'd never been born."

"Jareth, please!" I beg, my heart breaking in agony. "This isn't your fault! You can't blame yourself for what Pyrus has done!"

"Not my fault?" he cries, his voice filled with disbelief and scorn. "I'm the Master. The Blood Coven general. The one vampires count on to make the right decisions and keep them safe no matter what. But what I do instead? I let my emotions—my personal connections—color my decisions. I let them cloud my judgment and allow me to make foolish choices." He scowls. "Magnus told me that he would rather die than see his people harmed. And yet I willfully put them in danger, in order to save his life. Because he was my . . . my friend." He shakes his head. "What is the saying? 'With friends like these' . . ."

"Jareth, please," I beg. "I know you're upset. But you must come with me. We have to stick together. I can't make it without you!"

He looks up at me with bitter eyes filled with resolve. I shiver under his gaze. "Well, you're going to have to try," he whispers hoarsely. "Because after today, you'll never see me again."

14

Don't ask me how I made it back up to the streets of New York City. I wouldn't be able to tell you. And don't ask how many days and nights I wandered those streets—without sleep, without blood—with only my grief and anger to keep me company. Those hours are lost forever in a nauseous haze as my mind worked overtime to replay all the could-have-beens. The ones that might have given us all a chance at a happily ever after.

But unlike in video games, real life has no do-overs. You can't restart from your last save point; you can't begin all over again. In real life, my sister—my other half, my best friend in the world—is gone forever. And nothing I can do will bring her back.

I try to remember the good times, but truth be told, it's

much easier to remember the bad: the ones where I let her down or messed up her life. Or wasn't there when she needed me. That first night at Club Fang plays over and over again on a nonstop loop. What if I hadn't dragged her there? What if I didn't make her wear the BITE ME shirt? What if Magnus hadn't mistaken her for me?

Would she still be alive right now, living the happy-go-lucky normal life she so deserved?

How am I going to tell Mom? Heather? Stormy? How am I going to go back to Vegas and face Slayer Inc. and Vice President Teifert? Will they know somehow that I murdered Bertha? Will they be forced, under Pyrus's directive, to nano me? And, more important, do I really even care if they do? After all, what is there to live for now? Sunny's gone. Jareth's left me forever.

My stomach twists and turns, as if knotted up by rusty barbed wire. I dimly realize I haven't eaten for days. The hunger inside me blurs my vision as I wander down the streets of Manhattan's Lower East Side. Only a few people are still out at this hour—the kind of people, I note, whom most wouldn't miss if an empty shell of a vampire made them her dinner.

I shake my head. No. I can't go there. These people may seem pathetic and lost, but hell, am I really so different? They may be down on their luck, but they still have brothers and sisters and mothers and fathers. Who am I to steal them away from their loved ones simply to satisfy my vile emptiness?

Then again, a little voice inside chimes in, why should they be spared when my sister was not? They're untouchables—drug dealers, murderers, alcoholics, abusers, child molesters—the lowest of the low. Why should they walk the streets, thumbing their noses at the law and hurting innocent people? Why should they be allowed to live, when my innocent sister had to die?

I watch in the dark shadows as a scantily dressed woman stumbles into the alleyway, her fingers grasping a bottle wrapped in brown paper. Hunger surges at the sight of her. If I could just take one sip . . . I know it would soothe me. Take the edge off the unbearable pain that smothers me like a heavy blanket. Just one sip—she wouldn't even miss it. She wouldn't even remember the next morning that I'd come to her, in the dead of night, seducing her with my vampire scent before indulging in her essence.

After all, why should I be so empty, when she is so full?

I take a step forward and my nose catches a whiff of her scent. Sweat mixed with alcohol and spicy perfume. But it doesn't matter. Her blood will be sweet. Sweet and soothing.

"Hello," I say, stepping into the glow of a nearby streetlight after wiping away my blood tears. My voice sounds strange, after having not spoken for so long and I know I must look a mess. But it doesn't matter. I could be the Crypt Keeper himself and she'd still only see a beautiful, immortal she can't help fall in love with.

Sure enough, her eyes widen and she clumsily falls to her knees, looking up at me with a hollow face full of rapture. "Are you an angel?" she whispers. "Have you come to save me?"

Guilt knots in my stomach at her questions. An angel. Sunny was the angel. A perfect creature of light with feathery wings and a beautiful soul. I'm more like a dark demon, set upon the world to cause pain and suffering to those who dare try to love me.

"Sure, yeah, an angel. You should have seen my wings," I mutter, forcing the guilt back down inside. After all, there's plenty of time to worry about regret later—after my meal. I lower myself to the ground, pulling her close to me and cradling her in my arms, stroking her hair. As she closes her eyes, my fangs slide easily from my mouth and I lower my head to take that first juicy bite of her.

But before I can make the puncture, my eyes fall upon the tattoo seared into her shoulder. More precisely, a tattoo of Race Jameson, vampire rock star.

My cohort in rehab.

I shove her away and she goes flying across the alleyway, her bony body taking the brunt of my horror. What am I doing? I'm not this person anymore. I went through the twelve steps—I'm clean. I'm sober. I can't go back to what I used to be: a blood-hungry monster who stole Corbin's mortal life and forced him to live a nightmare, so I could have a mid-afternoon snack.

It takes three attempts to wrestle my phone from my pocket, my hands are shaking so badly. But somehow, eventually, I manage to do it. To call the number I was given on the day I left rehab. The number they promised would give me help if and when I needed it.

And, oh boy do I need it now!

"Please!" the woman begs, crawling back toward me, blood dripping from a cut on her forehead. "I beg of you. Don't leave me."

My stomach roils at her pleas even as it growls at the sight of her thick, syrupy blood. I force myself to avert my eyes, disgusted at my weakness. "Please, just go away," I beg her, reaching into my pocket and thrusting a wad of bills in her direction. "Go find yourself something to eat or something. Leave me alone."

But she doesn't. She's too sucked in to my vampire scent. She just sits there, quavering before me, crying her eyes out, begging me to take her, to give her my eternal kiss.

I've never felt so low in all my life.

"Hello?" the English-accented voice chimes from the other end of the phone.

Thank God. I let out a sigh of relief. "Race? It's Rayne McDonald. I need your help."

15

It's very lucky for me that Race is currently in town for a concert at Madison Square Garden and not halfway around the world. But even so, it seems like an eternity waiting for him to show up in his limo. In the meantime, it's not easy fending off the advances of the woman in the alley, who's begging and sobbing without relent. I do my best to keep my distance, to act like an upstanding member of Blood Coven society, but I feel like a drunk in a bar with a fistful of hundred dollar bills. I could sate my hunger in an instant, but could I live with myself in the morning?

"One day at a time," I whisper, over and over again until a shadow looms in the alleyway and the woman looks away from me for the first time since I vampire scented her.

"Race? Race Jameson?" she cries, her eyes widening. "Oh

my God. You're really here. I've got all your albums! Well, I mean, I did. Once upon a time, before my mom kicked me out of the house."

I cringe. In the haze of my bloodlust she looked old and wrecked, but now, as the limo's light shines into the alleyway, I see she's probably not even seventeen. What did I almost do?

Race smiles his rock star smile, leaning down to kiss her softly on the forehead. "Thanks for the support, luv," he says, taking her hand in his own. His bodyguard hands him a Sharpie and he scribbles his name up her dirt-caked arm.

"Oh my God!" she cries, looking down at her arm, then up at her idol. "I'll never wash this arm again."

As if she would have anyway . . .

Race gives her another charming, devil-may-care grin then drops her hand. "I hope not," he replies, his hot purple eyes burning into her. "Now why don't you run along, luv, and let me have a little chat with Rayne here?"

The girl nods, bowing before him before scrambling to her feet and running down the alleyway, fast as her skinny legs can carry her. Race shakes his head, watching her go. Then he turns to me.

"Lunching on my fans," he says, giving me a scolding *tsk*, *tsk*. "For shame. After all, you know as well as I do, most people don't tend to buy records—or download iTunes for that matter—once they're dead. And I really need *Blood on the Wind* to go platinum so I can beat out that Justin Bieber bastard. That freaking mortal thinks he's God's gift to music. And everyone who's anyone knows that title should always belong to me."

I try to pull myself to my feet but my legs refuse to work properly. Race catches me as I start to tumble back to the ground, holding me with strong, steady hands.

"You okay?" he asks, dropping his teasing tone.

"I didn't bite her," I manage to spit out.

He shrugs. "Doesn't matter if you did—I was only joking. Hell, if I had a dime for every Race Jameson fan I drained dry, I wouldn't need platinum records to become a billionaire." He chuckles. "Of course, that was in the good old days. Now I'm painfully reformed, like you, taking it one day at a time."

I attempt to nod, but it takes a lot of effort. I still feel like I'm this close to passing out. Race gives me a critical once-over.

"So, I don't want to be rude or anything," he starts, "but, darling, your perfume is saying *eau de raw sewage* right about now. So how about you come back with me to the tour bus and we'll get you all cleaned up? I've got a nice, pleasantly plump groupie who's signed all the blood donor consent forms and I'd be happy to share her if you're so inclined."

My mouth waters involuntarily at the suggestion and I find myself following him out of the alleyway and into the limo. Ten minutes later we're boarding the tour bus, and I'm standing in the shower, letting the hot water stream over me, ridding me of blood and filth.

"There she is!" Race cries as I emerge about twenty minutes later. He's sitting on a plush purple velvet couch and has changed into an orange silk bathrobe. He hands me a large wine goblet, filled to the brim with red liquid. "O-positive," he pronounces. "From what I remember in rehab, that's your favorite."

I take the glass from him with shaky hands, trying not to spill any as I bring it to my lips. I start to gulp it down, but Race holds up a hand to stop me.

"From the looks of you, you haven't drunk in days," he says. "Take it slowly, so you won't throw it up."

I do as he says, though it's painful. Eventually I manage to drain the glass dry. Setting it down on the table in front of me, I suck in a long, deep breath, trying to regain my senses. Already the blood is doing its magic—warming my insides and soothing my mind.

"Thank you," I murmur, then cringe as more details of the night start flooding back to me. I can't believe I let Race see me like that—at my ultimate worst. But then, I remember, he's been there. He, of all people, should understand.

He waves me off. "Don't fret about it for a moment," he says. "You should have seen the scrapes I got myself into before that third trip to rehab. Hell, VH1's *Behind the Music* stopped filming me at some point because the producer couldn't stop throwing up when viewing the daily footage."

I give him a wan smile, not knowing whether to be relieved or horrified.

"But enough about boring, little old me," Race says, reaching over to pour another glass of blood. He fills my goblet after his own. "What about you? You always struck me as much more sophisticated than that. What made you go down that long, dark alleyway road? I mean, sure, I know you're supposed to be the bad twin and all, but still! Doesn't seem like your style." He pauses, then adds, "And speaking of your better half, where is she? Where is that delectable fairy tale morsel—that Sunshine of my life?"

At Sunny's name, I burst into tears.

"What? What did I say?" Race asks, his mocking tone gone and his face full of confusion. "I'm sorry. I didn't mean to make any insinuations about your dear, sweet sister. You know I'd never touch a single blond hair on her pretty little head. Well, not unless she gave me permission, of course." He grins wickedly. "Then I'd make a vow to touch nothing else, as long as we both shall live."

I don't want to tell him. But at the same time I don't want to keep it inside anymore. I've been wandering around for God knows how long, trying to keep from exploding with guilt and grief. Maybe talking about it will help somehow.

And so I tell him the whole story, ending with Jareth pushing me away. "Why is it that every time I try to do something right, it ends up so horribly wrong?" I ask as I finish my sordid tale. "I am such an idiot."

"No you're not," Race scolds, swapping couches to come sit next to me, putting an arm around my shoulder and hugging me close. I know I should pull away—I've heard too much about his past with women, after all—but, I find, today his embrace feels nothing more than brotherly. And so I allow myself to collapse a little, leaning in and soaking up the strength he offers me, since I have none left of my own.

"It's obvious you had the best of intentions," he soothes, stroking my hair. "You did everything you could to save her."

"But instead, I killed her."

"No. Slayer Inc. killed her. Or that dreadful Pyrus," Race corrects. "And he would have found a way to do so anyway, whether involving you or not." He frowns. "Trust me, those bloody bastards don't stop at anything when they're on a mission. If it wasn't now, it would be later. And there would have been nothing you could do to stop them."

"That doesn't change anything. Sunny's gone and she's not coming back. I've lost my sister forever."

Race seems to consider this for a moment, pursing his lips. Then he releases me from his hold and rises to his feet, heading to the back of the tour bus. At first I wonder if he's just picked a really inopportune time to go to the bathroom. But then I remember vampires don't have to pee. A moment later he returns, accompanied by a tall, thin older man, dressed in skinny jeans and a leather vest.

"Rayne," he says, "this is my drummer, the Prim Reaper."

I look up at the gaunt giant, looming above me. "Don't you mean the Grim Reaper?" I find myself asking. As if it matters at a time like this.

"No, he means Prim," the man corrects in a haughty tone. "You're thinking of my brother. He's the grim one. I'm actually quite jolly most of the time, I'll have you know. Well, at least at times when my beauty rest is not being so rudely interrupted by a certain self-centered immortal singer who likes to stay up all night and bug me."

Race rolls his eyes.

"Oh." I take in the information. "I'm sorry. I didn't realize there were two of you."

He sighs dramatically. "No one ever does," he says, waving a dismissive hand. "That's why I decided to retire from the whole 'Death' gig and fulfill my lifelong dream of joining a band." He shrugs. "It was getting far too messy anyway."

"Messy?"

"Have *you* ever tried to drag someone down to Hell?" He fans his face. "Let me tell you—it's murder on one's manicure." He flashes me a set of perfectly French manicured nails, then shakes his head in disgust.

"Well, it's . . . nice to meet you," I reply, not sure what else to say. I mean, hello? Grieving vampire here? Not really in the mood for the old meet-and-greet.

"Listen, Prim," Race says to his drummer, his eyes suddenly shining with enthusiasm. "This girl has a twin sister—a fairy twin sister—and she was murdered the other day."

"You don't have to sound so freaking excited about it," I mutter, wishing the two of them would leave me alone with the bottle of blood.

"So?" Prim asks, stifling a yawn. "Should I alert the media?"

"So," Race continues, ignoring his jab. "Remember that time a few years ago when I hooked up with that Dark Court fae and accidentally drained her dry?" He throws me an apologetic look. "Pre-rehab," he qualifies before turning back to Prim. "You told me that fairies and other otherworld creatures don't go to the same Heaven and Hell that mortals do, right?"

I sit up in my seat, suddenly intrigued as to where this is going.

"That's correct," Prim replies, still sounding bored and put out. "The souls of the fae and vampires and others are sent to a much more classic Underworld."

"Classic Underworld? What the hell does that mean?" I demand.

Prim rolls his eyes. "Let me guess: You flunked out of Greek mythology."

"I got a D-minus, I'll have you know. Which is a totally passable grade."

He pats me on the head. "Of course it is, darling. In any case, the Underworld was most accurately described back in the day by the ancient Greeks. It's run by the god Hades, who's not such a bad fellow, when it comes down to it all. Certainly more reasonable than that beast, Lucifer, who rules the human Hell. Why, I remember one time I worked forty-eight hours straight after a big shipwreck off the coast of Boston. I'm talking grueling work—icy waters and dragging bloated bodies for miles on end. But did Lucifer give me time and half for my troubles? Even when I agreed to work through Memorial Day weekend? Um, that would be a no."

Race rolls his eyes. "I know it's hard, but do try to focus, Prim."

Prim scowls at him. "ANYWAY," he continues. "Like I said, Hades is a bit more reasonable. Don't get me wrong—he's got an ego the size of a towering inferno. But usually his little wifey is able to knock him down a peg or two."

"You mean Persephone?" I asked, scrambling to remember what I learned in school.

Prim nods approvingly. "Maybe you did earn that D-minus after all."

"Nah, she just saw that Percy Jackson movie," Race butts in.

"So what are you saying?" I ask, rising to my feet, trying not to get too excited, even as hope surges through me.

"That it's not completely undocumented for a petitioner to head down to Hades and request an audience with his majesty. Talk him into freeing one of the souls he's got imprisoned," Prim replies. "In fact, several folks have swung by over the years. Hercules, Odysseus, one of the real housewives of Orange County . . ."

"So you think he'd let Sunny out if I asked him? Bring her back to life?" I can scarcely believe my ears. Now my stomach's churning with anticipation.

"I'm not saying he will or he won't. Or that it would be an easy journey to get there in the first place. But if you can figure out a way to somehow arrive alive and convince the guy that your sister's death was an unjust one, well, you may have a fighting chance. Of course, you have to do it within a certain amount time—before she faces her final judgment and is sentenced to her eternal punishment or reward. After that, she's trapped there forever."

"Oh my God." I can't even breathe. "This is great. This is so great!"

"It may not work," Race cuts in. "And if it doesn't, you could get stuck there forever yourself."

"I don't care." I square my shoulders. "I would go to the

ends of the earth and back if it meant a chance to save my sister's life."

"Well, that's very admirable," Prim says with a small snort. "But luckily for the rest of us, who evidently wear far more ill-fitting shoes, the entrance isn't as far as all that."

"No?"

He shakes his head. "No. Just take the One up to Port Authority and jump on NJ Transit 137. You'll be at the Seaside Heights shuttle in a couple hours."

I do a double take. "So wait. You're telling me the entrance to hell is at the Jersey Shore?"

"Are you really that surprised?"

I laugh. I actually laugh. If you had told me ten minutes ago I'd ever laugh again in my life, I probably would have . . . well, laughed . . . at the idea of it even. But now hope is fluttering in my chest. Could I still have a chance to make this right? Could I get my sister back—alive?

Could we actually have a happily ever after, after all?

I have to find Jareth. Now.

16

"He's still holed up in the same tent," Cinder informs me as she and I walk through the remains of the refugee camp the next morning. It took me way too long to find this place a second time. I should have dropped bread crumbs or something on my way out. The camp looks nearly vacant—with most of the surviving supplies packed up and ready to move. The vampires who are well enough to walk around are busy pulling down tents and clearing debris, while those still too wounded to move lie around the fire, moaning softly. I wonder how they plan to make their big pilgrimage to the next safe spot with so many still down and out.

"He won't drink, he won't sleep. He just lies there, staring up at the ceiling. It's starting to get on the camp's nerves," she confesses. "After all, there are many vampires here who still blame him for the massacre. I try to tell them it wasn't his fault, but . . ." She trails off with a shrug. "It's hard to convince anyone of that, when he, himself, believes it to be true."

"I understand," I assure her. "So you're leaving? Do you know where you'll go?"

She shakes her head. "There's supposedly another safe house deep in the wilds of Mexico. But how we'll manage to get there with so many injured . . . I don't know." She sighs, the weight of the world on her thin shoulders. "If only Drake hadn't died in the attack. He always knew what to do."

"Well, maybe this will help a little." A reach into my heavy sack and pull out the first bag of blood. Cinder's eyes widen.

"Is it human?"

I nod. "One hundred percent rock star groupie." Race had been more than willing to part with some of his supply when I told him about the group's predicament. After all, he never has much of a problem getting fans to part with their bodily fluids. I hand her the sack. "I think there's ten bags in there—all I could carry. But if you can send someone up to the surface tonight after dark, you can get the rest from his bodyguards." I hand her a piece of paper with the meet-up address.

"Oh, thank you, Rayne!" she cries, throwing her scrawny arms around me in a huge hug. "Even a few drops of human blood can make all the difference to our wounded. And this is so much more than that! I can't even begin to tell you what this will mean to us. We'll be able to leave quicker and get somewhere safe. Maybe even make it all the way down to Mexico." She pulls away from the hug, eyes shining with blood tears.

"Your kindness means the world to me. I only hope I can repay it someday."

"You already have, by keeping Jareth safe," I assure her.

She releases me and gestures to the closed-up tent in front of us. "Here he is," she says. "I hope you're able to talk to him."

Me too, I think. I thank her, then pull the worn flap aside, crawling into the darkened tent. "Jareth?" I call out, blinking to get my eyes to adjust to the darkness. The place smells rancid. No wonder it's setting the other vampires on edge.

I hear a loud sigh from the far side of the tent. "I thought I told you to go away."

"Well, I thought you knew by now I'm not one to follow orders."

At first there's silence. Then, "What do you want?"

"I want you to come with me."

"There is no place on Earth I want to go right now."

"Well, that's no problem actually, considering this particular place is not *on* Earth."

Another deep sigh. "Rayne, please stop talking in riddles and tell me what the hell you're scheming now? I'm really not in the mood."

I frown, annoyed at his stubbornness. Reminds me too much of my own. "I've met up with some people," I tell him. "And I think we've figured out a possible way to bring Sunny back to life."

In the darkness I see his silhouette shift. Good. He's interested, despite his best intentions. "That's impossible," he says, though I can hear a shred of hope, laced with despair, in his voice. He wants me to tell him he's wrong. Which is exactly what I came here to do.

So I start my story, telling him about meeting up with Race and Prim. About the entrance to Hades at the Jersey Shore. About bargaining for my sister's soul. "There are no guarantees, of course," I finish. "But if there's even the slightest chance I could convince Hades . . ."

"You make it sound very simple," Jareth says slowly. "But Hades is a god, Rayne. You can't just smile and wink and vampire scent the guy and expect him to send your sister on her merry way. The man in fiercely protective of each and every soul he's acquired. And even if you can somehow convince him of your good intentions, he's going to want something pretty big in return for such a favor."

I wave him off. "Don't you think I know that?" I ask. "It doesn't matter what he wants. Because whatever it is, I'll give it to him." I look at him pleadingly. "Don't you understand, Jareth? I have a real chance at rescuing my sister here. I'm going to make the most of it—no matter what it takes." I pause for a moment, trying to gather up my nerves. "I would think of all people, *you* would understand."

Jareth winces, my words hitting home. "And so why did you come to me? You obviously have already made up your mind. And I know you never ask for permission . . ."

"Because I want you to come with me!" I cry. "This is going to be the toughest thing I've ever had to face. And I don't want to face it alone." I stop, my voice quavering as I push down the sobs that threaten to burst from my throat. "Please come with me. Please help me. I need you. Sunny needs you."

Jareth is silent again and for a moment I think he's going to refuse me. But at last he nods his head. "Very well," he says in a dull, resigned voice. "I will come with you. I suppose it's the least I can do, seeing as my bad judgment is responsible for this mess." He pauses, then adds, "But, Rayne, you must understand, this changes nothing between us. My coming with you does not mean we're getting back together. I stand by my initial vow—to remain alone from this day forward. I'll help you find your sister, but whether we succeed or fail, when we are finished with this quest, I will be gone."

Everything inside of me aches at the pain in his voice—the anguish he's trying so desperately to hide. Tears well up in my eyes and I'm grateful, suddenly, for the darkness.

"I understand," I manage to spit out. "I just want your help with Sunny. That's all." The lie burns at the back of my throat but I know it's for the best. It will take time for him to come around. And all I can do is be patient and not force him to accept what he's not ready to admit.

Because, in the end, he can pretend to be cold and unyielding and cruel all he wants. I know the real Jareth. I know how much he hurts.

Because I hurt that much, too.

But I will be there for him, no matter how long it takes. No matter how hard he tries to push me away. I will never give up on him, just as I won't give up on my sister. And someday I'll be able to prove to him that love is worth even the most immense amounts of pain.

Someday . . .

"Come on," I say, reaching out to take his hand in mine and pull him from his dark, self-imposed dungeon. "Let's go get my sister."

17

During the summer, New Jersey's Seaside Heights is a bustling beach community, home to a boardwalk, amusement park rides, cheesy clubs, and sometimes an MTV reality show. But in the chill of winter, it's very much a ghost town, with only a few shady locals wandering down the otherwise empty boardwalk of boarded-up shops and bars. A fittingly gloomy location, I suppose, for the entrance to Hell.

We park outside a small nondescript cottage, like hundreds of others lining the narrow streets, a few blocks away from the beach. Prim exits the limo first, pulling a long, golden key from his pocket. He's changed from his hipster drummer duds to the more fitting "black gown of death" uniform, complete with requisite giant scythe.

"Right this way, folks," he says in the low, menacing voice

he's adopted since beginning the tour. "To the gates to Underworld!"

I guess it's all part of the show, but still, I can't help it as a small shiver trips down my back. *The gates of the Underworld.* It sounds so ominous. And the magnitude of what we're about to do is starting to kick in big time. We're leaving the world—the Earth as we know it—to purposely travel into the fiery pits of Hell.

Where I plan to make a deal with the devil. Literally.

I glance over at Jareth, wishing I could reach over and slip my hand into his as I so often used to do. But he's barely acknowledged my presence since we left the underground vampire encampment and is currently staring vacantly off into the night sky, an empty shell of the boyfriend I love so much. And as much as right now I want to bury myself in his arms and find comfort in his cool, strong embrace, I know for a fact that if I reach out, if I try to make a move toward him, I'll only end up pushing him further and further away. For now, I must content myself with the fact that he is here—at least a part of him—ready to help me save my sister. Anything beyond that will have to wait.

Prim opens the cottage door and leads us through a dusty, cobweb-draped living room, the seventies-style, flower-patterned furniture all wrapped up in plastic. Guess no one has used this particular gateway to the Underworld in quite a while. We step into a dark and silent kitchen, then through a creaky screen doorway leading out onto the cottage's back patio. There, amongst the requisite glass-and-wicker furniture, my eyes fall upon a large

Jacuzzi in the center of the yard. Unlike everything else in the cottage, which has clearly sat unused for years, the Jacuzzi is lit up with rotating red, green, and purple lights, the steam from the hot water rising up into the night air. I glance over at Prim.

"Hot tub time machine to Hell?" I query.

He chuckles. "Something like that."

"Classy."

"Well, it does help people *warm* up to the idea," Race says with a laugh. "Get it? *Warm up?*"

I roll my eyes. "Wow. You totally missed your calling as a comedian."

He grins wickedly. "Well, let's get to it, shall we?" he suggests, pulling down his skinny jeans and revealing a pair of Union Jack–themed boxer briefs. Then he starts wrestling with his shirt. "Party in the hot tub!" he calls as he flings the shirt aside, then plugs his nose with his fingers before cannonballing in to the tub.

I leap back to avoid getting splashed, tumbling right into Jareth, who I didn't realize was standing so close behind me. I flail, losing my balance. He grabs me just in time—saving me from a nasty bruise on the patio floor. His strong hands, gripping my arms, send a longing chill down my spine.

I turn to give him a grateful smile. "Thanks," I say, looking up into his eyes. I realize he hasn't let go of me yet and it's all I can do not to cover his tormented face with kisses and tell him everything will be okay.

He blushes, dropping his hands quickly as if I'm a hot potato, taking a step back and putting distance between us. "I didn't want you to fall," he mutters, dropping his eyes to the floor.

"Well, I appreciate that," I say, giving him a sad smile. It's nice to know, at least, when push comes to shove, he can't help but care. Then I turn back to the hot tub. "Well, here goes nothing," I say, kicking off my shoes and readying to pull off my shirt. I don't relish the idea of skinny-dipping alongside Death, my sponsor, and my ex-boyfriend, but I'm pretty sure all the swimsuit shops are closed at midnight.

Out of the corner of my eye, I catch Race raising an amused eyebrow.

"What?" I demand.

He chuckles. "As much as I do admire your willingness to strip down to your birthday suit in order to save your sister, I would feel remiss in failing to mention it's not entirely necessary in this case."

I look up, surprised, dropping my shirt back down. "Oh?"

"These are magical waters," Prim explains. "They won't drench your clothes."

"Um, okay. So why are you in your boxers then?" I query, gesturing to the pile of clothes Race left behind on the deck.

"Bad habits die hard, baby."

I snort. "Oh I see. Rock stars and Jacuzzis. Really, Race, isn't that a little cliché even for you?"

"Please. If you looked up *cliché* on Wikipedia, you'd find this bloke's picture," Prim interjects.

Race frowns. "Only because you uploaded it there and I haven't a bloody clue how to take it down."

"Well maybe you should have thought of that before you drained our last webmaster dry."

Race looks over at me with mock exasperation. "See what I have to put up with, my little Rayne drop?" he asks, shaking his head. "And yet I do it all willingly, for you and your lovely, lovely sister!"

I'm about to reply but a growl erupts behind me. "Why are you even here?"

I whirl around, eyes widening. Jareth is staring at Race with venom in his eyes, his hands clenched into fists.

"Ooh, the brooding one speaks at last!" Race crows. "I was beginning to think you were a mute, mate."

Jareth scowls at the gleeful rock star, the hatred radiating off his body in waves. "I'm not your mate. And we don't need you here," he barks out. "You're not a part of this. So why don't you just go home to your groupies and leave us alone?"

Race shrugs. "Because at this hour, all good groupies have gone to bed with other rock stars," he says impishly. "And I, for one, hate to sleep alone. Besides, I'm little Raynie Day here's personal rehab sponsor. And she might need some moral support."

"Since when were *you* able to support anything moral?" I snort, unable to resist.

Race gives me a mock offended look. "You slay me, Slayer."

"Be careful what you wish for."

A loud shattering sound interrupts our banter. I turn just in time to see the patio table crash to the ground, glass flying everywhere. Whoa. Did Jareth do that? A quick glance at his bleeding fist gives me the answer before I can ask.

"Okay, okay!" Prim cries out hastily. "Let's not muck up my entire security deposit in one night, shall we? Everyone who's going to Hell, get in the hot tub, pronto. Charon's Ferry closes at two and I for one do not want to be sitting on the banks of the River Styx all night long, thank you very much."

"Fine," Jareth grumbles, wiping his hand on his pants and climbing into the tub. I follow, trying to meet his eyes, but he refuses to look in my direction. I sigh. Race chuckles to himself, observing the scene. A moment later I feel a hand on my knee. I slap it away, giving him an annoyed look. He just laughs again. Jareth shoots him a suspicious stare, at which he grins widely and starts humming the theme song to *The Love Boat*.

I shake my head. *Men!* But secretly I'm pleased. Maybe a little rock star flirtation is exactly what I need to get my boyfriend back.

"That's better," Prim says, sliding into the waters behind us. "Now let's get this baby bubbling."

18

For those of you who have never experienced travel by way of hot tub (which, I'm assuming, is the majority of you) let me just say now it's not exactly the most pleasant experience known to mankind. I mean, sure, if someone gave me the choice between, let's say, a hot tub time machine trip to the Underworld and a kick in the teeth, I might choose to go hot-tubbing. But it's certainly not as pleasant an experience as eating ice cream or dancing the night away at your favorite Goth club. More like being shoved into a dryer on spin cycle.

Luckily, it doesn't last too long and soon I find myself hurtling to the ground on the other side, slamming my butt against a piece of brimstone on impact. I suppose I should thank my lucky stars I didn't break anything in the process, as I'm guessing Hell doesn't take United Healthcare.

Soul Bound

"You know, you might want to consider fine-tuning the trip," I suggest bitterly as I scramble to my feet, rubbing my sore butt. "It's a bit bumpy."

"What did you expect?" Prim replies in a haughty voice. "It's a trip to Hell, not a Carnival cruise."

I suppose he's got a point. And hey, at least we're here. I look around, taking in my surroundings. We seem to have landed at the bottom of a deep, dark pit. So deep, in fact, that when I try to look back up the shaft, I can barely make out the glimmers of red, green, and purple from the hot tub waters far above us. And there are no convenient ladder or handholds, leading back up to the surface lands.

I swallow, the realization of what we've done hitting me hard and fast. I mean, I've put myself in some hairy situations before, but nothing like this. We've willingly dropped down into the world of the dead. And if I don't manage to impress the master of this literally godforsaken place, we might find ourselves stuck here forever. I look up longingly at the faint flickers of light far above, wondering if I've made a mistake.

At least I have Jareth, I remind myself, stealing a glance over at my ex-boyfriend. I'm not here alone. And no matter how much he tries to act impassive, I know deep inside he's still committed to my well-being.

"Come on," Prim instructs impatiently, gesturing for us to follow him down into a narrow, low-ceilinged tunnel that stretches off into total blackness. "We're running out of time."

I bite my lower lip, working to gather up my courage. I try to tell myself I've done the dark tunnel thing before—hell, just

137

yesterday I was deep down in the New York City sewers. But something about this particular tunnel scares me to the bone. Maybe it's the creepy glowing purple tendrils that climb the cavern walls. Or the red-hot blast of heat. Or perhaps it's the stench of sulfur assaulting my nose.

No, actually it's probably that piercing scream of pain echoing through the tunnel that has me most worked up.

"It's okay," Jareth's voice whispers in my ear. I startle—I didn't realize he was standing so close. "I'll be right behind you," he assures me.

I look back to give him a grateful smile, but he's already turned away. Still, I can't help but feel a little better as I take those first hunched-up steps into the darkness. In the distance my ears pick up more moans and groans from the permanent residents of this establishment. I gulp, picking up the pace, reminding myself that as frightening as this place is for me, my sister is probably ten times as scared right about now. And maybe even in pain—like that screamer. I can't let my own fear paralyze me from doing what needs to be done.

"No! I can't do it!"

I shuffle back around to see Race standing at the edge of the tunnel, a panicked look on his face.

"What's wrong, *rock star*?" Jareth asks, his voice filled with contempt.

Race scowls at him, running a hand through his messy hair. "Nothing. I simply don't like cramped spaces, okay?" he confesses, his face turning beet red. I can tell the admission of this little fact is killing him. Especially in front of Jareth. He must be super claustrophobic to say it aloud.

Jareth smiles smugly, looking happier than I've seen him all night. "I told you that you didn't need to come," he reminds him. "I mean, what did you expect? A yellow brick road?"

"Hey, AC/DC promised us a highway at the very least," Race mutters. "Not a freaking dirt path clearly built for hobbits." He sucks in a breath, searching the sky. "Is there a way back up? 'Cause I think I left my curling iron on back at the bus. And I'd hate for the whole thing to burn down, especially seeing as my manager already thinks I'm a closet arsonist and—"

"Sorry." I snort. "I'm pretty sure this was a one-way ticket. The only way out is to continue on ahead."

"Don't worry, rock star," Jareth adds, "I've got your back."

"Yeah, that's bloody comforting," Race mutters. "Just don't stick a stake in it, will you?"

"No promises."

"All right, all right!" I interrupt, realizing this could go all night. "Race, come on. I'll hold your hand, okay? Will that make you feel better?"

He considers this. "It'll make my hand feel better. What about the rest of me? Maybe if you—"

I roll my eyes. "That's my final offer. Take it or leave it."

Race grabs my hand tightly and I drag him through the tunnel, Jareth following close behind. The place is cave-dark and I can't even see my hand in front of my face, never mind Prim's movements some ways ahead. But finally, after what seems an eternity, there's a pinprick of red light in front of me. I press forward, relieved as the light grows larger and larger and the narrow tunnel eventually opens up into a gigantic red-rock cavern.

I breathe a sigh of relief as I straighten back up and take a look around. The place resembles some kind of demented theme-park attraction, with hundreds of people hanging out at the shores of a bloodred river. A long ferryboat sits at a rickety dock, waiting to take on passengers. It's manned by a tall, attractive looking older gentleman, dressed in a snappy three-piece suit.

"There he is," Prim exclaims. "Charon the Ferryman."

"That's Charon?" I question, raising an eyebrow. "I thought he was supposed to be a skeleton or something." I mean, I'm no expert in ancient mythology, but I did totally kick the ferryman's ass in the God of War video game. "And where's his oar?"

Prim smirks. "It's a wonder what they can do with reconstructive surgery these days, isn't it?" he asks. "A quick wellness retreat to Russia a few years back and he's good as new." He pauses, then adds, "And as for the oar, this is the twenty-first century, not ancient Greece. Back in the nineties he retrofitted that ferry with a sweet Marine Tech Navigator. Lazy bastard didn't like all that rowing."

Huh. I take another look at the ancient ferryboat. Sure enough, there's a sleek black motor attached to the back. Well, what do you know?

"Is that the line?" Race interjects, glancing at his watch. "If all those people are ahead of us, there's no way we're crossing tonight."

"Oh, no, no," Prim says, dismissing the crowd with a wave of his hand. "Those are all the people who can't pay." He shakes his head. "It gets worse every year, let me tell you. It's like no one remembers to bury their loved ones with the appropriate ferry fare anymore."

I scan the crowd of fairies and vampires and other otherworld creatures, all milling about, looking quite miserable. "So what happens to them?" I ask.

"They hang out on the shores for a hundred years," Prim explains. "If they can make it that long, then they're eligible for a free ride."

"Man, that's rough. Maybe the guy should consider putting out a Groupon once a decade or something," I say. "Give people a freaking break."

We head down the hill, toward the dock. The Ferryman looks over, taking one look at Prim and shaking his head. "Well, well, look what the imp dragged in," he says in a deep, grating voice. "Slumming it, are we?"

"Great to see you, too, Char," Prim says stiffly, looking a little offended.

"I expected to see your brother tonight. He e-mailed me about an hour ago, saying he was on his way with a whole boatload of German tourists."

Prim rolls his eyes. "Well, you know Grim. He's probably gotten wasted on *Weizenbier* and lost track of time. I've told them a hundred times not to assign him to the Berlin borough. He can't resist the beer and bratwurst."

"Of course." Charon groans. "And he'll show up here drunk and gassy, seconds before I'm ready to close up for the night, as always."

"Sounds about right."

"So what are you doing here again?" the ferryman asks. "And who are these people? I thought we had a long talk about giving Hell tours to the living after you showed up last time with that girl you were trying to hook up with."

"Well, technically we're not living," I point out. "We're undead."

Charon sniffs. "If you haven't been staked, burned, or decapitated, then you're classified as living beings down here. That's just the way of it."

"And how do you know we haven't?"

He gestures to the people at the shore. "No purple haze."

I follow his finger and take a closer look at the nearby dead. Sure enough, each of them has a weird purplish glow around them and they're also a bit see-through. Kind of like what you'd imagine for a ghost. I guess he's right. We don't exactly blend.

"Okay, okay, admittedly the last time was weak," Prim protests. "But this time we have serious business with the big guy downstairs. This girl's sister here was unjustly murdered and she wants to beg for her soul."

"Yeah, good luck with *that*." Charon grunts derisively. "But whatever. Not my business anyway. As always, if you've got the coin, I've got the transport." He holds out his hand, palm up, in my direction.

Prim turns to me. "Okay, Rayne, pay the guy."

I stare at him in confusion. "Wait, what?"

"A ride across Styx isn't free. Pay him."

"But you didn't tell me I needed money." I reach into my pockets, already knowing they're empty. I spent my last few bucks back in New York.

"Of course I did," Prim huffs. "Are you saying I don't know how to do my job?"

"Race? Jareth?" I ask, turning to the other vampires, praying they're more financially responsible than me.

Jareth gives me a rueful look. "Sorry, Rayne. I would have hit the ATM in Seaside, had I known . . ."

"And my manager never lets me touch money," Race adds. "He says I'll blow it all on strippers and blood."

"You would," Prim agrees, looking at us all in dismay. "So not one of you has a dime to your name?"

All three of us shake our heads. "I don't suppose he takes MetroCards?" I ask.

Charon rolls his eyes. "Does this look like the MTA to you?"

"Come on!" I plead to the ferryman, panic surging through me. "Give us a break, huh? We'll pay you later, I swear."

"Sorry, boss's orders," he says with a helpless shrug. "I mean, have you ever experienced the boss from Hell? 'Cause I have him. Literally."

I swallow hard, my mind racing for ideas, but coming up blank. I can't believe we got this far, only to get stuck right at the front gates. I turn to Prim. "So what do we do now?" I ask. "Go back up to Earth and go to the ATM, then return?" I hate wasting the time—not to mention going through another hot tub trip—but if it's the only way . . .

Prim shakes his head. "Sorry, but this is kind of a one-way thing," he explains. "You're going to have to wait with the others."

I stare at him, then at the refugees at the shore. "I'm not waiting for a hundred years!"

"I don't actually think you have much of a choice in the matter," he replies, not sounding as sympathetic as he should, seeing as this whole thing is really his fault. "Anyway, sorry it didn't work out. I did try." He starts walking back down the dock.

"Wait, where are you going?"

He looks back, surprised. "Home, of course. You think I'd wait here for a hundred years? Who would feed my cat?" He turns to Race. "I'll check on that curling iron thing for you, too," he adds, before continuing on his way.

Oh my God. I want to smack him so hard. "So you're just going to leave us? That is so unfair."

"Yeah, well, welcome to Hell," he replies, before waving his hands and vaporizing into thin air.

Race scowls. "I hate it when he does that."

I stare at the empty space that moments before held the Prim Reaper—our only guide to this crazy place. Did he really just *poof* himself away? Leave us here all by ourselves on the banks of Hades for the next hundred years?

I slowly turn to the two vampires, terror washing over me. "What are we going to do now?"

19

Reluctantly, we head back down the dock, toward the shore, where the masses are watching us with intent scrutiny. There's quite a motley crew here—vampires, fairies, werewolves, mermaids (who, hello!, you'd think could swim across the river instead of waiting for a ferry ride!), dragonkin, nymphs, and even a few bogeymen. A practical who's-who guide to the supernatural. And while most of them still seem pretty well put together body-wise (considering they were most likely killed in a pretty extreme fashion and should, for all intents and purposes, look like the waiting room in *Beetlejuice*) they all have that strange purple translucency that makes us stick out like sore thumbs.

"Do you mind?" I ask, kicking a leprechaun who's currently sniffing my leg. Beside me, Race shoves away a curious Puca who's shape-shifted into a giant rabbit while Jareth stares down a particularly ugly troll.

"Leave her alone, Iggy!"

I startle as a strangely familiar female voice cuts through the dead chatter. I look through the crowd, my eyes widening as I see a girl, dressed all in black, pushing through the masses to reach us. When she does, she throws her arms around me and gives me a huge hug.

"Rachel!" I cry in surprise, as the vampire pulls away, giving me a big fanged grin. "Oh my God. Is that really you?"

I stare at her in disbelief. It seems like only yesterday the poor vampire sacrificed her life at Riverdale Academy so Corbin and I could make our escape. Of course, had I known what Corbin would choose to do with his second chance at life, I probably would have tried to save Rachel instead.

"Rayne! It's so good to see you!" she says, hugging me again. "Come on over here. I want to hear everything." She leads me over to a small makeshift fire pit at the center of the encampment. Race and Jareth follow some bit behind, still being tormented by the eager dead, a few of them, it turns out, big fans of the rock star. "Why are you here?" she asks as we sit down on a couple of large stones. "You're not dead, are you? I mean, you don't look dead. You look great, in fact. Really great."

"Thanks," I say. "And, uh, yeah, I'm still technically alive. Or undead. Or whatever. Unfortunately, I can't say the same for my sister." I give her the short version of the story. "So we came down here to talk to Hades about getting her released." I take a quick glance around camp, cataloging each face. "I don't suppose she's here, is she?" I ask hopefully. Maybe she didn't have ferry fare either . . .

"She was," Rachel confirms. "I saw her a couple days ago when she first arrived. But lucky for her, she had exact change to cross the river, so she got to jump ahead in line."

Of course. Leave it to my former Girl Scout twin to be prepared . . . even down here.

"How did she look?" I ask eagerly as Jareth manages to shake off a banshee to sit down beside me. "Was she sad? Scared? Did she say anything about me?" I really, really hope she isn't blaming me for her death . . .

Rachel purses her lips, thinking back. "She seemed okay," she says at last. "I mean, a little shell-shocked, like most people are when they first arrive. And she was super worried about Magnus. Wouldn't stop asking people if they'd seen him. She looked pretty relieved when no one had."

"Yeah, he's not dead," I reply. "At least not yet."

From beside me, Jareth grunts, and I suddenly realize I've said the wrong thing. Before I can clarify, the vampire rises from his seat and walks away from the fire pit, staring intently at one of the nearby rock structures. Ugh. When I am going to learn to keep my big mouth shut?

"Wow, was that Jareth?" Rachel asks, watching him go. "He's here to help Sunny, too?"

I nod. "Unfortunately, he seems to think he's responsible for this whole mess," I reluctantly explain. "That if it wasn't for him, my sister would still be alive."

"Well, if it makes him feel any better, I'm pretty sure Sunny wasn't holding any grudges," Rachel replies. "In fact, she was pretty cool about the whole thing, all things considered. I think she was mostly looking forward to seeing your dad."

If I had a beating heart, it would surely skip a beat right about now. I hadn't even considered the fact that my dad would be down here, too. Would I be able to track him down if we were able to get beyond the river?

"So you've been here all this time?" I ask, looking around the decrepit refugee camp. To be honest, it doesn't look much better than the camp below the streets of New York City. A few patchwork tents, some refrigerator box shacks. Certainly nowhere I'd want to spend the night, never mind a hundred years.

Rachel nods. "It's really not too bad though," she says. "There are plenty of cool people to hang out with. And let's face it, not everyone's excited to face that final judgment across the river. In fact, some of us might be better off spending the next hundred years here, compared to what we'll likely get assigned to for eternity. We even have free Wi-Fi now, ever since one of the vampire executives at AT&T Wireless got staked by a slayer who was angry about that whole crappy 3G network thing."

"But, Rachel, we can't stay here a hundred years," I tell her. Even if the idea of free Wi-Fi does make it a bit more palatable. "We've got to get across somehow and find Sunny."

"Right." Rachel considers this. "Well," she says, "he'd probably never admit it, but I've heard there have been times when Charon has made an exception to the exact change rule. You might want to ask our eldest member, Torrid. He's been down here the longest. Ninety-nine years, eleven months, seven days.

He gets his free ride in just over three weeks. Lucky stiff." She shakes her head. "He's seen just about everything. If anyone were to know of a way to get across, he would."

Half of me wants to mention that if Mr. Torrid really did have a way to get across, perhaps he would have seen fit to use it in the last ninety-nine years. But hey, who knows, maybe he really likes having free Wi-Fi.

"Where is he?"

Rachel points to a small hut at the very edge of the river-bank. It's nicer than all the others, with real glass windows and an actual door. "As the oldest here, he scores the best digs," she explains.

"Great." I thank her and scramble to my feet, gesturing for Race, who's currently surrounded by purple glowing groupies, to follow me. Together we walk over to where Jareth is pretend-ing with great interest to study a very uninteresting rock. I give them the lowdown on Torrid that I learned from Rachel. "If anyone knows how to get past Charon, he will," I finish.

"Well, I'm ready to try anything at this point," Race says. "Before the groupies tear me apart."

"I continue to be in awe of the rough life you live," Jareth mutters.

"Hey, it's not my fault I'm all about winning!" Race pro-tests, in his best Charlie Sheen.

"Come on, boys!" I interrupt. "Let's go talk to Torrid."

Somehow I manage to corral them and the three of us head over to the small hut to knock on the front door. At first there's no answer and I wonder, for a second, if Torrid is off doing errands. Then I remember it's past one A.M. on the shores of the River Styx. I'm guessing he's not likely picking up his dry cleaning.

So I knock again, this time a little louder. Finally a deep voice emerges from behind the door. "I guess you're not going to go away if I simply ignore you."

"Please, Mr. Torrid!" I beg. "We really need to talk to you!"

Silence and then . . . "Come in. It's unlocked."

I push open the door and step inside the hut. It's much larger than it appears to be on the outside and actually pretty posh, considering we're in Hades and all, with beautifully woven Persian rugs on the floor, authentic-looking Ming vases displayed on marble pedestals, and brightly colored tapestries draping the walls. I wonder how he imports all his stuff down here.

A boy, who appears to be about fourteen years old, is sitting with his back to us, at a computer desk, eyes glued to his laptop. My ears pick up the familiar sounds of World of Warcraft coming from the speakers. "Sorry," he says, not turning around. "We're in the middle of taking down Fandral Staghelm. State your business please."

"Wow, you get video games down here, too? Sweet." Maybe this one hundred years thing isn't such a bad gig after all. No job, no homework, never-ending gaming sessions?

"Of course," he replies. "While Charon doesn't take credit cards, Amazon.com does. And now that I've signed up for their Prime membership, I can get everything shipped down here for free."

I glance over at Race and Jareth, shaking my head in disbelief. Will the wonders of Hell ever cease? "So um, anyway, we were wondering if you could help us out. We need to cross the river."

"So does everyone else. I suggest you get in line. Don't worry. The hundred years passes pretty quickly down here," he says as his troll mage lets loose a rainstorm of frostfire down on his enemy. I have to admit, he's pretty good. I wonder what server he plays on.

"Yeah. I'm sure it flies by. But you see, we're not dead. We came down here to talk to Hades about my sister. We need to get her out of here before she's processed into the system. A hundred years from now will be too late."

Torrid doesn't reply, back to his game. I don't try to press him—after all, I know how annoying it can be to be interrupted during a boss fight. In any case, it doesn't take long for the big fiery dude they're all fighting to take a major swipe at the main tank, knocking him to the ground, dead.

"Nooooo!" Torrid screams at the screen. "You noobs!"

The beast turns on the rest of the group—including Torrid's troll—engulfing them in flames. One by one they fall.

Game over.

Torrid swears, then spins in his chair to face us. It's then that I realize, for the first time, that he's actually a troll in real life, too, complete with horns sticking out of the sides of his cheeks. It's a little unnerving to say the least.

"So what do you want from me?" he asks.

I draw in a breath. Here goes nothing. "I was told that there have been times when Charon has made exceptions to the exact change rule. I was wondering if you knew what those were."

Torrid nods. "It has been done," he says. "But it's very rare." He gives us a skeptical once-over. "I'm not sure any of you would have what it takes to get him to agree."

I feel my hackles rising. Who does this troll think he is? "Try us."

"Well, the first person to do it was Hercules, son of Zeus," Torrid explains. "It's said he beat Charon in a test of strength, overpowering him and stealing his oar. Of course, these days the ferryman uses a motorboat, so that won't help you much. And he keeps the key on his person always. So you'd pretty much have to take him down to get it."

"Right," I say, glancing out one of the windows, watching the ferryman busy himself with closing up shop for the night. He doesn't look that tough. Pretty skinny, actually. Maybe if all three of us got the jump on him . . .

"Don't even think about it." Torrid snorts. "I've met Hercules. And you, my dear, are no Hercules."

Sigh. I suppose he's right. I turn back from the window. "What else?"

"Well, there was a Trojan hero known as Aeneas," he continues. "They say he was the son of Aphrodite. He was able to bribe Charon with a golden bough—which is basically like the Willie Wonka golden ticket down here in the Underworld." He smirks. "I don't suppose you have anything like that on you, do you? Maybe a Chia Pet, perhaps? The ferryman's pretty fond of foliage . . ."

I let out a frustrated breath. "Of course we don't," I say. "Come on, there must be something else. Something that doesn't require god-like strength or landscaping expertise."

Torrid thinks for a moment. "There was this one other time," he says at last. "When Orpheus came down to Hades to rescue his wife, Eurydice. He brought his lyre with him and with his music he was able to charm Charon into giving him passage across. As they say, music soothes the savage beast."

Huh. I consider this. "Well, I don't play any instruments, but I suppose I could sing," I suggest, launching into a rousing rendition of My Chemical Romance's "Welcome to the Black Parade."

Torrid and Jareth cringe and block their ears. Race puts a hand over my mouth. "We want to charm him, luv," he reminds me. "Not cause permanent hearing loss."

"Fine," I growl, offended by their obviously over-exaggerated reactions to my tuneage. "Well, then what about you, Mr. Rock Star? You think you could make yourself useful? Charm the socks off the ferryman?"

Race grins. "Now you're talking. Of course it'd have to be a capella. I didn't think to bring my guitar with me. And I have no idea what a lyre is."

"You might want to hit up some of the others," Torrid suggests. "A lot of people on the banks here are dead musicians who were buried with their instruments." He shrugs. "Now if you'll excuse me, I need to get back to my game. I only have three weeks left to level cap, before I'm forced to head across the river and face eternal damnation. I need to get moving." He grabs his mouse. "You can see yourselves out. Good luck."

Summarily dismissed, Race, Jareth, and I head out of the cabin, closing the door behind us. Race turns to me, his eyes shining with excitement.

"Honey, we're getting the band back together!"

20

By about three in the morning, Race has somehow managed to recruit a heavy-metal guitar-playing ogre, an Elvin harpist, an imp drummer, and a fairy who must have died circa 1983, judging from his Casio synthesizer. The makeshift band has gathered around the fire and is currently arguing over what kind of tune will best charm the ferryman. There seems to be some debate on whether he digs Goth, classical, or Osborne Family Christmas carols. And unfortunately, everyone seems to be trying to play their best guess all at the same time.

I try to stay out of the way, sitting down by the water, as far from the so-called "music" streaming from their instruments as possible. Unfortunately, I'm pretty sure there are ninety-nine-year-old deaf women in Siberia blocking their ears right about now, moaning in pain, and I'm getting worried on whether this plan will actually work.

A shadow crosses over me and a moment later Jareth sits down beside me in the sand. "I don't think I've ever heard anything this terrible," he exclaims.

"Me neither," I agree. "And I've sat through an entire John Mayer concert with Sunny." I grab a handful of crimson-colored sand, running it through my fingers. "I don't understand it. Race is an internationally known rock star. And yet he's as bad as the rest."

"Yeah, but remember, there's no Auto-Tune down in Hades."

"Good point." I frown. "At this rate, it's going to take them a hundred years to get good enough to play."

Jareth gives me a rueful look and the two of us fall silent. But somehow the silence is comforting rather than awkward. And even the terrible music currently sound tracking the scene can't put a damper on the fact that the vampire has chosen to come sit next to me of his own free will. I steal a glance at him, wanting to say so much, but at the same time I don't want to push him away again. I realize this is a big step for him, and I don't want him to regret making it.

"Remember that first night we sat on the beach?" I dare to ask at last, keeping my eyes glued to the water ahead of me. "Right after we staked the vampire Maverick during my first slayer mission?"

Out of the corner of my eye, I can see his slow nod. "You were poisoned by the blood virus," he remembers. "You told me you'd be dead in a few days."

"I know. I was pretty freaked out. Maybe it wouldn't have been so bad, had I known about the free Wi-Fi . . ." I can't help but joke.

Jareth doesn't laugh. "I remember thinking . . . I barely know this girl," he continues instead in a dead-serious voice. "How can I already love her so much?" He shakes his head. "It scared me to death, to tell you the truth."

I swallow hard, thinking back to that fateful night. I'd finally met the one guy I could allow myself to love. The one who understood the walls of protection I'd built around myself for all those years, afraid to let anyone see the real weak and powerless me. I knew Jareth had the power to help me tear down those walls once and for all. To love the real me, despite her flaws.

And now that I'd done it, now that I had finally embraced Rayne McDonald, warts and all, the vampire who'd helped me get there no longer wanted to be a part of my life.

"You saved me," I remind him. "When no one else could."

"Did I?" Jareth's voice turns suddenly bitter. "Or did I damn you to the life of a monster? Sometimes I wonder."

"What do you mean?"

"I don't know," he says with a small shrug. "If I had only let you go . . . allowed you to pass peacefully into a happy afterlife with free Wi-Fi and video games . . . would it have been better in the end? Was I really saving your life when I bit you? Or was I just being a selfish monster, not able to bear letting you go?"

I stare at him in disbelief. Is that what he really thinks? That I should have died rather than become a vampire?

"So what you are saying?" I ask, not able to help the undercurrent of anger in my voice. "That everything we've shared, everything we've said, means nothing to you? That if we had to do it all over again, you'd rather let me die?"

Jareth stares down at his feet, his eyes rimmed with blood tears. "I'm just saying I think you would have been better off if you never met me," he says at last, his voice tortured and broken. "Or if I'd never walked the Earth at all."

I open my mouth to protest—to tell him he's being crazy, ridiculous—that my life is three thousand million times better because he's been a part of it and I wouldn't change it for the world. But before I can speak, I hear a shuffling behind us. Whirling around, I see Charon standing above us, dressed in a pair of Superman silk pajamas, a big frown on his face.

"What the hell is going on here?" he demands, gesturing to the ruckus up by the fire pit. "I've never heard such obnoxious noise in all my millennia! It's four in the morning, for Hades's sake!"

I grimace. I was afraid this might happen. Here we are, trying to charm him and instead we've only managed to piss him off. I hope Torrid lets me take over his WoW account when he finally crosses the river. Otherwise it's going to be a long hundred years . . .

"Sorry," I say, rising to my feet. "I'm really sorry. We didn't mean to wake you. I'll tell them to lay off for the night, okay?" I start toward the band, but Charon grabs me by the arm.

"What, so they can begin again tomorrow morning?" he

demands. "Absolutely not. I will not tolerate another nanosecond of this blasted noise on my shores."

I'm about to apologize another hundred times, but suddenly an idea strikes me. It's a risk, of course. But those who dare, win, right? "Oh, well, good luck getting them to stop," I say breezily. "Race told me they plan to practice every day for the next hundred years. Evenings and weekends, too."

The ferryman stares at me with horror. "But they can't!" he protests. "I need my beauty rest. Eight hours a night, the reconstructive surgeons said, or I could end up back with my old skeleton face. I paid too much money for this skin to have it flake away from exhaustion."

I feel Jareth rise to my side. "Sorry," he says, looking the distraught ferryman right in the eyes. "But you know how musicians are. I doubt you'll be able to do anything to stop them." He pauses, then adds, "I mean, as long as they're here, on this side of the river, that is." He gives him a meaningful look and it's all I can do not to grin widely.

Charon crosses his arms over his chest, glaring at us. "Okay, okay," he says at last. "I'll take you troublemakers across to the other side. Let Hades himself deal with you. But I'm telling you now, Prim is in big trouble the next time he dares show his face down here. Bringing the living to Hades," he grumbles. "What's next? Honeymoons? Bachelorette parties?"

"So you'll take us?" I ask, trying not to reveal my total excitement. "Even though we don't have any coins?"

"Yes, yes," he agrees impatiently. "Just don't tell anyone,

okay? If Hades finds out, he'll dock my pay again. And I'm try-ing to save up to have my chin done." He involuntarily reaches to his chin, which I notice, does indeed look a tad too pointy. "I'll ready the boat. You get them to stop that noise." And with that, he storms over to the dock, leaving Jareth and me alone.

I turn to my ex-boyfriend, practically jumping up and down with excitement. "We did it!" I cry. "We actually did it!"

Jareth nods, unable to hide a small smile at the corner of his lips. "I guess we did," he admits, looking pleased, despite him-self. "Now, let's go tell Race the good news before we both lose our hearing permanently."

21

f someone had asked me, before this whole adventure, what I thought the Underworld would look like, I'd probably have spouted off some nonsense about fire-and-brimstone, red rocks, bubbling lava, narrow, crumbling bridges. Suffering people, horned demons cracking whips, lakes of fire—you get the idea.

But, turns out, I would have been wrong. By a long shot. You see, the real Hades looks a lot more like middle America. (Which, I imagine, to some, might be a hell in and of itself.) And not the nice, homey middle America with farmhouses and town squares and quaint little soda shops left over from the 1950s. I'm talking the kind right off the interstate—packed with strip malls and chain motels and crappy restaurants. Nothing unique or interesting or artsy as far as the eye can see.

To make matters worse, there's no sun or blue sky down

here deep underground, and so the colors all seem super muted—almost like we've stepped into a living, breathing sixties sitcom. (Without the breathing, obviously. Or the living, for that matter.) Everything is black and white, with the exception, of course, of the glowy purple people floating from shop to restaurant with bored looks on their faces.

"Ugh," I remark as I step off the ferry, glancing over at Race and Jareth. "I'd almost rather go for the lake of fire at this point. At least it would be colorful and interesting."

Race nods. "Prim told me about this place. They call it the Way Station. Souls hang out here until their lives have been judged and their punishment decided. Then they're shuffled off to other areas of Hell. Pits of brimstone, cells of sulfur, or maybe, if they're lucky, an address in the elite Elysian Fields subdivison."

"It used to be a lot worse, too," adds Charon as he readies the ferry to go back across the river. "A few years back, Hades got some stimulus money from the gods and decided to spruce up the place. Added a few office buildings, warehouses. He figured if people were going to be sitting around for months on end, they might as pull their own weight."

I do a double take as a soul floats by, carrying a briefcase. "So wait, you're saying when you die you still have to work?"

"Afraid so," Charon says, restarting the boat's motor. "The real estate investments the boss made down in Florida went underwater big time during the recession. So he needed some quick cash. And what better way to get it than put all these lazy souls on the payroll?" He snorts. "In fact, China's outsourced about thirty-three percent of their labor to Hades in the last couple years. Course, they still put 'Made in China' on the label. Otherwise people might start asking questions."

I make a face. "Sweatshops from Hell? Remind me never to die." In fact, the whole waiting around on the riverbank for a hundred years is seeming more and more an attractive option.

"So where does Hades live?" Jareth interjects. "We need to seek an audience with him."

"Yeah, good luck with that," Charon replies. "Your best bet is to head over to the Pearly Gates."

I raise an eyebrow. Charon shrugs. "Hades thought it'd be amusing to call it that," he explains. "You'll find he has a weird sense of humor." He hands me a map. "Take one of the free buses down to Demonia Lane and then take a right onto Spirit Avenue. You can't miss it—looks exactly like Graceland."

I look down at the map. "Okay, sounds easy enough."

Charon steps into his ferry and pushes it away from the dock. "Good luck," he says as he floats down the river and into the night. "And watch out for the Demon Patrols."

"Wait, what?" I cry after him, running down the dock. "What Demon Patrols?" But it's too late, he's already disappeared. I bite my lower lip, looking up and down the street, searching for anything remotely demonic.

"Come on," Jareth says, pointing to an approaching bus. "Let's get a move on."

We board the bus and it takes off down the dreary streets, puffing nasty-smelling smoke from its exhaust. I peer out from the greasy windows, watching all the souls we pass, hoping to see Sunny. I know it's like a needle in a haystack, but what else do I have to do?

The bus pulls up outside a wrought-iron gate, covered with black pearls. Above it reads: ABANDON HOPE, ALL YE WHO ENTER HERE. Guess this is the place. We scramble off the bus, locating a little guard shack, to the right of the gate. As we start to approach, we're suddenly cut off by a dog, straight out of Harry Potter—with three heads' worth of dripping fangs and a tail lined with spikes.

I look over at Race and Jareth. "Cerberus," I whisper, recognizing the infamous guard dog from Hell. They nod, both looking more than a little worried.

"Who goes there?" demands the dog's left head, snapping its teeth. As if he wasn't scary enough without making threatening mouth movements in our direction.

"Um, hey, Cerberus," I try, wishing I'd brought some dog biscuits with me. "My name's Rayne. And this is Jareth and Race. We're here to meet with Hades. Do you know if he's in, by any chance?" I feel a little ridiculous, addressing a dog, but when in the Underworld . . .

The beast's third head rolls its eyes. "Living," it snorts derisively. "I don't know how you got past Charon, but I can assure you that you won't get past us."

"At least not without the proper authorization," adds Head #1. Head #2 growls in apparent agreement.

"Proper authorization?"

The first and third head look at one another, sigh deeply, then turn back to us. "If you want an audience with His Majesty, you must submit your request in triplicate to the Ministry of Audience," explains Head #1. "There, the request will be heard by six committees. If all of the committees approve your request, then it gets sent up to the main office, where the master himself will consider it."

Ugh. "And how long will that take?" I ask worriedly. After all, we need to talk to him before Sunny gets judged and becomes a permanent resident. We have no time for bureaucracy.

Head #3 does some quick mental calculations. "On a good day? Maybe a month? But if any of the six committees finds an error on your application, which, let's face it, sixty-six percent of the time, they do, you'll have to wait another six hundred and sixty-six days to reapply."

Head #1 gives us a smug look. "Our best guess in your case?" it says, giving us a critical once-over. "You're probably in for a three-year wait at the very least."

"Three years?" I cry. "That's crazy!"

"*If* Hades decides to grant your request at all," adds Head #3.

Head #2 utters a self-satisfied growl that almost sounds like it's laughing at me. I give it a dirty look.

"It's better than the alternative," Head #1 reminds us. "Which is an eternity."

Okay, this is not good. Time for some creative problem solving here.

"Listen, Dude . . . Dudes?" It's hard to know whether I should be speaking in plural to the three-headed beast. "We're all adults here. Let's talk about what we need to do to make everyone happy. Maybe I could swing by the butcher and grab you some meat? A nice, big juicy steak perhaps? Or maybe three? Would that help . . . speed along my application?"

All three heads give me a horrified look. Head #2 growls menancingly.

"A steak?" cries Head #1. "Are you kidding me?"

"Don't you know we've been vegan since 1994?"

"Are you *trying* to mess with our cholesterol?"

I sigh. "A head of lettuce maybe?" This is not going well.

"Tsk, tsk," scolds Head #3. "Attempting to bribe an officer of the court. Just for that, your application will be denied."

"What? But I haven't even submitted one yet!"

"Well, then you'd better get on that, don't you think? Time's a wasting."

"Why you little—" I make a threatening move toward the beast, but Jareth and Race grab me and hold me back. Probably a good idea, in hindsight. Those sharp teeth may be vegan, but I have no doubt they'd be happy to tear me apart then spit me out, given half the chance.

"Come on, Rayne," Jareth says firmly, dragging me away from the dog house. "Let's go find the office and fill out the application."

"What, so these guys can play fetch with it?"

"Don't worry, we'll figure something out."

22

After some wandering, we do manage to find the application building, but, of course, it's closed for the weekend and a bored-looking attendant suggests we come back Monday. Discouraged and exhausted, we head back down the street wondering what to do next. Jareth suggests perhaps finding a motel room where we can crash and then regroup. (*Three* motel rooms, he clarifies after Race starts asking about who's sharing what bed.) Luckily, unlike the ferryman, many of these establishments advertise taking American Express. So we agree and head through the parking lot, and enter the first place we see. It's not five-star, by any means. Heck, if it got one star, I'd be shocked. But at this point none of us feel particularly picky.

We walk into the lobby, which is just as dreary and sad as the rest of the Way Station. The air is overwhelmingly musty and the furniture is ancient and filled with holes. There are cobwebs hanging from the ceiling and even the plastic plants seem wilted. The old clerk behind the counter is fast asleep. We walk up and ring the bell and he grunts as he wakes and looks up at us.

"No room," he mutters, looking only half conscious.

"What? What do you mean, no room?" I ask.

"Last flash flood flooded the place," he says with a big yawn. "We're all booked up for months while people wait for judgment. You'll find the same everywhere you look. The Way Station is bursting at the seams right now."

Jareth frowns. "Surely you have something," he presses, after noting my dismayed face. "We've come a long way. And this poor girl is about to drop with exhaustion."

I nod, doing my best to look pathetic, which isn't hard considering I haven't slept in days. "Please, good sir," I beg. "Maybe even a broom closet?"

The innkeeper frowns, straightening up and adjusting his tie. "Even if I did, you'd be last in line to get it," he huffs after giving us a critical once-over. "I run a proper establishment here. Dead only." He points to a sign on the wall, as if to prove his point. Sure enough, it reads: Living Need Not Apply.

"Isn't that a little racist?" Race demands indignantly. "After all, it's hardly our fault we haven't been properly staked yet."

But the innkeeper has already plopped his head back down on the desk and only snores in response. Reluctantly, we give up and head back outside and continue on down the street, looking for some place that might take us in. Unfortunately, each establishment seems to have the same policy, with signs ranging from DEAD OR DON'T EVEN THINK ABOUT IT to NO SHOES, NO GLOW, NO SERVICE to even NO LIVING ALLOWED—YES, HERCULES, THIS MEANS YOU!

"What are we going to do?" I ask the boys, dismay knotting in my stomach. "I mean, no one's going to take us in. But if we stay out in the open, we run the risk of running into one of those Demon Patrols Charon was talking about. And while I'm desperate for a bed, I do not want to sleep in a Hades jail cell, thank you very much."

Jareth nods, rubbing his chin with his hand. "I think we best keep moving," he says, looking up and down the desolate street. "If we stay in one place too long, we're bound to be noticed."

So we keep trudging forward, through the darkened streets, looking for some kind of shelter. I'm so exhausted and discouraged at this point, I can barely stand and I manage to trip over my feet twice. Luckily, both times Jareth catches me and helps me back upright.

"Thanks," I murmur, giving him a grateful glance.

But he only grunts in response, looking at me with sad eyes, then turning away. I know what he's thinking: If it wasn't for him, we wouldn't be here. I'd be safe in my bedroom playing Vampires vs. Zombies. I wish there was some way to convince him that I don't blame him for what happened and that I'd rather be here with him than anywhere on Earth alone.

"What was I thinking?" Race grumbles on my other side. "I should have never come. This place sucks. There's not even any groupies around to—"

"OH MY GOD—RACE JAMESON? IS THAT YOU?"

Seemingly out of nowhere, a blond, buxom vampire leaps into our path, her glowy purple eyes dancing with excitement. She throws herself at the vampire rock star and hugs him tight. "Oh my God, I can't believe you're here! You're really here! I wrote to your record company at least fifty times, trying to get you to come down here for a gig. But I never heard back! I'd been ready to give up hope!" She burrows her face in Race's chest. "I'm Amanda. Your biggest fan. When did you die? I checked your Hellbook status this morning and it said you were still living. What happened? Blood OD? Pyrotechnics gone bad?"

"Whoa, whoa!" Race says, trying to pry her off of his body. "I'm not dead. I'm just down here visiting with some friends."

She looks him up and down. "Oh right. Of course. I should have known. You don't have that new soul glow, do you? Sorry, I was just so excited to see you. I mean, I've been waiting for you to die forEVER so we can get some of your music down here. There's, like, no one at the Way Station that's half as good as you."

"Well, thank you. That's very . . . flattering. But I think I still have quite a long life—"

"What's a HellBook?" I interrupt curiously. "Is that like Facebook in Hades?"

Amanda turns and glares at me suspiciously. "Who are you?"

"She's with me, luv," Race reassures her. "I mean, not *with me*, with me," he adds quickly as the girl's eyes narrow. "She's just a friend."

"Oh!" The groupie's face clears. "Okay!" she cries. "Any friend of Race's is a friend of mine." She pulls out a glowy purple iPhone from her pocket. "Here, check it out. It's pretty cool." She loads up the app and then hands me the phone. Sure enough, it appears to be a social media site for the dead, go figure. Mark Zuckerberg sure has a long reach.

"Wow, that's pretty cool," I say, scrolling through her profile. Evidently she's been dead for twelve months, waiting for judgment. Her blood mate is still alive on Earth and her latest status says she's pissed because she believes he's hooking up with another living chick.

"It's super popular," Amanda assures me, as she takes the phone back. "I mean, in addition to keeping tabs on the living—though we can't write on their walls or anything—it also serves as a directory of who's down here and where. Hades is a huge place, and it used to take hundreds of years sometimes to find someone you know. Now you can look up your past loved ones in the directory and connect with them in an instant."

I stare at her, wide eyed. What a great idea. I grab the phone back from her and type Sunny's name into the search bar, my breath lodged in my throat. Would she be here? Could we finally track her down?

>>NO SUCH RECORD.

Damn. That would have been too easy. Guess she hasn't signed up for an account yet. Or maybe she doesn't want to. I know the girl was always kind of anti–social media or anything computer related.

"It takes a month or two to get listed," Amanda adds, catching my disappointed face. "The bureaucracy in this place is mind-blowing."

"Tell, me about it," I reply glumly, handing her back her phone. At this rate we're never going to find the girl, never mind actually have a chance to get her out.

"Wait a second, can I see that?" Jareth suddenly interjects. After glancing at Race and getting his nod of approval, the girl dutifully hands over her phone to him. Jareth's brow furrows as he attempts to use the touch screen. (Being old school—super, super old school, that is—he struggles with technology sometimes.) But he eventually gets it and then hands the phone back to me.

"Take a look," he says with a small smile.

I stare down at the screen, doing a double take, my jaw dropping in amazement. My sister may not be listed . . . but my father is! I look up at Jareth. "Oh my God!"

"Find someone you know?" Amands asks hopefully as Race signs her arm with a Sharpie.

"Yes!" I cry. "How do we go about contacting them?"

"Well, you could write on their wall, but then it would look like it was coming from me. Your best bet might be to use Google Maps. Click on their location and it'll bring it right up."

I do as she instructs and, sure enough, a moment later I have a map with my dad's house pinpointed. I breathe a sigh of relief. Maybe there's hope for us after all!

"Do you know where this is?" I ask Amanda, showing her the map.

She squints at the screen. "Hmm. It's not in the Way Station. He must have already gotten judged and been given a permanent address. I don't know how to get there, unfortunately. But I'll write it down for you. Maybe someone else can help." She grabs the Sharpie from Race and turns my hand over to scribble the address. "There you go."

"Thank you so much!" I say, relief flooding through me. "I cannot tell you how helpful you've been."

"Just remember," she says, giving Race a knowing look. "When you die I want tickets to your first Underworld show."

"Absolutely," Race agrees. "As far as I'm concerned, you can have front-row seats."

I wait for her squeal of delight. But strangely, instead, she suddenly shrinks back in fear, her eyes glued on something behind us. I whirl around to see what's gotten her so frightened, and my eyes fall upon a six-foot glowing green demon guard, stepping out from the darkness.

"What the . . . ?" I whisper, turning back around. But Amanda has already fled.

"Put your hands up," the demon instructs in a deep gravelly voice. "You are under arrest."

23

On instinct, I grab for my stake, once again lamenting I don't have something more suited for non-vampire slaying on hand. If I ever get out of this mess alive, I'm so going to make Teifert give me the key to the real weapons closet. After all I've been through, I think I more than deserve a slightly sharper stick in my arsenal.

The fat, pockmarked demon takes one look at my "weapon" and sneers, lowering his spear in my direction and taking a menacing step forward. "Oh, you want to fight, do you?" he says in a throaty growl, his extreme enthusiasm for my non-surrender more than a little disconcerting. I suddenly realize I have no idea the extent of the prowess of the creature I've picked a fight with.

"Rayne . . ." I can hear Jareth say behind me, his voice tight with worry.

"I've got this," I mutter back to him, keeping my eye on the demon, stake raised and ready. *I am slayer. Hear me roar.*

I consider firing some Buffyesque-style banter back at the demon, but then decide, in this case, actions speak louder than words. With a solid, roundhouse kick, I slam my foot against his spear, succeeding in knocking it from his unsuspecting claws. His eyes widen as it goes clattering down onto the pavement. *Yeah, baby!* Guess he wasn't expecting someone so *leet* amongst the living.

"You like that, big boy?" I ask, deciding now that I've disarmed him so easily I have the right to a little gloating. "Well, there's plenty more where that came from."

I lunge at him, throwing my full weight against his meaty frame. He stumbles backward and for a moment I think I have him down, but at the last minute he manages to keep his balance. He grabs my shoulders and I bite back a shriek as his ragged claws dig into my flesh. (Guess manicures aren't so big in the Underworld.) With an über-powerful thrust, he shoves me backward and I find myself flying through the air, my back slamming against one of the concrete buildings behind me. My head hits hard; I see stars as I crumple to the ground.

As I struggle to stay conscious, I watch as Jareth springs into action, his left fist connecting with the demon's head followed by his right fist slamming into its stomach. Green blood spurts from the demon's bulbous nose and the creature grunts in agony as it tries to hit Jareth back with weakened limbs. But my vampire ex-boyfriend is too strong, too quick, dodging his blows while raining down more of his own. I grin, pride swelling inside me as I watch his technique. Sometimes I forget he's been a vampire general for hundreds of years. His prowess in battle is awesome.

I feel movement above me and realize Race is holding out a hand, ready to help me to my feet. I take it, pulling myself up and preparing to help Jareth out with the guard—not that he probably needs it. But just as I manage to take that first stumbling step back into battle, the bloody, beaten guard manages to pull a whistle from around his neck and put it to his lips.

Suddenly, five more demon-shaped shadows emerge from the darkness from all sides.

Uh-oh.

The largest of the new demons—a seven-foot-tall monster—grabs Jareth by his shirt and yanks him off the guard he'd been fighting, as if he were nothing more than a pesky fly. I gasp in horror as he locks my ex-boyfriend in a crushing embrace and points a stake straight at his heart. The other guards surround us, spears pointed and ready.

"That's enough!" the giant guard cries. "Surrender now or he will die!"

I slowly raise my hands and Jareth and Race do the same. What else can we do? One false move and Jareth will become a permanent resident of this place. I let out a frustrated breath. What was I thinking, going after that guy like that? Once again, I'm too brave for my own good and have put people I love in danger.

"Look," I try, taking a cautious step forward, wanting desperately to atone for my idiocy, "we're not here to cause any harm. We tried to check in with your boss, but Cerberus turned us away. Trust me, we don't want to be here, wandering around, any more than you want us to be."

"And what business do you have with the Master?" one of the other guards demands, grabbing his spear and poking it uncomfortably in my direction. What happens when one gets staked here? I wonder wildly. Do you go back to the other side of the river and start all over again? 'Cause I'm guessing Charon won't be too excited about giving me another free trip. Especially since he *did* warn me about the patrol . . .

"We only wanted to pay our respects," I try. No need to bring up the whole thing about my sister. "You know, bow to him, seek out his wisdom, all that jazz?" I take another cautionary step forward, trying to keep a brave face.

Big mistake.

The guards react, surrounding me and suddenly I have spears pointed at pretty much all my extremities. "Sorry, sorry!" I cry, holding my hands up higher. "I didn't mean to—"

"You will surrender to us now," the head guard states in a flat voice. "Or we shall drive you through."

"But—"

"Rayne!" Jareth interrupts, still pinned by the other guard. His face is white and filled with fear. "How about we do as the nice gentlemen say, shall we?" he suggests in a taut voice.

Right. Of course he's right. Just shut up, Rayne. For one second, just shut the hell up.

"Fine," I resign, dropping my hands. "We surrender, I guess."

The head guard drops his stake from Jareth's chest and the others retract their spears. Three of them pull out cords of silver rope and begin roughly tying our wrists together behind our backs. The silver burns at my skin in the most itchy, painful way imaginable and I squirm as one of the guards tightens my restraints. "Okay, okay, I'm bound and helpless already. Enough!" I cry. Not that I'm under any delusion that my protests will do any good.

Once we're all tied up, the head guard barks an order to his men in some weird demon language, and one of them shoves me so hard in the back that I almost trip over my own feet again. Guess that's our cue to start walking. I shuffle forward, doing my best to keep my balance with my hands tied behind my back. From the windows of the buildings surrounding us, I can see curious eyes, watching the scene attentively. Ugh. Don't they have anything better to do? And won't anyone here try to help us?

Suddenly, as if in answer, a loud, almost primal cry crashes through the streets. The giant guard looks up in surprise, just in time to have a huge boulder—dropped from somewhere above— slam down hard on the top of his head. He lets out a groan of agony before collapsing to the ground in a dead faint.

As the other guards clamor around him, trying to make sure their leader is okay, I look up, trying to figure out where the rock had come from. It's then that my eyes fall upon a blond, tanned, total meathead of a man, swooping down from a high hotel balcony, using a clothesline the way Tarzan would have used a vine. He drops down in front of the other guards and whips a sword from his belt, waving it menacingly in their direction. Ah, now there's a weapon suited for demon slaying!

The demons—confused and disorganized without their fearless leader—scramble for their spears. But in the chaos, they mostly end up jabbing each other instead of our rescuer. The blond Adonis, who seems to possess the skills of a Samurai and the flexibility of a member of Cirque du Soleil, works quickly, slicing and dicing, and before you know it, there are five bleeding demons piled all around us, utterly incapacitated. Damn, this guy is good!

"Wow," I cry, looking up at our rescuer, more than a little impressed. "Thanks!"

"My pleasure," he says, flashing us a brilliant, white-toothed grin. It's then that I realize he's different from the others. No purple haze, no green demon glow. He's alive. Just like us!

With a deft flick of his sword, he breaks through my restraints, then moves on to help Race and Jareth. Once we're all free, he beckons for us to follow him. "Come on," he urges. "They'll be more of them coming. We must get out of here."

We don't need a second invitation. When he takes off, we run after him, exhaustion eclipsed by adrenaline. Down the dark streets, through alleyways and back roads, up stairs and down, until we come to edge of a wide black river, with a small rowboat pulled up to the shore. As I lean down, hands on my knees, gasping for breath, the man pushes the boat into the water, then gestures for us to all get in.

"Let's go," he says, looking beyond us, searching the streets with an anxious look on his face. But there's no one coming. We're safe for now.

We climb into the boat and our rescuer scrambles in behind us, pushing off from the shore and into the dark, black waters of the river. As we float downstream, the ugly lights from the Way Station fade behind us until they're only a mere glimmer.

"Is everyone okay?" our rescuer asks, looking us over carefully as he rows.

I nod, then glance over to Jareth and Race. They nod, too, though they both look pretty shaken. "Who were those guys?" I ask.

"The Demon Patrol," the man explains. "Mercenaries, paid by the Big Ugly to police the streets of Hades. Not that there's usually much to do—most people are so shell-shocked when they get here, they tend to keep in line. So when these guys come up against a real bona fide threat like the living, they tend to get a little . . . enthusiastic."

"And what would they have done to us?" Jareth asks. "If you didn't arrive?"

Hercules shrugs. "Depends on their mood. If they felt like following the rules, they would have thrown you in prison and allowed Hades to dictate your fate. Or they might have decided to make you permanent residents and take their time doing it. Like I said, they're pretty bored. And they love carnage."

I shudder, neither scenario sounding much better than the other. "Well, we really, really appreciate you rescuing us," I tell him. "You came just in time."

He flashes me another big grin. "I would have liked to have

found you earlier. Less messy that way. I started hearing rumors of a group of living vampires wandering around, asking questions. I'd been trying to track you down all night before the patrol found you. I was seconds too late."

"And who are you again?" I ask.

He gives a small bow. "Hercules, at your service."

I raise my eyebrows. "Hercules? You mean like the legendary Greek god Hercules? Son of Zeus?" Wow. I guess that explains the super muscles . . .

"That's my name, don't wear it out," he jokes. "Lucky for you I was down here to pay a visit to my girlfriend. Otherwise, I'm not sure things would have worked out so well for you, no offense."

"Well, we definitely appreciate it," Jareth says. "Thank you."

Hercules waves him off. "My pleasure. So what are you doing down here, anyway? This isn't exactly a great spot to vacation, you know."

"We were trying to get an audience with Hades," I explain. "To get him to agree to release my sister's soul before she's judged."

Hercules nods knowingly. "Ah, yes, the old soul-release attempt. We get people down here at least once a decade trying to get their loved ones out." He gives me a sorry look. "I hate to break it to you, but Hades is pretty stingy with releasing them these days—ever since his little frenemy, Lucifer, knocked him out of the *Guinness Book of Hell Records* for number of captured souls. He's been desperate to catch up and very stubborn about releasing any he's already gathered."

I bite my lower lip. That doesn't seem good. "But it's still possible, right?" I ask, not ready to give up hope.

"Anything's possible. You have to go in there with something he wants," Hercules explains. "Oh, and get an appointment to begin with. That's tough in and of itself." He drags his oar down on the ground, slowing the boat. "So where would you like to go in the meantime?" he asks. "Any friends or family that might be able to take you in while you're figuring things out? Otherwise the Demon Patrol is going to find you again. And this time I won't be there for the rescue."

I draw in a breath. "My father," I tell him, showing him my hand with the address. "Do you know how we can find him?"

Hercules studies my hand for a moment, then gives me an impressed look. "Nice location," he tells me. "Over on the outskirts of the Elysian Fields. He must have been a pretty good guy on Earth to score such a killer address."

My mind flashes back to my father, on the ground, dying of iron poisoning after saving my life. "Yeah," I agree. "He was." From the corner of my eye, I catch Jareth shooting me a sympathetic look.

Hercules releases the oar and the boat starts floating down into a dark tunnel, under a sign that reads: ENTERING THE CIRCLES.

"Circles?" I question.

"Not up on your Dante, are you?" Hercules asks. "Well, no matter. These are the Circles of Hell. Depending on how you sinned during your life, you might end up stuck in one of these for eternity." He shudders. "Trust me, once you see them for yourself, you'll never want to sin again." He points over to a small island on the port side of the boat. "See that? We're passing through Lust right now. A neighborhood dedicated to those who couldn't keep it in their pants."

I lean over the side of the boat to look. At first glance, the place looks like some kind of Grecian fantasy island, with beautiful, angelic-looking creatures sashaying around with barely any clothes covering their perfect bodies.

"What's so hellish about that?" I ask.

"Look closer," Hercules directs as we glide by. "Do you see the souls?"

I take another look, this time realizing there are purple-tinged spirits also wandering the island. Each spirit is chained up with a nasty looking collar around their necks. When one of the spirits happens to glance at one of the goddesses passing by, he jerks violently, then crumples to the ground.

"Was he electrocuted?" I ask in horror, watching the man writhe in apparent agony.

Hercules nods. "Afraid so. The punishment for those who give in to their lust on Earth is to be stuck with unfulfilled desire for eternity. If these poor schmucks even dare look at one of the beautiful ones, they're given a healthy zap for their troubles."

"Bloody hell," Race says with a grimace. "If I ever get out of here, I'm becoming revirginized for sure. No groupie is worth that."

I turn away, not wanting to watch anymore. As we round a bend, a few raindrops splash on my head. Hercules reaches into the boat and hands us some umbrellas.

"It gets a little wet around Gluttony," he apologizes, pointing to the opposite shore. I turn to look, not sure I want to see. My eyes fall upon a group of obese, anguished creatures, stuck in deep piles of gooey sludge, moaning miserably as the rain pours down on their heads. All around them are banquet tables piled with mountains of food, but not one of those stuck in the mud can reach any of it.

I grimace, turning away. "So they have to stare at the food for eternity and never eat?"

"Enough to turn you off Twinkies for life, right?" Hercules jokes. "Or, you know, blood." He gives us a pointed look, then gestures to the shore. There, I catch sight of a group of vampires surrounded by a lake of blood, but none of them are able to take a sip. Their mouths drip with saliva and their fangs look dry and brittle. They moan and cry as the bloodlust consumes them endlessly.

I swallow hard, remembering the scene in the alleyway. I'd come so close to stealing innocent blood. Could I have ended up here, too? Hungry and alone for eternity? I shiver and Jareth reaches out and squeezes my hand, making me feel a little better.

"So what's up next?" he asks. "Circle of Greed, if I remember right?"

"Yeah, if we kept going this way. But we're going to take a little shortcut through the Special Circles." Hercules steers the boat off to a side passage.

I'm about to ask what he means by "special circles," but my words are drowned out by the sounds of loud talking. I look over to the next island we're approaching and see a group of souls screaming in pain, hands over their ears, trying to drown out the incessant nonsensical conversation that surrounds them.

"This is the Circle for people who talk during movies," Hercules yells over the din. "They disturbed people in life. Now they will spend eternity being disturbed by others."

I can't help a small grin at this one. What a great punishment to fit such an annoying crime.

"And over here," Hercules adds, pointing to the opposite shore, "is the special Circle of Hell devoted to teachers who give out too much homework."

Sure enough, the island is filled with purple scholarly souls chained to desks with piles of work in front of them. Demons stalk the rows and every time one of the souls completes an assignment, three more assignments are plopped down in front of them.

"They have to work for eternity," Hercules explains. "They will never have a moment of free time."

"Nice," I say, wondering if any of my old teachers were secretly fairies or trolls or otherworld creatures. Because I'm pretty positive some of them would be eligible for this particular hell.

"What's that circle over there?" Race asks, pointing to the next approaching island. At first, the place looks more like a paradise than a torture chamber, filled floor to ceiling with bookcases stacked with books. But then I take a closer look at the residents and realize, with horror, that each and every one of them has had their eyes gouged out. They wander around blindly through a forest of books, unable to read a single one.

"Those are the e-book pirates," Hercules explains solemnly and suddenly I'm very glad I always paid for my Kindle downloads.

Finally, we head out of the Special Circles and down another branch of the river. A sparkling sign lets us know we're entering the outskirts of the Elysian Fields. I look around, drawing in an impressed breath. The place is gorgeous—alive with color in direct contrast with the dreary Way Station we recently left. There are rolling green hills, colorful birds chirping in blossoming trees, even a fake blue sky above us, complete with warm, shining sun. Everywhere I look there are souls hanging out, having picnics, swinging on swings, laughing, and basically having a great old time.

"Wow," I say with a low whistle. "It really pays to follow the Golden Rule doesn't it?"

Hercules grins. "Now according to my map, your father should be right around here." He pulls the boat over to a cotton candy colored dock. "Just walk down Happiness Lane and take a right on Paradise Cove."

We step off the boat, then turn to thank our guide. "I can't even tell you how great this has been," I tell him, giving him a big hug. "We really appreciate the ride. And, you know, the 'rescue from certain death' thing."

Hercules bobs his head modestly. "Eh, that's what heroes do," he replies with a saucy grin. "Now, if you'll excuse me, I've got a hot date with my girlfriend, Persephone."

"Wait a second. Persephone?" I cock my head. "Isn't that . . . ?"

"Hades's wife?" Hercules laughs. "Well, technically speaking, yes. But what the big guy doesn't know won't hurt him, right?" He puts a finger to his lips. "Good luck. Be careful. Watch out for the Demon Patrol." He pushes the boat away from the dock and floats down the river, seemingly without a care in the world. *"Adios!"* he calls out after us. *"Sayonara!"*

I watch him go, shaking my head. He'd better be careful, hooking up with the boss's wife like that. Or I'm guessing he'll end up with a very special circle all his own someday. If anyone can ever catch him, that is.

"Well, what are we waiting for?" Race interrupts my thoughts. "Let's go see your dear old dad!"

24

We head in the direction that Hercules suggested and soon come to a small but cute split-level home, painted in a pretty powder-blue color. It's not as McMansion as the other houses on the block, but it's got a quaint little white-picket fence and a beautifully maintained flower garden out front. Not exactly living large in Vegas, as my dad did while mortal, but certainly not a bad place to spend eternity, especially considering the alternatives we saw in the Circles neighborhoods.

I feel a little sick to my stomach as I force myself to walk up the front steps and knock on the door. The last time I saw my father, he was dying of the iron poisoning he got when saving my life. I hope he has no regrets about making that sacrifice, or this reunion is going to be more than a little awkward. And what if he's heard about what happened to Sunny? Will he blame me for her death?

I stop halfway up the front steps. "I don't know if I can do this," I say, turning back to Race and Jareth, who stand at the bottom of the steps, awaiting my move. "What if he's furious with me?" After all, Dad and I haven't always had the easiest father-daughter relationship. What makes me think this will be any different?

"Well, you won't know until you knock, now, will you?" Race says impatiently, glancing up and down the street. "And hey, better a furious pop than a Demon Patrol, right? So find a backbone and ring the bloody bell before we all get dismembered."

"Hey, lay off," Jareth snarls at him, baring his fangs at the rock star. "You don't know what she's gone through." He looks up at me, his eyes filled with sympathy. "You don't have to do this if you don't want to," he assures me. "We can figure out something else."

I swallow hard, grateful to him for giving me a choice. But, deep in my heart, I know what has to be done. "No," I say. "I'll do it." I turn back to the door and lift my hand to knock. A moment later, a very familiar voice tells me he'll be right there, bringing tears to my eyes. It's him. It's really him.

The door swings open and I almost fall over backward as I catch sight of my dad on the other side. He's like the rest, with the weird purple glow, but underneath the translucency, it's him. My dad. My father. I never thought I'd see him again.

His mouth drops open. "Rayne?" he cries. A moment later he's hugging me so hard I'm pretty sure he's going to knock me over. I squeeze him back, rejoicing at his warm arms around me.

"Oh, Dad," I cry, the tears streaming down my cheeks. "I'm so glad to see you!" The exhaustion and stress, the doubt and fear, all of it seems to fall away at our embrace. And when he pulls away to look at me, all I can see is love in his eyes. No damnation, no regrets. Just happiness.

"Oh, Raynie, my Raynie," he whispers in a hoarse voice, choked with tears. "I can't believe it's really you." He steps away from the door and ushers us inside. "But what are you doing here? You're not dead, are you? I mean, you don't look dead. Are you still . . . ?" he trails off, his voice filled with hope.

"I'm alive, Dad," I assure him as we walk up the interior steps into a clean, nicely furnished living room and take seats on the couch. I want to tell him about Sunny, about why I'm here, but the words freeze in my throat. He's happy to see me. Will he still be happy when he finds out what happened to his other daughter?

"Nice digs," Race says, checking out some of the photos on the mantle. "How does one score an address like this? We saw some bad neighborhoods on our way out here."

"This is the Self-Sacrifice subdivision," my father explains. "Anyone who gives up their own life to save someone else's is eligible." He glances over at me and gives me a sheepish smile.

"Well, I'm glad you got something out of the deal," I mutter.

"I got the chance to save my precious daughter's life," he

says pointedly. "The three-bedroom in the 'burbs is simply an added bonus."

The tears spring to my eyes again. "Oh, Dad," I start to say, then find I can't continue.

"I was a lousy father in life," he continues. "Letting my fear always control my actions and stop me from having a relationship with you girls. I'm lucky I had the chance to do something for you before I died."

I stare at my feet, emotions coming fast and furious. "I just wish it didn't have to be like this. You stuck down here . . ."

"Are you kidding?" my father cries. "This place is great. I mean, I miss my family, of course. But I finally get to have some peace. No more stress, no more worry, no more running for my life. I get to spend warm, sunny afternoons tending my flower garden. It's like the ultimate retirement." He gives me a smile. "Don't feel guilty, Rayne. I'm actually quite happy down here. And someday—though hopefully not anytime soon—you'll come join me. And we'll finally be able to make up for lost time." He reaches over and squeezes my hand.

It's too much. I need to tell him about Sunny. But how can I destroy the happy look on his face? He died to save my life. And yet I failed to do the same for my sister.

"Sunny . . ." I try to choke through my tears. He has to know. I have to tell him.

"Oh! Of course!" he interrupts. "What was I thinking?" He rises to his feet and walks down the hall. "Hey, Sun?" he cries. "We've got company!"

I look up, my eyes bulging out of my head to see my sister, translucent and glowing, step into the living room. Her wings are unfurled and she looks more beautiful than I've ever seen her before.

"Rayne!" she cries, diving onto the couch and throwing her arms around me.

"Sunny! You're here? You're actually here?"

"Of course I'm here! Where else would I go to hang out while waiting for Judgment Day? Certainly not one of those fleabag motels at the Way Station!"

I look up at my father in disbelief. "You knew all along . . ." I murmur.

He grins. "Of course. Sorry, I guess I should have told you. But I was feeling a bit selfish. Wanted a moment with you all to myself."

A rush of love washes through me as I gaze in wonder at my family. I suddenly realize all the issues I've had with them over the years mean absolutely nothing. I love them. And they'll be a part of me forever, no matter what happens. Even death itself can't destroy the bond we share.

"I can't believe you're all here!" Sunny says, looking from me to Jareth to Race. "I mean, I hope I don't sound too selfish, being overjoyed that you've died, too. But I'm so thrilled to have you back. Wandering through that Way Station alone was brutal. All I could do was wonder how you made out with Bertha. Did the refugee camp survive? What happened to Magnus? He's not with you, so I assume that he's still living. Did he manage to evade Pyrus? Is he still hiding out somewhere?" Her questions come too fast and furious for me to answer. I hold up my hands, begging her to stop.

"If you close your mouth for two seconds, I promise I will tell you all," I inform her. She laughs then clamps her hand over her mouth.

"*Gohead,*" she tries to say through sealed lips. I can't help but giggle. It's so good to have her back.

"First of all, Jareth, Race, and I aren't dead. Notice we don't have that purple glow?"

"Not dead?" My sister drops her hand. I knew the silence couldn't last. "But that's impossible! No one living is allowed down here."

"Which is why it's taken us so long to find you," I reply wryly, giving her the story of Prim and the hot tub, Charon, and finally the Demon Patrol and Hercules. "But we made it," I finish. "We're all here now."

"But . . . why?"

"To save you, of course."

My sister's eyes bulge. "To save me? From what? I'm already dead!"

"Exactly. We want to make you undead. I mean, not undead like a vampire, but, back to life completely. We're working to get an audience with Hades and are going to speak to him on your behalf. Explain to him that your death was unjust and should have never happened. There's still a chance, if we can convince him before your Judgment Day."

Sunny stares at me in disbelief, gnawing her lower lip. A sudden worry worms through my insides. "You do want to be saved, right?" After seeing how happy she is down here with my father, I'm starting to wonder.

"Well, yeah. I mean, I think . . . ?" She glances over at Dad with a guilty look on her face. Yup, I nailed it.

Luckily, my dad catches it, too. "Sunny," he scolds. "You have eternity to come back here and hang out with me. If you have a real chance to go back to Earth and finish out your life like you're supposed to, you need to take it. Think of Rayne and your mother. How could your mother go on without her daughter?"

"But you'll be alone . . ."

He reaches over and kisses her on the head. "And I appreciate you thinking about me. But I'm fine here. I've settled in nicely and am enjoying the peace and quiet. And when you someday come back to me, I'll have this place all fixed up and ready for you. Remember, time passes differently here. A month on Earth could be a single day in Hades. So I know you'll be back before you know it."

Her shoulders droop in relief and she smiles widely, absolved of her guilt. "Well, then, let's do it," she says, turning back to me. "After all, it sounds like Magnus is still in trouble. We need to go help him."

I nod, for once not even minding that she's more concerned with her boyfriend than her family. That's just my Sunny.

"I can't believe you guys came all this way," she continues. "Just for me. Rayne, you truly win Sister of the Year this time. How can I ever repay you?"

"I'm sure I can figure out a way for you to make it up to me," I tease. "But don't count your chickens yet. I haven't had any luck getting close to the big boss here. And it seems even if I do, he might not be so amenable to my oh-so-clever plan."

My father rubs his chin thoughtfully. "I may be able to pull some strings," he says at last. "Maybe get you an audience in a few days? Does that sound okay?"

"Perfect," I exclaim. "Then I get to spend some time with you, too." Excitement wells up inside of me. This day is getting better and better.

Sunny drags me and my dad together, and we give each other a big family hug. The warmth and love inside the circle is almost overwhelming and for a moment I truly believe everything is going to be okay.

Our hug is interrupted as the front door bangs shut. I look up, confused. It takes a moment to realize Jareth's missing. I glance over at Race, who's clicking through the TV channels, looking a little bored.

"He just got up and walked out," he explains with a shrug. "Maybe too much happiness clogging the air for Mr. Emo?"

My joy evaporates as I realize what must have happened. Poor Jareth. Here I am in a happy family moment and he's still suffering. I thought finding Sunny would make him happy—or at least alleviate some of his guilt, but I guess it only reminds him of his own pain. I get to hug my sister—maybe save her from damnation. He'll never see his again.

I rise from my seat, giving Sunny and my dad an apologetic

look. Sunny reaches out and squeezes my hand, as if to say she understands. "Go get him, Rayne," she whispers, giving me a secret smile.

I thank her, then head out the front door to find my ex-boyfriend.

25

Jareth is sitting on the porch swing outside the house, staring listlessly into space. My heart aches because I can see the pain practically radiating from his body as he works overtime to pretend he doesn't care.

"Hey," I say, daring to sit down next to him. The swing creaks a little from under my weight. My nose picks up the smell of fresh flowers and I can hear some early morning birds chirp from a nearby tree. "You okay?" Even in this paradise, he looks like hell.

He shrugs, not looking over at me. "Sure."

I study his impassive face. "I thought maybe you'd feel a little relieved to find Sunny," I venture. "I mean, we're so close now to accomplishing our mission. We'll get her back, safe and sound, and you won't have to feel guilty anymore. Doesn't that make you even the tiniest bit happy?"

"Of course," he says in the saddest voice ever. "I'm overjoyed."

"Mm-hmm. Sure you are. Except that, you know, you look like someone burned your favorite Batman shirt."

He leans back against the swing, letting out a long sigh.

"Come on, Jareth," I press. "Tell me what's bothering you now. You know whatever you say will be between the two of us. You can trust me, remember?"

He's silent and, at first, I'm pretty sure he's not going to speak. I almost give up and go back inside. But just before I start to stand, he opens his mouth.

"It's just . . . watching you in there," he says in a voice filled with agony. "Reunited with your sister . . ." He shakes his head. "You never had any doubt, did you? You weren't scared. You knew what needed to be done and you did it, with no thought to your own safety . . ."

"Of course I was scared," I protest. "I was scared out of my freaking mind. But Sunny needed me. And so I did what I had to do. Like my dad did for me back at Fairyland. That's just what family does for one another." I look at him helplessly. "I mean, you did the same for your family, right? When Slayer, Inc. attacked, you did what you could to save *your* sister . . ."

Jareth cringes, rising from the seat so quickly I almost fall off myself. He walks to the opposite end of the porch and stares off into the neighborhood. I rush after him, turning him to look at me, surprised to see the blood tears shimmering in his eyes.

"What aren't you telling me, Jareth?"

He hangs his head. "I lied to you," he whispers.

"What?"

"I didn't tell you the whole truth. Of what really happened the night my sister died. All these years, I've made it sound like I did all I could. That I tried my best and still failed."

I stare at him, horror growing inside me. "What are you saying?"

He's silent for a moment. "When those first slayers broke through our defenses, one of them recognized me," he says at last. "He knew I was one of the Consortium members who voted them into power. Who'd given them the right to police vampires and slay those who didn't conform to their rules. Like my sister and brother."

"So?"

"So he told me if I fought back—if I harmed even a single hair on the head of one Slayer Inc. operative, he'd consider that a breach of contract. Basically an act of aggression between two parties who were supposed to be on the same team." Jareth lets out a frustrated breath. "He said I would give them the right to sever the agreement altogether and go after our entire organization. Slaying them one by one until vampires were eradicated off the face of the Earth."

"Ouch." I grimace.

"I could choose to save my family," he concludes in a broken voice, "but it would be at the expense of the entire vampire race. And so I hesitated," he continues. "Trying to figure out what I should do. I would have gladly died to save those I love.

But I didn't want to betray my people either. The vampires trusted me; they'd placed themselves under my leadership. How could I willingly sacrifice them when they'd done nothing wrong?"

"I can't even imagine having to make that decision," I whisper. "And in a split second, too." I place a hand on his arm, trying to comfort him. But he only jerks it away.

"Sure you could. That's what I'm trying to say. You wouldn't have had one moment of doubt. You're a fighter, Rayne. You would have dove in, saved your family, and then continued to fight until you'd saved every last vampire on Earth." He hangs his head. "I, on the other hand, hesitated too long, my feet stuck in the mud, unable to move or act. And as I struggled with the decision, that same slayer stabbed my sister in the heart with his stake." A lone tear slips down his cheek, splashing down onto the white-painted porch. "I'll never forget the look she gave me before bursting into oblivion. She knew in her heart, somehow, that I was the one who'd betrayed her."

I grab him and turn him to face me, not taking no for an answer. "Jareth, look at me," I command. "You were put in an impossible situation. I'm sure your sister doesn't blame you for that. She knows your heart was in the right place. That you wanted what was best for everyone."

Jareth frowns. "That's easy for you to say. But you can't prove it. We'll never know for sure. And I will live with this guilt for all of eternity." And with that, he storms off the porch and into the night. I wonder if I should follow him, chase him down, and try to assure him that it wasn't his fault. That he doesn't have to live with the guilt. But I know that it won't do any good. The only person he'd ever believe right now would be his sister herself. And she's too dead to—

Oh my God. A lightbulb idea suddenly goes off over my head. I rush back inside the house, up the stairs, to the living room where Sunny's trying to not to laugh at Race's rakish charm.

"Come on," he's urging her. "It'll be like a big sleepover! Makeovers, pillow fights . . ."

"Go to bed, rock star," I say as I shove him aside. "Sunny and I have more important business to discuss."

"More important?" he cries in mock horror. "But what could be more important than me showering honor and affection on the most beautiful fairy to ever set foot in Hades itself?"

I snort. "Good night, Race."

He releases a long, exaggerated sigh, then hops off the couch, taking Sunny's hand in his and bringing it reverentially to his lips. "Good night, sweet princess," he says sadly. "May your beauty and grace enchant my dreams tonight and forevermore."

Sunny giggles. I roll my eyes. He is seriously too much.

"Fine, fine," Race says, catching my look. "I guess I'll go join your father downstairs for a little HADES-TV. Hopefully *he* won't reject me." And with that, he heads down to the lower level of the house.

Once he's gone, I turn to my sister.

"Is Jareth okay?" she asks. "He doesn't seem himself. Are you two in a fight or something?"

I quickly give her the rundown of what had happened.

"Wow, I can't even imagine having to live through eternity with that much guilt," Sunny commiserates. "No wonder he's always so dark and brooding."

"No kidding," I reply. "But what if we found his sister for him? She was a vampire—she's got to be down here, somewhere, right?"

My sister's eyes widen. "Of course," she agrees. "In fact, I bet his whole family is down here. You could find out where they're living and show up at their front door. Then they can tell him they don't blame him whatsoever for what he did and absolve his guilt once and for all."

"Unless they *do* blame him . . ." I make a face. "I mean, we don't really know what happened, right? They could be whiling away eternity pushing pins in a Jareth-shaped voodoo doll for all we know."

"Yeah, but they're his family," Sunny reminds me. "I mean, even when I'm super mad at you, I always get over it in less than a hundred years."

"Please. You can't stay mad at me for five seconds."

"We'll see about that, next time you piss me off."

I snort. "But the point is, Jareth's family might be living at 666 Lake of Fire Drive right now, being burned alive and cursing the day Jareth was born. How do we know? And is it worth the risk? If he sees them suffering, he's going to hate himself ten times more than he already does."

Sunny considers this. "What about that Hellbook thing?" she asks. "Maybe we could look them up on that! Figure out what their life is like by reading their walls."

"That's a great idea!" I jump up from my seat on the couch, diving for my dad's computer. "If they seem to be happy, we'll risk it. If not, we won't mention it at all."

"Sounds like a plan!"

I look back over at her, sitting on the couch, smiling at me. A sight I never thought I'd see again. My sister, back in my life. It's like a dream come true.

And now it's Jareth's turn to wake up from his nightmare.

26

"I don't know if this is a good idea," Jareth grumps as I drag him onto the No. 777 bus later that evening, after we've all had our first real sleep in ages. "Going out and about like this, we risk running into the Demon Patrol again. And this time there will be no Hercules to save us." He gives me a disapproving look. "You're this close to scoring an audience with Hades and rescuing your sister. Do you really want to risk being dismembered right about now? Just so you can have dinner?"

I withhold a smirk; I've got him completely fooled. "Hey, I haven't enjoyed real food in almost a year," I remind him. "I'm so not missing out on my one chance to chow down on a veggie burger."

When my father had informed us that even vampires could eat food down in the Underworld, I realized it was my perfect excuse to get Jareth out of the house to see his family. After all, there was no way he was going to agree to the mission if I told him the truth. But after Sunny and I had perused his family's Hellbook wall and discovered they lived about a mile away from Dad in the super-uppity Elysian Hills neighborhood, we knew it was vital I make this family reunion happen while there was still time.

"Besides, what else do we have to do today?" I continue. "I mean, Dad's still got to set up our meeting with Hades. Might as well take advantage of all the Elysian Fields has to offer while we're waiting. And I hear the chef came from a five-star place in Manhattan before he died in a tragic flambé accident."

Jareth leans back in his seat, staring out the window. "I suppose it will be nice," he admits. "I just don't want you to get sidetracked here."

I smile at him, appreciating the sentiment. He came back about an hour after storming off from my father's house, full of apologies. It wasn't my fault, he admitted. And he didn't want to distract me from my mission. From now on, it was all about Sunny.

Except that it wasn't. Not that he needed to know that right now. Didn't want to scare him away again.

The bus pulls up to the side of a pristine, tree-lined street in a gated community with huge mansions that makes my dad's place look like a small shack. The grass is so plush and green here that it almost looks fake and the gardens are overflowing with the most exotic, colorful flowers I've ever seen.

"Here we are," I say, grabbing Jareth by the arm and dragging him off the bus. We step down the stairs and the doors close behind us as the vehicle pulls away. Jareth looks around the neighborhood with puzzled eyes.

"Are you sure this is the right stop?" he asks. "It doesn't look like Hell's Kitchen . . ."

"Trust me," I say, leading him down the street, following the directions Sunny printed off Hellbook. As we walk, I take a closer look at the houses we pass. Unlike the subdivisions back home, where every house looks cookie-cutter, here, they're all completely different. Different styles, different generations. I guess everyone built the home that they felt most comfortable in, in the same style that was popular when they lived or died. There are adobe forts, Victorian mansions, New England salt-boxes, and . . .

. . . one big, old, honkin' castle at the very end of the cul-de-sac.

Jareth stops in his tracks, his eyes bulging from his head. "That castle," he murmurs. "It looks just like . . ." He glances over at me, his expression full of fear. "You're not taking me to dinner, are you?"

I shake my head. "Not exactly, no." I try to grab his arm, to get him to continue to walk. But he seems frozen in place. "Come on," I urge. "We're almost there."

"Rayne," he says in a strained voice. "No. You shouldn't have done this."

"Yes, I should have. After all, you've spent years and years missing your family. Are you going to tell me you're going to voluntarily give up a chance to finally see them again?"

"Well, no. I mean, I don't want to. But what if they . . ." He trails off, looking miserable. "What if they don't want to see me? I don't think I can live with that."

"Well, I don't think you get to make that decision," I say, grabbing his arm again and dragging him a few feet closer. But he digs his heels into the pavement. Argh. Stubborn vampire.

"Rayne, don't think I don't appreciate what you're trying to do here," he says. "But I don't think it's a good—" He stops, eyes widening at something behind me. I whirl around in time to see a petite, purple-glowing woman with hair down to her waist, running across the castle drawbridge as fast as her slim legs can carry her.

"Jareth!" she cries in an English-accented voice. "Is it really you?"

Jareth's nails dig into my arm, so hard they draw pinpricks of blood. "Sarah?" he whispers.

It must be, because a moment later, the girl has thrown herself into his arms, squeezing him with wild abandon. "I can't believe it!" she cries. "You're here. You're actually here! I heard the rumors but I didn't believe it!" She buries her face in his chest and hugs him even tighter. "Oh, Jareth, it's so good to see you at long last!"

It takes a moment for my shell-shocked ex-boyfriend to find his voice. "Sarah," he says at last, pulling her away to look her over. "You've grown up."

She giggles. "I had an extreme makeover at one of the Elysian salons down here. It's one of the benefits of being truly dead—you can pick whatever you want to look like. Of course, most people choose to go younger—shave off ten years or so. But after living in the body of a ten-year-old for a couple hundred years, I figured it was time to try life as a teenager."

She turns to me, her eyes—so much like Jareth's—shining brightly. "Oh, Rayne, thank you," she says. "Thank you for bringing my brother back to me. And for taking such good care of him."

"I try," I say with a small smirk. "It's not always easy, let me tell you. That brother of yours is one stubborn vampire."

"Don't I know it," Sarah replies, looking lovingly at her older brother. "Now come on! David's out playing baseball— he's a complete sports addict these days—but Mom and Dad are inside! We're just about to have dinner. You have to join us. Dad grills a mean porterhouse steak."

"See? I didn't lie! We are going to dinner," I point out to Jareth as Sarah drags him toward the castle. Somehow he manages to make his feet work, but he's still not saying too much. I hope he's okay. I mean, I meant to surprise him, not put him in a coma.

We step over the drawbridge and through the main gate. While on the outside the castle looks totally medieval, I'm surprised to see on the inside it's warmly decorated like a Pottery Barn catalog and has all the modern conveniences of the twenty-first century. A woman who appears to be in her early forties, with blond hair and blue eyes, stands at the sink, washing dishes. She grins widely as she sees Jareth, yanking off her rubber gloves and walking over to give him a huge hug.

"My son," she cries, kissing him soundly on both cheeks.

"It's so good to see you. We were starting to worry that you wouldn't be stopping by." She turns to me and gives me a big hug, too. "I hope I'm not being too forward," she apologizes. "It's just . . . I've wanted to meet you for so long now, Rayne."

I beam, liking her already. "I never thought I'd have the chance to meet Jareth's parents," I admit.

"How . . . did you know I was even here?" Jareth interrupts, still sounding dumbfounded by the whole scene. "And how do you know about Rayne?"

"Are you kidding? We keep very close tabs on you, my boy," announces a deep, booming voice from the next room. A moment later, a handsome man in his early forties—who looks startlingly like an older version of my boyfriend—steps into the room. He slaps his son on the back affectionately. "We know everything you've been up to these last few years."

"But how . . . ?"

"HADES-TV," his sister explains, pointing to their sweet sixty-inch flatscreen hanging above the fireplace. "We started subscribing a couple years ago. It's a closed-circuit television system that allows you to tune in to relatives you might have back on Earth." She gives Jareth an impish look. "We know what you're up to anytime—day or night."

Jareth stares at the TV, then at his eager family. "And you've been watching me?"

"Of course!" Sarah cries. "I mean, you're still my brother, you know. I need to keep an eye out for you—make sure you're okay."

"I can't tell you how happy we were the day you met Rayne,"

his mother adds. "After all those years of being alone—finally you had someone to care for you." She gives me an endearing look. Oh yes, I like this woman a lot!

"Hope you don't mind, Rayne," Sarah says. "But I always wanted a sister."

I smile at her. "Not at all. I think it's great."

Jareth sinks down onto the red slip-covered sofa, rubbing his face with his hands. "I can't believe this," he says, half to himself. "I'm sorry. I . . . I need a moment."

"Take all the time you need. We have eternity." His mother leans down and kisses him on the top of his head, the gesture sending trills of happiness all through me. Ever since I met Jareth, he's been such a loner. Never warming up to people, never able to relax and share with anyone except maybe me—and then only once in a while. To see him in a home setting, surrounded by people who love him as much as my family loves me—well, it's surreal to say the least.

No matter what happens, I'm so glad we did this. It can't help but make things better.

"I'm going to finish up dinner," Jareth's mom tells us, heading back around the breakfast bar. "Honey, will you check on the steaks?"

"Absolutely, dear," Jareth's father agrees, walking to the back of the castle and pulling open the sliding glass door. The delicious smell of barbeque wafts through the room.

I plop down on the couch next to Jareth, trying to catch his eye. "This is your chance," I hiss at him. "You've waited so long to talk to your sister. Now here she is. Don't blow this. It's an opportunity I'm pretty positive will never come again."

Jareth is silent for a moment, then nods slowly. "Sarah?" he calls out. "Can I talk to you?"

"Of course!" Sarah bounces onto the seat across from him. "What's up?"

As Jareth leans forward to take her hands in his own, I slip off the couch to try to give them some space to talk alone. Still, I can't help but stay close enough to overhear the conversation.

"I just . . . I just wanted to apologize," he says, stumbling over his words. "I'm sorry for what I did to you back at our castle, the night Slayer Inc. broke through the walls."

Sarah squints her eyes at him, looking puzzled. "Wait, what did you do to me?"

Jareth rakes a hand through his hair, a tormented look on his face. "I failed you. I let you die. I hesitated when you needed me most and that slayer struck you through the heart." He hangs his head. "It's my fault you're here. That you never got to live out your life."

I hold my breath, waiting for Sarah's response. Will she forgive him? Or tell him it's too late to say sorry?

To my surprise she does neither. Instead, she bursts out laughing.

"What?" Jareth demands, looking annoyed. "What in Hades could be so funny?"

"Sorry, sorry!" she cries quickly. "It's just—is that why you've been so emo all these years? You think you were responsible for my death?" She shakes her head, looking at him with loving, clear blue eyes. "Oh, Jareth," she murmurs. "You remember it all wrong. You told me to stay back, remember? You even had a hiding spot for me. But I wasn't about to back down against those bastards. I may have looked like a little kid, but I was already a hundred years old. I knew exactly what I was doing when I ran out there and took on Slayer Inc."

"But I could have stopped you . . ."

"No. You couldn't have." Sarah shakes her head. "Even if you wanted to."

"What are you talking about?"

"I never told you my vampire power, bro. I guess I figured if you knew, you'd find a way to stop me from using it."

"I don't understand. What power? And how could it have made any difference?"

"Jareth, I can bend people's wills," she explains. "It's something I've been able to do ever since I first turned into a vampire." She shrugs sheepishly. "That night, well, I knew you'd go in there, fangs blazing, trying to take them all out yourself— even if it meant your own death. So I placed a hold on you. I suggested you stay in one place. I mean, you had all those other vampires in the Consortium to worry about. I couldn't rightly let you sacrifice yourself for me."

Jareth stares at her, shaking his head in disbelief. "So I didn't leave you?"

"Not of your own free will, anyway. There was no way on Earth you could have resisted the power of my suggestion," she assures him. She reaches out for her brother's hands again, finding his eyes with her own cool green ones. "Jareth, you didn't cause my death. I saved your life."

Her admission is too much. Jareth bursts into tears. His sister climbs over to the couch and hugs him close, rubbing a reassuring hand up and down his back. "Oh, big brother," she murmurs. "I'm so sorry I did that without telling you. I can't believe you've been walking around all these years feeling guilty over something you didn't do." She pulls away, giving him a rueful smile. "Can you ever forgive me?"

He swallows hard, wiping the tears from his eyes. "Only if you forgive me first."

"It's a deal! Shake on it?" She holds out her hand. He grabs her into another hug.

"Oh, Sarah. Thank you. Thank you so much."

"No, big brother. Thank *you*. I'm just glad you don't blame me for what I did. Now I don't have to feel guilty, either."

"I would never, ever blame you."

As the siblings hug, I look over to the kitchen where Jareth's mom and dad, who have come back in from outside, are both standing. Mom gives me a thumbs-up. I grin. Victory at last!

But just as I'm about to do a little dance of joy, a loud siren erupts over the chamber. What the . . . ? Jareth's parents swing into action, checking the video monitors by the door then turning to us, unable to hide the panic on their faces.

"What is it?" I ask, my breath catching in my throat.

"Demon Patrol," Jareth's father announces grimly.

"Here?" Oh God. Not here. Not now. Not after we're this close for a home-run-happily-ever-after ending. I glance over at Jareth, wide-eyed. How did they find us? And what are we going to do now?

"They must have followed us somehow," Jareth says, rising to his feet, his face white and his hands clenched. "I'm sorry. We shouldn't have come. We've put you all in danger." He grabs me by the hand. "Come on, let's go out the back door."

"No, wait," his father interrupts. He rushes to a nearby floor-to-ceiling built-in bookcase and pulls out a book, seemingly at random. The case swivels, revealing a small dark room beyond. "Get in," he instructs. "You can hide there until they're gone."

"But—" Jareth starts to protest. But his sister cuts him off.

"You either do it of your own free will, or I'll make you do it with my mind," she informs him in a tight voice that leaves no room for argument.

Jareth bites his lower lip, thinking for a moment, then seems to make up his mind. "Okay," he says, leaning down to step into the small chamber. "But I'm not staying here if things get bad." He gestures to me. "Come on, Rayne."

I don't need a second invitation. As soon as I'm beyond the books, Jareth's father replaces the tome and the bookcase slides shut again. We wait, holding our breaths in the darkness, as a loud, ugly voice echoes through the castle.

"We know you're in there, so open up," the demon leader demands. "Otherwise you will be charged with aiding and abetting the living, according to Edict 432543-2. You will surrender them—or be prepared to face the consequences of your disobedience."

I look over at Jareth with anxious eyes. Even in the darkness, I can see his distraught face. "What are we going to do?" I whisper.

27

There's a banging on the front door—so loud it practically shakes the entire castle. "Open up!" the demon guard demands. "Or we will break this door down!"

"Oh, no need for that. Just getting my key," Jareth's father says quickly. We hear a click in the lock and a creak as the heavy wooden door slides open. Jareth winces at the stampede of heavy feet trafficking over his family's beautiful carpets.

"Where are they?" the demon demands. "A neighbor reported seeing them enter this house not ten minutes ago."

Ugh. Sold out by the neighbors. So not cool.

"Sorry," Jareth's sister says. "Where is who? We don't know what you're talking about."

"Maybe this will jog your memory."

There's a thud, then a squeal of pain and a loud *thump* to the ground. Jareth cringes, shooting me a look.

"Now, now," Jareth's father cuts in. "There's no need for violence. We're citizens of good standing here and we're happy to assist you in your search. But we need more information. Who is it you're looking for again? And why do you think they might be here?"

"Don't play dumb with me, vampire. You're already all in deep trouble. If I find out you're aiding and abetting wanted fugitives, you will be charged with treason. Kicked out of your little castle here and sentenced to a thousand years in the Lake of Fire prison."

Jareth turns to me. Even in the darkness, I can see his ashen face. "I can't let them do this for me," he whispers. "They already died once on my account. I can't just sit here and let them take another punishment for my sake." He reaches out and brushes my cheek with a soft hand, searching my face anxiously. "You understand, right? I mean, you'd do the same if it were your family?"

I nod, swallowing back my tears. As much as I don't want him to go out there and face the demons, I know he has no choice. In his mind, this is his one last chance at redemption. I can't stand in his way.

"I love you," he whispers, leaning down to kiss the top of my head. "I love you so much. And I'm so sorry for everything."

My heart aches at the agony in his voice. "I love you, too,

Jareth," I whisper, covering his face with kisses. "And I'm so proud of you. I can't even tell you how much."

He gives me a sad but pleased smile, then presses his hand against the back of the bookcase, forcing it to slide halfway open, then slipping out the crack before closing it behind him. Leaving me trapped in the darkness, practically drowning in fear.

"Leave them alone," I hear him say. "I'm the one you want. If you agree to spare my family, I will go with you without a fight."

The pride in his voice sends chills down my spine, even as I burst into tears. While half of me wants to storm out from the hiding spot and demand they take me, too, so I can at least spend a few more minutes with the vampire I love, I know that doing so would negate his sacrifice. He's doing it for his family, but he's also doing it for me. So I can stay safe and rescue my sister. And, as much as it kills me, I have to let him.

My heart breaks at the scuffle that follows. The grunts of pain that escape my boyfriend's lips. I dig my fingernails into my palms so hard they draw blood, hating to just stand here and wait and not try to save the day.

"Where are you taking him?" I hear Jareth's father demand. "As citizens of Elysian Hills, we have the right to know."

"And don't try to do anything stupid," his mother adds. "We are witnessing this arrest. If he's not treated in a lawful manner, we will report your patrol to the proper authorities."

"Don't get your panties into a bunch," the demon sneers. "We're taking him to the Lake of Fire prison, nice and legal

like. You can file an application to visit once he's been processed."

"We will do that. And I better not see a hair on his head out
of place when we do."

I can't help a small smile at Jareth's mother's bravery. Standing up to slimy demons can't be easy. But she loves her son. I
can hear it in her voice. And I'm pretty sure she'd stand up to
Hades himself to protect him.

It's not long before I hear the heavy front door slam shut
behind the demons and their voices fading off into the distance.
The bookcase slides open and Jareth's family peers in at me.
"Rayne?" Sarah calls. "Are you okay?"

How do I even answer that question? I emerge from my hiding spot, my whole body still shaking. Jareth's mother pulls me
into a warm hug, stroking my hair. "I'm sorry," she whispers. "I
wish he hadn't done that. He didn't have to."

I pull away from the hug. "Actually," I tell them, "I think he
did. But don't worry. I'm not going to give up until I get him
out."

"Oh, Rayne, I'm so sorry!" Sunny cries, as I tell her and Race
the story later that evening back at my father's house. "You
must be totally freaking out."

I flop back on the couch, staring up at the ceiling. "Freaking
out doesn't even begin to cover it. I can't believe I just stood
there and let them take him away. Without even a fight. What's
wrong with me?"

"What good would it have done to have both of you in jail?" Race points out. "This way at least you have a chance to save him."

"But how?" I moan. "I mean, I can't exactly storm a Hades prison and break him out. Even with Hercules's help, that would be impossible."

"Maybe when you talk to Hades about me you can ask him to free Jareth as well?" Sunny suggests hopefully.

"But then what about you? You think he's going to let you both go?" I scowl as I realize the position I'm in. Will I really have to choose between my sister and my boyfriend? How could I possibly make that choice if I can only save one?

"There's got to be another way," Race reasons. "If only we could get in touch with Hercules. Maybe he could help us out. I mean, I know the prison-storming thing is out. But the guy's pretty clever. He might have another idea up his sleeve. After all, he's been hooking up with the boss's wife for hundreds of years and still manages to keep his head somehow." The rock star's voice is full of admiration.

I look at him, my mouth dropping open in excitement. "That's it!" I cry, bouncing up on the couch. "That's totally it!"

Race and Sunny give me puzzled looks. "What's it?" my sister asks.

"Hercules's girlfriend. Hades's wife. Persephone. I bet she has the power to spring someone from jail. And I'm sure she's listed in Hellbook."

"But why would Mrs. Hades help us?" Race questions. "I mean, unless Hercules mentioned us to her, she doesn't know us from a hole in the wall. Why would she stick her neck out for some random non-dead strangers?"

"Because," I say, my eyes shining my enthusiasm. "These particular random, non-dead strangers know about her secret love affair. And I'm guessing she'd pretty much do anything in the world to avoid us mentioning this little tryst to her husband . . ."

Sunny stares at me in disbelief. "Are you serious? You want to blackmail the Queen of the Underworld?"

"If it means getting my Jareth out of the Lake of Fire? Abso-freaking-lutely!"

28

"He's over here, Your Majesty," the green-skinned demon jailer announces, jingling his keys as he leads the beautiful Persephone and me down a narrow, rocky path along the shores of the Lake of Fire the next day. The goddess, dressed in a pair of skinny jeans and blinged-out tank top instead of the Grecian toga I'd imagined her in, wipes her sweaty brow as she gingerly steps over a boulder in strappy Louboutins.

"Finally," she mutters. "This heat is going to ruin my complexion."

I'm not enjoying it much either, but I'm too happy to complain. Thank the gods that when I first contacted Persephone—"Call me Percy"—over Hellbook, she was more than happy to help me out. Especially once I explained the situation. Turns out Mrs. Hades isn't too fond of the Demon Patrol either, as it's always trying to mess up her opportunities to see her boyfriend. And she's a sucker for stories of forbidden love. So when I told her of their actions and how I needed to get my own boyfriend back, she was more than happy to throw her weight around to spite her husband's guard and give us a happy ending. As a bonus, she also agreed to bring us to the palace afterward for a personal meet-and-greet with the husband. And we didn't even have to blackmail her for the privilege.

"Ugh. I hate this place," the goddess mutters as she pinches her nose with delicate fingers to ward off the stench of rot and sulfur. "I cannot wait until winter is over and I can go back up to Earth for the next six months." She glances over at me. "I'll look you guys up when I get back. Maybe we can try that new Mario Batali restaurant that just opened. It's supposed to be to die for." She giggles at her pun. "Get it, to die for?"

"Um, sure. That sounds . . . great?" Okay, she's a little annoying, but I think her heart is in the right place. Guess it can get pretty lonely down here for the living.

"Here we are," the jailer announces, stepping in front of a room literally made of pillars of fire. Thank goodness as a vampire, I don't have to be concerned with smoke inhalation. I try to squint past the flames to catch a glimpse of my boyfriend. I gasp as I find him lying on the ground, bruised and battered. I guess the demons didn't keep their promise not to rough him up. Bastards.

"Jareth!" I cry as the guard slips his key in the lock and the fire door slides open. He looks up, confused and dazed. Then his eyes lock onto me.

"Rayne!" he cries, scrambling to his feet. He rushes over to me and gives me a huge hug. "You found me. You actually found me."

"Of course I did, silly," I say, hugging him back. "You think I'd leave you down here?"

He looks at me, then at the jailer. "But how . . . ?"

"Jareth, meet Percy. As in Persephone, Queen of the Dead. She totally hooked us up."

Jareth bows low to the goddess. "I am forever in your debt, Your Majesty."

But Percy waves him off with a laugh. "Don't mention it," she says. "It's the least I can do for true love." She looks over at me with a smile. "You've got quite a lady here," she tells Jareth. "You'd better hang on to her tight."

"Oh, I will," Jareth replies, his eyes shining. "You'd better believe it."

And that's how we find ourselves, sometime later, in a large, luxurious one-bedroom suite in the castle of Hades himself, waiting for our audience with the big guy. Percy said it might take a while for her to pull some strings, and in the meantime, she wanted to make our reunion as sweet as possible. The room is decorated entirely in white and the bed linens are made of the softest silk. As I step out of a nice, hot steamy shower, wrapped in an Egyptian cotton robe, I find Jareth propped up in the king-sized bed. He gestures to me with a smile and I join him, curling up into his body and resting my head on his shoulder.

"You're amazing," he whispers, stroking my back, looking down at me with love in his eyes. "You never give up. You always find a way for a happily ever after."

"You're pretty amazing yourself," I remind him, rejoicing in the feel of his hands on me. Happy I'll never have to leave his arms again. "I mean, what you did for your family . . . For all you knew, you could have been stuck in that jail cell for eternity. And yet you had no reservations."

"I would have been, if it wasn't for you," he says, leaning down to kiss my cheek. "Oh, Rayne, I've been such a jerk. Such an idiot. I pushed you away when all you wanted to do was help me. And yet, you didn't give up on me. Not even after I told you I never wanted to see you again."

"Yeah, well, I can be just as stubborn as you," I reply stoutly. "And you're my blood mate. You're stuck with me—no matter how far you try to run."

"I promise I will never run again," he assures me, gazing into my eyes with affection. "How can I ever repay you?" he asks. "For what you've done for me and my family?"

"Well, you can start by forgiving yourself," I tell him. "No more Mr. Emo."

He chuckles. "Can you believe that?" he asks softly. "All this time I've held onto such guilt for destroying my sister's life. Little did I know she's a lot more grown up than I gave her credit for." He rubs his chin thoughtfully. "Seeing her down here, with my family, so glowing and happy, I realize I've wasted too many years wishing I could change things, when things are actually pretty great, just as they are."

"Absolutely," I agree. "And now we've just got to save my sister and live happily ever after."

"I like the sound of that," he agrees, pressing his lips against mine. "And I promise, no matter what happens, I'll always be there for you. I'll never push you away again."

"Ditto," I murmur, dissolving into his kiss, our mouths finding and loving one another with a passion I never thought possible.

29

For some reason, I thought Hades's palace would look like something out of a *Clash of the Titans* movie. You know, all Acropolis looking, with marble floors and lots of white pillars and the like. Maybe even some royalty types lying on couches, being hand-fed grapes by their slaves. And, of course, lots of togas. But, as I should know by now, real life is nothing like the movies. And here is no exception. Instead, the palace is done up in a completely postmodern style, with crimson leather couches, glass tables, and art-deco chandeliers. Pretty sweet, I have to admit.

"You have a lovely home," I say politely to Percy as we pass through yet another opulent living space on our way to meet her husband the next day.

"Please. You should have seen the disaster it was when I first moved in," she replies, fanning her face with a well-manicured hand. "The place was totally Gothed out to the max. For some reason, my dear old husband had the idea that the Lord of the Dead should be a Hot Topic frequent shopper. He painted all the walls, floors, and ceilings black and even had a specially commissioned coffin couch. A *used* coffin couch." She shudders. "I had my poor decorator murdered the moment I arrived so I could begin a total top-to-bottom makeover. It's been years and it's just starting to shape up now . . ."

Wow. I totally take all my compliments back. Coffin couches? Black walls? How cool is that? Hades sounds like my kind of bad guy.

We come to a small waiting room with two antique couches alongside each wall. On the far wall is a set of extremely ornate double doors with depictions of demons and other nightmarish creatures carved into the wood.

"See?" Percy points to the door. "There are obviously some things that still need to be replaced." She pushes open the two doors and we follow her into a small, dark study. On the far side of the room, covering nearly the entire wall, sits the biggest TV screen I've ever seen. Beneath the TV, sits a nondescript, little old man, sporting two miniature horns on top of his balding head. My eyes widen as they take in his wrinkly, liver-spotted hands and grandpa trousers. Is this the big bad everyone's so scared of?

And is he . . . I do a double-take . . . actually playing Vampires vs. Zombies?

"Um, hi, sweetie," Percy addresses her husband in a saccharine-sweet voice. Now I can see why she's hooking up with Hercules. "This is—"

"Damn it to hell!" Hades screams as a zombie proceeds to grab his vampire character and chomp its head off. He throws the controller across the room, where it smashes into about a hundred pieces. He whirls around in his cushy, black leather chair, giving his wife a death look. "How many times have I told you never to interrupt me when I'm playing my video games?"

Percy rolls her eyes. "About as many hours as you spend playing them," she growls back, obviously not afraid of him. I cringe a little, waiting for his response.

Instead, the god just laughs and pats her on the arm. "Touché, wifey," he replies before swiveling back around and taking a brand-new controller from the white-togaed slave who presents it to him. I wonder how many of these things he goes through in a week.

"I'm sorry, maybe you didn't hear me," Percy says louder. "I've brought some friends to talk to you."

"They'll have to come back," Hades replies absently. "I've decided not to speak to anyone until I pass level twelve." He hits "continue" on his game and the monitor springs back to life. His vampire reappears in the mall, hacking at the oncoming zombies with a machete. I remember this level from back home. It's a real bitch.

Percy steps in front of the monitor, obscuring her husband's view. "But, darling," she says through clenched teeth, "you've been on this level for three weeks now. And the minions are starting to get restless."

Hades screeches as a zombie grabs him and takes a huge chomp out of his leg, spewing blood everywhere. There goes another controller. I hope he has stock in PlayStation.

"I don't care if Zeus himself wants to come for tea," he screams back at her. "Now get out of here before I have the lot of you beheaded." He grabs yet another new controller from his slave with such force the poor boy almost gets knocked over.

"Fine. Whatever. See if I care if they overthrow you from power," Percy shoots back before storming out of the room. I glance over at Hades again but he's completely back to the game. Reluctantly, Jareth and I retreat after Percy.

"Sorry," she says with an apologetic look. "As you can see, my husband is a bit . . . occupied . . . right now." She rolls her eyes. "You're welcome to wait." She glances at her diamond-studded Rolex. "Now if you'll excuse me, I have to go meet . . ." She giggles. "Well, you know who."

And with that, she skips down the hall, disappearing from sight. Jareth sinks down onto one of the couches with a sigh. "Well, at least the furniture here is more comfortable than at the Lake of Fire prison," he says, trying to stay optimistic.

"Yeah, sure," I mutter, peeking through the office doors, still immersed in the game play. I'm just in time to see Hades get killed again, this time by a trap laid by humans in the ice cream parlor. "But this could take a while. I mean, it took me three days to get past this level and I'm totally *leet*. In fact, it wasn't until I looked up online and learned about the shotgun hidden in the toy store that I really—" I break off, an idea coming to me. "I'll be right back," I inform my boyfriend.

"Where are you going?"

But I don't bother to answer. Instead, I push through the double doors again and into Hades's chamber. A bold move, I know, and one liable to get my body separated from my head if his threats are to be believed. But those who dare, win. Especially when it comes to video games.

"I thought I told you to go away," the god grinds out, not looking up from his TV as he guides his character through the mall, avoiding a hungry zombie to his left. He's actually pretty good, I observe, and might eventually be able to master the level without my little trick. But we don't have time, in this case, to wait and see.

"Go left," I instruct him. "Into the toy store."

He whirls around at my voice, almost losing it to an oncoming zombie.

"Watch out!"

He turns back to the game, just in time to take out the creature. Saving his life and quite possibly my own head.

"Toy store," I repeat, adrenaline kicking up a notch. I have a feeling if I can't get him through this, it'll be game over for me. Permanently.

Thankfully, he does as I say, swinging a left into the toy store and cutting down a zombie cashier at the entrance.

"Head down the toy gun aisle," I instruct, heart in my throat. Will he make it? Will I? "Then search the lowest shelf under the Super Soaker display."

Hades obeys, making a right, then a left through the Barbie aisle, past the Hot Wheels section, narrowly missing being chomped by a child-sized zombie on a three-wheeler. I watch, breathlessly, as his character searches the shelf in question and . . .

"Shotgun acquired," the game announces.

Yes! I jump up and down in excitement as Hades locks and loads. A zombie clown comes barreling toward him, but he easily blows it out of the water. He looks back at me with a big, toothy grin and I clap my hands appreciatively. Maybe I'll save my head just yet. And my sister's soul, too.

"Now head to the roof," I tell him. "The helicopter's waiting."

He follows orders, storming the mall, shooting everything in sight. His points rack up higher and higher as he ascends the back stairs and steps out onto the roof. Sure enough, the helicopter is waiting for him and a moment later, he's flying away, with the game auto-saving his place before moving him on to level thirteen. From the side of the room, I can see his slave boy breathe a sigh of relief.

Hades sets down the controller and rises to his feet, turning to me with a big smile on his wrinkled face. "Good trick," he admits. "I never would have found that."

I smile back at him, trying to look braver than I feel. "Yeah, well, that level is total hell," I reply. "Um, pardon the pun." Oops. Hopefully he's not sensitive about that kind of thing.

But luckily, the god just laughs, sitting down on a nearby sofa and patting the cushion for me to join him. "So tell me, gamer girl," he says. "Who are you and what do you want?"

30

And so I dive in, telling him the whole sordid tale. And when I'm finished, he makes me go back further. Then even further. Until I come to that first night at Club Fang. When, because of my actions, my sister fell down the rabbit hole and lost her innocence forever.

"So you believe that if you didn't drag her to this night-club," Hades concludes when I'm finished, "none of this would have happened."

"Well, Sunny wouldn't be mixed up with vampires, that's for sure," I reply, wondering what he's getting at. Is he trying to make me feel guilty about the whole thing? 'Cause if so, he's a little late. "I take full responsibilities for my own actions. I made my choices and I knew the consequences. But Sunny just wanted to be normal. And I stole that from her." I stare down at my hands, remembering that fateful night. The first time I saw those two tiny puncture wounds on my sister's neck. At the time, she'd thought it was all a big joke. Little did she know . . .

"Sometimes I wish I could go back," I mutter. "Do it all over again."

Hades sits up on the couch, his small, beady eyes locked on me. "What would you do differently?"

I shrug. "I don't know. Everything? I mean, it's hard to say, right? I certainly wouldn't let Magnus bite my sister without explaining the whole deal to her first. I'd want her to at least be able to make an educated decision on what kind of life she wanted to lead."

Of course, even as I'm saying the words, I wonder. Sure, if Sunny knew the truth, she might not let Magnus bite her. But then she would have never fallen in love with him either. And as much as their relationship has been tumultuous, to say the least, he's also been her rock. Her soul mate without a soul.

Is it better to have loved and lost? Or never loved at all?

Hades rubs his graying goatee thoughtfully. "This could be fun," he mutters, half to himself.

"What?" I cock my head in question. "What could be fun?"

He turns back to me. "Well, my dear, I'm sure you realize that I can't just release your sister's soul out of the blue like this," he explains. "I mean, death is death. There's no coming back. Unless it's as a zombie. And zombies are trouble, as you saw. You don't want your sister to become a mindless brain muncher, do you?"

I shake my head. That's one supernatural creature I never

want to see in real life. "But you're Lord of the Underworld," I protest. "You have the power to bring people back to life."

"Honey, we can't change the rules midstream or make exceptions—even for sisters of very talented gamer girls. What would people think if the dead suddenly started coming back to life? It'd be anarchy. It'd shake the very foundation humanity is based on."

My heart sinks. This is so not what I wanted to hear. At all. "Please. I came all this way," I cry. "Isn't there something you can do? I can't live life without my sister. And I'll do anything to save her. She didn't deserve to die." I pause, sucking in a breath. "Can we make an exchange? My soul for hers?"

Hades chuckles. "You're a vampire, remember?" he reminds me. "You gave up your soul a long time ago."

Crap. I'd forgotten about that little technicality. I'd already willingly tossed aside the one thing that could have saved my sister. For what? Riches? Power? I am truly too stupid to live.

"There has to be some way to save her," I beg, not ready to give up. "Please. She's my sister."

Hades considers this for a moment, then gives me a sympathetic pat on the knee. "Well, there is one possible way," he ventures. "But I don't think you're going to like it."

"Anything!" I cry, hope surging inside of me at his words. "Anything in the entire world."

"Very well," the Lord of the Underworld says. "Let's play a little game. I'll call it Operation Do-Over."

I stare at him, confused beyond belief. "What the hell is that?"

"I can't bring Sunny back from the dead. But we could go back to a time when she's still living," he says slyly. "After all, you told me you'd do things differently if you had a second chance, right? That night at Club Fang? You'd let Sunny choose her destiny."

I stare at him, my head spinning, feeling as if I'm going to pass out right then and there. "You want us to go back in time?"

"In a sense," Hades says thoughtfully. "We'll reset the clocks, sending you and your sister back to the time before she was bitten by a vampire. Like returning to the save point in your video game. The two of you will still retain the knowledge and experiences you've gained over the last year. But everyone else will be exactly how they were. This way, you and your sister will have the chance to play it out, all over again. To make new choices, armed with what you know now about the consequences of those choices.

I force a hard swallow. "And no one will know this has happened—except us?"

Hades grins. "That's right. Just you and Sunny against the world."

But that would mean . . . Horror engulfs me as I glance over to the double doors, where Jareth waits in the next room. That would mean . . .

"No. I can't," I say, shaking my head with vehemence. "I can't leave Jareth like this." After all we've been through. After all we've said to one another. After he gave me his heart and I promised him eternity. How can I walk away now? Leave the love of my life behind? To go back to a time when he won't even recognize me?

"Typical." Hades clucks, as if disappointed. "Everyone always says they'd do anything." He gets up from the couch. "Until that *anything* is presented to them."

"Come on! There has to be another way!" I plead, my heart feeling as if it's breaking in two. I try to imagine a life without Jareth. No, worse—a life where he's there but doesn't know me from a hole in the wall.

The god heads back to his recliner, grabbing the joystick off the table. "That's my proposition. Take it or leave it." He glances at his watch. "I'm going to work on beating level thirteen now. You need to have made your decision before I complete it."

"But level thirteen's just a bonus round!" I cry. "You'll beat it in no time!"

"Well, then I suggest you start deciding," he says, tipping his head to me before turning back to the game. He un-pauses it and then starts playing.

And I head out with heavy feet and heart to talk to Jareth.

31

I stumble out of the room, my eyes blurred with bloody tears. Somehow I manage to fall into Jareth's arms, clinging to him with desperation, wanting to feel his embrace one more time before our lives change forever. His cool arms wrap around me, stroking my back as he tries to soothe my choking sobs.

"He said no, didn't he?" my boyfriend concludes, leading me back over to the sofa and sitting me down. "I was afraid of that. I didn't want to discourage you. But from all I've heard about the guy—"

I shake my head furiously. "I almost wish he had," I reply. "It would have made things a lot easier." I give him the whole story from beginning to end. "I don't know what I'm going to do," I finish. "I mean, how am I supposed to make this decision? If I turn down his offer, I'm basically condemning my sister to death." I hang my head. "She deserves another chance. A chance at the happy, normal life she's always wanted for herself. The one I stole from her that night at Club Fang. If I agree, she has another chance to find that. To grow up, become a journalist, get married, have children—everything that she always wanted. Who knows what she can accomplish if given a half a chance?"

I start choking and have to stop. Jareth pats my back, looking at me with tender eyes. "It would be great," he agrees. "To bring her back to life. To allow her another chance at happiness."

"But then what happens?" I cry, breaking away from his grasp, feeling ready to explode. "If I accept his offer—if I go back time . . ." I squeeze my eyes shut in agony, imagining the scene. "That's it for us. You won't even know me anymore. You won't . . . love me. You won't be mine. It'll be like we . . . like we never met."

Jareth grabs me in his arms, crushing me in his strong grip. I can barely breathe, but it doesn't matter. At the moment I don't care about anything but his hands on me, holding me tight. And I wildly beg for this moment to freeze in place forever.

Can I live without Jareth? My true love? Can I accept an existence without him by my side? Can I go back to a life where I'm totally and utterly alone?

"I finally got you back," I whisper hoarsely. "How can I just walk away? How can I just leave all we have behind?"

Jareth looks down at me tenderly, brushing a lock of blood tear–stained hair out of my eyes. "Rayne, I spent a lifetime feeling guilty for letting my family down. And it's a torture I wouldn't wish on my worst enemy." He sighs. "If you turn down Hades's offer, you're going to have to live with that decision for the rest of your life. You'll be tormented by the idea that you could have saved her, could have given her a chance at new life but you chose your own happiness instead. It'll haunt you every day until you go mad, wondering if you made the right decision." He pauses, looking down at me with the saddest eyes I've ever seen. "And then you'll start to resent me. Because I held you back. I kept you from saving your sister."

I stare at him in horror. "But I'd never—"

He holds up a hand, interrupting me. "You say that now. But are you sure you'll always feel that way? Because as much as I love you to death, I don't think I could live with being the cause of such all-consuming pain and guilt. I know what it feels like. I know how it can so easily destroy your life."

I moan. This is all so hard. So, so hard.

Jareth reaches out, lifting my chin with his hand, forcing me to stare into his beautiful eyes. "Sweetheart, darling, my Rayne," he murmurs. "You told me our love could stand the test of time. Well, now we're faced with that test. I won't be gone. I may not remember you, but I'll still be there, waiting for you, even though I don't know it. You made me fall in love with you once. You helped me break down the walls of the emotional prison I'd trapped myself in. Don't you think you could do it all over again?"

I nod slowly, my heart overflowing with emotion. "But what if you don't fall for me this time around?" I manage to choke out.

He presses his lips against my forehead with such tenderness

I can barely stand it. "How could I not fall in love with you? You've brought me more happiness than I ever thought possible. And besides." He quirks his mouth into a grin. "I know you. And I know you won't take no for an answer."

I crawl back into his arms, wishing there was a way to burrow inside of him. I want to memorize every touch. Every caress. Save it all deep in my heart until the time I can feel it again.

Because I know he's right. We're bound together by a force stronger than time itself. And there is nothing in the universe—on Earth or in Hades itself—that has the power to break us apart.

"My little soldier," Jareth soothes, stroking my hair with gentle fingers. "You fought so hard. It's now time to go and accept your victory."

"I'll find you again," I gurgle against his warm chest. "I'll make you love me. Even if I have to hit you over the head with a brick!"

"I have no doubt," he replies. Then he kisses me.

Our very last kiss.

At least for now . . .

Epilogue

Sunny

"Sunny! Rayne! Are you two still in bed? It's almost time for school!"

I rub my eyes groggily, confused at the sound of my mother's voice waking me from my slumber. Is this some kind of dream? I sit up in bed and look around.

Oh yes, definitely a dream. I'm back in my old bed at home in Oakridge, Massachusetts. My familiar posters still on the walls and the patchwork quilt, made by my fake grandma down in Florida, folded at the end of my bed. (Or was it made by my actual fairy grandmother and Mom fudged the truth?) In any case, this particular blanket is long gone by now in real life.

And I'm long gone, too. Stuck in Hades for eternity. Unless my sister can pull me out somehow.

My mother sticks her head into the room. She's wearing

some kind of long, colorful hemp skirt and peasant blouse, just like she used to before becoming Queen of the Fairies. I smile. What a lovely dream. Life as it used to be. Nice and normal.

"Sunny! Get up, now!" she commands. "You're going to be late for school!"

"Yes, Mom," I say agreeably, rolling out of bed, enjoying the feel of my favorite Victoria's Secret flannel pajamas against my skin. I look out the window and see blue skies and sunshine and I yawn, hoping I don't wake up too soon and spoil the rest of this beautiful dream day.

Mom nods, satisfied she's woken me, then heads out of my room, presumably to wake up my sister. A moment later I hear a scream. What the—? I run into Rayne's room. She's got her covers pulled up to her chin and she's staring at Mom with wide, frightened eyes.

"Oh my God, it worked! It really worked!" she's babbling over and over again.

"What worked?" I ask curiously. Her gaze swaps to me and she leaps out of bed and throws her arms around me. She's dressed in her Emily the Strange nightgown and, I realize she still has blond hair, like before she dyed it. We're identical twins, all over again. This dream gets better and better.

"Whoa! Watch the smothering sister love!" I protest, pushing her away. But she clings on tight. From the corner of my eye I can see Mom roll her eyes.

"The bus will be here in fifteen minutes," she announces. "I suggest you both get dressed." And with that, she walks out of the room.

"Ohmigod, ohmigod!" Rayne cries, bouncing on the bed with excitement. "I can't believe it. It's crazy!"

"What are you talking about?" I ask, starting to get a little annoyed.

"Don't you remember? Oh, please say you remember! At the very least I need you to know what's going on!"

"Remember what?"

She swallows hard. "Hades," she whispers.

"Well, of course I remember. I'm still there, right? I mean, this is just a dream."

"No, Sunny, it's no dream. We've been given a second chance."

"Wait, what?" I stare at her with a growing feeling of horror creeping into my bones. "What are you talking about?"

"Hades wouldn't free your soul. But he agreed to send us back in time. Before any of this happened." Rayne dashes to her computer. "See, it's April fifteenth."

My jaw drops to the floor. "April fifteenth . . ." I look at the calendar she's pulled up, swallowing hard as my eyes catch the year. "Oh my God."

"One month and one week before prom," she announces solemnly. "And . . ."

"One month before that night at Club Fang," I realize with growing dread. "One month before Magnus bites me by mistake." I stare at her, the implications of her words hitting me hard and fast.

He doesn't know me. He's never met me. He's never fallen in love with me . . .

Terror seizes my heart, squeezing it tight. "Oh, Rayne," I cry, looking at my sister with horrified eyes. "What have you done?"

"I've given you a second chance," she says stoutly, crossing her arms over her chest. "A chance to choose your destiny once and for all. Are you ready to take it?"

I swallow back the bile rising to my throat. I guess I'd better be.

~ TO BE CONTINUED ~

Turn the page for a special excerpt
from the next Blood Coven Vampire novel . . .

BLOOD FOREVER

*Coming soon from
The Berkley Publishing Group!*

resist the nearly irresistible urge to reach up under my black and red-trimmed corset to give my belly button a good solid scratch. Seriously, I don't know how the heck Rayne wears this Goth stuff everyday of the week. It is so majorly uncomfortable, what with the thick black lace rubbing my armpits raw and the corset bones digging into my waist, making it nearly impossible to take in a full breath. And that's not even mentioning the smoosh factor going on with my already admittedly small breasts. Seriously, give me a pair of Old Navy boot-cut jeans, tank top, and flip-flops any day of the week, thank you very much. Sure, they may not qualify me to rock a runway, but at least I'm able to take advantage of my full lung capacity.

But unfortunately tonight my own "uniform" just won't cut it. Not if I want to fool the vampires down at Blood Coven

University into thinking I'm my twin sister, that is. Rayne wouldn't be caught dead in jeans, which means that I must suffer through the agony and humiliation of sneaking out of the house in full-on Goth gear, complete with fluffy tulle skirt, ripped fishnets, and black boots with six-inch platform soles, all dug out of her jam-packed black-on-black-on-black closet.

I know, I know. I shouldn't be doing this. And Rayne would freaking kill me if she found out I was. (Even before she learned it was in her clothes.) After all, the whole point behind this life "do-over" my sister arranged with the Lord of the Underworld was designed to give us the opportunity to go back to living a normal, vampire-free life. And if Rayne—the girl who loves vampires more than anything in the universe—is able to simply walk away from her vampire-in-training class, what the heck am I doing, choosing to attend in her stead?

But let's be honest here; what would *you* do if you had the opportunity to catch a glimpse of your true love one last time? Could you just walk away—go see a movie instead? Yeah, I don't think so. And hey, it's not like I'm going to go make out with the guy and declare my eternal devotion or anything. I'm just going to gaze upon him, quietly, from across the room. Take one last, longing look before I go back to my pathetic, normal, Magnus-free life, forever.

Besides, it's not like I could do any more than that, even if I wanted to. This Magnus, the one who exists in this time period, doesn't think of me as his girlfriend. He's not in love with me. He doesn't want to be with me. And, if we do happen to cross paths, he's just going to assume I'm my sister. So no big deal.

Except, of course, it kind of is. It's kind of the biggest deal ever.

No. I shake my head. *I won't go there.* What we're doing is for the best. Like my sister said, if I never befriend Magnus, we'll never end up together. He'll never have to make the choice between the Blood Coven and me and thus none of the badness that has happened over the last year will happen. I won't die. He won't be tried for treason. And the Blood Coven won't be kicked out of the Consortium. Everyone will live happily ever after.

And I'm totally down for all that to happen. After I get my one last look.

The vampire-in-training class is being held right outside Saint Patrick's Cemetery—just a few blocks from the Blood Coven HQ, not that I'm supposed to know that. The location of the vampire crypt is strictly classified until you become a full-blooded member. So instead they hold classes in a nearby former church, which seems a totally weird option, until you learn that this particular church has been long ago de-holy-ized and put out of official commission. Meaning the ground is no longer hallowed and perfectly fine and safe for vampire feet to walk over.

I head up the wooden front steps and through the front door, resisting the urge to roll my eyes at some of Rayne's fellow vampire-in-training classmates who are standing outside smoking. I mean, hello? Could you be any more stereotypical if you tried? Every single one of them is dolled up in their Gothy best, complete with black (and/or hot pink) hair, pancake-white makeup, and an inordinate amount of piercings. Seriously, doesn't anyone outside the Goth scene want to become a vampire anymore? I mean, you'd think with the whole *Twilight* phenomenon we'd get a few Bellas out here at the very least.

"Name, please?"

I glance down at the bored-looking receptionist sitting at a card table just inside the front door. My eyes widen as I realize it's none other than Marcia herself, Magnus's former secretary. Of course right now, I guess, she's his future secretary, still working for Lucifent, who's currently Master of the Blood Coven. It's not 'til Bertha slays Lucifent and Magnus takes over his leadership gig that she starts working for her new boss. (This time-travel stuff can be very confusing even if you are paying attention.)

"Um, are you deaf?" she demands, her face twisting into a scowl. "I said, what is your name?"

Yup. She's exactly the same. I bite back a frown, pinning my arms to my sides so as to avoid my hands reaching out and involuntarily strangling that haughty look right off her face. Bitch. After all, it's because of her that Pyrus learned of our secret location under the streets of New York City. Because of her that I'm dead in the future. But what can I do? Accuse her of a crime she's yet to commit? That'll be sure to go off well. And besides, seeing as she's a vampire and I'm just a puny mortal, I admit I might have a tough time cutting off her air supply using nothing more than my bare hands.

Gotta live and let live, I suppose. At least for now.

"S—I mean Rayne McDonald," I reply instead, trying my

best to sound as bored as she. She scans her list and checks me off, snapping her gum in an apparent effort to let me know how insignificant I am to her existence. If only she knew.

"You can go and sit over there," she informs me, pointing a perfectly manicured finger to the left side of the church, where another group of Goths have congregated. Across the aisle, I notice a much more mainstream crowd hanging out chatting. The vampires themselves, I realize. Unlike their trying-too-hard mortal trainees, the vampires are dressed casually. Jeans, T-shirts, sundresses . . . and . . . I do a double-take . . . is that really the same pink BITE ME tank top I ended up wearing on that fateful trip to Club Fang? The one that started all the trouble in the first place? I remember Rayne telling me she borrowed it off some vampire she met in training . . .

As I make my way over to the mortal section, I suddenly catch a glimpse of a door at the front of the church swinging open. I stop in my tracks, my heart skipping a beat, as a lone vampire steps out into the sanctuary.

Magnus.

My world spins off its axis as I watch him stop and stand just behind the altar, scanning the room with disinterested eyes. He looks bored, a little annoyed, and totally and utterly hot. My mind treats me to a vivid flashback of that first night we met at Club Fang. He was dressed in simple but elegant Armani, just like today, and I remember thinking he looked exactly like Orlando Bloom from the first *Pirates* movie, with his shoulder-length chestnut-colored hair tied back with a simple leather strap.

Tonight his hair hangs free, falling into his elfin eyes, brushing against his perfectly sculpted cheekbones and ending just short of his sensuous mouth. Suddenly I find myself unable to think of anything else in the world except for him taking me into his arms and pressing those full, soft lips against my own with a reverence and worship I've never fully deserved.

Oh Magnus . . . I find myself stepping forward, my heart aching in my chest. *Oh my love* . . .

He turns, raking a hand through his hair and clearing it from his face. His gaze locks onto mine, his eyes zeroing in on my own. I swallow hard and find myself giving him a small, hopeful wave and smile. But instead of smiling back—instead of his eyes lighting up as they fall upon my face, he merely raises a perfectly arched eyebrow, his beautiful lips curling into a small sneer as he gives me a critical once-over before turning away.

My heart plummets as reality comes crashing back down on me. He doesn't know me. He doesn't love me. All he can see is some stupid overdressed vampire wannabe stranger, just like the rest, making googly eyes at him from across the room. Ugh. What possessed me to dress like my sister tonight? I've only succeeded in repulsing my own boyfriend with a tacky outfit that isn't even me.

Which is a good thing, I try to remind myself. The last thing I want is for him to be attracted to me when I'm supposed to stay far, far away.

But still, it hurts. Especially as I watch him watch him walk over to one of the other vampires—the girl in the BITE ME tank—and whisper something in her ear. She turns and looks over in my direction, chuckling. Are they really making fun of me? My face burns in a mixture of embarrassment and fury.

What am I doing? Why am I even here? I should have stayed away—then I could have lived out the rest of my life, only remembering Magnus gazing upon me with adoration and love. Now I'll be forced to remember his look of scorn and derision until my dying day.

I stumble toward the exit, my eyes blurring with tears. I need to get out of here and fast. Before I dissolve in a pathetic puddle of lovelorn goo.

Unfortunately my escape attempt does not go as smoothly as I planned—mostly because I'm just not used to running around in boots with six-inch soles. So instead of slipping out the door and vanishing into the night, I find myself stumbling head over heels, crashing into a standing candelabrum before becoming one with the marble floor.

The room, predictably, erupts in laughter. And here I thought my face couldn't get any redder.

"Are you okay?"

I look up toward the sound of a familiar female voice. My eyes widen as I find none other than Charity herself—one of Magnus's blood donors—looming above me, a worried look on her face. Without waiting for me to answer, she helps me up and leads me over to a nearby pew. I can feel the amused stares of all the vampires and mortals as I collapse onto the bench, but I force myself to ignore them.

"Thanks," I say, letting out a long breath. "Sorry, just lost my footing there for a moment."

She plops down beside me and reaches into her bag, pulling out a large chocolate chip cookie. "Eat this," she instructs. "I find a little sugar helps when you're all weak in the knees."

I take the cookie gratefully. After all, she should know about weak knees, being a blood donor and all. She's probably used to living life a pint or two short. And I appreciate her kindness—it's more than I can say about anyone else in the room. "Thanks," I say, taking a bite of the cookie. "I appreciate it."

"I'm Charity," she says, holding out a hand. "I assume you're one of the trainees?"

I nod. "I'm Sun—I mean, Rayne McDonald," I say, shaking her hand.

Her eyes widen with interest. "Rayne McDonald?" she repeats. "So you're—"

A shadow looms above us, cutting her off her question. "There you are, Charity. You're wanted in the back. Rachel tells me it's time for your draining."

Oh God. My throat goes dry. I'd know that deep, English-accented voice anywhere. If it were a thousand years since I'd heard it, I'd still know it better than my own. My hands start shaking uncontrollably and I quickly shove them under my thighs.

Don't look up. Whatever you do, don't look up. Keep your eyes glued to the floor until he walks away and out of your life forever.

But, of course, there's no way I can do that.

And so I find myself gazing upon his beautiful face, my eyes falling helplessly into his own sapphire ones, framed by thick, black lashes. *This is just Magnus,* I try to scold my quickly melting heart. *You've spent hours and days locked in his embrace. It should be no big deal to look at him.*

But it is. It's like the biggest deal ever.

"I'm so sorry, Master," Charity says, rising to her feet and lowering her gaze in deference to the vampire. "I will go do that right away. I know you must get very hungry on a night like tonight."

Her words startle me out of my trance. "Night like tonight?" I find myself blurting out, realizing I have no idea what people actually do here at vampire-in-training school. What could Magnus be up to that would require an extra pint of blood or two?

Magnus gives me a hard look. "Bite night," he replies stiffly, as if it's a burden to even lower himself to speak to me. He starts turning back to Charity.

"Magnus," the blood donor hisses in a distinct stage-whisper. "This is Rayne McDonald. Your, well . . ." She pauses, biting her lower lip, looking from her master to me. "You know . . ."

"Your future blood mate," I finish, rising to my feet and giving him awkward smile. "At your service."

Magnus's face goes stark white. He looks at Charity, then at me, then back at his blood donor. I know exactly what he's thinking. *You're telling me I'm going to be stuck with this tacky fashion victim for all of eternity?* If it wasn't so tragic, it'd almost be comical.

The silence that follows is suffocating. My heart feels as if it's been squeezed in a vice. "Maybe I should go," I stammer. "This was a bad idea." *On so many levels.*

I turn away so he won't see the tears spring in to my eyes. I should leave. I should bolt out of this old, decommissioned church and never look back. But as I take that first step, I feel a strong hand on my arm. I turn back to see Magnus's sheepish face.

"Wait," he says, his voice filled with guilt. He always was a softie—underneath that tough exterior. "I'm sorry. I think we've gotten off on the wrong foot. Please forgive me." He releases my arm and bows his head reverently. "It is lovely to meet you, Rayne McDonald," he says. Almost as if he actually means it.

"Yeah," I manage to reply, though it's quite an effort getting any words past the lump in my throat. He must think I'm a total freak. "Um, great to meet you, too." Out of habit, I stick out my hand. I can't believe I'm actually giving my soul mate a friendly handshake. What the hell was I thinking coming here in the first place? This is torture worse than any fiery circle of Hell.

In response, he slips his hand into my own, squeezing it with tempered vampire strength. My whole body explodes at his touch, and it's all I can do not to cry out loud.

Oh Magnus. My love . . .

He drops my hand like a hot potato and my first reaction is to be offended all over again. But then I catch the shadow crossing his face, the glimmer of confusion in his eyes. Ha! He feels it, too. Despite his best efforts, he feels something of the magnetic attraction between us. Just that simple fact makes me feel a little better.

I watch, breath in my throat, as he swallows hard, then turns to Charity, who's watching the scene with apparent amusement. "Why the hell are you still here?" he demands angrily, taking out his confusion on the only target he can.

"I'm not! I'm gone!" she assures him, dancing down the aisle and toward the back door, leaving me alone with Magnus again. My heart pounds in my chest as I search for something intelligent to say.

"So, um, Bite Night?" I try. "What's that?" It's all I can come up with on short notice with my body still humming from his touch.

He shakes his head before replying, as if trying to regain some semblance of control over his traitorous body. "Well," he says, "as you know, in one month, when you complete your vampire training, the two of us will share one another's blood, bonding as blood mates . . . for eternity."

"Right," I reply, nodding. "I know that part." Of course unbeknownst to him, by then I'll be far, far away. Forgetting he even exists for the good of all humanity and vampire kind. I wonder what he'll think when he finds out I bailed. Will he be disappointed? Relieved?

"Well," he continues, clearing his throat. "On Bite Night we practice."

"Um, what?" My pulse picks up all over again as I give him a questioning look. "Practice what?"

His cheeks pinken into a blush, and for a moment I think he's not going to explain. But then he shrugs and looks up, piercing me with his hot blue eyes and melting me all over again.

"Why, biting you, of course."

JOIN THE BLOOD COVEN!

Do you want . . .
Eternal life?
Riches beyond your wildest dreams?
A hot Blood Mate to spend eternity with?

We're looking for a few good vampires! Do you have
what it takes to join the Blood Coven? Sign up online to
become a Vampire in Training, then master your skills at
Blood Coven University.

You'll go behind the scenes of the series, receive exclusive
Blood Coven merchandise, role-play with the other
vampires, and get a sneak peek at what's coming up next
for Sunny and Rayne.

BLOOD COVEN VAMPIRES
Check out all the Blood Coven Vampire titles!

Boys That Bite
Stake That
Girls That Growl
Bad Blood
Night School
Blood Ties
Soul Bound

And don't miss the next Blood Coven Vampire novel

Blood Forever

Coming Fall 2012 from Berkley!

www.bloodcovenvampires.com

penguin.com

T125.1211

The Blood Coven Vampire Novels
by Mari Mancusi

Boys That Bite

Stake That

Girls That Growl

Bad Blood

Night School

Blood Ties

Soul Bound

"Delightful, surprising, and engaging—
you'll get bitten and love it."
—Rachel Caine, *New York Times* bestselling author

Don't miss *Blood Forever*, the next book in the Blood Coven Vampire
series, coming Fall 2012 from Berkley!

www.bloodcovenvampires.com

penguin.com

T126.0511